Who will answer the challenges and questions of the future?

Sometimes they will be young people, caught in unexpected, unimaginable situations; demanding quick reflexes and fast thinking, or simply a young person's freedom from preconceptions.

Such situations and such young people are the subject matter for the fresh, vivid, thought-provoking stories that Roger Elwood has assembled here—stories that explore all the excitements, challenges and rich experiences of the future, faced by young people with the urge to live life to the full, and learn from it.

Avon Books by Roger Elwood

DEMON KIND
YOUNG DEMONS

EDITED BY ROGER ELWOOD

AVON
PUBLISHERS OF BARD, CAMELOT, DISCUS, EQUINOX AND FLARE BOOKS

This is the first publication of
FUTURE QUEST in book form.

AVON BOOKS
A division of
The Hearst Corporation
959 Eighth Avenue
New York, New York 10019

Published by arrangement with the editor.

First Avon Printing, September, 1973.

AVON TRADEMARK REG. U.S. PAT. OFF. AND FOREIGN COUNTRIES, REGISTERED TRADEMARK— MARCA REGISTRADA, HECHO EN CHICAGO, U.S.A.

Printed in the U.S.A.

ACKNOWLEDGEMENTS

DULL DRUMS by Anne McCaffrey—Copyright © 1973 by Anne McCaffrey. Reprinted by permission of the author.

SECOND NATURE by Chad Oliver—Copyright © 1973 by Chad Oliver. Reprinted by permission of the author.

TAPPING OUT by Barry N. Malzberg—Copyright © 1973 by Barry N. Malzberg. Reprinted by permission of the author.

HOW TO BE ETHNIC IN ONE EASY LESSON by Poul Anderson—Copyright © 1973 by Poul Anderson. Reprinted by permission of the author.

WEEP NO MORE, OLD LADY by C. L. Grant—Copyright © 1973 by C. L. Grant. Reprinted by permission of the author.

CITY'S END by Mack Reynolds—Copyright © 1973 by Mack Reynolds. Reprinted by permission of the author.

MOONCHILD by Tom Purdom—Copyright © 1973 by Tom Purdom. Reprinted by permission of the author.

PET by Raymond F. Jones—Copyright © 1973 by Raymond F. Jones. Reprinted by permission of the author.

Contents

FUTURE QUEST

DULL DRUMS

Anne McCaffrey

The trouble with student issue clothing was not its neutrality, thought Nora Fenn, but its instability. Did the suppliers think students doddered about the academic cloisters like sedentary pensioners? She fingered together the rent across her hip, hoping that no one would brush against her and widen the tear. She must have overstressed the fabric when she stampeded from Con's last night. Wouldn't you know it'd be on the left side because that's where her tights had run this morning?

Doggedly she continued through the pedestrian way, toward the Metropolis' Main Computer Block, twisting and dodging through the clumps of slower citizens.

It had been such an honor to qualify for the special cybernetics course, given by Master Scholar Siffert himself. Nora didn't mind the twenty-minute commute from the University Complex to the Computer Block no matter how the others in the class complained. (Not much suited them anyhow!) Even after nearly a year, she reacted to the stimulus of metropolitan living with added alertness. Just to walk the pedestrian ways, to look at the variety of faces and costumes and shops was a treat for a Farm Complex-bred girl. She usually started for this class early so she'd have time to window-shop and people-see. Then Con's mean words leapt to her mind.

"Yeah, you say you like people, Nora Fenn, but I never saw anyone communicate less in my life."

"Just because I'm not always gibbering," she'd said in self-defense.

Con had thrown back his head and howled. "The very notion of you . . . *you* . . . gibbering! May I be around to see the day!"

There was nothing wrong, Nora told herself stoutly, with taking pleasure in just being among people. You didn't have to participate actively.

But last night's scathing accusations rang in her ears.

"You can't be a parameter cloddie forever, Nora. You'll never really know what life is about until you start communicating and experiencing actively. And don't tell me you're in computer programming because that's your aptitude. That's your cop-out so you won't have to live and feel. If your Guidance Officer had one wit about him, he'd have phased you out of Computer Science and shoved you into the Humanities. And opened wide holes in your father's home-brewed homilies."

"My father—"

"Your father"—and Con was so incensed the cords stood out in his neck—"your father is a throwback to all the parental autocracies, the narrow-minded, sex-blocked, inhibiting, maladjusting, martyrizing, egotistical possessiveness that our present system of social harmony is supposed to correct!"

"How dare you say such things!"

"Because *you* have! Only you're still too much under your father's domineering influence to realize how much you resent him."

"I don't resent my father. I understand his—"

"Understand?" Con threw his arms up in dramatic frustration. "Understand why he's refused to give you any credit allowance? By the printed circuits which feed us, every other Complex Manager would do without so he could budget *something* for any youngster his unit can send on to Academic Advancement! Wake up, Nora. Your ever-loving father has never forgiven you, his daughter—much less the Educational Committee for letting you go on to the University instead of the male, his son."

"I don't need credit allowances." Nora tried to sound convincing but she'd been hurt and confused by her father's parsimony. "I got an academic bonus of a hundred credits first term . . ."

Con shook his finger right under her nose.

"You can fool yourself, Nora Fenn, but you sure as 0 x 0 is 0, don't fool me! Your paternal parent has royally screwed you and why you persist in trying to prove you're worth his disdainful notice even if you are female, I don't understand. He isn't worth it."

Con had stepped forward then, his expression hard and angry as he grabbed her arms and gave her a good shaking. His manner was frighteningly different from the jovial, joke-cracking clown pose he usually affected.

"About the computer courses, Nora. Get into Humanities. Take some behavioral psych. See objectively how futile it is to try and win your father over. And then grow up and live as Nora Fenn instead of Herbert Fenn's unwanted female child."

"Thank you, Connor Clarke, for your lecture and your advice. Send me the bill! But don't try my number. I'm programming you out from now on."

She grabbed her cloak and strode from his room, racing down the hall to the anti-grav shaft. She'd entered it fast—that's probably when she'd torn her tunic—and cried all the way down the a.g. shaft to her own level, cursing Con under her breath and desperately trying to forget what he'd said.

But his words haunted her as she walked into the shadow cast by the Computer Block. It was cold out of the sun's direct rays and Nora pulled her shabby cloak tighter around her. It had been the one piece of complex issue clothing which she'd been able to bring with her. Not that her father had ever let his family use more than farm issue.

"No need to put credits into fancy fabrics and silly clothes you wear once a month. People should take us for what we are, not what we wear. It isn't needful for us to show our status."

'Needful.' That was her father's operative word. What was needful was procured instantly and ordered in the best quality, regardless of the cost. What was unnecessary was given scant consideration.

It hadn't been needful for Nora to have any credit allowance from the Fenn Farm Complex. Her father had solemnly announced that she would have student quarters at the University Complex, adequate food (because students did not eat subsistence level but ate a high calorie diet), and sufficient clothing to cover her decently. If Nora were as good a student as the Educational Committee (which had passed her for Advanced Study instead of Nick) had said, then she would earn credit bonuses with those brains of hers, wouldn't she? Privately, Nora had vowed she'd earn a bundle. And she had. But now she regretted her diplomacy—no, her subservient conciliatory gesture, as Con would say—in permitting her father to select a heavy comp sci program for her first year.

"That way you'll qualify as Computer Technician. Grade II by spring instead of wasting your time on unnecessary trimmings," her father had said.

Nora knew now, what he meant was it wouldn't be needful for the Fenn Complex to pay the salary of the Grade II, comp tech for the spring planting.

Six months at University and Nora knew that she wouldn't be able to go back to the Farm. It wasn't simply the knowledge that her father's basic ecological orientation was limited, but the realization that she'd hated her existence there, from fattening geese to the bone-jarring tractor work which all the automation in the world couldn't completely eliminate. The glitter of bright lights and vapid entertainments in the Metropolis didn't attract her half as much as the crowds of people, the antithesis of the lonely farm complex with its rigid society, seasons, and the so-well-known personalities.

She was gregarious, but she didn't have to be verbose the way Con was to enjoy a group situation. She didn't need to maul people with sweaty hands; she could enjoy the sound of voices, the play of emotions on faces. She could sense the interaction in brand-new combinations.

Deep in thought, she had arrived at the great Computer building and had crossed the magnificent inner hall without gawking at the famous sculpture depicting man overpowering the Laeconia of science. She'd passed by without re-examining the tridex models reviewing the significant events leading to the Dicta "Ecology, Economy, and Society" in which the technical sciences had swung violently to the aid of the crushing social problems and the conservation of dwindling natural resources. She had marched quickly past the programming desks with their lines of applicants and petitioners.

Every citizen had the right to bank storage. Every citizen could apply for additional space, for more programming time, for reprogramming—these were as much their rights as subsistence, shelter, and education. It was these rights of use that had ended citizen fear of a computer-assisted society. Man had proved to the doubtful that science worked for his good, not his extinction.

Nora took the grav shaft up to the storage banks

where the class was being held, and despite her depressing reflections, she experienced a curious sense of elation, of purpose, that usually gripped her on her way to class.

She knew that she was incredibly lucky as a first-year student to be in Research Scholar Siffert's special course. Master Siffert was *the* man in Computer Programming. Each student had to be especially recommended by his or her Mentor and then passed by Siffert himself. (Nora had lost pounds anticipating that interview.) Their integrity had to be above reproach because the course included lift-lock previleges. All the laboratory work involved the erasure of private records to clear storage drums for current usage but the lift-lock meant the unharmonious could have access to any records.

To clear drums, the students had to cross-check references with Housing and Obituary—audit the drum, checking off a variety of items on income, profession, and use of and referral to the individual's programming rights. The last chore was to provide statistical proof on a fair apportionment of storage space to citizens. Nora wasn't certain of the exact goal of the course although she'd learned a lot from the labs about data retrieval and erasure. Research Scholar Siffert was known for his eccentric methods, so undoubtedly, all would be clear in the final lecture.

The one factor she disliked about the course was the attitude of the other students. Granted they'd all had the same integrity clearance but she did feel their approach to the lab work was improper. It had become the fashion to try to top each other with ridiculous anecdotes drawn from their auditing. Callous and cruel, Nora thought, to ridicule the dead for their shortcomings and petty follies.

As she entered the Data Erasure room, she heard the inane caw of Larry Asher's laughter above the general chuckles.

"Haven't you heard any good ones, Fenn?" Asher asked her as she slipped into her chair.

She shook her head.

"Fenn apparently has hit the dull drums," Clas Heineman said with a twitch of his lips for the pun.

"On the contrary," Nora replied, raising her voice above the laughter as she remembered Con's jibes, "I've had some very interesting ones. But I don't think they're ludicrous."

"Fenn also has no sense of humor," Clas remarked with a rueful grin for Nora's lack.

"Humor has nothing to do with your quips, Clas Heineman. It's easy to mock something you've not the sensitivity to appreciate."

"O-ho, Fenn's got opinions, too," Larry Asher said, chortling because he sensed a verbal tiff between the two. Heineman was not only an upper classman with a high scholastic average, but was also one of the University's dominant personalities. "Tell us more, Fenn."

Clas Heineman dared her, his eyes sparkling. The rest of the class waited, all too eager to see Heineman score her down.

She took a deep breath and stolidly addressed Clas.

"What you don't appreciate, Clas Heineman, is what a panorama of the human condition you've been auditing."

"Go on," and Clas used that poisonously quiet tone she'd heard him use before he changed the state of some unwary lower classman.

"I know what you'd find hilarious: the woman who recorded her husband snoring so she could prove that he did. After he died, she'd have that played back every night so she could get to sleep." Someone guffawed and she glared in his direction. "That isn't *funny*: it's human. So's the man who programmed a report of his luxury credit-standing to wake him up every morning and put him to sleep at night. Then he won the Index Lottery and cancelled the instructions. Or the fat woman who had the words 'think thin' played back all day just below the audible level. It must have worked because three months later there's a stop order. Of course, you're all so grand and well-adjusted that you won't need to program such things. And all those would-be poets . . . *why* are they so laughable? *You* all pinion your friends and make them listen! At least the dead poets only bored themselves." She knew that the frustration and anger in her voice was not for the class alone but for her own personal situation. But she'd started to let go all those pent-up feelings and she'd hit the target. "And I'd just love to be around when someone, a hundred years from now, starts auditing your storage drums. I wonder what would be risible to him."

The smirks had faded from some faces but Clas

Heineman's smile remained as fixed as his glittering eyes on her.

"And for all your scholastic honors, I don't think you've realized just what all these so-funny incidents show."

"Since you're so acute, suppose you tell the rest of us obtuse clowns," Heineman's voice was deadly now and Nora was suddenly as scared as she'd been when she confronted her father and insisted on her student rights.

"The subtle change of fear and suspicion of his neighbors to fear and suspicion of the computer-based society, then a gradual acceptance of computer-assistance. We all started with drums beginning in 1990 when the main Comp Banks were switched on in this Metropolis, so you should all see what I meant. By mid-century I noticed a definite drop in the incidence of recorded paranoia, and the incidence and repetition of psycho-chem therapy. It's noticeable because people began inputting the most deeply intimate secrets. They realized that no one could break a privacy seal . . . until we come along with our sophomoric mentalities."

"Oh come now, Nora," a girl said from the back of the room but she sounded embarrassed, "so much of it's pretty damned dull."

"I don't agree. I think it's fascinating to watch a saner mental outlook emerge . . ."

"Thank you for the lecture, Miss Fenn," Larry Asher said with a jeer.

"Thank you indeed, Miss Fenn," repeated a deep voice.

The entire class swiveled about, startled. In the doorway was the substantial figure of Research Scholal Siffert. The students leapt to their feet. "Thank you, class. Remain standing, Fenn."

She felt the hopeful aura of the class as they watched Master Siffert approaching her. She felt utterly miserable, but she held her chin up and her shoulders back. She was damned if she'd let anyone see her change state.

The Scholar approached her, with each step looming more and more forbiddingly. He isn't at all like Father, she told herself, halfheartedly. She steeled herself to look him in the eye and then realized that Master Siffert was by no means grim. His lined face was suddenly cut by an enormous grin. He seized Nora by the shoulder and turned her toward the expectant students, one arm proprietarily draped over her shoulder.

"Nora Fenn has just earned a scholarship bonus of 300 Luxury Credits and a Distinctive Honors Scholastic Credit."

There was an astonished mass gasp. Nora closed her mouth with a snap when she realized that her jaw had dropped open. Three hundred L.C.'s? He couldn't possibly mean that! And a D.H.? What on earth had she done?

"We will dismiss the rest of you from today's auditing. I do not believe you would be able to keep your mind on your work after Fenn's astute summation. And then, too, you will need considerable time for the essay, the length of which I leave to your judgment"—and he swept the room with a stern glance—"on the pyschological trends noticeable in personal programming in the early twenty-first century. I believe that most of you have penetrated the fifty-year mark of that era. Nora Fenn"—and he gave her a paternal hug—"has spared you what I imagine would have been an unwelcome surprise at term end when this essay would have been duly announced. You are dismissed."

The group rapidly dispersed. Nora made an attempt to follow but the Scholar's heavy arm remained about her shoulders and to disengage herself would be improper.

When the room had cleared, the Scholar released her, gesturing toward a chair. He seated himself next to her, crossing his legs and beaming at her.

"I don't really deserve—"

"Nonsense, my girl. Not many students outsmart Siffert." His beam took on additional radiance.

Nora felt the blush rising to her cheeks. He chuckled and patted her hand.

"Now, now. You were using your mind and your heart, which all too few computer programmers do. They tend to regard people as bits to be recorded or changed as to state, instead of as thinking humans with emotions—with all the pettiness and vainglories of the human condition." He chuckled. "I had rather relied, you know, on the notorious student irreverence toward the task to obscure the ultimate goal of the course."

Nora groaned, realizing that she had undone some very careful manipulating.

"I do so enjoy the look on their faces when these young scuts have to change state to the proper polarity. There ought to be some very stimulating essays. And"—his eyes twinkled at Nora—"to have a student capable of some independent evaluation . . . outguessing a Research Scholar . . . delightful!" He beamed. "Really delightful!"

There was no question that she'd pleased him and Nora began to relax though she still couldn't believe in her good fortune. With an alacrity at odds with his physical size and age, the Scholar rose and strode to the master panel that dominated the classroom. Nora heard his lift-lock slide and the click of rapidly depressed input keys, the almost negligible pause before the print-out occurred. Master Siffert grunted and turned, leaning against the control board and eyeing her thoughtfully.

"Really diverting. But my dear Fenn, whatever are you doing in Computer Sciences?" He waved a print-out sheet at her. "You'd be wasted on a Farm Complex. What on earth is your Complex Manager about? Not to say your local Guidance Officer? And why on earth have you been permitted to continue in a cross-aptitudinal course? Really, I shall have quite a deal to say to your Tutor. How ever could he encourage you in this gross misdirection of ability?"

"Sir, I applied for Comp Sci."

"What? How's that again? Comp Sci with your personality index? Good heavens, no! Wouldn't do! I'd be going against the precepts of the Educational Act to condone that!" He strode over to her. "Don't look so woebegone, my dear. Do some serious re-evaluation yourself. I'd say you'd be much happier in Socio-Psycho Dynamics, for instance. Can't imagine how you've continued almost a full year in the wrong field. I shall definitely have a word with your Tutor."

"Please, sir. It's not his fault. My Complex Manager needs a good computer technician."

"You'd be wasted on a farm, my dear Fenn. Wasted. Surely your parents have seen your real aptitudes . . ."

"Sir, my father is the Complex Manager and it's my wish to—"

Scholar Siffert pinned her with such an astonished stare.

"Your father . . . is the Complex Manager and—good heavens, I thought such situations couldn't happen anymore." Siffert blinked and regarded her with outright horror. Then his expression softened. "You appear to me to be a very level-headed young lady, Nora Fenn."

"The situation has been difficult, sir. You see, my twin brother, Nick, opted for animal husbandry. He wasn't qualified for Academic Advancement, just Vocational." Nora knew she was expressing things badly and stammered on. "Father'd always expected that Nick would be the Computer Technician and, well, it wasn't socially harmonious to do anything else just then . . ."

Siffert regarded her sternly. "The situation is outrageous. Parents cannot be permitted to live vicariously through their children. Can't be permitted. You should not be in Computer Sciences. You're excused from the rest of the course."

"I'd really like to continue . . ."

The Scholar made a rueful noise and then smiled kindly at her. "Well, it wouldn't be good for class morale for you to stay on, my dear. Besides, you've already accomplished what the course was designed to effect: an understanding of the human condition behind the bits and states. No, my dear. Use this course time to find out where you really belong. Consult your floor Psychman." He gave her a warm reassuring smile. "I've registered your scholastic rating and bonus. Why don't you ring up your boyfriend and sport him to a real meal? And I warn you, I shall have a few words with your Tutor. In person." He wheeled to the master panel, his scholar's robe billowing behind him, in effect dismissing her. As she left the room, she heard him typing, heard the printout chatter a rebuttal.

She couldn't believe what had happened. A fantastic credit bonus and a Distinctive Honors. Just wait until she told Con! And she could feed him—and then she realized she couldn't tell Con for a very good reason: Scholar Siffert supported Connor Clarke's opinion that she shouldn't be in Comp Sci at all.

"Nora . . ."

Clas Heineman blocked her path.

She ducked and ran to the grav shaft, entering it

fast. If Con was the last person she wanted to see right now, Clas Heineman was next to last. She whipped out of the grav shaft on the ground level and dodged through the throng in the Main Hall. She underestimated Heineman's determination to intercept her.

He caught up with her at the entrance, grabbing her hand and when she wrenched free, he caught at her tunic and all but ripped the student issue clothing from her.

"Hey, I'm sorry," he cried, dismayed. Before Nora could protest, he'd wrapped her tightly in his own cloak and bustled her onto the fast-pedestrian way, speeding toward the edge of the Metropolis. She couldn't struggle with her clothing in shreds and only his cloak saving her from an immodesty citation.

Shaken by the morning's events and last night's scene, Nora began to cry.

"Hey, don't get in that state, Fenn," Clas said, concerned. "I'm not polarized. In fact, I owe you an apology. Two." Clas Heineman grinned at her, his eyes kind and anxious. His arm tightened reassuringly, his fingers pressing into her waist under the cloak. When he felt her bare flesh, he politely took a new hold. "I didn't mean to tear your dress. This student issue isn't worth a discarded bit, is it? Good thing you've got 300 L.C.'s."

Clas reminded her in a nice way that people were looking at them, even if they were on the fast belt and speeding by. It wasn't good manners to publicize intimacy.

"Oh, Clas, it's so far back to the U."

"Back to the U? For more student issue? Don't be silly, Fenn. We're transferring . . . now!"

He half lifted her to the moderate speed belt and then, with a second warning, to the slow one. At the next shopping center, he guided her off and straight into the clothing section.

"I've always wondered what you'd look like in a decent outfit," he said, conversationally, as he steered her into the shop. He gave her an appraising look. "Deep red . . . like that outfit, for instance."

"Oh, no! That's fourteen credits," but Nora couldn't help coveting the smart tunic suit with its silver piping, the deep sleeves and the matching garnet cape. It did seem to be a tightly woven durable material, though.

"A first-year student who has copped a D.H. in Siffert's course cannot appear back on campus in tatters," Clas told her and before she could protest, he dragged her up to the shop's computer and shoved her wrist ID disc in the slot, punching out a data request. She wasn't certain if Clas had made a deliberate or an unconscious mistake in data retrieval. A credit balance was all that the shop required but he'd punched for a credit check. The entries made a distressing picture of her economic status. There was the student bonus from her mid-term and the shocking allowance of ten credits from her Complex.

"Clas, that's not fair."

His eyes were thoughtful as he looked at her.

"You got a lousy Complex, girl. Well, you can tell

'em to feck off if that's all they can scrape up for a student with your ability. Why, my Complex—change state! Let's get you dressed, girl."

The attendant had arrived, prompted by the use of the computer panel. Clas erased all but the credit balance and the attendant's smile was correspondingly affable.

"If you're going to feel guilty about spending for clothes, Nora Fenn, I'll drag you to the nearest psych machine," Clas Heineman said as they emerged, socially apart, from the shop.

"I shouldn't have let you talk me into buying so much," Nora said but she smiled at him. He'd overridden her objections and, neatly reinforced by the shop attendant who had visions of a respectable commission, talked her into buying not only the garnet red suit but two other changes and some pseudoleather boots: all completely unneedful since Nora had maintained that the one good outfit would do for social occasions and she could, after all, do well in student issue for classes.

"A D.H. has a certain position to maintain, Nora," Clas informed her and told the attendant to airshoot the rest of the purchases to Nora's student quarters.

"Now, I'll do the spending," he said and steered her to the nearest eating house.

He didn't consult her, just punched out a high protein lunch, definitely luxury class.

"If I asked you what you wanted, you'd probably insist on ordering basic standard and this is not the day to be basic or standard. Not after your class performance."

That reminded Nora of what she'd directed at him and, abashed, she stared down at her hands. He started to laugh.

"Nora," he said in a wheedling tone which surprised her into looking up. "Do you know the real aim of Siffert's courses?" Then, before she could speak, he shook his head. "No, not the humanistic approach to computer programming. Think again."

Nora shook her head, too confused by the day's events to be able to think logically.

"It's to puncture the pomposity of computer programmers. You were the only one"—and Clas waggled a finger at her—"who wasn't trying to figure out what *technical* trick Siffert had up his sleeve this semester. The trick was not technical, of course, and the rest of us smart ape *d.h.* student programmers have been neatly deflated to size. By you and by Siffert. Oh, for the love of little apples, Nora Fenn, will you stop blushing? Ah, here's food. Real food! Not student pap or subbie wad."

Nora ate with as much relish as Clas, although she was shocked at such profligate expenditure of credit on food. Clas was amusing company, too, completely unlike Connor whose single-minded intensity in ingesting food left no time for conversation. Naturally, they discussed the course and Clas urged Nora to expand on her observations. Although it seemed to Nora that she was monopolizing the conversation, Clas gave no indication that he was bored by what she had to say. It wasn't until the sodium lights began glowing on the walkways, that Nora realized how late it was.

"I've got to get back to my Dormblock. I've an assignment to research," she said.

"Say, it is rather late. And I've work for tomorrow. And that essay next week."

"Well, you've more than enough material now to get an honors grade on Siffert's essay," Nora said as she settled her new cloak about her shoulders, smoothing the fabric with an appreciative hand. Then she noticed Clas staring at her in a guilty fashion.

"Did you think I'd—"

"Why not?" Nora was puzzled. "I was afraid you'd be furious with me for what I said in front of the class. And then you gave me this lovely treat . . ."

Why on earth did Clas look so stunned?

"Fenn . . . Nora, you've an alarming habit of changing state when no one expects it." He scrambled to his feet.

It was difficult to talk on the fast belt back to the University Complex but Clas kept one hand firmly about her waist and whenever she looked up at him, he smiled down at her and gave her a little squeeze. When they finally hopped over to the University Plaza, he took both her hands in his.

"What's your call sequence?"

She stammered it out, because she certainly hadn't expected him to ask for it. He gave her hands another squeeze.

"You'll be hearing from me, Nora Fenn. After I've turned in that essay."

And somehow, to her surprise, she believed him.

She had to take the cross campus belt to her dormitory quad, a trip she'd found rather chilling in the old cloak with the wet spring winds knifing around the corners. She pulled the new, wind-proof cloak more tightly around her, secure in its warmth and in the warmth of the day's miracles. Just wait until she showed Con . . .

The day's pleasures diminished. It'd been gratifying to have Clas Heineman interested in her, prod her into buying more clothes than were really needful, and luxuriating in a high-credit meal, but she'd rather have been able to share her triumph with Con. He'd shared her miseries.

She was half-tempted to go to the Commons and see if, by any chance, he might be about. But he wouldn't want to see her, not after the way she'd stormed out of his place yesterday. She'd even told him she'd cancelled his number from her program. She hadn't, of course, but he wouldn't know that.

She cudgeled her brain to think of some way of apologizing to him, of making amends. She couldn't help him with any of his courses because he was in a different Discipline. She'd darned all his socks and patched his good cloak where the fastening had torn. She'd . . .

"Hey, don't you speak to old friends now you're a *d.h.* with a 500 credit bonus?"

Con's bony fingers clutched her arm and swung her

about. She searched his long doleful face, with the shock of bird's nest hair, the rather ludicrous black handlebar moustache and saw only comic dismay in the rather wide-set intelligent grey eyes.

"You mean, you're still speaking to *me*?"

"Whaddaya mean? Am I still speaking to you?" He frowned and then, seeing they were attracting attention, pulled her out of the walkway into the angle of the building. "You mean, because of last night?"

She nodded, swallowing anxiously, watching the shift of expression on his mobile face. He was no Clas Heineman for looks but she felt much more comfortable with Connor Clarke. He took her by both arms now and gave her a rough shake, his thin fingers biting into her flesh.

"Aw, Nora," he said in a cajoling tone, his eyes tender, "friends can get mad at each other, you know, without printing out a major disaster. Besides," and he recovered himself with a characteristic shrug, "I was right and you ought to know it today. Say, gal, have I been strutting for you since I heard. A *d.h.* and 500 L.C.'s? And you scored off Clas Heineman and all those wire-brained plug-in artists . . ."

"The bonus was only 300 and Clas Heineman—"

"You watch that soft-soaper, Nora," and with one of his sudden switches, Con was in a sober phase again, "he may come trying to pick your brains 'cause he's got to maintain his . . ."

"He already has," Nora said, giggling. Now she knew what had disconcerted Clas Heineman in the food shop. He'd laid the charm on thick and figured he'd taken her in when he was pumping her about her drums. Only it had never occurred to her that that wasn't a fair exchange for the way she'd talked to him in class and for the meal he'd bought her. She did know more about people than programming.

"He has?" Con was nonplussed.

"He waylaid me after Siffert excused me and—"

"He didn't—"

"And"—Nora giggled again, twirling on her toes to show off her cape and the tunic suit underneath—"he made me spend money on new clothes. D'you like them? The student issue just tore right off me . . ."

"Huh? Oh, yeah, nice—tore right off you!" Con looked angry enough to take Clas Heineman apart bit by bit.

"Mind your thoughts, Con. Really, you're overreacting. Besides which, you caused the first rip in my s.i. last night. All Clas wanted was to pump me and, well, after the way I rounded on him in front of the class . . ."

"Nora!" Con roared her name with a most measuring possessiveness in his tone. "Nora . . ." Then he deflated with misery. "Nora, I was wrong last night. You don't have to gabble like me to relate to people. You *know!*"

"No, Con, *you* were right. And I am out of Comp Sci. Master Siffert is ordering me out," she said, patting Con's face to reassure him and grinning affectionately at his miserable expression.

"Well, then"—and Con brightened immediately, putting his arm around her waist and drawing her over to the cross campus walk—"since that's settled, let's go eat and you can tell me all about it. Mind you, I've heard some state-changing versions that don't sound like my Nora at all." He stopped in his tracks, so that she all but tripped over his feet. "That is, if you want to . . . after the way I treated you last night . . ."

Nora smiled up at him. "Oh, go tell it to the computer. It has to listen to you!"

SECOND NATURE

Chad Oliver

The rain came down, hard. It was an earthlike rain, a tropical rain: fat and heavy drops that fell almost in solid sheets, splashing into the muddy ground and forming shallow puddles and sudden, tiny streams. The rain was warm, if you monitored it from the ship and believed your instruments.

Paul Edmondson stood outside in that rain, his hands on his hips, and he didn't like it. His screen protected him but the water poured down the edges of his field and he could feel the damp chill. His boots were thick with mud.

Behind him towered the ship, an immense metallic cylinder that thrust with featureless precision upward into the gloom. The ship was a gigantic thing, dwarfing the rain-soaked plain on which it stood. Even shielded as it was, with only bright yellow beams of floodlights stabbing from its glistening hide, it hummed with power. There was more available energy in that ship, Paul knew, than could be mustered by the entire planet that provided its temporary resting place.

Ahead of him, caught between the lights and the

gray backdrop of the rain, the scene was very different. It was as though, in the space of a few hundred yards, time itself had slipped and become unjointed. Familiar as it was to him from many seedings on many worlds, Paul had never gotten used to the stark contrast. On the one hand, the ship—a monument to the technological creativity that had carried men to the stars. And on the other—

Animals?

No, something more and something less . . .

They stood there uncertainly, naked in the driving rain. There were fifty of them, half males and half females. They huddled together, wet and miserable. There was nothing about them that suggested intelligence or purpose. They did not speak, of course. They did not move. They simply stood there in the mud, facing the lights, waiting.

Two legs, two arms, one head. Wetly gleaming skin that had never known the sun. Two eyes, a nose, a mouth. Hands that clenched, feet that balanced and supported. A generous forehead masked by plastered hair. Cold and naked, they all looked alike unless you studied them closely; even the sex differences didn't amount to much without personality and individuality. They were all young—all precisely seventeen years, two months, and six days old. They were all equally unmarked by experience.

Human?

Well, maybe. Paul Edmondson tried to think of them that way. He was not always successful. They had human bodies, human brains. They could hunger and hurt. They could die. If you cut them open, they were human enough—bone for bone, organ for organ.

The trouble was, they were empty.

Blanks.

Potentially human, certainly. Born of man and woman, or at least grown from their fertilized sex cells. But then different. Nurtured in fluid-filled tanks, developing in mechanical wombs. Meat in a vat. Exercised electronically, watched by instruments, fed, cleaned. Stimulated, after a fashion. Asleep much of the time. The rest of the time—call it non-sleep.

The blanks were good at waiting. It was all they had ever known.

Paul stared at them. Impatiently, he dug out his pipe and fired it up. *He* was not built for waiting. He turned and looked back at the ship.

"Let's get on with it," he muttered.

As if on cue, the ship became active. There was no increase in the subdued humming sound that pulsed from somewhere within it, but its shining metallic flanks blurred in several places. What had been smooth and unbroken was suddenly pocked by fuzzy spots that seemed to swirl and flow in the rain. Circles of color appeared, indistinct at first and then strong and firm. Green, red, yellow—living tubes of color telescoped from the sides of the ship and bonded themselves to the muddy ground.

"It's about time," Paul said. Actually, the tubes were right on schedule.

The tubes of color blurred at their bottom ends and men and equipment moved out into the rain. Paul waved to Tino Sandoval and splashed across to him.

"Hey," Tino said. "This is a swamp. How are they doing?"

Paul clamped down on the stem of his pipe. "They love it. Soupy. Just like their little private fishbowls."

Tino shook his head. "There ought to be a better way. It's enough of a shock for them to come out of the tanks. Standing around like this—"

Paul shrugged, hiding his own concern. "They've got to get used to it, and the sooner the better. If they can't handle a little rain they're in for a short future."

"Yeah, and if we don't start pumping the goodies into them *we're* in trouble. Remember that Procyon foul-up. A couple of hours can make a big difference."

Paul smiled and knocked his pipe out against the palm of his hand. "I was waiting for you, friend. Let's go."

They got to work, moving with the precision of a well-drilled team. The mechanics of the operation were not complex. All of the tough stuff had been done months ago, before the ship had left the earth. The memory banks were stored and ready. The patterned circuits had been checked and rechecked. The computers were primed. All that remained was hooking up the electrodes and doing a little force-feeding.

Nothing to it.

Just a matter of pouring a lifeway into full-grown infants.

Just a small problem of creating a culture from scratch: language, symbols, dreams, values, experience, know-how.

Just a minor miracle: turning non-functioning animals into human beings.

The blanks were perfect subjects. They neither resisted nor tried to help. They stood where they were placed, unmoving, uncaring. Their eyes were empty. The rain pelted their naked bodies and it meant nothing to them.

Not for the first time, Paul wished that all this could be done aboard the ship. But the experiments done half a century ago, when the seeding program had started, had been conclusive. The conditioning worked better when the blanks were in what was to be their natural environment. The difference was not great, but it was significant.

They needed all the breaks they could get.

The technicians worked smoothly despite the mud and the rain. The blanks were connected, put to sleep. The bodies were dragged to grassy hillocks and arranged to eliminate the danger of drowning.

The machines were turned on. The transfer began.

Not just a culture. A new culture, designed for this world. A variant lifeway, part of the mosaic to enhance the potential of the human animal. A fresh beginning, one of many spread throughout the galaxy.

It would take many long hours to complete the transfer, of course. After that would come the months of observation, the rechecks, the necessary corrections. There were always bugs, subtle problems, unanticipated conditions . . .

The machines had not run five minutes when the alarm siren sounded from the ship. The screeching wail was sudden and overwhelming. The noise cut through the rain like a screaming knife.

Paul jerked upright, his heart hammering. He felt an icy dread. He knew what to do; they had all been drilled in this countless times. That siren *never* went off unless the danger was immediate, urgent, and definite.

Disconnect.

Abandon project.

Return to ship and prepare for liftoff.

Hurry!

There was no time to think, no opportunity for reflection. That would come later, if they were lucky. The blanks were doomed. They wouldn't have a chance—

Murderer.

Paul pulled the switches, started his machine skimming back. He sprinted toward the green tube, his boots sticking in the mud.

It was bedlam with the siren screaming and men cursing and equipment locking into place. Still, it was efficiently done. In minutes the tubes of color retracted into the ship. The floodlights went out.

With a barely perceptible surge of controlled power, the great ship lifted on her anti-gravs. Higher she went through rainy skies, up beyond the clouds—

A flash of light, a roar of thunder as the drive cut in.

The ship was gone.

On the planet's surface where the ship had been, the deep night shrouded the grassy plain. The blanks slept in terrible isolation, the rain washing their naked bodies.

They dreamed no dreams.

There was only one possibility, and that made that part of it simple. Paul Edmondson knew what had happened; he had known when he had first been jolted by the siren.

No ship ever abandoned its seed cargo except under precisely specified conditions. It was not a decision that could be lightly made, and the captain's discretionary powers were severely limited. The choice had to be the ultimate one. Them or us. A shipload of nearly three hundred functioning human beings or fifty blanks. People or bodies.

The blanks could not be reloaded on the ship. Once they had been removed from their tanks there was no reversing the process. They could not survive out of the tanks on the ship. There was no way to program them for that lifeway.

And the ship had to be saved; that was basic. Too much was at stake to risk the ship. Too much engineering, too much hard-won knowledge, too many secrets. The balance was delicate.

Man was strong, but he was not alone. The universe was vast, huge beyond comprehension, and it was not Man's private playground. There were Others.

Call them aliens, call them monsters, call them the stuff of nightmares. The names didn't matter. They were lifeforms so different from men that there was no basis for communication. They were destroyers, their motives unknown and unknowable. They fought and killed and obliterated anything different from themselves. They were tough, powerful, and relentless. Their starships were the equals of any made on Earth.

They were the Others. In a rational universe, perhaps they would not have existed. But they were there.

If they caught a ship on the ground, unprotected by the defense systems that ringed the earth and her primary bases, that ship was finished. When the presence of the Others was detected, there was one command that overruled everything else: *get into space.*

There, maybe, you had a chance.

Paul knew that the odds were no better than even on his own survival now. The ship might make it and it might not. He was faintly surprised to find that he felt no consuming terror. He was afraid, yes, but he had often known fear in space. The thing was somehow too impersonal to create horror; it was as remote and uncaring as the universe itself. And the two ships might maneuver for months before anything happened . . .

The rough part, actually, was that there was nothing that he could do. He had become a passenger and that was all. Like the other behavioral scientists, biologists, and medical personnel, Paul's job was to oversee the introduction of a new social unit, a new culture, on Capella V. He was an anthropologist, not a spaceman. There was no chance for him to be a hero, even in the sense of prodding the right answers out of the computers that were directing the ship.

He was excess baggage.

He could only wait it out.

He walked slowly through a passageway and took the lift down to the level where the blanks had been kept. He did not know why he went; something impelled him. He pressed the combination on the sealed door and entered the vault. The chamber was deserted. There was no sound except for the throbbing of the ship.

The empty tanks—surgically antiseptic sarcophagi shining under the white lights—were strangely still. The life-support systems, so carefully monitored on the outward voyage, were shut down. More than ever, the moisture-beaded tanks looked like swollen coffins in a forgotten necropolis. Paul reached out his hand and touched one. Cold, cold and clammy . . .

"Well, friends," he said, "you deserved something better." His voice was small and lost in the silent vault.

He wandered aimlessly through the chamber. The blanks had been his children, in a way; he had been responsible for them. He felt a gnawing sense of failure. To carry them across the light-years, half-alive, and then to dump them like so much inconvenient garbage—

Them or us. Yes, that was the theme of all human history, wasn't it? And prehistory too, for that matter. But it wasn't good enough. After all, the blanks were human too.

Almost.

"Damn," he said.

He wanted to *do* something. His own fate was out of his hands. The blanks were gone, sleeping under the rains that fell from a distant sky. They didn't have a chance, of course.

But still—

Paul turned abruptly and left the vault. The heavy door swung shut behind him. The lock mechanism whirred into place and the chamber was sealed again.

"Look," he said, loading his pipe with fresh tobacco and lighting it with an old-fashioned wooden match. "Are we absolutely dead sure the blanks can't make it?"

"Dead sure," Tino Sandoval said. "And the operative word is *dead*."

They sat around a small table in a comfortable lounge—the five of them. Paul Edmondson, lean and graying, his long legs stretched out in counterfeit relaxation. Tino Sandoval, the sociologist, his dark eyes bright and attentive. Art Embree, psychologist by trade, argumentative by temperament, a balding little man with sheer energy bubbling out of his ears. Kitemu Nzioki, biologist, his slender hands fiddling with a drink. And the doctor, Rick Bordie, slouched, skinny, quiet as a spider.

Art Embree snorted. "I'm not that certain about anything. I've seen too many pretty theories blow up in my face. I'll write them off when I see their bones, not before."

"But they're *blanks*," Tino said. "Facts are facts."

"Not quite blanks," Kitemu said quietly. "Remember, the transfer had started. That is a fact. They had a five-minute input. And the term *blank* is inaccurate anyway. They get some conditioning in the tank. Nothing much, but something."

"If it comes to that," Art pointed out, "they're *born* with something—or hatched, or whatever the word is. They come from fertilized sex cells. Genetically, they're no different from us. Culture and learning aren't the whole story, you know. Have you forgotten Lorenz and Tinbergen? The genes carry a good deal of coded information."

"Nuts," Tino said. "You'll be giving me the racial memory bit next."

Paul jabbed with his pipe, trying to convince himself, "Man is an animal. He may be a peculiar kind of an animal, but that's an animal body he lugs around with him. There ain't no such thing as an animal that begins life with *nothing*. It may take time to mature, it may need specific stimuli to bring it out, but it's there. You don't have to teach a cat to purr or a dog to bark or a fish to swim. And there's plenty built into the human animal, too. We're not just empty pots waiting for the miracle fluid of culture."

"Okay," Tino said. "I went to school. So what's in the blanks?"

They kicked that one around, scribbling on notesheets, trying out ideas on each other. It was a session similar to countless others that all of them had known; it was as much a part of their lives as eating or drinking. The fact that the discussion took place in a starship that was fighting to survive made no difference. Indeed, it heightened the pleasure they all took from wrestling with an interesting problem. It was a lot better than staring at the walls and counting the seconds.

So what *was* in the blanks?

To start with, they had whatever was inborn in man. They had a capacity for culture, a capacity for language, a capacity for symbolic thinking. Capacity: that was a weasel word. It was more than that. The principles were still far from clear, but at the very least the human animal had tendencies to develop along present lines . . .

There was more. There were rudimentary things that were necessary to any functioning human animal anywhere. Scientists did not know how much of this was carried genetically. It was, however, essential no matter what particular form the lifeway was to take. Therefore, it was fed in, over the years, while the bodies grew in the tanks.

Simple things.

Food versus non-food. Danger, safety, caution. Facial expressions. Young-old. Male-female. Darkness and light. Territory. Security, comfort. Grasping, standing, walking. Sensitivity to temperature. Vocal sounds. Avoidance of pain.

Nothing much.

And what had the five-minute input contained, while the machines had run?

Pitifully little. Just a kind of prologue, a preparation for the actual transfer of concrete data and invented experience. An animal awareness, an awakening of the individual. And curiosity, a stimulation of the brain to make it receptive to the knowledge it was about to receive.

The knowledge that had never come.

No real *content.* No culture, no language, no tricks of survival painfully acquired over the millennia.

"So what we've got," said Art Embree, "is a manlike primate starting out from scratch. An ape that's got a good brain with nothing in it."

"It sounds like a recipe for oblivion," Tino said.

Paul smiled and poured himself a drink. "The apes did pretty well until we came along," he pointed out. "They had some advantages the blanks don't have—social experience, for instance. But they didn't have human brains. Maybe that's the equalizer."

Kitemu frowned. "You really think they have a chance?"

Paul looked at him. "Maybe they've got a better chance than we do," he said quietly.

"Doc," asked Art Embree, "what's the medical prognosis? Can they live?"

Rick Bordie spoke slowly, choosing his words with care. He was not a man enchanted by the sound of his own voice. "Physically, they are healthy seventeen-year-old males and females. They are completely free from disease; their environment has been sterile. Right now, they are very strong—stronger than any of us here. They need to learn how to use their bodies, but they have been exercised in the tanks. Their reflexes are good. They are quick. They have had their protective injections. The danger is that they may encounter an unknown disease for which they have no immunity. I think that danger is slight, but it is real —that's why they should have been monitored in the usual fashion. However, they *can* survive physically if they can find food and water. My opinion is that they will."

Tino stood up nervously, easing his cramped leg muscles. "Dammit, you guys are optimistic to the point of lunacy. Those blanks are *not* apes, and they're not lions or termites either. They are plain old human beings *without* any of the advantages that men have had—without any of the things that have turned men into powerful animals. They don't even have a spear, to say nothing of a bow and arrow. They don't even have the *idea* of a spear. They have no fire, no nothing. Don't give me that jazz about inventing significant human culture in a week or six months or a generation. It's impossible, and you know it."

Paul drew on his pipe and aimed a neat smoke ring at the ceiling. "As an anthropologist, I have to agree with you, Tino. But you're forgetting a few things. To start with the obvious, what about the first men, wherever you draw the line? *They* had no real culture either—no more traditional knowledge than a band of apes. They made it, somehow. If they hadn't, we wouldn't be here. And creatures like the Australopithecines were not big husky brutes, either. They probably weren't as strong physically as we are."

"Okay," Kitemu said. "You started with the obvious.

What else have you got? I'd like to be convinced—so would Tino— but it's going to take more than rosy hopes to pull those blanks through."

"Try this," Paul said, his mind racing. "Consider the situation they face. They don't have to worry about the Others; our voracious friends are chasing *us* and they never bother non-technological settlements on the ground. To them, the blanks are just so many grasshoppers or rabbits. With me so far? Capella V is an essentially earthlike planet; that's why it was chosen. There are no people there, of course—the planet never developed an intelligent culture-bearing species or it would have been closed to us under the Charter. So all the blanks will have to cope with are the normal hazards of existence: the environment, sickness, other animals."

"And themselves," Art Embree said. "Don't forget that. Most of man's troubles have always come from other men."

Tino laughed with exasperation. "Is *that* all? Just storms and cold and wind? Just their own natures, which may be unique to say the least? Just hunger, with no way to get food? Just carnivores that can rip their defenseless hides to shreds? Come on!"

Paul shook his head. "I know I'm pleading a case. I feel guilty; we all do. But there *is* a case. Look, they can't be natural prey for any animal on Capella V—that's true by definition."

"That doesn't mean they will never be attacked," Art Embree objected. "A man is not natural prey for a lion, either—or a snake. Just the same, lions have killed men, and eaten them, too. Snakes have struck. Even non-carnivores can get into the act; a fair number of Kitemu's ancestors were killed by elephants, for instance. And the blanks—assuming that they live for awhile—are totally helpless."

"Are they? I've heard that one all my life." Paul clenched his fist and slammed it down hard on the table. "Who says man is so weak and defenseless without his weapons, anyway? Isn't that a myth like so many of the ideas we have about the human animal?"

"It's no myth," Tino said. "Go wrestle a gorilla sometime—or even a chimpanzee."

"I don't believe it." Paul stroked his pipe to calm himself down. "What kind of men are we talking about? College professors who write books telling us how feeble we are? Invalids? Babies? Businessmen who push paper all day? Those blanks are young and healthy. Look, I've heard all the stock lines. I even believed them once: man isn't as strong as a gorilla, he can't fly like a hawk, he can't see like an eagle, he doesn't have claws like a tiger or teeth like a lion, he can't run like an antelope or dig like a mole or swim like a tuna or climb like a gibbon. So what?"

"So he's weak and defenseless," Kitemu said. "That's what you're saying, isn't it?"

"No, that's *not* what I'm saying. Can't you see the fallacy in all those statements? You take the human animal and match him against the very best in specialized categories; of course he doesn't look good. But try it another way. He's a lot stronger than most animals his size, and he has more endurance. He can outrun a rabbit. He can swim a heck of a lot better than a horse or a rhino—let's see them try the English Channel sometime. He's got superb eyesight. He can out-climb a bull anytime. He can kick, he can choke, he can tear, he can punch. His teeth are plenty good enough to bite a small snake in half. And that's not all."

"There's more?" Art Embree smiled.

"Yes, there's more. All these comparisons always match *one* man against some other animal. Why? Man is a pack animal and always has been. He lives in groups, he hunts in groups, he fights in groups. There's nothing startling about that, but it does make a difference. It's one thing to catch a man alone, and something else to tackle ten or fifteen. There's still more. He can throw—rocks, sticks, anything. Just let him pick up a rock and he is a deadly fighting machine."

"Isn't that culture?" Tino objected. "Doesn't man have to be taught?"

Paul shrugged. "I don't know. Nobody *knows.* Some of it is probably instinctive, if I may use that dirty word. I suspect that pack animals are pretty much born that way, if they are not inhibited by some fancy experiment. There's no doubt that a chimpanzee will pick up a stone on occasion or brandish a stick of wood if it is threatened. Call it culture if it makes you feel better, but why can't a blank do the same? And he's got a brain, remember. He's got a better brain than anything else on that planet. He may not have any experience yet, but he's not Joe Stupid."

"So we can all relax," Tino said. "Man wins again. It's very reassuring."

"No, I don't say that. I just say they've got a chance, just like we do. That's all."

"All of our technology may not save *us*, friends," Art Embree said. "But if we could just make it—go back and see what happened—help out the survivors and get them started in the right direction . . ."

The five men looked at nothing, their fingers toying with writers and pipes and glasses. They became aware again of the throbbing ship around them. They sensed the immense power of the interstellar drive that twisted them through the smoky gray folds of space prime.

They felt the cold that was beyond temperature.

They felt the sweat that dampened their hands.

And they felt the presence of the Others, out there somewhere, probing, seeking, following . . .

He opened his eyes. There was brightness, pain. He closed his eyes, stirred. He felt heat on one side of him. On the other, cold. Cold and damp.

He lay where he was, waiting. He had always waited. He did not know what he was waiting for. Nothing happened.

He was still, quiescent. Time passed. The sensation of heat increased. It was not comfortable. He waited. He was not eased. That was strange. Always before, he had only had to wait if something was wrong and the something went away.

He felt . . . different. There was no buoyancy. Fluid

did not touch his skin. Something rough and sharp dug at his cold side. There had been nothing hard in his world.

He waited. Nothing happened.

He began to hurt. Slowly, he moved. He moved away from pain. He turned, rolled. His hot side cooled, was soothed. His damp side warmed. That was better.

He sighed. He waited again. He dozed. The discomfort came back. He felt empty, depleted. He turned again. There was a brief easing and then more pain.

He opened his eyes a second time. He was more careful now. He did it slowly, a little at a time. The brightness returned. Not as bad this time, not as harsh.

He had seen light before, but not like this. The light was above him. It was huge. It was hot. It hurt.

His mind engaged the problem, uncertainly. The light was hot. It was hurting him.

Move.

Away from the light.

He struggled up on his hands and knees. He stood up, swayed, fell. He lay there, waiting. Not good. Pain. He stood up again. It took him a long time.

Strange. Different.

He stood there, a creature without a name. Very slowly, he shaded his eyes with his hand. He turned in a circle, staring at the world in which he found himself.

He saw colors that he had never seen before. He did not know what they were. They assaulted his senses, stabbing him with vividness. One color above, surrounding the bright glare of hotness. Other colors down where he was. Many colors, but one most of all. A cool color that rested his eyes. He drank it in, tasting wetness in his mouth.

Textures that were new to him, and yet half-remembered. A stirring against his skin. Not fluid, very slight. Another sensation against his feet. He knelt down, clumsily, and felt it with his hands. Different things. Some stringy, not hard. Some damp and yielding. Some sharp things. Hard.

He stood again. He noticed . . . forms . . . sprawled on the surface. Many forms. He studied them. They were unlike other things that he saw. They seemed . . . something that he knew . . .

He looked at himself, touching himself with his hands. He looked at them. He compared. He grunted, satisfied. Yes, they were like him. He lost interest.

He alone stood. That made him different.

The pain returned. He was hot. His skin hurt. An emptiness gnawed at his belly. He did not know what to do. He stood motionless, waiting. There was no relief.

He used his eyes, searching. The glare bothered him. He saw an area of non-brightness. It was a cool color. It looked soft and damp. His mouth watered again and he licked his lips. He had no real concept of distance or of movement. He was where he was. The cool place was not-here.

Puzzled, he shuffled his feet, turning. The pain did not go away. He groaned.

He made no conscious decision. He began to move, walking uncertainly. He was drawn by the cool-colored place. He stumbled more than once, but he did not fall. He kept going through the bright hotness. The cool area got bigger. He could feel it.

He touched it. The walking became difficult. Things scraped at his skin. Hard, sharp things. Almost as high as he was, but not rigid. They gave when he pushed through them. He could smell wet coolness. He heard a fluid gurgling sound. He went toward it, staggering.

The glare . . . stopped. He was less hot. Tall things around him now, big cool things, reaching up. He saw liquid. Much of it, moving. More than in the world he had known.

He smiled. He knew about fluid. He walked into it and fell, trying to pull it around him.

He screamed. Cold. The shock numbed him. He felt betrayed. The liquid should have been warm—warm and soothing . . .

He twisted, crawled, clawed his way out. He sprawled, gasping. He waited, breathing hard.

Slowly, he eased his efforts. His skin dried. There was no glare. He was cooler. He had swallowed some of the fluid. It hurt, but it was a good hurt.

Cautiously, he extended his hand. He touched the liquid. It was still cold, but it did not surprise him now. He wet his hand, his arm. He touched the hot places on his skin. He wet his hand again. He licked it. It was sweet. *Good.*

This is a good place.

He relaxed, dozed. He put more fluid in his mouth. His head cleared. He felt a sense of well-being, almost of pride. He had done something. *He* had done something.

He stood, looked back the way he had come. He could see the glare outside the cool place. He felt a sudden unease.

Something . . .

He remembered.

Out there. Where he had been. Forms, shapes. Like him. Down, not moving. Heat.

He shook his head. He was confused. This was a good place. That was not.

A new idea: *why*. They were like him. They were where he had been. This was better. Why did they stay there?

He puzzled over it, worried it. He could not let it go. He did not like it. He wanted to wait, to enjoy. But he kept thinking . . .

The unease overcame the comfort. Again, there was no conscious decision. He moved, going back.

The glare and the heat stopped him for a moment, but it was familiar to him now. He knew he could get out of it by retracing his steps. That made it easier. He moved on. He moved more quickly, more certainly. He knew where he was going.

He found them. A few stood, as he had done. Some were down, with their eyes open. Others were still; their eyes closed. He studied them, checking. Yes, they were like him.

Heat. Pain. He did not know what to do. He stood there, waiting. They ignored him. The pain increased.

Go back.

He turned, thinking of the cool place and the fluid that sounded. He started, stopped.

They were like him. This was not a good place. The cool place was better. If—

Another new idea: *how.* And another: *together.*

He knew what he wanted to do. He did not know how to do it. He waited, but not for long. *No. Waiting will not work, not any more.*

The glare and the heat irritated him. He had to do something. Move, action, not alone . . .

He went back, walked up to one of the standing ones. He reached out to touch him. The standing one growled and raised his hand.

He turned away, puzzled. He knelt and touched one of the forms that was down. It twitched but did not pull away. Eyes looked at him.

He moaned. He did not know what to do. He hurt.

Together.

His hands grasped, held. He pulled. He lifted. The form came up, stood. He clutched it.

He walked, holding it, taking it with him. When it fell, he picked it up. He kept it moving. Small pleasure sounds came from his throat. It was harder than walking alone, but it was better.

It took him a long time, but time was nothing to him. He half-carried it to the cool place, the soft place. He put it down next to the moving liquid. He drank.

He saw another. It had followed.

Yes.

He went back, through the bright light and the hotness. He was tired, but it was easier now. His body responded to him. He moved with more assurance. He felt—strong.

He had a good feeling.

He would get them all.

Sleep came, despite the emptiness within him. He slept deeply, not moving. He dreamed images. His mind worked while he slept, absorbing, storing, sorting . . .

Cold. He awakened, opening his eyes. He saw grayness. The bright glare above the shading screen was gone. There was something else. Smaller, cooler. It was hard to see, but it was not really dark. He was not alarmed. He liked the color of gray. It reminded him of something a long time ago—

He listened. Sounds. A murmur of liquid moving. A whisper in the shading things. Rustlings near him. Other sounds he could not identify. A sharp, penetrating call from somewhere. Repeated. He shivered. He felt a prickling sensation on his head.

He was very cold. He ached. His skin burned through the cold, making him shiver. The emptiness cramped him.

This time, he did not wait. He crawled to the moving fluid. He drank. It did not help much. It was cold in him.

He sought warmth. There was only one source. The

like-hims, sprawled there in the grayness. He went to them. He lay down next to one. He held it in his arms. Soft. Warm. It sighed and stirred, then was quiet. He made a pleasure sound.

Better.

He slept again.

When he opened his eyes, the bright hotness was above him. He could feel it through the shade things. He could see clearly in the shadows. There were colors in the world.

He moved his arms, releasing the other. He looked at it, studying it. Like him, but not quite the same. There were differences. He saw that now.

He was not interested. The emptiness in him was everything. It twisted him. It demanded.

He got up. He used his eyes, searching. The ache almost blinded him, but he kept looking. He did not know what he was after. He frowned, trying to think. When he was cold, he sought warmth. When he was hot, he sought coolness. When he thirsted, he drank. When he was empty . . .

He remembered. It had been taught to him long ago, in that other world where he had waited. Food and not-food. Food was for emptiness.

He felt excitement at the thought of food. That was what he needed. Yes, but where was it? What was it?

He kept using his eyes, seeking. It did not work. There were so many things, so many colors. He could not decide.

He used his hands and his mouth and his tongue.

He tried substances. Hard, soft, wet, dry. He spat them out. Not-food. He crawled and he walked. He pulled things, broke things, licked things. He whimpered.

He saw a bright color, bright but cool. Up, not down. Hanging in the shade-things. He touched it. Soft. He ripped at it, crushing it between his hands. It was wet but not fluid. He smeared it on his mouth. He licked it.

It tasted sweet. He swallowed some. It was in him. He reached up and grabbed another. He crammed it in his mouth and swallowed it whole. Food. Food was for emptiness. He ate another and another and another.

He began to hurt. He crawled back to the moving liquid and put his face in it. He gagged, choked. He pulled himself out of the fluid and collapsed in the shade.

This time, he waited. He could not move. The cramping was worse, then subsided. The emptiness was gone. He felt a subtle, growing strength.

He was drowsy. He felt easy and relaxed.

He closed his eyes, resting. A faint smile played at the corners of his sweet-stained mouth.

There was brightness and grayness. Sometimes there were two brightnesses at once, one of them much larger than the other. Sometimes the grayness did not come and it was dark. It was a definite cycle, however; there was regularity to it. It could be known, anticipated.

The rhythm of change continued. Glaring light and gentle gray glow. Blackness speckled with tiny points of light. Heat and cold. Wind that blew and rain that fell.

It was less strange, now. It was a part of them.

The cycle went on.

He learned and the strength within him grew. He knew who he was and discovered pride. He had been the first. The first to walk, to seek, to drink, to eat. He had led the way. He was the First One.

He knew his companions. They were all the same and all different. Some were males, as he was. Others were females. Some were strong and some were not. Some could climb better than others. Some were quick, others slow. Eyes were different, and hair.

One male never awakened. He was very still. His skin was cold. After a time, he smelled. First One dragged him away and left him.

He learned many things. He knew about the water; he found its bubbling source and followed its moving trail. He knew about fruits and berries and nuts and roots. He knew the difference between trees and grass and bushes. He understood that the rain that fell was like the water in the stream. He knew how much sunglare he could take and when to avoid it.

He knew who would help him and who needed help. He knew where to find comfort and when to growl. He knew that being First One meant responsibility.

He knew that there were other things in his world.

Things that were not-us. He saw and heard them in the trees and in the sky. He heard calls in the night. Once, out on the grassy plain where he had first awakened, he saw some big things moving. He ran from them. They did not follow.

He knew colors. He recognized the blue of the sky, the green of the grass, the redness of fruit. He was still astonished by colors. He drank them in, learning them.

He knew so much. It was incredible to him how empty he had been. He relished his new knowledge, all of it. He knew the joy of living.

He did not yet know tears.

A day came, like other days. First One and three of the people had wandered a long way, leaving the grove of trees. It had been growing colder and they were searching for a warm place, a warm place with water and food.

They had crossed the level grassland and worked their way up a rocky hill. It was hard going and it was not good. It seemed that the higher they climbed the colder it became. The wind blew against them, whining. The shadows lengthened.

First One braced himself and rested. He was pleased to find that he could see a long distance. There was nothing to block his eyes. He could even see the trees that had sheltered them, and they were far. It was, he decided, a place to come to examine his world, sometime. But now it was cold and night was on the way.

They started back, wearily. First One was annoyed that he had not found warmth. It did not occur to him that he might never find it.

They descended the hill and walked across the grassland. It was getting darker but he could still see. Long before they reached the trees, he sensed that something was wrong. There was a difference, a feeling.

Unease . . .

Danger!

He broke into a run. He was First One. He should be there, where the danger was. He could do something.

Just as he got to the trees, he heard a deep hissing growl. It was not a people noise. He heard a scream, suddenly choked off. That was one of his kind. It was a female. He knew her.

He went to the sounds, crashing through the bushes. His breath came hard and fast. He shouted a new noise.

He saw them. A snarling furry thing, bigger than he was. A tail, lashing. Teeth that flashed, claws that tore. The female, down. Red fluid on her skin. One arm—off.

He did not hesitate. He charged, teeth bared, arms swinging. He hurled himself at the thing. He caught it. He felt power—

Pain. Hurt. Shock.

He was thrown back, down. His head hit something. There was wetness on him. The furry thing was all over him. Strong, strong. He smelled him. He felt claws that ripped.

He rolled, kicked. He tried to crawl away. He was not fast enough. The thing was on him. He cried out.

The three who had been with him came. They attacked, growling. The thing turned to face them, its great tail twitching. It roared.

First One staggered to his feet. He learned. He knew now he must not get in close. He grabbed a stick to make his arm longer. He swung it, as hard as he could. One of the men was down now, red on his chest. Another picked up a rock, threw it.

More people came out of the trees, shouting.

The furry thing whirled, hissed. It was not hurt but it was confused now. It ran, moving in great gliding bounds. It disappeared into the gathering darkness of the grasslands.

First One could not stand. He fell to his knees. He touched the sticky redness on him. Warm. His warmth. There was no pain. Only weakness, depletion.

And shocked surprise.

He had been strong. He had tasted success, many times. He had not known that he could fail.

He collapsed, shaking. He felt hands on his body, lifting him. He knew he was being carried. He felt it when they washed him with cool water. He knew the smell of his own nest.

He shuddered. He had no strength. He was cold.

A form came into his nest. Warm. Soft. He knew her. She made comforting noises. She held him.

He could not hold on, could not think. He slipped away, falling . . .

He slept.

The starship maneuvered through the gray reaches of space prime, its computers plotting vectors and strategies. There could be no mistakes, not here. Mistakes were fatal. There were no second chances.

Controlled power is not infinite and sealed systems must ultimately have renewal. There came a time when evasive action was not enough.

The ship made its move.

It attacked with maximum surprise and force. Beams lanced out, ice-white and hot-red. Raw concentrated energy pulsed from the transmitters. The great missiles were launched: spacecraft in their own right, locked on their target, warheads set.

The ship of the Others was not caught napping. That awesome shape-changing fish of the deeps responded. Screens flickered into being, beams flashed. But the ship of the Others was late, a fraction of a second late.

It was hit, hard.

It glowed, expanded—and burst, a brief and temporary sun where there could be no suns.

It was gone.

The starship was damaged, but not critically. It could function, and did.

It drove through the folds of space prime. It seemed to go on forever in nothingness.

In time, the ship wrenched joltingly back into normal space. It was battered and clumsy and it emerged perilously close to its own family of planets.

But it made it.

It set its course for home, limping in.

It was nearly three years before the new starship returned to the binary system of Capella. The giant yellow primary burned against the blackness of space, almost obscuring its smaller companion sun. Capella V, a world of blue and white and green, waited.

The ship was loaded and ready. A full complement of blanks floated in the nourishing vats, neither awake nor asleep. The voyage could not be wasted. There were alternate targets, but Capella V was the obvious choice. The Capella system was forty-two light-years from Earth. Even utilizing the folds of space prime, that was no casual jaunt. The experts at home had virtually written off the first abortive seeding attempt.

They had to try again, and this time complete the job. A man without a culture was nothing; he had no chance. The ship had the fresh blanks. It had the detailed lifeway, stored and ready for transfer.

The seeding *had* to succeed, not only here but in many places. There was no more room on Earth. The home culture was static, stagnant, feeding on itself. The trouble with a single planet-wide culture was that it tended to freeze. There were no alternatives, no variants, no new ideas.

But those variants could be tried on other worlds.

Human beings could be seeded—not as helpless babies, but as strong young men and women. A culture could be fed in—any culture. Hunters, farmers, industrialists. A thousand lifeways, each with its own potential.

Man could survive with promise, even when Earth was old.

That was the reason for Capella V.

Of course, the starship could not proceed blindly. It could not assume too much. There *had* been a seeding here, however strange it had been.

If any of those people were still alive . . .

They would have to check *very* carefully.

Paul Edmondson would see to that.

The starship rested in orbit, a huge metallic cylinder that floated on the thin edge of space. The autoscouts went down through the sky. Gleaming spheres, they probed and searched and recorded. It did not take them long. They knew what they sought, and they knew where to look.

They returned, docked, and disgorged their data.

And the five men sat again around a table in a quiet room aboard a starship. This time they were not playing a game of make-believe. This was more than an intellectual puzzle to distract the mind. They had a decision to make, and the authority to make it.

"It's incredible," Kitemu Nzioki said. "As a biologist, I hardly know what to say. There are forty-five of them left, plus eight living infants. They have *increased* their population."

Doc Bordie smiled his thin spider smile. "I *told*

you they were healthy young animals. There's not a one of them that's twenty-one years old yet, remember. And those injections are effective, we know that."

Tino Sandoval threw up his hands. "I was wrong. Okay. What do we do now? We can't seed again with them there; it's against regulations. We can't just leave them. And, dammit, they're not quite blanks anymore. Can we adapt a lifeway design to what they already have, build on it? That's never been done before. That's why we use blanks."

"We can do it," Art Embree said. "They haven't got much. We could catch them easily enough, recondition them. That isn't the question. *Should* we tamper with them now? *That's* the question."

"I'm with you." Paul Edmondson fired up his pipe. "Look at what they've done in three years. Kitemu used the right word: incredible. Do we just step in and take it all away from them? Do we just muscle in with some prefabricated culture that *we* happen to like? I don't think so."

"Take *what* away from them?" Kitemu asked, shuffling through the data sheets. "They have no language. They have no fire. They have no real shelters—just piles of thorny brush with nests hidden in them. They have no effective weapons. They can't even hunt. They're just—scavengers."

"They have survived," Art Embree said quietly. "They have reproduced. They have cared for their young. They have worked out the rudiments of a social order. Who are we to sit in judgment? Are our own lifeways all that great?"

Paul Edmondson stood up, nervously. He paced the floor. "Look," he said. "The whole purpose of the seed program is to create new ideas, new directions. This is a real opportunity. If *we* dream something up, we use the old ideas, no matter how we modify them. Our thinking flows through familiar channels; it has to. If we let them alone, anything can happen. Cultural evolution does not have to repeat itself; there's nothing foreordained about it. These people may come up with something we've never dreamed of."

"Yeah," said Tino. "Anything can happen. That includes extinction. They don't *have* a culture yet, for my money. We can't just abandon them."

"I don't know." Art Embree rubbed his balding head. "I just don't know."

"Some of *our* cultures haven't worked," Kitemu reminded them. "We don't have all the answers."

Paul Edmondson groped for words, trying to express what he believed. He felt that he had betrayed those people once. That time, the choice had not been his. This time, it was. Those people had beaten fearful odds. They had earned a crack at their own destiny, whatever it was. He recognized the irony in his choice. He wanted to leave them again.

But this time it was different. *They* were different. Perhaps he too had changed.

"Look," he said. "Those are our kids down there, in a way. All these years, all these countries, all these thousands and thousands of years, we have tried to figure out what was best for them. We were the elders. We meant well, sometimes we did well. But now, maybe for the first time, we can see what *they* can do. I say let's step aside and give them their chance. Don't they deserve it, on just one world in all the universe?"

There was a long silence.

"I remind you that there are alternate targets," Art Embree said finally. "We will have to proceed elsewhere in any case, to seed our blanks. The choice concerns what we do here. Do we build a lifeway for them, or do we let them go it alone? We'll need a vote, I think. Are we ready?"

The men nodded.

The vote was taken.

Tino Sandoval alone voted for interference.

The starship would not land.

First One had returned to the high rocky hill, where the cool wind blew and the sights were long. He went there often. It was a good place to think.

He seemed taller now, and leaner. His weathered body was hard and scarred. The cunning of experience was in his eyes.

He could see the grove of trees where his people were. He knew that they were safe. He thought of his mate and his young one. The memory warmed him.

He heard the distant thunder of the departing starship above the sky. The sound faded. It meant nothing to him.

He smiled with a happiness he could not name. He stood there on the hill, a rock in his fist, looking out at his world.

TAPPING OUT
Barry N. Malzberg

I

The machine is merciful. I must remember that. The process, though painful, is essentially kind and leads only to the most reasonable of ends. Deep in the drugs and sensors link, I descend and at the end of that flight find my father. He is pretty much as I remembered him although somewhat older with a thin taint of incompetence oozing from him—incompetence and fear. This is the way it should have been.

"No," he says, gesturing, "you cannot do that." We are having another one of our meaningless arguments about my career or my late hours or perhaps, simply, about our inability to bear one another. The issues are not important. "I will not permit it," he says, backing up a step and teetering against the wall of our living room. "Not at all."

"Yes, you will," I say, coming right to the point. "Yes, you will; you *will* allow me to do that because I am more important than you and I am not afraid of you—and your whole life is worthless anyway," and with surpassing ease I lean forward, close the gap between us (I seem to be moving through gelatin) and begin to throttle him by his wizened neck. "I can do anything I want to do because I am no longer afraid," I say and my father says, "*ulp*" and dissolves underneath me to the floor and he gasps, "*yes, you're right, I'm sorry*" and flaps helplessly beneath me. I feel the strength, the strength and the triumph building: I have at last conquered my father. As I take in my first breath of power, watching him struggle below, I begin to feel better, better than I have in months, but before I can truly appreciate and enjoy this, I am yanked away. At growing speed, I move far away from there and surface, as always, to the technicians who lean over with gloved fingers to take the leads away. I feel electrodes imploding within and at some pity in the technicians' gestures, shame as well.

Nonetheless, I sense that I am progressing.

II

At the new session with my doctor we agree that I have made strides and am showing a new maturity and am well on my way to a full discharge from the Institue; nevertheless, he warns me that I must take nothing for granted. "The process is risky, still experimental," he says. "In the fantasies, you are assuming a far more purposeful role in relation to these authority figures but too much cannot be taken for granted. The test will come when you must live in the world again. Whether you will be able to carry over the reconstructed to the real." *Reconstructed to the real.* My therapist is a bird-like man with displaced eyes who insists upon talking to me in this way. We have never had what might be called a relationship. "You are becoming far more dominant in these fantasies," he says, "and this is all to the good, but transfer is vital. You are only seventeen years old, however, and there is much promise. A younger person such as yourself has more of a chance. Later on, one rigidifies."

One rigidifies. It is really impossible to take my therapist seriously. But our sessions are mandatory. It is the machine that will make me well and I will come out of here in due course and live my life with gentle power.

The first thing I will do in my new life is to tell my father how I hate him. Then I will say the same to my mother and after that—how I look forward to it!—I will take care of all the others.

III

At the next process, locked in the sensors again, I reconstruct a girl I barely remember who once turned me down for a date. In this reconstruction I launch myself upon her like a bird and have my way with her without resistance: at the end she cries my name and I pitch over the edge to find myself once again throttling my father.

IV

"You have got to modify your responses," the therapist says. He looks slightly worried but on the other hand, it may only be a gastric disturbance: I refuse to be sensitive to him. "The point of the process is re-enactment not indulgence. We want you to be able to review your relationships—the relationships you have had, I mean to say—in light of what you should have done but we do not believe in impossible aggression." He shakes his head, considers certain records before him which presumably contain the content of my activities under the machine. I really did not expect these to be secret but it is somewhat dismaying to realize that everything I have done under the privacy of the sensors is, in a sense, public record. "This is very expensive treatment," my therapist says vaguely. "You are costing your parents a great deal of money; I tell you this frankly so that you will treat the opportunity with the respect it deserves. You are here not to indulge yourself but to get well. If you do not cooperate and use the process in the way it is intended you are abusing it." He taps his desk, looks at the wall, turns back to me. "You have a schizoid condition," he says. "I know you know that. You have a chance for a complete cure but you must cooperate and do better."

I promise him that I will, looking at his blotched, shrunken neck and thinking of other things.

V

"You must cooperate and do better," my therapist in the sensors says and I say, "Go to hell, Jack," and fling myself upon him, screaming, attempting to choke the life out of him. He is much livelier than my father and it is difficult but at length I succeed. It feels good to have killed my therapist and I am enjoying the various sensations of power and fulfillment. But before

I can truly luxuriate, I feel myself being yanked to the surface rudely, struggling like a fish in sand, and when I come to myself I am lying on the table under wires, as always, and the technicians are looking at me in a terribly unfriendly fashion. I wonder if I have displeased them.

VI

My father comes to visit me and, after a while, says that I am not doing very well. I have not responded to treatment. Further treatment is contraindicated and I am being discharged. I will be sent to the state hospital tomorrow for more conventional treatment and, of course, my father is sorry. Also, it appears to be my fault. According to reports my father has heard, I have never cooperated.

I do what I always did with my father in difficult moments: I collapse against him and beg forgiveness but all the time behind my closed eyes, I see the images of how in the machine I killed him, and knowing this—knowing that I have done it—I know that I will never truly be the same again. Nor will I be different. Schizoid condition the therapist said. I am seventeen years old.

HOW TO BE ETHNIC IN ONE EASY LESSON

Poul Anderson

Adzel talks a lot about blessings in disguise, but this disguise was impenetrable. In fact, what Freeman Snyder handed me was an exploding bomb.

I was hard at study when my phone warbled. That alone jerked me half out of my lounger. I'd set that instrument to pass calls from no more than a dozen people, all of whom I'd told shouldn't bother me about anything less urgent than a rogue planet on a collision course.

You see, my preliminary tests for the Academy were coming up soon. Not the actual entrance exams—I'd face those a year hence—but the tests determining whether I should be allowed to apply for admission. That policy can't be blamed on the Brotherhood. Not many regular spaceman's berths become available annually, and a hundred young Earthlings clamor for each of them. The ninety-nine who don't make it . . . well, mostly they try to get work with some company that will someday possibly assign them to a post somewhere outsystem, or they grit their teeth and save their money till at last they can go as shepherded tourists.

At night, in my car out by the ocean, away from city glow, I look upward and am ripped apart with longing, too. As for the occasional trips to Luna, last time—several months ago when the flit was my sixteenth birthday present—I found my eyes running over at sight of that sky.

But now tensor calculus was giving me trouble. The phone announced: "Freeman Snyder."

I couldn't refuse my principal counselor. His word has too much to do with my evaluation as a potential student for the Academy. "Accept," I gulped, as his lean features flashed on. "Greeting, sir."

"Greeting, Jim," he said. "How are you?"

"Busy," I hinted.

"Indeed. You are a rather intense type, eh? The indices show you're apt to work yourself into the ground. A change of pace is downright necessary."

Why are we saddled with specialists who judge our lives on the basis of a psychoprofile and a theory? If I'd been apprenticed to a Master Merchant of the Polesotechnic League, *he* wouldn't have given two snorts in vacuum about my "optimum developmental strategy." He'd have told me, "Ching, do this or learn that;" and if I didn't do it satisfactorily, I'd be fired—or dead, because we'd be on strange worlds, out among the stars.

No use daydreaming. League apprenticeships are scarcer than hair on a neutron and are mostly filled by relatives. I was an ordinary student bucking for an Academy appointment, from which I'd graduate to service on regular runs and maybe, at last, to a captaincy.

"To be frank," Freeman Snyder went on, "I've worried about your indifference to extracurricular activities. It doesn't make for an outgoing personality, you know. I've thought of an undertaking which should be right in your orbit. In addition, it'll be a real service, it'll bring real credit, to—" he smiled afresh, feigning humor while he intoned "—the educational complex of San Francisco Integrate."

"I haven't time!" I wailed.

"Certainly you do. You can't study twenty-four hours a day, even if a medic would prescribe the stim. Brains go stale. All work and no play, remember. Besides, Jim, this matter has its serious aspect. I'd like to feel I could endorse your altruism as well as your technological abilities."

I eased my muscles, let the lounger mold itself around me, and said in what was supposed to be a hurrah voice: "Please tell me, Freeman Snyder."

He beamed. "I knew I could count on you. You've heard of the upcoming Festival of Man."

"Haven't I?" Realizing how sour my tone was, I tried again. "I have."

He gave me a narrow look. "You don't sound too enthusiastic."

"Oh, I'll tune in ceremonies and such, catch a bit of music and drama and whatnot, if and when the chance comes. But I've got to get these transformations in hyperdrive theory straight, or—"

"I'm afraid you don't quite appreciate the importance of the Festival, Jim. It's more than a set of shows. It's an affirmation."

Yes, I'd heard that often enough before—too dismally often. The line of argument the promoters used: "Humankind, gaining the stars, is in grave danger of losing its soul. Our extraterrestrial colonies are fragmenting into new nations, whole new cultures, to which Earth is scarcely a memory. Our traders, our explorers push ever outward, ever further away; and no missionary spirit drives them, nothing but lust for profit and adventure. Meanwhile, the Solar Commonwealth is deluged with alien—nonhuman—influence, not only diplomats, entrepreneurs, students, and visitors, but the false glamour of ideas never born on man's true home. We grant we have learned much of value from these outsiders. But much else has been unassimilable or has had a disastrously distorting effect, especially in the arts. Besides, they are learning far more from us. Let us proudly affirm that fact. Let us hark back to our own origins, our own variousness. Let us strike new roots in the soil from which our forebears sprang."

A year-long display of Earth's past—well, it'd be colorful, if rather fakey most of the time. I couldn't take it seriously. Space was where the future lay, I thought. It was where I dreamed my personal future would lie. What were dead bones to me, no matter how fancy the costumes you put on them? Not that I scorned the past; I wasn't so foolish. I just believed that what was worth saving would save itself, and the rest had better be let fade away quietly.

I tried to explain to my counselor: "Sure, I've been told about 'cultural pseudomorphosis' and the rest. Really though, Freeman Snyder, don't you think the shoe is on the other foot? Like, well, I've got this friend from Woden, name of Adzel, here to learn planetology. That's a science we developed; his folk are primitive hunters, newly discovered by us. He talks human languages, too—he's quick at languages—and lately he has converted to Buddhism and—Shouldn't the Wodenites worry about being turned into imitation Earthlings?"

My example wasn't the best, because you can only humanize a four-and-a-half-meter-long dragon to a limited extent. Whether he knew that or not, Snyder wasn't impressed.

He snapped, "The sheer variety of extraterrestrial influence is demoralizing. Now, I want our complex to make a decent showing during the Festival. Every department, office, club, church, institution in the Integrate will take part. I want its schools to have a leading role."

"Don't they, sir? I mean, aren't projects under way?"

"Yes, yes, to a degree." He waved an impatient hand. "Far less than I'd expect from our youth. Too many of you are space-struck—"

He checked himself, donned his smile again, and leaned forward till his image seemed ready to fall out of the screen. "I've been thinking about what my own students might do. In your case, I have a first-class idea. You will represent San Francisco's Chinese community among us."

"What?" I yelped. "Bu—but—"

"A very old, almost unique tradition," he said. "Your people have been in this area for five or six hundred years."

"*My* people?" The room wobbled around me. "I mean . . . well, sure, my name's Ching and I'm proud of it. And maybe the—uh—the chromosome recombinations do make me look like those ancestors. But . . . half a thousand years, sir! If I haven't got blood in me of every breed of human being that ever lived, why, then I'm a statistical monstrosity!"

"True. However, the accident which makes you a throwback to your Mongoloid forebears is helpful. Few of my students are identifiably anything. I try to find roles for them on the basis of surnames, but it isn't easy."

Yeh, I though bitterly. *By your reasoning, everybody named Marcantonio should dress in a toga for the occasion, and everybody named Smith should paint himself blue.*

"There is a local *ad hoc* committee on Chinese-American activities," Snyder went on. "I suggest you contact them and ask for ideas and information. What can you present on behalf of our educational system? And then, of course, there's Library Central. It can supply more historical material than you could read in a lifetime. Do you good to learn a few subjects besides math, physics, xenology . . ." His grimace passed by. I gave him marks for sincerity. "Perhaps you can devise something—a float or the like—something which will call on your engineering ingenuity and knowledge. That would please them, too, when you apply at the Academy."

Sure, I thought, *if it hasn't eaten so much of my time that I flunk these problems.*

"Remember," Snyder said, "the Festival opens in barely three months. I'll expect progress reports from you. Feel free to call on me for help or advice at any time. That's what I'm here for, you know: to guide you in developing your whole self."

More of the same followed. I haven't the stomach to record it.

I called Betty Riefenstahl, but just to find out if I could visit her. Though holovids are fine for image and sound, you can't hold hands with one or catch a whiff of perfume and girl.

Her phone told me she wasn't available till evening. That gave me ample opportunity to gnaw my nerves raw. I couldn't flat-out refuse Snyder's pet notion. The right was mine, of course, and he wouldn't consciously hold a grudge; but neither would he speak as well as he might of my energy and team spirit. On the other hand, what did I know about Chinese civilization? I'd seen the standard sights, I'd read a classic or two in literature courses, and that was that. What persons I'd met over there were as modern as myself. And as for Chinese-Americans . . .

Vaguely remembering that San Francisco had once had special ethnic sections, I did ask Library Central.

It screened a fleet of stuff about a district known as Chinatown. Probably contemporaries found that area picturesque. (Oh, four-armed drummers who sound the mating call of Gorzum's twin moons! Oh, wild wings above Ythri!) The inhabitants had celebrated a Lunar New Year with fireworks and a parade. However, I couldn't make out details—the photographs had been time-blurred when their information was recorded—and was too disheartened to plow through the accompanying text.

For me, dinner was a refueling stop. I mumbled something to my parents—who mean well but can't understand why I must leave the nice safe Commonwealth—and flitted off to the Reifenstahl place.

The trip calmed me a little. I was reminded that, to outworlders like Adzel, the miracle was this earth. Light glimmered far out over the great sheen of bay and ocean; often it fountained upward in a many-armed tower, sometimes giving way to the sweet darkness of a park or ecocenter. A murmur of machines beat endlessly through cool, slightly foggy air. Traffic control passed me so near a bus that I could see that the passengers were from the whole globe and beyond: a dandified Lunarian, a stocky blueskin of Alfzar; a spacehand identified by his Brotherhood badge; a journeyman merchant of the Polesotechnic League who didn't bother with any identification except the skin weathered beneath strange suns, a go-to-hell independence in his face, which turned me sick with envy.

The Riefenstahls' apartment overlooked the Golden

Gate. I saw lights twinkle and flare, heard distant clangor and hissing, where crews worked around the clock to replicate an ancient bridge. Betty met me at the door. She's slim and blonde and usually cheerful. Tonight she looked so tired and troubled that I myself paid scant attention to the briefness of her tunic.

"Sh!" she cautioned. "Let's don't say hello to Dad right now. He's in his study, and it's very brown." I knew that her mother was away from home, helping develop the tape of a modern musical composition. Her father conducted the San Francisco Opera.

She led me to the living room, sat me down, and punched for coffee. A full-wall transparency framed her where she continued standing, in city glitter and shimmer, a sickle moon with a couple of pinpoint cities visible on its dark side, a few of the brightest stars. "I'm glad you came, Jimmy," she said. "I need a shoulder to cry on."

"Like me," I answered. "You first, however."

"Well, it's Dad. He's ghastly worried. This stupid Festival—"

"Huh?" I searched my mind and found nothing except the obvious. "Won't he be putting on a—uh—terrestrial piece?"

"He's expected to. He's been researching till every hour of the mornings, poor dear. I've been helping him go through playbacks—hundreds and hundreds of years' worth—and prepare synopses and excerpts to show the directors. We only finished yesterday, and I *had* to catch up on sleep. That's why I couldn't let you come earlier."

"But what's the problem?" I asked. "Okay, you've been forced to scan those tapes. But once you've picked your show, you just project it, don't you? At most, you may need to update the language. And you've got your mother to handle reprogramming."

Betty sighed. "It's not that simple. You see, they—his board of directors, plus the officials in charge of San Francisco's participation—they insist on a live performance."

Partly I knew what she was talking about, the rest she explained. Freeman Riefenstahl had pioneered the revival of in-the-flesh opera. Yes, he said, we have holographic records of the greatest artists; yes, we can use computers to generate original works and productions which no mortal being could possibly match. Yet neither approach brings forth new artists with new concepts of a part, nor do they give individual brains a chance to create—and, when a million fresh ideas are flowing in to us from the galaxy, natural-born genius must create or else revolt.

"Let us by all means use technical tricks where they are indicated, such as for special effects," Freeman Riefenstahl said. "But let us never forget that music is only alive in a living performer."

While I don't claim to be very esthetic, I tuned in his shows whenever I could. They did have an excitement which no tape and no calculated stimulus interplay—no matter how excellent—could duplicate.

"His case is like yours," Betty had told me when

we were first getting acquainted. "We could send robots to space. Nevertheless, men go at whatever risk." That was when I stopped thinking of her as merely pretty.

Tonight, her voice gone bleak, she said, "Dad succeeded too well. He's been doing contemporary things, you know, letting the archives handle the archaic. Now they insist he won't be showing sufficient respect, as a representative of the Integrate, for the Human Ethos unless he puts on a historic item, live, as the Opera Company's share of the Festival."

"Well, can't he?" I asked. "Sure, it's kind of short notice, same as for me. Still, given modern training methods for his cast—"

"Of course, of course," she said irritably. "But don't you see a routine performance isn't good enough either? People today are conditioned to visual spectacles. At least, the directors claim so. And Jimmy, the Festival is important, if only because of the publicity. If Dad's part in it falls flat, his contract may not be renewed. Certainly his effort to educate the public back to real music would be hurt." Her tone and her head drooped. "And that'd hurt him."

She drew a breath, straightened, even coaxed a smile into existence. "Well, we've made our précis of suggestions," she said. "We're waiting to hear what the board decides, which may take days. Meanwhile, you need to tell me your woes." Sitting down opposite me, she said, "Do."

I obeyed. At the end I grinned on one side of my face and remarked, "Ironic, huh? Here your father has to stage an ultra-ethnic production—I'll bet they'll turn handsprings for him if he can make it in German, given a name like his—only he's not supposed to use technology for much except backdrops. And here I have to do likewise, in Chinese style, the flashier the better, only I really haven't time to apply the technology for making a firework fountain or whatever. Maybe he and I should pool our efforts."

"How?"

"I dunno." I shifted in the chair. "Let's get out of here, go someplace where we can forget this mess."

What I had in mind was a flit over the ocean or down to the swimmably warm waters off Baja, followed maybe by a snack in a restaurant featuring out-system food. Betty gave me no chance. She nodded and said quickly, "Yes, I've been wanting to. A serene environment . . . do you think Adzel might be at home?"

The League scholarship he'd wangled back on his planet didn't reach far on Earth, especially when he had about a ton of warm-blooded mass to keep fed. He couldn't afford special quarters, or anything near the Clement Institute of Planetology. Instead, he paid exorbitant rent for a shack down in the San Jose district. The sole public transportation he could fit into was a rickety old twice-a-day gyrotrain, which meant he lost hours commuting to his laboratory and live-lecture classes, waiting for them to begin, and waiting around after they were finished. Also, I strongly suspected he was undernourished. I'd fretted about him ever since we met in a course in micrometrics.

He always dismissed my fears: "Once, Jimmy, I might well have chafed, when I was a prairie-galloping hunter. Now, having gained a minute measure of enlightenment, I see that these annoyances of the flesh are no more significant than we allow them to be. Indeed, we can turn them to good use. Austerities are valuable. As for long delays, why, they are opportunities for study or, better yet, meditation. I have even learned to ignore spectators, and am grateful for the discipline which that forced me to acquire."

We may be used to extraterrestrials these days. Nevertheless, he was the one Wodenite on this planet. Take a being like that: four hoofed legs supporting a spike-backed green-scaled golden-bellied body and tail, arms in proportion, and torso rising two meters to a crocodilian face: fangs, rubbery lips, bony ears, wistful brown eyes—you take that fellow and set him on a campus in his equivalent of the lotus position, droning "*Om mani padme hum*" in a rich basso profundo, and see if he doesn't draw a crowd.

Serious though he was, Adzel never became a prig. He enjoyed good food and drink when he could get them, being especially fond of rye whiskey consumed out of beer tankards. He played murderous chess and poker. He sang, and sang well, everything from his native chants, through human folk ballads, on to the very latest spinnies. (A few things, such as *Eskimo Nell*, he refused to render in Betty's presence. From his avid reading of human history, he'd picked up anachronistic inhibitions.) I imagine his jokes often escaped me by being too subtle.

I was tremendously fond of him, hated the thought of his poverty, and had failed to find any way of helping him out.

I set my car down on the strip in front of his hut. A moldering conurb, the feverish reflections off thickening fog cast it into deep and sulfurous shadow. Unmuffled industrial traffic brawled around. I took a stun pistol from a drawer before escorting Betty outside.

Adzel's doorplate was gone, but he opened at our knock. "Do come in, do come in," he greeted. Fluorolight shimmered gorgeously along his scales and scutes. Incense puffed outward. He noticed my gun. "Why are you armed, Jimmy?"

"The night's dark here," I said. "In a crime area like this—"

"Is it?" He was surprised. "Why, I have never been molested."

We entered. He waved us to mats on the floor. Those, a couple of cheap tables, and bookshelves cobbled together from scrap and crammed with codexes and reels, were his furniture. A fake Japanese screen hid that end of the single room that contained a miniature cooker and some complicated, specially-installed plumbing. Two scrolls hung on the walls, one showing a landscape and one the Compassionate Buddha.

Adzel bustled about, making tea for us. He hadn't quite been able to adjust to these narrow surroundings.

Twice I had to duck fast before his tail clonked me. "I am delighted to see you," he boomed. "I gathered from your call, however, that the occasion is not altogether happy."

"We hoped you'd help us relax," Betty replied. I myself felt a bit disgruntled. Sure, Adzel was fine people, but couldn't Betty and I relax in each other's company? I had seen too little of her these past weeks.

He served us. His pot held five liters, but—thanks to that course in micrometrics—he could handle the tiniest cups and put on an expert tea ceremony. Appropriate silence passed. I fumed. The custom might be charming; still, the Oriental traditions had caused me ample woe.

At last he dialed for *pipa* music, settled down before us on hocks and front knees, and invited: "Share your troubles, dear friends."

"Oh, we've been over them and over them," Betty said. "I came here for peace."

"Why, certainly," Adzel answered. "I am glad to try to oblige. Would you like to join me in a spot of transcendental meditation?"

That tore my patience apart. "No!" I yelled. They both stared at me. "I'm sorry," I mumbled. "But . . . chaos, everything's gone bad and—"

A gigantic four-digited hand squeezed my shoulder, gently as my mother might have done. "Tell, Jimmy," Adzel said low.

It flooded from me, the whole sad, ludicrous situation. "Freeman Snyder can't understand," I finished.

"He thinks I can learn those equations, those facts, in a few days at most."

"Can't you? Operant conditioning, for example—"

"You know better. I can learn to parrot, sure. But I won't get the knowledge down in my bones where it belongs. And they'll set me problems which require original thinking. They must. How else can they tell if I'll be able to handle an emergency in space?"

"—or on a new planet." The long head nodded. "Yes-s-s."

"That's not for me," I said flatly. "I'll never be tagged by the merchant adventurers." Betty squeezed my hand. "Even freighters can run into grief, though."

He regarded me for a while, most steadily, until at last he rumbled: "A word to the right men—that does appear to be how your Technic civilization operates, no? *Zothkh.* Have you prospects for a quick performance of this task, that will allow you to get back soon to your proper work?"

"No. Freeman Snyder mentioned a float or display. Well, I'll have to soak up cultural background, and develop a scheme, and clear it with the local committee, and design the thing—which had better be spectacular as well as ethnic—and build it, and test it, and find the bugs in the design, and rebuild it, and—and I'm no artist anyhow. No matter how clever a machine I make, it won't look like much."

Suddenly Betty exclaimed, "Adzel, you know more about Old Oriental things than he does! Can't you make a suggestion?"

"Perhaps, perhaps." The Wodenite rubbed his jaw,

a sandpaper noise. "The motifs . . . let me see." He hooked a book off a shelf and started leafing through it. "They are generally of pagan origin in Buddhistic or Christian art . . . *Gr-r-rrr-m* . . . Betty, my sweet, while I search, won't you unburden yourself, too?"

She twisted her fingers and gazed at the floor. I figured she'd rather not be distracted. Rising from my mat, I went to look over his shoulder . . . no, his elbow.

"My problem is my father's, actually," she began. "And maybe he and I already have solved it. That depends on whether or not one of the possibilities we've found is acceptable. If not—how much further can we research? Time's getting so short. He needs time to assemble a cast, rehearse, handle the physical details . . ." She noticed Adzel's puzzlement and managed a sort of chuckle. "Excuse me. I got ahead of my story. We—"

"Hoy!" I interrupted. My hand slapped down on a page. "What's that? Uh, sorry, Betty."

Her smile forgave me. "Have you found something?" She sprang to her feet.

"I don't know," I stammered, "b-b-but, Adzel, that thing in this picture could almost be you, what is it?"

He squinted at the ideograms. "The *lung,*" he said.

"A dragon?"

"Western writers miscalled it thus." Adzel settled happily down to lecture us. "The dragon proper was a creature of European and Near Eastern mythology, almost always a destructive monster. In Chinese and related societies, on the contrary, these reptiloids represented beneficent powers. The *lung* inhabited the sky, the *li* the ocean, the *chiao* the marshes and mountains. Various other entities are named elsewhere. The *lung* was the principal type, the one which was mimed on ceremonial occasions—"

The phone warbled. "Would you please take that, Betty?" Adzel asked, reluctant to break off. "I daresay it's a notification I am expecting of a change in class schedules. Now, Jimmy, observe the claws on hind and forefeet. Their exact number is a distinguishing characteristic of —"

"Dad!" Betty cried. Glancing sideways, I saw John Riefenstahl's mild features on the screen, altogether woebegone.

"I was hoping I'd find you, dear," he said wearily. I knew that these days she seldom left the place without recording a list of numbers where she might be reached.

Her fists clenched.

"I've just finished a three-hour conference with the board chairman," her father's voice plodded. "They've vetoed every one of our proposals."

"Already?" she whispered. "In God's name, why?"

"Various reasons. They feel *Carmen* is too parochial in time and space; hardly anybody today would understand what motivates the characters. *Alpha of the Centaur* is about space travel, which is precisely what we're supposed to get away from. *La Traviata* isn't visual enough. *Götterdämmerung*, they agree, has the Mythic Significance they want, but it's *too* visual. A modern audience wouldn't accept it unless we supply a realism of effects, thus drawing attention away from the live performers on whom it ought to center in a production emphasizing Man. Et cetera, et cetera."

"They're full of nonsense!"

"They're also full of power, dear. Can you bear to run through more tapes?"

"I'd better."

"I beg your pardon, Freeman Riefenstahl," Adzel put in. "We haven't met, but I have long admired your work. May I ask if you have considered Chinese opera?"

"The Chinese themselves will be doing that, Freeman—er—" The conductor hesitated.

"Adzel." My friend moved into scanner range. His teeth gleamed alarmingly sharp. "Honored to make your acquaintance, sir . . . ah . . . sir?"

John Riefenstahl, who had gasped and gone bloodless, wiped his forehead. "Eh—eh—excuse me," he stuttered. "I didn't realize you—that is, here I had Wagner on my mind, and then Fafner himself confronted me—"

I didn't know those names, but the context was obvious. All at once Betty and I met each other's eyes and let out a yell.

Knowing how Freeman Snyder would react, I insisted on a live interview. He sat behind his desk, surrounded by his computers, communicators, and information retrievers, and gave me a tight smile.

"Well," he said. "You have an idea, Jim? Overnight seems a small time for a matter this important."

"It was plenty," I answered. "We've contacted the head of the Chinese-American committee, and he likes our notion. But since it's on behalf of the schools, he wants your okay."

"*We?*" My counselor frowned. "You have a partner?"

"Chaos, sir, he is my project. What's a Chinese parade without a dragon? And what fake dragon can possibly be as good as a live one? Now we take this Wodenite, and just give him a wig and false whiskers, claws over his hoofs, lacquer on his scales—"

"A nonhuman?" The frown turned into a scowl. "Jim, you disappoint me. You disappoint me sorely. I expected better from you, some dedication, some application of your talents. In a festival devoted to your race, you want to feature an alien! No, I'm afraid I cannot agree—"

"Sir, please wait till you've met Adzel." I jumped from my chair, opened the hall door, and called: "C'mon in."

He did, meter after meter of him, till the office was full of scales, tail, spikes, and fangs. He seized Snyder's hand in a gentle but engulfing grip, beamed straight into Snyder's face, and thundered, "How joyful I am at this opportunity, sir! What a way to express my admiration for terrestrial culture, and thus help glorify your remarkable species!"

"Um—well—that is," the man said feebly.

I had told Adzel there was no reason to mention his being a pacifist. He continued, "I do hope you will approve Jimmy's brilliant idea, sir. To be quite frank, my motives are not unmixed. If I perform, I understand that the local restaurateurs' association will feed me during rehearsals. My stipend is exiguous and"—he licked his lips, two centimeters from Snyder's nose—"sometimes I get *so* hungry."

I whispered in my counselor's ear, "He is kind of excitable, but he's perfectly safe if nobody frustrates him."

"Well." Snyder coughed, backed away till he ran into a computer, and coughed again. "Well. Ah . . . yes. Yes, Jim, your concept is undeniably original. There is—" he winced but got the words out—"a certain quality to it which suggests that you—" he strangled for a moment—"will go far in life."

"You plan to record that opinion, do you not?" Adzel asked. "In Jimmy's permanent file? At once?"

I hurried them both through the remaining motions. My friend, my girl, and her father had an appointment with the chairman of the board of the San Francisco Opera Company.

The parade went off like rockets. Our delighted local merchants decided to revive permanently the ancient custom of celebrating the Lunar New Year. Adzel will star in that as long as he remains on Earth. In exchange—since he brings in more tourist credits than it costs—he has an unlimited meal ticket at the Golden Dragon Restaurant and Chop Suey Palace.

More significant was the production of Richard Wagner's *Siegfried*. At least, in his speech at the farewell performance, the governor of the Integrate said it was significant. "Besides the bringing back of a musical masterpiece too many centuries neglected," he said pompously, "the genius of John Riefenstahl has, by his choice of cast, given the Festival of Man an added dimension. He has reminded us that in seeking our roots and pride, we must never grow chauvinistic. We must always remember to reach forth the hand of friendship to our brother beings throughout God's universe [who might otherwise be less anxious to come spend their money on Earth]."

The point does have its idealistic appeal. Besides, the show was a sensation in its own right. For years to come, the complete Ring cycle will be presented here and there around the Commonwealth; and Freeman Riefenstahl can be guest conductor and Adzel can sing Fafner—at top salary—any time they wish.

I won't see the end of that, because I won't be around. When everything had been settled, Adzel, Betty, and I threw ourselves a giant feast in his new apartment. After his fifth magnum of champagne, he gazed a trifle blurrily across the table and said to me:

"Jimmy, my affection for you, my earnest wish to make a fractional return of your kindness, has hitherto been baffled."

"Aw, nothing to mention," I mumbled while he stopped a volcanic hiccough.

"At any rate"—Adzel wagged a huge finger—"he would be a poor friend who gave a dangerous gift." He popped another cork and refilled our glasses and his stein. "That is, Jimmy, I am aware of your ambition to get into deep space, and not as a plyer of routine routes but as a discoverer, a pioneer. The question remained: could you cope with unpredictable environments?"

I gaped at him. My heart banged in my breast. Betty caught my hand.

"You have convinced me you can," Adzel said. "True, Freeman Snyder may not give you his most ardent recommendation to the Academy. No matter. The cleverness and, yes, toughness with which you handled this problem—those convinced me, Jimmy, you are a true survivor type."

He knocked back half a liter before tying the star-spangled bow knot on his package. "Being here on a League scholarship, I have League connections. I have been in correspondence. A certain Master Merchant I know will soon be in the market for another apprentice and accepts what I have told him about you. Are you interested?"

I collapsed into Betty's arms. She says she'll find a way to follow me.

WEEP NO MORE, OLD LADY

C. L. Grant

During the past few weeks, I have been struck with an almost desperate feeling of empathy with anyone who is or has been imprisoned. I imagine I know exactly what it is like to be stripped naked of whatever freedoms there may be, to be forcibly placed in a room so isolated that it precludes any meaningful communication with the so-called "outside world". It does happen, of course, and in fact happens quite often. There are various kinds of prisoners and different types of wardens. In my case, I suppose, there should really be some attempt at formulating a distinction in order that I not be confused with, say, a prisoner of war. I myself have tried on one or two occasions to do just that. But it's awfully hard to be objective.

You see, in this . . . cell such decidedly unpleasant and even morbid thoughts come easily, most of the time unbidden and usually from reacting over-emotionally to my predicament and indulging in a tasteless bath of self-pity.

But I cannot be sure that I'm not lowering myself

to rationalizing when I eventually get hold of myself and contend that I'm not a prisoner at all. Not all the time, anyway.

In fact, this place is as comfortable as a small room can be. When I begin to forget things, I stretch out on the floor and re-establish its length and width at nine and ten feet, respectively. By standing squarely in the center of the room and raising my hand and arm over my head, estimate the height at approximately eight feet. There's a wonderfully soft double bed that waits within one wall—if you look carefully between the animal patterns on the wallpaper, you can just make out the almost invisible lines which mark its place. It really is comfortable. And I sleep quite well at night, except when I have nightmares.

There's a bookcase that hides one complete wall and has been thoughtfully stocked (by me?) with a generous mixture of fact and fiction, though nothing too steep for my purposes. The only flaw here is a collection of Gideon Fell novels slipped in by some sadistic son-of-a-bitch—I believe they're called locked room mysteries. I have read none of them. I never will. Among the others I have my favorites, but I am afraid that they will pale soon.

Perhaps I shall be free by then.
But dammit, I'm not a prisoner!
I'm a Brain-Child.

It's easy to dream. And less than easy to do something about your dreams.

When I tend toward petulance in irrational moments, I lay the blame for my condition on my parents. Justifiable in some ways, but not wholly so. As intelligent as I am, I should have been able to foresee something like this happening.

Father was not really an extraordinary person: a professor of Ancient History who had a fondness for dry sherry, leather upholstery, the Boston Red Sox and Rex Stout. He enjoyed being alone. Mother, on the other hand, was a joiner—a president of so many women's clubs that often, when I was younger, I would read in a newspaper something like "President Visits Brazil" and would run through the house crying because she didn't say goodbye to me. She had a fondness for cognac, blue satin draperies, the Boston Bruins and Ellery Queen.

I have dreams of fairies and goblins and elves and visions of sugar plums and the Big Rock-Candy Mountain.

My parents were beautifully matched and I was their only child. Occasionally they were mistaken for brother and sister, and I often wondered what I was to be then—their distorted mirror? I am blond, have brown eyes, am barely perceptively buck-toothed, gently hook-nosed, slightly on the heavy side and—though I try to hide it—painfully pigeon-toed.

But they were handsome and I am not. They were my parents and I am their son. They caused my being; they molded me; *they* were the ones, rightly or not, who fed me with knowledge and saw to it that my potential as a genius was exploited.

And it is very hard to try to undo all that which has been done.

And Jesus, it's lonely.

Special schools (public schools and public children apparently could not handle me) and special tutors with the damnedest educational theories were the forces that drove me headlong out of my early years. And through it all were the binding webs of ecology, astronomy, philosophy, geology and mathematics. Not to mention theology, entology, biology and oceanography. Freedom of choice. Study what I wanted. Even now, I grin a little remembering the expressions on my teachers' faces when I soared past them so rapidly that my incessant "Whys" and "Hows" toppled their egos and crushed them. Of course, I was too young to know that then, they merely looked humorous to me.

Dreary, difficult and frustrating. I must have cried myself to sleep a thousand times for the understanding I was unable to achieve in depth because of my age and lack of experience. And then I began to think myself ugly and refused to allow mirrors in the house. Father used to tease me about being a vampire and it frightened me. Scared me. God, but I was scared.

God, I'm scared.

God, I'm lonely.

Sometimes I dream of gazelle and lions and tigers and elephants and Batman and the Lone Ranger.

Did I tell you I was a Brain-Child?

I am, you know.

I'm sleepy.

But it's not time for the bed to come. Not now. Later. At eight o'clock. It's the experiment, you see. But don't tell anyone. It's a secret.

Then there was the Time of Crisis (as Mother calls it in her book which was twenty-three months on the *Times* best seller list. The names were changed, but that still made me rather famous to those in the know. The book is supposed to be fiction. I hate her for that). It became readily apparent that even geniuses of my particular ilk had their limits of absorption. Father's wobbly little Renaissance Man was turning out to be just another bright kid who peaked a few years before anyone else. Mother was only disappointed, but Father's face would redden and his voice fairly thundered throughout the house when I was totally unable to assimilate another iota of material. And he damn near cried when I began forgetting things. My paintings became static, my compositions stale, and together we pronounced my academic future as bleak as an English moor in autumn. I hated that, I really did, and I raged and threw tantrums and even wept at my helplessness—one of the few childlike things I ever did.

Enter, the Government, which shares the blame and I cannot forgive them for they knew exactly what they were doing—the bastards.

I never saw the President or a Cabinet member or even an assistant to an Assistant Secretary. For me the Government was Mr. Bernard Polaisky, as plain a man you'll never see. He appeared out of nowhere and I used to sit on the bottom step in the hall and fall asleep to the drone of his monotonous voice. He came once a week, then every night, talking and listening and arguing for about an hour or so, and then there would be nothing left of him when he'd gone. No feeling, no atmosphere, no odor—no memory of him. It was just as if he had never been. I doubt seriously that I'd know him if he walked through the door this moment (only there is no door, or windows. Just several hidden shafts that bring me food and air and an ice cream cone or two).

However, what turned out to be the final conversation did finally involve me. We were introduced and Mr. Polaisky smiled warmly as he shook my hand. I remember that because it was obvious he recognized my abilities and treated me as an equal.

"You're a fine young lad," he said, and I grinned so idiotically I couldn't answer. I believe I spent the rest of the evening by Mother's chair, clutching her arm—and grinning.

"Richard," Father said to me, "this gentleman would like very much to assist us . . . rather, assist you with your problem. Your Mother and I have done all that we can, and I think you're intelligent enough to realize that without some further, perhaps even artificial guidance, you'll remain just about where you are now."

"Yes, Father." I was grinning—did I say that already?

"Do you know what your problem is?" That question, naturally, was for the benefit of the Government man. Father loved to show me off. He was kind of proud.

"Yes, Father," I said, but did not move away from Mother's side. "To put it very, very simply, it seems like I'm all stored up. As if there's no place for anything to go anymore; partly because I've concentrated on all subjects instead of one; partly because I am unable to tap unused areas of my brain for further storage and recall. And what portions are being utilized are overburdened because they cannot strengthen themselves to handle the load. I am starting to forget things. It's kind of like a solution which has so much salt dissolved in it that eventually the salt begins to re-form and precipitate."

Yet it was all play-acting, nothing more. Father was proud of me and wanted me very much to be chosen for something he felt would be a great honor.

Did he think of me?

I was picked, of course, and so undramatically that I was quite disappointed. Every two weeks I was carted off to a dingy office in Boston where all I got were *pills!* I could hardly believe it. Pills, for crying out loud. After so many stories and articles I had read about experimental surgery and serums and injections —all to 'give you' knowledge, and all of them so tragically resolved. Pills! When I first saw them I thought they were aspirin. Mother and Father were terribly excited and so let down when I was unable to share in their enthusiasm. But believe me, there's nothing at all exciting about pills—which I took. And they worked.

So I climbed from my stagnant plateau and continued to reach greedily for more. I specialized in nothing and recalled everything, and eventually the price was paid.

The price was me.

My parents loved me, you see, and let me go. I saw the wisdom in this move, and since they were allowed to come and see me regularly (until I began this experiment and forbade it), there was little of the pain of parting. Tears, mostly, and effusive promises to write.

They drove me all the way to Princeton where I was to live and study. Father was cheerful, as indeed he should have been. His only son was at the top and still climbing for the fame no professor could realize. It was a beautiful day—the fall, if I remember correctly—and even though Mother tended to sniffle and wipe her eyes once in a while, she laughed too and was beautiful. And Father sang. Badly (does he still?) but gustily. He had never brought himself to learn more than one line of a song, and that not always correctly. I knew them all, but never helped him. You understand?

So it was "Weep no more, old lady" a million times from Connecticut to New Jersey. And when we were finally alone in the car in the shadows of a hundred trees as old as the country, Mother hugged me and Father shook my hand. He told me I was a man. I wanted to cry.

I dream of ankles and thighs and breasts and lips and Raggedy Ann and Mamie Stover.

When he left he was still singing, only now as if he were going to a funeral. So melodramatic when I can remember it—but then Father was a great actor.

It was nearly two years before I discovered exactly what the Government wanted with me. Although they had moved me to Princeton, had given me my own cottage and let me go my own way, not once did they express more than a passing interest in my various inventions, scientific studies, paintings or musical compositions. But, while I was puzzling their intentions and swallowing that miserable aspirin in varying amounts at staggered times, I was in an earth-bound heaven. For a short time I experienced great concern over the side-effects of those pills, but soon realized the dangers were minimal, if they existed at all. Meanwhile, I prepared myself physically, embarking upon a program of rigorous exercise: push-ups, one-two (buckle my shoe), walking and jogging to keep limber and nimble (Jack be quick), isotonic and isometric interludes to break the routine of my work.

I almost wished I had permitted mirrors so that I could have seen myself grow.

But obviously the Government was not treating me as an Anglo-Saxon Leonardo for purely altruistic reasons, and eventually I tired of my being placed on exhibit, however limited. I began brooding and complaining. I baited every visitor and demanded explanations (when my Mother cried from the moment she saw me on her last visit, Father kept her away. Or did I forbid them to come?). I am quite obviously the means, I would say. So what the hell are the ends? I became obdurate in my refusal to do anything at all. I allowed myself to grow slovenly and crude in my daily progress reports: Today I developed a self-flushing toilet and mastered Kama Sutra #56.

I threatened to run away.

And lo and behold, but didn't Mr. Bernard Polaisky pop out of the woodwork and ask for a moment of my time.

"Time is a man-made fabrication," I said. I loved being pompous and obtuse, though pomposity in a sixteen-year-old is bound to be ludicrous. I know he thought so because he was about to lose his grip on his anonymity and slap me.

"Sit down," he ordered.

I did. The grass was warm in August and I was spending most of my time outside in the backyard.

"Richard, we're all pretty proud of you, you know."

I knew it, of course, but I had a good, heated feeling in my cheeks and chest on hearing it.

"You've proven a number of things for us."

"I'm ever so glad," I said as caustically as I could.

He ignored me. "For, more than having merely a photographic memory—if you'll pardon the layman's term—you have also developed a power of reasoning, albeit a limited understanding, which has kept a remarkably even pace with your memory. The pills don't work on everyone, you see." This was the first confirmation I'd had that I wasn't alone. But at the time it was no consolation. "In fact, Richard, you're the only person with extraordinarily high intelligence that has benefited more than just a little from the experiment."

I was grinning, even though I knew it was an immature way of covering my embarassment. He didn't seem to notice. He rambled along in the same vein for several minutes, floundering in a sea of platitudes and eventually running out of words. He smiled, and stared at me.

"Okay," I said. "So?"

"So what? That's it, Richard. You wanted to know what was going on, didn't you? You were observed. You were tested. Though the pills will continue to increase your memory and ability to learn, the cumulative effects from now on will be so small as to be practically negligible. If you must have it crudely, Richard: you worked."

I . . . worked. Like a rat that can run the maze and avoid the shocks and answer the bell and slap the lever. I worked. Worked, like a goddamn new machine.

Mr. Polaisky was distressed. He smiled as he patted me on the shoulder and tousled my hair. "You see," he said—because obviously I didn't—"several important people were concerned that those pills would make everyone in the country a genius and thus leave no one left for the actual manual labor so vital to any society's viability. But you and the others have proved this worry to be without foundation. There is a limit, Richard. For everyone. Even you. Each person can go just so high, and no higher.

"Do you remember that saturated solution you told

me about when we first met? Well, even with the pills, the analogy fits. A little bit frightening, I guess, isn't it? But you'll be allowed to stay here and work if you want. Remember, though, you'll eventually reach the same problem you had before we came into the picture.

"So you see, son, you worked. You're a hero. A bona fide hero, and your country is grateful."

I remember screaming at Polaisky and even throwing a well-aimed, perfectly unexpected punch to his mid-section.

I dream of silver bells and cockle shells and Dante's Hell and wishing wells.

To be truthful, I behaved like a fool. I even vowed eternal revenge until I realized how silly it was. Instead, I continued my work and this time, an active interest was exhibited toward my projects. I also consented to live in Princeton (what a lovely community; I think it's in New Jersey), and when I grew tired of remembering it all I went on a trip across the country.

And came back.

Because I have a new experiment. Women.

Have you ever sat in a park or walked in a forest or waded in an ocean with a girl who, at that particular moment, is the most beautiful creature in the world, and found you could not keep from commenting sagely on the gold content of salt water, or the average life-span of conifers versus deciduous trees, or the advantages of sod over seed?

Have you ever tried to make friends with another kid who can't understand a word you're saying and ends up either laughing at you or beating you up?

When you're seventeen, a man, a genius, you are—I am—a bore.

You are lonely.

You can't be scientific playing a scratch game of baseball. You can't be wise at a Junior Prom.

Oh hell.

But in this cell . . .

It has dolls and cut-outs and comic books and bubble gum and trading cards; electric trains and television and a radio and college pennants and model cars and a baseball glove and a football. A record player. A tape recorder.

My favorite record was made especially for me. It's Dad singing "Weep no more, old lady" over and over and over again. Once in a while I think I can catch Mom laughing in the background.

The Government pays me a pension. I built the room myself. I'm a genius, you see, and tend to act a bit weird sometimes. The new experiment is what I told them. I'm trying very hard to remember and forget.

But I'm seventeen. And that's a very long time.

There are no mirrors (did I tell you how Dad tried to kid me about being a vampire and how it scared me?), and I keep telling myself that my hands are awfully rough from all my work, and that I don't really have any wrinkles. Or gray hair.

I'm only seventeen.

Do you understand?

I'm only seventeen—I think.

CITY'S END
Mack Reynolds

Bobby was a baboon. He didn't know why they, the mainlanders, called them baboons. Perhaps it was because baboons are animals that live in a jungle and Bobby lived in a jungle. His jungle was the ruins of what was once New York City.

He didn't have a last name, or at least if he did, he didn't know what it was. He had become separated from his parents during the gigantic riots which finally led to the all but complete destruction of the city and its abandonment. He had been so young that when the woman who temporarily rescued him asked his name, all he could say was, "Bobby."

He didn't know his age now, but he figured that he was somewhere in his early teens because he was growing so fast that every couple of months he had to steal new clothes from the abandoned shops and department stores.

Well, perhaps steal wasn't quite the word. He had to *find* new clothes. Mr. Thompson, old Fred Thompson, the only real friend he had, had explained it once.

"It's not stealing if it doesn't belong to anyone. The

food and clothing and other things that we scrounge out of the ruins no longer belong to anybody and nobody cares. The former owners will never come back—those that are still alive."

Right now, Bobby was disgusted. He glared down at the portable Library Booster screen which sat on his small desk in the living room of his apartment. There was nothing wrong with the set. He had found it in the ruins of the Macy-Gimbels department store and he had an ample supply of the tiny power-pack batteries to keep it in operation for years. The trouble was that as a baboon he had no priority whatsoever. It was as though he were a criminal, a mental defective, a dangerous subversive, or someone on relief, collecting Guaranteed Annual Income.

Without priority, he could only dial books and other information from the Library Banks of the National Data Banks, on the very lowest level. Try to dial any book on the Booster screen that was the least bit advanced and the computer voice immediately demanded his identity and priority rating.

How in the dickens was he ever going to educate himself if he had no priority to dial anything beyond children's books?

He decided to go and consult Fred Thompson. The old man had told him once, "Boy, I'm no font of wisdom. Don't ever believe that hogwash about wisdom coming with age. I sometimes suspect that I'm not nearly as smart as I was fifty years ago. But there's one advantage I have over a young feller such as yourself. I've had the time to accumulate a lot of experience.

You haven't been around long enough. So if there's ever anything you need advice about, you might try me."

All right, he'd go over to Mr. Thompson's. He picked up his .22 sporting rifle and slung it over his shoulder by the strap and headed for the trap door he had cut through the apartment floor and through which he could lower himself to the floor below.

He knew that the light rifle wasn't much gun. And he suspected that if he ever had to defend himself against one of the more vicious baboons on the island he'd be lucky if he even dented the man. However, every adult—and you were more or less an adult when you reached your teens—living in the ruins of the city carried at least one weapon, and some, two or three. Even the few women remaining carried guns. As soon as he gained a few more pounds and inches he'd be able to handle a heavier caliber and feel more secure.

Bobby had selected his apartment with care and more with an eye to defense than comfort, although he had furnished it quite well by pirating things from other abandoned flats. It was a house whose front had been demolished by cannon fire from National Guard tanks, trying to put down the rioters. There was no way of gaining entry from the street directly. It was a matter of going down to the basements, then through a hole in the wall to the cellars of the adjoining apartment house. From there you could climb the stairs and emerge in an alleyway and hence make your way to the street.

He had stumbled on the place, quite by accident, while prowling the buildings in the vicinity seeking some kind of stove that would operate on the only kind of fuel available in the city—gasoline taken from the tanks of abandoned cars, buses and trucks. He doubted very much if anyone else had ever been in his building since the riots many years ago. So far, he had been safe here.

However, when he reached the head of the alley, he carefully unslung his rifle and peered up and down East 55th. The once swank residential street was a mass of rubble, overturned cars, cars rammed up onto the sidewalks, odds and ends of personal belongings abandoned by the fleeing population, a baby carriage, small trunks and suitcases, even an antique mirror. It was a mess.

Bobby could see no signs of movement. Had he seen anyone at all, he would have faded back into the alleyway. He didn't want anyone to know where he lived. It was a precaution taken by most baboons, but he had another reason for secrecy. He didn't want to be caught and made a monkey.

The coast clear, he stepped out and started up 55th Street toward what had once been Park Avenue. He customarily left his bicycle in a ruined sports shop there. There was no danger of it being stolen. But if it were, he would simply appropriate another new one from some sports shop. There were thousands of bicycles on Manhattan, more than enough for all. Actually, they were the only practical means of transportation around the island. It would have been easy enough, if you had mechanical ability, to fix up one of the abandoned automobiles. But there were few, if any, places on Manhattan where you could have driven. The city was as if it had been leveled in an all-out air raid.

He had reslung his .22 over his shoulder, the better to make his way over the wreckage. Now a hulking brute of a man stepped out from behind a burned-out car. He said, "Hold up, kid. I want to talk to you."

He was about fifty and must have weighed at least two hundred pounds. He was very well dressed in sports clothes, including a tweed jacket that had probably originally been meant to sell in some swank shop for at least two hundred dollars. There was no reason why he shouldn't be well dressed, Bobby knew, all you had to do was steal . . . scrounge . . . new things from the best shops, once your clothes became soiled or you wearied of them. However, the man's face and hands were dirty. He was obviously too lazy to bother hauling water for himself for bathing from one of the springs in the subway or the park.

Bobby knew him. Or, at least, knew of him. He was called Moose and he was possibly the most notorious keeper of monkeys on Manhattan. There were few children on the island and those that did remain, for whatever reason, were almost all appropriated by some vicious adult as soon as they had become old enough to work. They were forced to fetch and carry, to hunt for the food and other requirements of their baboon. If they tried to escape him, he would beat them. Some were even chained at night, or any other time the baboon couldn't keep his eye on them. If they did escape, invariably they fell into the hands of some other baboon who could be even worse than the one before.

Bobby had been a monkey for almost two years before achieving his independence and running off to live by himself. He had been lucky enough to have had a fairly kindly baboon as his master, but his independence, his frantic desire for freedom, finally led him to the step of escape. He never regretted it.

But this Moose who now confronted him! He had heard of Moose, one of the baboons on the island who remained because the police authorities on the mainland sought him. Since he had no Universal Credit Card—even if he had, and used it, the computers would have been on him like a flash and notified the police of his whereabouts—the only place in the country where Moose could live was in one of the abandoned cities.

His reputation was the worst. His last monkey had evidently been beaten so badly that he had become worthless to Moose (who allowed him to go to the Grand Central Terminal jet-metro station, the only one maintained on the island and ask to be sent to the mainland hospital). The boy had only been about ten.

He repeated, "Hold it, sonny. I want to talk to you."

Bobby shook his head. "No. I don't want to talk to you, Moose. Goodbye."

The other leered at him, displaying broken teeth. It was one of the many shortcomings of being a baboon in the ruins of New York. You might appropriate the most expensive canned foods and clothing on the island, and live in a former mansion, but you had no dental care and only such medical care as you could provide yourself from the medicines in drugstores.

He said, "If you got good sense, kid, you'll become my monkey. I need a new monkey."

Bobby had not survived long years in the jungle of the ruined Manhattan by being a coward. There were no cowards on the island. They had long since fled or perished.

He shook his head again and unslung his small gun. "I'd rather die than be a monkey for you, Moose."

The other laughed scornfully. He carried a semiautomatic carbine, and a heavy automatic pistol on each hip. Then he growled, "Kid, I'd hate to see you have to start off your first day for me with a beating. So far as that peashooter you're carrying is concerned, I bet you don't even know how to shoot well. I'll betcha I can put a slug through your leg or arm before you can hit me with it. Not that it would make much difference if you did hit me. That's a .22, ain't it? Kid, I've been hit with .45s in my time and I'm still around. Tough, see? Now cut out all this crud and come along with me."

Bobby was in his early teens, quick and nimble, and he knew this neighborhood as though he had been born in it. All of a sudden, he blurred into motion—zipped around the back of a car, slewed around a burned bus beyond, and jumped through the broken window of a store.

A voice behind him yelled in rage, "Come back here, you little rat, or I'll shoot!" He could hear the lumbering footsteps of the other chasing him.

He had to laugh inwardly. He knew these houses and ruined stores like a mouse knows the labyrinth beneath a warehouse. He could have run through here almost with his eyes closed. When the house-to-house fighting had taken place between the police, the National Guard and the rioters and criminal gangs, they sometimes blew holes in the walls between the buildings to allow themselves to get through to the rear of their opponent. Bobby knew every hole.

He was three buildings up, scurrying along like a lizard, through the debris, through the wreckage, almost as fast he he could have gone along the street. The sounds of pursuit behind him disappeared.

All right. But did he dare appear on 55th Street again, to get his bicycle?

Yes, he did. By this time, Moose might be anywhere.

He carefully stuck his head out of a doorway, the door itself having long since disappeared.

There was no sign of Moose.

He hurried out and up the street, taking care to use the shelter of abandoned vehicles to the greatest extent he could. He didn't know it but he was using the same tactics as his ancestors in the caves had used fifty thousand years and more before him, when they were eluding a saber-toothed tiger in the wilderness that later became Europe.

He hustled into the sporting goods store, wanting to get out of sight as soon as possible. And, yes, here was his bicycle. He looked at the tires critically. All the glass and rubble were awfully hard on tires. And it was sometimes hard to find new ones in good shape. They were so old that the rubber was beginning to rot.

He wheeled the bike out onto the sidewalk, mounted, and headed down Park Avenue. It was usually easier going on the sidewalk than the street, since there was less refuse.

He came to a sudden halt, dismounted and pushed the bike behind a car. He peered around the side of it. Two blocks ahead, he could see a man. A man dressed in khakis and high leather boots, with a safari hat on his head and rifle in hand.

A hunter! The first one Bobby had seen in months.

There was no law on Manhattan. No police, no courts, no judges, no jails. In short, no law at all.

If anybody was foolish enough to remain on the island he could expect no protection whatsoever from the authorities. If you were robbed, hurt, or even killed, it was your own bad luck. Hence it was that the ruined cities, such as New York, Chicago and Los Angeles, were possibly the only places in the world where a thrill-seeker could actually kill someone for the sport of it and never be apprehended.

The hunters took advantage of this. They would get permission to visit the island on the excuse of attempting to find some object in one of the museums, the library, a private home, or perhaps some record lost in a law office. They would fully arm themselves with the latest weapons, and wear bullet-proof clothing. Then they would come seeking victims. Victims to kill for the fun of it, the thrill of it.

Bobby couldn't imagine more disgusting human beings.

But the problem now was getting past this particular one. He was certainly having bad luck today. First Moose and now a hunter. He must take it carefully. Hunters almost always came in a group, at least two or three, for mutual protection against the baboons. Most baboons went around singly, as did Bobby, and were seldom a match for hunters in a group.

Waiting until the other's back was to him, Bobby quickly remounted his bike and returned to where East 53rd cut over to Fifth Avenue. He peddled over to Fifth and carefully looked around the corner before entering it.

No one in sight. He peddled on.

This was a route he didn't usually take, due to the fact that quite a bit of the fighting had taken place at Rockefeller Center and the rubble of that once fabulous complex of buildings made the street just short of impassable. He would have to push his wheel through it.

When he reached the public library, something came to him. He dismounted and pushed the bicycle up the steps, past the shattered stone lions, and into the building. He left it just inside the crumbled doors, where no one would see it, and headed for the rooms with the shelves of books. There weren't too many of these rooms left undestroyed, but he thought he knew what he was looking for. So far as Bobby knew, he was the only baboon on the island who ever came in here. Few of them were the type who did much reading, and those who did had Library Boosters and could dial their low-level reading material from the National Data Banks, just like respectable citizens throughout the rest of the country.

Sure enough, he found the two books he had in mind without too much difficulty, and headed back for his bicycle.

Fred Thompson's apartment wasn't too much further now. On East 37th, to be exact. The old man lived on the eighth floor, which made it a hard climb for a man his age, but it afforded him quite a bit of protection from his fellow baboons and from hunters. There was only one stairway intact and most of the way up it was quite dark. Thus Fred Thompson could rig the way with various little warning devices, so if anyone started up, without shouting his identity first, Fred could take his shotgun and fire a few warning shots down the stairwell. That invariably warned them off.

Bobby stopped a few moments at the nearby grocery store and selected a dozen or so cans of pork and beans and corn, and another dozen of sardines. It would save his friend a load the next time he wanted to replenish his supply of canned goods. The old man was fond of beans and had a plentiful supply available, since most baboons were inclined to steal more luxurious foods from the ruins of the grocery stores. Bobby also picked up a few cans of fruit juices. He put the things in a plastic shopping bag.

He pushed his bike into the ruined foyer of the apartment house his friend lived in, went over to the stairway and started up, yelling as he went, "Mr. Thompson! Mr. Thompson. It's me. Bobby!"

By the time he got to the fourth floor a weak voice called down to him, "Come on up, Bobby."

Fred Thompson's apartment was the only one on the eighth floor that had survived sufficiently to be habitable. Bobby had been there so often that he knew the place almost as well as his own. Sometimes when he got caught by the night he stayed, rather than risk returning home in the dark.

He put his parcel of food on the kitchen table and returned to the living room where the old man was seated in a comfortable chair. Like Bobby, Fred Thompson had pirated excellent furniture from other apartments and was thus well equipped.

He said, "Well, how've you been, son? Haven't seen you so far this week."

"I've been trying to study," Bobby said.

Fred Thompson had gotten to that period in life where he looked as though he might be anywhere between seventy and ninety. His hair was still full but completely white, his hands trembled a bit, and his voice was wavering. Otherwise he seemed to be in reasonably good shape for his years.

Bobby walked over to the one window that still had glass in it—the others were boarded up with cardboard. He stared down at the street, not expecting, really, to see the hunters this far away from where he had spotted them, but one never knew. They sometimes had hover cars or even helicopters and could travel much faster than someone on a bike.

He said, "On the way over, that big one called Moose tried to grab me. Wanted me to be his monkey. Then I spotted a hunter on Park Avenue."

"This town gets more dangerous, not less, as time goes by," the old man grumbled.

From this height, Bobby could see over a considerable section of this part of the city.

He said softly, "Was it pretty in the old days, Mr. Thompson? New York, I mean."

"Eh? Pretty?" the old man scratched his chin. "Why, I suppose so. This part of town, at least. A lot of the nice buildings, nice homes were around here. Up where you live, too. But there were a lot of parts of town that were terrible. Harlem and so forth."

Bobby left the window and went over and sat at the table near his friend. He knew the story, more or less, but he said, "Mr. Thompson, what happened?"

The other knew what he meant. He pursed his aged lips before answering. "Why, I suppose a lot of things, son. The big cities were doomed for years before they finally collapsed. For one thing, poor people from the South, from Puerto Rico, and other places where it was hard to make a living, moved to the cities to get on relief. So the better-to-do people moved out into the suburbs where they could have better schools, better police protection and so forth. The cities had to raise the taxes so they could support those on relief. So more of the better-paid people moved out, to escape the taxes. So did a good many businessmen, with their businesses. And that meant even less work, and more people on relief. Crime went up and the city couldn't raise enough money to pay more policemen. The population of the slums increased but the city couldn't raise enough money for more teachers to educate the kids, more and more of whom dropped out and got in trouble in the streets."

Bobby said, "But I mean, how did the final riots start?"

"Actually, over a period of time. There were smaller riots, between blacks and whites, students demonstrating against their schools, riots between pro- and antiwar folk, demonstrations of people on relief who wanted more money. Everybody was up-tight, everybody was frustrated.

"Then came the water shortages and the breakdown in the supply of electricity. The city went broke. Police, firemen, garbage collectors and the rest went unpaid. Many of them quit their jobs and left town to get work somewhere else. Then all of a sudden it popped. Everybody who could afford to, for all practical purposes, had left to live in the suburbs or smaller towns. The big fires started and there weren't enough firemen, and the water supply broke down. Half the city had no electricity. Mobs of unemployed kids and criminals began prowling the streets. Some of them broke into gun stores and stole guns. Some of them mobbed police stations and took the guns. Before you knew it, thousands and then tens of thousands of people were trying to get out of town. Hundreds of gun fights were going on. The subways stopped—too many of the employees had joined the people escaping the city. The traffic lights went out. Traffic piled up until the whole place was clogged. People left their cars and, hysterically, started walking, heading for the bridges. The fires got worse and worse, and then the looting. Practically everybody seemed to be looting. The National Guard was brought in, including aircraft to drop first, tear gas then, high explosives on areas where the gangsters, the rioting kids, the looters had taken over completely. And still the fires got worse.

"It lasted for a couple of weeks, I suppose, and finally, even the police deserted the city. There was no city left. No water, no transportation, no electricity—no people. Only we baboons remained."

"Why?"

The old man shrugged. He didn't mind talking about it. He liked company and Bobby was his only visitor, these days.

"Why, some were criminals. Some were mental cases. Some liked the looting." He pursed aged lips again. "I suppose possibly I come under that heading. I'd never had much money, son. I lived in the poorest neighborhoods, ate the cheapest food. All of a sudden, I was able to move into a swank apartment, scrounge the best food available from the gourmet stores. I'd never tasted caviar before, for instance. I got myself the fanciest of clothes. For the first time, I was living it up. Of course, there were disadvantages. No lights, so I had to find camping lanterns in the sport stores that burned gasoline. No water in the plumbing, so it had to be hauled up from the springs that busted out in the subways. And no fresh food at all, so I had to supplement my canned food with vitamins and minerals from the drugstores. But it was kinda fascinating. In a way, I suppose I'm sorry to see it all end. I'm afraid I'm going to have to go back to the mainland like so many of the older baboons have to sooner or later. I don't think I can spend another winter with this kind of heating."

The old man looked at the boy. "How about you, son?"

Bobby put his chin in his hand and his elbow on the table. "Well, I was just a child when it happened. I suppose I got separated from my parents, or they were killed. I can't remember. An old woman picked me up and took me to her place. She lived in a cellar at that time. I can barely remember it. Later, we moved to an abandoned apartment. Now I realize that she was crazy. Her mind must have slipped in the rioting. She died, just a few years ago, and then one of the adult baboons made me his monkey and I worked for him for about two years before I escaped. Then I found the place I'm living in now. I guess that's about it."

"No, I meant, why didn't you go back to the mainland? Most of the folks who remained dribbled back over the years. Living is too tough here. And the only new recruits we get are either criminals hiding from the police, or aliens who aren't eligible for Guaranteed Annual Income and this is the only place they can make a living—scrounging in the ruins."

"Oh," Bobby said. He thought about it. "Well, when I was living with the old lady, I didn't know about anything else. Then when I was a monkey, I couldn't escape. Now, I'm in kind of a pickle."

"How do you mean?"

"Well, suppose I went back to the mainland. I have no parents. They'd put me in some sort of an institution. They wouldn't let me have the kind of freedom I have now. But besides all that, I haven't the education that others my age have. I wasn't even able to read until three years ago, when I met you and you helped me."

"You've sure done a lot since."

"Yes. But if I went back, I wouldn't know the things that kids are taught in the schools over there. I'd have to start in where five-year-olds are. They'd make me. I'd never catch up to the point where I'd learn enough to hold down a job."

"Yeah," the old man said unhappily. "However, there's a lot of advantages to getting the kind of education you are getting. You're getting your own, studying what you want; you're not on a treadmill."

Bobby said, scowling, "That's what I wanted to talk to you about. Listen, why am I not able to get any book I want from the National Library of the National

Data Banks? The computers won't let me because I have no priority rating."

The old man frowned, too. "I know," he said. "It's kind of a long story, son."

Bobby waited.

"Well," the old man said, "the way I figure it, it's because The Establishment, the powers that be, or whatever you want to call it, don't want anybody to rock the boat."

"The Establishment?"

"That's a word they used to use maybe thirty years ago. It meant the men at the top, the men who run things. You see, son, all down through the ages the men on top have fought change. They don't want their applecart upset."

"I don't understand."

"Well, along about the end of the Second World War, about fifty years ago, the second industrial revolution came along. Automation and computerization and the knowledge explosion. At first, it led to a lot of new jobs, building new factories and new machines. But then it hit. Half a dozen technicians can run a factory now, where it used to take thousands of men. As far back as the 1950s, when I was still fairly young, we began to have unemployment and one of the think-tank men predicted that by the year 2,000, two percent of the labor force would be all that was needed to produce everything the country needed. Well, he was right. They had to bring in Guaranteed Annual Income—sometimes they called it Negative Income Tax—to keep the unemployed going. They merged all local relief with Social Security, old age pensions, Medicare, and all the rest, and practically everybody wound up on it."

"But what's that got to do with me not being able to get advanced books?"

"Son, the present-day Establishment, the two percent who do work and get fabulously high pay, want to remain in that spot. And they want their children to, as well. So the children of the present well-to-do get the best educations available but the children of those on Guaranteed Annual Income are given a ridiculously inadequate education, most of it devoted to keeping them from thinking about changes—about changing or reforming the government. Not only schools they attend, but the books they read, the TV shows they see, even sometimes the sermons they hear—all are devoted to making them conformists, happy with things the way they are."

"What changes are you talking about?"

The old man looked at him questioningly. "I don't know, son. And perhaps I'm too old to have an opinion. But I'd say that when a nation has ninety-eight percent of its population on what amounts to relief, and only two percent of the population works at all, then something very basic is wrong with that country and it'll never really progress. Idleness isn't good for individuals and it isn't good for a nation."

"What should I do to help change it?"

Fred Thompson shook his head. "That's not for me to say, son. It's for you to find out on your own. I was born in 1920. It was my generation who gave our country the Great Depression and later the Second World War. The next generation gave the Asian wars to us, pollution of our country, the race riots and the chaos in the schools of that time, among other things. Obviously, we didn't do so well."

He thought back to the time when he was younger. "In my day, the kids used to have a slogan. You can't trust anybody over thirty. At the time we either laughed at the kids, or got mad at the way they refused to do things the way we always had. But you know, Bobby, I've about come to the conclusion that they were right. We weren't to be trusted."

He looked at the books the boy had laid on the table. "*Collected Works of Thomas Jefferson* and *The Speeches of Abraham Lincoln.*" Fred Thompson nodded. "Were these some of the books you couldn't get on your Library Booster screen?"

"Yes."

The old man shook his head. "So they've got to the point where they consider even the two greatest presidents the country ever had to be subversive, eh? Afraid that if the common people read what they had to say, they might start thinking about real freedom and real liberty, instead of the gobblydygook the politicians hand out these days."

"Then you think these books would be worth my reading?"

"They're certainly as good a place as any to start. Bobby, one of these days, when you're a few years older, you're going to have to return to the mainland. And when you do, you're going to be confronted with the same problem the rest of your generation has: How to get the country back on the path of progress. Not just material progress. Real progress. Like I say, I can't tell you how to do it. My generation didn't. We failed."

Bobby picked up the two books. He said, "I'd better get along, Mr. Thompson. I want to start wading into these, if they're not too hard."

The old man saw him to the door. "I suspect that they won't be too hard, Bobby. And that before the year is out, nothing will be. The person who has the thirst for knowledge can somehow manage to find drink. The public library isn't the only source of your material, you know. Half of the old mansions in town that have remained comparatively whole, have big private libraries. You might try scouting around in them when there's something you want."

"Goodbye, Mr. Thompson. Thanks a lot." Bobby started down the stairs.

The old man looked after him. "Thanks for what?" he said softly. "Your generation is the hope of the country. If we don't get out of this rat-race soon, mankind will disappear."

Bobby found his bike where he had left it, put his books in the luggage rack and wheeled it out onto the street. He looked up and down carefully for hunters or other baboons. Ordinarily, the baboons on the island didn't bother each other. There was no reason to and so there was an armed truce. But since he was in the ideal age group to be made a monkey, he couldn't take any chances. He was growing rapidly but he was still too slight to resist one of the burly toughs such as Moose. And, actually, most of the men remaining on the island were large, strong specimens. The weaklings had been weeded out long ago.

The return to his own place was uneventful. To make doubly sure he would avoid the hunters, he went over to the Avenue of the Americas before heading north. As he peddled, it came to him that in this whole day, the only living things he had seen were Moose, the hunter and Fred Thompson. He hadn't spotted, even at a distance, another baboon. There must truly be few left. How many? Nobody knew, but he suspected that there were less than a couple of hundred on Manhattan. Each year some returned to the mainland, due to age or whatever, and each year some died, particularly in view of the lack of medical care. And few indeed were the newcomers.

He thought over what the old man had said and he realized that in one respect his way of life was an advantage. Except for the members of—what had his friend called it? The Establishment, he was one of the few in the whole country who had access to what The Establishment considered dangerous books. Real books were no longer printed. The rest of the country depended on the National Library of the National Data Banks. And you were only allowed to dial for your home screen those books that they thought suitable for you to read. Bobby didn't know it, but the system was one of the most effective systems of censorship the world had ever seen. But he, Bobby, was able to beat it. He wasn't dependent on the National

Library. In the ruins of New York, he had real books at his disposal.

He reached 55th Street and turned right, being doubly cautious now. He was entering the vicinity where the hunters had been and where Moose had accosted him that morning. He prayed inwardly that Moose hadn't seen the alleyway from which he had emerged.

So far, so good. He reached the corner of Park Avenue and wheeled his bike into the sports shop. He began to leave, but then hesitated and looked at the gun rack. Some of the rifles and shotguns that had originally been there had been taken, particularly the heavier caliber ones. But there were still some of the lighter models. He took down an automatic chambered for the .22 Magnum bullet. It wasn't much heavier than his own .22 Long Rifle gun. He searched about and found a couple of boxes of cartridges and loaded the gun. To make sure it was still in working order, he emptied it into the wall, then reloaded it. It was still in order all right, and he liked the feel of it, and realized that its high velocity made it almost as powerful as a higher caliber. He left his own gun in the rack and turned to go.

The way was clear, but he approached his apartment house very slowly, so as not to be surprised. Moose might be waiting for his return. He might be behind any burnt out vehicle or in any doorway.

But he wasn't.

Bobby reached his alleyway, looked up and down again to check if there was anyone who might see him enter. Then he hurried up it, gun now slung over his shoulder, his books in hand.

The reason Moose had not been seen on the street was because he was in the basement of the apartment house adjoining that of Bobby. He was sitting on a wooden crate, next to a furnace, and his carbine was held on his lap, ready for action.

There was no retreat; Bobby was past Moose and had his one exit cut off before he saw the man.

Moose grinned nastily and said, "Hello, kid. I told you not to run this morning, but you did. That means you're going to start out being my monkey by taking a beating. First of all, drop that gun. From now on you don't carry no guns. If you need any protection, Moose'll protect you."

Instead of dropping the gun, Bobby dropped the two books. He took a deep breath and said, "Moose, a friend of mine, Fred Thompson, once told me that no man has to become a slave if he doesn't want to. He can die first—and a dead man isn't a slave."

"Don't be crazy, kid. I don't want to kill you. But if you give me any trouble I'll put a slug in your leg. It'll lay you up for awhile, might even cripple you permanently. But that'd just make you easier to keep herd on. So drop that little peashooter and come along."

Bobby unslung the gun and the other must have thought he was about to drop it, as ordered. But that was where Moose made his final mistake.

Bobby shot him three times. *Bang. Bang. Bang.*

Once in the upper chest, once in the throat and once square in the middle of the forehead.

The big man doubled forward, his reddish eyes popping surprise, even as he died.

Coldly and efficiently, Bobby dragged him out into the alley. The man was heavy, and it was difficult, but he managed. He could take him no further, he didn't have the strength, but he knew it wasn't necessary. When night came, the other inhabitants of Manhattan, other than the baboons, would take care of the problem of disposal; the wild cats, the wild dogs, and, above all, the rats.

Bobby turned and made his way back into the interior of the building. He took up his gun and the books, and through the devious holes and passageways, returned to his apartment.

He was feeling very empty. He had never hurt another person before in his life, even in self-defense. He did not believe in harming other human beings. But he believed even more strongly that everyone has a right to his freedom and must be willing to fight and die for it.

He leaned his gun up against the wall and took his books over to his desk. He sneered at the Library Booster sitting there and, instead of activating it, opened one of the books—*Jefferson's Collected Works*—at random.

He came upon the first inaugural address and the first lines that hit his eyes were:

. . . let us hasten to retrace our steps and to regain

the road which alone leads to peace, liberty and safety.

He knew that old Mr. Thompson was right and that there was hope.

Surprised, he reached up to wipe away some tears.

MOONCHILD
Tom Purdom

Ten minutes after his brother left the apartment, Harvey Oliver picked up his big wooden recorder and started warming it between his hands. He had been playing the tenor recorder for nearly three years now and he was getting pretty good at it. His big hands could handle the long stretch between the finger holes, and the structured, measured music of the Baroque period had always appealed to him. The music had been written in a century when there had still been country roads on Earth and no one had dreamed there would ever be cities on the Moon, but something in his personality had always responded to it.

The recorder is a wind instrument, however. The pitch is controlled by the performer's control of his breath pressure. A harsh, raspy note leaped out of the instrument before he was halfway through the minuet and he pulled it away from his mouth and turned away from his music stand.

It had now been fourteen minutes since Ted had slipped through the door. It would take Ted twenty minutes to walk down to King Garden and another five or ten minutes to look it over and make sure they could plant the containers without dodging too many mid-afternoon strollers.

His father raised his head and smiled thinly. "I'm afraid I'm not feeling particularly calm myself," Dr. Oliver said.

"It's just tension," Harvey said. "I felt the same way the night before the election."

"Why don't we get the stuff out of the closet and get it set up?"

Harvey pulled the recorder apart and reached for the long swab he used to wipe out the moisture after he finished playing it. His father stood up and Harvey watched his thin, stooped back as he opened the closet and bent over.

"It's a good thing we aren't trying to do this with bombs," his father said. "I'd probably be sitting here thinking they were going to go off accidentally every time somebody walked past the door."

Harvey chuckled politely. His father turned away from the closet and laid a belt and three plastic containers on a stone coffee table.

"All in order," Dr. Oliver said. "All primed and ready to go."

Harvey stood up and untied the sash around his waist. His father was wearing shorts and a belted judo jacket, but students all over Earth and the Moon had been wearing long, brilliantly colored robes for the last two years. His father was going to plant the containers in the park, but he and his brother were going to tote them there.

His father stuffed the containers into the pouches on the belt and he stepped up to the table and picked it up. He had helped his father make the chemicals in the containers but he didn't feel any sense of accomplishment when he looked at them.

"It's the only way we can do it," Dr. Oliver murmured. "We aren't going to get anywhere sitting around waiting for the next so-called election."

Harvey pushed back his robe and buckled the belt around the turtleneck body shirt he wore underneath it. His father had said that a dozen times already, but Harvey knew he was really trying to convince himself. He was only fourteen but he had been studying modern psychology since he had been in kindergarten and he understood most of the dynamics of normal human behavior. His father was just as troubled by this as he was. Every time Dr. Oliver made one of his little speeches, he was really telling his sons he wasn't sure he was doing the right thing.

I thought about this for a long time, Harvey. I've never done a violent thing in my life. This is the only alternative we've got to breaking out the guns and knives. We tried to beat them at the polls, and they proved we aren't going to win them over that way. No ruling class has ever given up its privileges until it is forced to. They'll know somebody sabotaged their life support system as soon as they get a look at the results. They'll know we can do it again anytime we want to. There's no place on the Moon for people who are willing to wallow in luxury while the rest of the people in their community are doing without a necessity. People are too dependent on each other on the Moon. It's too easy for somebody to deprive you of something vital. They've forgotten they're vulnerable but they aren't fools. They'll come to their senses as soon as they get a little reminder. This will probably be the one and only time we'll have to do something like this.

"We'll be all right," Harvey said.

"It'll probably be the easiest thing we ever did."

"We'll probably be back here before we know it."

The phone buzzed. Dr. Oliver's shoulders jerked. Harvey settled his robe over his belt and turned on the phone screen.

Ted's face filled the screen. "I've just been taking a little stroll around the park, Harve. Why don't you two music addies get out of that prison cell and stretch your legs?"

"We'll be right there," Harvey said. "Where do you want us to meet you?"

"I'll probably be hanging around the fountain. There's some nice looking hits sitting around the edge."

"Have fun."

The screen blanked. Harvey turned away from the phone and fiddled with the knot on his sash.

"It looks like we got ready just in time," Dr. Oliver said.

"He didn't waste any time."

Half a dozen children were playing tag in the long

corridor that ran past their door. Two of Harvey's friends were playing chess in an alcove. A fat man was pulling a shopping wagon loaded with groceries and three or four other people were strolling along the corridor on various errands. It was three o'clock in the afternoon, according to the twenty-four-hour cycle people used on the Moon, and most of the people in this part of Freedom City were safely tucked away in their offices and labs.

Two girls raced past them with a five-year-old boy yelling at their heels. His father stopped and watched them trample down the corridor and Harvey stopped a couple of steps in front of him and waited. He knew what his father was thinking without being told. The Duvalis process.

This process had been developed on Earth only six years before and it had become a global issue overnight. For the first time in the history of mankind, every human child could grow up with an IQ in the 200's. The proper combination of drugs and carefully planned environments could put every child on Earth and the Moon in the genius class. The drugs and the environments had to be tailored for every child, however. Parents and teachers had to receive special training. If every child were to receive the benefits of the process, every nation on Earth would have to increase its educational expenditures by a factor of six.

Two major nations had already decided the investment would give them a population that would dominate the world economy, and would therefore be worth every sacrifice they had to make. The rest of the governments on Earth were dragging their feet, as usual. A complete Duvalization program would require massive increases in taxes—and the people who would have to put up the money would naturally be the wealthiest and most powerful people in each society. Most of the countries of the world were already using the Duvalis process on some of their children, but it was obviously going to be a long time before they started giving it to everybody. Somebody always lost when the world changed—and the people on top always resisted when they thought there was a good chance they might be the losers.

The political conflict in Freedom City was a microcosm of the struggle taking place on Earth. The independent colony had been founded by one of the leading genetic researchers on the Moon and the independent research stations still dominated it economically and politically. Their research on genetic engineering and artificial ecologies brought in most of the wealth the city attracted from the outside; the sterile, isolated deserts of the Moon were the best place to experiment with new microorganisms and with modifications in the ecology of Earth, and many of the best researchers in the world had left the bases owned by their nation states and joined the independent colony. Earth needed the research facilities located in Freedom City and it was willing to pay for the services of the men who controlled them. The rest of the people in the colony, however, were primarily farmers and small businessmen; they had left the planned societies of Earth because they wanted more personal freedom, and they knew they would have led impoverished lives on the Moon if they hadn't been associated with the men at the research stations. And the people in the research stations naturally felt they should get the lion's share of the colony's resources.

"You can't have every advantage you had on Earth," the Chairman of City Council, Dr. Nathan Gibson, had told a delegation of parents. "This is the Moon. We don't have the resources they have on Earth. Pioneers can't live like the people who stayed behind in civilization. This is a land of opportunity and it's a place where you can call your mind and soul your own—but it isn't Earth. It will be a long time before you can have all the comforts of Earth."

As far as Harvey's father was concerned, however, the parents had been asking for a necessity, not a luxury, and they weren't getting it because Dr. Gibson and his colleagues were being selfish and greedy. "We could do it if some of us would give up some of our fancy incomes," Dr. Oliver had said. "We could double the number of children we could give the treatment to, even if we couldn't give it to everybody. But they won't do it. They'll let children grow up with their intellectual potential stunted before they'll give up some of the money they spend on toys for their own children."

Dr. Oliver turned away from the children in the corridor. He straightened up as if he were stepping onto a speaker's platform, and Harvey lowered his eyes.

"Let's go," Dr. Oliver said.

The light in the hallway varied from section to section as they walked along. The walls were decorated with long brightly colored murals and windows in the ceiling let in filtered sunlight every couple of hundred meters which focussed on big potted plants. The sun was hammering on an airless desert outside, but Freedom City was a sealed oasis of life, color, and warmth. The crowded underground cities of Earth tended to be sterile and colorless, but the citizens of Freedom City had tried to create an environment in which there would be room to stretch your arms, and food for all your senses. They hadn't crossed 240,000 miles of empty space merely because they wanted to re-create the sterile, dull environments they had left on Earth.

Martin Luther King Garden was a good example of the lunar colonist's fondness for bright colors and lush vegetation. It was the life support system for a big section of Freedom City but it had been laid out so it would be a pleasant place to visit, too. Fountains danced among the big-leaved plants that produced most of the oxygen. Narrow, winding paths twisted through the shrubbery. Tropical birds chattered and twittered in the branches of small trees. Oversize dragonflies darted through the dome and preyed on other insects.

The bio-engineers who had developed the organic life support systems had been 240,000 miles away from the nearest large supply of free air and water. They had wanted a system they could trust and they had known that the living organisms in the system would still be subject to the laws of nature. The microorganisms in the system would still be mutating and evolving as they adapted to their environment and competed with each other. Humans would still be arriving from Earth, their bodies full of germs. If the lunar colonists populated their domes with one or two species of plants and food animals, a single new disease might spread through the whole system and wipe out most of their supply of food or oxygen before they could cope with it. An organic life support system had to be a complete, self-sustaining artificial eco-system and it had to be as varied as the natural eco-systems of Earth. If a new disease attacked a plant, there had to be other species of plants that could form a barrier between the disease and its next victim—or that could take the victim's place and fill in the gap if the disease wiped out a whole species. And you couldn't add new species of plants without adding new species of insects and microorganisms, and all the other creatures they needed to support them and keep them in balance.

Nothing lived alone. Every living organism was supported by a web of life. You could build a new web under a lunar dome but it still had to be a web.

Ted was lounging against a jumble of rocks beside the main fountain. He was talking to a freckle-faced girl in a long black and yellow robe. Another girl was sitting on top of the rocks with her arms around her knees.

The spray from the fountain touched Harvey's face.

He raised his hand in greeting and Ted grinned and waved back.

"It's about time you bolts got here," Ted said. "I knew you'd get here just when I found some decent company."

Dr. Oliver's face darkened for a moment. He smiled at the girls and the freckle-faced girl smiled back. The other girl nodded her head and turned back to her contemplation of the fountain.

"We've got a little family business we have to talk about," Ted said. "I'll probably be back in about twenty minutes."

"I'll still be here," the freckle-faced girl said.

"I hope so."

Ted pushed himself away from the rocks and fell in beside his father. The three of them turned a corner and moved down a narrow, winding walk.

A yellow bug landed on Harvey's arm and he pushed it off without hurting it. The soft, low sound of a pair of recorders reached him from somewhere in the shrubbery. Two girls in their early twenties were strolling about ten meters ahead of them.

Dr. Oliver's face looked tense and sober. He was holding his long, thin arms close to his sides and walking as if his joints were surrounded by a rigid, invisible space suit.

"That girl Natasha really lights me up," Ted said.

Dr. Oliver swallowed. "The girl in the black and yellow robe?"

"Right."

"Have you known her very long?"

"I just met her last week. Her father owns a farm in a little dome about twenty kilometers out. She only gets into town when she can hitch a ride with somebody."

They turned a corner and entered a little clearing in which a small fountain was dancing between two stone benches. The two girls had disappeared around a bend twenty meters ahead.

Dr. Oliver stopped at the edge of the clearing. He touched his chin with his hand, and Ted and Harvey glanced at each other.

Dr. Oliver stepped into the center of the clearing. He looked up and down the path and studied the bushes on both sides.

"All right, Harvey."

Harvey stepped down the walk and looked around. He pulled a container out of his robe and his father grabbed it and held it against his side with his hand covering most of it.

"Watch the other end of the walk," Dr. Oliver said. "Stay there, Ted."

Harvey stepped across the clearing and positioned himself beside a bush. He glanced over his shoulder and saw his father dropping to his hands and knees and crawling into the bushes.

The container in his father's hand had a small black tab on one side. When Dr. Oliver pulled on the tab, a powder and a liquid would combine inside the container and an odor would spread through the surrounding area as the compound evaporated. No human nose could detect the odor, but it would have a serious effect on a small black and red beetle. Like most insects, the beetles located their mates with their sense of smell; their chemical senses could detect the correct odor if only a few molecules were present in every cubic foot of air—and the chemical in the containers would increase the number of molecules per cubic foot by nearly six hundred percent. The beetles would become confused and their birth rate would be significantly affected.

The beetles were the specific control for a bug that ate the roots of certain plants and kept their population under control. The bugs would begin to increase and there would be a gradual decrease in the number of plants in three different species. Within six Earth months, if Dr. Oliver's calculations were correct, the plant population in the artificial eco-system would be much less varied than it had been.

The change wouldn't be detectable for most of those six months. Three Earth months from now, Dr. Oliver would return to the life support system and spread a virus he had already developed in his home lab. The virus would spread through a species of plants that had exceeded its normal population density and huge areas of oxygen-producing vegetation would be blighted and put out of action. At the very minimum, oxygen production would be reduced by twenty-five percent. If any unexpected side effects took place and the thing got out of hand, it might be reduced by fifty to seventy-five percent.

Nobody in the area served by the system would be killed. Oxygen could be pumped into the area from other systems. The damage would probably be repairable. Dr. Gibson and his chums would merely be getting a warning message in the only language they seemed to understand. They had rigged the electoral system in their favor and there was nothing anybody could do about it; you couldn't vote the rascals out when they had set up the political system and had made sure it included a lot of nice little items, like the rule that all employees of research stations had to cast their votes at their places of employment. But that didn't mean they could ignore the anger of the people they lived with.

Dr. Oliver backed out of the bushes on his hands and knees. He glanced at both ends of the path as he stood up and Ted nodded reassuringly.

"Five more to go," Dr. Oliver murmured.

The six containers had to be scattered around the park. The exact locations weren't important but they had to be sure the odor would cover most of the area.

A girl laughed behind Harvey's back. He turned around as if he had been jabbed with a pin and saw a girl and a young man five steps behind him. He had turned his head when his father had crawled out of the bushes and they had apparently rounded the bend and walked up on him before he had seen them.

Dr. Oliver turned toward a rose bush behind a bench. Ted stepped off the walk and raised his head as if he was examining the top branches of a tree. The couple walked across the little clearing with their arms around each other's waists and Dr. Oliver turned away from the rose bush and stalked toward Harvey.

"Keep your eyes on the damned path, Harvey," Dr. Oliver whispered. "Don't worry about me."

"You were already standing up when they came up behind me. They didn't see a thing."

"Keep your eyes on the path. We aren't playing games."

Harvey's face reddened. Ted came up behind his father and shrugged.

"Where to next?" Ted said.

Dr. Oliver shook his head. He put his hand on Harvey's shoulder and Harvey smiled wryly and punched him on the biceps.

"I can think of a lot of other things I'd rather be doing right now," Harvey said.

"You're doing fine," Dr. Oliver said. "Let's go."

A middle-aged couple were sitting in the next open area. Dr. Oliver, Harvey, and Ted trudged across it without saying anything and Dr. Oliver turned left when they came to a branch in the path.

"There's another little clearing about thirty meters ahead," Dr. Oliver said.

A woman was sitting in the clearing with a baby in her arms. A boy and girl were playing hide-and-go-seek in the bushes.

"I was afraid it would turn out like this," Dr. Oliver murmured.

"It went off fine the first time," Harvey said.

"It looks like we had beginner's luck."

They stepped out of the clearing and rounded another bend in the path. Dr. Oliver gestured with his hand and his sons stopped in their tracks.

Dr. Oliver looked around him. His whole body stiffened. He gestured at Harvey and Harvey reached inside his robe and handed him another container.

Dr. Oliver lowered his head and ducked into the dark, hedge-like bushes beside the path. Ted and Harvey faced each other and watched the path by looking over each other's shoulders.

Ted stiffened. Harvey turned his head and saw a square, muscular man in a red beret coming down the path.

"I should have known we'd run into one of them at a time like this," Ted said.

People could prowl around in the bushes near the fountains and the clearings, but the areas beside the paths were off limits. Martin Luther King Garden was a life support system, not just a park—and you didn't let people tramp around inside a life support system just because they thought it might be fun. Dr. Oliver would be in trouble even if the man from the Peace Watch never suspected he was trying to sabotage the system.

Harvey's face reddened again. The peaceman's eyes slid across his face and Harvey turned back to his brother and tried to look innocent. Every nerve in his back was tingling.

Should Ted ignore the peaceman and pretend he was talking? Should he say hello and give him a wave? Did his father know the peaceman was there?

Ted looked tense, too. He turned his head toward the bushes and Harvey's fists clenched.

Branches brushed against the peaceman's clothes. "How's it going, men?"

"Fine," Harvey blurted.

"Seen any good-looking hits around today?"

Ted turned his head. The peaceman was rocking on the balls of his feet and smiling pleasantly.

My father's hiding in the bushes. He's planting a chemical that can wreck a life support system.

"There's a big bunch of them by the main fountain," Ted said.

Leaves rustled in the bushes. Ted jerked his head around.

A moth and two small birds leaped into the air. A big praying mantis hopped across a bush. The birds landed on a branch on the other side of the path and the moth rose into the air with the dream-like, lazy strokes of a creature flying in the low lunar gravity.

He's probably got the container in his hands right now. You'll catch him red-handed.

The peaceman's eyes narrowed. He glanced at the two faces in front of him and Harvey's mind blanked. They had talked about all the things they could do in different situations and now he couldn't remember one thing they had said.

Ted smiled. "It sounds like there must be a bear running around in there."

"We've been having a real problem with bears around here lately."

"It's our father," Ted said. "He wanted to look at something in there."

"He's a bio-engineer," Harvey blurted. "He saw

something interesting and dropped into the bushes before we knew he was gone."

Leaves rustled near the hem of Harvey's robe. He stepped back and his father crawled out of the bushes with all the care of a man who valued every leaf in the system. Dr. Oliver looked up at the peaceman and then he stood up and brushed himself off.

The peaceman shook his head. Most peacemen were students who were working their way through school, but he looked like he was the kind of man who would have been a policeman on Earth, too.

Dr. Oliver held up a pocket microscope. "I was just looking at some of the soil in there. I made some improvements in the soil system here four years ago and I couldn't help taking a look at it on the spur of the moment."

The peaceman's face clouded. "They're getting pretty strict about people going into the off-limits zones. A lot of people are getting so self-confident nowadays they're beginning to forget we've got reasons for those rules."

"I don't do it very often," Dr. Oliver said. "I could get a permit but I just yielded to impulse."

"May I see your ID please?"

Dr. Oliver colored. Harvey started to step back and then caught himself and stayed where he was.

Dr. Oliver reached inside his jacket and took out his wallet. He flipped it open and the peaceman leaned over and studied it.

"Dr. Oliver! I thought I knew you from somewhere. I'm sorry! I was standing guard outside the council room when you made that statement three months ago."

"The statement I made at the meeting about the Duvalis process? It wasn't a very effective statement, I'm afraid."

"It was a pleasure just to hear somebody from the blasted labs was standing up for us ordinary bolts. My oldest daughter's getting the Duvalis treatment right now but I'll be damned if I can see why she should get it and my son shouldn't."

"That's exactly the point I was trying to make," Dr. Oliver said. "They're going to be living on the same world for the next sixty or seventy years. How can we have some of them grow up with 200 plus IQ's and the rest of them only be normal?"

"It's too bad a few more of the voters couldn't have seen it that way. I would have given up three months rations if it would have helped some of Petri's people get on the Council."

"We'll just have to try again next time. Sooner or later people have to see it's the only way."

"I hope so."

Harvey shuffled restlessly. Dr. Oliver held out his hand and clapped the peaceman on the shoulder.

"They will," Dr. Oliver said. "It's going to take longer than I'd hoped it would, but I'm certain they will."

They backed away with Dr. Oliver in the lead and disappeared around another bend. Ted sagged against a tree trunk and rolled his eyes at the top of the dome as if he were going to faint.

"Buck up," Dr. Oliver said.

"He knows who you are," Harvey murmured. "He'll remember you were here."

"It can't be helped, Harvey. We'll just have to go ahead and hope for the best."

"They'll know we were doing something in the bushes if one more peaceman catches us like that."

"I couldn't let him catch me in the bushes with the container. He would have been suspicious right away if Ted hadn't told him I was there."

"I wish you'd come out sooner," Ted said. "I didn't know what to do there for a minute."

"You aren't the only one. I would have stood up two minutes earlier if I hadn't been scared stiff."

"They'll just have to spot us like that one more time," Harvey said. "That's all it'll take."

Dr. Oliver stared at his son's face. The path was empty in both directions but they were all talking in whispers.

"Do you want us to go on without you, Harvey? Do you think it's too dangerous?"

"He knows your name, Dad. He knows you're one of the people who've been fighting the Council. He'll remember you were here as soon as they find the container and start asking questions."

"It'll be six months before they start looking. They can't prove we put it there even if he goes against his natural inclinations and happens to remember he saw us."

"It'll just take one more incident. They'll know it wasn't just a coincidence if one more peaceman happens to see us."

Dr. Oliver's gentle, scholarly face hardened. "You'd better give Ted your last container, Harvey. We'll go ahead without you."

A man and a woman came into view at one end of the path. Ted pushed himself away from the tree trunk and studied his brother's face.

"It doesn't matter whether I go with you or not!" Harvey said. "You're the one they'll persecute."

"We don't have time to argue, Harvey. Give Ted your container."

The couple were about twenty meters away. Harvey sucked in a deep breath and stepped toward his brother.

"Don't let him do it, Ted. He can't do it if you won't help him."

His voice cracked with emotion. He had been scared before but he was on the edge of panic now. His father trusted him. They had gotten along well for fourteen years. They had worked side by side on election day and they had come out of the experience with a real respect for each other. He had showed his father he could hold his own in a rough situation and his father had given him a vivid picture of a mature man's anger at selfishness and injustice and his concern about the people who were the victims of other people's callousness.

Ted's eyes shifted from his brother to his father. He glanced at the couple coming down the walk and frowned.

"You can get the containers as soon as they go by," Dr. Oliver murmured.

The couple came down the walk with their hands gesturing and their attention obviously concentrated on their conversation. Harvey and his father both stepped closer to Ted to give them room to pass. They went on by without a glance and another couple came around the bend on the other side and walked by.

"Don't let him do it," Harvey whispered. "They'll kill him if they find out he did it."

Fingers dug into his shoulders. Rough hands spun him around. His father's red, contorted face glared down at him.

"*Give him the container!* Give him the container and shut up!"

The fingers squeezed his shoulders like a set of clamps. His father's eyes were glaring at him like the eyes of a madman.

The angry mask glanced up and down the path. Dr. Oliver reached inside the robe and jerked the container out of Harvey's belt. He swung on Ted and Ted grabbed the container away from him and shoved it under his belt.

Harvey stepped away from his father and rubbed his aching shoulders. Dr. Oliver stalked down the path and Ted shook his head and followed him. Ted looked back once and then turned away with his eyes on the ground.

Harvey slumped against the tree trunk. Three voices chattered on the other side of the bend and he stood up and tried to look composed.

Three young girls ran around the bend. They ran

past him without a glance in his direction and he slumped against the tree again.

More voices rose on the other side of the bend. He pushed himself away from the tree and trudged around the bend as if he were walking through a fog.

Two boys his own age had dropped onto a bench and started arguing about an international chess game they had seen on television. They looked up when he came around the bend and turned back to their argument.

A big moth fluttered past his ear. He waved it away without touching it and a flash of red caught his eye.

His right hand slid along the top of the bushes as if he were resting it on a bannister. People flowed past him as if in a dream. A man and a woman looked at him strangely.

The peaceman was standing by a fountain with a pair of girls. He looked relaxed but his eyes were watching every side of the clearing as he talked. He jerked his hand at Harvey and gave him a wink as soon as Harvey entered the clearing.

"How's it going?" the peaceman said.

Harvey stopped ten steps from the peaceman. One of the girls turned her head and eyed him curiously.

The peaceman frowned. The other girl turned her head and raised her eyebrows.

"I've got something I have to tell you," Harvey said. "Can I talk to you alone?"

The peaceman ran his hand across a girl's shoulder and stepped toward him. "Sure. What's the matter?"

"We'll still be here when you're finished," one of the girls said.

The peaceman stopped in front of him. Harvey looked around the clearing and the peaceman pointed down a path. "Let's go that way."

The peaceman strolled down the path and Harvey found himself moving with him. They stopped beside a big, flower-covered bush and the peaceman studied Harvey's face.

"What's the matter, son? What can I do for you?"

Harvey's fists clenched. He was standing on one side of a huge canyon and his father and Ted were standing on the other side. His father had grown up on Earth and lived there most of his life. Ted had been five years old when their family had moved to the Moon.

"I need some help with my father," Harvey said. "He's getting himself in a lot of trouble. Somebody has to help me stop him before he gets into trouble."

"He's doing something illegal again?"

"He's trying to make the council change its policies. He thinks he can scare them into giving more kids the Duvalis treatment."

The peaceman frowned. "He thinks he can *scare* them?"

"He's trying to damage the garden. He can't do it if you're watching him."

The peaceman's eyes narrowed. He stepped back and looked Harvey over.

"You're trying to tell me a man like your father would damage a life support system?"

"He thinks it's the only way we can get any justice. He's so angry he doesn't care what he does."

"That's a pretty big accusation, young man. You're certain you aren't trying to have a little fun with a poor stupid cop?"

"He's doing it right now. He'll be all done in another fifteen or twenty minutes if you don't help me stop him."

"One man can't destroy a life support system all by himself. What's he going to do? Set it on fire?"

"He's hiding a container that contains a chemical he developed himself. It's like a poison. He knows exactly what to use. He's already planted two but he has to plant four more. He'll have to stop if he sees you watching him."

The peaceman unhooked the radio on his belt. He pressed a button on its control panel and raised it to his mouth.

"This is Johnson," the peaceman said. "I've got a situation here we'd better look into. Look out for Dr. William Oliver and his oldest son—a thin man in his mid-forties, about 188 centimeters tall, type twelve face, bald, white tunic, black turtleneck shirt, accompanied by a teenager, about eighteen, type six face, in a blue robe with yellow embroidery. They may be planting containers with some kind of poison in them. Don't let them dump anything they're carrying. Hold them right where they are if you catch one of them climbing out of the shrubbery."

Harvey stepped back. The peaceman lowered the walkie-talkie and looked down at him.

"He's breaking the law, son. I can't help him break the law."

"He can't do it if you're watching him."

"That's not my job. He's breaking the law and you and I both know it."

"He doesn't know what he's doing. He's only doing it because he's worried about your children."

"We can't have any kind of law here if I decide I'm going to enforce the law some of the time. You knew I might send out the alarm when you told me about this. You did everything you could to protect him. You know we can't let people do things like this. He couldn't do anything worse than this."

The walkie-talkie buzzed. The peaceman raised it to his ear and nodded. "I'll be right there," he said.

He lowered the intercom. "They caught him coming out of the bushes. They're waiting for me now."

His father and Ted were standing by a bench with three peacemen standing around them. A dozen curiosity seekers were standing near them. More people were coming down the path.

Harvey stopped twenty steps away and rested his hand on a bush. Johnson barked an order as he moved in and a young peaceman started searching Ted's robe.

The peaceman pulled out the belt with the containers. He handed it to Johnson and Johnson looked over the two prisoners.

Dr. Oliver's face was scarlet. He had drawn himself up to his full height and he was looking down on the peacemen as if he were standing on top of a mountain.

He turned toward Harvey and their eyes met across the heads of the peacemen.

Harvey's eyes blurred. He turned his head away from his father and two middle-aged women stepped between them.

A huge moth landed on his bare hand. The touch of its feelers sent a shiver up his arm. He brushed it off without hurting it and it flew across the bushes and landed on a flower.

A life support system was a sacred object. Nobody should damage a life support system. Not for any reason.

PET
Raymond F. Jones

Expelled!

Jeremy Carter stared at the slip of paper in his hands. It hadn't happened. He knew it was impossible. But the blue slip would not go away. He sat down on the edge of his bed and glanced across the room at his space pet, Aristotle. The off-world animal rolled about his pen with complete lack of concern for Jeremy's predicament.

Jeremy was convinced the featureless ball of fur was somehow connected with his plight, but he didn't know exactly how. If only they had given him a little more time—

He heard the expected knock on his door, and his father entered without waiting for Jeremy to answer. His father's face was hard and lined with seriousness.

"I heard," said Whit Carter. "The School Director called me at my office today."

Jeremy shuffled his feet and spread his hands. "I'm sorry, Dad. I didn't think I was being deliberately out of line. I disagreed, and tried to explain to everybody what I thought, and what my reasons were. They acted like I was crazy or something. Is it really the end of any chance at a Space Apprenticeship? Did Dr. Haslam say anything about that?"

Whit Carter shook his head. He sat down on the bed beside Jeremy and folded his big hands across his knees. Jeremy's father was a big man all over. He was Chief Engineer for Inter-space Lines, and to Jeremy he had always seemed as big and powerful as the atomic space liners he tended. "Let's start at the beginning and you tell me just how this thing got started anyway."

"You know most of it, Dad," said Jeremy miserably. "It started right after we got Aristotle."

"Yes, I know." Whit Carter's voice was bitter. "How I wish we'd never seen that beast."

"Dad, you don't understand! Aristotle's my friend. He wouldn't do anything to harm me—"

"Yet you've done it to yourself because of him."

"Dad, don't—"

"Let's go back to the beginning."

Jeremy thought back to that day when they'd bought Aristotle at Sam Haskins' Off-world Pet Shop. The round ball of fur that rolled almost unceasingly about the cage had been moved to a far corner of the shop. People were fascinated by the creature for a little while. Then its aimless movement became tiring and they wandered off to more exciting pets.

The animal was about the size of a basketball, with no features except a small white patch of fur amid all the brown. It seemed to regard that white patch as its bottom, for that was where it came to rest at long intervals between its almost ceaseless, aimless rolling. There was a sense of discomfort produced by that completely featureless body. People needed eyes to look back at them with curiosity, appeal, humor, or even hostility. They needed something resembling a nose to indicate which was front and which was back. Some kind of appendages for locomotion—like legs.

Here—nothing.

Jeremy remembered how he had felt. Almost instantaneously. It wasn't pity; it wasn't sympathy. It was, he guessed later, something like falling-in-love with something or someone. He said to his father, "I want this one."

And Whit Carter had done his best to divert Jeremy's attention to more conventional animals in the pet shop. But Jeremy refused to be put off. He had to have an off-world pet to report on for his Biological Adaptibility class in two weeks. There was nothing else in the pet shop that interested him.

On the way home he had decided on the name Aristotle.

"It was that night," said Jeremy. "I had an assignment to do a spaceport design with the use of the engineering computer they furnish to us at the beginning of the year. I got the idea of a spaceport in the air, keeping all the commotion and waste products out of the atmosphere of a city and yet being close to it. It seemed to me that it could be supported on columns of light if a way could be found to concentrate enough beams to provide sufficient radiation pressure.

"I checked the computer for the idea and it buzzed

almost all night before it came up with a design and some equations that showed a light-beam support could be devised. And it was all so real—it was just like I could see it in my mind. I knew just how it could be. It was just like I had been in such a place."

"That's what you told Dr. Haslam?" asked Jeremy's father quietly. "You told him you knew it was right because you had been there?"

"I guess I did." Jeremy hung his head, then looked up to his father in sudden appeal. "But that's the way it was, Dad! The idea was so real to me—it did seem just like I had been there!"

"But, of course, you hadn't. You know that."

"Yeah—I know that. But *he* had—" They both looked toward the silent, rolling furball.

"So you still think that animal has been communicating something to your mind in a way you don't understand?" said Whit Carter wearily.

"I know I'm getting something from it. You said yourself that these things I've come up with are impossible, but they wouldn't be impossible if Aristotle were feeding them to me."

"But you can't hear it. You have no evidence whatever that there is any communication from the animal."

"No. But there's something—I know there is—"

"You know that electro-psychometric tests, required to import such an animal, showed it completely dormant intellectually—along with the absence of any life hazard, which is required to permit its importation."

"If I could just have a little more time. I know I could find some line of communication with Aristotle that I could demonstrate to you and Dr. Haslam."

"You told him about your belief regarding the animal?"

Jeremy nodded. "That was the final straw, I guess. He really blew up when I tried to tell him I thought Aristotle was influencing me with these ideas."

"I don't blame him," said Whit Carter. "I don't blame him one bit. As to the equations, I hoped that you might be right, but when Haslam called me, I got hold of your paper and had some of the best men down at the shop take a look at them. They're nothing but GIGO—Garbage In, Garbage Out. The expressions in your so-called equations are meaningless."

"They're not," said Jeremy doggedly. "They mean something. I don't know what, but they mean something."

"Then there's that simulation of an off-world society. You came up with a set of environmental factors and social customs that was utterly impossible, yet you argued with the professors that it was right because you knew such a situation existed. You said they wouldn't know a real-life situation if it fell on them. That made Dr. Morton and Dr. Howard mad."

"So they throw me out because I made them mad by showing up their stupidity!"

"They are throwing you out because they believe you are either having hallucinations or else you are so obstinate you contradict authorities who have spent their lifetimes learning their professions. I don't know what's happened to you, Jeremy. But I know the result, and so do you. There'll be no Space Apprenticeship. Is it worth that sacrifice to be so obstinate and rebellious?"

Jeremy pressed his lips tighter. "Do I have to let them call me stupid and a daydreamer just to make sure I get the Apprenticeship?"

"Yes—if that's what's required. Your goal is to get into space. Does anything else matter?"

"Honesty matters. Integrity matters."

"It's not a question of honesty or integrity, can't you understand that? These men aren't frauds. They've spent a lifetime in their professions. Your opinions are based on a few wild hunches. Theirs are based on years of solid study and experience."

"I don't agree, but I won't argue with you, Dad. Is there any chance for me, or am I out?"

"I told Dr. Haslam I'd have a talk with you. I think he left the door open, and I'll see what I can do. I'm to call him again tomorrow. He may want to come to see you. If he does, remember he holds the key to whether you get to space or whether you don't."

It was a sleepless night for Jeremy. He lay on his bed staring into the darkness.

He should never have tried to tell them about Aristotle. That was his biggest mistake. He had thought they would be excited and welcome the idea that he was somehow being helped by the strange, seemingly inert bit of life from out of space. Instead, they were repelled by the idea.

He didn't understand it. But there were endless numbers of things he didn't understand. He didn't understand why his father would require him to submit to the dishonesty and shortsightedness of such men as Morton and Howard—and Haslam. Yet, in a way, it made sense if you accepted the dishonest values of the world he lived in. Morton, Howard and Haslam controlled Jeremy's future. It was the rules of the one-sided game that was being played. If he didn't like the rules he could get out of the game. But getting into space was part of that game.

It maddened and confused him and he tried to sleep—and couldn't. Or maybe he did, he thought a bit later, because he was dreaming that someone was talking to him. He heard a voice say, "I'm sorry to have caused you so much trouble, Jeremy Carter. I was only trying to help you. I seem to have done it all wrong."

He awoke with a jerk and smashed on the light. He felt a moment of terror because it had been so real—and he knew there was no one with him in the room.

He was standing beside his bed, staring groggily around at the room in which he was alone.

Then he heard it again. "I'm sorry, I didn't mean to hurt you, Jeremy. I hope you will forgive me."

The back of his neck prickled, and a chill shot the length of his spine. He turned to the brown ball of fur, which he had released from its cage as he did every night. It was motionless on the floor near the far wall.

And he knew it had been the voice of Aristotle.

The animal had spoken to him, in words he could understand. The thought was staggering. After the days and hours he had spent studying his pet in preparation for his paper he had found no response to any stimulus he had been able to provide. Sound of all frequencies, heat, cold, light, darkness—nothing had produced response from the creature.

Now . . . it spoke. It said again, "I'm truly sorry, Jeremy. Is there anything I can do to repair the damage I have caused you?"

He sank down on the edge of the bed and stared. Aristotle was quiet and motionless—the longest time Jeremy had seen him unmoving. Jeremy tried speaking, and it seemed ridiculous even to be addressing the faceless ball of fur. "How am I hearing you, Aristotle? How can I hear your words in my mind when I know there's no sound?"

"You don't even believe I'm talking to you," said Aristotle accusingly. "Well, I don't blame you. I didn't intend to do so, except that I've gotten you into so much trouble I must take some direct action to get you out of it. But I'm so confused by your rules and customs that I can't really see what I can do."

"You're right," said Jeremy. "There is nothing you can do. I don't know what your world is like, but surely it can't be as crazy as this one. How are you speaking to me? How can I understand your words?"

"Direct mental contact is a simple thing," said Aristotle. "No words are needed. You supply your own in response to my mental stimulus. I understand you in the same way, except that to me such things as words do not exist. Now, tell me what I can do," the creature insisted.

Jeremy lay back on the bed and switched off the light, the better to think and to converse. He told Aristotle the substance of his problem, his threatened expulsion from school because of his insistence that the problem solutions given him by Aristotle were correct.

"I shouldn't have done it," Aristotle said sadly. "I should not have interfered."

"But I'm glad you did!" Jeremy exclaimed. "I don't care what happens, I'm glad you showed me something of your world. Now, show me more, please!"

"No, not tonight. Not until we get you out of the predicament I have caused you."

"What do you think I ought to do?"

"Do exactly what your father suggested. Apologize for antagonizing your teachers. Your time will come."

"Tell me of your world," Jeremy begged.

"No. That is all for tonight. I will be silent now."

Try as he would, Jeremy could arouse no further response from his pet.

Pet?

He had to get rid of that term in his mind. Whatever Aristotle was, it didn't fit the word pet. But what was Aristotle? Jeremy's mind churned wih fantastic thoughts. If Aristotle had inspired the intricate engineering designs, the details of a culture that was beyond imagining—if this represented Aristotle's world, how had he permitted himself to be captured and treated as a mere pet, an animal?

Something was wrong. Something didn't fit. Jeremy fell asleep at last, fighting for an answer that wouldn't come.

He stayed home the next morning instead of going to school, but his father advised him to expect a visit from one of the school authorities, probably Dr. Haslam himself.

Jeremy's sisters left for their classes, and his mother went to her room, which was a part of their living quarters, where she was employed as a computer terminal operator. It was a highly privileged position. Jeremy realized he mustn't disturb her by his own problems. He didn't know whether his father had spoken of his expulsion from school. His mother didn't mention it that morning and neither did Jeremy.

Alone in the dominium, he wandered through the rooms and stared out the windows over the expanse of the city. He found himself hating it more intensely than ever before. He had never walked down into the deep canyons, which were only a short distance away, but he knew they were filled with ugliness and filth and the crawling poor, which were not visible from here. His father's position assured his family of green card status, which provided dominium dwelling in the highest levels and unlimited selection of food and clothing.

He turned back to his own room and Aristotle, who was rolling about the floor, free of his cage, but not going beyond the limits of the room. He tried to talk to the creature, but Aristotle offered no response.

Jeremy almost began to wonder if the conversation of the night before was strictly from his imagination.

He turned to his studies, reviewing the work that he would have been presenting in class if he had attended this morning. It seemed futile. They would never let him return. He would never get to space now. He would never even qualify for a green card on Earth. The only future for him lay in those jungles in the canyons at the bottom of the city. But he wouldn't submit to that, either. He knew there were still far-away places at the ends of the Earth where some men lived in some degree of defiance and freedom from the hated cities. Fearful tales were sometimes told of the life that went on in those places, but the worst of them could not be as bad as enduring the city jungles. Those places were where he would go.

He hadn't the faintest idea how to get there.

At mid-morning he heard the outer door open, and voices spoke in strained tones. One of them belonged to his father. He recognized the other, too. Dr. Haslam.

Jeremy's heart jumped a beat. He was filled with a confused mixture of hope and hate. Dr. Haslam and the school represented his hope of escape to space, but he hated nearly everything they forced him to do to get there. Not the studies—he loved them. It was all the other stuff—like apologizing for being wrong when you knew you were right.

"Jeremy!"

"In here, Dad."

He moved to the door to meet them, but the two

men were already at the entrance to his room. They came in and Mr. Carter offered the School Director a chair. Dr. Haslam instantly spotted Aristotle, who had stopped rolling and retreated to a far corner. Mr. Carter followed his glance.

"Put it in the cage, Jeremy," he directed.

Jeremy obeyed. He picked up the silent, motionless furball and laid it gently in the cage and fastened the wire door.

"Dr. Haslam and I have had a talk," said Jeremy's father. "There may be some possible consideration of reinstatement for you. I'll let Dr. Haslam tell you how he feels."

The Director cleared his throat and looked severely at Jeremy. "We have concluded, Jeremy," he said, "that your behavior was possibly motivated by external and very unusual circumstances which placed a psychological burden upon you that you were not prepared to deal with. Your father has related to me the circumstances of the past two weeks, involving the acquisition of this pet of yours, and it appears there has been some psycho influence, not detectable by the screening required for import, which has been wholly detrimental to you. We have encountered this thing a number of times before. If this turns out to be the case we can offer you reinstatement without prejudice, provided your attitude and behavior with respect to school authority return to normal."

Jeremy glanced at his father, who was staring at him with lips pressed together and eyes hard. "I'll be glad to do anything required," Jeremy said. "And I apologize for my offensive attitude."

Dr. Haslam beamed. "Excellent, Jeremy! Excellent!" Jeremy thought for a moment he was going to reach out and pat him on the head. That would have been too much, he thought. He would have turned and run before he would have submitted to that, regardless of the advice of his father or Aristotle.

But Dr. Haslam refrained. He continued beaming and said, "One more thing, then, will be required. This pet must be done away with immediately."

Jeremy felt a sickness inside. He looked at his father again. "Must we return him to the pet shop?"

Dr. Haslam interrupted before Whit Carter could answer. "Not returned," said Dr. Haslam. "I said, 'done away with'. This beast must cease to exist so that your psychological separation may be utterly complete."

"You mean, kill—?" Jeremy cried.

"It will be painless," said Whit Carter quickly.

"It's done all the time, you know," said Dr. Haslam. "Perhaps you don't know, but there is an extermination agency for disposing of these repulsive off-world animals that are brought in as pets and which breed and become surplus. It's become quite a problem down in the city, you know. You can take this animal to the agency. They will take care of it for you. But I must have your assurance that it will be done before a return to class. You will see to that, will you not, Mr. Carter?" He turned to Jeremy's father.

"Yes, of course. That's agreeable to you, isn't it,

Jeremy?" The tone of his voice implied to Jeremy there was only one answer to the question.

Jeremy was seized with panic. He thought of the conversation only last night, in which Aristotle revealed himself as an intelligent being of another world. He must be utterly helpless and defenseless or he would never have been caught and sold as a pet. There had to be some way—some way to help him.

"It *is* agreeable to you, is it not?" said Jeremy's father again with a severity that Jeremy had never heard before.

Jeremy's mind blurred. "Yes—yes, of course it's all right. It's just—let me have one more night—we'll do it tomorrow, the very first thing."

"I'd advise you not to delay," said Dr. Haslam severely. "You are jeopardizing everything you hope to attain every minute you persist with that beast. However, it is up to you. I will give you until the end of the week to apply for reinstatement. Beyond that time there can be no further consideration. Good-bye, Jeremy. Good day to you, Mr. Carter."

Jeremy's father saw the School Director to the door and then returned. His voice was softer now. "I know it's hard, Jeremy. You get attached to a creature like that. I remember a dog I had when I was a kid—"

Jeremy's eyes were filled with tears. "It's all right. I'll be o.k. Just let me have one more day and then I'll do it."

Whit Carter punched the boy on the shoulder. "Sure, I know. We'll take it down tomorrow." He started for the door and then paused. "Just between us, I don't like that guy Haslam any better than you do. But what can you do when he's the key to your whole future?"

Alone, Jeremy smashed his fist against the wall and swore in his agony of frustration. Do away with Aristotle—the world would be better off without Haslam!

But whatever the cost, he was not going to murder Aristotle because of Haslam.

Without a need for material food, Aristotle's requirements for survival were simple. But what could be done with him? Where could he be hidden? It was impossible, yet a way had to be found.

Would his father cooperate in protecting Aristotle if he knew the creature was an intelligent being, apparently representing an advanced culture and civilization? Jeremy wasn't sure. His father was a kind and compassionate man, yet Jeremy's future meant more than anything else right now to Whit Carter. Jeremy knew what a blow his threatened expulsion had been, and he knew how difficult it must have been to persuade Haslam to reconsider.

The risk was too great to take a chance on his father's reaction. Whatever was to be done, Jeremy had to do it alone.

He had been in the living room, staring out the windows to the ugly city below. Now he heard a voice in his mind again. That same clear, golden voice he had heard the night before.

"Jeremy—Jeremy," Aristotle said. "Will you help me? I need your help."

Jeremy raced into the other room. Aristotle rested quietly in the center of the room. Jeremy's eyes turned to the cage in which he had left the creature and stared at what he saw. The wires were burned away as if a welding torch had cut through them with intense heat. There was a space just big enough for something about the size of a basketball to roll through.

"I need your help," said Aristotle again. "Will you help me?"

"Of course." Jeremy continued staring at the burned wires of the cage. "What can I do?"

"I heard your father and the other man. I see I can stay with you no longer. I thought I might go elsewhere on Earth for a time, but I think there is no further purpose in my staying. I shall go home to my people."'

"How?" Jeremy asked in bewilderment. "How can you get back?"

"There is a ship not far away. I have been in communication with them. They will come for me tomorrow, but I must get to a place where they can reach me."

The thought was staggering. Aristotle—a member of a race that had accomplished space travel—this creature he had thought to be no more than an animal, a pet. Yet the implication had been there in the things Aristotle had taught him. The mystery remained, however: why had the creature been so easily captured as an alien pet?

Jeremy wanted to ask, but Aristotle was hurrying on.

"There is something more, Jeremy. I want you to come with me. You want to see space, visit other worlds, and know other peoples. Come with me and I will show you more wonders than you ever dreamed of!"

"Go with you—" Jeremy stared at the little furball, breathless with the implications of the invitation. "Could I get back?"

"Probably not. Our ships do not come this way very often. But what does it matter? What is there here for you?"

The creature's question was like a knife that seemed to suddenly sever all ties that Jeremy had with Earth. What, indeed, did he have here?

A lifelong battle to obtain and keep a green card so that existence would be bearable, so that there would be enough food to eat and shelter to protect. A joyless existence whose greatest goal was the privilege of going into space. He would miss his father, most of all. His mother had been part of the machinery of the city civilization for so long he scarcely knew her. His sisters were following their mother's pattern. He had little to hold him.

"Yes—let me go with you!" he said breathlessly.

And suddenly, a giant panorama of alien world unfolded to his mind, as if a great screen were unrolling before him. He saw blazing suns of yellow, blue and white; planets of glory with alien, struggling creatures striving to fulfill their destiny. For a moment he caught a glimpse of their hopes and fears and ambitions. He sped through the darkness of space between the galaxies and the super-galaxies, out to the very edge of the Universe itself. For a moment he understood the very purpose of existence. And then it was gone.

He knew Aristotle had opened his mind to this burst of glory. It was only a glimpse of the things the creature could show him.

"Yes—" he said again. "I want it. I want to go with you. Show me the way!"

"First, we must get out of the city into the open country. How can this be done?"

Jeremy shook his head. "It can't. The city is fenced to keep out nomads. I couldn't get through the guard gates."

"There must be a way. My ship can't approach except in the open. I can't be picked up unless we can get out there."

Jeremy knew an attempt to get through the city gates would only draw attention and rouse suspicion, and then his father would be called to account for him. Where could a space ship from another world land to pick up Aristotle?

Where do space ships land? he wondered.

They land at space ports.

And the city had a space port. That was it. That had to be the way, the only way.

"Our own ships land about twenty miles from the city," Jeremy said. "There's a subway shuttle for passengers and visitors, which we can ride if there's a schedule we can use."

"And if there isn't?"

"Let's find out."

Jeremy went to the information panel in the next room and punched the buttons which would give him the space port shuttle schedule. The timetable showed one for that afternoon.

"If we leave in an hour we can do it," Jeremy told Aristotle.

He wandered through the rooms of the dominium, the familiar rooms in which he had spent his whole life. He would never be seeing them again, and though there was nothing he wanted to take with him, he felt as if he wanted his eyes to absorb everything he could see so that he would never forget it.

He thought of writing a long letter of explanation to his father and made a couple of starts. Then he gave it up. What was there to say? Did anyone ever miss someone who just disappeared? He didn't know. There were constant stories and rumors of persons, both children and grownups suddenly disappearing and being seen no more. It was always said they were assaulted by the denizens of the bottom of the city. But no one ever seemed to miss very much the ones who disappeared.

He didn't know how to write a letter to his father. He gave up trying.

"I'll take a small bag," he said to Aristotle. "That's all I can take without looking suspicious. I'll pack a few clothes and squeeze you in with them. Is that all right?"

"It's very good," said Aristotle soberly.

Jeremy didn't know whether it was very good or not. He felt shaky even though going out to the spaceport was perfectly acceptable and should arouse no suspicion. His bag was a little narrow, but Aristotle was capable of some accommodation by squeezing in his sides. Jeremy punched in an application for a shuttle ticket and received it printed out and charged to his father's green card. With a last look around he picked up the bag and closed the dominium door behind him for the final time.

No one paid any attention to him in the halls or in the elevators. He left the building and went through the mall toward the city shuttle that would take him to the spaceport shuttle terminal. No one along the entire way would ever remember seeing him. No one paid any attention to anyone else.

At the spaceport shuttle entrance, he presented the ticket to the gate attendant. The man glanced at the ticket and then at Jeremy. The boy felt a quiver of hesitation.

"What is your business?" the man said.

"I'm going out to the port."

"There's no flight."

"The shuttle is scheduled."

"It's a work shuttle. Only port employees take this one. You an employee?"

Jeremy shook his head. It was hopeless to try to pretend he worked at the port. "I'm writing a paper at school," he said. "Operation of port facilities. I didn't know this wasn't a regular passenger shuttle, but I would like to go if there's no objection, so that I can get my class material."

The attendant was not satisfied. "You've got a bag,"

he said. "You need a bag for going out to get your paper?"

"Just some things—" said Jeremy vaguely.

"Let me see."

Jeremy hesitated. What was the use? He was going to get turned back no matter what he did. He'd have to think of something else. "I guess I'll have to wait for the regular passenger shuttle, then," he said. "I didn't know this was just an employee shuttle. You ought to put that information into the computer. It doesn't tell people what to expect."

"Let me see what you've got in the bag," the attendant demanded.

"I told you I'll come back."

The attendant reached for the bag. Jeremy tried to withdraw it, but he couldn't cope with the man's reach and strength.

The voice of Aristotle burst in his mind. "It's all right, Jeremy. I'll take care of him. Let him open the bag."

Jeremy stood back as the man roughly undid the clasp and raised the top half. Nestled among the clothing was the silky brown furball that was Aristotle.

"What the—" the attendant began. Then his face suddenly grew passive and his eyes glazed over. He closed the bag as if in a trance, his hands white and cold like those of a corpse. "Move on," he said in dead tones.

Jeremy felt a chill at the back of his neck. He had believed Aristotle utterly passive and helpless, incapable of contending with the environment and civilization of Earth. He remembered the burned wires of the cage back in his room, and he thought of the dead eyes of the space shuttle attendant. What depth of unknown powers lay within that small ball of fur?

He knew he was no longer leading, but that he was being led as Aristotle spoke again. "Hurry, Jeremy. The ship will arrive in a moment. It cannot remain long. Your people will be investigating."

Jeremy walked faster, then ran, as if some power beyond his own mind were driving his muscles. He raced through the entrance building where idle clerks and freight handlers paid no attention. Aristotle guided him now as if on old familiar territory, and Jeremy wondered how much the alien needed him at all. Aristotle could probably have found his way alone over open country to any meeting place his people selected.

His lungs were fiery with the strain of his exertion as he neared the end of the long concourse leading to the arrival pads. He ran through the doorway leading to the thick concrete apron. No one entered here without tickets and proper authority, but Jeremy felt a blanket of subduing force was radiating in all directions about him—emanating from the ball of fur cramped into the bag he carried.

He reached the area of the most distant pad and Aristotle directed him to stop. He saw nothing. Above was the clear summer sky, and the air was fresh here, free of the perpetual gray shroud that cloaked the distant, ugly city.

Then he felt a stirring in the mind of Aristotle and looked upward into the sunlight. After a moment he saw it, a great silver torpedo moving out of the sun, dropping Earthward at suicidal speed. A blast of hot, furious air touched him while the ship was still high. Dust swirled. And then the ship slowed, lowered without visible force to retard it until it sank gently to the surface of the pad a quarter of a mile away.

"Hurry!" Aristotle demanded.

Jeremy knew he could not resist that demand. He raced toward the waiting ship. His lungs burned again from the flood of air he sucked in as he ran.

The ship was not a large one by Earth standards. It lay on its side, rather than the end. It appeared no more than a hundred-and-twenty-feet long and thirty in diameter.

As they neared, a panel slid aside near the center. "Inside, quickly!" Aristotle commanded.

Jeremy hesitated a moment as he stepped over the metal threshold. He looked back at the space port. A few figures were gathered now at the end of the concourse, gesturing toward the alien ship as if in great confusion. In a moment, a car would be bringing them out to investigate.

On the distant horizon were other cities whose names Jeremy knew, but which he had never visited. And there was his own familiar city. It was his last glimpse of it. He wondered for a moment if he were doing the right thing. Did he really want to abandon Earth and the meager birthright it offered for unknown adventure among the galaxies with Aristotle and his people?

He turned and moved down the corridor amid alien light. The panel clanged shut behind him.

Aristotle asked to be released from the bag now. Jeremy opened it and let the alien out. Aristotle rolled ahead, leading the way through the long corridor and down passages that became increasingly smaller until Jeremy was stooping. Side passages that opened from time to time were utterly small for him. They were about the size for a basketball to roll through.

"We have come through the freight entrance," said Aristotle. "Most of the ship will be too small for you to enter, but we will go to the central control chamber. The ship's officers must give judgment as to whether you can go with us, but I have already had assurance they will approve."

They came abruptly into a small chamber about twenty feet across and about half as high. It was U-shaped, and they entered from the open end. Opposite, from floor to ceiling, were tiers like the tiers of seats of some great playhouse. In cushioned recesses within these tiers reclined scores of furball creatures similar to Aristotle.

Some of the creatures were larger than Aristotle; none were smaller. On some, the hair was of varied colors, not the smooth homogenous brown that Jeremy was familiar with on his pet. Some were gray, as if with age, although Jeremy had no way of knowing whether age changed their color or not.

Immediately Jeremy sensed a flood of communication between the assembly and Aristotle. Aristotle was being questioned and was telling the story of all that had happened to him since Jeremy encountered him in the pet shop. Jeremy understood his appeal that they confirm their previous agreement that Jeremy could come with them.

He sensed age and wisdom here in this gathering. He sensed their vast experience in a hundred-thousand worlds. Yet it was alien and it chilled him, although there was no unfriendliness here. Could he give up all human companionship in exchange for the gifts these alien strangers might give him?

He listened as best he could to their swift debate. There was no antagonism, no hostility. They accepted him. One, who seemed to be among those in highest command, seemed especially agreeable. He was commending Aristotle on his desire to bring Jeremy along.

"He will be a most excellent—" the alien commander said.

Jeremy struggled for comprehension of the word or phrase the alien used. And then he froze.

There was no mistaking the word.

There was no mistaking the thought.

The alien had said a thing that could only be interpreted as the Earthmen's word pet.

Jeremy stared at the assembly and at Aristotle. He could have a life among these brilliant aliens as a pet.

He would be no more to them than Aristotle had

originally been to him—an interesting animal of another species.

A pet.

But he had no hidden qualities as Aristotle had, to lift him above the level of a pet to them. Never, as long as he remained with them would he ever be more.

Aristotle read his sudden alarm and panic. "It's not like that. He didn't mean what you think. It was the wrong word. I'll always take care of you. I'll show you all the worlds I promised."

But Jeremy knew there had been no mistake. "How did we get you?" Jeremy demanded. "You weren't helpless in being captured by our traders. Why did you let them take you? Why did you come to Earth?"

"I had a project—in school—just like yours. I had to conduct an experiment and make a report on an experience among an alien group. You see, I am what you would call a schoolboy among my people, just as you are among yours. I was doing with you almost the same thing you were doing with me. But I meant no harm. Come with me, Jeremy. Stay with me. You can go everywhere with me. We'll see a thousand-million worlds in a million galaxies. Come with me."

So that was it. Aristotle was like him, an adolescent in an adult world he didn't understand and that didn't understand him. Aristotle would like to regard Jeremy as an equal and a companion, but in the eyes of the adults of that alien world he would never be anything but a pet, a child's pet.

And Aristotle would grow and become an adult himself. Nothing he could do would change the adult view of Jeremy, the Earthling, as a pet. And Aristotle would mature and tire of the strange pet from Earth . . .

Jeremy turned and ran in terror from the chamber of aliens. Aristotle rolled swiftly behind him, and then surged ahead.

"Jeremy! You'll always belong to me. You'll have everything you want."

There was a sudden faint whisper of vibration within the ship, as if it were prepared to lift off.

"No!" Jeremy cried. "Let me go, please! I can't be your pet. If I am not equal, then I can't live with you!"

The panel slid open in the side of the ship. He was free to go. They had no desire to hold him prisoner. Jeremy leaped to the concrete pad. In the distance a pair of cars started toward the alien ship.

"I'm sorry," said Aristotle. "You're right. It wouldn't have worked. You couldn't have equal rights among my people. Just as I could never be accepted among your people. How can we ever bridge what lies between us?"

"Can we talk?" Jeremy begged. "Can you reach me over whatever distance lies between?"

"Not entirely. Only a few thousand light years. Whenever we come that close, I will reach out to you. Listen for me. You will know when I call."

The panel slid shut. The silver torpedo rose. And Jeremy Carter was hurled to the ground by the air waves of the swift departure. He lay there sobbing on the dusty concrete of the pad.

His story was easily accepted: He had been overwhelmed by the mental influence of the creature from another world, and he had escaped being kidnapped at the last moment by the skin of his teeth. As a result, a ban was placed on all off-world pets, and those in existence were rounded up and exported to their home worlds or similar ones.

Jeremy returned to his former life. With quiet diligence, he drove to the top of his class and became the outstanding Space Apprentice.

His reputation as an original and creative student rose rapidly. Some of his ideas at times seemed out of this world, but he could always back them up very carefully.

He often speaks of building bridges, not over canyons or rivers, but over the gaps between people and worlds. He sounds a little confused on this subject; no one is entirely sure what he is talking about. But this is considered a youthful enthusiasm that he will outgrow in time.

He is known, too, as a loner. He has few close friends, and often, when he thinks no one is near he seems to be listening to a voice that no one else can hear, and see visions that no one else can see.

pauline frommer's

LONDON

spend less see more

2nd Edition

by Jason Cochran

Series Editor: Pauline Frommer

Wiley Publishing, Inc.

Published by:

Wiley Publishing, Inc.
111 River St.
Hoboken, NJ 07030-5774

ISBN 978-0-470-30869-1

Editor: Jamie Ehrlich
Production Editor: Jonathan Scott
Cartographer: Roberta Stockwell
Photo Editor: Richard Fox
Interior Design: Lissa Auciello-Brogan
Production by Wiley Indianapolis Composition Services

For information on our other products and services or to obtain technical support, please contact our Customer Care Department within the U.S. at 800/762-2974, outside the U.S. at 317/572-3993 or fax 317/572-4002.

Wiley also publishes its books in a variety of electronic formats. Some content that appears in print may not be available in electronic formats.

Manufactured in the United States of America

5 4 3 2 1

Contents

List of Maps

About the Author

Jason Cochran was awarded Guide Book of the Year by the North American Travel Journalists Association for this book. He also wrote *Pauline Frommer's Walt Disney World & Orlando* and *Pauline Frommer's San Francisco.* He has written for publications including *Budget Travel* (as senior editor); *Entertainment Weekly;* the *New York Post, Daily News,* and *Times; Travel + Leisure* and *T+L Family;* and *Newsweek*. His writing has been awarded the Golden Pen by the Croatian government and was selected to appear in a permanent exhibit in the National Museum of Australia. He also devised questions for *Who Wants to Be a Millionaire* (ABC). As a commentator, he has appeared on CNN, WOR, Outdoor Life Network, and MSNBC.com.

Acknowledgments

Among the countless people who helped shape this book, several were particularly instrumental, including Jacqueline French and Rachel Kelly from Visit London; Paul Chibeba and Andrew Weir from Visit Britain; and, of course, my vigilant series editor, Pauline Frommer, whose passion for even the most minor details is contagious. The contributions of two witty Londoners transformed the book: Jennifer Jellicorse and Robin Oakley, whose bottomless well of appreciation gave me more ideas than I could use. Thanks also to Arthur Frommer for being a gracious teacher. A deep bow for Mark and Derek Ellwood, to whom I'll always be grateful. I also can't express enough gratitude to my family and friends, who always strike the right balance of laissez-faire and cheerleading—that includes Michael for his strings-free support, Julie for nursing me between battles, and my mother Tracy, who sent me to London first.

An Invitation to the Reader

In researching this book, we discovered many wonderful places—hotels, restaurants, shops, and more. We're sure you'll find others. Please tell us about them, so we can share the information with your fellow travelers in upcoming editions. If you were disappointed with a recommendation, we'd love to know that, too. Please write to:

Pauline Frommer's London, 2nd Edition
Wiley Publishing, Inc. • 111 River St. • Hoboken, NJ 07030-5774

An Additional Note

Please be advised that travel information is subject to change at any time—and this is especially true of prices. We therefore suggest that you write or call ahead for confirmation when making your travel plans. The authors, editors, and publisher cannot be held responsible for the experiences of readers while traveling. Your safety is important to us, however, so we encourage you to stay alert and be aware of your surroundings. Keep a close eye on cameras, purses, and wallets, all favorite targets of thieves and pickpockets.

Star Ratings, Icons & Abbreviations

Every restaurant, hotel, and attraction is rated with stars ★, indicating our opinion of that facility's desirability; this relates not to price, but to the value you receive for the price you pay. The stars mean:

No stars: Good
★ Very good
★★ Great
★★★ Outstanding! A must!

Accommodations within each neighborhood are listed in ascending order of cost, starting with the cheapest and increasing to the occasional "splurge." Each hotel review is preceded by one, two, three, or four dollar signs, indicating the price range per double room. Restaurants work on a similar system, with dollar signs indicating the price range per three-course meal.

Accommodations		Dining	
£	Up to £75/night	**£**	Meals for £5 or less
££	£76-£110	**££**	£6-£8
£££	£111 to £150	**£££**	£9-£11
££££	Over £151 per night	**££££**	£12 and up

In addition, we've included a kids icon (kids) to denote attractions, restaurants, and lodgings that are particularly child friendly.

Frommers.com

Now that you have this guidebook to help you plan a great trip, visit our website at **www.frommers.com** for additional travel information on more than 4,000 destinations. We update features regularly to give you instant access to the most current trip-planning information available. At Frommers.com, you'll find scoops on the best airfares, lodging rates, and car rental bargains. You can even book your travel online through our reliable travel booking partners. Other popular features include:

- Online updates of our most popular guidebooks
- Vacation sweepstakes and contest giveaways
- Newsletters highlighting the hottest travel trends
- Podcasts, interactive maps, and up-to-the-minute events listings
- Opinionated blog entries by Arthur Frommer himself
- Online travel message boards with featured travel discussions

a note from pauline frommer

I started traveling with my guidebook-writing parents, Arthur Frommer and Hope Arthur, when I was just 4 months old. To avoid lugging around a crib, they would simply swaddle me and stick me in an open drawer for the night. For half of my childhood, my home was a succession of hotels and B&Bs throughout Europe, as we dashed around every year to update *Europe on $5 a Day* (and then $10 a day, and then $20 . . .).

We always traveled on a budget, staying at the mom-and-pop joints Dad featured in the guide, getting around by public transportation, eating where the locals ate. And that's still the way I travel today, because I learned—from the master—that these types of vacations not only save money but offer a richer, deeper experience of the culture. You spend time in local neighborhoods, meeting and talking with the people who live there. For me, making friends and having meaningful exchanges is always the highlight of my journeys—and the main reason I decided to become a travel writer and editor as well.

I've conceived these books as budget guides for a new generation. They have all the outspoken commentary and detailed pricing information of the Frommer's guides, but they take bargain hunting into the 21st century, with more information on using the Internet and air/hotel packages to save money. Most important, we stress "alternative accommodations"—apartment rentals, private B&Bs, religious retreat houses, and more—not simply to save you money, but to give you a more authentic experience in the places you visit.

A highlight of each guide is the chapter that deals with the "other" side of the destinations, the one visitors rarely see. These sections will actively immerse you in the life that residents enjoy. The result, I hope, is a valuable new addition to the world of guidebooks. Please let us know how we've done!

E-mail me at editor@frommers.com.

Happy traveling!

Pauline Frommer

Pauline Frommer

1 London the Lionhearted

The best the city has to offer

WHETHER YOU REALIZE IT OR NOT, LONDON HAS AFFECTED YOUR DESTINY. There's hardly a quarter of the globe that it hasn't changed. The United States was founded in reaction to London's edicts. Australia was peopled with London's criminals and later, with settlers looking for a better life away from England's hardships. Modern Canada, South Africa, and New Zealand were cultivated from London. India's course was irrevocably changed by the aspirations of London businessmen, as were the lives of millions of Africans who were shipped around the world while Londoners lined their pockets with the profit. You're holding proof in your hands of London's pull: that you bought this very book, written in English somewhere other than in England, is evidence of London's reach across time and distance.

London is inexhaustible. You could tour it for months and barely know it at all. Few cities are home to such a cross-section of people living together in remarkable harmony. That diversity makes London like a cut diamond; approach it from a slightly different angle each day, and it takes on an entirely fresh shape and sheen.

That's the goal of this book: to encourage you to take one step sideways, off the beaten tourist track, and see the city from a different perspective. Don't see it only for its misty rains, its lilting accents, or its monumental buildings of stone. See it like a South Asian immigrant in East Ham, who spends Wednesday nights at the Bollywood movie house and worships in the largest Hindu temple outside of India. Or like the Jamaican-born Brixton resident who spends each morning shopping for exotic greens at a street market that's been running for well over a century. See it like a twenty-something whose weekly highlights are the quiz night at the local pub and the Saturday breakfast at the local caff. Step sideways and see another London. And then another.

After all, their London is your London.

THE SIGHTS YOU SIMPLY CAN'T MISS

For all the years during which London was the capital of a globe-spanning empire, treasures flowed into the city, so it possesses some of the finest collections of international art and antiquities on the planet. London deserves its reputation as an expensive city, but people overlook that its finest museums cost nothing to see: The relics of **The British Museum** (p. 135); the comprehensive holdings of **The National Gallery** (p. 145) and **The National Portrait Gallery** (p. 153); the little-seen but phenomenal small collection of **The Courtauld Institute of Art Gallery;** and the rare clothing, art, and decorative arts at the **Victoria and Albert Museum** (p. 150) are just four enormous collections, each of which could absorb you for an entire cost-free day.

London in a Nutshell

Population: 7.5 million (12.5% of the entire U.K. population)
Ethnicity: More than 30% of the population is non-white
Languages spoken: More than 300
Area: 1,584 sq. km/612 sq. miles (30% of that is parkland or open space)
Total English land area occupied by London: 1.2%
Median weekly gross pay: £581 (£462 for England as a whole)
Source: Visit London and London Councils

London is also a nerve center for cutting-edge modern art, and the free display in the soaring industrial caverns of **The Tate Modern** (p. 146), on the bustling riverside promenade of Bankside, has quickly become a requisite stop during a visit. **The Saatchi Gallery** (p. 182) in Chelsea, assembled by a renegade art fan, is a favorite for feats of modern, monumental artistic daring, and the world's top art aficionados convene on the many **galleries** (p. 182) and freely exhibiting **auction houses** (p. 269) to augment their collections. Wealth has always created architectural showpieces: The distinctive two-level **Tower Bridge** (p. 180) over the River Thames was a great engineering feat of the Victorian era, and across town on the same water, the handsome observation wheel called the **London Eye** (p. 137) was embraced by the city quickly after its 1999 erection, proving that modern architecture can be just as iconic. The rounded tower at **30 St. Mary Axe,** nicknamed the Gherkin for its pickle-like profile, and the ovoid **City Hall** (p. 198) are the latest evolutions on a skyline that has continuously reinvented itself.

As a magnet for the world's sophisticates, London has peerless **shopping areas** (including Oxford St., Regent St., Piccadilly, and Spitalfields Market), although given the power of the pound, you'll probably be more inclined to window-shop. London's **theaters** (p. 285) have been setting the aesthetic bar for more than 500 years. You won't experience the depth of London's culture without spending at least one night in front of one of its stages. You can also witness unique performances at **Shakespeare's Globe** (p. 187), a faithful re-creation of an Elizabethan theater, or at one of the city's many casual **pub theaters** (p. 296), from which spring movie stars, stand-up comics, and household names. And, of course, the productions at the **Royal Opera House** (p. 298) are among the world's most acclaimed. To get around, take the city's **Underground** (p. 8), or Tube, parts of which opened as the world's first subway system in the 1860s.

THE FINEST HISTORICAL SIGHTS

Many spots where bygone famous names conducted their business have been carefully preserved, and visiting some of these ancient sights can boggle the mind and inspire the imagination. The world's most famous castle, **The Tower of London** (p. 142), has stood sentry on the Pool of London since 1068, and has been used as a keep, a prison, a zoo, and now as the repository for the legendary Crown Jewels. **Westminster Abbey** (p. 140) has been the location of every coronation since 1066, and is the final resting place of the bones of more than a dozen monarchs including the steely Elizabeth I. **St. Paul's Cathedral** (p. 151), in the oldest quarter of the city, has been a symbol of London since it was designed by the impossibly prolific Sir Christopher Wren in the late 1600s. Many royal homes are open for public inspection, including the ancient **Hampton Court Palace** (p. 163), **Windsor Castle** (p. 321), **Kensington Palace** (p. 160), and their junior sister, **Buckingham Palace** (p. 161).

The day-to-day operation of the United Kingdom is still undertaken around Whitehall, where the finely decorated **Houses of Parliament** (p. 181) are proclaimed by the clock tower containing the famous bell **Big Ben.** Nearby is the prime minister's home, **10 Downing Street** (p. 237), whose Georgian facade appears humble but actually masks a virtual citadel of power.

BEST AFFORDABLE ACCOMMODATIONS

Many visitors put off their dream trips to London simply because they don't think they can afford to go. Hotel costs receive much blame. Yet the reality is that the least expensive places to stay often yield the most exciting visits. Many London residents maintain spare homes or rooms expressly for international visitors. Most are located in the same areas where the most popular hotels are found (p. 43). Better yet, by renting an entire apartment (p. 28), you'll pay roughly the per-night cost of a moderate hotel room, yet you'll get far more space, including a kitchen.

One of the least expensive but most rewarding accommodations options is to rent a room in a family-owned B&B, which are usually located in historic Georgian or Victorian town houses, complete with sweeping staircases and basement-level kitchens where the owners prepare you a hot breakfast as part of the bargain. Three such home-grown inns are the **Jesmond Hotel** (p. 49), the **Alhambra Hotel** (p. 46), and the **Celtic Hotel** (p. 52), all within walking distance of the West End. Your rooms will be clean and simple, but affordable, leaving you money to spend on what you came to do—see London.

For more cash, smartly designed **B+B Belgravia** (p. 79), **Base2Stay Kensington** (p. 61), **Hotel La Place** (p. 66), and **Number Sixteen** (p. 61) heighten the B&B concept with fashion-sensitive style that bridges the gap between a guesthouse and a hotel. If more traditional hotels are your preference, it's possible to find a room within a sensible budget. **The Hoxton** (p. 73) and the **Southwark Rose** (p. 69) provide amenities you'd see in a more expensive corporate hotel but with more attentive management and for less money. A few chain hotel brands also provide comfortable rooms, spacious enough for families, at acceptable prices; if you stay at the **Premier Inn London Southwark** (see p. 69), you'll take your breakfast overlooking the Thames.

DINING FOR EVERY TASTE

London's cuisine reflects its diversity. Asian cooking is particularly prevalent, having supplanted fish and chips as England's go-to casual meal. One of the best Indian meals of my life was served at the long-running **Punjab Restaurant** (p. 110) in Covent Garden, although I also appreciate the modern, innovative Indian flavors of **Imli** (p. 107). The all-you-can-eat vegetarian buffet at **Veg Bhelpoori House** (p. 96) is one of the city's greatest bargains.

Contemporary Southeast Asian is also in vogue; the communal wooden tables at the many locations of the **Wagamama** (p. 99) chain are terrific places to chat with strangers over a flavorful bowl of noodles, and the winning formula is repeated at **Busaba Eathai** (p. 106). Hard-to-find Asian cuisine is well represented on London's widely multicultural scene, including at **Mandalay** (Burmese, p. 125) and **Kandoo** (Persian, p. 125). Skilled vegetarian cuisine is something carnivores and herbivores alike appreciate, and you'll always find crowds at **Govinda's Restaurant** (p. 106), student hangout **Food for Thought** (p. 109), and the diner-like **Eat and Two Veg** (p. 101).

Of course, traditional cooking is back in fashion, and you'll be hard-pressed to find a table where English cuisine's dowdy reputation is upheld. **S&M Cafe** (p. 116) celebrates sausage; **The Fryer's Delight** (p. 115) is perhaps the prototypical "chippie" making fish and chips. **Frontline** (p. 128), a hangout for foreign correspondents, typifies the current trend toward upscale versions of comfort food that a British mum might prepare. Several chefs are intent on providing gourmet preparation and top-notch ingredients for affordable prices, including celebrity chef Gordon Ramsay at his "gastropub" with a view, **The Narrow** (p. 115), and the award-winning proprietors of Soho's **Arbutus** (p. 108), where you can have a multi-course, award-winning meal for well under £20. Combating the high price of sit-down meals, the **triangle sandwich** (p. 90) is the ubiquitous London lunch, consumed on the go by seemingly everyone. And the so-called "beigels" of Spitalfield's 24-hour **Beigel Bake** (p. 114) are the unique missing link between the Polish originals and the breadier "bagels" of North America.

THE BEST SPORTS & "OTHER" EXPERIENCES

Londoners revel in learning and in sharing experiences—call it another byproduct of a city raised on diversity. Be one of them. Take a chance and leap out of the tourist rut so that you can experience what London life is really like. Team up with armchair trivia experts at one of the many **pub quizzes** (p. 214). Stroll the restaurants and stores that cater to the daily errands of foreign-born immigrants in one of the city's many **ethnic neighborhoods** (p. 199). Watch elected leaders, including the prime minister, snipe at each other at the raucous **Question Time** (p. 198). Kibbutz with East End salt of the earth at the Victorian steam baths of **York Hall Leisure Centre** (p. 218) or with Marylebone doyennes at the ritzy **Porchester Spa** (p. 218); dig around in the sediment of the river for buried treasure with **Thames21** (p. 209); learn how Big Ben and America's Liberty Bell were made on a step-by-step tour of their birthplace, the family-run **Whitechapel Bell Foundry** (p. 202). Hear one of the world's great choirs at a service at **Westminster Cathedral** (p. 211) and one of the world's best organs at **Brompton Oratory** (p. 211). In a city full of ghosts, hold a séance for spirits in the old town house owned by the **Spiritualist Association of Great Britain** (p. 212) or track Jack the Ripper's victims on a **walking tour** (p. 193).

There are fewer pursuits more integral to an Englishman's sporting life than attending a British **football match** (p. 227); or a **cricket match at the Oval** (p. 228). Spend the evening in the **Dennis Severs' House** (p. 165), a thoroughly authentic 19th-century town house whose sights, sounds, and smells trick visitors into believing they have gone back in time. Dress up as a nun and talk back to the silver screen at the **Sing-a-Long-a *The Sound of Music*** (p. 216); give the universe a what for at **Speakers' Corner** (p. 219); drink away your Sunday with a British brew at one of the countless pub **roasts** (p. 214); or go on a graffiti safari for work by the maverick artist **Banksy** (p. 185).

2 The Lay of the Land

How London's jigsaw fits together

FEW GREAT MODERN CITIES ARE AS MULTILAYERED, INTRICATE, AND YES, *messy* as London, and that's because history was knitted into its very layout and never removed. Nearly half the housing in Paris was pulled down in the 1800s so Napoleon II could indulge his fantasy of wide avenues of parks. Chicago took advantage of a massive fire to reshape itself in the image of classic Europe. But London's modern makeup is mostly the haphazard product of blind evolution, which piled up over successive generations to produce the complicated metropolis that exists today. One could say that London simply happened.

As recently as the early 1800s, London—and by London, I mean what we now call The City, between St. Paul's and the Tower—was a compact, teeming monster where many lives, birth to death, were carried out within the same few blocks. Within that frenzied cluster, districts developed out of logic or bias—the smoke of industry was banished downwind, for example, and kings lived near the Thames for easy transportation. All around The City were dozens of villages, many of which retain their original names as modern neighborhoods, and often, a whiff of their original personalities.

Quickly, London swelled to swallow much of its current territory. Yet because of ancient echoes, neighborhoods remain surprisingly small—many are just minutes across by foot, and all but the most crucial streets can change names several times within a few blocks. It's still possible to stroll along and, within a block, sense a sudden shift in energy and character. In many ways, London is still a complex system of hundreds of hamlets. It's one of the many delights that makes it so surprising. It also means it can take a lifetime to scratch its surface.

Your first purchase, which can be made at any newsstand or bookstore, should be a map. Don't bother with the simplified map your hotel might offer—the inferior maps leave off side streets. The most cherished variety is the ***London A-Z*** (www.a-zmaps.co.uk), first compiled by the indefatigable Phyllis Pearsall, who walked every mile of the city for the 1936 debut edition and commanded the resulting cartography empire until her death 60 years later. The A-Z includes every street, hospital, post office, and train station, no matter how obscure, and although it comes in many sizes, your prime concern should be that your hotel's street is somewhere in it. I prefer the ***London Mini Street Atlas*** (£4.95), a booklet that fits into a jacket pocket and can be consulted discreetly. Just be sure to call it an "A to Zed" or you may get a funny look; in England, the last letter in the alphabet is, quite sensibly, pronounced to not rhyme with eight others.

For mail delivery, London is chopped into geographic parcels, and you'll see those **postcodes** on street signs and hear them in conversation. The heart of the city, in postcode terms, is near the Chancery Lane Tube stop. From there, areas are given a compass direction (N for north, SW for southwest, etc.) and a number (but

Where Is It?—Use the Code

Every address in this book includes its postcode, which corresponds to the neighborhood in which you'll find it. Don't worry—you won't need to memorize these because each listing also includes the nearest Tube stop to help you quickly place locations on a map. Here are some of the most common postcodes:

WC1 Bloomsbury
WC2 Covent Garden, Holborn, Strand
W1 Fitzrovia, Marylebone, Mayfair, Soho
W2 Bayswater
W6 Hammersmith
W8 Kensington
W11 Notting Hill
SW1 Belgravia, St. James's, Westminster
SW3 Chelsea
SW5 Earl's Court
SW7 Knightsbridge, South Kensington
SE1 Southwark
SE10 Greenwich
EC1 Clerkenwell
EC2 Bank, Barbican, Liverpool Street
EC3 Tower Hill
EC4 Fleet Street, St. Paul's
E1 Spitalfields, Whitechapel
E2 Bethnal Green
E14 Canary Wharf/Isle of Dogs
N1 Islington
NW1 Camden Town
NW3 Hampstead

ignore that, since a number greater than 1 doesn't mean the area is in the boonies). In the very center of town, addresses get an extra C for "centre," as in WC1, which is where Covent Garden is located. These codes are useful for orienting yourself.

GETTING AROUND

There are three practical methods for getting around sprawling London: by Tube (historic and enchanting, but expensive); by bus (less expensive and less glamorous, but more edifying and often quicker); and by foot (the best method, but not always possible). Taxis are overpriced, and driving your own car is madness.

Untangling the Tube

Don't be daunted. The Tube operates a 24-hour information line that answers even the silliest questions: ☎ 020/7222-1234. Or visit www.tfl.gov.uk, an elaborate site that contains more maps, jplanners, and FAQs than a normal person can use.

As endearing as the Tube is, it is not a perfect system. You need to be prepared for a few things:

1. **Stairs.** Most stations are as intricate as anthills. Passengers are forever being corralled sadistically up staircases, around platforms, down more staircases, and through still more staircases. The Victorians must have had some sexy legs. Yours might hurt after a day of touring. Even stations equipped with extremely long escalators (Angel has the longest one in the system—59m/194 ft.) perversely require passengers to climb a final flight to reach the street. So if you bring luggage into the Tube, be able to hoist your stuff for at least 15 stairs at a time. (This is where backpacks make sense.) The only tourist-area stations in zone 1 or 2 that have lifts all the way to the street are at Earl's Court, Hammersmith, Brixton, and everything on the Jubilee Line from Westminster east. A sorry list. The entire DLR is accessible, though. For more info, contact **Transport for London Access & Mobility** (☎ 020/7941-4600; www.tfl.gov.uk).
2. **Delays.** When you enter a station, look for a sign with the names and colors of the Tube lines on it. Beside each line, you'll see a status bar

THE UNDERGROUND

More culture shock: It's not called a "subway." In England, when you see a sign for a "subway," the word just signifies a foot passageway under a busy street.

Instead, Londoners call their 405km (252-mile) metro system the Underground, its official name, or just as commonly, "the Tube." Its elegant, distinctive logo—a red "roundel" bisected by a blue bar—debuted in 1913 as one of the world's first corporate symbols, and it remains one of the city's most ubiquitous sights.

There's no older system on Earth—London's Metropolitan Railway was not only the first, which took no small leap of imagination and engineering, but it also gave the world the standard coinage for subway, "metro." The first section, running from Paddington to Farringdon, opened in 1863—when Americans were still fighting the Civil War. That was 33 years ahead of the next European city (Budapest), 34 years before Boston, and 41 years before New York—indeed, the original snippet that opened then is still in use today. The Tube's most recent major addition, in 1999, was the £3.5-billion Jubilee Line extension from Westminster to Stratford. Now underway for 2010: extensions to the East London line.

The Tube is an attraction unto itself. I'm fascinated by Tube history, and seeking out vestiges of the early system (1907 tilework on the Piccadilly Line; the fake reading "Good service," "Severe delays," or the like. Trust this sign—it's updated by staff every 10 minutes because lines close without warning. If you note "Minor delays," don't worry, because you probably won't notice the extra wait (unless the situation degenerates after you're through the turnstiles). Not only are Londoners hypervigilant about reporting things like suspicious packages, which suspends service for unpredictable chunks of time, but also remember the Tube system is older than dirt. It was left to languish in benign neglect for much of the twentieth century, and now engineers can't keep up with the breakdowns, signal failures, and track issues that keep cropping up. Should your desired lines be out of commission, plan another route using other lines, or by walking or taking the bus.

3. **Heat.** Especially in the summer, the network can be stuffy and hot.
4. **Tough weekends.** London's system was experimental, so it had to be built on the cheap, which means each line gets only one set of tracks per direction, unlike more modern systems which generally have two sets in each direction. When tracks need maintenance, lines simply must shut down. Weekends, by and large, are when this happens, and never a weekend goes by when there isn't a list of roving closures to contend with. Check with staff in the ticket hall to see what's shut down, because something will be.

house facades built at 23-24 Leinster Gardens to hide exposed tracks; abandoned stations like the one at Strand and Surrey St.) is one of my favorite activities on a visit. If such "urban archaeology" fascinates you, visit the London Transport Museum in Covent Garden (p. 159), one of the city's family-friendly highlights. The Tube is also much more dignified than most American systems. In fact, its seating is upholstered.

Operating Schedule

The Tube shuts down nightly, mostly because it has to in order to maintain its tracks. Although exact times for first and final trains are posted in each station (using the simple 24-hr. clock), based on when they arrive in Central London, the Tube generally operates Monday to Saturdays from 5:30am (0530) to just after midnight (0000), and Sundays 7am (0700) to 11:30pm (2330). If you plan to take the train near the starting or ending times, you should always check the schedule beforehand to make sure you won't be locked out because of a mistake.

What happens if you do miss the last train? Don't worry—you're not stranded, although your trip may take a little longer or cost more. Just turn to the city's network of 100 Night Bus routes (p. 15). Or, as a last resort, take a taxi (p. 15).

How the Tube Works

There are 12 named lines on the Tube network, plus a light rail system (the Docklands Light Railway, or DLR, serving Docklands, Greenwich, and Southeast London) and a tram line, which together serve nearly 300 stations. On an average visit, you'll become familiar with a dozen or so stations. Lines are color-coded: the Piccadilly is a peacock purple, the Bakerloo could be considered Sherlock Holmes brown, and so on.

Navigating is mostly foolproof. Riders look for signs pointing them to the color and name of the line they want. Pretty soon, more signs separate them according to the direction they want to go in, based on the Tube map. So if you know the name/color of the line you want, as well as your final station destination, the multitude of signs will march you, cattlelike, directly to the platform you need.

If you need to change trains (and you will, now and then), the follow-the-signs method repeats until it's time to look for the "Way Out," which is Undergroundese for "Exit." You'll shuffle through a warren of ancient cylindrical tunnels, many of them faced in custard-yellow tiles and overly full of silent commuters, and you'll scale alpine escalators lined with ads for West End musicals.

One of the groovier things about the Underground is the electronic displays on every platform that tell you how long it'll be until the next train. Knowing how long you'll have to wait (it's never that long) takes a huge amount of frustration out of a commute.

The most confusing line for tourists is the Northern Line (black on the maps), which takes two paths because it was cobbled together from several independent train lines. One travels through The City, and one travels through Bloomsbury. Both legs meet up at Euston, so you can switch between them there, or else you can use one of six other Tube lines to cross between the two paths. To make things more confusing, the Northern Line forks again north of Camden Town station; the western leg visits popular Hampstead, and the eastern leg goes via Highgate. Know which train you're getting on, or you'll have to backtrack to fix your mistake.

Owing mostly to the petty backbiting and poor planning of the Victorians who built these lines as individual businesses, the District Line, which serves many budget hotels in West London, can also be tricky—trains veer off on different branches to several final destinations. You can handle it. Final destinations are clearly noted.

If you ride the DLR (and you should—it provides a lovely rooftop-level glide through the brickwork of the old East End and the monolithic towers of Canary Wharf), note your train's final destination as you board it, since the system is rife with forks in the routes. (The system is also rife with opportunities to change for the right train, so don't be put off.) Most DLR stations are aboveground, and thoughtfully, carriage doors don't open to let cold air in until a passenger needs to go through them. Push the button on the door to open it.

Fares

Oy. Here we go.

London Underground gives more than a billion rides a year, and seemingly every passenger pays a different fare. The LU system is so unnecessarily complicated that I can only assume its architects designed it that way on purpose to

Finding "Mind the Gap"

As you gloss through London's tackier souvenir stands, you'll often see a peculiar catch phrase reproduced on bumper stickers, shirts, and brass-plated key chains: MIND THE GAP. The phrase has nothing to do with brainwashing customers into an allegiance to a certain denim chain. It's what you hear on some London Underground trains when they pull into curved stations. Wherever a chasm of a few inches might appear between carriage and platform, a recorded admonition is played. You'll hear "Mind the gap" around the system, but if you want to be sure to catch it (and gain street cred over the tourists who just bought the T-shirt), try these stations:

- Aldgate
- Bank (Central Line)
- Embankment (Northern Line)
- Monument
- Tower Hill
- Wapping
- Waterloo (Bakerloo Line)

bewilder travelers into paying more than they have to. The fare guide is 36 pages long. Never mind. I'll walk you through it and make it as simple as I can.

Start with the concept of zones. The center of town—basically everything the Circle Line envelops, plus a wee bit of padding—is zone 1. Heading outside of town, in a concentric pattern like a target, come zones 2 through 6. Most tourists stick to zones 1 and 2; very few popular sights are outside those (Wimbledon, Hampton Court, and Kew being the main exceptions). Your fare is calculated by how many zones you go through, and the lower the zone number, the less you pay. Where the zones lie won't come as a surprise to you because every station lobby has a giant map showing the boundaries. If a station appears to be straddling two zones, you'll always pay the cheaper zone's price.

Important: Keep your ticket handy because you'll need it to get back out through the turnstiles. (If you can't find it, you'll have to fork over the maximum rate.) On the DLR, you must remember to touch your Oyster card (if you have one; see below) to a yellow reader dot both before you board *and* after you get off. Inspectors regularly check passengers' tickets with hand-held computers and they won't hesitate to fine you.

Astonishingly, **kids under 11 travel for free** when accompanied by an adult. Adults must buy their own ticket and then ask the staff to wave Junior through the entry gate. Kids 11 to 16 can travel with an adult for £1 all day after 9:30am with a Child Day Travelcard.

There are essentially three ways for adults to pay for a trip, which they can do at automated machines or at staffed ticket windows. Cash and credit cards both work. One-way tickets are called "singles" and round-trips are "return."

The Tube Map Lies!

Although the Tube's handsome map, first seen in 1931, is a marvel of elegance (its draughtsman, Harry Beck, is a demigod among graphic designers for his restrictive use of angles and color), it tells filthy lies. Tourists who take it at face value will, to their pocketbooks' peril, believe that some stations are miles apart and only accessible via circuitous journeys. In truth, many are extremely close. Leicester Square and Covent Garden are 255m (837 ft.) apart; Charing Cross and Embankment less than 300m (984 ft.). Do you wanna spend £4 on *that?* In many instances, two stops that appear to be on distant, inconvenient detours are actually neighbors. Don't waste time and money just because the Tube map makes something look hard-to-reach. These surprising station pairs are 450m (1,476 ft.)—or less—from each other.

Tottenham Court Road—Covent Garden
Farringdon—Chancery Lane
Barbican—St. Paul's
St. Paul's—Blackfriars
Moorgate—Bank
Bank—Mansion House
Liverpool Street—Aldgate
Aldgate East—Tower Gateway
Waterloo—Lambeth North
Euston—King's Cross St. Pancras
Baker Street—Marylebone
Great Portland Street—Warren Street
Regent's Park—Great Portland Street
Paddington—Lancaster Gate
Bayswater—Queensway
Monument—Mansion House
Earl's Court—West Brompton

A) **Per ride.** Only fools (or tourists) buy per ride. Why? I'll put it in perspective: It costs about $6,500 in winter to fly the 3,500 miles from London to New York City in First Class on British Airways, or about $1.85 per mile. But to travel a mile in zone 1 on the London Underground, the cash fare stands at £4, or about $8. So it costs four times as much to go a mile on the Tube than it does to go a mile in transatlantic First Class. Buses aren't much better: £2 a ride in cash. Only choose to pay by cash per ride if you need to travel a single time on a single day. (For short trips, though, you may find sharing a cab costs just as much.) Otherwise pick option B.

B) **Via Travelcard.** This is an unlimited paper pass for 1, 3, or 7 days on the Tube, bus, and the DLR. There are "Peak" Travelcards good for all hours (£6.80), but the "Off-Peak" ones cost roughly 25% less (£5.30) for zones 1 and 2), with the only caveat being that they're good after 9:30am, after the morning rush clears out; they're still valid for the evening rush. You're likely to still be eating breakfast at 9:30am, so the Off-Peak is the better choice of the two types. The card is also good for stations on the Overground and National Rail railway network, which covers huge sections of South London that the Tube doesn't. If you find you have to pop into a zone that isn't covered by your card, buy an extension from the ticket window before starting your journey; it's usually £1 to £1.80 more. If you're staying for more than 5 days, Option C will save you a little money.

C) **Via Oyster.** This credit card–size pass, which you just wave over a yellow dot at the turnstiles, offers the lowest fares, but it's hardest for tourists to use. Basically, it's encoded with what you've paid. You can put the equivalent of a week-long Travelcard on it, or you can pre-pay rides with a wad of cash that debits from your account. Just wave it over the yellow plate at the turnstiles and keep moving. No matter how many times you ride the Tube (debited at £1.50 in zone 1), bus (debited as 90p after the morning rush), and DLR (£1.50), the maximum taken off your card in a single day will always be 50p less than what an equivalent Day Travelcard would cost (so, £4.80 for zones 1 and 2). Translation: Oyster day passes cost 50p less than a Travelcard. But getting an Oyster requires a £3 deposit unless you're buying rides for more than a week. Before you skip town, any Tube ticket office can refund your unused money as long as it's under £5, but if they owe you more than that, it's tough to get your money back; London Underground only mails deposit refunds to U.K. addresses (gee, thanks). Pre-paid Oysters don't cover Mainline rail stations; you have to pay a surcharge to get to those before starting your commute. Still, you can lend your card to someone else when you're not using it. If you're staying more than 5 days and riding the Tube and bus hard, Oyster's a pearl.

Whichever method you choose, the Tube's still an expensive proposition. I do everything I can to plan days during which I don't have to take it at all. A significant aspect of that strategy is choosing a hotel that's within walking distance of lots of the things I want to do. Fortunately, that's not hard to do because the city's very walkable. Trains go so slowly (34kmph/21 mph is the *average* and has been for over 100 years); you can watch the tunnel walls creep by, and in the center of town, stations are often close together. In fact, if your journey is only two or three stations, you can often walk the distance in the same amount of time.

NATIONAL RAIL

These are the commuter rail lines (sometimes called mainline rail or, if you hate admitting Maggie Thatcher is gone, BritRail) that extend into the city but aren't operated by the Underground. These lines are generally still covered by Travelcards as long as you stay in town. This category includes the newly designated Overground, a London-only system of routes that essentially girdles North London but doesn't cut through The City. These lines are particularly useful for reaching South London, where marshy soil (and politics) prevented Victorian engineers from tunneling traditional Tube lines. Tube trains don't serve Hampton Court, for example, so you may end up using National Rail at least once.

There are many termini, but you don't have to hunt for the right one by trial and error. No one carries timetables anymore. They just call the 24-hour operators at **National Rail Enquiries** (☎ 08457/48-49-50; www.nationalrail.co.uk). You can't book with them, but they will tell you where you can. Alternatively, each station posts timetables. Schedules are listed by destination; find the place you're going, and the departures will be listed in military time.

National Rail stations accept discount cards for certain folks. Each card costs £24 for a year and requires proof of eligibility (i.e. passport, ISIC student ID), but since they can be used for trips to distant British cities, they pay for themselves quickly if you're doing lots of rail-riding. Get them at rail stations:

- The **Senior Railcard** (www.senior-railcard.co.uk) snares discounts of about 33% for those 60 or over.
- The **16-25 Railcard** (www.16-25railcard.co.uk) gets those 16 to 25, plus full-time students of any age, 33% discounts. It requires a passport-size photo, which may be uploaded from a computer. If you're applying in the U.K., bring a passport photo for that purpose.
- The **Family Railcard** (www.family-railcard.co.uk) is for at least one adult and one child aged 5 to 15, with a maximum of four adults and four kids on one ticket; at least one child must travel at all times. It awards adults 33% off and kids 60% off. But know that two kids under the age of five can travel with an adult for free at all times, even without this card.

BUS

The buses in your city may not come very often, but London's are frequent (every 5 min. or so on weekdays), plentiful (some 100 routes in central London and 700 in the wider city), and surprisingly fast (many operate in dedicated bus lanes).

And let's admit it: Sitting on the second level of a candy-apple red double-decker, watching the scrolling landscape, is one of London's priceless pleasures. A few routes are truly world-class, linking legendary sights. With routes like these, you won't need to splurge on those tedious hop-on, hop-off tour buses:

- The **15 bus,** which crosses the city northwest to southeast, takes in Paddington Station, Oxford Street, Piccadilly Circus, Trafalgar Square, Fleet Street, St. Paul's Cathedral, and the Tower of London.
- The **12** links Notting Hill, Kensington Gardens, Regent Street, Trafalgar Square, Whitehall, Big Ben, the London Eye, and Waterloo Station.
- The **10** passes Royal Albert Hall, Kensington Gardens, Knightsbridge (a block north of Harrods), Hyde Park Corner, Marble Arch, Oxford Street, Goodge Street (for the British Museum), and King's Cross Station.
- The **14** is for the Victoria and Albert Museum, Harrods, Hyde Park Corner, the grand shops of Piccadilly, Piccadilly Circus, the theaters of Shaftesbury Avenue, and the northwest corner of the Covent Garden area.

Best of all, the bus is much cheaper than the Tube. An all-day pass costs £3.50, no matter the zone, and that's £8.90 less than what you'd pay for the same access on the Tube. Single trips cost £2 in cash. Travelcards and Oysters yield the best fares (the per-day cost is capped at £3), but cash users can get a 33% savings if they buy "Bus Saver" booklets of six bus tickets for £6. If you can't find an automated ticket machine that sells them, duck into the nearest Tube station and buy them from the cashier there.

Some shelters have automated ticket machines (cash only, and don't expect change), but all have easy-to-read maps of the vicinity that tell you where to catch the bus going in your direction. Many shelters even have electronic boards that approximate the arrival time of the next bus. Board by the driver, who operates the ticket machine, and get off via the door at the middle. Press one of the yellow buttons on the handrails to request a halt at the next stop.

Routes that start with N are Night Buses, which tote the clubbers home after the Tube stops. Bus passes and Travelcards expire at 4:30am the day after you buy them, so if you have one for the day, you probably won't have to pony up money that night to get home; the cash fare is £2, as usual.

FERRY

Londoners are only just now beginning to fall back in love with their river, the Thames. Using it to get around is impractical on a regular basis because, of course, it only goes east and west while the rest of the city sprawls in all directions. But planning a single day of sightseeing along its banks is easily done; there are 16 ferry stops in the tourist zone between the Tate Britain and the O_2 dome in Greenwich, including stops outside the Tower of London and the Tate Modern.

A variety of companies provide service, and they are all contracted to the same rate for the same distance. Fares depend in how far you're going, but for a trip from Westminster to Greenwich, expect a one-way fare of £7.50. You will always save money if you buy a return trip instead of two one-ways (say, £7.80 round-trip instead of £12.80 for two singles). **Thames Clipper** (☎ 087/0781-5049; www.thamesclippers.com) fast catamarans go every 20 minutes during the day. Passes that allow you to take as many trips as you want on a single day are called River Roamer passes, and they cost £8 for adults and £4 for kids (these tickets stop short of Greenwich). Unfortunately, fares are not covered by your Oyster card, although those with Travelcards loaded into their Oyster cards can score discounts of about £2.80 for adults and £1.40 for kids on a Day Roamer pass. Two adults and two kids can all use the same Roamer ticket for £18.

TAXI

Even Londoners think taxis are crazy expensive. Personally, I use them exactly twice on any trip: once when I arrive from the train station and once when I leave. And that's *only* if my luggage is too heavy to lug into the Tube.

It's not the fault of the cabbies. They're the best in the world. Before they're given their wheels, every London taxi driver (there are some 24,000 of them) must go through a grueling training period so comprehensive that it's dubbed, simply, "The Knowledge." They arrive inculcated with directions to every alley, mews, avenue, shortcut, and square in the city, and if they don't know, they'll find the answer so discreetly you won't catch the gaffe. And then there are those adorable vehicles: bulbous as Depression Era jalopies, yet able to do complete U-turns within a single lane of traffic.

Crosswalk Cheat-Sheet

Central London's authorities are big on erecting waist-high fences along the sidewalk ("pavement") to corral pedestrians toward crosswalks ("crossings"). After you press the button at these so-called "pelican" (**pe**destrian **li**ght **con**trolled) crossings, the light can take so long to turn that it feels timed to match the tides. Then, when it finally turns, you have to hustle. For two-way streets, your allotted crossing time may be so short that you'll only make it to the protected median. If that annoys you, be grateful for two true concessions made for pedestrians:

- "Zebra" crossings (pronounced ZEH-bra) are your best friend. They're marked by alternating white bars painted across the road and tall, flashing orange-yellow lamps (called Belisha beacons) on both pavements. Here, you have the right-of-way, and if it can, all oncoming traffic must stop for you (which explains why the cover of the *Abbey Road* album doesn't show a pile of Beatles roadkill).
- You'll often see "Look Right" or "Look Left" painted on the street to tell you where the traffic's coming from. It's helpful unless you're like me, and you absent-mindedly read the *other* side of the street's upside-down message.

But for this admittedly peerless carriage, you'll pay a £2.20 minimum. Trips of up to 1.6km (1 mile) cost £4.40 to £8 during working hours; 3.2km (2-mile) trips are £6.80 to £10.60; 6.4km (4-mile) trips are £11 to £18; and trips of around 9.6km (6 miles) hit you for a painful £17 to £27. Rates rise when you're most likely to need a taxi: by about 10% from 8pm to 10pm, and roughly another 10% from 10pm until dawn. Mercifully, there is no charge for extra passengers or for luggage. It has become customary to tip 10%, but most people just round up to the nearest pound. Some taxis accept credit cards, but mostly, they are a cash-only concern.

Taxis are often called "black cabs," although in fact 12 colors are registered for them, including "thistle blue" and "nightfire red." If you need to call a cab, **One Number** (☎ 087/1871-8710) pools all the companies, with a surcharge of £2.

RENTING A CAR

Don't. Rare is the local who drives in central London, where there's a mandatory daily "congestion charge" of £8 (don't believe me? See www.cclondon.com), and where daily parking fees are several times that. Streets, many of which were cramped even back in medieval times, aren't much improved today, and are dogged with one-way rules. You'll go crazy and broke, so why do it?

LONDON'S NEIGHBORHOODS

The beauty of so many of London's neighborhoods is that they were laid out and named during a period of wagon and foot traffic, when districts were defined in narrower terms than we define them today; indeed, for centuries people often lived complete lives without ever seeing the other side of town. Addresses sometimes reflect this helter-skelter improvisation; a building is numbered 75 on one side of the street while the one directly across might be 32. Good thing that very few streets last for more than a few blocks before being renamed something else.

Ironically, the Tube has done much to divide these districts from each other; since visitors are more likely to hop a train between them, they don't often realize how remarkably close together they really are. There's no reason someone staying in, say, King's Cross, couldn't traipse over to the West End or Marylebone, or why a person in South Kensington wouldn't amble blithely into Victoria.

Are these the only areas of interest? Not even close. Literally hundreds of fascinating village clusters abound, many with names as cherishable as Ponders End, Tooting, and The Wrythe. But I've chosen places where foreign visitors are likely to spend time, and a few more where I think they should.

BLOOMSBURY & FITZROVIA

Best for: Museums, affordable inns, residential streets, universities, and homewares and electronics shops on Tottenham Court Road

What you won't find: Evening entertainment, nightclubs

It's important to remember two things about Bloomsbury: The British Museum and Gower Street. The former is London's most popular attraction, and the latter is one of the best avenues for low-cost accommodations, made even more desirable because it's within walking distance of the West End, Oxford Street's shopping, Covent Garden—and the British Museum, London's most popular attraction.

Bloomsbury's dark-brick, white-sashed residential buildings and leafy squares date mostly from the Georgian period, when the district became the first in a chaotic city to be developed; in later epochs, Victoria, Chelsea, and Kensington took up the same dignified layout using a more ostentatious architectural language. Bloomsbury's refined air must have been like oxygen because it attracted the intelligencia nearly from the start, and its two universities are both 19th-century institutions. The first surgery to use anesthetics, a leg amputation that took 30 seconds, was conducted at University College in 1846.

Bloomsbury became a place of remembrance as the neighborhood that bore the brunt of the bombing attacks of July 7, 2005; of the 52 who died that day, 26 perished underground on a Piccadilly Line train between King's Cross and Russell Square stations, and 13 were killed on a double-decker bus passing through Tavistock Square, 2 blocks north of Russell Square. But Londoners are hardy and forward-looking, so you won't find much evidence of that dark day.

Bloomsbury's showier sister Fitzrovia, similar in character but devoid of major attractions, lies on the western side of Tottenham Court Road. Famous residents include George Bernard Shaw and Virginia Woolf, who both lived (at different times) at 29 Fitzroy Square. Charlotte Street, in the shadow of British Telecom's Tower is one of the West End's more happening places for restaurants.

KING'S CROSS

Best for: Budget hotels, trains heading north (and soon to Paris), alternative/down-and-dirty nightlife, student housing, take-away counters

What you won't find: Top-notch restaurants, parks, shopping

London Neighborhoods

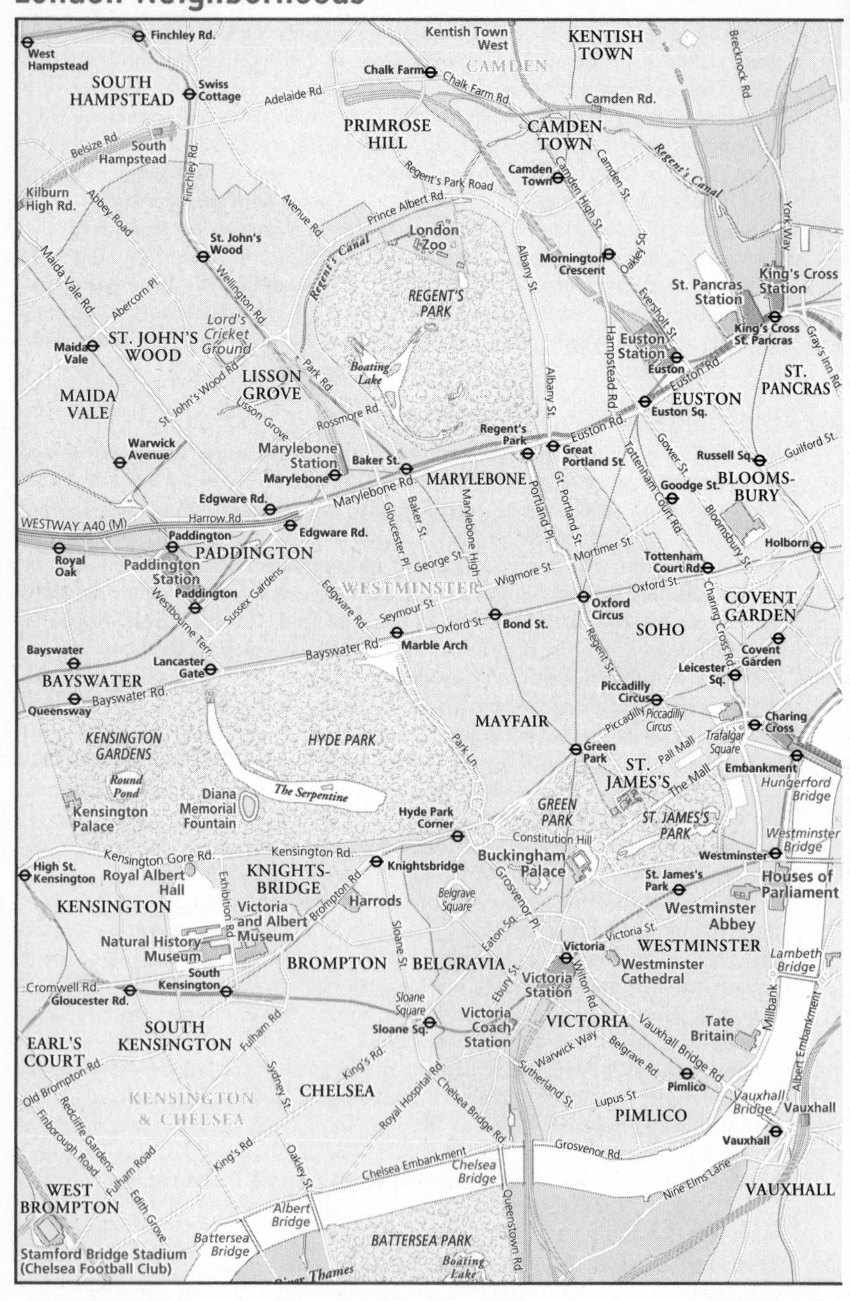

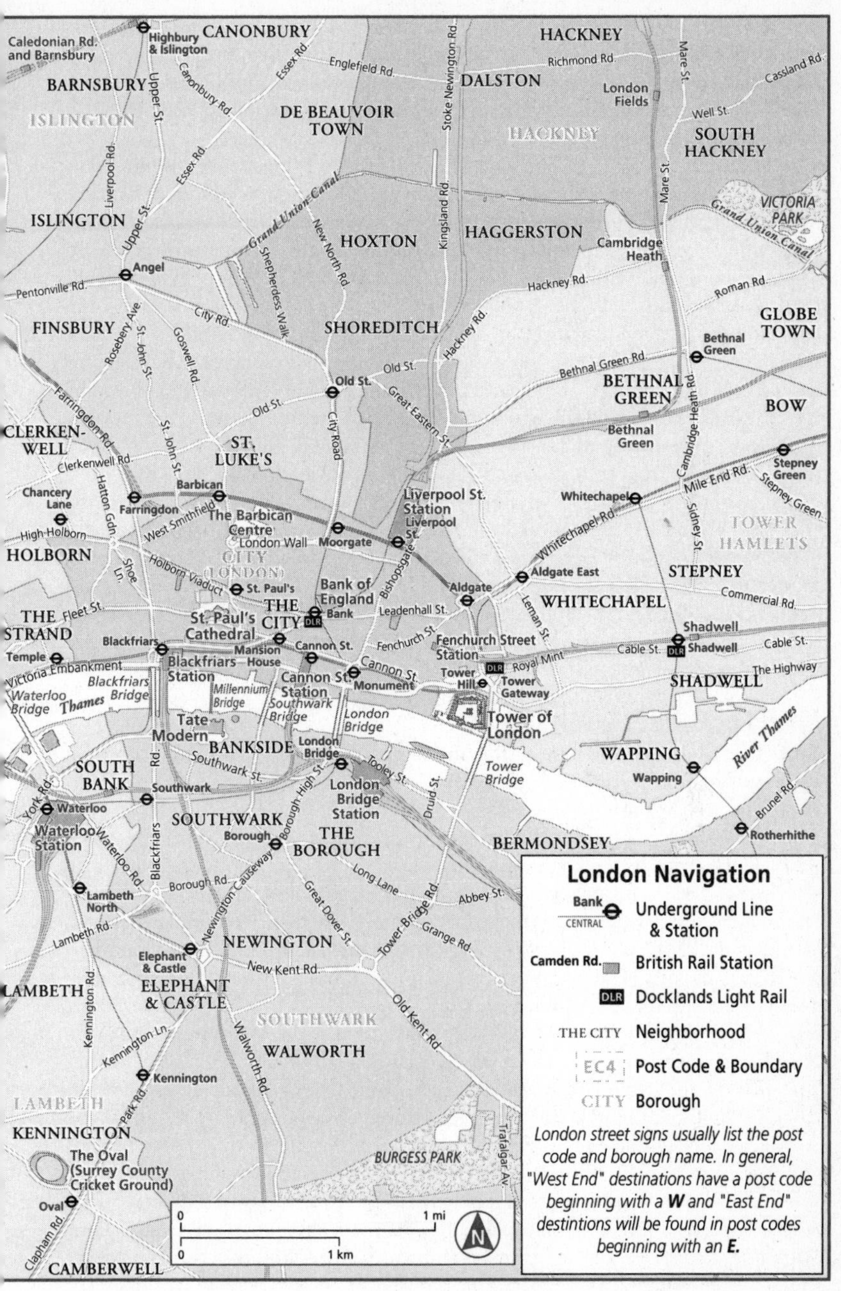
London Navigation
Underground Line & Station
British Rail Station
Docklands Light Rail
Neighborhood
Post Code & Boundary
Borough
London street signs usually list the post code and borough name. In general, "West End" destinations have a post code beginning with a **W** and "East End" destintions will be found in post codes beginning with an **E.**
CANONBURY
HACKNEY
DALSTON
DE BEAUVOIR TOWN
BARNSBURY
ISLINGTON
SOUTH HACKNEY
VICTORIA PARK
HOXTON
HAGGERSTON
FINSBURY
SHOREDITCH
GLOBE TOWN
BETHNAL GREEN
BOW
CLERKEN-WELL
ST. LUKE'S
HOLBORN
STEPNEY
TOWER HAMLETS
WHITECHAPEL
THE CITY
THE STRAND
SHADWELL
WAPPING
SOUTH BANK
BANKSIDE
SOUTHWARK
THE BOROUGH
BERMONDSEY
NEWINGTON
LAMBETH
ELEPHANT & CASTLE
WALWORTH
KENNINGTON
CAMBERWELL
BURGESS PARK
The Oval (Surrey County Cricket Ground)
Tower of London
Tate Modern
St. Paul's Cathedral
Bank of England
The Barbican Centre
River Thames
Grand Union Canal
1 mi
1 km

Recently, the area around King's Cross station was an unsavory tenderloin of porn stores, flophouses, and warehouses. Its turnaround, currently in play, has been just as dramatic, as millions of pounds are poured into its derelict industrial infrastructure. Now, brick warehouses built for produce and coal are more likely to house boutique media companies.

Until the mid-1800s, the area was known as Battle Bridge, after a Roman skirmish that occurred here. Stern-looking King's Cross station, which took its name from a short-lived monument to George IV, opened in 1852. Legend (surely apocryphal) says the Celtic queen Boudica rests somewhere near Platform 8. Fans of Harry Potter know that the young wizard boards the Hogwarts Express at the (fictitious) Platform 9¾; the movie versions have shot at Platforms 4 and 5 but used prettier St. Pancras station, right next door, as a stand-in facade.

Change came, as it often has in English history, from France. The Channel Tunnel Rail Link opened at St. Pancras station (a palatial facade with a shopping mall inside) in autumn 2007, replacing Waterloo as the starting point for Eurostar train trips to France and beyond. Now, an estimated 50 million people pass through King's Cross each year, and the area serves as both a city showcase and a prime bolthole for tourists. Seemingly overnight, once-grotty B&Bs cleaned up their act to cater to international tourists who spend the night before or after a Continental rail journey. For now, the Cross is still appealingly scruffy and well-located for access: Six Tube lines convene beneath its streets, and a few of the most stroll-worthy districts lie within 20 minutes' walk, including bookish Bloomsbury to the south, army-booted Camden Town to the north, and cafe-cultured Islington to the east.

MARYLEBONE & MAYFAIR

Best for: Shopping, hotels, restaurants, small museums, strolling, access to Regent's Park and Hyde Park, embassies

What you won't find: Historic sights

The middle-class hubbub of Oxford Street west of Regent Street divides high-hat Marylebone from its snobbish southern neighbor, Mayfair. Both areas are lined with warm 18th-century town houses, and both play host to upscale shopping and several fascinating, if overlooked, museums, but there the similarities end. World-famous Mayfair, typified by hyperluxe bauble shops and blue-blood heritage (the present Queen was born on Bruton St.), has a high opinion of itself as a starchy enclave of wealth and, aside from the eateries of Shepherd Market, it has less to offer the casual tourist—although admittedly, the window shopping on New Bond Street may be the best on the planet. (Trivia to impress your friends: The title of the famous musical *My Fair Lady* is witty wordplay on how its Cockney heroine, Eliza, would have pronounced "Mayfair lady.")

Marylebone (MAR-le-bun), on the other hand, benefits from convenient Tube and bus connections, affordable hotels nestled in antique dwellings, and lively sidewalks crowded with evening celebrants, particularly around James Street. Also, thanks to a territorial local authority, its main shopping drag (Marylebone High St.) remains one of the last important streets in London that isn't awash with the same corporate chain stores that you'd find everywhere in the country. Miraculously, Marylebone retains a village atmosphere that has set it apart from central London for centuries.

They were cut from the same cloth, but one neighborhood turns its back on outsiders who press their faces to the glass while the other raises a glass with them.

SOHO, COVENT GARDEN, OXFORD STREET & CENTRAL WEST END

Best for: Shopping, restaurants, theater, cinema, nightlife, opera, free art (National Gallery and National Portrait Gallery), star sightings

What you won't find: Elbow room, hotel values, silence

London's undisputed center of nightlife, restaurants, theater, and swanky nightclubs, the West End seethes with tourists and merry-makers 24 hours a day, but the vibe changes hour by hour. The day shift comes for the bookstores of Charing Cross Road and Cecil Court; after work, the pubs and restaurants of Old Compton Street and Covent Garden (pronounced with the "o" sound of "covered") overflow with workers catching up with friends; by 7:30, the theaters and two opera houses are pulsing; by midnight, the action has moved into the dance halls of Leicester Square and lounges of Soho; and in the wee hours, you might find groups of partiers trawling Gerrard Street, in teeny Chinatown, hunting for snacks.

Oxford Street is the city's premier shopping street; the western half between Oxford Circus and Marble Arch is the classier end, with marquee department stores such as Selfridges, Debenhams, and Marks & Spencer, while the Oxford Circus–to–Tottenham Court Road end is more for knockoff luggage and mobile phones. A trot down Oxford Street on busy weekends quickly becomes a crawl.

Prim Trafalgar Square, dominated by the peerless National Gallery, has often been called London's focal point. On a sunny day, you'll find few places that exude such well-being and gratitude.

WESTMINSTER, INCLUDING ST. JAMES'S

Best for: Historic and government sights, river strolls, St. James's Park

What you won't find: Affordable hotels, a wide choice of restaurants

This is near the central West End, but its energy is markedly different. It's a district tourists mostly see by day. South of Trafalgar Square, you'll find regiments of robust government buildings but very little in the way of hotels or food.

You'd think this neighborhood would be stacked with hotels, because it's near the things visitors want to see (and hear), including Westminster Abbey, the Parliament House (and Big Ben), the Cabinet War Rooms, and Buckingham Palace. Yet it's more for government buildings, and has been since antiquity, when Whitehall was the location of (the now-lost) Whitehall Palace, the King's main residence, and Trafalgar Square was his stables. One of the few souls who dares to sleep here does so out of duty: The prime minister's home at 10 Downing Street is protected by a garrison of gun-toting bobbies behind impregnable gates.

Whitehall's severity doesn't spread far. Just a block east, its impenetrable character gives way to the proud riverside promenade of Victoria Embankment, overlooking the London Eye, and just a block west, to the greenery of St. James's Park, which is, in effect, the Queen's front yard. North of the park, the staid streets of St. James's are even more exclusive than Mayfair's, if that's possible, with few stores or restaurants to enjoy.

Whenever a state event is held at Westminster Abbey (coronations, funerals), the royal retinue usually emerges from the Palace, heads east up The Mall, detours through Horse Guards Parade (the de facto "front door" of the Palace), turns onto Whitehall, and proceeds south to the Abbey—the official processional route.

THE CITY

Best for: Old streets, the Tower of London, St. Paul's, financial concerns
What you won't find: Old buildings, nightlife or weekend life, affordable hotels
Technically, this is the only part of London that's London. Other bits, including the West End, are under the jurisdiction of different local governments, such as Westminster or Camden. Shocking as it is to realize that the Queen herself doesn't technically live in The City of London, the soothing reality is that the greater city is still considered to be London, no matter what the borough borders say.

The City, as it's called, is where most of London's history happened. It's where Romans cheered gladiators. It's where London Bridge—at least 12 of them—have touched shore. It's where the Great Fire raged. And, more recently, it's where the Deutsche Luftwaffe focused many of its nocturnal bombing raids, which is why you'll find so little evidence of the preceding two millennia of events. Eager to put the war behind it, the city threw up blocks of undistinguished office towers, turning the so-called "Square Mile," which until medieval times was protected by stone battlements, into a business-and-banking wilderness of plate glass, lobby security desks, and suits. Although 320,000 work here, scarcely 7,200 call it home. Outside of working hours, the main thing you'll see in The City is your own reflection in the facade of corporate offices on weekend lockdown.

Although this is where you'll find such priceless relics as the Tower of London, St. Paul's Cathedral, the Tower Bridge, the Bank of England, and the Monument, some of the most authentic remnants are underfoot, since much of the spider-web of lanes and streets dates back to the Roman period. Buildings have come and gone, but the veins of the city have pumped in situ for thousands of years.

The district of Clerkenwell is northwest, and it hosts meat markets and media lofts by day and some of the city's cooler nightclubs and restaurants by night.

SOUTHWARK & BOROUGH

Best for: Museums, memorable pubs, strolls, gourmet groceries, and wines
What you won't find: Shopping, parks
Revisit your old textbooks and look up a map of London from 400, 300, or even 90 years ago. Southwark is barely there. Although it lay just a few hundred feet across the Thames from one of the world's most dynamic cities, Southwark was outside city walls and out of mind. The neighborhood, considered until the 19th century as part of Surrey, not London, was where respectable Londoners sojourned to misbehave—it was the place of Chaucer's pilgrims, Shakespeare's stages, bear-baiting amphitheaters, rowdy pubs and brothels, and pleasure gardens for wayward couples. Eventually, grimy warehouses, breweries, and factories took over, and the district's unsavory character was cemented.

The devastation of World War II and the collapse of river-borne trade caused the city to take a new look. During Southwark's rehabilitation, a blighted power station became one of the world's greatest museums (the Tate Modern). A master playwright's theater was re-created (the Globe). A supreme riverfront path (the Jubilee Walk) replaced the coal lightermen's rotting piers with pleasing waterfront pubs, and a dramatic showpiece (the National Theatre) was erected. Now, the South Bank, which stretches from the London Eye east to Tower Bridge, has reclaimed its status as the city's pleasure garden, and the dank under its once-dank railway viaducts have been filled with wine bars, museums, and reasonable restaurants. It's gratifying to see that some things never change, though; Southwark Cathedral has risen above the changing scenes for 900 years, and Borough Market, which attracts gourmet foodies from around the world, is the direct descendent of the market that fed the denizens of that medieval skyscraper built over the water, London Bridge.

VICTORIA & CHELSEA

Best for: Boutiques, low-cost lodging, attractive town homes, wealthy neighbors
What you won't find: Transit options, street life, museums

Victoria as a name doesn't technically apply to the neighborhood around the eponymous train station—Belgravia (to the west) and Pimlico (south and east) take those honors—but generations of tourists have learned that some of the city's most affordable hotels are found within walking distance of Victoria station, and the shorthand stuck. Most of the area, which is residential, was developed starting in the 1820s in consistent patterns of white stucco terraced homes. Then, as now, it's a lovely place to spend the night, but it doesn't wake up much during the day.

Chelsea, though, has a history of well-heeled bohemianism—Oscar Wilde, James McNeill Whistler, the Rolling Stones, and the Beatles all lived here—although today it's known more as one of the most exclusive communities in the city, and a stroll past the boutiques and high-end furniture stores of the King's Road (sadly, turning ever-more corporate and indistinct) leaves little doubt about the elevated tax brackets of their intended patrons. Chelsea's exclusivity is guaranteed by the insulation that comes with being a 15-minute walk to the Tube.

> *"London is on the whole the most possible form of life. . . . It is the biggest aggregation of human life—the most complete compendium of the world. The human race is better represented here than anywhere else, and if you learn to know your London you learn a great many things."*
>
> —Henry James

KENSINGTON, KNIGHTSBRIDGE & EARL'S COURT

Best for: Museums, shopping, French pastries, hotels, celebrities
What you won't find: Historic sights

If you want to spot England's most famous faces—the ones who appear at the business end of a paparazzo's lens in English gossip rags like *Heat* each week—hang out around Kensington. Here, one expensive neighborhood bleeds into another as they press against the soothing greenery of Hyde Park and Kensington Gardens. South Kensington and Brompton draw the most visitors with the Victoria & Albert, the Natural History Museum, Royal Albert Hall, and the Science Museum; and Knightsbridge, put succinctly, is home to Harrods and

Harvey Nicks. Privilege has long had an address in Kensington—that's a reason those edifying institutions were located here to begin with, away from the grubby paws of the peasants. Kensington Palace, at the Gardens' western end, was where Princes William and Harry were raised by their mum, Diana.

The upscale character of each nook differs in marginal ways. South Kensington is notable for its contingent of French-speaking expats and when school lets out each afternoon, Kensington (often referenced by its Tube stop, High Street Kensington) morphs into the domain of football mums. The orphan among this opulence is Earl's Court, the only area deprived of a contingency to the park, and consequently a frumpy, slightly tattered zone good for cheap eats and sleeps. As King's Cross rises as a dependable transit and budget-lodging center, Earl's Court, dependent on the Tube, has been slumping.

BAYSWATER & PADDINGTON

Best for: Inexpensive lodging, ethnic food, well-preserved Victorian thoroughfares
What you won't find: Attractions, non-chain stores, street life
Its whitewashed, terraced houses were briefly the most fashionable in the city (Churchill and Dickens were residents), yet today, something is missing in Bayswater. Perhaps the fault lies with the sizable transient population, including tourists, that quickly passes through the neighborhood, depriving it of sustained energy. In recent decades, the area has borrowed some identity from new immigrant communities from Greece and Middle Eastern and Arab countries (Edgware Road is a magnet for Halal cuisine). One exception to the muddle is Queensway, a popular shopping street crowned by Whiteleys, a gorgeous 1911 department store edifice converted into an urban shopping mall in 1989.

Although Paddington station is one of London's most beautiful train hubs (it was built by the legendary architect Isambard Kingdom Brunel in 1838), because of lame Tube links, it's also the most inconvenient. The disused 19th-century canal behind it is being revitalized for condos and shopping, so within a few years the area may rediscover a portion of its fashionable cachet, but it will not see its pinnacle again in our lifetimes.

DOCKLANDS

Best for: Gleaming developments, ancient warehouses, super-cheap chain hotels
What you won't find: Street life, nightlife
Most of East London along the north side of the Thames is ignobly called by a single, sweeping name: Docklands. Yet Captain Cook set off on his explorations from here, and its hand-dug basins once teemed with ships bearing goods from around the planet. Docklands made colonial Britain successful—and thus America, Canada, Australia, and South Africa, too.

Adolf Hitler swept most of that away, and after a fallow generation, East London's hand-dug pools have been resettled by corporations in stacks of fluorescent-lit office cubes. If Tower Bridge represents the apotheosis of Victorian British engineering ingenuity, surely the Canary Wharf area, which contains One Canada Square, the tallest building in Britain, symbolizes the heedless economic prowess of modern-day Britain. Developers are working to sweep the rest of the area's dilapidated relics away and build new facilities here for the 2012 Olympic Summer Games (www.london2012.com).

Away from the river, in salt-of-the-earth neighborhoods like Bethnal Green, Stratford, and West Ham, the city's Pakistani and Indian populations flourish, with marvelous food and shops.

OTHER GREAT LONDON NEIGHBORHOODS

Mostly because of iffy transit connections (for example, service by a single Tube line that, should it go on the blink, would derail your vacation), I haven't included these areas in my list of prime places to stay. But there's no doubt that they'll enrich your time abroad, and many count among my favorite places in the city.

Islington

Best for: Antiques, music shops, gastropubs, theater, street markets, cafes, strolls
What you won't find: Museums, hotels
Few neighborhoods retain such a healthy balance between feisty bohemianism and groomed prosperity, and almost none retain streetscapes as defiantly mid-century as Chapel Market. Islington's leafy byways are dotted with charming puppet theaters, antiques dealers, hoary pubs with backroom theater spaces, beer gardens, and most pleasingly on a sunny day, pedestrian towpaths overlooking Regent's Canal. Why more tourists don't flood Islington is a mystery—and a blessing.

Camden

Best for: Alternative music, massive street markets and food markets, punks, pubs
What you won't find: Refined company, hotels, upscale restaurants
Name a British tune that got under your skin, and chances are it received its first airing in the beer-soaked concert halls of Camden Town. London's analogue to San Francisco's Haight-Ashbury District, it was big in the countercultured '60s and '70s, but is now powered mostly by its old reputation. The area's margin-pushing markets, which hawk touristy hokum in the former warehouses and stables serving Regent's Canal, are so thronged with weekend sightseers that the inadequate Tube station only serves one-way traffic on Sunday afternoons. Watch for pickpockets, mate.

Greenwich

Best for: Museums, antiques and food markets, river views, strolls, pubs
What you won't find: Hotels, bustle
More than any other place near central London, Greenwich, on the south bank across from the Canary Wharf development, retains the vibe of an untouched village; if you can't get into the countryside to sample England's little towns, a day trip here (sun is good, for the markets) will more than satisfy. Such lovely insularity exists because the Tube (well, the DLR) didn't connect it to the greater city until 1999—all the more remarkable when you consider the town's illustrious pedigree as a royal getaway (it's got the oldest royal park in London), as a scientific citadel,

and as one of the world's most crucial command centers. If it all sounds like a living museum, it is: On top of largely being a UNESCO World Heritage Site (Maritime Greenwich), the village is literally the center of time and space, since it inhabits the exact location of Greenwich Mean Time, and of longitude 0° 0' 0". From the hill in Greenwich Park, you can get a prime view of New London (the Canary Wharf district) from one of London's oldest royal hunting grounds. Set away from town there's the colossal O_2 dome, the city's iconic concert venue.

Whitechapel & Spitalfields

Best for: Nightclubs, live music, South Asian food, galleries, clothing, and crafts
What you won't find: High-end restaurants, hotels
If Mayfair is London's champagne, Whitechapel has always been its hangover. For centuries it was an impoverished, squalid slum. When you think of obscene Dickensian depravity—of Jack the Ripper slashing or The Elephant Man suffering jibes—this is probably where it happened. That's all in the history books now. By the last century, the gallery-clogged area (which blends seamlessly with equally edgy Spitalfields [SPIT-all-fields], just north) settled into anonymity as a refuge for immigrants, first Jewish and now Pakistani and Indian—the so-called "Bangla Town" around Brick Lane is the city's most popular drag for curry meals. Prostitutes and orphans have been replaced by artists, fashion designers, and hipsters. The Whitechapel Art Gallery, founded in 1901, is among Europe's best fringe modern art exhibition spaces; and Old Truman Brewery, once a mire of industrial gloom, is now a complex of cafes and stages. You may have heard that Camden is the place to be, but the cool kids are here now.

Notting Hill

Best for: Markets, a village vibe, restaurants, pubs, touristy strolls, antiques
What you won't find: Well-priced shopping, museums, Hugh Grant
Thanks partly to Hollywood, this westerly nook of London, once known for its race riots, appears high on many visitors' checklists. Its Saturday Portobello Road market, the principal draw, is fiendishly crowded and the stuff for sale is cynically pitched to the gullible, but some authentic charmers can be uncovered, including the fabulous Electric Theatre, which dates to silent film but now seduces movie buffs with loveseats that have built-in wine buckets.

Brixton

Best for: Caribbean and Indian food, markets, nightclubs, decaying Victoriana
What you won't find: Upscale shopping, hotels
Once upon a time, when Victoria was Queen, Brixton was a sparkling new neighborhood of matching homes, and respectable families flocked to live near the incandescent lights of Electric Avenue, which in 1888 became one of London's first shopping streets lit by electricity. But within 100 years, hard times moved in. Although the grim days of the 1980s and 1990s (recession followed by riots) are in the past, Brixton remains rough, which is perhaps why so many alternative music clubs fit in here. By day, to explore the glazed awnings of Brixton's markets, with meat and exotic spices, is to walk through a portal to Jamaica, India, or China, and to be reminded that London, like few others, is a truly worldly city.

Hampstead

Best for: Cafes, parks, pubs, historic homes, high-end shopping
What you won't find: Unique shops, hotels
In hilly North London, the rich come out to play on weekends. The little houses and hidden mews are adorable, but it all feels like a very wealthy, very insulated bubble, or at least like a party to which you weren't invited. Fortunately, Hampstead's wooded green space, the Heath, is enough to make anyone forget the slight, and its stately brick homes impress.

Primrose Hill

Best for: Strolls, views of the city, cafes, bookstores
What you won't find: Easy transport links, a wide shopping selection
Enviable townhouses, winsome French-style cafes, prams stuffed with plump yuppie offspring, and frivolous, obedient dogs—Primrose Hill, which is secreted between Camden and the top end of Regent's Park, is the pseudo-suburban paradise to which recently moneyed Londoners aspire. A panorama of the city bows down from its eponymous hill, at the southern end of Regent's Park Road.

3 Accommodations, Both Standard & Not

All the options, from spare cots in private apartments to comfy digs in boutique hotels

LET'S CUT TO THE CHASE: THE MOST EXPENSIVE PART OF YOUR TRIP IS going to be lodging. You're going to a pricey city carrying a currency that wilts like Earl Grey tea leaves in the steaming presence of the pound. You should admit it, you should embrace it, but you shouldn't let it stop you. Because although, yes, London is an expensive city, bargains can be found.

Part of the secret is understanding the culture you're walking into. When you know what qualifies as a good value in London, you'll know when you see one. The other half of the puzzle is actually finding those bargains. And for the next chapter, I'm going to throw as many lifelines your way as I can.

STAYING IN A PRIVATE APARTMENT

It's a tradition in the Pauline Frommer series to lead off with the most illuminating, most edifying, and most economical way to see any city in the world. Well, no, I'm not talking about staying with friends, although that's a really good idea, and if you can arrange that, you're way ahead of the game. Kindly skip this chapter.

I'm actually talking about renting an apartment, or a *flat,* as the British usually say. If you've stayed in a hotel lately, you'll know why I have such a high opinion of flat rentals. These days, when you check into even a middling hotel run by a well-known company, you start by paying a great deal for what amounts to a single smallish room. From then on, everything you do or say ends with a huge charge on your bill. Parking. Laundry. Lots of places even add "resort fees" for using the pool or the gym—the very perks that drew you to a hotel to begin with!

When you calculate the per-day cost, flats are often a fraction of the price of hotels. If you don't believe me, read on and do the math for yourself. Visit London, the official tourism organization for the city, recently quoted the average London hotel room rate as £110. Yet:

- The nightly price to stay in a B&B room in the same town house where Virginia Woolf grew up, and where she published some of her earliest writing (a household newsletter called *The Hyde Park Gate News*), is £85 for two, or around £43 per person, including a breakfast prepared by a gourmet chef.
- In the heat of July, when even the bare-bones inns charge £80 a night, Living London Apartments can find you a home with a kitchen near the British Museum that sleeps two for £67 and studios for singles for as little as £32. And that's with air-conditioning, a rarity in Britain.

Where to Bunk: Basic Training

Because tourists are enamored of the Underground and tend to remain in its orbit, some of the least crowded, and consequently least expensive, accommodations are found in neighborhoods nearer to a National Rail commuter rail station than a Tube stop. Choosing one of those doesn't mean you'll have to take the equivalent of Amtrak to get to the heart of the city. British trains are still among the best in the world, and millions of Londoners rely on them daily in the same way North Americans rely on highways. Why some areas are better served by Tube and some are better served by National Rail stations is usually the product of complicated histories involving 19th-century railway company building rights and the engineering challenges of digging through South London's soft soil.

In truth, National Rail stations are only marginally less convenient than Tube stations, since trains are regular. And it doesn't make much difference in cost: When you buy a Travelcard for the Underground, you must always select which zones it's good in. That Travelcard will include all rides to *both* Tube and National Rail stations within the zones you choose, so you can use the same ticket to get from your local commuter-rail station to the Tube, ride the tube and buses all day, and come home by the same commuter station, all for the same price. (The trick doesn't always work when you use an Oyster card, so you should ask your potential host if their local station is included. The entire Tube system's fare structure is explained starting on p. 10.)

Before you sit down to sort through the options that these flat-rental and homestay companies throw at you, I strongly suggest that you visit the **London Underground's website** (www.tfl.gov.uk/tube/maps) and download the free "Tubes, Trams, and Trains" map. On it, all the stations and zones in both networks will appear on the same page, making it easy to know where your prospective flat will be and, if your agency hasn't already told you, which zone it's in. The site also has some terrific simplified bus maps that show you only the routes from the neighborhood you'll be in (www.tfl.gov.uk/tfl/gettingaround/maps/buses). The website www.streetmap.co.uk will further help you pinpoint addresses. When you see how close to town some of those discounted flats really are, you'll be much more likely to pounce on one.

- Six people sleeping on a luxury duplex houseboat on the Thames, rented by Coach House Rentals, would split a nightly bill of £225, or about £38 each. Even if two people hogged it for themselves, they would pay £103 each, which is still less than the average hotel rate.
- The weekly rate for a simple, freshly renovated studio apartment near the Paddington area from Price Apartments is £490, or £70 a night. Split that between two, and you're paying just £35 a night to be in Central London and to possess a kitchen.

All right, so flats can save you money. But there are more bonuses to flats in a city like London: First of all, you can cook. That's not a poke at British cuisine (hey, it's come a long way), but a reference to the city's dozens of markets that sell fresh meats, vegetables, and spices. You can't bring that stuff home—Customs won't let you—and so if you want a taste of it, let alone a crack at cooking something exotic for a change, you have to have a kitchen.

If you're traveling with kids, flats have doors that close on them when they give you a headache, or when you take a look at your spouse and realize a headache is the furthest thing from your mind.

Flats often have history. You might even find a place that was once a country cottage on a rustic village green before London's swelling sprawl caught up with it many years ago. Flats may have neighbors, too, who might be open to making friends and sharing the secrets of their neighborhood with you. In short, flats give you more room to be yourself, as well as a vehicle for opening yourself up to local influences, which is presumably one of the reasons you travel.

The British love renting flats when they go on vacation and, culturally speaking, that's important, because it means they have lots of them available back home, and you have a long, long list of potential places to pick through.

There are actually two kinds of flats, and I give resources for each below.

HOSTED FLATS

In many places, staying in a quaint private room usually corresponds with a huge uptick in price. But English B&Bs and hosted flats have been one of the world's great travel bargains for many lifetimes. Instead of being hosted by semiretired lawyers and marketing executives, like in typical Vermont or Northern California establishments, they're usually hosted by interesting working-class folks who'd like to make a few extra pounds where they can.

One potential hidden advantage of this sort of stay comes if you've got a car—for example, if you're stopping in London during a drive round the island. Staying with a family in zone 3 or 4 may enable you to park your car cheaply. After all, driving into the city incurs a £8-per-day congestion surcharge (p. 16), and that's *before* parking fees.

What's included? At the minimum, a bed and breakfast—yes, stays like these are how the term "B&B" got started. Everything else depends, since homestays are as unique as the hosts themselves. Your hosts may allow you to make free local calls, or they may ask that you use a prepaid card. They may have wireless Web access, or they may think toaster ovens are the cutting edge of technology. They probably won't clean your room; many of them are far too observant of privacy to do that. Since no industry standard exists, prepare a short list of what you think you'll need. Armed with a wish list, your broker should be able to pair you with suitable options. Just keep in mind: B&B agencies categorize their homes according to their amenities and their convenience, so every extra request might bump you into a higher nightly rate (though still not a rate that will break your bank). Don't make even a verbal agreement until you've found your best match.

The following agencies specialize in booking visitors in private homes—what used to be called bed-and-breakfasts. The people who run the homes they represent are generally pleased to meet tourists (otherwise they wouldn't have opened their doors to them), and their continued good standing is dependent on their treatment of you. Many flats require a minimum stay of at least 2 or 3 nights, and weekly rates result in the best discounts.

Maggie Dobson has personally selected the homes that make it into the stable of **At Home in London** (☎ 020/8748-1943; www.athomeinlondon.co.uk) since 1986. "About 50% of my decision is based on the attitude of the hosts," she says. So confident is she in their quality that she submitted every property to be assessed by Visit Britain's official inspection team. Her 60-odd properties are in the tourist areas of West London, near the Tube, and are priced accordingly: £60 (Fulham, Hammersmith) to £66 (South Kensington, Belgravia, Knightsbridge). A few of its most prime locations (Mayfair, Westminster) are priced closer to £95 a night for doubles, although one property at Buckingham Gate is just £83, a steal for the area. Thorparch Road in Vauxhall is owned by an opera singer, and goes for £80 for doubles, £56 for singles. Hyde Park Gate (£85 doubles, £65 singles) is the house where Virginia Woolf spent the first 18 years of her life; its owner, who happens to be a professional cook and prepares a colossal breakfast, will pull out the Woolf mementos for anyone who asks. Dobson makes an effort to set up tourists with compatible hosts, and she's also sensitive to the worries of first-time homestay customers: "Some people are concerned that they'll have to talk to the host too much, that the host will be intrusive, or that they'll have to be back at a certain time or risk annoying their host. Nobody does that anymore." She even puts out a free online newsletter designed to bring customers up to speed on how her service works and what's worth doing in London. Prices include service fees, taxes, and nearly always, breakfast.

Bulldog Club (☎ 020/7371-3202; www.bulldogclub.com; stay@bulldogclub.com), around since 1988, aims to provide a luxury experience in the kind of home you might see spotlighted in a decorators' magazine. Guests are greeted on arrival by their host, who'll have been approved for their willingness to help visitors acclimate. One double bedroom, located in a 160-year-old house near the famous Portobello Road market, comes with a claw-foot bathtub and a walk-in shower, plus access to a private roof terrace. It costs £80 for a single or £95 for a double room, including breakfast. Another, in the Limehouse section of the historic Docklands area, just east of the Tower of London, is in a private wing of an apartment that's been slotted into a spacious 19th-century shipping warehouse—think exposed brick and vaulted timber ceilings. In the morning, you can watch boats ply the Thames from your breakfast table. The cost is £125 a night. More properties are on offer, of course, at similar prices, and most have a 2-night minimum stay. All are nonsmoking and come with a full English breakfast.

London Bed and Breakfast Agency (☎ 020/7586-2768; www.londonbb.com) is another agency that personally inspects all of its properties (Victorian, modern, Edwardian—about 40 at last count) and gives the heave-ho to hosts who don't pull their weight. One of its properties, in the chi-chi northern suburb of Hampstead, is hosted by a film actress well-known in England. The three operators of this firm are women, and because they frequently host single female travelers, they pay special attention to listing safe neighborhoods with trustworthy hosts. Its price structure is based on how close to the center of London you want to stay. Category A homes are in zones 1 and 2 (the most central, most urban zones) and cost £74 to £114 for doubles, usually £42 to £60 for singles. B category homes are in zones 2 and 3, which is to say they're 20 to 30 minutes by Tube or bus from the center of town in average neighborhoods, and they're £56 to £66 for doubles, depending on whether you get your own bathroom, and £50 to £60 for singles. The C categories are situated in London's many bedroom communities: zones 3 and 4, where few tourists usually go. That's why they're £50 for doubles and £27 for singles. No kids under 5 are allowed (a good rule of thumb for any homestay, I'd say). A £5 fee is added to the total.

ROCK-BOTTOM HOME STAYS OUT OF THE CENTER

The tradition of paying to stay in spare rooms goes back a long, long way in Britain. The following agencies see things the old way. That is, their main concern is placing you in a home at the price you can afford. I can't promise that your hosts will bend over backward to show you the city (which may actually suit more private travelers), but I can promise low prices:

You can tell that **London Homestead Services** (☎ 020/7286-5115; www.lhslondon.com), in business since 1985, is an old-fashioned concern by taking a look at the landlords' monikers—all are referred to by their initials, as in Mr. and Mrs. R., who offer a £22 double room in their home at Wembley Central. The budget category is incredibly cheap (£20 is the average fee for both doubles and singles), but that's usually because they're located in commuter neighborhoods a good half-hour train ride from town, within small, traditional homes. Staying in one of these rooms feels a lot like visiting a distant relation whom you'll want desperately not to disturb, but on the other hand, you'll be spending what you would at a hostel for a dorm bed, in authentic London neighborhoods (old-fashioned grocers, markets, and so on) that few tourists bother to explore. Loosely speaking, the agency's "budget" properties are in smallish semidetached homes; its "standard" ones in slightly larger houses; and its "premier" options are in some of the largest homes (though they're still not palatial by suburban standards). Remember that you will have to pay a little more for trains to reach those neighborhoods, but if you stick to a weekly Oyster pass, adding a zone only costs a few extra quid. "Standard" rooms are generally £25, and "premier" class is typically £30 to £35. Although this company inspects all its offerings, ultimately it acts as a clearinghouse for hooking tourists up with places to stay; the running of the accommodations is up to the landlords.

Established in 1992, **Happy Homes** (☎ 020/7352-5121; www.happy-homes.com) specializes in rooms in southwest London, about a 25-minute commute to the West End. Its catalog also offers fairly typical, old-fashioned, middle-class homes, which is why its rates can be stupendously low. Unfortunately, its clunky website means you have to call to hash out where you're going to stay. Two types of rooms are offered: Short Term (4–13 nights) and Long Term (2 weeks and over), plus a one-time fee of £25 per person. For short term, singles are £25 and doubles are £40. Long-term prices for a single room are £120 per week, with a £60 administrative fee, and for a double, it's £195 per room per week, with a £90 fee. If you pay with a credit card, you'll incur a surcharge of 3%—perfectly legal here.

If you're scraping the linty depths of your wallet, you'll do well to stay farther from the action in the center of town, such as in Wimbledon, Clapham, or Putney—all about 30 minutes away from the West End by Tube or train. For those subdued but money-saving areas, try **Annscott Accommodation Service** (☎ 020/8540-7942; www.holidayhosts.free-online.co.uk). The price of a single room with shared bath arranged by Annscott (in business under one name or

Pauline Frommer Says: Questions to Ask Your Potential B&B Host

Though most in-apartment B&B stays are fun, carefree holidays, sometimes . . . well, things can go mighty wrong. It's extremely important to find out what sort of person you may be sharing your vacation with and what the apartment is like before you put down a deposit. Call your potential host or the agency to go over any concerns you may have before committing to a hosted stay. You may want to ask your potential host or agency the following questions:

1. **What is the host's schedule?** Some hosts will be in the apartment for most of the day, while others work outside the home, meaning that you'll have the place to yourself for large chunks of time.
2. **Where does the host sleep in relation to the room you'll be using?** Another privacy issue: Will your host be in the room right next door, eavesdropping, intentionally or not, on your every sigh or snore? Or will there be a room or two between your two bedrooms? In some extremely rare cases, cash-crunched hosts have been known to rent out their own bedrooms and take the living room couch for a week. If the listing is for a one-bedroom, you may want to find out if this is the case, as that can be an uncomfortable situation, especially if you have to walk through the living room to get to the bedroom or bathroom. (From what I understand, this is not a common scenario, but hey, it's better to ask.)
3. **Is the bathroom shared or private?**
4. **Are there pets in the house?**
5. **Are children welcome as guests?**
6. **Are there any rules the host has for his or her guests?** Whether or not guests can smoke in the apartment is obviously a common issue, as is the guest's use of the shared space (I once met a host who only allowed the guests she liked to venture into the living room). Most hosts do not allow guests to cook, except to reheat prepared foods, so if this is an issue for you, bring it up. And sometimes the rules can be even more unusual—I know of a Kosher hostess who requires guests to separate the plates used for dairy products and meat products (not an easy task).
7. **What does the bedroom face?** Does the room get a lot of sun in the morning? Does it face a busy street, or a quiet back courtyard? For light sleepers, these questions are key.

another since the early 1990s) goes as low as £17, topping out at £40. Doubles are £34 to £65. Don't expect the red carpet—just someone's spare room done up nicely, as if they were expecting a visiting school chum. Homes closer to town (Chelsea, Knightsbridge, Belgravia) go for £36 to £54 for singles and £58 to £90 for doubles. The management personally inspects all homes, and a minimum stay of 2 nights is required. Rooms all come with breakfast, TV, and tea and coffee facilities. At press time, the website could not perform secure bookings, so you'll have to call after you peruse the choices.

SERVICED APARTMENTS

The following agencies specialize in renting someone's home or second home. When you arrive at these homes (which you'll have to yourself), you'll often find a helpful folder that schools you in the best local shops and restaurants, and you may encounter helpful neighbors keeping an eye on the place and on your welfare (at one property I know of, the owner herself pops round and pretends to be a helpful neighbor), which is an advantage if you want to learn more of the city's secrets. Many properties have minimum stays of 5 to 7 nights, but that varies by property; a few have no minimum stay at all. You're also more likely to find the cheapest places in West London around Earl's Court or Bayswater.

For a good range of homes from mid-range to fantasy, the well-established **Coach House Rentals (☎ 020/8133-8332; www.rentals.chslondon.com)** shines brightest in Chelsea, around Hyde Park, and in the bedroom communities southwest and west of town, such as Wandsworth. All flats are selected and approved by the bosses, Meena and Harley Nott, and are owned by Londoners who are out of town much of the time; calendars reflecting availability are posted online. The Notts supply every incoming guest with a starter pack for the first morning's breakfast plus a handbook detailing what's worth doing around their temporary home. The company's namesake is a converted carriage house tucked behind a home in Wandsworth that belongs to the Notts themselves. It's a detached building with its own entrance and an atmospheric beamed bedroom, and it fits up to five people. In the morning, you cross the garden to the main house, where breakfast is served by Meena, who uses the time to coach you on how to fill your day. That room can book up 6 months in advance and is £150 for two or three (£50 per person), sliding to £175 for five (or £35 per person).

Other properties are simply furnished flat rentals and don't come with breakfast. Typical of what's available: A one-bedroom sleeping two or three that's on the seventh floor of a modern apartment building near the Tate Modern, with across-the-hall access to terrace views of St. Paul's and the city for £120 a night (6 or fewer nights) or £105 a night (more than 6 nights). One of its swishier homes is an honest-to-goodness duplex luxury houseboat (original sculptures, central heating, four-poster bed, and use of a nearby pool and fitness center—the works) moored in the Thames; that's £225 a night, but it fits six. Many properties have free high-speed broadband. Maid service is weekly, and most properties are non-smoking. The website is plainspeakingly honest.

The operators of **Loving London Apartments (☎ 020/7096-8871; www.lovinglondonapartments.com)**, a clearinghouse for a wide range of flats in around 50 disparate buildings, visit every property themselves, often as frequently as once every 3 months, and their attention to seeing things from a guest's eye-view has fed their company's quick rise as one of the city's most reliable renters. What began in 2003 as a booker for Spanish vacation villas spread to London in 2005, run by Brits. Its website is the most versatile of all short-term apartment renters, giving you the option to search according to a slew of attributes you select (having air conditioning, for example, or a washing machine), by price, or using calendars that are clearly color-coded by price changes. You can even use an interactive street map that shows you exactly where each place is located. The lowest prices are around £500 to £650 for a week (that's £35 a night per person, sleeping two, though many places sleep more) for simply decorated quarters dedicated to hosting short-term travelers—these places are investments, not second homes—with kitchens you can cook in, and often with perks like DVD players. In low periods, you can find "hot deals" on its site, signified by pink days on the availability calendars; using those, I've found single rooms with air conditioning near the British Museum for just £32 a night, and £67 doubles, both in the peak of summer. The firm's £10 booking fee, charged just once, is lower than many of its competitors'. The company, which gains and deserves trust by carefully disclosing any potential drawbacks of a given unit (say, if the kitchen has a microwave but not a burner) from the very first step, also operates in other markets (Loving Barcelona, Loving Prague . . .).

Although it was initially set up in 1995 to help gay and lesbian travelers find temporary apartments in friendly neighborhoods, **Outlet 4 Holidays (☎ 020/ 7287-4244; www.outlet4holidays.com)** welcomes bookings from anyone. Be thankful they're inclusive—this company's flats are better-located for tourists than perhaps any other firm's. The Outlet's locations are around the 'hood of Old Compton Street, above the thriving Soho cafe-and-club scene, smack in the West End. The location will save you a pile on Tube fares. The properties are mostly owned and decorated by sophisticated, worldly professionals, who may only use them themselves for a month a year and rent them out the rest of the time. They're equipped with free Wi-Fi, linens, and towels, and they're given some pretty campy code names, such as Cleopatra, Bette, and Diana. Prices range from £63 to £169 for Soho rooms for one to three, with prices around £110 the norm. All of the London properties have been inspected and approved. Make a note of when your flight arrives, because there are £15 to £25 fees for checking in outside of office hours or on Sundays. This is on top of a mandatory booking fee of about £15. Should trouble arise, each flat has its own property manager, and the company's office is in Soho, so you won't have far to go for assistance.

BUILDINGS OF SELF-CATERING FLATS

Finally, London boasts entire buildings that are dedicated to self-catering flats. Often, you may book these directly with the property, which is why I've listed them separately (although you may also find them represented through an agency, so comparison shop your quote in case the building itself is offering a lower rent). A little bit like hotels, they usually have a front desk offering standard hotel services (concierge, for example) and pretty much everyone staying there is a temporary resident. As such, choosing one is not a good way to meet locals. However, you'll have privacy, a kitchen, and more space than a normal hotel room provides. This class of lodging is popular with long-term travelers such as businessmen and West End actors, but short-term tourists are almost always accepted, too. In some cases, there's a minimum stay of a week.

The cream-colored town house of **Vancouver Studios** ★★ (30 Prince's Square, W2; ☎ 020/7243-1270; www.vancouverstudios.co.uk; Tube: Bayswater or Queensway) is so crisp and homey inside, you instantly wonder why all low-cost lodgings in Bayswater can't rise to the same standard. Although flats aren't huge and have power showers but not bathtubs, they're well equipped with a microwave, toaster, two burners (or "hobs"), utensils and pans, crockery, wireless Internet, TV and DVD player, membership to a nearby gym, and daily maid service. There's a private ivy-lined garden with a gentle fountain out back for guest use. The owners keep rooms ship-shape but are not afraid to be eccentric in the common spaces: Scented candles frequently permeate the lobby, and two friendly cats have the run of place. It's a happy environment. Singles cost £85, doubles are £125 (doubles with a mini balcony over the street are £155), and triples are £170. Whack 10% off those prices if you're staying for a week or more.

The handsome, stone **Astons Apartments** ★★ building (31 Rosary Gardens, SW7; ☎ 020/7590-6000; www.astons-apartments.com; Tube: Gloucester Road) is just south of the Gloucester Road Tube station, about 10 minutes west of the Victoria & Albert Museum, and is completely given over to self-contained flats with simplistic, hotel-style furniture and decor, satellite TV, kitchenettes, and modern bathrooms. Their unremarkable and well-used furnishings, combined with the town house–style building unfashionable among big-spending business travelers, may not be splashy, but they get the job done, making Astons one of the better values in terms of flat buildings. Studios with shower and WC (tiny bathrooms) are £72 for singles, £99 for doubles, and £107 for twin beds, and they are slightly larger than a standard hotel room. If you have more than two people, you're in the family apartment category, which costs £138 for three and £183 for four. Want an extra bed in there? That's £10 more. Ask for a unit on the first floor and facing the front, which have small balconies. Weekly rates net a (weak) 5% discount.

About a 7-minute walk east from the Tower Hill Tube station (you skirt the Tower of London to get there), **Hamlet** (UK) ★★ (☎ 800/504-9851 or 01462/67-80-37; www.users.globalnet.co.uk/~hamlet_uk) rents a few one-bedroom apartments in 1970s buildings with full kitchens and broadband. One-room apartments that sleep up to four (two on a sofabed) are £645 per week in summer and £580 in the off season. Its two-bedroom apartments, sleeping up to six if you pull out the sofabed, are £835 a week during the summer, and £775 a week during off-season. Some of its apartments have a view of the marina at St. Katherine's Docks, with the Tower Bridge in the distance.

The building housing **Chelsea Cloisters** (Sloane Ave., SW3; ☎ 020/7589-5100; www.chelsea-cloisters.co.uk; Tube: South Kensington) went up in the 1930s, and in the 1980s, it became one of London's first serviced apartment buildings, with some 600 units. Picture something faceless and in danger of becoming run-down in a year or two, but do-able. The battery-hen apartment building has high guest turnover and a detached staff, but also has an enviable South Kensington location about 10 minutes by foot south of the big museums and 15 minutes southwest of Harrods. Studios with paid wireless Internet are around £616 a week and sleep two, while one-bedrooms, which also sleep two, supply an extra living room for £875 a week. If your stay is shorter than that,

The Gallic Alternative

The French-owned chain **Citadines** (www.citadines.com) is devoted to cheap, private, apartmentlike quarters (they call them "apart'hotels"), light on the service but often conveniently located. Nightly rates are set at one level for stays of 1 to 6 nights and generally drop about 10% for stays between 7 and 29 nights. You get a pull-out couch (in studio apartments, it's your bed, but the mattresses are thicker than on a standard pull-out couch), king-size bed (in apartments), desk, kitchen with microwave, small fridge, hot water kettle, bathtub and shower, modem jack, a stereo (in most units), TV, private telephone number, safe, and at least two sockets. Extra beds are around £12, and laundry (wash and dry) is about £7 in a laundry room. Room cleaning is weekly, but extra once-overs are around £15, breakfast £10, parking around £20 a day. The prices below fluctuate depending on availability, but they're typical.

Found just up the block from the Tube, the French-run **Citadines London Barbican** ★ (7-21 Goswell Rd., EC1; ☎ 020/7566-8000; www.cidatines.com; Tube: Barbican) is on an ugly, windswept street, which may account for its below-market rates, but it's near enough to the action to consider. It's located in a modern 129-unit building. Just west are the nightclubs and restaurants of hip Clerkenwell. Studios that fit two start at £106, and one-bedrooms that fit four start at £150.

Citadines London Holborn-Covent Garden ★★ (94-99 High Holborn, WC1; ☎ 020/7395-8800; www.citadines.com) boasts a terrific location near Covent Garden and on the Central Line. Of 192 units, 40 are one-bedrooms, and the rest are studios, which are adequate; imagine hotel rooms with kitchenettes. Those on the front face a noisy street, but also overlook the magnificently ornate facade of the Renaissance Chancery Court. Studios fitting two start at £108, and one-bedrooms fitting four start at £169.

The 92-room **Citadines London South Kensington** (35A Gloucester Rd., SW7; ☎ 020/7543-7878; www.citadines.com; Tube: Gloucester Road) is found farther from the West End than any other Citadines in London, but its advantage is that it's nearer to Kensington Gardens and Hyde Park than almost any other economy property in the quarter. Studios that fit two start at £116 and one-bedrooms that fit four start at £170.

The best-located Citadines property, **Citadines London Trafalgar Square** ★★ (18-21 Northumberland Ave., WC2; ☎ 020/7766-3700; www.citadines.com), with 187 units, is a quick trot toward the Thames from Trafalgar Square, in the heart of tourist's London. That's why its prices are the highest among the chain's London properties, but its sensationally easy Tube connections may make it worth the extra price, especially if you've got kids in tow. Studios that fit two start at £115, one-bedrooms sleeping four start at £190, and two-bedrooms fitting six start at £230.

The Pleasures (and Perils) of Packaged Hotels

What if I told you that you could spend 6 nights in London, airfare and all hotel nights included, for $749 including airline fuel surcharges in spring and fall? Or for around $850 over New Year's Eve? Even in summer, when airfare by itself can cost $1,100 and many people put off visiting London, air-hotel packages can cost about the same—but with hotel, breakfast, and often a tour or two thrown in. With math like that, it's as if the hotel stay is free. How do they do it? Contracted rates and bulk buying.

I love air-hotel packages. There's often no cheaper way to get to London. And unlike escorted tours, with air-hotel packages you don't have to amble around the city on a bus full of tourists—you get your air ticket and your hotel voucher, and off you go to explore. The lowest prices leave from eastern American cities such as New York and Boston, but for a few dozen dollars more, you can leave from just about any other American city. You can also often extend the return airfare by as much as a month without having to buy more hotel nights (although you can do that, too).

The king of affordable air-hotel deals is **Go-Today.com** (☎ 800/227-3235; www.go-today.com), which usually offers 3-, 4-, and 6-night packages to London, often paired with other European destinations such as Paris or Rome, including local flights between the cities (as low as $1,000 for six combined nights in winter). Other big brokers can share the same inventory, so options might be similar among them: **EuropeASAP** (☎ 415/750-5449; www.europeasap.com) has prices that are competitive with Go-Today. **Virgin Vacations** (☎ 888/937-8474; www.virgin-vacations.com), the air-hotel wing of funky Virgin Atlantic Airways, does 3-, 4-, and 6-night

expect rates of about £103 for studios and £152 for one-bedrooms. The kitchens are better equipped than most, with plenty of cutlery, a fridge, microwave, toaster, kettle, and hot plate, plus a washing machine and a dryer. All stays are subject to a £71 "tenancy agreement fee," whatever that is, and I have heard reports of this property taking its sweet time in returning deposits after vacations are over. Perhaps it pays for the 24-hour concierge you're probably not going to use.

ACADEMIC ROOMS

Wait, don't skip this section yet!

Staying in an empty dorm room is actually an ideal option. After all, given the size of London's hotel rooms—even the pricey ones—you're not going to get much more space than a college student, anyway. Besides, by summertime, when the dorms open to the public, the students are long gone and every square inch has been polished to a glare by custodial staff, so it's not like you're going to deal with student filth or sleep under posters of Pete Wentz.

deals. The best deals from **British Airways Holidays** (☎ 877/428-2228; www.baholidays.com) are its 3-night air-inclusive vacations, but some of its packages are priced higher than others on the air-hotel market. Also beware of its airline sales that come with hotel rooms, because sometimes, companies like Go-Today can beat those prices, too. **Gate 1 Travel** (☎ 800/682-3333; www.gate1travel.com) most often offers packages that include London and one other European city, and it sometimes sells 4-night packages as "6-day trips." **E.E.I. Travel** (☎ 800/927-3876; www.eeitravel.com) is Go-Today's corporate cousin, so deals can be similar at its lowest end. **Auto Europe** (☎ 888/223-5555; www.autoeurope.com) sometimes adds London to its offers, but unlike its cars, its hotels are not at the cheapest rates.

The catch with package deals is this: Although all air-hotel deals give you a range of hotels to pick from, many of the least expensive ones ("budget" and "tourist") are pillow mills that have seen better days. Depressing but true. So what can you do about this? First of all, don't give up on air-hotel packages. The money you save could make or break your trip, and besides, you'll only endure even the worst hotel for a few minutes before you sleep and for an hour or two after you wake up. The rest of the time, you'll be touring or unconscious.

For a little more peace of mind, you could also opt for a slightly more expensive "superior" or "deluxe" property. Another good idea: hit Internet message boards and see what others have said about the place you're about to pick. **TripAdvisor** (www.tripadvisor.com) has active London boards, as does **Frommers.com.**

There are 24 universities and colleges in town with 350,000 students, and schools nurture this lucrative sideline with detailed websites on which you can book rooms. For summer, reservations are accepted starting in March or April.

At all of them, you should expect a wood-frame bed with linen, a desk, a dresser, an in-room sink, windows that open, nightstands, the possibility of an equipped kitchen (although it might be shared), an en suite bathroom (shared situations are noted), laundry facilities, breakfast (often at a reasonable charge), and phones in the room or in the hall. A few even have TV lounges. And all of them have round-the-clock security.

London School of Economics ★★★ (☎ 020/7955-7575, www.lsevacations.co.uk). Check these rooms out first. They're in terrific condition, with modern furnishings and the dignity that you'd expect of a school that trains the world's future power players in business. Generally, rooms rent cheaply for July, August, and the first chunk of September. School's not in session around Christmas, either, but LSE only opens

Rosebery then. Some (in Carr-Saunders, Passfield, and Rosebery) are also available around Easter.

Northumberland House (Edward VII Rooms, Northumberland Ave., WC2; Tube: Embankment) opened in summer 2007 and has a formidable location near Trafalgar Square. However, there are only singles (£55) and doubles (£79), and breakfast isn't served.

Grosvenor House Studios (141-143 Drury Lane, WC2; Tube: Covent Garden). These rooms, just a few years old, have microwaves, grills, and hot water kettles. Singles run from £59, twins from £89, and one-bedroom flats with kitchens from £99. Accessible for travelers with disabilities.

High Holborn (178 High Holborn, WC1; Tube: Holborn) offers £35 singles, £54 twins, £79 twins with en suite, and £89 triple with en suite. Summers only. Accessible for travelers with disabilities.

Carr-Saunders Hall (18–24 Fitzroy St., W1; Tube: Warren Street). Singles cost £32 and twins with shared bath £50. This one usually opens around Christmas and Easter, too.

Bankside House (24 Summer St., SE1; Tube: Southwark). En suite rooms: £48 singles, £70 twins, £89 triples, £99 quads. Some singles share baths, and they're £39. This is the only spot on this list without kitchenettes. Accessible for travelers with disabilities.

Passfield Hall (1-7 Endsleigh Place, WC1; Tube: Euston Square) got a refurb in late 2006. It's got £33 singles, £52 twins, £65 triples. Some units have shared bathrooms.

Rosebery Hall (90 Rosebery Ave., EC1; Tube: Farringdon). Shared bath: £32 singles, £52 twins, £62 triples. Some twins are en suite and cost £64. Accessible for travelers with disabilities. You can often score rooms here around Christmas and Easter, too.

Butler's Wharf (11 Gainsford St., SE1; Tube: Tower Hill) has £34 singles, £55 twins, £151 nightly/£1,000 weekly for five, £185 nightly/£1,190 weekly for six. This one doesn't have guaranteed en suite bathrooms or breakfast.

A few more options, ordered within each list from most central to least central:

City University London ★ (☎ 020/7040-8037; www.city.ac.uk/ems): Two of its dorms are open from mid-June to the first week of September:

Finsbury Residences (15 Bastwick St., EC1; Tube: Barbican): Singles only (£32) with shared bathrooms, en suite doubles £60, both with shared kitchen without utensils.

Peartree Court (15 Bastwick St., EC1; Tube: Barbican): Singles (£25) with one bathroom per four to six people and kitchen without utensils.

These following two options have a higher standard and are mostly open year-round.

> **Francis Rowley Court** (16 Briset St., EC1; Tube: Farringdon): Three singles conjoined with a shared kitchen and bathroom (£36 per bed), with TV. Closed late August to mid-September and over the December holidays.

> **Walter Sickert Hall** (29 Graham St., N1; Tube: Angel): Hotel-style singles (£32) and twins (£60, both en suite. No kitchens during the summer, but there is a cafeteria.

University College London ★ (☎ 020/7631-8310; www.ucl.ac.uk/residences). Its dorms are less prestigious than LSE's, but they still fit the bill and aren't depressing. From mid-June to mid-September, its seven residences are available for public use, but four of them only accept groups. The three that accept both individuals and groups (act quickly) are:

> **Astor College** (99 Charlotte St., W1; Tube: Goodge Street): Singles from £29 and a few twins from £53. Shared bath.

> **Campbell House** (5-10 Taviton St., WC1; Tube: Euston): Singles from £22 and twins from £43. There are 15 kitchens for 180 bedrooms. Shared bath.

> **Ifor Evans Hall** (109 Camden Rd., NW1; Tube: Camden Town): Singles from £26 with kitchens, or £32 with breakfast, or £37 with breakfast and dinner. Shared bath. Accessible for travelers with disabilities.

King's College (☎ 020/7836-5454; www.kcl.ac.uk/kcvb): Open July through mid-September. It opens four dorms, but only three are in central London (its King's Hall location is only accessible by commuter rail in the south-central area of Camberwell). The candidates, all with kitchens that lack tools of any kind (a disappointment that diminishes their utility), are:

> **Stamford Street Apartments** (127 Stamford St., SE1; Tube: Waterloo): All singles, en suite, with a small fridge (£35), and wheelchair accessible.

> **Great Dover Street Apartments** (165 Great Dover St., SE1; Tube: Borough): Mostly singles (£33), all en suite with small fridge. Accessible for travelers with disabilities.

> **Hampstead Campus** (Kidderpore Ave., NW3; Tube: Hampstead): Mostly singles (£27), some twins (£45), all with shared bath and continental breakfast.

> **King's College Hall** (Champion Hill, SE5; Mainline rail: Denmark Hill): All singles (£20), all with shared bath and cooked breakfast.

International Students House ★★ (229 Great Portland St., W1; ☎ 020/7631-8300; www.ish.org.uk; Tube: Great Portland Street): Part dorm, part subdued hostel. Rates are £27 in a gender-separated dorm, mid-£30s singles, £30 twin. Most of the year, it's full of students from around the world, but in summer, it has the

A London Lodgings Glossary

When you're booking your bed, you're going to hear some terminology that you might not understand. Don't pretend like you know what they're talking about, because the English are too polite to presume that you need explanations. Here's a cheat sheet:

Twin vs. double: Twin rooms have two single beds, like the ones the Cleavers might sleep in. A double room almost always has a big bed for two in it. Because London rooms are so often small, single rooms usually come with just a single bed. If you want to sleep alone in a double bed, you'll probably have to pay for a double room unless occupancy is light and you score a free upgrade. (Be nice. It happens.)

En suite vs. shared: En suite is just a fancy way of saying you'll have your own toilet, or "WC" (which is "water closet," a polite British term for the john) attached to the room. Shared (or "standard") rooms mean your toilet will be a short pad down the hallway. "Private" facilities may be down the hall, but they will only be used by you. Many old-fashioned rooms also have a sink in them. Don't despair that you're in a dump if you have to share a WC, because there's a long tradition of shared facilities in Europe. Even the Waldorf Hotel on Aldwych opened in 1908 with 176 bathrooms for 400 bedrooms, when it was one of the city's finest hotels.

First floor vs. ground floor: The English call street level the "ground floor" and start counting up from there, so the first floor is what many Americans might call the second floor. If you're lucky, there will be a "lift" (elevator) to it.

Pub hotel vs. guesthouse: "Pub hotels," which are located upstairs over a pub, are descended from inns of the past that supplied travelers with one-stop food and lodging. "Guesthouses" are usually the same as bed and breakfasts.

Full English vs. continental breakfast: "Continental" generally means breads (toast, croissant, muffin), maybe some yogurt and fruit. "Full English" is a plate of cooked food. Both will come with tea or coffee. If you find a place that does full English for free (usually eggs, bacon, beans, mushrooms, cooked tomatoes), consider yourself lucky because most hotels are cutting back or throwing down a surcharge for it. And if you find something like tattie scones or black pudding on your plate, rejoice, because extras like those are rare indeed. (Although you may stop rejoicing when you're told that black pudding is actually blood sausage.)

space to admit short-stay visitors. Bathrooms are shared, and some are co-ed but partitioned. The rooms boast modern furniture and are notably clean, but other academic rooms listed above are cheaper and more private.

If you're still stuck after plowing through this list, try contacting **Venuemasters** (☎ 011/4249-3090; www.venuemasters-london.co.uk), an organization that helps tourists locate and book academic accommodations in the U.K. for free.

LONDON'S HOTELS & FAMILY-RUN INNS

I understand that out of habit, some people might prefer to check into a hotel rather than an apartment or a homestay. Fortunately, because of London's long tradition of privately operated B&B hotels, going the hotel route doesn't preclude you from having an authentic English experience. London has more than 100,000 rooms, but I've whittled down the choices for you considerably. Hotels are listed by neighborhood starting with the cheapest and moving upward.

London essentially has three varieties of hotel: family-run inns that provide B&B, traditional hotels, and hostels. In case you were leaning against the family-run B&Bs, be assured that they're more private than you might think. Because times are hard for little businesses, it's now unusual for proprietors to live on-site. It's more economical to rent out the rooms that, in years past, the family would have occupied. There's also this: If you stay at a family-run B&B, you'll be privy to the owners' personal counsel about what's worth doing and what's not. These days, many higher-end hotel desk clerks are actually from continental Europe, and many of them know London only barely better than you do. But people who run family inns have often been on top of the tourist scene since their parents taught them. This is changing rapidly, as many budget properties are being taken over by new immigrants on their way up the British economic ladder.

Times are hard for the family-run B&B in London. Because of rising lease rates, competition from economy chain hotels, and a tightening economy, many have recently closed. Many others have been forced to jack their rates 15% to 20% in the space of 2 years, far above the rate of inflation. Combined with poor exchange rates, the cost of accommodations in London, particularly around Victoria, is often some 30%higher now than it was just a few years ago. It now behooves you to compare price quotes with economy hotel chains you might not have otherwise considered, or to look harder at academic rooms or flat rentals.

When it comes to researching prospective hotels, don't get caught up in the star rating (or for guesthouses, the diamond ratings). In Britain, the difference between no stars and one star has nothing to do with the quality of the linens, for example, or the size of the bathroom. The extra star comes because the establishment will serve you food. Distinctions like that aren't important to tourists who are in town to see the sights. In fact, the more stars a place has, the more likely it is to charge for using its amenities, so focus instead on the price and the quality of the rooms.

In many of the hotel write-ups, you'll read a range of prices. London's non-corporate hotels are pretty good about sticking to their posted rates; in fact, every property is required by law to post them in the lobby. When you're quoted a price, rest assured it will never go higher. Hotels may charge more if there's a rare major event happening, such as the London Marathon (Apr) or a giant trade show, but even then, the increase will usually be limited to one or two neighborhoods.

Accommodations are subject to a Value Added Tax (VAT) of 17.5%. Happily, almost all small B&Bs include taxes in their rates, so you don't have to think about it for most of the places below. However, more expensive hotels (those around £150 or more) tend to leave it off their tariffs, which can result in a nasty surprise at check-out. It never hurts to ask about it before you commit.

Where are the luxury hotels? Trust me, London has some unforgettable ones, and places that have been the settings for important historic events. But I figured you don't want to spend £450 a night to hide out in a velvet box and that you'd rather use your funds to get underneath the skin of the city. But there's a little help in the box on p. 70.

SOHO AND COVENT GARDEN

Let there be no doubt: This, the West End, is the middle of London. The part of town that offers everything you need outside your door. Also the one with streets crawling with inebriated 20-year-olds singing drinking shanties as you press your pillow to your sleepless head. Hotels around here, by virtue of the location, can slide by with lesser quality than others in town, but you may not care. I wouldn't, because staying centrally can save on Tube fare more than it costs in shoe leather.

£–£££ No affordable hotel in the central Covent Garden area will offer much space, but we'd be in good shape if they all offered the throwaway charisma of **The Fielding Hotel** ★★ (4 Broad Court, Bow St., WC2; ☎ 020/7836-8305; www.thefieldinghotel.co.uk; AE, MC, V; Tube: Covent Garden or Holborn), set in perhaps the most peaceful alley within a square mile. In this early 19th-century warren of tight staircases and fire doors, most of the 24 rooms face Crown Court and the blank building about 4.5m (15 ft.) across it. The management (at it for some 40 years) has taken the unusually helpful step of posting local suggestions for restaurants, laundromats, and Internet cafes in every room. Very small singles (about the size of a double bed, and somewhat airless) are £85; appealingly cramped and creaky doubles and twins run £105 to £125 (for a slightly larger one). Room 10 (£150) is a double with a sitting area that catches lots of afternoon light thanks to its corner position and copious windows. Everything's en suite (but shower only). Trivia: Oscar Wilde was convicted of gross indecency in the Bow Street Magistrates' Court next door, which closed in July 2006 to await rebirth as—what else?—a high-end boutique hotel.

££–£££ Fans of the **Seven Dials Hotel** (7 Monmouth St., WC2; ☎ 020/7681-0791; www.sevendialshotellondon.com; AE, MC, V; Tube: Covent Garden) generally praise its top-drawer location and ignore its shortcomings, and if you can do the same, you'll think it's a fine, central choice. Rooms aren't big; a few have furniture and bathroom doors that appear to be duking it out for space. Still, there's usually enough storage space, a TV mounted on an armature, a writing desk, clean bathrooms, and firm beds. Count out wireless access, though (a cafe next door has it for free). Forget all the ways it's average. Its situation on Monmouth Street, steps from a rainbow of pubs, shops, and bars clustering around Covent Garden, is

King's Cross to Covent Garden Accommodations

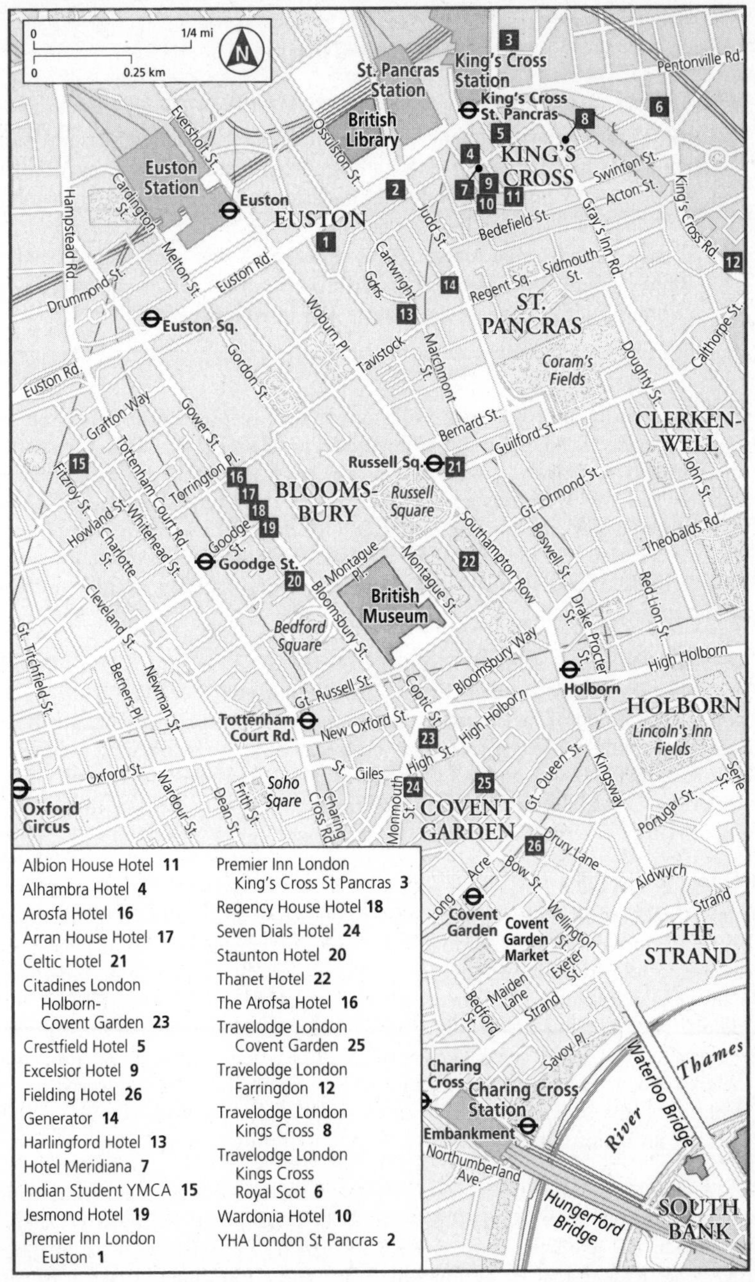

All in the Timing

To save money on guesthouses and inns, remember two simple rules:

1. **Off-season is cheaper.** Many hostels and big hotels have two seasons: April through September and October through March (excluding holidays). Prices will be 10% to 25% cheaper during the latter period. Interestingly, very few family-owned B&Bs and inns bother with this system.
2. **To save pounds, stay longer.** While researching this book, I didn't find a family-run hotel that wasn't willing to lower its prices for anyone who stayed for 5 or 6 nights. Chances are that applies to your vacation.

without compare and will enable you to take quickie power naps and drop off shopping bags. You can pop out at any hour, no planning or public transportation required, and walk to many of the city's most important sights; everything from St. Paul's to Westminster will take you less than a half-hour to reach. For that, I'd gladly pay £75 for singles and £85 for doubles, all with a buffet breakfast. For a shared bathroom, subtract £10 and prepare to climb to the top floor. Because of its busy location, all guests must use the door buzzer to enter, no matter the time of day.

££–£££ Only one economy chain has made inroads around Covent Garden and Soho: **Travelodge London Covent Garden** (10 Drury Lane, WC2; ☎087/1984-6245; Tube: Holborn), where prices are around £100. You can pay less for B&B doubles around here, but if you snare the special £29 rate by booking months in advance, you'll have scored big for a prime locale. It's a three-minute walk northeast of the Covent Garden action in a mood-alteringly ugly concrete tower. For a description of Travelodge amenities, see p. 51.

KING'S CROSS

King's Cross is quickly becoming a prize area for tourists on a budget. The newly opened terminal for Eurostar's high-speed trains to continental Europe has given the area a lift, and the once-pervasive sleaze is rapidly ebbing away. Gradually, many inns surrounding St. Pancras station, practically next door to King's Cross station, are changing from junky B&B catastrophes favored by construction workers to good-value cheapies favored by international tourists. What's more, the area is better situated than Victoria or Bayswater, given that it's served by six important Tube lines and is within closer reach of dozens of prime sights. From here, the attractions of the West End are just a 20-minute walk away.

£ A family-run spot of which I've grown fond, the well-kept, comforting **Alhambra Hotel ★★★** (17-19 Argyle St., WC1; ☎ 020/7837-9575; www.alhambrahotel.com; MC, V; Tube: King's Cross St. Pancras) can't claim to be stylish, but there's no denying that it's an inn with heart, and a top value. In fact, it dispels the myth that B&Bs in the classic mold must also be depressing. Its proprietors work hard, and they keep the prices low. They also like Americans; they often go to New York for vacation. Picture simple but dignified rooms (LCD TVs but no phones, always spotless) squeezed into old spaces and freshened up with bright bedspreads; cream pinstripe wallpaper; inviting blue carpeting; and, often, built-in desks with chairs. Frank, the patriarch, does the cooking, and he dabbles in art, too; in the basement breakfast area, check out the pastel still life he drew to illustrate what's included in his generous full English breakfast. His Portuguese son-in-law handles the hotel's maintenance and modernization, such as the addition of free Wi-Fi, and his two baby daughters can often be found playing around the front desk. If you share a bathroom (there are plenty to go around), singles are £45, doubles and twins are £55, and triples start at £55. Add £10 to singles and doubles if you want a shower but not a toilet, and add £20 to £25 if you want both a shower and a toilet. Weekends see a £5 price bump, and using a credit card incurs a 3% surcharge. Although it's close to the King's Cross Tube and seething Euston Road, it's remarkably quiet. The same family runs an annex across the street that has the same high standards.

£ Yes, it calls itself a "hotel," but it's really a low-cost B&B that's been groomed by someone with a sense of affordable style: **Albion House Hotel** (29 Argyle Square, WC1; ☎ 020/7837-0571; www.albionhousehotel.com; MC, V; Tube: King's Cross St. Pancras) has only 13 rooms, but they're bright, perky, and en suite. The same brother-and-sister team, Patrick and Cherie Parekh, control the 28-room **Excelsior Hotel** (42 Argyle Square, WC1; ☎ 020/7837-0571; www.excelsiorhotel.co.uk; MC, V; Tube: King's Cross St. Pancras), located steps away on the west side of the same square, and both were given a similar design makeover a few years back. The two compact Georgian town houses were remade into perky B&Bs with orange accent walls and geometric rugs, wood floors, beds with deep duvets, heated towel rails, radio alarm clocks, and a tiny but social breakfast room at the Albion (serving an unexciting continental only) outfitted with custom-made tables. Are rooms small? Yes, but they compare with many other budget properties', and few other bargain hotels at this price are as gloom-free. The weak spot is the staff—if you want a homey reception, look elsewhere. Rates at the Albion run from £60 for singles, £75 for a double or twin (a "junior suite" comes with two single beds and a futon bed for £14 more), £95 for triples, and £125 for a quad. Doubles and singles at the Excelsior are about £5 higher; you're paying more to have an on-site office, since both hotels' reception areas are there. That makes solving problems at the Albion time-consuming. Caution: These two show up a lot on deal websites such as Laterooms.com, where the property is often listed as four-star (it certainly isn't), and guests who booked that way have found themselves re-booked elsewhere without advance warning.

£ In 2006, anticipating the 2007 opening of new Eurostar terminal at nearby St. Pancras station, the **Wardonia Hotel** ★ (46-54 Argyle St., WC1; ☎ 020/7837-3944; www.wardoniahotel.com; MC, V; Tube: King's Cross St. Pancras) underwent a full renovation, giving it a fresher look than many of its neighbors. The inn posts floorplans of its rooms online, and its TVs offer more than 30 channels, both of which are unusual for the city. The rooms' style is less unusual—very simple in blue and white fabrics and plain brown wainscoting, bathrooms with showers but not tubs—although the rates charged are something to write home about.

Everything's en suite: singles are £40, doubles £65, and triples £70. Those are quite low, but it doesn't seem like the owners have cut many corners to deliver them apart from not serving breakfast. When you pair them with a staff that is friendly but not obsequious, the Wardonia is plainly a value contender. Prices may dip about £10 lower in winter.

£ Prices are remarkably low at **Hotel Meridiana** (43-44 Argyle Sq., WC1; ☎ 020/7713-0144; www.hotelmeridiana.co.uk; MC, V; Tube: King's Cross St. Pancras) and to an acceptable degree, you get what you pay for: The walls can be thin, the bathrooms truly teeny, the breakfast room so small as to sometimes force you to wait (at least the queue is for a proper cooked breakfast). But on the flip side of that, this is one of the cleaner, brighter budget inns in a neighborhood more known for one-night crash pads and workman's flophouses. Heating and hot water are reliable, too, which isn't always the case in buildings of this age, and some rooms have drawers, another relative curiosity. If you just want a place to sleep where you'll have no regrets about hygiene or price, this no-frills B&B is a decent choice. You're unlikely to get as much value for the price: singles just £32 with shared bath or £45 with one, doubles £45 shared bath or £58 en suite. Family rooms for four are just £80.

£ Southeast of King's Cross station (not at Farringdon, as the name implies), the chain hotel **Travelodge London Farringdon** (10-42 King's Cross Rd., WC1; ☎ 087/1984-6274; Tube: Farringdon or King's Cross St. Pancras) furnishes no-frills, standardized rooms. Rooms run £81 a night unless you grab its Web-only £29 early-bird specials. If that one's full, you might consider **Travelodge London Kings Cross Royal Scot** (100 King's Cross Rd., WC1; ☎ 087/1984-6272; Tube: King's Cross St. Pancras) at the same prices. It isn't as appealing as the Farringdon location, but it does a cooked breakfast. The third location in the area is **Travelodge London Kings Cross** (Willings House, Grays Inn Road; ☎ 087/1984-6256; Tube: King's Cross St. Pancras), which is about three minutes' walk closer to the Tube and occupies a pretty, old brick building. That costs £4 more without the Web special; and because its dining area is located in a historic room, cooking is forbidden, so dinners aren't offered at this property. Rooms on the front, which you can request but can't guarantee, have floor-to-ceiling windows. For a description of Travelodge amenities, see p. 51.

£–££ The 52-room **Crestfield Hotel** (2-4 Crestfield St., WC1; ☎ 020/7837-0500; www.crestfieldhotel.com; MC, V; Tube: King's Cross St. Pancras) stands out for holding itself to a higher standard than most of its neighbors. It may be on the basic side, but it's not grim; yes, it's an old guesthouse, but it boasts a lovely iron gate and genteel blue trim. Rooms are tiny, freshly painted in canary yellow and done up with lace curtains, have glass-topped bedside tables (a sign of trust for budget guests if ever there was one), and there are generous touches such as baskets of potpourri. Rooms also boast TVs (albeit teeny ones), but no phones. There's a back terrace where breakfast is served in nice weather, otherwise you eat in the basement dining room. Bathrooms (most rooms have their own, with toilet) are essentially tiled cubicles with drains in the floor, but some have their own windows, which is unusual for town house hotels. Room 9, a double, is located on a landing facing the back, so it's even quieter than most. The licensed bar area proves that the owners are trying for a hotel, not a hostel, image. Singles are £40 to £50, doubles and triples are £65 to £85, and quads are a dead-cheap £100, with unlimited continental breakfast. If you're only staying on weekdays, ask for a special deal, because the hotel sees a lot of weekend trade. Although the owners are gradually adding private facilities to all rooms, some still share bathrooms; you'll pay £10 to £15 less for those.

£–££ Found in a modernized brick building out the eastern side door of King's Cross station, **Premier Inn London King's Cross St Pancras** ★★ (26-30 York Way, N1; ☎ 087/0990-6414; www.premiertravelinn.com; Tube: King's Cross St. Pancras) has an open, glassy atrium that belies its budget rates. The cafes of Islington are a 15-minute walk east. In peak season, rooms are £110 weekdays and £90 weekends, and they are around £90 when it's slow. The other Premier in the vicinity, **Premier Inn London Euston** (1 Dukes Rd., WC1; ☎ 087/0238-3301; www.premiertravelinn.com; AE, MC, V; Tube: Euston), is in a drab office-building rehab beside the infernal traffic of Euston Road. That said, you won't suffer noise, since windows are well buffered, and you won't want for Tube connections (six lines run nearby). Expect to pay £110 on weekdays and £90 on weekends and during low season. For a description of Premier Inn amenities, see p. 50.

BLOOMSBURY

If King's Cross has the personality of a genial but uncouth warehouse worker, Bloomsbury is a clean-shaven college student. After all, the area's prime institutions are the British Museum and two universities, and much of its cultural pop history is literary. That doesn't mean the neighborhood is staid: Bloomsbury's chocolate-colored Georgian town houses lie within a 20-minute walk of Soho and Covent Garden, and they make it easy to take the Piccadilly Line in from Heathrow. To be honest—and let's spill a dirty secret here—these places are better located than many of London's most expensive hotels.

Beware the 1,600-room Royal National Hotel, a beastly concrete colossus brimming with noisy school groups but little charm. Because it's so big, it often appears as a budget hotel option in packages, but you can do better. So does the nearby Imperial Hotel, which also won't deliver many warm-and-fuzzies.

£ I confess a soft spot for the **Jesmond Hotel** ★★★ (63 Gower St., WC1; ☎ 020/7636-3199; www.jesmondhotel.org.uk; MC, V; Tube: Goodge Street), because I stayed here when I was a young backpacker just getting to know London (I stayed in number 3, a cozy single on the rear landing—still there, still snug). Back then, the Beynon Family, who took over the Jesmond in 1979, had a young son Glyn. Today, Glyn is the man in charge, and he's doing a solid job of updating the family business far beyond the expectations of his tariff range. He recently installed new bathrooms with all-new piping (accounting for the larger-than-average showers), he soundproofed the front windows to keep out the roar of Gower Street's bus traffic, and he converted the house's 18th-century coal chute into a kitchen where full English breakfasts are prepared and served in a cellar breakfast room that doubles as a day lounge—check out the free Internet and DVD player with movie library. The back garden provides welcome respite and is cultivated with daffodils and a

The Deal with Those Economy Hotel Chains

Love them or hate them, chains are here to stay, and they're a viable accommodations option for folks who prefer some predictability in a topsy-turvy town. London's budget-hotel landscape has shifted with the proliferation of corporate brands that are chipping away at the city's already suffering B&Bs. At these cookie-cutter economy hotels, the desk will mostly be staffed by distracted young people from other European countries, so don't expect much local expertise or service. But rooms, while hardly oozing charm, are brightly designed, well cleaned, and reliable—there's not much difference between one Ibis room and another. These places aren't necessarily a talisman for savings. Many have become so popular that when they're most busy, they may charge £20 to £50 more than the family-run B&Bs down the block. All offer both smoking and non-smoking options, all charge by the room and not per person (unless you squeeze in more people than the prescribed limit), all can furnish hair dryers, and all take the major credit cards.

Parents should pay special attention to these places, because most properties have up-sized family rooms that sleep four (two on a pull-out) for the same price—a lifesaver. (Ibis' London properties can only fit three.) They all have cafes that serve up sandwiches, soups, beer, and the like. I have not included all of the options in the listings of this guide—just the most competitively priced or the best-located ones. Because of Web deals, you're best off booking online directly with each company.

Premier Inn (☎ 087/0242-8000; www.premierinn.com; AE, MC, V): This is my favorite of London's economy brand hotels, not just because its rooms feel the most upbeat, but also because it constructs attractive buildings that fit in with their surroundings. Weekend rates (Fri–Sun) are lower than weekday rates. You get a king-size bed, bathtub and shower

birdbath. He also converted the former parlor, with its antique (non-working) fireplace, into room 2, a spacious double. It's simple, it's friendly, and it's still one of London's last "they're charging *how* much?" values. The prices vary by shared/en suite: singles are £45 to £55 (most are on the top floor, where it's quietest); doubles are £70 to £85; triples are £90 to £115; and quads are £100 to £125. Pay for 6 nights, and you can stay for 7. Don't confuse this place with the Jesmond Dene, a decent B&B on Argyle Square in King's Cross—it's fine, but not as central as the Jesmond.

£ Another solid value, **The Arosfa Hotel ★ kids** **(83 Gower St., WC1; ☎ 020/7636-2115; www.arosfalondon.com; MC, V; Tube: Goodge Street)** is distinguished by the antique lacquered sign out front that still advertises its old telephone exchange: "Museum 2115." A long-running, non-smoking, 15-room hotel that's with all-purpose shower gel, climate control, tea- and coffee-making facilities, TV, phone, iron, paid Wi-Fi access, at least three outlets, and a desk. Full breakfast costs £7.50, continental £5.25, and up to two kids (under 15) eat free. Londontown.com often discounts rates by a quarter.

Ibis Hotel (www.ibishotel.com; AE, MC, V): This French chain is distinguished by its trademark 3-foot-square windows, its just-off-the-margins locations, and its bare-bones but cheerful decor. You'll get a double bed, bathroom with shower, climate control, tea- and coffee-making facilities, TV, phone, paid Internet access, at least one outlet, and a built-in desk. The breakfast charge varies per property (£6.50's usual), but food is usually served from 4am, making this a smart choice if you need to catch an early flight or train. The fresh-baked breakfast baguettes are delicious—hey, it's French.

Travelodge (☎ 087/0850-950; www.travelodge.co.uk; AE, MC, V): Go online right now, because rates here start at a head-slapping £26 if you book many months ahead. That more than makes up for having the thinnest amenities of the economy brands. Signing up for its e-mail sale alerts can also pay off handsomely. Expect king-size beds, bathtub and shower, tea- and coffee-making facilities, TV (but no toiletries or phone, which can present a problem), paid wireless Web access, paid in-room movies, a wardrobe, at least one power point, and a desk. "Family rooms" have a pull-out couch for two kids but cost the same as a double. A continental "breakfast bag" to go is £4, while full English and table-served continental breakfast charges vary per property (£7.50—too much—is common). It's nicer than the American Travelodge brand, which is a separate beast entirely.

operated, as of 2008, by new but equally attentive owners who are gussying it up with fresh perks (like LCD TVs), it's equipped with double-glazed windows, a garden for guest use, bright red carpet, powerful showers, English breakfasts, carefully selected lounge furniture (not too common in the hand-me-down world of B&Bs), and a smattering of fabric flowers to enliven the mood. Singles go for £60 and generally lie behind fire doors on the stairway landings, away from the other rooms. Doubles or twins are £90; triples are £102; and quads are £120 (like room 5, a family room that still has its rich-looking carved fireplace, now filled in). If there's a downside, even at this sensational price point, it's the prefabricated plastic bathrooms that were inserted into all the rooms in lieu of actual contractor-built booths. I think the full English breakfast makes up for those. Across the street, you'll find one of the city's largest Waterstone's bookstores, patronized by students from neighboring University College London.

£ Gower Street's streak of admirable budget lodging continues at **Regency House Hotel** ★ (71 Gower St., WC1; ☎ 020/7637-1804; www.regencyhouse-hotel.com; MC, V; Tube: Goodge Street). Victor Gilbert, the proprietor since 1977, makes and fixes almost everything himself because, he laments, workmen are no longer willing to come into the city due to tolls. He's got good taste—the cornflower blue–striped wallpaper and golden embellishments go a long way to approximating (not replicating) this town house hotel's bygone glory days as a private home. Showers have doors, not curtains, plus rooms have matching bedside tables, two chairs for the desk (many places just supply one), and Gilbert also lays out plenty of towels. There are 14 rooms; number 17, a double, has an exceptionally large bathroom for a town house B&B, and number 5 boasts an intricately carved marble fireplace that has been insured for £10,000. You can enjoy it for £99, the price of a double room. Singles are £62, triples are £125, and full English breakfasts are included. In peak season, prices crawl upward, but not by much. Rooms on the top floor have smaller windows.

£–££ Whoever waved a magic wand over the once-dreary Gower Street B&Bs didn't neglect **Arran House Hotel** ★★ (77-79 Gower St., WC1; ☎ 020/7636-2186; www.arranhotel-london.com; MC, V; Tube: Goodge Street), which continues the street's streak of affordable, high-quality B&Bs. Here, prices are a notch higher than at its neighbors, but you're paying for perks like hair dryers, matching pillows and carpet, phones and—unusual for a B&B—access to a shared refrigerator. Flooring and much of the furniture are warm and wooden, done up in a sort of rustic country style unusual for London. The bathrooms are less heartwarming; private baths are mostly tiny molded-fiberglass units. The exceptional beds make up for that—the thick white duvets have a nearly magnetic pull. The ground-floor lounge has a gas-powered fire in the winter, which is also rare. The English-style rose garden is open to guests. Shared-bath rates are as follows: singles £55, doubles £82. En suite rooms are: singles £65, doubles £105. Unusually, Arran House also offers a minidorm, in the cellar but at the front by the street (windows are soundproofed), with four bunks for £23 without breakfast or £27 with breakfast. There's free Wi-Fi if you're lucky enough to lodge in the basement or on the ground floor, and breakfast is full English (included in the non-dorm rate). The owner, John Richards, mostly leaves the running of the place to a slate of businesslike young Europeans, but he loves the theater and opera, so if you spot him, pigeonhole him for viewing advice.

£–££ In 2007, the Duke of Bedford evicted a beloved budget B&B, the legendary St. Margaret's Hotel, after a residence of half a century. Its premises were swiftly converted to yet another unnecessary boutique hotel. "We were swindled!" declares the woman behind the desk of the **Celtic Hotel** ★ (61-63 Guilford St., WC1; ☎ 020/7837-6737; www.celtichotel.com; MC, V; Tube: Russell Square), where the St. Margaret's operators, the eccentric but dedicated Marazzi family, have shifted their efforts to continue the good work. The Celtic was until recently a shabby town house inn, but the Marazzis, sadder but wiser, are making quick work of its rehabilitation. The Marazzis started by renovating every bathroom, securing a steady supply of hot water, and they are gradually rehabbing the rooms in easy pale colors (ask for a renovated room; only a few are en suite, but all have sinks), which should give the place a more coherent look than the old place ever had. Few other budget hoteliers put as much heart into making sure guests are acclimated to London by answering questions, obliging special dietary requests, and filling bellies with a cooked breakfast that's so enormous (try the banana yogurt) that lunch might become optional. To keep attracting longtime regulars, many of whom know staffers by name, the Celtic retains the features that made Maggie's a quirky stalwart: rooms do not have TVs or phones, furniture is endearingly mismatched, and the lounge remains a hub for socializing with fellow guests, many of whom are students. And, oh yes, the sensational prices: £45 for singles, £65 doubles, £85 triples, and £95 quads. Bitterness apart, the upside is that the Celtic is even better located than St. Margaret's was: in the thick of restaurants and pubs, and very near the Tube.

£–££ The values of the owners of **Thanet Hotel** (8 Bedford Place, WC1; ☎ 020/7636-2869; www.thanethotel.co.uk; AE, MC, V; Tube: Russell Square) become evident when you observe the details: a classic blue awning distinguishes the building from the rest of the (quiet) street, bathrooms were recently renovated, and original architectural details such as transom fan windows and carved fireplaces are lovingly highlighted. It's a little non-smoking hotel with the usual small rooms, but it's friendly and run with care. Probably because its neighbors also command high rates, its prices are a little higher than similar hotels along Gower Street: singles are £78, doubles or twins £104, triples £120, and quads £130. The location around the corner from the British Museum is choice, which accounts for the slight inflation. It's owned by Richard and Lynwen Orchard—she's to thank for the flowers in the lobby. Breakfast is full English and filling. LateRooms.com often discounts this one by around £15.

££–£££ Styled as a boutique inn, **Harlingford Hotel** ★ (61-63 Cartwright Gardens, WC1; ☎ 020/7387-1551; www.harlingfordhotel.com; AE, MC, V; Tube: Russell Square), with a facade that crawls with ivy in the summer months, succeeds on many levels. Its design takes a cue from its logo: an easy chair with a pillow emblazoned with an H. All beds are piled with just such a pillow, and bedspreads match curtains in an array of purples, golds, and creams. It doesn't hit you over the head; it's simply all-around nice, as are the newly spruced-up bathrooms with seafoam-green tilework, slender spigots, and green-glass bowl sinks. Granted, all of this tastefulness is imposed on typically small town house–hotel quarters. The staff, who serve a free full English breakfast in the ground-floor breakfast room, loans keys to the tranquil semicircular park out front. It's a contemporary twist on a fairly average B&B, and prices, which are about £20 higher than nearby competitors with fewer sartorial gifts, reflect the spin: singles are £85, doubles and twins are £110, triples are £125, and quads are £135. It would have been nice if they had granted free Wi-Fi the way cheaper hotels around here do. The owner's family has run this place for three generations.

£££–££££ Though not as cheap as its Gower Street neighbors, which makes it a second-rung choice, the 17-room **Staunton Hotel** (13-15 Gower St., WC1; ☎ 020/7580-2740; www.stauntonhotel.com; AE, MC, V; Tube: Goodge Street) is an admirable, welcoming, small B&B. Even though it's situated in a pair of 230-year-old town houses on the corner of two loud streets (Store and Gower), windows have been double-glazed and adorned with treatments, which tamps

The Lowdown on Town House Hotels

Many B&Bs operate inside antique town houses, and their owners will proudly proclaim that they're "listed" buildings. What does that mean, and why should you care? It means that the authorities have deemed the building to be of historical or architectural importance—it's a surviving example of a fine Georgian home, for example, or it occupies a stately Victorian terrace. To keep unsentimental developers from knocking down a gem, "listed" buildings are protected by the government. Changing just about anything, down to the color of the paint, requires permission, and permission is tough to come by.

Why should you care? Because if you're staying in a listed place, your host inherited an aging building with traditions of its own. When first arriving in a city like London, many tourists, used to new buildings with lots of elbow room, must learn to let go of expectations and to embrace the peculiarities of their new temporary home. That hotel is not a dump! It's just carrying the torch of historic hospitality.

Ceilings get lower as you go higher. Until the 20th century, the floors of fashionable town houses served distinct functions. The cellar was for kitchens and coal storage (coal was delivered through a hole in the sidewalk). The ground floor was usually used for living rooms. The first and second floors were reserved for bedrooms, and the top floor was for servants and for the children's nursery, which accounts for the slightly lower ceilings there. If you book a top-floor room, you won't feel like Alice in Wonderland—ceilings are 2.1m or 2.4m (7 or 8 ft.) tall.

Rooms are small by American standards. Look up in almost any room of a town house B&B, especially on the lower floors, and you'll see vestiges of carved molding disappearing asymmetrically into blank walls. Yes, those walls were added to subdivide large rooms after the house was built, but no, the current owners had nothing to do with it. Most room subdivision

down a bit on aural clutter. Well-appointed rooms also have safes, satellite TV, firm beds, AC with remote control, modem ports, luggage racks, and strong showers. I imagine the owners are charging more for the slightly larger-than-usual quarters, as well as the formidable location within walking distance of the entire West End. Doubles are £140; "trebles" are £175. If you can, secure room 103—it's larger than a standard double.

KENSINGTON, EARL'S COURT & SOUTH KENSINGTON

These family-oriented, generally well-to-do residential neighborhoods, which hug the southwest corner of Kensington Gardens, have been hallowed grounds for budgeteers for generations. Reaching the energy of Piccadilly Circus may take was done in the mid–20th century to fill a housing gap after many of the city's big hotels were destroyed in the war, and now, even removing those slapped-up walls requires civic approval, which is nigh impossible. You are unlikely to have a closet and in some rooms, particularly singles, suitcases can be hard to open without using the bed. Hotel managers may be able to give you a larger room if you need one. Here's a tip: The largest rooms in such B&Bs usually face the front.

Bathrooms are even smaller. In the old days, all guests shared bathrooms, but to suit changing tastes, landlords have slotted compact booths containing the staples (toilet, shower, sink) into rooms that weren't designed to have them (remember, they're not allowed to bash down any plaster), which naturally cuts down on floor space. Adding bath cubicles makes for smaller rooms, but it's one of the reasons why town house B&Bs are so much more affordable than standard hotels.

Don't expect an elevator, or "lift." It takes years of begging and a small fortune to convince the council to allow the destruction that elevator construction brings, so few hotels have them. Assume you're going to have to use the stairs. They may be narrower than you're used to, especially the ones leading to the cellar, but on the bright side, the banisters are pretty. The trade-off is that rooms on higher floors receive more light, less noise, and fewer patrons, so you'll get a better view and more privacy.

Not all windows are double glazed. The councils enforce all sorts of arcane rules about changing windows, too. You think it's loud now? Imagine how it must have sounded when horses and carriages were clattering up the cobbles at all hours. If you're a light sleeper and your chosen B&B doesn't have double glazing, simply ask for a room at the back. Rooms on back stairway landings often don't adjoin other rooms, either, which takes care of much ambient noise.

about 20 minutes on the Underground from here, and that remove from the action has traditionally fueled the low-priced competition. Unfortunately, things are changing. As rents rise, fewer family-run hotels can afford to stay open in neighborhoods such as Earl's Court, while others can barely make ends meet. The area is still the right choice if you want to stay within walking distance of the park, and there are plenty of inexpensive dining options.

£ The English know all about the cheap-and-basic ethic behind **easyHotel South Kensington** ★ (14 Lexham Gardens, W8; www.easyhotel.com; MC, V; Tube: Earl's Court or Gloucester Road), because its founder, Stelios Haji-Ioannou, has made himself a minor celebrity by creating budget brands (easyJet, easyCruise)

Kensington Accommodations

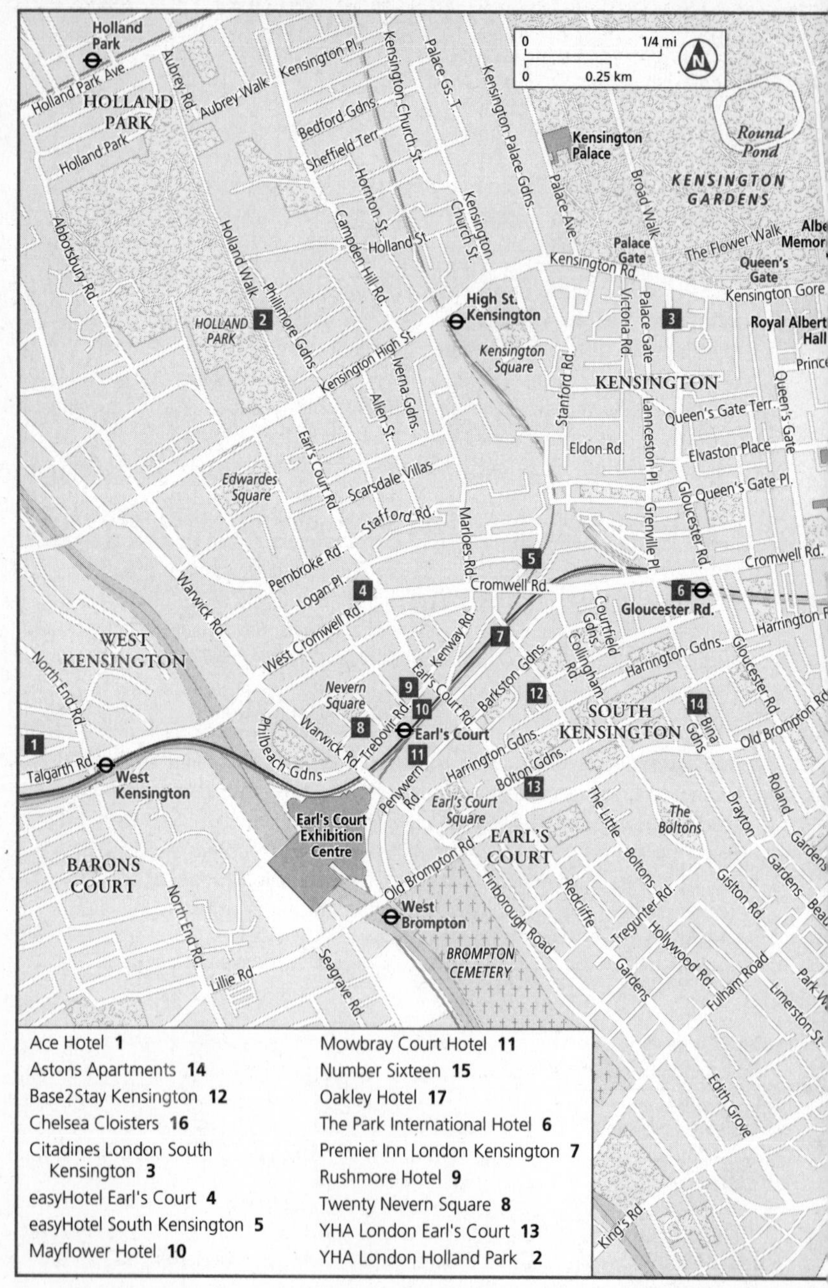

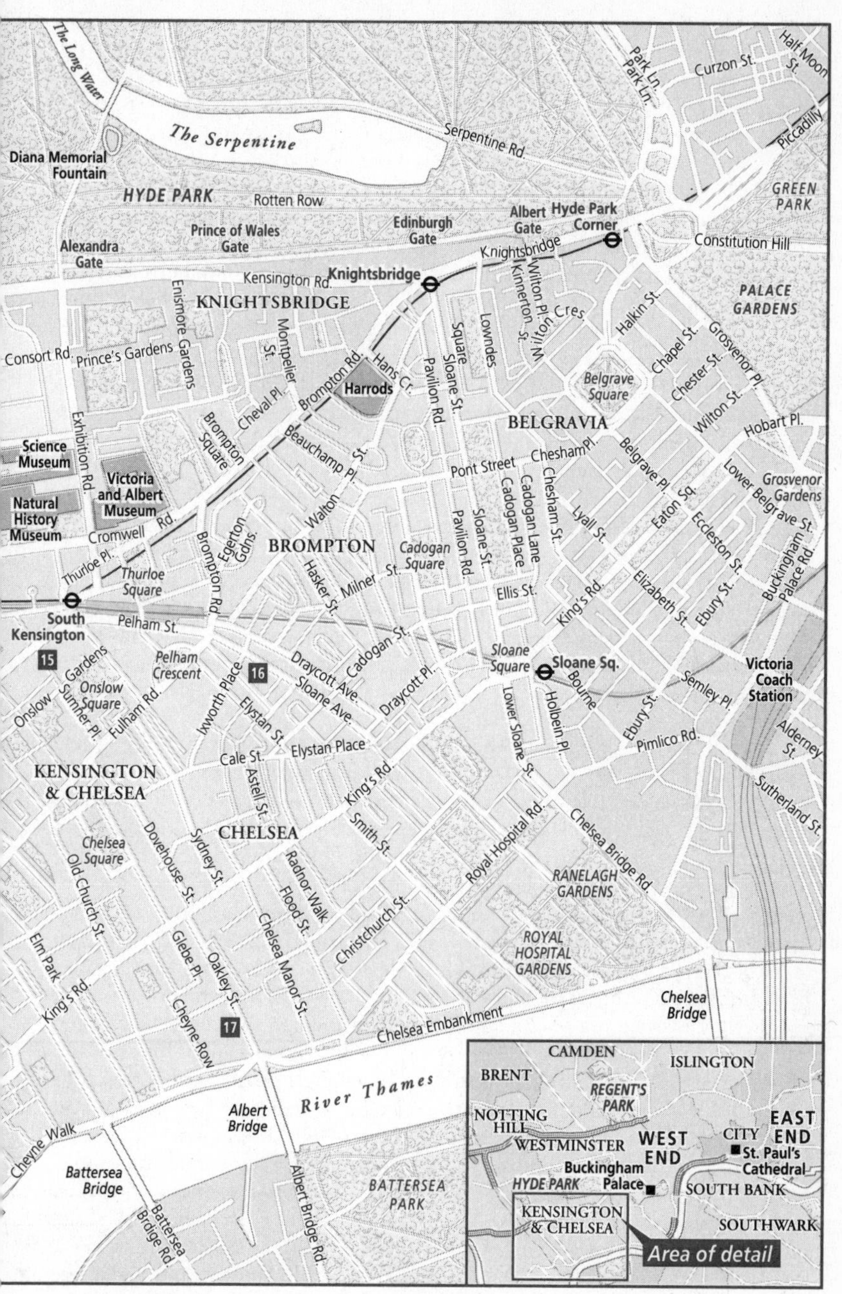

The Long Water
The Serpentine
Serpentine Rd.
Diana Memorial Fountain
HYDE PARK
Rotten Row
Prince of Wales Gate
Edinburgh Gate
Albert Gate
Hyde Park Corner
Alexandra Gate
Kensington Rd.
Knightsbridge
KNIGHTSBRIDGE
Park Ln.
Curzon St.
Half Moon St.
Piccadilly
GREEN PARK
Constitution Hill
PALACE GARDENS
Consort Rd.
Prince's Gardens
Ennismore Gardens
Montpelier St.
Brompton Rd.
Hans Cr.
Harrods
Pavilion Rd.
Sloane St.
Square
Lowndes
Kinnerton St.
Wilton Pl.
Wilton Cres.
Halkin St.
Chapel St.
Chester St.
Grosvenor Pl.
Belgrave Square
Wilton St.
BELGRAVIA
Hobart Pl.
Exhibition Rd.
Science Museum
Natural History Museum
Victoria and Albert Museum
Cheval Pl.
Brompton Square
Beauchamp Pl.
Walton St.
Pont Street
Chesham Pl.
Cadogan Place
Cadogan Lane
Chesham St.
Belgrave Pl.
Lower Belgrave St.
Grosvenor Gardens
Cromwell Rd.
Egerton Gdns.
BROMPTON
Cadogan Square
Lyall St.
Eaton Sq.
Eccleston St.
Buckingham Palace Rd.
Thurloe Pl.
Thurloe Square
Brompton Rd.
Hasker St.
Milner St.
Ellis St.
King's Rd.
Elizabeth St.
Ebury St.
South Kensington
Pelham St.
15
Onslow Gardens
Onslow Square
Sumner Pl.
Pelham Crescent
Fulham Rd.
Ixworth Place
16
Elystan St.
Draycott Ave.
Sloane Ave.
Cadogan St.
Draycott Pl.
Sloane Square
Sloane Sq.
Bourne
Holbein Pl.
Lower Sloane St.
Semley Pl.
Victoria Coach Station
Ebury St.
Pimlico Rd.
Alderney St.
Cale St.
Elystan Place
KENSINGTON & CHELSEA
Astell St.
King's Rd.
Sutherland St.
CHELSEA
Smith St.
Royal Hospital Rd.
Chelsea Bridge Rd.
Chelsea Square
Dovehouse St.
Sydney St.
Old Church St.
Radnor Walk
Flood St.
RANELAGH GARDENS
Chelsea Manor St.
Christchurch St.
Elm Park
Glebe Pl.
Oakley St.
ROYAL HOSPITAL GARDENS
King's Rd.
Cheyne Row
17
Chelsea Embankment
Chelsea Bridge
River Thames
Albert Bridge
Cheyne Walk
Battersea Bridge
Battersea Bridge Rd.
Albert Bridge Rd.
BATTERSEA PARK
CAMDEN
BRENT
ISLINGTON
REGENT'S PARK
NOTTING HILL
WESTMINSTER
WEST END
CITY
EAST END
St. Paul's Cathedral
Buckingham Palace
HYDE PARK
SOUTH BANK
KENSINGTON & CHELSEA
SOUTHWARK
Area of detail

that cost less when you book early and more if you reserve at the last minute. So it goes here, where reservations are accepted only over the Web, but typically cost £25 for double rooms if you book 5 to 6 months ahead, and £50 to £70 if you procrastinate. (You've got to act months in advance to beat other tourists to the lowest prices.) Stelios' other revelation: prefabricated room units in day-glow orange and white that differ only in how little floor space you're given. Beds, which are double-size with white duvets, are near the ground on pedestals and rarely have an inch of space between mattress and wall. In a "standard room," (the hotel's terminology, not mine), you may find a long ledge on which to pop a travel alarm clock, but bathrooms aren't more than plastic cubicles combining a shower, toilet, and sink in one water-splashed closet. "Small" rooms won't have much space to even turn around. The cheapest rooms don't even have windows, and forget about hair dryers, baby cots, safes, phones, and laundry. Want to watch TV? You'll pay £5 for 24 hours (for ten channels), but you'll get a remote control you can take home. Now you know what easyHotel is good for: Clean, no-nonsense crash pads for someone who wants to pay hostel prices without putting up with hostel mayhem. You can get a more human double elsewhere for less than easyHotel's full price, but its early-bird deals are terrific. Shockingly, it's also one of the few truly disability-friendly budget hotels in town; there are a few "special needs" rooms, there's a lift to get over the stoop, and Earl's Court station, its main Tube stop, is also accessible. There's a 10-night maximum, and no smoking is permitted. Very nearby, the 70-room **easyHotel Earl's Court** (44-48 West Cromwell Rd., SW5; www.easyhotel.com; MC, V; Tube: Earl's Court) was recently installed on a busy thoroughfare. Given a choice, I'd pick the easyHotel South Ken, which is on a more pleasant side street.

£ You can say what you want about **The Mowbray Court Hotel** ★ (kids) (28-32 Penywern Rd., SW5; ☎ 020/7373-8285; www.mowbraycourthotel.co.uk; AE, MC, V; Tube: Earl's Court). It's world-weary. It's not even slightly trendy. It needs not just a face-lift but a whole-body lift. But it's also remarkably inexpensive and delightfully clean, and parents won't find many places cheaper than can fit all their brood. And the Dooley family, who runs this basic "tourist class economy" choice, puts effort into making sure its guests are comfortable even though they don't pay a lot. The Dooleys' patriarch emigrated from Ireland in 1959 with £50 in his pocket, and the hotel is named for the road he raised his family on. His sons Peter and Tony now direct the show, folding fresh towels in a playful origami style, and striving to keep the phone rates lower than calling card–company charges. Singles are £55, doubles £69, triples £84, and family rooms £96 for four to £132 for six—those are with facilities, but if you're willing to share, and if you don't need a TV, you'll dock about £9 off the price for a "standard" room. There's an honest-to-goodness lobby bar for draught beer (which almost no rock-bottom hotel has), and Earl's Court Tube station, which links directly to Heathrow, is literally behind the hotel. The Mowbray, which consists of four former town houses with bright Southern exposures on the back, is one of those struggling places doing what it can to update without much cash. I dread the inevitable day when, thanks to skyrocketing rents, we no longer have no-frills, family-run bargains like this to rely upon.

£ An incredible find. The rates at the **Oakley Hotel** ★★ (73 Oakley St., SW3; ☎ 020/7352-5599; www.oakleyhotel.com; AE, MC, V; Tube: Sloane Square or South Kensington), like the homey vibe, channel a bygone era: £39 for singles and £55 for doubles or twins without bathrooms, £75 with. But there's a trade-off: It's a 20-minute walk to the Tube or an eight-minute bus ride from Victoria Station. Choose among twelve rooms, six of which have their own facilities (shower only), and six of which share bathrooms (although there are so many WCs that you won't have to wait even if everyone else has just consumed a pork vindaloo). No rooms have phones. The compact 1850s house, one of the oldest on a block that includes the former home of the poet Carlyle (now a museum), has seen grander days, but since the mid-'80s owner Brian Millen has kept the facilities in fine condition and built entire new areas with his own two hands. When I showed up for an unannounced inspection, he was covered with wood dust and paint from a guest-room renovation, which is always a good sign. He's got some gorgeous furniture, much of it older than the house itself, and he's not stingy about sharing the treasures in the guests' rooms. Rooms on the front face noisy Oakley Road and have only single-glazed windows. The double with a four-poster bed is £85, and it was a favorite of the late, dissolute football superstar George Best, who regularly stayed here, presumably on his London binges. Guests can use the kitchen like it's their own, and about 90m (295 ft.) outside the front door, you'll find the tranquillity of the Thames River and, across the cast-iron Albert Bridge, soothing Battersea Park.

£–££ An odd duck, **Rushmore Hotel** (11 Trebovir Rd., SW5; ☎ 020/7370-3839; www.rushmore-hotel.co.uk; AE, MC, V; Tube: Earl's Court) is a standard town house inn that was inflicted with an ill-advised makeover in classical themes. Corridors are adorned with murals of Mediterranean and Roman iconography (fig trees, anyone?), making the place feel like the butt of a design joke that the staff, friendly as they are, don't seem to be in on. But that kitschy art doesn't make staying here awkward because its 22 rooms meet expectations, done in a fading Regency style, and have their own shower and bath equipped with plugs for U.S. razors. The bright dining room, in a garden conservatory, boasts a much savvier tone involving blue glass, black metals, and cacti as tall as basketball players; sadly, only continental breakfast is served. All in all, it's reasonably priced and good enough on all counts, and just quirky enough to be someone's favorite. The prices run from singles £69 to £79, doubles £89 to £99, and a few triples and quads for £115 to £139, with the usual concessions for low season and long stays. The family room is on the fourth floor, and there's no lift.

££ Hidden in a residential back street off noisy Cromwell Road, **Premier Inn London Kensington** (11 Knaresborough Place, SW5; ☎ 087/0238-3304; Tube: Earl's Court) occupies an ugly '70s box distinguished by poo-brown panels and ample windows. It links via pedestrian bridge to a building shared with a Marriott charging £100 more. Neither annex is larger or quieter, but rooms on the southern sides get more sun (some also overlook Tube trains hurtling to and from Earl's Court station—they're not jarringly noisy). Prices are £96 on weekdays and £84 on weekends, with prices around £87 in slower times. Londontown.com sometimes discounts those an additional £12. For a description of Premier Inn amenities, see p. 50.

££ As soon as you step into **Twenty Nevern Square** ★★★ (20 Nevern Square, SW5; ☎ 020/7565-9555; www.twentynevernsquare.co.uk; AE, MC, V; Tube: Earl's Court), on the south side of the square of the same name, you can tell it's not your run-of-the-mill economy hotel. It may reside in an old English town house, but its heart is in colonial Malaysia. Bedrooms are warmly done in carved wood headboards, wood wardrobes, and richly colored window treatments. Toiletries are concealed in mini chests in the marbled bathrooms, each room has a CD player, and TVs are wide-screen. Although all rooms feel cloistered and inviting, room 11, a double, may suit romance most, given that it's on its own private landing and has windows on two sides. At the continental breakfast, which is served beneath the cathedral-like rafters of the ground-floor conservatory (also a bar), you can choose from types of honey from around the world. Considering all the amorous set dressing, the prices are not too much higher than simpler properties: singles are £89; doubles £99; and the Pasha Suite, with a king-size four-poster bed and a terrace overlooking the square, is £170. Those rates are flexible; check the website's "Offers" section for discounts of £10 to £20. Rooms have showers, bathtubs, or both, and if you're a light sleeper, request not to be placed in a basement room, which are privy to footsteps from the lobby's wood flooring. The owners, originally South African, also operate the Mayflower around the corner. There's a lift, and the front desk has a key to the private gardens in the square.

££ For those who just want a cheap, fairly large hotel, there's **The Park International Hotel** (117-125 Cromwell Rd., SW7; ☎ 020/7370-5711; www.parkinternationalhotel.com; AE, MC, V; Tube: Gloucester Road), which is unremarkable in most ways, but inoffensive in as many more. It takes up five interconnected town houses, four stories high, just west of the big South Kensington museums. Its rooms, lobby, and even the TVs are noticeably larger than the area average, but the interior design smacks of *The Golden Girls.* The overworked staff, mostly Eastern European transplants, do what they can to be professional but are mostly too harried to be effective. Rooms are standard-issue and aging, if carefully serviced, and have air-conditioning, minifridges, and safes big enough for a laptop. Wi-Fi is strongest in one part of the hotel, so if you want it, ask, and the nonsmoking rooms are on the higher floors. Singles are £75, doubles £89, although in summer, prices can pop up to £140 and if you snare an "early booker" deal online, doubles can sink to £62. Because of its size (117 rooms), this hotel also crops up among air-hotel discounters. Continental breakfast is a ridiculous £8, but you can get it thrown in for free if you book directly, and besides, there's a Waitrose grocery store about 2 blocks away.

££–£££ Like its sister hotel, Twenty Nevern Square (see above), the 47-room **Mayflower Hotel** ★★★ (26-28 Trebovir Rd., SW5; ☎ 020/7370-0991; www.mayflower-group.co.uk; AE, MC, V; Tube: Earl's Court) was transformed a few years back by tasteful inflections to become an economy town house property (read: small rooms) with exceptional value. The little touches, like something out of *The Jungle Book,* impart dignity and exotica to a stay, from antique doors mounted on the walls as art, to dark rattan furniture, to a silvery fountain behind the front desk, to the open sensation of wood flooring throughout. Rooms come with TVs with 50 channels, CD players, marble desks, and a few complimentary magazines. There's also a lovely back garden. A quibble: Its bathrooms, though marbled and sleek, could use better ventilation. Singles cost £85 (but are often upgraded to double rooms), doubles run £99 (regular double beds) to £115 (king-size beds), triples are £109, and the family room is £160. I like room 18, a deluxe double (£135), with its little outdoor terrace over the quiet street; its peaked, carved headboard; and its farmhouse-style rafters overhead. There's a lift, albeit one the size of a shower stall, and a bar.

££-££££ A relative newcomer to the budget-boutique scene, **Base2Stay Kensington** ★★★ (25 Courtfield Gardens, SW5; ☎ 020/7244-2255; www.base2stay.com; AE, MC, V; Tube: Earl's Court) may look from the outside like another stucco town house, but inside, it's a thoughtfully and intelligently designed, Zen-like oasis (charcoals, woods, gentle stripes) that, like the Hoxton Hotel (p. 73), aims to deliver low prices without sacrificing a sophisticated atmosphere. The founder calls the concept "luxury limited service." Customers have been wild about the place, and I love it, too. There's a good range of room types, from singles (£93) to bunk-bed doubles good for kids or scrimping friends (£97, and they connect to doubles if you want) and doubles from £107, which are all well appointed with fancy "aromatherapy" toiletries: flatscreen TVs; free Internet; a free music library; air-conditioning; some oversized showers; safes; lots of outlets; plenty of storage space; and, most helpfully, mini-kitchens with fridges, microwaves, and a kettle, so you can prepare simple meals. Rates are a little high for the westerly Earl's Court area, especially since you'll have to rely on the Tube for most of your sightseeing, but there's little doubt that you're getting elevated design for your extra cash, and that kitchen makes a big difference—in fact, the owners publicize Base2Stay as an "apartment hotel" because of them. The neighborhood has plenty of restaurant and grocery options, and the genuinely interested staff is truly helpful.

££–££££ Another admirable boutique hotel at the top end of our range is stylish **Number Sixteen** ★★★ (16 Sumner Place, SW7; ☎ 020/7581-4045; www.numbersixteenhotel.co.uk; AE, MC, V; Tube: South Kensington), belonging to the Firmdale Hotels group, whose husband/wife designer/owners, Tim and Kit Kemp, are fixtures on the city scene. I count it as one of the loveliest B&B experiences in the city that comes closest to supplying a movie star's pampering at less-than-Hollywood prices: singles are £120, doubles £165 to £200, with slight discounts on weekends. The lowest prices are available in winter and from late July to early September (when business travel drops off). For those prices, expect all the trappings of a luxury hotel, only in a series of very well refurbished town houses in an updated English country style. Every available space is adorned with displays of forward-thinking British art from the owners' considerable collection, and all rooms, which are individually designed and truly beautiful, come with huge, come-hither beds (laid with more pillows, skirting, and spreads than most people have at home), safes, voicemail, and ample polished-stone bathrooms (with bathtub and shower). On the ground floor, a library and a drawing room with an honor bar are at your disposal. In the morning, sunlight pours across the verdant back garden (accented by a soothing ornamental pond) into the conservatory where continental breakfast is served. There's a lift, a doorman, a professional staff, and the location off restaurant-rich Old Brompton Road, near the banner museums, ranks high for quiet.

Avoid the Tangled Web

You may be used to booking through sites such as Expedia.com or Travelocity.com for the best prices, but when it comes to London, think again. Many London hotels, particularly the most affordable ones, are privately owned, and many of them are represented on the Web by third-party travel agents and booking engines that pad the price with a few extra bucks, which they'll skim off for themselves as commission. So if you call the hotel directly for your bookings, you'll not only get the lowest price, but you'll also have the power of negotiation.

Another danger of making an online reservation: There are heaps of lousy budget hotels in London, particularly around Bayswater and King's Cross, that post misleading images on the Web, and it's easy to end up in a seedy one if you don't first take some independent advice.

Of course, if you want to stay in a corporate hotel, all bets are off. Online searching works for those. These sites will help:

Mobissimo.com, Sidestep.com, and **Kayak.com** are three "aggregator" sites that scan dozens of sites for deals and pull them all together.

Visit London, the city's official tourism office, also has an area on its website (www.visitlondon.com) for discounted hotel bookings, although it's maintained by an outside travel agent. The **British Hotel Reservation Centre** (www.bhrc.co.uk) also sports some discounts, as does **LondonTown.com,** where I've seen £85 rooms (mostly from chain hotels) marked down to £59.

Lastminute.co.uk is one of the most popular booking sights in the U.K., so you may find bargains there that you won't find on the American sites. Other popular offshore hotel sites include **Booking.com, Venere.com, Eurocheapo.com, Cheaphotel.eu,** and **HotelsCombined.com.**

And **Priceline.co.uk** works just like its American counterpart; most of its hotels are corporate-owned. As with all bid-for-travel sites, you could end up with a deal, but remember that when you stay at hotels with more stars, there are more extra charges to contend with during your stay.

MARYLEBONE

For visitors who want a balance of central location and residential vibe, Marylebone's the place. A 10-minute walk takes you to the "smart" end of Oxford Street and Mayfair to the south, the wide-open fields of Regent's Park to the north, and the shops and cafes of Soho to the southeast. Add to that one of the most attractive shopping thoroughfares in the city (Marylebone High St.) and a cluster of affordable restaurants (on James St.), and you've got the makings for an ideal tourist stomping ground. Why bother with Earl's Court?

Bayswater, Paddington & Marylebone Accommodations

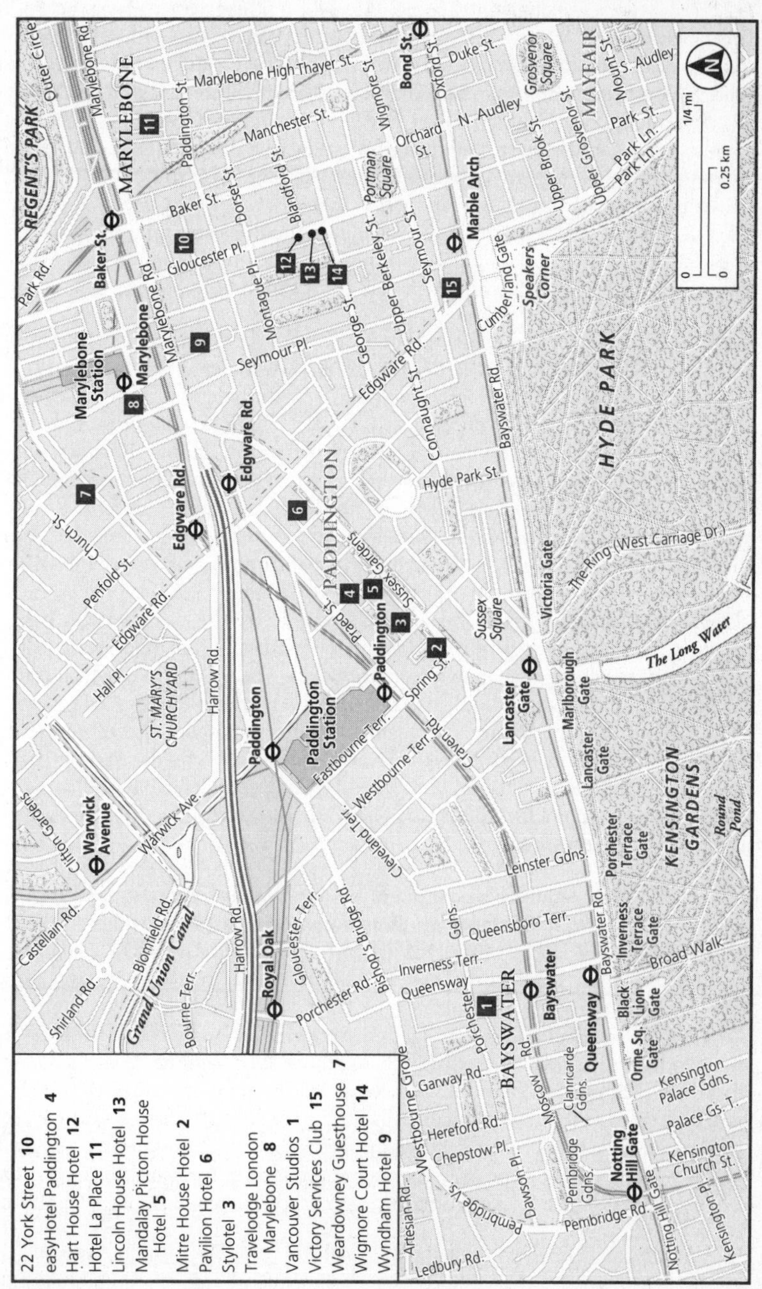

£ What can I say about the **Wyndham Hotel** ★ (30 Wyndham St., W1; ☎ 020/7723-7204; www.wyndhamhotel.co.uk; AE, MC, V; Tube: Marylebone or Baker Street) except that it's wee and plain and sweet? Well, it's an old-fashioned inn (recently redecorated) in an old-fashioned neighborhood, and it's one of the most solid values that London has. All rooms have shared bathrooms, which is why it's fairly cheap: £59 for singles, £85 for doubles or twins, £95 for triples. You won't get much space to wiggle around the bed in a double room. That said, I am utterly charmed by the Wyndham. The staff is young and attentive (how could they not be with just 10 rooms?), the cleanliness is exemplary, Wi-Fi is free, and it's on a quiet residential street. I also love the neighborhood: It's five minutes' walk west of Baker Street, with its shopping, 10 minutes' walk from Edgware Road's Middle Eastern restaurants, and 10 minutes' walk from Paddington Station.

£–££ Because it's been in the same family for years, the **Wigmore Court Hotel** (kids) (23 Gloucester Place, W1; ☎ 020/7935-0928; www.wigmore-hotel.co.uk; MC, V; Tube: Marble Arch) hasn't been renovated much. As you might imagine, that's both a curse and a blessing. The decor doesn't dazzle. Think powder-blue rubberized wallpaper, mirrors bolted to the wall beneath yellowing fluorescent tubes, and a fair share of veneered wood and random cigarette burns. But along with the telltale signs of downmarket digs, plenty of vestiges of the house's glorious Regency past remain, including generally commodious rooms and bathrooms that make this inn, which has no lift, a cut above its price competition. Over the double bed of room 1, a triple on the (noisy) front road, hangs a gold-colored crest of a classical maiden. The spacious room 2, a double on the (quiet) back, has an expansive curving back wall overlooking the garden; it's popular with elderly guests because no stairs separate it from the street. The fourth floor, which is normally a little shorter in buildings of this era, has been modified to boast higher ceilings. The staff is attentive and adaptable—they even allow guests to use the kitchen. Factoring in its convenient location, this place could certainly charge more for its 16 en suite rooms than £65 for singles, £92 for doubles or twins, £135 for triples, and £145 for quads. There are just two rooms that share a bath: a single (£52) and a double (£55).

££ A budget guesthouse where old-fashioned British hospitality and modern hip fashion intersect, **Weardowney Guesthouse** ★★★ (9 Ashbridge St., NW8; ☎ 020/7725-9694; MC, V; Tube: Marylebone) charms guests with its quaint, stylish underpinnings. Literally: Its owners, former models, run a sweet fashionista's knitwear boutique on the ground floor, which was once a pub. The rooms (£84), in a delightfully ancient building, are light on the amenities—only two of the seven, all doubles, have their own bathrooms (making those £96)—but heavy on homespun charm, as each one has been individually designed. Some drip with fabric, others have beds piled with pillows, but all evoke old-school British coziness without feeling dead, and the room count is so low that breakfasts can be customized. The owners have published books on knitwear and offer knitting classes in their shop. The roof terrace is open for relaxing, and there's a kitchen for cooking your own meals.

££ As affordable inns go, **Lincoln House Hotel** ★★ (kids) (33 Gloucester Place, W1; ☎ 020/7486-7630; www.lincoln-house-hotel.co.uk; AE, MC, V; Tube: Marble Arch) is in extraordinarily good condition—or, as Londoners might say, "in good nick." Each of the 24 rooms has a private bathroom, so that's easy, but the rates are byzantine, subcategorized by bed size. For example, a single "budget" is £69 because it has a twin bed, but there's a "single plus" with a 4-foot-wide bed that goes for £79. Doubles are "budget" (meaning they have a double mattress that won't suit basketball players) for £85, or "standard" (meaning they have a queen-size mattress) for £95. Two twin beds are £115, triples are £125, and family rooms for four are £135. Forget all those prices now because the owners regularly lop off 25% if it's not busy or if you book months in advance. Half the fun of Lincoln House, which has been in the same family for more than 30 years, is the nautical theme, which recurs in unexpected ways (portholes as mirrors, antique barometers as art). Handmade paneling in the hallways adds warmth, and there's 24-hour security. Larger rooms are equipped with wardrobes and minifridges, and Wi-Fi is free. Five types of breakfasts are served: continental, full English, vegetarian, vegan, and—refreshingly—Mediterranean. The one bummer is that the bathrooms are prefabricated fiberglass units, but if you've ever been on a cruise ship, you'll cope.

££ For the corporate-hotel route, the newly opened **Travelodge London Marylebone** (kids) (Harewood Row, NW1; ☎ 087/1984-6311; AE, MC, V; Tube: Marylebone) is so popular that the chain's ultra-low advance deals aren't available here. Rates are from £80 to £90. There are no sights of note within walking distance, but there's plenty of shopping and restaurants, and Regent's Park isn't far, either. For a description of Travelodge amenities, see p. 51.

££–£££ When you want to check into **22 York Street** (22-24 York St., W1; ☎ 020/7224-2990; www.22yorkstreet.co.uk; AE, MC, V; Tube: Baker Street), you'd better know where you're going, because it's not marked. The owners, Michael and Liz Callis, discourage riffraff by refraining from advertising. When I showed up unannounced and walked into the spacious kitchen, I thought at first that I'd knocked on the door of a private home of some wealthy doctor or lawyer. Inside, the couple is going for a farmhouse feel, with warm wooden floorboards, plenty of antiques and oriental rugs, and large bathrooms, almost all of which have tub/shower combinations. Guests get their own keys and are let loose to treat the premises as their own, which in the town house next door (part of the B&B), includes a drawing room with a grand piano and plenty of tea, coffee, and biscuits for munching. Adding to the home-away-from-home feel, guest rooms aren't numbered. Breakfasts, served in the kitchen at a communal country table where you meet your fellow guests, are continental but, as Michael succinctly puts it, "quite substantial" (including yogurts and true Cheddar cheese). Singles are £89 and doubles are £120, although doubles sometimes run £100. Although they're not explicitly banned, kids may not feel comfortable.

££–£££ Andrew Bowden has been part of **Hart House Hotel** ★★ (51 Gloucester Place, W1; ☎ 020/7935-2288; www.harthouse.co.uk; MC, V; Tube: Marble Arch or Baker Street) since he was 6 years old, when his family took it over, so he knows his nonsmoking, fully en suite hotel—and his city—very well. He runs his perfectly lovely inn extremely professionally, with a consistency that you might expect of a posher place. He outfits chambermaids in black frocks with white trim, and stocks rooms with top-quality furniture, built to last. He has even thought to put power outlets near the desks. Showers tend to the tiny side (what else is new?), but towels are plentiful and the rooms themselves are well cared for, embellished with little sculptures, mild putty-colored paint schemes, and reading lights for each bed, which are being fitted with thick duvets instead of blankets. Singles cost £95; try for room 11 at the front (it has a 4-ft.-wide bed). Doubles and twins are £135; triples are £160 (room 9, on the back, comes with an enormous bathroom located in its own nook); and quads are £185.

££–£££ Everything about **Hotel La Place** ★★★ (kids) **(17 Nottingham Place, W1; ☎ 020/7486-2323; www.hotellaplace.com; AE, MC, V; Tube: Baker Street)** is nicer than it has to be. It's run by Hal Jaffer and his French-born mom, who spent time in Tennessee and Texas learning hotel management. The Jaffers, who bought this town house building as a derelict dump in 1988 and shaped it into the property you see today, grasp the exacting demands of the American market. So although it's priced a bit higher than standard budget hotels (singles £99–£115, doubles £129–£149), you'll find a pile of extras that are more in keeping with chain hotels, starting with a proper full English breakfast, and including ice machines; mini-bars; double beds that are genuinely king size (rooms with smaller, 5-ft.-wide beds are £4 less); a cafe-cum-wine bar in the lobby offering 24-hour room service; free Wi-Fi; plenty of electrical outlets for charging stuff up; widescreen LCD TVs into which you can plug your laptop; and even a lift. Beds are given particular attention, with orthopedic mattresses and testers (fabric canopies) that match the pillows and spreads. Bathrooms are done up in granite and marble, nearly every window is dressed, and rooms classified as doubles or higher boast air-conditioning. Room 102 (£160) is good for families, since it's got two side-by-side double beds, Holiday Inn–style.

BAYSWATER & PADDINGTON

Although you may have heard that this neighborhood is prime ground, that news is old. As the budget hotel scene gravitates back to central London, you'll find fewer reasons to choose Bayswater aside from decent Underground connections. There are no tourist sights, save Hyde Park and Kensington Gardens, within reasonable walking distance. Strolling down street after street of regal, impossibly identical terraced houses does conjure up some serious *Mary Poppins* fantasies. Still, some visitors prefer to stay near Paddington merely out of a sense of tradition, perhaps, or merely because the Heathrow Express train alights there. Choose your hotel carefully, though, because there's plenty of fading flophouse chaff among the cut-price wheat. Sussex Gardens has been known as a drag for prostitution, but police have aggressively pounced on the problem and the area is safe.

£ Before brothers Barry and Paul Charalambous got ahold of the family business, it was a forgettable inn, Ruddiman's. But now, those forward-looking chaps have given the old digs the *Star Trek* treatment, and by late 2005, **Stylotel** ★★ (kids) **(160-162 Sussex Gardens, W2; ☎ 020/7723-1026; www.stylotel.com/stylotel2.swf; AE, MC, V; Tube: Paddington or Lancaster Gate)** was one of the city's wildest budget properties. Rooms are standard London size, but they've been profoundly transformed with dimpled sheet-metal walls, blonde wood floors, pristine beds with duvets and royal blue padded-vinyl headboards, frosted lightboxes that double as side-tables, and ample slab mirrors to reflect back your hypermodernist room in all its angular, stainless-steel glory. The cellar buffet breakfast room, with its military rows of jagged high-backed chairs creating a virtual blade garden, is perhaps Paul's masterpiece. I'll bet the Germans love it. Single "stylorooms" are £60, doubles or twins are £85, triples ("trios") are £105, and quads (er, "quatros") are just £120; sometimes 3-day minimum stays are required. The lobby bar pours free coffee and hot chocolate, and breakfast is selected from a 30-item cooked menu. It's easy to be grateful to the Charalambous boys (who also give top advice on London nightlife) for bringing some swagger and couture to the low-end of the lodging market.

£–£££ The newest, and thus far lowest-priced, local link of its brand, **easyHotel Paddington** (10 Norfolk Place, W2; www.easyhotel.com; MC, V, Tube: Paddington or Edgware Road) opened in late 2008. It's pressed from the same prefab mold as its three sisters (rooms and advance-purchase discounts are described on p. 55/easyHotel South Kensington listing), and prices start at £25 to £35 a night in all types of rooms, both with windows and without. That's a good lowball price, but you might pay more than double that when things are busy, and in that case, a B&B will have more freebies for a similar outlay.

£–££ As the tides of tourism swirl out of Bayswater, the neighborhood has been left with scads of dried-up B&Bs that thoughtlessly slap pillows down for undiscriminating short-term workers and recent immigrants. Clean, well-run places are no longer the norm, and the survivors have been forced to keep prices ultra-low to compete, which explains the head-turning prices at **Mandalay Picton House Hotel** kids (122 Sussex Gardens, W2; ☎ 020/7723-5479; www.mandalayway.com; MC, V; Tube: Paddington). Its enthusiastic managers, the Ally family, also run the excellent Burmese restaurant Mandalay (p. 125) nearby. There's no use pretending that this two-star property is anything but a tidy, low-priced place to get a good night's sleep as you explore London, but this cheap bedder (stashed, like all of Sussex Gardens' establishments, in a cramped, old building) stands out for its attentive details that other budget properties often ignore; towels are changed daily and the breakfast includes cooked items, not just breads. Doubles with a tiny bathroom are £65, a delightful price for anywhere in London, but if you're willing to share a bathroom down the hall, you can save another £10. Family rooms are also cheap: £105 for four or five, with a bathroom. Rooms even come with TV and hair dryer.

£–££ Let's face it: In another decade, the interior of the family-friendly **Mitre House Hotel** (178-184 Sussex Gardens, W2; ☎ 020/7723-8040; www.mitrehousehotel.com; AE, MC, V; Tube: Paddington or Lancaster Gate) could be included among the V&A museum's design artifacts, it's so rooted in the early '80s. We're talking walls and carpets in bleary rose-and-rust tones, hallways lamely gussied up with outdated theatrical posters, mismatched furniture in pressed wood and wicker, and a slouching bar in the lobby. But it's spotless, the owners are old hands at the value-hotel game, and there's a lift (although, weirdly, it's upholstered). Of the 69 rooms, singles are generally the equivalent size of a double bed, and cost £70, doubles and twins are much more generous and cost £90, and triples (here

Should I Wait to Book till I Get There?

In many European cities, you can pretty much roll off the train, waltz into the tourist's office, and book a room on the spot. Can you do that in London? Sure, but I wouldn't. Summertime (June–Sept) is extremely busy, and you might get shut out or totally hosed. It's also not very kind to turn up at a family-run hotel at 11pm just to browse rooms. But if you insist on booking last-minute, these resources work:

Britain & London Visitor Centre (1 Lower Regent St., south of Piccadilly Circus, SW1; ☎ 020/7839-4891; www.visitlondon.com), the city's official tourism branch, has staff that will help you find a place according to your ideal price and your selected area, and they'll do it for free. You can also search online at its website. It's open Mondays 9:30am to 6:30pm, Tuesday to Friday 9am to 6:30pm, and Saturdays and Sundays 10am to 4pm. In summer months, Saturday hours are 9am to 5pm.

At Heathrow and Gatwick, stop by the **British Hotel Reservation Centre** (Heathrow: ☎ 020/7592-3055; Gatwick: ☎ 01293/50-24-33; www.bhrc.co.uk), which also books for free online. Lines are open Monday through Friday 7am to 7pm and weekends 9am to 6pm.

Two websites proficient at last-minute bookings are Lastminute.co.uk and Laterooms.com; both light on the very cheapest options. It's better not to go online at the extreme last minute, though, lest your reservation fail to transmit to the front desk in time.

called "trebles") are £100. You can combine rooms, such as 101 and 102, to form a "family suite" with a bathroom, for £130. Corner rooms such as 303 (a twin) have bigger bathrooms, lots of light, and views up and down Sussex Gardens. If you need a bathtub, request one, because not all rooms have them. A few "standard" rooms share bathrooms, and those are £70. All in all, it's a decent value, but not someplace you'll want to linger.

£–££ Like Stylotel, the 29-room **Pavilion Hotel** ★ (34-36 Sussex Gardens, W2; ☎ 020/7262-0905; www.pavilionhoteluk.com; AE, MC, V; Tube: Edgware Road) distinguishes itself from the grubby Sussex Gardens rabble through elaborately themed rooms, dreamed up by the owners, who've had the place since 1989. Casablanca Nights, one of the most popular and largest doubles, faces busy Sussex Gardens but compensates with a preposterous design of rich cobalt drapes, leopard-print fabric, and ostensibly Moroccan furniture. Other popular gag rooms, embellished with amusingly mismatched accoutrements are: War and Peace (military), Quiet Please (a library), and Monochrome Marilyn (a single reimagined with Warhol's Ms. Monroe). Of the doubles, Enter the Dragon (Asian themed) is a bit larger than its brothers, but disco-era Three's Company and Honky Tonk

Afro are more requested. The decor, which can get racy, enlivens an otherwise slightly tired B&B. Singles are £60, doubles £100, triples £120, and quads £130. Is all this silliness worth the extra £20 a couple will pay compared to others on the same street? That depends on your sense of fun.

SOUTHWARK & WATERLOO

You won't find many hotels in this area, despite the sensational location. Since medieval times until about 15 years ago, "respectable" Londoners wanted nothing to do with this once-industrial area, which explains the proliferation of anonymous apartment blocks and the overabundance of railway viaducts. The same Londoners are wishing they'd bought property now. It's actually a terrific place to dwell in good weather, when the area comes alive with walkers, booksellers, pubgoers, and playgoers reveling in the nearby re-creation of Shakespeare's *Globe* theater.

££ If I had to pick one property from one chain to recommend, it would be the **Premier Inn London Southwark** ★★★ (Anchor Bar, 34 Park St., SE1; ☎ 087/0990-6402; Tube: London Bridge). The neighborhood is atmospheric, cobbled, and historic (the walking tour on p. 242 passes right by it), and although the hotel structure is new, it blends seamlessly with the adjoining historic Anchor pub, where guests take breakfast overlooking the Thames. Rooms are £88 in low season and £110 in high season, but book far in advance, because the secret's out. **Premier Inn London County Hall** ★ (County Hall, Belvedere Rd., SE1; ☎ 087/0238-3300; Tube: Waterloo) is also in the vicinity and commands a stellar location yards from the London Eye and shares a palatial building on the Thames with a high-end hotel. Although few of the sizable rooms offer the slightest glimpse of the river (in fact, most overlook a large air shaft), you'll be in the thick of many top sights. Prices are the highest for the chain: £117 weekdays, £104 Fridays and Saturdays, and an excessive £134 in busy seasons. A less convenient, third property below the river, **Premier Inn London Tower Bridge** (159 Tower Bridge Rd., SE1; ☎ 087/0238-3303; Tube: London Bridge) is a 10-minute walk from the Tower Bridge or the Tube and is priced between £88 and £104. Meanwhile, **Travelodge London Southwark** ★ (202-206 Union St., SE1; ☎ 087/1984-6352; Tube: Southwark), opened in 2008, is a 5-minute walk south of river near an atmospheric Victorian railway viaduct (windows are soundproofed). Its 202 rooms cost £49 if you book way early, but usually hit you for around £100, normal for this area. If you can't get into the nearby Premier Inn, this one gets you very close to Tate Modern and the Globe. For a description of Premier Inn and Travelodge amenities, see p. 51.

££–£££ A modern addition to one of London's oldest neighborhoods, the **Southwark Rose Hotel** ★★★ (43-47 Southwark Bridge Rd., SE1; ☎ 020/7015-1480; www.southwarkrosehotel.co.uk; AE, DISC, MC, V; Tube: London Bridge or Southwark) gets a lot right for a design hotel. First, it doesn't charge snob rates. You'll be told that doubles and twins cost £180 (that's too much even considering the location), but online, you'll regularly find prices as low as £90 for Friday, Saturday, and Sunday, when the business folk go home. Its six-story, 84-room, purpose-built home is entered via a garagelike lobby hung with cauldronlike lamps that doubles as a progressive art gallery. Upstairs, rooms are a bit smaller

Blue Light Specials at Blue-Blood Hotels

When the briefcase brigade retreats home for the weekend (Fri–Sun nights), rates at expensive hotels plummet. Sure, the downside of changing hotels for the weekend is that it undercuts your ability to negotiate lower prices for longer stays during the rest of the week. And even with the discounts, you'll rarely pay less than you can at a two-star B&B. But the upside is that you can experience another part of town and kick back in a luxury property for a democratic rate. Almost every corporate hotel, especially in The City or Docklands, will hack tariffs over the weekend, so play around on their websites to uncover prizes like these:

Apex City of London Hotel ★★★ (1 Seething Lane, EC3; ☎ 013/1666-5124; www.apexhotels.co.uk; AE, MC, V; Tube: Tower Hill): During the weekend, when The City is deader than Old Marley (good luck even finding a sandwich), the Apex becomes a peaceful urban retreat. It's handsomely designed by chic Scots, with huge rooms done in hardwood and walnut, and bathrooms larger than many B&Bs' guest rooms, including walk-in showers. It's literally steps from the Tower of London. Weekday rate: £165 (City King room). Weekend rate: £80 to £122.

Swissôtel the Howard ★ (Temple Place, WC2, ☎ 020/7836-3555; www.swissotel.com; AE, MC, V; Tube: Temple): Strangely, London has precious few hotels situated on the Thames. But here, above Temple Tube stop, many rooms boast the most flabbergasting views of the river imaginable—from St. Paul's dome all the way to Parliament and the London Eye. You won't want to close your eyes, and to help you, all rooms have their own Lavazza espresso machine for free unlimited use. Weekday rate: £310. Weekend rate: £145 (rates fluctuate, so you may have to check its website a few times to find this level).

Andaz ★★ (40 Liverpool St., EC2; ☎ 020/7961-1234, or ☎ 888/725-3755 in the U.S.; http://london.liverpoolstreet.andaz.com; AE, MC, V; Tube: Liverpool Street) This Hyatt spin-off is a modern art-crammed, sleek business hotel with a difference: You won't be bled by extra charges. Local

than the American hotel norm (tip: rooms ending with 06 are a touch larger), but are also well conceived for the price, with large, cushy white beds piled with pillows; backlit chair rails and headboards; motorized blackout curtains; and, behind a curving wall, a smartly designed bathroom (showers only) that maximizes minimal space with clever triangular sink spaces and plenty of mirroring. Safety is well observed here, since key cards are required to use the elevators and room doors are extra-sturdy and have peepholes. The top floor is devoted to a spacious bar/restaurant with a sunny western exposure.

phone calls, laundry, in-room movies, breakfast, Wi-Fi, a minibar of juices and water—it's all included in the price. The building, an 1884 railway terminal hotel, is also cool. Weekday rate: £230. Weekend rate: £110.

And although I don't recommend blowing a pile of cash on a five-star hotel, there's no question that some people—honeymooners, for example, or history buffs—may want to spend at least a single night of fantasy fulfillment at a legendary property. For them, there's one I'd pick over the pompous Ritz, stuffy Claridges, or the nouveau riche Dorchester:

Brown's Hotel ★★★ (30 Albemarle St., W1; ☎ 020/7493-6020; www.brownshotel.com; AE, MC, V; Tube: Green Park) epitomizes the classic Mayfair hotel (est. 1837), albeit with cool, updated interiors that won't make commoners feel out-of-place. The first-ever phone call was placed from its ground floor, and Mark Twain scandalized the press by appearing on its stoop in his bathrobe. While staying here, Rudyard Kipling finished *The Jungle Book* and Stephen King started *Misery*. Weekday rate: A crazy £415. Weekend rate: £275 (still crazy, but closer to your reach). Of course, you can simply avail yourself of the atmosphere at its afternoon tea, probably London's finest, for under £40.

By the same token, a few upscale hotels have been known to fill rooms by offering the same rate in American dollars that's normally offered in pounds. So a £199 room becomes $199. That's still more than you have to pay to stay in London, but if getting a deal on a posh place interests you, poke around these hotels and see if they're offering something: **Hazlitt's** (☎ 020/7434-1771; www.hazlittshotel.com; Tube: Tottenham Court Road); **The Rookery** (☎ 020/7336-0931; www.rookeryhotel.com; Tube: Farringdon); **The Gore** (☎ 020/7584-6601; www.gorehotel.com; Tube: South Kensington); **The Mandeville** (☎ 020/7935-5599; www.mandeville.co.uk; Tube: Bond Street); **The Athenaeum** (☎ 800/335-3300; www.athenaeumhotel.com; Tube: Hyde Park Corner).

££–£££ A pub hotel that bills itself more as a borderline mainstream hotel, **Mad Hatter Hotel** ★★ (3-7 Stamford St., SE1; ☎ 020/7401-9222; www.fullershotels.co.uk; AE, MC, V; Tube: Southwark or Blackfriars) could easily seduce guests into lingering in its gorgeous Victorian-styled bar, part of the sizable Fuller's chain. But upstairs, soundproofed from the typically English frolic but close enough for a quick pint, the sizable rooms feel like they were lifted from a business hotel. Think decent-size bathrooms with tub/showers, rose-colored bedspreads matching painted accent walls, a lift, and ice machines—rare as diamonds in the U.K. The rack rate for its 30 rooms with breakfast is £145 for singles or doubles, which I think is a bit high, but outside of busy summertime, you're more likely to be quoted £10 less than that online, and even less on the weekends (£95 isn't unusual, with discounts granted for stays of three nights or longer). Just five minutes from the Tate Modern or the National Theatre on the Thames, the ideal location may be its best feature. Some rooms can be conjoined for families, or extra beds can be added for £12.

THE CITY

Because the so-called "square mile" essentially shuts down after work, tourists will find that amusements and family-run hotels are both in short supply. Although rooms in The City are often dramatically cheaper during the weekend and you'll be in the oldest part of London, come Saturday, you'll have to forage for a coffee like a Sioux hunting for buffalo. The exceptions are Clerkenwell (pronounced "CLARK-en-well"), a seat of hip hotels and nightclubs, and the artsy hoods of Spitalfields and Whitechapel east of Liverpool Street station.

£–££ Ibis London City (5 Commercial St., E1; ☎ 020/7422-8400; Tube: Aldgate East or Aldgate) is on an off-putting white block, but it's close to the bohemian galleries, ethnic takeaways, and clubs of Whitechapel and Spitalfields, and the Tower of London isn't far off. The hotel has 348 rooms, which means there's usually availability—or a line for the elevators. Rooms go to £105 for weekdays, but weekends and low periods see discounts of about £25. For a description of Ibis amenities, see p. 51.

££ Hemmed in by modern office buildings near Liverpool Street station, the six-story **Travelodge London Liverpool Street** ★ (1 Harrow Place, E1; ☎ 08701/91-16-89; Tube: Liverpool Street) overlooks a sleepy pocket park, which means no traffic will keep you awake. The area is lifeless after work, although happening Spitalfields is just 5 minutes northeast. The rate is £85, plus £6.95 for a breakfast buffet. No one can get in without swiping a key card. Travelodge has also opened a few other very new properties in The City: **Travelodge London Aldgate East** (6-13 Chamber St., E1; ☎ 087/1984-6406; Tube: Tower Hill or Aldgate East), which requires crossing too many busy streets for my tastes, and **Travelodge London City Road** (7-12 City Rd., EC1; ☎ 087/1984-6333; Tube: Old Street), close to Shoreditch's nightlife and galleries but not much else. For a description of Travelodge amenities, see p. 51.

££–££££ The sort of place that has its own style magazine with articles extolling the merits of top-shelf tequila, the 97-room **Malmaison** ★★ (18-21 Charterhouse Square, EC1; ☎ 020/7012-3700; www.malmaison-london.com; AE, MC, V; Tube: Barbican) is the sole London branch of a burgeoning British design chain. Rooms are hyperbolic in their heavy-handed but frivolous design (slender art lamps, earth tones and metallics, and machine-like lever handles on everything from the sinks to the doors), but the beds don't suffer from the same preening. They're giant, just soft enough, and inviting, and the modernist bathrooms have both showers and tubs along with sinks like oversize noodle bowls. There's a buzzing brasserie and bar in the basement, but you'll find plenty of equally stylish

Watch the Clocks and Book the Hox

Opened in late 2006, **The Hoxton** ★★★ (81 Great Eastern St., EC2; ☎ 020/7550-1000; www.hoxtonhotels.com; AE, DC, MC, V; Tube: Old Street) quickly made a name for itself as a hot place to stay. Its stated goal was to give affordable hotels some modern style, and it delivers. You'd swear you were in a much more expensive place. Its 205 rooms brag exposed brick walls, rain showers, and industrial-chic furniture of metal and stained wood. Breakfast is delivered to you each morning, minibar prices are fair, and even a phone call to America is just 5p a minute. The public spaces, dominated by a huge carved fireplace and leather sofa, supply hangouts in their own right, as there's a glassy bistro, free computers to use, an on-site gallery, and works by brand-name artists like Christo and Jeanne-Claude. However, the Hoxton is famous for yet another perk: Its frequent deals. A few times a year, it sells five rooms each night for just £1. You have to get on its e-mail list for advance word or you'll be shut out within 20 minutes, but the savings are so extreme it's worth planning a London trip around a score like that. Otherwise, prices scale up steeply from £30 as bookings increase. For trips 6 months in the future, you stand a fair chance of reserving a place in this style haven for £59 to £99. That's as much as at a plainer B&B. Most times, though, you will be unlikely to pay less than £149 to £199, although weekends tend to be cheaper. All this in the revitalized post-industrial district of Shoreditch, somewhat stark but crawling with artists and nightlife, and within walking distance of the colorful East End and Spitalfields. No visitor on a budget, especially one who wants to sample the sophistication of modern London, should overlook this place.

nightlife right out the door around Smithfield Market. Doubles go from £185 on paper (don't fall for quotes that may be double that), but often cost £99 in reality, since the hotel routinely cuts deals, especially on weekends. Because it's not snooty, this full-service hotel has the right level of *Zoolander*-esque posturing. There's a gym, too, plus a lift.

£££–££££ For those who have to hang with the in-crowd, the current hot bedder is the 59-room **Zetter Hotel** ★ (86-88 Clerkenwell Rd., EC1; ☎ 020/7324-4444; www.thezetter.com; AE, MC, V; Tube: Farringdon), a former warehouse on a noisy street. Its restaurant attracts scenesters with its DJ nights, readings, and mixers. Its visual gag is described by some as "punk-chintz." If you don't think that's funny, this place, with its five-story atrium, isn't for you, because it translates into a quirky, sometimes overly angular symphony of sliding doors, wood shutters, Raindance shower heads, and butterfly stencils; you'll admire its chutzpah but may find it a bit prickly. On weekends, movies and Internet access are free, and

The City Accommodations

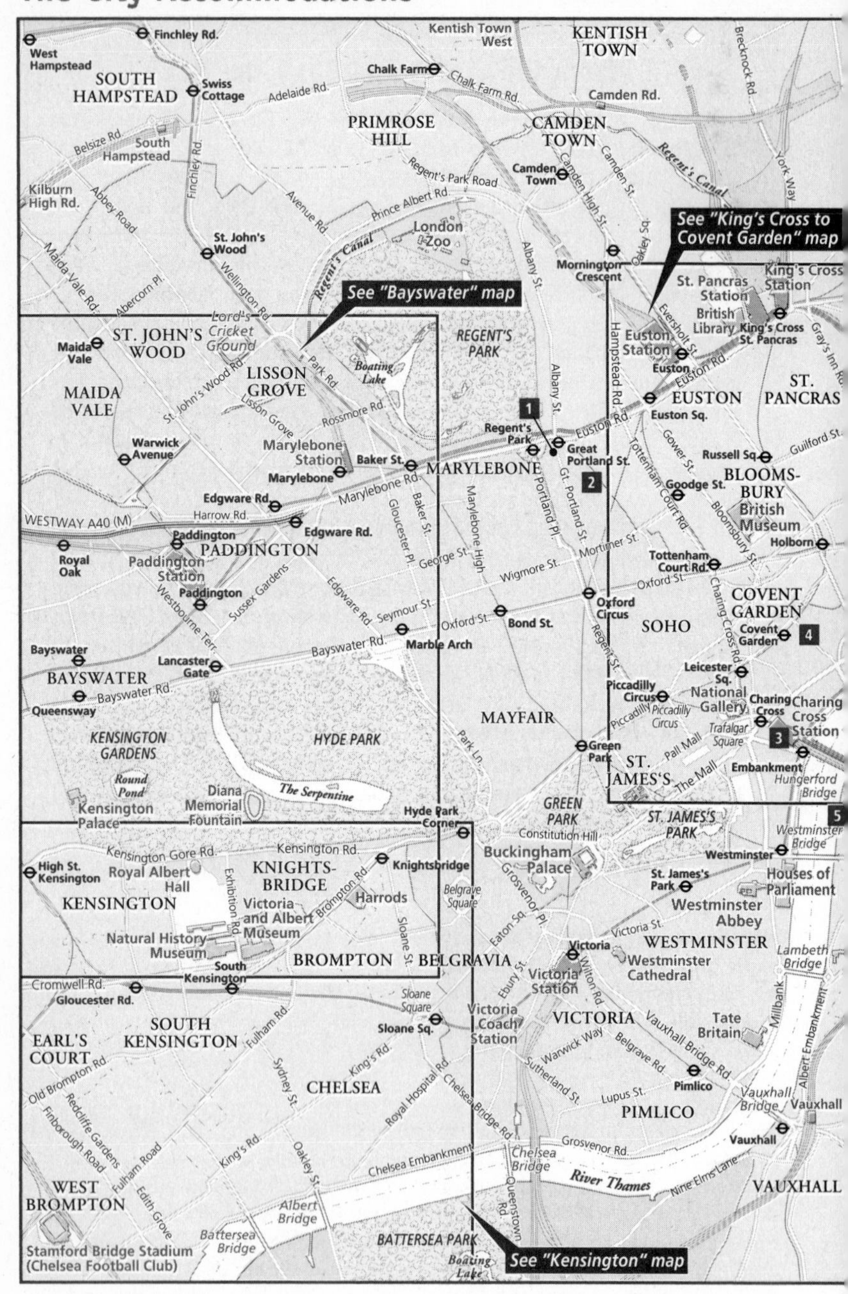

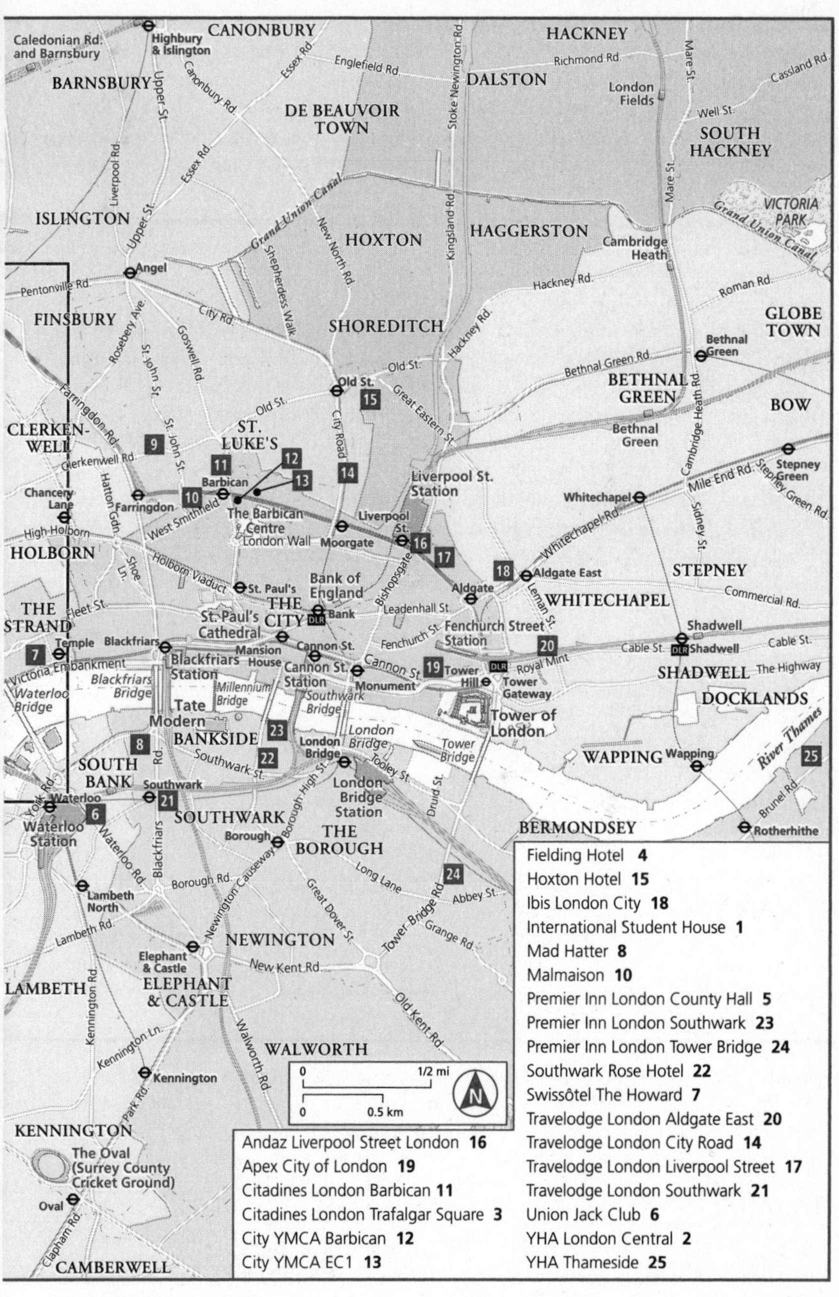
Fielding Hotel 4
Hoxton Hotel 15
Ibis London City 18
International Student House 1
Mad Hatter 8
Malmaison 10
Premier Inn London County Hall 5
Premier Inn London Southwark 23
Premier Inn London Tower Bridge 24
Southwark Rose Hotel 22
Swissôtel The Howard 7
Travelodge London Aldgate East 20
Travelodge London City Road 14
Travelodge London Liverpool Street 17
Travelodge London Southwark 21
Union Jack Club 6
YHA London Central 2
YHA Thameside 25
Andaz Liverpool Street London 16
Apex City of London 19
Citadines London Barbican 11
Citadines London Trafalgar Square 3
City YMCA Barbican 12
City YMCA EC1 13
CANONBURY
HACKNEY
BARNSBURY
DALSTON
DE BEAUVOIR TOWN
SOUTH HACKNEY
ISLINGTON
HOXTON
HAGGERSTON
FINSBURY
SHOREDITCH
GLOBE TOWN
BETHNAL GREEN
BOW
CLERKENWELL
ST. LUKE'S
HOLBORN
STEPNEY
THE STRAND
THE CITY
WHITECHAPEL
SHADWELL
DOCKLANDS
BANKSIDE
SOUTH BANK
WAPPING
SOUTHWARK
THE BOROUGH
BERMONDSEY
NEWINGTON
LAMBETH
ELEPHANT & CASTLE
WALWORTH
KENNINGTON
CAMBERWELL
River Thames
0 1/2 mi
0 0.5 km

in the winter, beds are adorned with hot water bottles and throws. The least expensive rooms (which is to say £136 in winter and on weekends, £160 in summer and on weekdays) are on the lower floors, while the fifth floor is given over to deluxe penthouse suites, with panoramic terraces (£225) that you and I can only dream about. Two-night weekend stays are sold for £320 including breakfast. London certainly has better-value hotels but not many that are cooler.

VICTORIA, CHELSEA & WESTMINSTER

The streets around Victoria Station, lined with proud mid-19th century houses as evenly spaced and white as a line of wedding cakes, were built for the rising middle class but have long hosted good low-cost lodging. The area is slightly less bustling than Bloomsbury and King's Cross, appealing to visitors with a yen for peace. Deals tend to flower the farther southeast you walk from the station along Belgrave Road, but be warned that some of the hotels on this stretch are becoming as grotty and dim as the flophouses of Bayswater (except for the ones I've chosen, of course). I prefer the B&Bs along Ebury Street, which sprouts southwest of Victoria Coach Station, because they're closer to the boutiques and cafes of Belgravia, such as along Elizabeth Street. Farther south, window shopping with the wealthy on Chelsea's King's Road is a fine weekend pursuit, and because of its relative remove from the Tube system (but not the bus routes), hotels and flats come cheap.

Times are getting tough in Victoria, especially along Ebury Street. The area's landowners have hiked lease rates, forcing the closure or shrinkage of several old reliables and resulting in the boutiqueification of others. In the past 2 years, room rates have been jacked up, in some cases by 35%. There are still some low-priced gems to be found, but Victoria, despite its decent location, is decreasingly a primary domain for savings. The starting point for most cross-country bus routes is at a terminal nearby.

£ Nothing more than a crash pad, **easyHotel Victoria** (36-40 Belgrave Rd., SW1; www.easyhotel.com; MC, V; Tube: Victoria or Pimlico) is a new 78-room conversion carved into what was once a 50-room budget hotel. Priced like the original South Kensington location (see p. 55 for how that place works), this joint isn't for everyone. Few rooms have windows or even space to properly prop up big luggage. But they're cheap, cheap, cheap if reserved way ahead, and if you're planning on being on the go during your trip, why pay more?

£–££ Because they started life as two separate hotels and were conjoined in the 1990s, you'll sometimes see the **Luna Simone Hotel** ★ (kids) (47-49 Belgrave Rd., SW1; ☎ 020/7834-5897; www.lunasimonehotel.com; MC, V; Tube: Victoria or Pimlico) called the Luna & Simone. Prices for rooms rise based on availability: Doubles go from £80 to £100; triples from £100 to £120; and the quad from £120 to £140. The only category in which not every room is en suite is the single category (prices start at £45 for shared bath and cap at £65). Internet access is free in a booth off the lobby. Although it's a protected building with old metalwork on the banisters and oddly sized guest rooms, the owners have taken pains to modernize with fresh, inexpensive furniture and modernist prints by Rothko

and Miró. Its two large morning rooms, done up like a diner, have a weird undulating blue ceiling that makes scooping your cereal feel a bit like doing the backstroke. Everything is in excellent condition, which is a bit of a surprise when you consider that the owners have been at it since 1970.

£–££ The **Melbourne House Hotel** (**79 Belgrave Rd., SW1; ☎ 020/7828-3516; www.melbournehousehotel.co.uk; MC, V; Tube: Pimlico**), was recently transformed by its owners of more than 2 decades, John and Manuela Desira, who lavished money and elbow grease on completely refurbishing the 17-room B&B. You can smell how well-scrubbed the property is the moment you enter. Units, all in an older town house per the London norm, now sport little flatscreen TVs (with 70 channels, some 65 more than at most inns) and fresh paint jobs, making this one a value for a standard guesthouse. Singles with shared baths (the only rooms here that share a bath) are just £42, one of the lowest prices in town, and doubles (go for room 1, which has both tub and shower and extra space) go for £95. Family rooms are £140, a little high, although the owners are open to bargaining. Breakfast is fully cooked on weekdays, but it's continental on weekends. Rooms in the back don't have next-door neighbors. The hotel, which is within walking distance to Westminster Abbey, will also strike deals in the winter.

Read This to Avoid Booking Blunders

Did you swap the date and month? In Europe, the month and date are usually written in the reverse order of how they're given in the U.S. So May 11, 2008 in America becomes 11 May 2008 when you're using a British booking engine, or 11/5/08. (Dates go from the smallest increment of time to the largest.) Check carefully or you may reserve for the wrong month!

Deals are better direct. In my experience, if you can find a room in a hotel for £100 through a discounter, you will always be able to find it for at least as little from the hotel itself. Probably lower, since if you book directly with the hotel, you won't pay commission. This goes double for London, where so many hotels are run by families, not rule-bound companies.

Make sure you're sure. If you don't like your hotel, you can change, but empty rooms hit tiny family-run places in the purse. Check the property's cancellation policy before you book—for example, is there no backing out within 48 hours of your reservation? Even if you think the joint's a pit, if you've missed a cancellation deadline, you won't get a refund.

Remember the time difference! If you need to call England to make reservations, make sure you know what time it is there first. Many of the inns listed in this book are run by everyday folks who may not appreciate receiving a phone call at 2am.

£–££ Every time I visit **Morgan House** ★ kids (120 Ebury St., SW1; ☎ 020/7730-2384; www.morganhouse.co.uk; MC, V; Tube: Victoria), I'm amazed by how chirpy the guests look. They treat this cramped Georgian B&B like home, lingering over breakfast to swap travel tales, or hanging out on the staircase in the foyer to warn each other of the bad plays seen the night before. There must be something extra special about this place, or its owners, Ian Berry and Rachel Joplin, for it to attract such friendly devotees. Maybe it's the low prices: £52 for singles, £72 for doubles, and £92 for triples. It certainly can't be the rooms, which are tight but adequate; only four of them have their own bathrooms (add £20 to the nightly bill if you want one of those), plus orthopedic mattresses and a peaceful communal garden with white iron furniture. The family room has a double, a bunk bed, and a bathroom for £132, which is a good deal. With only nine rooms (with too-thin walls between them, but what else is new in London?), there's no hubbub to contend with—indeed, breakfast, noted for its homemade museli, is only available in a 90-minute window each morning. Over a stay, you almost get the sense of what it must have been like to live in a mid-20th-century boardinghouse. This hotel is not to be confused with the Morgan Hotel, a perfectly nice, but doubly expensive, B&B/flat letter in the lee of the British Museum.

££ The typically British **Cartref House (108 Ebury St. and 129 Ebury St., SW1; ☎ 020/7730-6176; www.cartrefhouse.co.uk; AE, MC, V; Tube: Victoria)** is run by Sharon and Derek James, second-generation hoteliers who raised their two kids here and clearly care about their business. "Cartref" means "home" in Welsh, although since they entertain an 85% American clientele, you won't feel put off by a language barrier. Rooms are light but done up simply in gentle tans, with unadorned wood furniture. Unfortunately, the Jameses are feeling the squeeze of modern times; after they recently sold a second property across the street, rates leapt £15 in 2 years, bringing double-room prices to £95 and singles to £69. That's standard for budget hotels in this neighborhood, but £10 to £20 higher than in King's Cross or Bloomsbury, but you can be assured that for the expenditure, you'll be looked after by true professionals with a proven track record and a deep knowledge about their city. Rooms, which have free wireless Internet and often a wardrobe, are basic but cheery for the price, and a full English breakfast is taken in a quaint dining room of bentwood chairs and tablecloths. You may be able to bargain for lower rates in winter.

££ Until recently, **B+B Belgravia ★★★ (64-66 Ebury St., SW1; ☎ 020/7259-8570; www.bb-belgravia.com; AE, MC, V; Tube: Victoria)** was a cookie-cutter property with nothing to recommend it, but a group of forward-thinking investors gave the premises an extreme makeover. Although it follows the form of a typical town house hotel (rooms of various sizes, stairs instead of lifts), it dares to have a strong sense of style. An ocean of white paint has been applied to every surface, and a futuristic glass-floored bridge was constructed, no doubt at great expense, to link the ground-floor sitting area (enormous wall clock, free espresso machine) with the light-drenched kitchen and dining area. Once you've made your way to the kitchen, you get a high-end breakfast that includes French-press coffee and Wilkin & Sons jam. Rooms are of standard London size, meaning barely big enough for you and your luggage, but the bathrooms, with cylinder sinks and pleasingly detailed tilework, bear little resemblance to the dated closets on offer at the competition. You won't spot a yard of chintz in its 17 rooms, although Ikea is well represented. Your TV is flatscreen, and if you have a laptop, Wi-Fi is free; you can also borrow the laptop in the lounge, where coffee and hot chocolate are always free. Free bikes, DVDs, and books are loaned, too. Each night on your pillow, instead of chocolate, you may find a slice of "rock," a traditional British seaside treat. For this high-concept execution, catnip to penny-pinching business travelers, the rates are £99 for singles (typically in a double room), doubles £115, and family rooms for £145 (for three) to £155 (for four)—in winter, you can negotiate £10 or so lower. The "B+B" brand is expanding nationwide, having recently opened its second location in Weymouth, in Dorset.

DOCKLANDS & GREENWICH

Docklands, the wide zone showcased in the TV show *Eastenders,* is a terrain of offices and some of the city's best-priced chain hotels. Even though it takes about as long to get to The City from Canary Wharf as it does from, say, High Street Kensington, the prices in Docklands are competitive since the area is off most tourists' radars. On the plus side: If you stay here, you'll mainly commute using the above-ground DLR train (entirely accessible for travelers with disabilities), which lets you to see a lot more than on the Tube. On the negative side: There

Do You Need It?

Mind the culture gap. Don't let these quirks take you by surprise:

- Although all hotels include towels and linen, you'll find for the most part that travelers are expected to bring their own washcloths. Don't ask me why, because it's a mystery to me.
- Many beds have duvets but not top sheets. It's just a European style; locals would probably explain that the duvet cover *is* the top sheet. Many Americans, after riding through the initial sensation that they're in a naked bed, find the setup surprisingly comfortable.
- You may find that your bed is made each day but your sheets aren't changed. This, too, is normal, and it saves on water, electricity, and detergent. If you want them changed, simply request it.
- Nearly all rooms in the budget category have phones and TVs these days, but not cable, so expect only four or five broadcast (or "terrestrial") channels (BBC 1 and 2, ITV, Channel 4). Phones might only dial the front desk but not an outside line.
- Ask for a loaner hair dryer, because your non-British one probably can't handle the increased voltage. New non-British hair curlers fare better, although they may get hotter than they do back home.
- Your family-run B&B probably can't employ a porter but rare is the place that doesn't have at least one strong person to tote your baggage upstairs. It's yet another incentive—beside massive airline penalties for overweight bags—to pack lightly.
- Not every small hotel stocks irons, sometimes for safety reasons. If yours doesn't, steam your clothes using the hot water in the bathroom; at least there's one advantage to their puny size.
- Most places don't have air-conditioning because during a normal summer London doesn't get that hot. Even if it gets warm during the day, it almost always gets chilly again after sunset. If you do get hot, most town house hotels have windows that open, and they loan out table fans. A few also have ceiling fans. If all that fails, you could do worse than to retreat to the breezes of one of the world-famous parks.

aren't many places to eat outside of the Canary Wharf malls. You'll also have to bring your personality—these hotels don't have much of their own. Should you be quoted prices that are higher than the ones quoted here, it's probably because there's a major event happening at the nearby ExCeL convention center then.

£ As part of modern redevelopment around the docks, **Travelodge London Docklands** (Coriander Ave., off East India Dock Rd.; ☎ 087/1984-6192; Tube: East India DLR) can feel, like many Docklands chain hotels, a little windswept and lonely. Think of it as modernist Northern European, and you'll feel better. It's close to the DLR station, though, a 15-minute scoot into town. The £62 to £70

Docklands Accommodations

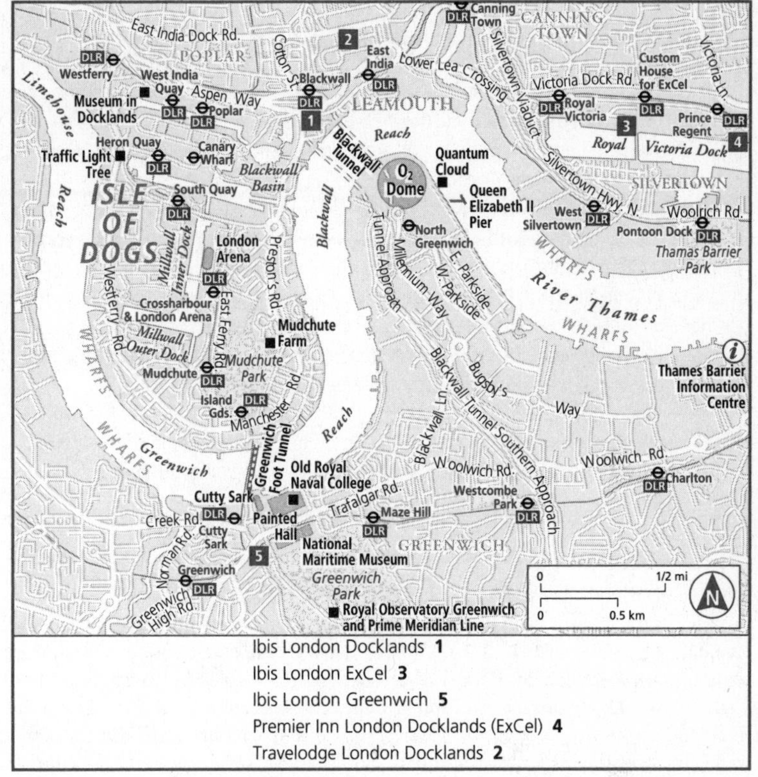

peak room rate becomes £29 if you book far ahead. For a description of Travelodge amenities, see p. 51.

£ A few steps south of the DLR station in a cul-de-sac haunted with cobbled vestiges of its dockworker past, the 87-room **Ibis London Docklands** (1 Baffin Way, E14; ☎ 020/7517-1100; Tube: Blackwall DLR) is good for a crash pad, but there's not much to do nearby. Fortunately, the price compensates: £90 on weekdays and a scandalous £70 on weekends—worth taking a 15-minute ride to the city. Also in the area, the **Ibis London Excel** (Royal Victoria Dock, E16; ☎ 020/7055-2300; www.ibishotel.com; Tube: Custom House DLR) sits in a Lego-like congregation of faceless hotels serving the ExCeL Convention Center. When shows aren't on, rates plummet to £65. For those marvelous savings, you'll have to endure a 10-minute walk to the DLR and then a 25-minute ride into the city. For a description of Ibis amenities, see p. 51.

£ The most easterly of the bunch, so requiring a slightly longer commute to town, the **Premier Inn London Docklands (ExCeL)** (Royal Victoria Dock, E16; ☎ 0870/0238-3322; Tube: Prince Regent DLR) also sports lower prices than any of its in-town brethren: £67 Fridays and Saturdays and £86 weekdays.

Staying Web Connected in Your Room

These days, even budget travelers are packing their laptops and keeping in touch with e-mail and free Internet-based phone calls such as Skype. (Hide those computers under your dirty socks, though, because most low-cost hotels don't have in-room safes.)

You can't judge Web availability by the room rate. About 50% of inns currently offer some kind of in-room high-speed Web access, almost always for free. Many more provide free service on terminals in their lobbies, and a few charge by the minute for lobby use. You should assume that if I don't mention Web access at a small hotel, then it hadn't been installed at press time; it's being added quickly these days at even the lowest-priced places, though, so ask when you're ready to reserve.

As for major hotels with more than 100 rooms, almost all of them have it, even if I don't say so. But unlike the little guys, they charge for it–around £10 is normal, although some places get away with charging more.

MILITARY HOTELS

A club hotel catering expressly to world servicemen, **Union Jack Club ★★ (Sandell St., SE1; ☎ 020/7928-4814; www.ujclub.co.uk; AE, MC, V: Tube: Waterloo)** was opened by King Edward VII in 1904 to shield soldiers from the wickedness of Edwardian London. Today, its vague modern furnishings and hotel-like amenities (restaurant, library, souvenir shop, bar) recall a much pricier hotel. It's certainly as large as a goliath hotel: 330 rooms rest in the 1975 tower. In addition to American and Commonwealth servicemen and women, it accepts commissioned officers, firefighters, policemen, and ambulance workers, too—although it frowns upon accepting officers; after all, they have their own clubs. It costs £25 to gain membership and £14 for a year, which is prorated as the year wears on. If you don't feel like paying that but you still qualify, your accommodations rate will be about 15% higher than the standard rates, which start low (£33 single, £62 twin) and rise if you want a bathroom (£45 single, £82 double). Family rooms have bunk beds for kids and cost £104. Flats for four to six people, with kitchens, cost £148 a night.

The Victory Services Club ★ (63-79 Seymour St., W2; ☎ 020/7616-8335; www.vsc.co.uk; AE, MC, V; Tube: Marble Arch) was established in 1907 to ease the homecoming of veterans of Britain's many wars and is only for those who have served in the military. It's open to retired personnel of the Crown, Commonwealth, or Allied nations, including NATO personnel. Once the £20 annual membership is paid (in advance by mail), you can crash in one of the Club's 220 rooms, which are more basic than those at the Union Jack Club. Prices are comparable to other budget hotels, but mingling with former British and international servicemen is an interesting experience. Rooms in the Old Club House (dating to 1948) are simpler, with shared bath, while rooms in the newer Memorial Wing (1954) are en suite. Depending on if you're in the old wing or the new, and if you want your own bathroom, it's £32 to £45 for singles and £59 to £85 for doubles, including a cooked breakfast. There's a cheap restaurant that gets playful on periodic theme nights (Curry Night, Best of British Night), and a lounge bar that segues from coffee to stronger stuff as the day ages.

HOSTELS & LOW-COST SPECIALTY HOTELS

Not all hostels are created equal. The two major players are **YHA** (once called Youth Hostel Association, 8 properties in central London; www.yha.org.uk; MC, V) and independently owned properties. Independents have no standardized protocol, so they're operated pretty much as the desk staff—often Australian visitors—see fit, and that includes dorms that sleep both sexes. Loosely speaking, hostels that are independently owned will attract a more social crowd and cost about a third less than those operated by the YHA network, but YHA properties, which usually divide guests into same-sex dorms, have standards that are reliably higher. (These are gross generalizations, I know. I've been in independents run with military accuracy and at YHAs where I've met lifelong friends, but use these guides as a rule of thumb.) If you don't have a YHA membership (it costs £16 a year for individuals, £23 per family), you're still welcome, but you'll pay £3 more per night. The more people you jam in your room, the less you pay, and those under 18 usually get about £5 lopped off the rate. When it comes to booking rooms for families, most hostels will rent out an entire dorm room, which almost always have an even number of beds; families of three or four would be assigned a four-bed room at the four-bed price, families of five would be assigned a six-bed room, and so on. Ask ahead if small children are welcome. YHA has a rotten online reservations system that changes the price slightly according to when you want to stay, but never by more than four or five pounds per person a night.

A third category is **Young Men's Christian Association** (YMCA; www.ymca.org.uk; AE, MC, V). Given that they're operated by a Christian charity, they have zero party potential, and sometimes barely more personality, but they're secure, tidy, gender-separated, and a top value, if occasionally lonely-feeling. You'll find long-term guests here, mostly foreign visitors who may even hold down honest-to-goodness jobs or academic schedules.

£–££ An independent, fresh-faced hostel that's cleaner and not as party-crazed as others, **Ace Hotel** ★★ (16-22 Gunterstone Rd., W14; ☎ 020/7602-6600; www.ace-hotel.co.uk; MC, V; Tube: West Kensington or Barons Court) is a good

---

What to Bring—& Not to Bring—to a Hostel

The good news: Hostels no longer require guests to do chores, bring bed linen, be under a certain age limit, or come home by curfew. Still, you'll need to bring:

- Earplugs (if you're a light sleeper)
- Your own padlock to secure your gear in lockers
- Toiletries and flip-flops for the shower
- Your own towel (although some hostels provide them)

20-minute ride from the West End on the Tube, but that commute buys you a quiet, secure street inhabited by everyday Londoners. There's a garden patio that's heated in the winter and that hosts barbecues in the summer, and the design is bright and contemporary. A pallid breakfast (toast, coffee) comes free, but no self-catering kitchen facilities are offered. Dorms come in three-, four-, six-, and eight-bed flavors, with prices from £17 to £26 depending on how many you shack up with and whether you want an attached bathroom. Simple private twins are £53 with a shared bath and £57 with a private bath. Prices scale downward to £18 the more people you're willing to share with, up to eight in a room. Doubles with bathrooms are £99, which aren't worth it when you consider what some budget hotels are charging in the middle of town. November through March, prices drop £2 to £4 across the board, and they rise by the same amount on weekends. Book early because it's gaining in popularity.

£ Instead of operating like an institutional charity, YHA now runs like a professional discount lodging concern where a customer can comfortably kick back in between day tours and crash in a single-sex dorm. If you want to be in the middle of everything and don't mind paying a few pounds more for a bed, pick the gleaming **YHA London Central** ★ kids (104-108 Bolsover St., W1; ☎ 087/0770-6144; www.yha.org.uk; londoncentral@yha.org.uk; MC, V; Tube: Great Portland Street), which cost £4.3 million to build, has boisterously colorful decor by a specialized interior design firm, and has been packed, often with kids, since opening in early 2008. Although facilities are new, the staff is as businesslike as you'd expect of an accommodations machine like this. The tariff starts at £22 for metal bunks, and although most rooms are advertised as en suite, in fact many have in-room basins but showers and toilets are at the end of the hall. Most rooms (opened by key-card) only house about four or six people (peaking at £144 per en suite, six-bed room), good for families but not couples. You have to pay to use the Web, but if you buy something at the in-house cafe, like the £4 breakfast, you get a free daily pass. The self-service kitchen, happily, is open round the clock.

£ One little-known property is practically on the Thames: the **YHA London Thameside** ★ (20 Salter Rd., SE16; ☎ 020/7232-2114; www.yha.org.uk; MC, V; Tube: Rotherhithe or Canada Water. Rooms are giant by hostel standards, and although designers took too much advantage of the space by triple-stacking the bunks, it's rarely full, which means you won't always be assigned roommates. There's a kitchen, a full English breakfast (included), and you can buy a picnic lunch for a few quid. All rooms, mostly four- and six-bunkers (£18–£21 a bed, £27 with breakfast) have bathrooms, even if you have to share them with whomever's bunking with you. Ten private twin rooms (£50–£54 a room) are also on hand. What keeps this property from massive popularity is its location well east of town (convenient for Greenwich and the Tower of London). The rebuilding of the East London line, which ends in 2010, means you'll have to walk 15 minutes to the Tube. This hostel was once known as YHA Rotherhithe, but that proved about as alluring as YHA Middle of Nowhere.

£ Homier and quieter than the student-packed Central location is the 181-bed **YHA London Earl's Court** ★★ (38 Bolton Gardens; ☎ 020/7373-7083; www.yha.org.uk; earlscourt@yha.org.uk; MC, V; Tube: Earl's Court), which recently received a top-to-bottom renovation after a devastating 2006 fire. From the intricate tile flooring in the foyer to its sweeping staircase, it has settled inside a grand single-family home within walking distance of the big Kensington museums. (Beatrix Potter was born and spent her formative years, raised mostly by servants, in a neighboring house, 2 Bolton Gardens.) Dorm beds start at £22, and couples can do a shared-bath double for £56. Four-bed rooms are £87, and six-bed rooms are £131. There's laundry, a kitchen, TV lounge, bike hire, and a simple back garden. It's tricky to find because there are so many streets named Bolton; from Earl's Court Road, go down the one with Caffe Mokarabia on the corner, and you'll find the hostel on the right.

£ There's no question that the **YHA London St. Pancras** (kids) (79-81 Euston Rd, NW1; ☎ 020/7388-6766; www.yha.org.uk; stpancras@yha.org.uk; MC, V; Tube: King's Cross St. Pancras) is in a convenient spot: across from the British Library, and within quick reach of six Tube lines. But this hostel, the second-newest YHA in town, doesn't have much personality. Still, it books up early. Rooms, most of which are four-bedded, are bigger than the norm, with the added luxury of a table and a few chairs and lots of storage space, and although the road outside is busy, security is tight and windows are triple-glazed. It's a good place to crash if you're catching a morning train from King's Cross station. Beds are around £25; the price includes a full English breakfast, which is unusual. "Premium rooms" come with either double beds or twin bunks and have a TV and bathroom (£60–£63, not much different than a King's Cross B&B). There are also similarly priced "family bunk rooms" holding two (£61) to six (£161) bunks; most include a bathroom, but you must check in with at least one child under 18. For five, that would cost £134 per room including breakfast. The maximum stay is 10 nights. There's a kitchen, air-conditioning, and a lift.

£ If you're a young person looking for a hostel where you can party all night, there's no bigger playground than the **Generator** (Compton Place, off 37 Tavistock Place, WC1; ☎ 020/7388-7666; www.generatorhostels.com; london@generatorhostels.com; MC, V; Tube: Russell Square or Euston), discovered down a cobbled lane opposite Kenton Street. By day, the mega-hostel appears like some kind of tanker ship stranded in the mews, and by night, when the socializing is in full swing, it's like the monkey house at the zoo. The Art Deco building was a police station in its younger years, but a makeover of sheet metal gave it a *Blade Runner* mood that's at distinct odds with the Roman proclivities of the clientele. You'll meet lots of young backpackers—with more than 800 beds, there's plenty of opportunity to make a new friend or twelve. Guests get access to a microwave and a toaster, but not a full kitchen, so you will have to eat out. The cafeteria, Fuel Stop, dishes up changing dinners like barbecue chicken and mixed vegetables for £4. The bar is open until 2am (happy hour, £1.50 pints), and for better or worse, many make heavy use of it. All rooms (standard metal bunks, nothing to shout about) have wash basins but share bathrooms, and with so many young people banging about, things get grimy. Everyone is assigned a backpack-size locker (bring your own lock), and there's laundry, a lift, and a lobby shop that sells everything from washing powder to discounted tours to Vegemite. Breakfast (cereal, toast, coffee or tea) is free. Private rooms are: singles £50 weekdays and £70 weekends; twins (no double beds) £25/£35 daily per person; you can almost always do better at a B&B, but you'll do without the beer bongs. Prices for mixed-gender dorms are £20/£25 in four-bed dorms, with discounts up to £5 possible if you choose a room with 8, 12, or 14 beds. Some eight-bed dorms are female-only, and there are a few triples and quads.

£ For a well-located, no-nonsense option, there's **City YMCA Barbican** ★ (2 Fann St., EC2; ☎ 020/7628-0697; www.cityymca.org; MC, V; Tube: Barbican), which occupies a dull-as-dirt concrete 14-floor high-rise at the northwest corner of the plain but safe Barbican development. Because of its off-putting landscape, most tourists overlook Barbican, which is probably why the prices have actually gone *down* slightly since the last edition of this guide: £212 for a week's stay in a single room, or £34 per night; and £182 for a week's stay per person in a twin room (no double beds), or £32 per night. That price includes a light breakfast and a cooked dinner, balanced but hardly gourmet, Monday through Friday. Rooms are cleaned daily (linens changed weekly), there's a TV lounge and lift, and all guests, many of whom stay for several months, are entitled to use the fitness center (weight training, cardio) for free. A supermarket is nearby, and so is the popular nightlife zone of Clerkenwell. You'll find similar prices at the nearby **City YMCA EC1** ★ (8 Errol St., EC1; ☎ 020/7614-5000; www.cityymca.org; AE, MC, V; Tube: Barbican or Moorgate), a 2-minute jaunt east down Fann Street, but the Barbican is closer to transit.

£ Perhaps because visitors assume it only welcomes Indians, not much attention is paid to the **Indian Student YMCA** ★★ (41 Fitzroy Square, W1; ☎ 020/7387-0411; www.indianymca.org; AE, MC, V; Tube: Warren Street). That's their loss and your find. Although it *is* popular with Indian students studying in London (in fact, it's operated by the National Council of YMCAs in India), you're welcome to stay here. Its lobby is as institutional as a 1950s airport lounge, but upstairs it's much more than advertised. Private rooms have blue carpet, thick red blankets, TVs, phones, and lamps that turn on and off with a tap. You could eat off the bathroom floor, but I don't know why you'd want to when the downstairs canteen, attended by staff in white uniforms and chef hats, serves delicious authentic Indian food at all three mealtimes for next to nothing (onion bhajia £1! veggie curry £1.35!). Four-bedded dorms are £25 per person, and private rooms come with a shared bath (singles £38, doubles £55) or an attached bath (singles £50, doubles £65). Those prices include breakfast and dinner but not the £1 surcharge for nonmembers. There's a lift, and let's not ignore the location: On a historic, pedestrianized square within walking distance of seven Tube lines, the British Museum, Oxford Street, and the West End.

£ The chief advantage of the 200-bed **YHA London Holland Park** ★ (Holland Walk, Kensington, W8; ☎ 020/7376-0667; www.yha.org.uk; MC, V; Tube: Holland Park or High Street Kensington) is its location within a Jacobean former mansion in a wooded area of Holland Park, which is like a western annex of Kensington Gardens. The chief disadvantage, besides the place's popularity with unruly school groups, is that the idyllic-seeming location actually places it about 10 minutes from the nearest Tube station, and both of those are about another 15 minutes from the West End. Single female travelers may not feel comfortable walking to the hostel at night through the park. But the facilities are strong, with clean rooms, generous lockers, individual reading lights, park views, a cafe, bike hire (£1.50 an hour or £9.50 a day), a kitchen, laundry, and cheap restaurant. There are only dorms (8–20 beds) costing £25 for adults.

4 Dining Choices

Guaranteed to please all tastes & pocketbooks

IN 1957, ARTHUR FROMMER VISITED LONDON'S BEST RESTAURANTS DURING research for his seminal *Europe on $5 a Day.* His report was dispiriting: "With great despair, this book recommends that you eat in these inexpensive chains while in London and save your money for the better meals available in France and Italy. Cooking is a lost art in Great Britain; your meat pie with cabbage will turn out just as tasteless for 40¢ in a chain restaurant as it will for $2 in a posh hotel."

Thankfully, the English palette has caught up with the rest of the world, and the residents of London now rightfully pride themselves on their advanced and multicultural cuisine. Your food will almost certainly not be tasteless, and cabbage has been banished from most menus. But eating in London is still a problem, and the best choices are still dominated by chain restaurants—albeit chains that will be new to you because they often don't exist outside of London.

The trouble is most kitchens here are shockingly pricey. That resurgence of British home cooking you've heard about—the rise of the gastropub—is a trend aimed at spendy diners. The blistering exchange rate makes those already costly dinners twice as expensive for visitors. Once you get to London and see the menus, you'll be amazed (and appalled) at how even basic food can set your budget back.

Eating out, as a pastime, is still gaining cultural traction. Remember that this is a place that was, as recently as the 1950s, still living on rations. It's in their bones to cook for themselves. London is also wallet-draining even for most of the people who live there. For Britons of an average income, going out to eat is a treat, and usually something done to catch up with friends or on special occasions. Although "take away" (to go) meals are common, ordering dinner for delivery is rare.

Now that the floodgates of E.U. bureaucracy have broken and the city is swarming with working people from all over the world, it's possible to find nearly every imaginable style of international cuisine, from Burmese to Belgian. But here's something you won't find much of: fish and chips. In central London (if less so than in suburbs and in the north of Britain), old fry-ups have been replaced, by and large, with Britain's new favorite comfort food, the Indian curry shop. You also won't find many pubs serving the classic definition of English cuisine, such as steak-and-kidney pie or Yorkshire pudding. Most pubs have followed changing tastes and have reduced old-fashioned menu choices to a few roast meats or unadventurous beef pies, in favor of ever-popular pizzas, sandwiches, and burgers.

Don't like meat? London's greenie culture is far more entrenched than in nearly any other Western city, and in addition to supporting a huge number of meat-free establishments that are considered cool by carnivores and herbivores alike, virtually every menu will have at least three or four—usually more—items for vegetarians to eat. The situation for vegans isn't quite as flexible, although most servers understand vegan dietary requirements and are likely to know which dishes comply. In short, good news for both human plant-eaters and farm animals.

THE AFFORDABLE RESTAURANTS OF LONDON

Most of these establishments also serve lunch, should you get sick of sandwiches or need to rest your legs for a spell, but since your hotel will surely serve breakfast, I won't waste space on morning eateries.

My focus is places charging around £10 or under for a main dish. Any more than that, and you'll be paying US$20 before you've added a starter, dessert, coffee, or tip—a full meal at those prices will hit you for £30. Do that twice daily, and you'll have lost more than US$100 a day to food alone! My prices are restrictive, but scaling it more liberally would make this list a lot less useful to you.

For each neighborhood, I list spots in order of cost so that it's easier for you to find something according to what you're willing to pay. When and if you find yourself ready to splash ou[illegible]e of pricier options vying for your palette; a few of my [illegible] for breadth.

BLOO[illegible]ROVIA

£ One of the most spectacular buys in the city, the **YMCA Indian Students Hostel** ★ (41 Fitzroy Square, W1; ☎ 020/7387-0411; www.indianymca.org; Mon–Fri noon–2pm and 7–8:30pm, Sat–Sun 12:30–1:30pm and 7–8:30pm; AE, MC, V; Tube: Warren Street), on the southeast corner of Fitzroy Square, serves truly authentic Indian food, not a Pakistani hybrid; not surprisingly, its clientele consists mostly of Indian students. Apart from having the personality of an airport lounge, this buffet-style cafeteria is welcoming to anyone, resident or visitor. Pay the clerk, who'll give you a receipt that you show to the cook (who wears an immaculate white chef's tunic), who in turn loads you up. Rices, chapatis, and fish curries make regular appearances, along with plenty of vegetarian options, many of them Punjabi. Get here right after opening for the best pickings (but don't BYOB, since alcohol is not allowed). And the price? Almost everything is under £3. Amazing.

The Five Rules for Eating Affordably

If you want to find good, inexpensive places to eat (beyond the places that I list later in this chapter, that is), follow these rules:

- Sandwiches, sandwiches, sandwiches (see "Save Your Bread at Sandwich Shops," below). And baked potatoes.
- The cheaper places are on non-touristy roads, such as one road behind the busiest streets.
- Asian cuisine—Thai, Malaysian, Indian—is key.
- London's beautiful parks are ideal for picnics using grocery items.
- If all else fails, drop by Marks & Spencer's Simply Food for prepared meals (p. 91) or the nearest pub, where menus are cheapish and filling.

When Restaurants Are Open

Lunch at family-owned restaurants is served from about 11am to 3pm, although a few may wind up at 2:30pm. Dinner starts at around 5:30pm and goes to 10:30 or 11pm. I've noted exceptions in the reviews that follow. At an increasing number of places, serving hours don't pause in the afternoon, but you may find that kitchens shut down about a half-hour before the posted closing time. In Britain, closing time often means the time staff clocks off, not the moment last orders are taken.

Most of London's cheapest restaurants aren't strict about defining their cuisine. You'll see pizza alongside noodles alongside roasts, and Thai fused with Chinese fused with Malaysian.

For sandwich shops, see p. 90; for pubs, see p. 129.

£–££ One of those secret cafes you have to have a friend tell you about, **Camera Café** (44 Museum St., WC1; ☎ 020/7831-1566; www.cameracafe.co.uk; Mon–Fri 11am–7pm, Sat noon–7pm; MC, V; Tube: Tottenham Court Road or Holborn) is a coffee house tacked onto the back of Aperture Photographic, a small shop near the British Museum specializing in lenses and SLR cameras; the walls are decorated with shots taken by local artists. Food (£3.50–£7) takes its sweet time in coming (at least there are lots of coffee-table books on art and Britain to borrow, plus a vintage Scrabble set) but arrives in a big way; the huge chow mein noodle bowls could serve two. The free Wi-Fi, plus the brewed coffees and teas, mean boho patrons tend to relax for hours.

£–££ It does business in a hideous slug of a concrete open-air mall, but **Hare & Tortoise** (11-13 Brunswick Shopping Centre, WC1; ☎ 020/7278-9799; daily 12pm–11pm; MC, V; Tube: Russell Square), peps up its surroundings with nonstop crowds of chatty young customers, who stream in until 11pm daily for noodle dishes. It's always a good sign when a place serving Asian cuisine is popular with native-born Asians. Its ramen bowls are a good deal—shrimp, chicken, or pork served in a deep bowl with soup and vegetables for £4.30 to £4.50; stewed chicken with spices, coconut milk and lemongrass is £5.25. Meats here are almost always served with Asian accompaniments and are usually moist and well-roasted. Gyoza dumplings are £2.80 for four, and more conventional dishes (chow mein, fried rice) span £5 to £6—servings are big. Lunch can be so busy that you may feel rushed.

££ You'd never know it from the sleepy avenue it is today, but Cleveland Street, which runs a block west of Fitzroy Square, was once one of the city's most notorious red-light districts, where many a writer fell afoul of his unchecked libido. On that now-peaceful road you'll find **Cavalleria Rusticana** ★ (124 Cleveland St., W1; ☎ 020/7383-7762; daily 11am–3pm and 5:30–10pm; AE, MC, V; Tube: Great Portland Street), an old-fashioned, homespun hole in the wall, Italian to the core, that's been going for years but is untouched by tourism. Service in this cafe-style storefront is unhurried and often doled out by a server with a real Italian accent,

Save Your Bread at Sandwich Shops

You'll go all day without crossing paths with a bobby or a true Cockney, but you can barely walk 3 blocks without passing a sandwich shop. Sandwiches are a cultural institution: Anywhere people work, you'll find sandwiches, soups, and "jacket potatoes" (£2–£4), which are baked potatoes stuffed with fillings such as cheese and bacon or tuna salad.

My advice is to eat like the locals do. Save the splashy meals for supper. Most of London's attractions are only open from about 10am to 5pm. That doesn't give you a lot of time to see what you came to see, so a marathon lunch will cost you precious hours. To dine like a true Londoner, have a big breakfast (your hotel probably serves it for free, so chow down), and at midday, grab a carb-laden bite (a sandwich, a jacket potato) and get on with your day. Dinner is the time for table service, long conversation, and adventurous cuisine—in fact, many sandwich places close in mid- to late-afternoon, dictating your choices for you.

You don't need my help finding sandwiches. They're everywhere. But I will tell you that the cheapest ones are what I call the **triangle sandwiches,** which are ready-made, sliced diagonally, and sealed into triangular containers. They are made fresh every day by the million. The British don't usually call them triangle sandwiches—they just call them takeaway sandwiches, undistinguished from a sandwich made to order—but the nickname fits. Triangle sandwiches range from £1.25 (for an egg salad/"mayo"

and the house wines are good. Pastas (there are 10) are but £6.95 to £9.95, and there are usually three risotto choices on the menu. All-day set meals are generously programmed: you get a starter such as avocado and shrimp salad or pan-fried mushrooms with goat cheese, and a main such as spaghetti with spicy meatballs or fried calamari, for £10.95. In good weather, the few sidewalk tables make for a fine vantage point on one of Fitzrovia's less busy streets.

££ Unlikely as it seems, one of London's growing niche cuisines is the all-you-can-eat meatless Thai buffet. **Joi Café (14 Percy St., W1; ☎ 020/7323-0981; daily noon–10pm; no credit cards; Tube: Goodge Street or Tottenham Court Road)** masters the genre with a pleasing steam table lined with constantly replenished lo meins, faux-beef stir fries, fried dumplings, and spicy Thai salads and curries, all for £5.50 at lunch or £6.50 Sundays and evenings. Stuff your face in the simple dining room for as long as you can stand it, or stuff a take-out box for £3. Partly because chefs furnish a hearty complement of spices and sauces, even die-hard carnivores have been known to appreciate this fare. It's located near the big campuses, so it's popular with students, and if you have a student ID, you get a free drink after 3pm. Buffets like this have mushroomed around the West End, but or other vegetarian selection) to about £3.95 (for triple-packs containing three sandwich halves with a variety of fillings).

Here are explanations of ingredients that will help you decode them:

- *Pickle* is a tangy vegetable spread that tastes a bit like steak sauce.
- *Cress* is slang for watercress.
- *Mayo* is like saying salad (i.e. "tuna mayo"), but "salad" listed as an ingredient usually denotes just a cursory pinch of lettuce.
- A *bap* is a round bread roll, and a "toastie" is a sandwich that's visited a sandwich press.

A few ubiquitous chains catering to the triangle sandwich trade are:

Boots (www.boots.com): The cheapest triangle sandwiches on the High Street, and a wide selection.

Eat (www.eat.co.uk): Its quality is right behind Pret, with a good selection of organics and whole grains.

Gregg's (www.greggs.co.uk): Its sandwiches are average in every way, but people also queue for its pies and hot meat rolls.

Marks & Spencer/Simply Food (www.marksandspencer.com): Lots of cheap stuff, well done.

Pret A Manger (www.pret.com): The highest-end sandwichier, with gourmet fixings in snazzy combinations.

this location was one of the first to popularize the form in a city where all-you-can-eats are unusual, and it's near the British Museum, where tourists can use cheap chow.

££–£££ Local Filipinos favor **Josephine's Restaurant** (4 Charlotte St., W1; ☎ 020/7580-6551; www.josephinesrestaurant.co.uk; Mon–Sat 11:45am–3pm and 6–11pm, Sun 5:30–10:30pm; AE, MC, V; Tube: Goodge Street or Tottenham Court Road), which is somewhat surprising when you take a gander at the schticky trappings (bamboo chairs, a slatted ceiling, basic canteen plates). Then again, it is the only Filipino place in the West End. The hearty food arrives via dumbwaiter from the cellar kitchen; eschew the Chinese dishes (which aren't terrific) for the more challenging "traditional" Filipino choices (which are), such as *rellenong pusit* (whole squid stuffed with seafood, chestnut, and spice), chicken adobo (tangy chicken with garlic; the Philippines' national dish), and crispy *pata* (deep-fried pork leg). At lunch, two courses cost £7, and three £9; dinner prices are fair, too. Try the cassava cake for dessert; it tastes like sweet potato with yam cream. Its website posts coupons good for things like a free glass of wine.

London-Wide Dining

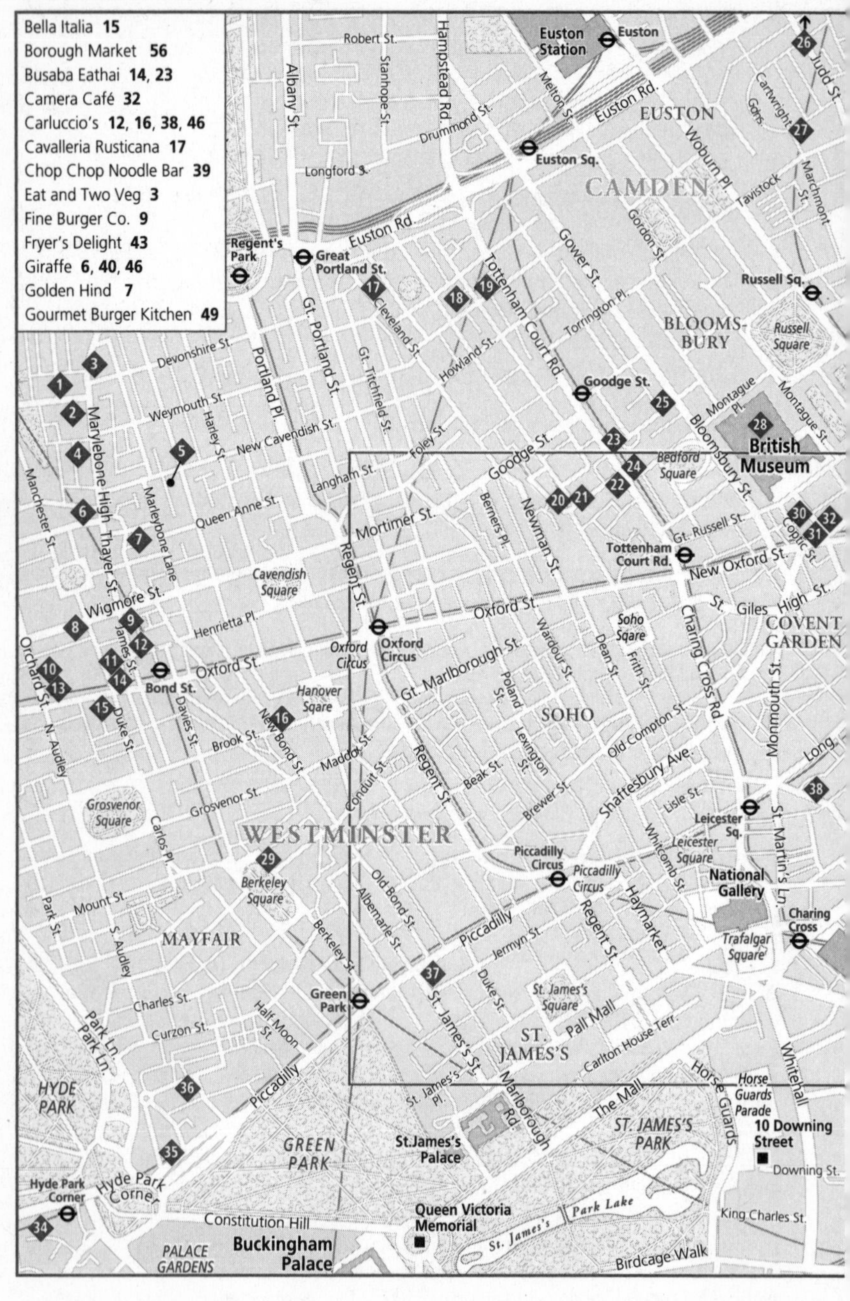

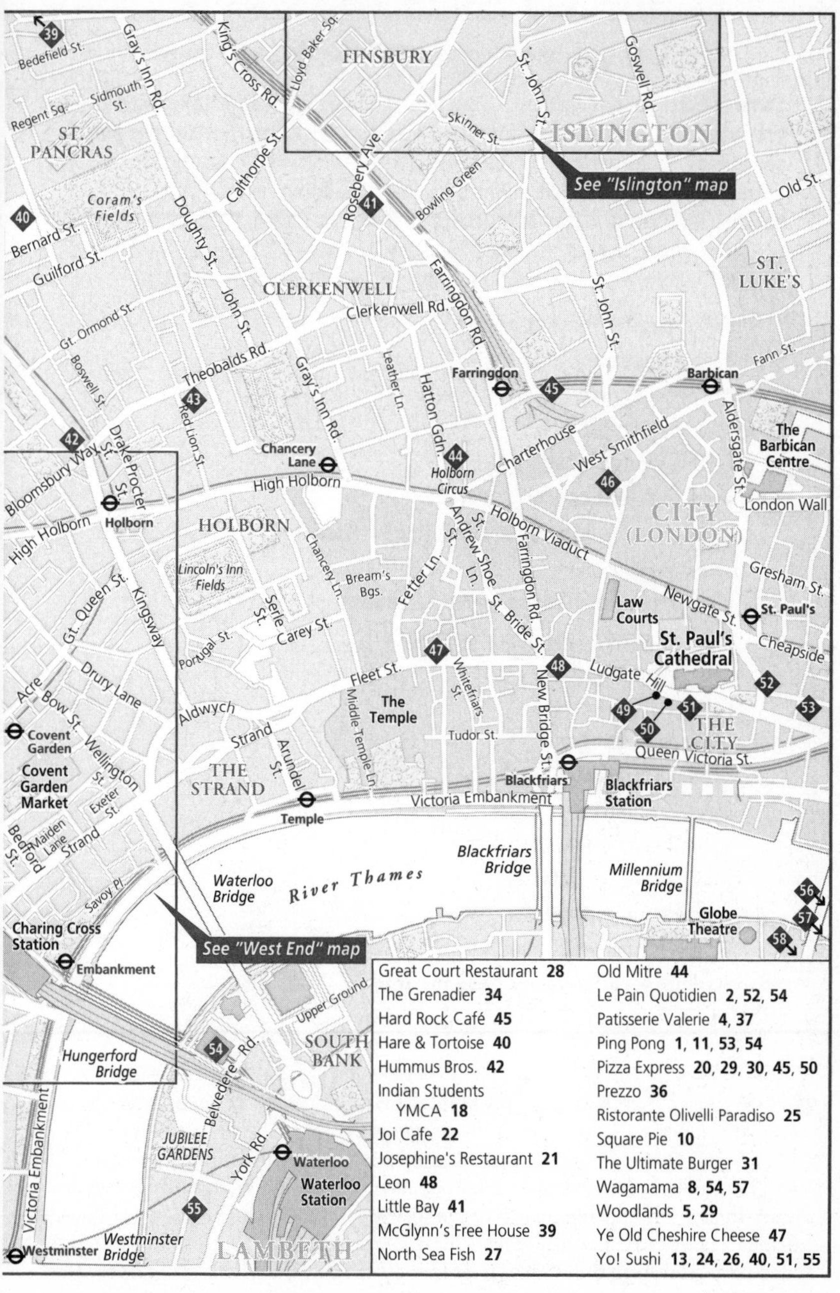

FINSBURY
ISLINGTON
See "Islington" map
ST. PANCRAS
Coram's Fields
CLERKENWELL
ST. LUKE'S
HOLBORN
Lincoln's Inn Fields
CITY (LONDON)
THE CITY
THE STRAND
The Temple
Law Courts
St. Paul's Cathedral
The Barbican Centre
Covent Garden Market
SOUTH BANK
JUBILEE GARDENS
LAMBETH
River Thames
See "West End" map
Bedefield St.
Regent Sq.
Sidmouth St.
Gray's Inn Rd.
King's Cross Rd.
Lloyd Baker Sq.
St. John St.
Goswell Rd.
Skinner St.
Calthorpe St.
Rosebery Ave.
Bowling Green
Old St.
Bernard St.
Guilford St.
Doughty St.
John St.
Farringdon Rd.
Clerkenwell Rd.
Gt. Ormond St.
Boswell St.
Theobalds Rd.
Leather Ln.
Hatton Gdn.
Fann St.
Red Lion St.
Aldersgate St.
Charterhouse
West Smithfield
Bloomsbury Way
Drake St.
Procter St.
High Holborn
Holborn Circus
London Wall
Holborn Viaduct
St. Andrew St.
Shoe Ln.
Chancery Ln.
Bream's Bgs.
Fetter Ln.
Gresham St.
Newgate St.
Cheapside
Gt. Queen St.
Kingsway
Serle St.
Carey St.
St. Bride St.
Portugal St.
Drury Lane
Fleet St.
Whitefriars St.
New Bridge St.
Ludgate Hill
Acre
Bow St.
Aldwych
Middle Temple Ln.
Tudor St.
Wellington St.
Strand
Arundel St.
Queen Victoria St.
Victoria Embankment
Exeter St.
Maiden Lane
Bedford St.
Savoy Pl.
Upper Ground
Belvedere Rd.
York Rd.
Farringdon
Barbican
Chancery Lane
Holborn
St. Paul's
Blackfriars
Blackfriars Station
Covent Garden
Temple
Embankment
Charing Cross Station
Waterloo
Waterloo Station
Westminster
Waterloo Bridge
Blackfriars Bridge
Millennium Bridge
Globe Theatre
Hungerford Bridge
Westminster Bridge
Great Court Restaurant 28
The Grenadier 34
Hard Rock Café 45
Hare & Tortoise 40
Hummus Bros. 42
Indian Students YMCA 18
Joi Cafe 22
Josephine's Restaurant 21
Leon 48
Little Bay 41
McGlynn's Free House 39
North Sea Fish 27
Old Mitre 44
Le Pain Quotidien 2, 52, 54
Patisserie Valerie 4, 37
Ping Pong 1, 11, 53, 54
Pizza Express 20, 29, 30, 45, 50
Prezzo 36
Ristorante Olivelli Paradiso 25
Square Pie 10
The Ultimate Burger 31
Wagamama 8, 54, 57
Woodlands 5, 29
Ye Old Cheshire Cheese 47
Yo! Sushi 13, 24, 26, 40, 51, 55

Speak the Right Tongue for the Right Flavor

Some people call dinner **tea.** If you need it to go, say it's for **takeaway.** If you want an American-style appetizer, you want a **starter.** French fries are sometimes called **chips,** but decreasingly so. What North Americans call entrees are **mains.** Dessert might be called a **pudding,** even if it's cake. A packet (such as for sugar or ketchup) is a **sachet** ("sash-AY"). To request your final check, ask for the **bill.** If you say "to-*may*-to," they say "to-*mah*-to." But before you call the whole thing off, we all say "po-*tay*-to."

baked potato = **jacket potato**
beet = **beetroot**
chicory = **endive**
cookie = **biscuit**
cotton candy = **candy floss**
eggplant = **aubergine**
ground beef = **mince;** but pie filling of dried fruit, etc. = mincemeat
Jell-O = **jelly**
juice drink (not fresh-squeezed) = **squash**
lemon-flavored soda pop = **lemonade**
molasses = **treacle**
potato chips = **crisps**
sausages = **bangers**
shrimp = **prawn**
squash = **marrow**
string beans = **French beans**
white raisins = **sultanas**
yellow corn = **sweetcorn**
yellow raisins = **sultanas**
zucchini = **courgette** or **baby marrow**

££–£££ Pizza Express ★★ kids (30 Coptic St., WC1; ☎ 020/7636-3232; www.pizzaexpress.com; chain-wide hours generally Mon–Sat 11:30am–midnight, Sun 11:30am–11pm; AE, MC, V; Tube: Russell Square) is so ubiquitous—some 300 outlets in the U.K., dozens in London—you could call it a modern British institution. In fact, since its rise, which began in 1965 (9 years before McDonald's first stuck its flag in English soil), it seems like half the casual restaurants in town have added knife-and-fork, thin-crust pizzas to their bills of fare. Money-saving tourists will certainly turn to pizzas at least once during their trip, and they would do well to dig in at this classy chain, where two dozen pizza varieties (£5.65–£9.10, but mostly around £8)—not too bready, well topped—rightfully keep the traffic coming. I favor La Reine (ham, olives, mushrooms, £7.45) and Veneziana (onions, capers, olives, sultanas/raisins, and pine nuts, £6.25), but there are 21 other varieties, plus six types of salad and six more of pasta. Service is almost always freakishly fast and cheerful. There are more than 70 branches in town. The location at 10 Dean St. is probably the best for evenings because it sometimes books concerts by important names like Van Morrison and Jamie Cullum (Reservations: ☎ 084/5602-7017; www.pizzaexpresslive.com; Tube: Tottenham Court Road). Other handy branches include 133 Baker St., by Madame Tussaud's (Tube: Baker Street); 9 Bow St. (Tube: Covent Garden); 80-81 St. Martin's Lane (Tube: Leicester Square); 25 Millbank, by Tate Britain (Tube: Pimlico); 7-9 Charlotte St. in Fitzrovia (Tube: Goodge Street); and Islington's 335 Upper St. (Tube: Angel).

££–£££ Back in the day, this trattoria was so well-known that the Marx Brothers chose to dine here during their only trip to Blighty. Today, **Ristorante Olivelli Paradiso** ★ (35 Store St., WC1; ☎ 020/7255-2554; www.pizzaparadiso.co.uk; Mon–Sat 10am–midnight; AE, MC, V; Tube: Goodge Street) is an unpretentious place for good Italian food in a setting popular with families and groups. It deserves props for its homemade pastas (£7.85–£8.95), which are a notch more creative than other kitchens' at this level: gnocchi sorrentina is savory with aged parmesan and pomodoro; and ravioli asparagi with stuffed with gorgonzola and walnut is satisfyingly rich. Save by ordering pasta as a slightly smaller spaghetti starter for £1 less. The menu has 13 types of wood-fired pizza, from £6.50, plus a slate of meats (£12–£17), and at least four fresh fish dishes (around £15). The pastas give the owners pride, but the chef also makes the ice cream from scratch.

££–££££ One of the last central London bastions of batter-fried fish and chips, **North Sea Fish** (7 Leigh St., WC1; ☎ 020/7242-4119; Mon–Sat noon–2:30pm and 5:30–10:30pm; AE, MC, V; Tube: King's Cross St. Pancras or Russell Square) isn't a linoleum-lined chippie, but a classy fish market-cum-restaurant, hidden on a lost-in-time side street. Every hotel manager within a 3.2km (2-mile) radius recommends it. Portions are huge, and there's always a selection of fresh fish (bream, trout, skate, halibut, and so on). Make sure you ask the cost when ordering because it's easy to get hit with a high market price (haddock and cod tend to be

Lunch Make a Deal

Lots of expensive restaurants advertise lunch and pretheater deals to boost business at slower times. Some are prix fixe, and some are low-price offers for a la carte courses. These are ever-changing, but as an example, Ebury Wine Bar, a refined bistro on Ebury Street south of Victoria station, charges around £15 for a main, but at lunch £16 gets you two courses and £19 gets you three. Check the menu boards at any restaurant that interests you—you are likely to luck out. After 7pm, these deals dry up.

Keeping the Bill in Check

Bear in mind these cultural differences while ordering and you'll avoid some nasty dining pitfalls:

Avoid Coke: It often costs £1.75, and you'll probably receive only a puny glassful without refills.

Avoid overtipping: Only tip if the menus say "service not included." Credit card slips often have a blank line for tipping even if your tip was built in. Restaurants double-dip when you double-tip.

Avoid rice dishes: It's customary to pay £1.50 to £3 for a side dish of plain rice, even if you order something you think should come with it.

Avoid eating in: Some counter-service establishments charge as much as 20% more if you decide to eat your purchases there.

Avoid water: Well, avoid bottled water. If you just order "water," many waiters may bring expensive sparkling water, so if you want it for free, specify "tap water."

Avoid starters: Even where mains are £6, starters can be £3 to £5.

Avoid cocktails: These are luxury items. Mixed drinks can cost a dizzying £8 to £11. If you do drink, stick to beer (£2–£3 a pint) or wine (around £4 a glass).

cheaper). If you need a healthier option, you can also get your fish grilled, and keep in mind that sitting down to eat will cost more than using the take-away desk. Try the terrific homemade tartar sauce, or, for fans of little fishies, sample grilled sardines with salad (£4).

KING'S CROSS & ISLINGTON

£ It ought to be protected by the National Trust. Not only is the **Indian Veg Bhelpoori House** ★★★ (92-93 Chapel Market, N1; ☎ 020/7833-1167; daily noon–11:30pm; cash only; Tube: Angel) meat-free, but it's also probably the best meal value in London. You pay just £3.95 for a giant all-you-can-eat-buffet in a city where plain rice usually costs nearly the same—that's enough to make this off-the-beaten-track, multilevel restaurant inkworthy. You'll get a mix of spicy choices, conventional choices (onion bhajis, which go fast but get replenished), and weird choices (like curried brussel sprouts). Its homey decor—the walls are coated with propagandist slogans and dubious bar graphs extolling the virtues of vegetarianism—make it even more of a must-see. Many a penniless student has survived thanks to the long-running deals. It even serves booze. There are other cheap no-limit buffets in town (a few are lined on Marchmont St. northeast of the British Museum), but no others come close in quality, range, or atmosphere.

£ On rainy days, the plate-glass windows of **Chop Chop Noodle Bar** (3 Euston Rd., N1; ☎ 020/7833-1773; daily 11am–midnight; MC, V; Tube: King's Cross St. Pancras) fog up, concealing the crowds of students, commuters, and tourists who favor this simple, quick eating hall over the many banal fast food chains that clog King's Cross. The menu's huge (98 items: noodles, soups, rice dishes, and fresh juices), and since it's up to customers to fill out their own order card, it's easy to

Islington Dining

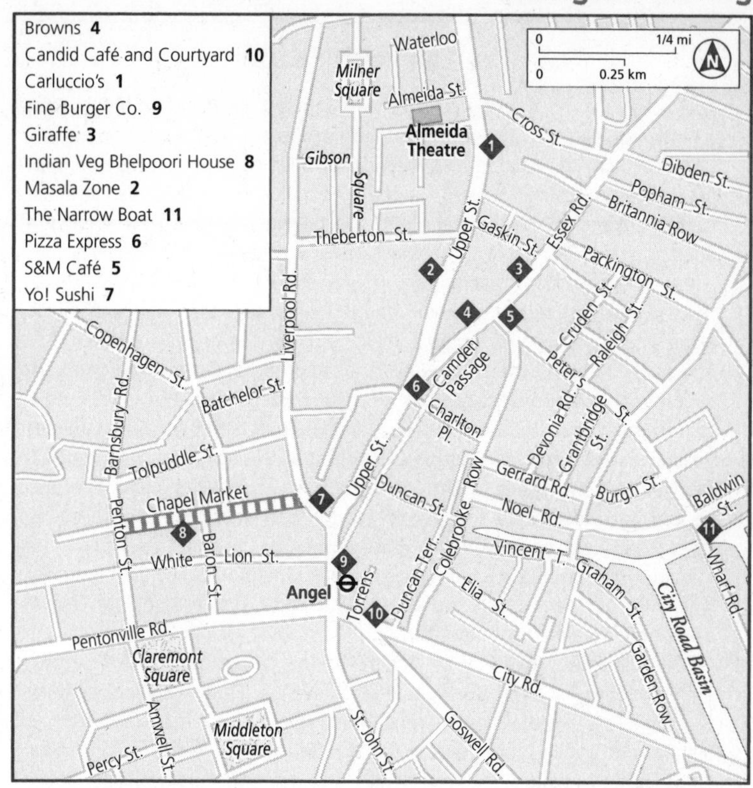

go crazy and order too much. I call it "Cheap Cheap": Most items are between £3.30 and £3.90. I'll guide you: the Singapore Laksa soup, big as a hot tub, strikes upon the ideal medley of creamy coconut, vermicelli, shrimp, and come-from-behind spiciness. Most London noodle bars wimp out on the zing, but Chop Chop doesn't do bland. Great for the money.

£–££ A hidden space to escape for a few hours, **Candid Café and Courtyard** (3 Torrens St., N1; ☎ 020/7837-4237; www.candidarts.com; Mon–Sat noon–10pm, Sun noon–5pm; AE, V; Tube: Angel) is on the second floor of Candid Arts Trust, a gallery-and-studio complex in a converted warehouse just east of the Angel Tube station. This time-warp cafe is a mellow, candle-filled hangout for reading, tea nursing, deep conversation and, if you're so inclined, admiration of the psychedelic paintings on the walls. Sandwiches (from £3) come with upscale fillings like brie, avocado, and feta, and the changing cooked meals (£5–£10) usually include organic meat and a few vegetarian dishes such as lasagna or mixed veggies in coconut sauce with couscous. Service isn't what you'd call sprightly; your waitress may have to set her own coffee down to fetch your food. Most customers just buy some cake and a coffee and linger. In the summer, the idle pleasures spread to the serene courtyard out back.

The Cabman's Shelter

As you roam, keep an eye out for curious kelly-green shacks no bigger than a horse and cart. Wooden, shingled, and peaked, fringed in simple gingerbread latticework, topped by a wee cupola vent, they're as cute as a hobbit's outhouse. Some balance in the median of an overcrowded avenue, some hunker like newsstands along the pavements. These are Cabman's Shelters, built by a charity between 1875 and 1914, when "respectable" classes were worried about cab drivers straying into the pubs. Here, instead of a pint, horsemen could find hot soup, tea, and other wholesome refreshments. Of the 61 original shelters, barely more than a dozen survive, and a few of those, against the odds, still contain teeny greasy spoons where cab drivers can pull over for a cuppa. Not all of them court custom from tourists, but if you're friendly and not with a group, you may hold your own with some garrulous cabbies at the counters. Simple meals (cooked as if by miracle on little more than a burner and a microwave) can be had for unbelievably low prices: tea for 50p, enormous English breakfasts for £5. The one on Temple Place advertises "pie, mash + liquor!"—a lax policy that would scandalize its original landlords. Some are closed for weeks on end, and hours are erratic, but when they're cooking, they're open from breakfast to mid-afternoon.

Chelsea Embankment, near Albert Bridge (Tube: South Kensington); Embankment Place at Northumberland Avenue (Tube: Embankment or Charing Cross); Grosvenor Gardens, west side (Tube: Victoria); Hanover Square, north side (Tube: Oxford Circus); Kensington Park Road, numbers 8–10 (Tube: Notting Hill Gate); Kensington Road, north side (Tube: South Kensington); Pont Street (Tube: Knightsbridge); Russell Square, west corner (Tube: Russell Square); St. George's Square, north side (Tube: Pimlico); Temple Place (Tube: Temple); Thurloe Place, opposite the V&A (Tube: South Kensington); Warwick Avenue at Clifton Gardens (Tube: Warwick Avenue); Wellington Place at Wellington Road (Tube: St. John's Wood).

MARYLEBONE & MAYFAIR

£ No one should leave Britain without having pie for lunch. The hand-held, meat-stuffed pastry parcels occupy a vital cultural position as a quick, satisfying lunch or snack. A top choice for a well-stuffed one is **Square Pie** (Selfridges Food Hall, 400 Oxford St., W1; ☎ 020/7318-2460; www.squarepie.com; Mon–Fri 10am–8pm, Sat 9:30am–8pm, Sun noon–6pm;AE, MC, V; Tube: Bond Street or Marble Arch), in the rear, ground-floor food hall at Selfridges. "Classic" pies weigh over half a pound and come in a dozen varieties including steak and cheese, steak and Guinness, jerk chicken, lamb with rosemary, and the infallible steak and kidney (all are £5 or less—cheaper to go). To be truly authentic, pair your pie with mashed potatoes, beans, or mushy peas (around £1 each; there may be a deal to include it for less). I always go with mushy peas (it tastes better than it sounds), which is also a traditional accompaniment to fish and chips. On Fridays, Fish Pie joins the lineup. There's a second store at 16 Horner Square, at Spitalfields Market (closed Sat; Tube: Liverpool Street).

£–££ Considering its organic breads and lush-looking pastries, it's no wonder journal writers and book readers never seem to vacate **Le Pain Quotidien** (72-75 Marylebone High St., W1; ☎ 020/7486-6154; www.lepainquotidien.com; Mon–Fri 7am–9pm, Sat 8am–9pm, Sun 8am–7pm; AE, MC, V; Tube: Baker Street). It functions as a patisserie or a cafe, depending on your mood. Selections are light but fresh, such as carrot and coriander soup (£3.50, with bread), juicy strawberry tarts (£3), and slices of pavlova (an Australian meringue, £3.50). The tartines (open-faced sandwiches, £5 to £6) are more substantial; get one with aged Gruyère and three mustards or tuna salad, capers, and anchovies. Or just grab a simple pain au chocolat (£1.20). There are other locations near Covent Garden (174 High Holborn), one east of St. Paul's (1 Bread St., closed weekends), at 9 Young St. (Tube: High Street Kensington), and within both the Royal Festival Hall and St. Pancras station.

££ All hail **Wagamama** ★★ kids (101a Wigmore St., W1; ☎ 020/7409-0111; www.wagamama.com; Mon–Sat 11:30am–11pm, Sun 11:30am–10pm; AE, MC, V; Tube: Bond Street)! It's impossible to overstate the addictive popularity of this sociable, modern noodle bar. There are 22 locations in town, each one more packed than the last. This one is tucked behind Selfridges at Duke Street, perfect for Oxford Street shoppers. Diners are seated at long, communal wooden tables, so you'll have ample opportunity to meet your neighbor, and orders are transmitted by handheld tablets straight to the kitchen. Part of the appeal is the varied menu that includes kare noodles, teppan, ramen, and chilli men, served in deep white bowls, no skimping on the ingredients or the spice. Mains fall mostly around £7 or £8, which pound-earning Londoners find marvelously cheap, but I think is high enough to be mostly a dinner option. Teens love it, and the kids' menu is all noodles because, as its cover proclaims, "Kids love noodles." Some of the best-located branches are at 4 Streatham St. (Tube: Tottenham Court Road); 1 Tavistock St., south of Covent Garden (Tube: Covent Garden); 10a Lexington St. (Tube: Piccadilly Circus); Tower Place, next to the Tower of London (Tube: Tower Hill); at Harvey Nichols, 109–125 Knightsbridge (Tube: Knightsbridge); and Royal Festival Hall (Tube: Waterloo).

££–£££ The solid-value minichain **Carluccio's** ★★ kids (St. Christopher's Place, W1; ☎ 020/7935-5927; www.carluccios.com; Mon–Fri 8am–11pm, Sat 9am–11pm, Sun 9am–10:30pm; AE, MC, V; Tube: Bond Street) apparently fashions itself after an Italian grocery from Manhattan's Little Italy; you enter through a little shop selling pastas and sauces and then beg for attention from the harried staff (just like the real thing). Pastas, which reach beyond spaghetti into the zone of fresh tomatoes, saffron, and ravioli, are well made and cost mostly in the £7 to £8 range, but there are salads, meat plates, and an extensive kids menu. The £10 "Massimo!" antipasto dish serves two. Polish off dinner with a £1.60 demitasse of cioccolate fiorentina drinking chocolate, but do resist ordering the "transporti": It's a £1,849 Vespa scooter. Carluccio's is genuinely popular with locals, and worthy of

High Tea, Low £

Nowadays, with a Starbucks on every British corner, only tourists and matrons with ice in their veins partake of afternoon tea. But I know, I know. That doesn't mean you wouldn't like to do it, especially since you're in London, right? The genteel Thames Room at the Savoy Hotel and the wood-paneled English Tea Room at Brown's Hotel (open since 1838) are steeped in lore—if you want to part with £38 per person. Just how much do little sandwiches cost to make, anyway? Instead, try these spots, generally from 3 to 6pm. It pays to reserve and to dress nicely:

Bramah Tea and Coffee Museum ★★ (40 Southwark St., SE1; ☎ 020/7403-5650; www.teaandcoffeemuseum.co.uk; AE, MC, V; Tube: London Bridge) is run by passionate people who know their Assams from their Oolongs. So their afternoon teas feature a properly chosen leaf and are assiduously brewed. Choose from Cream Tea (£7 with scones and clotted cream, an addictive dairy delicacy that I recommend) or Afternoon Tea (£9 with sandwiches and cake). The setting is plain, but you can visit the adjoining museum afterward, and you might even learn something.

Covent Garden Hotel (10 Monmouth St., ☎ 020/7806-1000; www.firmdale.com; AE, MC, V; Tube: Covent Garden) supplies a traditional afternoon tea in a well-appointed hotel, as is the custom, but for £24, £14 less than at the ritzy places, including The Ritz. You get sandwiches, scones, preserves, tarts, strawberries, a brownie—but no snooty attitude.

Great Court Restaurant at the British Museum (Great Russell St.; WC1; ☎ 020/7323-8990; www.thebritishmuseum.ac.uk; MC, V; Tube: Russell Square). Tea and a fruit scone with clotted cream and jam and finger sandwiches are £19. Or go simple with just tea and cookies for £5.50—all under the dazzling glass-and-steel canopy in the museum's courtyard, overlooking the famed Reading Room. It's not the best tea in London, but it's half the price of the hotel teas. And the setting is sterling.

Tea Palace ★ (175 Westbourne Grove, W11; ☎ 020/7727-2600; www.teapalace.co.uk; AE, MC, V; Tube: Westbourne Park), at the top end of Notting Hill, was set up as an alternative to high-priced tourist trap; it delivers the same upper-class frippery for £17 (although a single pot, without extras, costs a quarter of that). The tea is impeccably chosen, and it comes with plenty of scones, sandwiches, and organic jam.

its repeat clientele. The upstairs dining room is brighter but noisier; the cellar rooms are cozier but darker. Plenty of other branches are scattered around town, but the most convenient include 8 Market Place (Tube: Oxford Circus), Garrick Street (Tube: Covent Garden), the Fenwick store on New Bond Street (Tube: Bond Street), 1 Old Brompton Rd. (Tube: South Kensington), 108 Westbourne Grove (Tube: Notting Hill Gate or Bayswater).

£–£££ A cosmopolitan veggie place, **Eat and Two Veg** (50 Marylebone High St., W1; ☎ 020/7258-8585; www.eatandtwoveg.com; Mon 10:30am–11pm, Tues–Sat 9am–11pm, Sun 10am–10pm; no credit cards; Tube: Baker Street) somehow appeals to every taste with its juice-based cocktails, huge portions, and contemporary diner-inspired vibe. The soy-heavy food is serviceable, the wait staff less so, but the hangout quotient is through the roof—insist on one of its cavernous booths. The halloumi sandwich comes with homemade salad, coleslaw, and fries (£9), and Sunday after 1pm, the spinach and herb nut roast, served with a Yorkshire pudding and a gravy boat (£11), imitates the British tradition, but without meat, and packs enough energy to carry anyone through the day. The cocktails prove this is no fuddy-duddy greenie joint.

££–£££ Its huge selection of pastas (16 recipes) and pizzas (13), all at prices that mostly hold under the £9 ceiling, won't win it awards for creativity, but it does qualify **Prezzo** (kids) (17 Hertford St., W1; ☎ 020/7499-4690; www.prezzoplc.co.uk; AE, MC, V; Tube: Green Park) as one of Mayfair's rare contemporary bargains. Sure, it's a chain, but only in England, and because it makes an effort to purchase good-quality, seasonal pizza toppings and to adorn its dining room with fresh-cut flowers, it's a cut above. The kids' menu (main, dessert, drink) is £4, and the whole chicken, roasted on site and served with potatoes, serves three or four for £18.

£££–££££ I have little praise for **The Hard Rock Café** (kids) (150 Old Park Lane, W1; ☎ 020/7514-1700; www.hardrock.com; Sun–Thurs 11:30am–12:30am, Fri–Sat 11am–1am; AE, MC, V; Tube: Hyde Park Corner), located since 1971 near Hyde Park Corner. You'll find one in every town from Key West to Kuwait. Its burgers (though excellent and sizable) hover around an outrageous £10 to £12, much of the so-called memorabilia consists of instruments that big names played maybe once and tossed, and waiting up to 90 minutes for a table chews up time that could be used for more authentic touring. It's true that this Hard Rock was the world's first, but it's also true (and telling) that its corporate headquarters have moved to Orlando, Florida, and no rock star would be caught dead in here today. You can barely move for all the American tourists—there are so many that it accepts U.S. dollars. So why is it in this book? One, because some visitors demand to see it. Two, because rugrats often dig it. And three, its mini museum of rock lore, The Vault, is free and open to the public (see Slash's guitar, Madonna's bustier) daily from noon to 9pm, and that I applaud, even if it's just a come-on to funnel tourists through its merchandise store.

SOHO, COVENT GARDEN & THE CENTRAL WEST END

Everyone ends up around here, the dining and entertainment hub of London, for at least a day or two of their London odyssey. Naturally, a miasma of dining also-rans has sprung up, from junky steam-table buffets to the usual fast-food culprits to overpriced bistros that cook up a glitzy image better than anything they serve.

Soho's southern fringe hosts a meager Chinatown in the neon-tinted 2-block section between Leicester Square and Shaftesbury Avenue. The district survives mostly as a tourist attraction, and I don't think many of its restaurants are distinguished enough to single out. Many of them use MSG, too, despite public health currents.

£ Italians settled Soho in the 1940s, and before they decamped for the suburbs, they bequeathed the district with a set of mod, gleaming coffee bars and caffs. The most vibrant is **Bar Italia** ★ (22 Frith St., W1; ☎ 020/7437-4520; www.baritaliasoho.co.uk; daily 24 hrs.; AE, MC, V; Tube: Leicester Square), a haunt of slumming celebrities and artists, yet modest enough for the rest of us. While the place is busy all day—making simple sandwiches, delivering pastries—it swells with revelers after midnight. Even Rome doesn't have bars that steam, press, and shuffle cups of strong coffee with such gusto. "Like everything in this city that Londoners really enjoy, it reminds us of being abroad," quipped the *Guardian*. Whatever; it practically leaks hipness.

£ Strictly for quick Mediterranean bites—a common need if you're prowling the bars and clubs—**Maoz** (43 Old Compton St., W1; ☎ 020/7851-1586; www.maozveg.com; Mon–Thurs 11am–1am, Fri–Sat 11am–2am, Sun 11am–midnight; no credit cards; Tube: Piccadilly Circus) is a modern-looking, forward-thinking Dutch chain that fills the grease gap left by the withdrawal of the old fish-and-chippies. Its glassy Soho location is a falafel ball's toss from lots of pubs. There isn't much seating, but what there is offers a feast of people-watching. Complete meals—falafel, fries, and a drink—cost from £4.20, and Belgian french fries served in a paper cone go for £1.70. Just stuff your pita with the ingredients you like in its salad bar and then stuff yourself.

£ Although the communist theme is tasteless (Is the face of Lenin appropriate for a place that chooses ingredients for "no pain and suffering"?), the food is anything but. **Red Veg** (95 Dean St., W1; ☎ 020/7437-3109; www.redveg.com; Mon–Sat noon–10pm, Sun noon–6:30pm; no credit cards; Tube: Tottenham Court Road), perhaps compensating for the bloodshed fostered by Communism, serves no meat. Instead, you get inventive and remarkably flavorful tofu concoctions like the RedVeg burger (£3.65), the spicy ChilliVeg burger (£3.65), hickory smoked veg burger (£3.85), and vegwurst hotdogs (£2.95). Falafel sandwiches (£4.35) and fries (from £1.20) round out the healthy–fast-food experiment. Everything can be made vegan. If only the seating were so accommodating; there's barely enough space to turn around in.

£–£££ Mexican culture is relatively new to Londoners—I once had to explain burritos to an Englishman—so it's sensible to name a Oaxaca tribute restaurant phonetically: **Wahaca** (66 Chandos Place, WC2; ☎ 020/7240-1883; www.wahaca.co.uk; Mon–Sat noon–11pm, Sun noon–10:30pm; Tube: Leicester Square). Situated conveniently between Trafalgar Square and Covent Garden, this thriving, vibrant basement space with lime-green walls and wood-block tables specializes in affordable bites it calls "street food"—soft corn-tortilla tacos, tostadas, quesadillas, fresh guacamole with warm chips (all between £3 and £4), burritos (£6.50), and that Spanish stalwart, churros and chocolate (£3.40). Prices are kept low by cooking less with oil and more with hot ovens, as well as by sourcing ingredients locally—Lancashire sends cotija-style cheese, and chili peppers are grown in plastic greenhouses in Bedfordshire. The adaptation works, and Wahaca feeds a stream of chatty folks day and night.

West End Dining

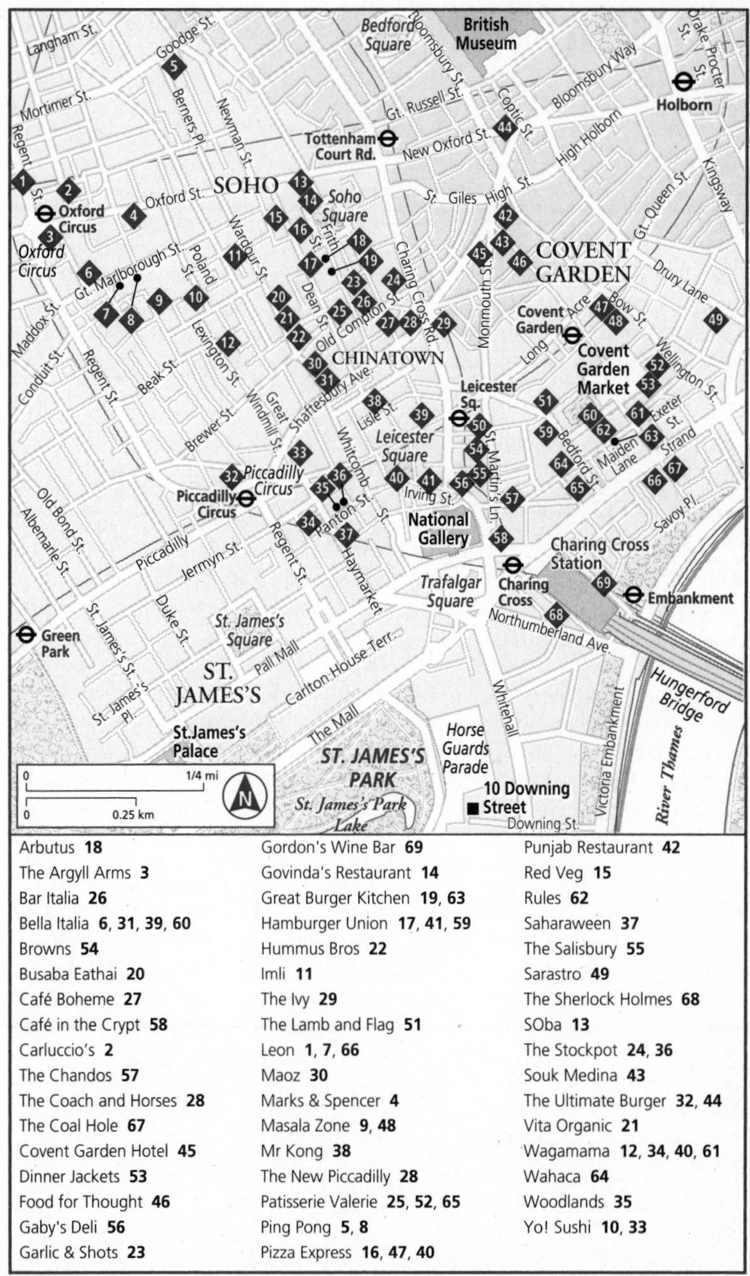

Arbutus **18**
The Argyll Arms **3**
Bar Italia **26**
Bella Italia **6**, **31**, **39**, **60**
Browns **54**
Busaba Eathai **20**
Café Boheme **27**
Café in the Crypt **58**
Carluccio's **2**
The Chandos **57**
The Coach and Horses **28**
The Coal Hole **67**
Covent Garden Hotel **45**
Dinner Jackets **53**
Food for Thought **46**
Gaby's Deli **56**
Garlic & Shots **23**
Gordon's Wine Bar **69**
Govinda's Restaurant **14**
Great Burger Kitchen **19**, **63**
Hamburger Union **17**, **41**, **59**
Hummus Bros **22**
Imli **11**
The Ivy **29**
The Lamb and Flag **51**
Leon **1**, **7**, **66**
Maoz **30**
Marks & Spencer **4**
Masala Zone **9**, **48**
Mr Kong **38**
The New Piccadilly **28**
Patisserie Valerie **25**, **52**, **65**
Ping Pong **5**, **8**
Pizza Express **16**, **47**, **40**
Punjab Restaurant **42**
Red Veg **15**
Rules **62**
Saharaween **37**
The Salisbury **55**
Sarastro **49**
The Sherlock Holmes **68**
SOba **13**
The Stockpot **24**, **36**
Souk Medina **43**
The Ultimate Burger **32**, **44**
Vita Organic **21**
Wagamama **12**, **34**, **40**, **61**
Wahaca **64**
Woodlands **35**
Yo! Sushi **10**, **33**

£–££ The bowls at finger-lickin' **Hummus Bros** ★ (88 Wardour St., W1; ☎ 020/7734-1311; www.hbros.co.uk; Mon–Wed 11am–10pm, Thurs–Fri 11am–11pm, Sat noon–11pm, Sun noon–10pm; AE, MC, V; Tube: Piccadilly Circus or Tottenham Court Road) are so tasty, and the service so merry, that it elevates the perennial appetizer to a meal. In a shared-table, airy eating hall, you pick your hummus bowl size (£2.80–£4 at weekday lunch, £4.70–£5.90 otherwise, including pita bread), then decide on the crowning pile of goodness: guacamole, mushroom (a portobello-button mix), chunky beef, chicken, or three other veggie options. The food arrives warm, accompanied by little dishes of chopped chili peppers and lemon juice, and you just scoop away with your pita. Save room for *malabi,* a light-tasting milk custard drizzled with date honey, for £2. Rich homemade brownies are £2. Everything is 50p to £1 cheaper before 4:30pm. This popular newcomer recently added a second location just east of the British Museum (37–63 Southampton Row, WC1; Tube: Holborn).

£–££ The meat-and-all options at **Leon** ★ (35-36 Great Marlborough St., W1; ☎ 020/7437-5280; www.leonrestaurants.co.uk; AE, MC, V; Tube: Oxford Circus; or 12 Ludgate Circus, EC4; ☎ 020/7489-1580; Tube: Blackfriars) are fashioned from a free-trade/organic shopping list, hooking young people and making this one of city's fastest-growing names. Its block wood tables and chairs are usually crammed with office girls grabbing a healthy, casual meal. If it's full (a likelihood), pack your meal in one of the cute brown folding boxes and eat al fresco on Carnaby Street. The menu is seasonal and gets heartier at dinner, but the best recurring options include Moroccan meat balls in plenty of red sauce (£3.50); grilled *halloumi* (£3.90); a "superfood" salad combining energizing ingredients such as beans (£4.95 at lunch); and organic chocolate bars. Drinks are sweetened with natural fruit sugar instead of refined sugar. Other locations are just north of Oxford Circus (275 Regent St.); at Spitalfields market; west of St. Paul's Cathedral (weekdays only; 12 Ludgate Circus); a few minutes' walk east of Trafalgar Square (73–76 Strand); and behind the Tate Modern (7 Canvey St.).

£–££ If you like fine pastry but your thighs like it more, you might want to keep your distance from **Patisserie Valerie** (44 Old Compton St., W1; ☎ 020/7437-3466; www.patisserie-valerie.co.uk; Mon–Tues 7:30am–8pm, Wed–Sat 7:30am–11pm, Sun 9am–8pm; AE, MC, V; Tube: Leicester Square). Its picture-window frontage, a tempting ballet of pastry, croissants, mousses, marzipan novelties, and other lush confections, will do no favors for your waistline. The cafe also does light meals and savories (club sandwiches, salad with quail eggs and ham) for £7 to £8. Its upstairs 50-seat cafe churns out popular English breakfasts (around £5). Valerie has eight locations, but it was in Soho first, since 1926. The most handy outposts are at 15 Bedford St. (Tube: Covent Garden), 37 Brushfield St. in Spitalfields (Tube: Liverpool Street); 105 Marylebone High St. (Tube: Baker Street); and 162 Piccadilly (Tube: Green Park).

£–££ Just steps off busy Oxford Street, the industrial-chic noodle bar **Soba** (11-13 Soho St., W1; ☎ 020/7287-7300; www.soba.co.uk; Mon–Sat noon–midnight, Sun noon–11pm; AE, MC, V; Tube: Tottenham Court Road) has a deal worth noting: mains are £5 all day Sunday. Outside of then, unless the discount is

Chains of Love

In many cities, restaurants run by corporations are the bane of authentic dining. But London is a different beast. Some of its best restaurant choices are part of local or British chains. Being part of one doesn't automatically mean the food is pre-frozen or machine-made. It often just means that a single restaurant became so popular that its owners decided to open more outlets in other parts of town.

In this guide, rather than duplicate a restaurant in every location where it's found, I've named each chain once followed by a list of other locations, organized by Tube stop. Below is a geographic rundown of the strongest chains in this chapter; where you see a name in italics, that chain's description is located in that neighborhood's section.

Bloomsbury and Fitzrovia: Ask, Busaba Eathai, Carluccio's, Giraffe, Hummus Bros., Ping Pong, *Pizza Express,* Wagamama, Yo! Sushi

Marylebone and Mayfair: Ask, Bella Italia, Browns, Busaba Eathai, *Carluccio's,* Giraffe, *Le Pain Quotidien,* Patisserie Valerie, Ping Pong, Pizza Express, *Square Pie, Wagamama,* Woodlands, Yo! Sushi

Soho and Covent Garden: Bella Italia, *Browns, Busaba Eathai, Hummus Bros., Leon,* Masala Zone, *Patisserie Valerie, Ping Pong,* Pizza Express, *The Stockpot,* Wagamama, *Woodlands,* Yo! Sushi

The City: Carluccio's, *Giraffe,* Leon, *Little Bay,* Patisserie Valerie, Pizza Express, *S&M Café,* Square Pie, Wagamama, Yo! Sushi

Southwark and Borough: Giraffe, Le Pain Quotidien, Ping Pong, Pizza Express, Wagamama, *Yo! Sushi*

Victoria and Chelsea: Bella Italia, Pizza Express, The Stockpot, Wagamama, Yo! Sushi

Knightsbridge, Kensington, and Earl's Court: *Bella Italia,* Carluccio's, Giraffe, Le Pain Quotidien, *Masala Zone,* Patisserie Valerie, Pizza Express, Wagamama, Yo! Sushi

Paddington, Bayswater, and Notting Hill: Carluccio's, Ping Pong, Pizza Express, S&M Café

Islington: Browns, Carluccio's, Masala Zone, S&M Café, Wagamama, Yo! Sushi

applied to weekday lunch (it often is), prices are several pounds higher, so time your visit. Soba's generous portions are dead-on Japanese, with stir-fry noodles (seafood yaki udon, chicken yaki soba), rice dishes (tofu black bean, chicken fried rice), and slightly more adventurous sides (salt and pepper squid, won tons).

££ The Stockpot ★★ (18 Old Compton St., W1; ☎ 020/7287-1066; Mon–Tues 11:30am–11:30pm, Wed–Sat 11:30am–midnight, Sun noon–11:30pm; no credit cards; Tube: Leicester Square), high on function and low on glamour, could qualify as a founding member of London's Budget Hall of Fame. It's been indispensable to scrimping visitors and families for years and got me through many a lean day of backpacking. A frequent appearance is made by the country pâté, as wide as a fist. Other common cameos are made by vegetarian moussaka, omelettes, and beef stroganoff. No dish will set you back more than £5.20, though a two-course set menu is £5.95, and all portions overflow their plates. A glass of house wine is £2.30, and the whole bottle just £9.60. On one recent visit, a brief power outage interrupted my dinner. "Just like the food," my neighbor inveighed, "it has a certain Eastern Bloc flavor." Although this one is in the most electrifying neighborhood, there are two more locations: one a few blocks south at 38 Panton St. (Tube: Leicester Square), and one at 273 King's Rd. in Chelsea (Tube: South Kensington or Sloane Square).

££ The "pure vegetarian" cafeteria **Govinda's Restaurant** (10 Soho St., W1; ☎ 020/7437-4928; Mon–Sat noon–10pm; AE, MC, V; Tube: Tottenham Court Road) is run by the Hare Krishna movement, which also operates the Radha Krishna Temple next door, so the staff is unsettlingly smiley—not all that common in mind-your-own-business Europe. The cooking style is "karma free" and Vedic, meaning no meat, onions, garlic, eggs, or mushrooms, which some diners mistake for unintentional blandness, and others cherish for its simplicity. Soho's vegetarian options have grown in number and in hipness since Govinda's first opened its doors, but its value has never changed. After 3pm but before the dinner rush, you can eat all you want for £6.95; during peak times, prices for a single plate are about a £1 less, Indian-style thali feast platters are £6.95, and pakoras are but 60p. If you have a religious issue with your dinner being offered to Lord Krishna before being served to you, skip this one. Also skip the desserts. They're boring and won't bring you any closer to the Creator.

££–£££ Founded by Alan Yau, the renegade who began the revolutionary Wagamama chain (p. 99) and London's celebrated Hakkasan restaurant, **Busaba Eathai ★★** (106-110 Wardour St., W1; ☎ 020/7255-8686; Mon–Thurs noon–11pm, Fri–Sat noon–11:30pm, Sun noon–10pm; AE, MC, V; Tube: Piccadilly Circus) duplicates its forebear's formula: a high-design dining area, convivial tables shared with strangers, and a Thai-inspired menu that abandons curry-and-rice banality. I've yet to sample a dish (generally £7–£9) that I couldn't say something nice about, be it the wok-prepared ginger beef with spring onion, the spicy *sen chan phad Thai* (noodles with prawn, peanut, green mango, and crab meat), or the butternut pumpkin curry with cucumber relish. This high-minded yet populist-priced supper has enchanted the masses, so you'll probably wait for a seat even though turnover is quick. The name is on the cusp on an expansion boom, but for now it's also at Marylebone (8–13 Bird St., W1; Tube: Bond Street) and Bloomsbury (22 Store St., WC1; Tube: Goodge Street).

££–£££ The agreeable, casual Parisian brasserie **Café Boheme** (13-17 Old Compton St., W1; ☎ 020/7734-0623; Mon–Fri 7:30am–3am, Sat 8am–3am, Sun 8am–midnight; http://cafeboheme.co.uk; AE, MC, V; Tube: Leicester Square) is where you should go for an unpretentious, noisy late meal during a night out at the bars. Little plates (£5–£9) include escargot and leek-and-cheese tarts, but I gravitate toward its substantial sandwiches, like chicken clubs with perfectly crispy frites, £9. A recent renovation of this old favorite priced main plates a bit too high for bistro fare (£11–£16 for sea bass, duck, and the like), but sandwiches and salads are ample and affordable, and few other establishments serve food so late. Weekends from 4 to 6:30pm, there's live jazz.

££–£££ A chic fusion of Chinese dim sum and cocktail lounge, **Ping Pong** ★ (45 Great Marlborough St., W1; ☎ 020/7851-6969; www.pingpongdimsum.com; Mon–Sat noon–midnight, Sun noon–10:30pm; AE, MC, V; Tube: Oxford Circus) boasts such a cutting-edge, glass-and-steel design (tip: check out the space-age toilets) that it appears at first to be one of the West End's many overpriced clubhouses for young, upper-class toffs. Yet it's affordable, with a service staff willing to walk newbies through the process. Baskets of piping hot dumplings (£2.90 for four pieces) arrive almost as quickly as they're ordered, and they're stacked in towers on your table as a trophy of your progress. The cocktails bear repeating, too (I like the vanilla, lemon, and vodka, served in a huge milk glass, for £5.85). If you can't decide, go for the "Dumpling fix" (£11), which buys 10 various pieces, sticky rice, and two scoops of ice cream for dessert. The Jasmine tea, made with a huge flower suspended in a glass, is just £1.95. The brand operates nine London locations including 10 Paddington St. (Tube: Baker Street), 29a James St. (Tube: Bond Street), the Southbank Centre (Tube: Waterloo); 48 Newman St. in Fitzrovia (Tube: Goodge Street); and 74–76 Westbourne Grove (Tube: Bayswater).

££–£££ The concept alone is compelling: Indian small plates. Springing from that good idea, **Imli** ★ (167 Wardour St., W1; ☎ 020/7287-4243; www.imli.co.uk; daily noon–11pm; AE, MC, V; Tube: Tottenham Court Road), an affordable, thoroughly modern spin-off of Mayfair's more exclusive Tamarind, innovates in flavors as well: Dishes are light, rich, sometimes refreshingly sour. This isn't the India of dowdy curries; it's the India of peppy spice, smoky overtones, cashew nuts, coconut, and avocado. Whereas traditional Indian sometimes bores or perplexes me, I clean my plates here, and the tapas imitation is ideal for India's richer cuisine. Although the menu suggests you order three or four £4-to-£6 dishes, allow me to push forward the excellent £16.50 tasting menu, which one person will be hard-pressed to finish alone and which allows you to tour the regular menu (it's sometimes sold as two-for-one on LastMinute.com). Even cheaper specials (sampler platters for £7.50, three-course menus for £10) are often trotted out, so ask about them.

££–£££ The latest fringe culinary trend to delight London is the subjective "superfood" movement, in which recipes are formulated according to how their ingredients react in the body once metabolized. The menu at Soho's vegetarian, carcinogen-free **Vita Organic** (74 Wardour St., WC1; ☎ 020/7734-8986; www.vitaorganic.co.uk; Mon–Sat noon–10pm, Sun noon–9pm; no credit cards; Tube: Piccadilly Circus) is annotated according to how each dish is thought to affect your chakras. At dinner, which is a crowded, slow-service affair conducted at communal tables under candlelight, three heaping buffet-style helpings (lots of bean-based casseroles, bakes, and salads) cost £6.90. Hearty soups—nine choices, including Orange Sweet Potato Dal and Parsnip Fennel Mushroom—cost £3.90.

£££–££££ I am repeatedly drawn to **Garlic & Shots** ★ (14 Frith St., W1; ☎ 020/7734-9505; www.garlicandshots.com; Mon–Wed 5pm–midnight, Thurs–Sat 6pm–1am, Sun 5pm–11:30pm; AE, MC, V; Tube: Leicester Square) despite its high prices. This stunt is too much fun. Everything at this scruffy bar and restaurant, run by tattooed Swedes and frequented late at night by Scandinavian headbangers (it sounds like I'm making this up, doesn't it?) is infused with doses of garlic. Seriously—it's even floating in the beer. Mains (£11–£17) are mostly versions of comfort food, such as XXX-Hot Texas Chili in a Pan (just what it says), spaghetti, and honey-roasted baby back ribs. The house clove even takes a final bow at dessert; the garlic honey ice cream is remarkably supple. As for the "shots," those are the 101 varieties of vodka shooters designed to put you (and your deadly breath) under the table, from the clever Bloodshot (vodka, tomato, garlic, chili), and the tummy-tangling Yellow Death (tequila, bananas, and rum). You'll be a social and sexual pariah for a while, and small children may flee on your approach—but you'll leave smiling.

££££ A pair of already celebrated chefs opened the exquisite **Arbutus** ★★★ (63-64 Frith St., W1; ☎ 020/7734-4545; www.arbutusrestaurant.co.uk; Mon–Sat noon–2:30pm and 5–10:30pm, Sun 12:30–3:30pm and 5–9:30pm; reservations recommended; Tube: Tottenham Court Road) with the intention of serving magnificent modern food at prices reasonable for the effort involved, and they have triumphed, winning a Michelin star for their efforts. The menu changes according to what ingredients are in season and top-quality, but British-styled dishes might include saddle of rabbit, English pea soup, Scottish organic salmon, or braised pig's head. Some of these may sound dauntingly adventurous, but deliciousness is not left behind—I have an aversion to fishy flavors, but I thought a recent mackerel dish was absolutely delectable. Definitely go between 5pm and 7pm for the pre-theater set menu, when three courses are just £18, which is the normal price for a single main later in the evening. Service is impeccable, and as another budget bonus, wines are available in carafes equal to a third of a bottle.

COVENT GARDEN & LEICESTER SQUARE

While the streets of Soho are suited to quick bites and after-hours noshes, the lanes around Covent Garden are best for sit-down establishments where you'd be more likely to pass an evening, especially on weekends.

£ Often overlooked because it lacks a building, **Dinner Jackets** (outside London Transport Museum, Covent Garden, W1; ☎ 020/7240-2677; daily 11am–6pm; Tube: Covent Garden) is a mobile kitchen stall that has been planted here for years, dishing out carb-rich stuffed baked potatoes ("jacket potatoes" in the U.K.) at lifesaving prices. That means a starting point of £1.80 and not much higher than £3.50 for a list of fillings including chicken curry, veggie chili, tuna mayo, and the like. Park yourself on one of the low stone steps surrounding Covent Garden, watch the many street performers, you've got yourself a cheap, satisfying, and memorably atmospheric on-the-go meal.

£–££ You gotta love the **Café in the Crypt** ★★ (Trafalgar Square, WC2; ☎ 020/7766-1158; www.stmartin-in-the-fields.org; Mon–Wed 8am–8:30pm, Thurs–Sat 8am–10:30pm, Sun noon–6:30pm; MC, V; Tube: Charing Cross), the most delicious graveyard I know. Under the sanctuary of the historic St. Martin-in-the-Fields church, atop the gravestones of eighteenth-century Londoners, one of the West End's sharpest bargains is served each day. The menu at this dependable cafeteria changes daily, but the satisfying options always include a few hot meat mains, a vegetarian choice, soups, and a traditional English dessert such as bread and butter pudding or apple crumble, all homemade—even the strawberries are topped with rich, fresh whipped cream. The soup-and-pudding deal is £5.75, and mains are £6.25 to £7.95, including three vegetables. Soup with bread is £3.85. As proof that this busy diner isn't stuffy (after all, it shares space with a gift shop and a brass rubbing center), it even serves wine for £2.95 a glass. Twice a month, it hosts evening jazz nights (£5–£8 entry) along with a £9 dinner (main, pudding, and wine).

£–££ A long-running vegetarian whole foods kitchen, **Food for Thought** (31 Neal St., WC2; ☎ 020/7836-0239; Mon–Sat noon–8:30pm, Sun noon–5pm; no credit cards; Tube: Covent Garden), feels like a commune, what with the mismatched plates, and a changing slate of three or four dinner items (casseroles, salads, stir-fries, bakes, couscous, etc.) that often run out after 6 or 7pm. The basement dining room is elbow-to-elbow—just eight tables. I find the offerings (spooned out in huge portions) to be heavy on the beans, and I make liberal use of the salt and pepper since the food is so "clean," but I also like the earthy, doing-right-by-my-body sensation I get after I wipe my plate here. There's no doubt the price is right, especially for the area. The fruity, sugary "scrunch" at dessert reverses some of the virtuous feelings. A full dinner tops out at £7, but most people will be satisfied with what £4.50 buys.

£–££ Strong in the pre-theater eat-and-run department, the West End standby **Gaby's Deli** (30 Charing Cross Rd., WC2; ☎ 020/7836-4233; Mon–Sat 11am–midnight, Sun noon–10pm; no credit cards; Tube: Leicester Square) makes a lame attempt at rustic decor—pinning ladles to the wall does not a design concept make—but it puts more effort into its singularly affordable bites. Grab stuff a la carte (falafel for £4, salt beef sandwiches for £5.50), or spring for the day's special (a typical sample: giant stuffed peppers served with falafel balls or a starter of tuna salad, £7). The vegetable fritters (£3.50 with hummus), big as saucers and stacked in the window, often stop passers-by in their tracks.

££ One of the Chinatown rabble worth pausing for, the cramped **Mr. Kong** (21 Lisle St., WC2; ☎ 020/7437-7341; Mon–Sat noon–2:45am, Sun noon–1:45am; AE, DC, MC, V; Tube: Leicester Square), across from the Prince Charles Cinema, works from a lengthy Cantonese menu, and works it well. It's not much to look at, and its steely waiters treat patrons as little more than business transactions, but it's one of the few establishments to supplement Western-style Chinese dishes with daring ones (starring eel, soft-shell crab with chilies, and the like, mostly in the £7 zone). In addition to laying claim to a following of Asian-born devotees, who order razor clams and scallops by the bowlful, it's kid-friendly and serves until the wee hours.

££–£££ In London, there's a Browns for fashion, and a Brown's Hotel, but the spacious cafe **Browns** ★ (82-84 St. Martins Lane, WC2; ☎ 020/7497-5050; www.browns-restaurants.com; Mon–Wed 9am–11pm, Thurs–Fri 9am–11:30pm, Sat

10am–11pm, Sun 10am–10:30pm; AE, MC, V; Tube: Leicester Square) is the Browns you can afford. Installed in the former Westminster County Courts, it serves updated English food and imported beer. The globe lanterns, enormous mirrors, and staff buttoned into crisp white oxford shirts impart the sense of a Gilded Age chop house. Expect lots of indulgently hearty dishes such as salad with watermelon and duck, sea bream garnished with fried beans and hazelnuts, and a nice fat bacon cheeseburger. Lunch specials are always posted on the blackboards, and the pre-theater menu gets you two courses for £13. Otherwise, many mains are under £12 and two-course kids' menus are £5. Come for a bistro-style afternoon tea (2pm–5:30pm), where you get the works for £6.75. There's another Browns at 47 Maddox St. in Mayfair (Tube: Oxford Circus), a riverside one southeast of Tower Bridge (Butlers Wharf; Tube: London Bridge or Tower Hill), and one at 9 Islington Green (Tube: Angel).

££–£££ The victuals are barely more than steam-table chow, but the atmosphere is matchless at **Gordon's Wine Bar** ★★★ (47 Villiers St., WC2; ☎ 020/7930-1408; www.gordonswinebar.com; Mon–Fri 8am–11pm, Sat 11am–11pm, Sun noon–10pm; AE, MC, V; Tube: Charing Cross or Embankment), London's oldest and friendliest wine bar. It was established in 1890 (when Rudyard Kipling lived upstairs) and, thank goodness, hasn't been significantly refurbished since. These crusty old cellars are wallpapered with important newspaper front pages from the 20th century—the Crystal Palace's destruction by fire, the death of King George VI—while ceiling fans threaten to come loose from their screws. Everything has been dyed a mustardy ochre from more than 42,000 past evenings of tobacco smoke. It's so resistant to change that tables are still candlelit, and music is not played—not that you could hear it over the din of conversation. Dozens of wines and sherries by the glass are around £4, and you can select from a marble display of English and French cheeses. Eats include port-drenched pork pie with salad (£7.50) and homemade Scotch eggs, a favorite (£6.95). The scene is unmissable. Come down well before offices let out to secure seating in the tight, craggy cellars, which tunnel intimately in vaults beneath pedestrianized Villiers Street.

££–£££ Ignore that it looks like every other curry shop sponging off the Covent Garden tourist trade. **Punjab Restaurant** ★★★ (80 Neal St., WC2; ☎ 020/7836-9787; www.punjab.co.uk; Mon–Sat noon–3pm and 6–11:30pm, Sun noon–3pm and 6–10:30pm; AE, MC, V; Tube: Covent Garden) has been cooking since 1947—it proclaims itself the oldest North Indian restaurant in the U.K. Beneath its golden twill wallpaper, you could end up sitting next to an elderly fellow who has his lunch there five times a week, or by editors finalizing the layout of their new children's book. The common bond, of course, is superlative cooking, light on the oil and *ghee* (clarified butter), and a staff of old fellas, many in turbans, who have worked here for decades. Meats (from £7.65) and tandoori (from £7.95) have been well marinated, and so they arrive tender. But what I dream about when I'm not in London is the *anari gosht,* or pomegranate-flavored lamb (£8.40). The flavors dovetail gorgeously with every bite, winding up with a slight spicy twang. The menu is cheeky, too: "If you have any erotic activities planned for after you leave us, perhaps you should resist this sensational garlic naan." (And, yes, resistance would be a mistake.) I have been threatened with bodily harm for revealing this find, but to share such bliss is worth it. Reserve ahead on weekends or face the queue.

Meat the Newcomers

As much as it irks Londoners to admit they're adopting any aspect of American culture, it's true that the humble hamburger is becoming a staple of the British scene. Not only does every pub now serve them, but a few quickly multiplying restaurants also specialize in replicating that delicacy of the Texas plains. Here are the biggest new chains and how their menus stack up:

££ Fine Burger Co. (50 James St., W1; ☎ 020/7224-1890; www.fineburger.co.uk; daily noon–10pm; AE, MC, V; Tube: Bond Street; or 330 Upper St., N1; ☎ 020/7359-3026; Tube: Angel). Regular: £5.45. With cheese: £6.45. Weirdest: American Deli, with salami and pickles, £7.25. Guiltiest pleasure: Peanut butter and banana milkshake, £3.45.

££ Gourmet Burger Kitchen (15 Frith St., W1; ☎ 020/7494-9533; Mon–Fri noon–11pm, Sat 11am–11pm, Sun 11am–10pm; Tube: Tottenham Court Road; or 13-14 Maiden Lane, WC2; ☎ 020/7240-9617; Tube: Charing Cross; or Condor House, St. Paul's Church Yard, EC4; ☎ 020/7248-9199; Tube: St. Paul's; or 107 Old Brompton Rd., SW7; ☎ 020/7581-8942; Tube: South Kensington). Regular: £5.75. With cheese: £6.85. Weirdest: Kiwiburger, with beets, egg, and pineapple, £7.95. Guiltiest pleasure: Oreo milkshake, £3.45.

£–££ Hamburger Union (4-6 Garrick St., WC2; ☎ 020/7379-0412; www.hamburgerunion.com; Sun–Mon 11am–9:30pm, Tues–Sat 11:30am–10:30pm; MC, V; Tube: Covent Garden; or 22-25 Dean St., W1; ☎ 020/7437-6004; Tube: Tottenham Court Road; or southeast corner of Leicester Square; ☎ 020/7839-811; Tube: Leicester Square; or 341 Upper St., N1; ☎ 020/7359-4436; Tube: Angel). Regular: £3.95. With cheese: £4.65. Weirdest: Blue cheese and vegetable sausage, £5.45. Guiltiest pleasure: Crème de Menthe cocktail milkshake, £3.95.

££ The Ultimate Burger (34 New Oxford St., WC1; ☎ 020/7436-6641; www.ultimateburger.co.uk; Mon–Sat noon–11pm, Sun noon–10pm; AE, MC, V; Tube: Holborn; or 36-38 Glasshouse St., W1; ☎ 020/7287-8429; Tube: Piccadilly Circus; or 98 Tottenham Court Rd., W1; ☎ 020/7436-5355; Tube: Warren Street). Regular: £5.65. With cheese: £6.55. Weirdest: The Sunday Roast, with Yorkshire pudding and hot horseradish, £6.95. Guiltiest pleasure: Chili fries, £2.95.

££–£££ Unbeknownst to many tourists, an oasis of fun restaurants awaits on the street south of Leicester Square, and one of its most enjoyable is **Saharaween ★** (3 Panton St., W1; ☎ 020/7930-2777; daily noon–midnight; MC, V; Tube: Leicester Square), which means "people of the Sahara." Relaxation sets in when you cross its threshold. In a dim, cool, two-level space, candles flicker behind lattices, fabric billows against the ceiling, and couples lounge on pillows eating off silver tables. (There are standard seats, too.) Start with the satisfying chorba soup (£4.50), a North African specialty as velvety as chili but without meat. Move on to couscous with chicken (£10) or, more theatrically, to the tagine casbah, a stew of minced meat, garlic, coriander, and cumin prepared in a clay pot and topped with egg, for £11; when it arrives, the waitress lifts its lid, releasing a flourish of steam. End with a hot cup of mint tea. Check for its off-weekend prix fixe of three courses and wine for £15. The service is relaxed, so set aside at least an hour—longer if you'd like to puff on the hookah pipe.

££–£££ A 30-strong international vegetarian chain, **Woodlands** (37 Panton St., SW1; ☎ 020/7839-7258; www.woodlandsrestaurant.co.uk; daily noon–11:30pm; AE, MC, V; Tube: Leicester Square) should be seen for what it is: a casual place for reliable South Indian food. It's decorated as if someone raided a Crate and Barrel, and the recorded smooth jazz is just as bland. Woodlands does a range of dishes, though, including snack-worthy *chaat* (crispy pastry rounds you stuff with chutneys, from £4.95), but its signature is the dosa, an enormous crepe made from soaked lentils and rice, formed into a cone, and stuffed with one of eight fillings. The onion *rava masala dosa* (£6.50), my favorite, has a crepe flecked with sautéed green chilies and a filling of potatoes, onions, and peas. Of course, when a dosa arrives, your table suddenly looks like an old gramophone. Order Kingfisher, an Indian beer (slogan: "most thrilling chilled"). It's also at 77 Marylebone Lane (Tube: Bond Street).

£££–££££ Keep your eyes peeled for celebrities at **The Ivy** ★ (1 West St., WC1; ☎ 020/7836-4751; www.the-ivy.co.uk; Mon–Sat noon–3pm and 5:30–midnight, Sun noon–3:30pm and 5:30–11pm; AE, MC, V; Tube: Leicester Square or Covent Garden); Britain's biggest stars (Look! Hugh Grant! Ooh! Simon Cowell!) come here to be seen while dining in its wood paneled, stained-glassed halls, which have been serving for nearly a century. The food is sumptuous, spanning Britain to Thailand to Italy, and served by some of the city's most professional waiters, but you will pay for the scene. Try the slow-roasted pork belly (£17), something off the vegetable submenu (get asparagus if it's on; the Ivy does it well), or a freshened-up view on fish and chips with deep-fried haddock served with minted pea puree and chips (£18). When it's in season, don't miss the stunner of a rhubarb pie. Its Sunday lunch set meal, for around £27 for three courses, is not a bad price for cooking of this level. Book way ahead—like, now.

£££–££££ What if Mozart went insane? He'd open the flamboyant **Sarastro** ★ (126 Drury Lane, WC2; ☎ 020/7836-0101; www.sarastro-restaurant.com; daily noon–11:30pm; AE, MC, V; Tube: Covent Garden), an over-the-top paean to the opulence of opera. Sarastro's every cranny has been gilded, sheathed in shimmering fabric, or filled with erotic statuary (you can't miss the self-pleasuring Diablo). Along the walls, ten intimate opera boxes, reached up precarious stairs, survey the silliness. You'd think that all this hammy folderol would come with tourist-trap prices, but amazingly, a standard two-course meal clocks in at around £18. The menu—like it matters amid such eye candy—is Mediterranean, though not as fun as the setting. The "chicken Princess," tender and savory with asparagus and red wine sauce, goes for £9.95, while lobster thermidor, among the priciest choices, is £18. On Sundays and on Monday evenings, opera singers serenade diners (the £25 entry price includes three courses).

£££–££££ If you want a West End restaurant experience that's both stylish and reasonably priced, **Souk Medina** ★★ (1a Shorts Gardens, WC2; ☎ 020/7240-1796; www.soukrestaurant.co.uk; daily noon–midnight; AE, MC, V; Tube: Covent Garden) plays the swinging Marrakech hideaway to the hilt—stairways are elaborately candlelit and winding; and romantic nooks are heaped with pillows and illuminated by silvery lamps. Cocktails (the aicha martini has vodka, watermelon, and vanilla), dispensed by fez-wearing bartenders, are priced below the London average (£4–£5.95). Couscous with chicken or *merguez* (lamb sausage) starts at £11, and clay-pot tagines start at £11 (I love the lamb with prune, apple, and almonds); plenty of vegetarian versions (£9.50) are also on hand. After dinner, share a pot-bellied, silver shisha pipe packed with mild, flavored tobacco, easy even for nonsmokers (from £7.50). The place is jumping on weekends, so reserve ahead. If you want a subtler Moroccan evening, try Saharaween on nearby Panton Street (p. 111).

££££ For a high-end kitchen that takes British cuisine seriously, **Rules** (35 Maiden Lane, WC1; ☎ 020/7836-5314; www.rules.co.uk; Mon–Sat noon–11:45pm, Sun noon–10:45; AE, MC, V; Tube: Covent Garden) is an iconic choice. In fact, it's London's oldest restaurant, having been cooking since 1798. Being a major stop on the tourist trail has gone slightly to its head, and its view of a dining experience is steeped in its own hype; beer comes in a "silver tankard," for example, and the dining rooms are an overdressed mélange of yellowing etchings, antlers, and rich red fabrics. But what's on the plate, much of it English-reared meat like venison and pheasant, suits the lofty set pieces: steak and kidney pie with oyster pudding (£18), grilled calves liver and bacon (£19), and roast rack of West Devon lamb (£24). For a real taste of country England, try a cool glass of Pimms No. 1 Cup (£11), an apertif of orange peel, Champagne, and the famous tonic made of herbs and quinine.

WESTMINSTER & ST. JAMES'S

I'll warn you now: Westminster may be where you find some of the city's top tourist attractions, but it's a dead zone for food. For more options, walk across Westminster Bridge to South Bank or up Whitehall to Leicester Square.

£–££ The mid-century "caff" diner, once a staple of London life, is rapidly being swept into Formica heaven by trendy bistros, coffee bars, and triangle sandwich sellers. As Edwin Heathcote puts it in his elegiac 2004 book *London Caffs,* "the increasingly sparse network of surviving refuges represents the dying, but still steaming, breath of a particular moment in the city's history." The precious few left in central London, some garish, some plain, are as "of their moment" as Bakelite, Rolleiflexes, and Edsels. Among the few holdouts in central London is the 1940s **Regency Cafe** (17-19 Regency St., SW1; ☎ 020/7821-6596; Mon–Fri

Head East, Old Man

As London accepts more working foreigners, American influence, and health-aware lifestyles, traditional British grub, which was tailored to workers who once burned far more calories, is on the decline. But traditional British cuisine isn't dead. You find it where style and flash have yet to entirely quash tradition—the East End.

£–££ Northeast of Spitalfields, **E. Pellicci** ★ (332 Bethnal Green Rd., E2; ☎ 020/7739-4873; Mon–Sat 6:30am–5pm; Tube: Bethnal Green) is a caff-style fry-up that's been run by the affable Nevio family for generations (some of them were born upstairs). The Deco interior, a mélange of sunburst icons and laminates, was designed just after World War II and is now protected by law. Besides serving as a hangout for artists (and once, for gangsters), many of whom have signed photos for the wall, meals are a steal: under £8, most often £5. Italian dishes are done, but you'd most want to come for its English breakfast, when heaping plates of beans, eggs, and chunky chips are flung about to assuage clubbers' hangovers. To call meals hearty would be more than accurate, although ironically, the heart would suffer the most from their regular consumption. Help yourself to the range of on-table condiments (the HP sauce, in the brown bottle, is my choice for potatoes). There's no more iconic caff in town.

££–££££ You may have heard about the so-called "gastropub" movement, in which old pubs are given new identities as gourmet restaurants. Unlike the pubs they have refurbished, most gastropubs are too high-priced for comfort, but there's at least one that retains a populist atmosphere—you can stop by anytime for a pint and sublime riverfront views of the old shipping lanes. Gordon Ramsay, the blustery celebrity chef, opened

7am–2pm and 4:30–7pm, Sat 7am–noon; Tube: Pimlico), an elegy to another age in black and white tiles. This isn't a gastronomic treasure (the fryer is in heavy use); it's an anthropological one. And an efficient one—meals are prepared with lightning speed, and when they're ready, your order is loudly announced by a throaty man so that you can come fetch it. It's an excellent value, too (average mains £6, all-day breakfasts £5). So rare is the caff nowadays that the Regency has a tidy sideline as a movie location. Have a cuppa while it's still steaming. For another marvelous caff, see E. Pellicci (above).

THE CITY, SPITALFIELDS & WHITECHAPEL

£ The city's most famous bakery, Jewish or otherwise, **Beigel Bake** ★★★ (159 Brick Lane, E1; ☎ 020/7729-0616; daily 24 hr.; no credit cards; Tube: Liverpool Street) never closes but there's always a line. The queue moves quickly, though, and it snakes past the kitchen, where you can glimpse the bakers using strange contraptions and wooden planks. The patronage is a microcosm of London, ranging from

The Narrow ★★★ (44 Narrow St., E14; ☎ 020/7592-7950; www.gordonramsay.com/thenarrow; Mon–Fri 11:30am–3pm and 6–11pm, Sat noon–4pm and 5–11pm, Sun noon–4pm and 5–10:30pm; AE, MC, V; reservations recommended; Tube: Limehouse DLR) to wild success in the spring of 2007. Here, in a skylit restaurant area, his henpecked minions deliver delicious, uncluttered British dishes (quiche, fish, steaks, pig's cheek, sticky toffee pudding) with a near-religious emphasis on high-quality seasonal ingredients for £8 to £16 per main—about as affordable as a gastropub gets. The bar area (no reservations) also serves light meals for around £7; try the ploughman's, a beloved farmer's snack of bread, rich cheese, and tangy "pickle" spread. Because of its culinary care and the chance to taste food created by an international talent, this is a top value, and the gastropub I'd choose.

As it happens, the Thames estuary east of London is a welcoming habitat for eels; so as far back as can be remembered, they've been an East End dietary staple. The most popular presentation has long been **jellied eels,** in which the slippery fish is stewed, cools until a jelly forms, and is often served with spicy vinegar. Although I like eels in sushi form, I detest this stuff, and so must lots of other people, because the East End is one of the only places you can find it. A few roving carts sell servings for a couple of quid (Tubby Isaacs appears near Goulston and Whitechapel High sts., by the Aldgate Tube). You can also find it served at a few "pie and mash" diners such as **F. Cooke's Pie and Mash** (150 Hoxton St., N1; ☎ 020/7729-7718; Mon–Thurs 10am–7pm, Fri–Sat 9:30am–8pm; Tube: Old Street). If you do partake, take care not to knock them back in disgust, because they contain bones. Yeah, a charming snack.

bikers to hipsters to arrogant yuppies to the homeless. Its beigels ("BI-gulls") are not as puffy or as salty as the New York "bagel" variety, and they even come filled for under £1.50. Its pastries are gorgeous, too: The chocolate fudge brownie, less than £1, could be nursed for hours. Watching the clerks slice juicy chunks of pink salt beef in the window, then slather it onto a beigel with mustard from a crusty jar (£3.50 and too much to eat), is an attraction unto itself.

£–££ In this age, no one would dare name their takeaway something as hydrogenated as **The Fryer's Delight** ★★★ (19 Theobald's Rd., WC1; ☎ 020/7405-4114; Mon–Sat noon–10pm; no credit cards; Tube: Holborn or Chancery Lane). Fortunately, this takeaway is not of this age. It's a true old-world chippy, where the fish is served crisp, chips come in paper wrappings, the wooden booths date to the postwar days, and the men behind the counter gruffly demand to have your order. Prices are anachronistic, too: Of the six types of fish (I like the cod), nothing's more expensive than £5 (takeaway; eat-in prices are about £1 more),

Brick Lane: 24-Hour Playground

Central London has few thoroughfares that are associated with a single ethnic group or nationality, but Brick Lane (so named for its medieval status as a source for bricks), once a Jewish area, has become so strongly identified with immigrants from the Indian subcontinent that its name has transcended geography to become a sort of shorthand term for England's South Asian population. In the span of just a few blocks, most of which have signage in both English and Bengali, lines of Indian restaurants jockey for business. No discerning Londoner would claim that any serve the city's best Indian cuisine—most of them are run by Bangladeshi or Pakistani entrepreneurs catering to the average Englishman's milder notion of northern curries—or even that there's much difference between them, but it's nonetheless a terrific place to stroll along, leverage competition, and shop for a bargain meal. (Bring your own wine, though, since most are run by Muslims who don't sell alcohol.) By day, the connecting Dray Walk is a short block of sophisticated boutiques and laid-back cafes. By night, Brick Lane morphs into a hipster habitat as a major street for music venues. On Sunday, it hosts a market for vintage clothes, produce, books, and art (www.bricklanemarket.com). Reach Brick Lane via the Aldgate, Aldgate East, or Liverpool Street Tube.

and most are around £4. Seamy? Not at all—it's just one of the last hangers-on from the lost fish-and-chips tradition, so get a taste while you still can. It's a 10-minute walk east of the British Museum.

£–££ England's country links rule **S&M Cafe** (48 Brushfield St., E1; ☎ 020/7247-2252; www.sandmcafe.co.uk; Mon–Fri 7:30am–10:30pm, Sat–Sun 8:30am–10:30pm; MC, V; Tube: Liverpool Street), also known as Sausage & Mash, opposite Spitalfields Market. Introduce yourself to the world of wieners and mash at one of its diner-style tables, covered with classic red checkered plastic: Cumberlands are pork with treacle; another is made of wild boar with apples; and there's one that mixes leek and Caerphilly cheese (see, vegetarians aren't ignored). They make Oscar Meyer look like a clown. Don't forget the mushy peas—a lurid green, cherished British side. Full breakfasts are £5.75, all day, and there's a kids' menu. Outposts are well located for shoppers: 268 Portobello Rd. in Notting Hill (Tube: Ladbroke Grove), and 4–6 Essex Rd. in Islington (Tube: Angel), while a third is at the O_2 (Tube: North Greenwich). The Islington one is in a fine old cafeteria, once the longstanding Alfredo's, full of 50-year-old tilework, fittings, and signs (such as "Ices 3d. 4d. 6d.").

££ Of my favorite restaurant finds, **Little Bay** ★★★ (171 Farringdon Rd., WC1; ☎ 020/7278-1234; www.little-bay.co.uk; Mon–Sat noon–midnight, Sun noon–11pm; no credit cards; Tube: Farringdon) is a quirky contender for the best value in town.

Spitalfields Dining

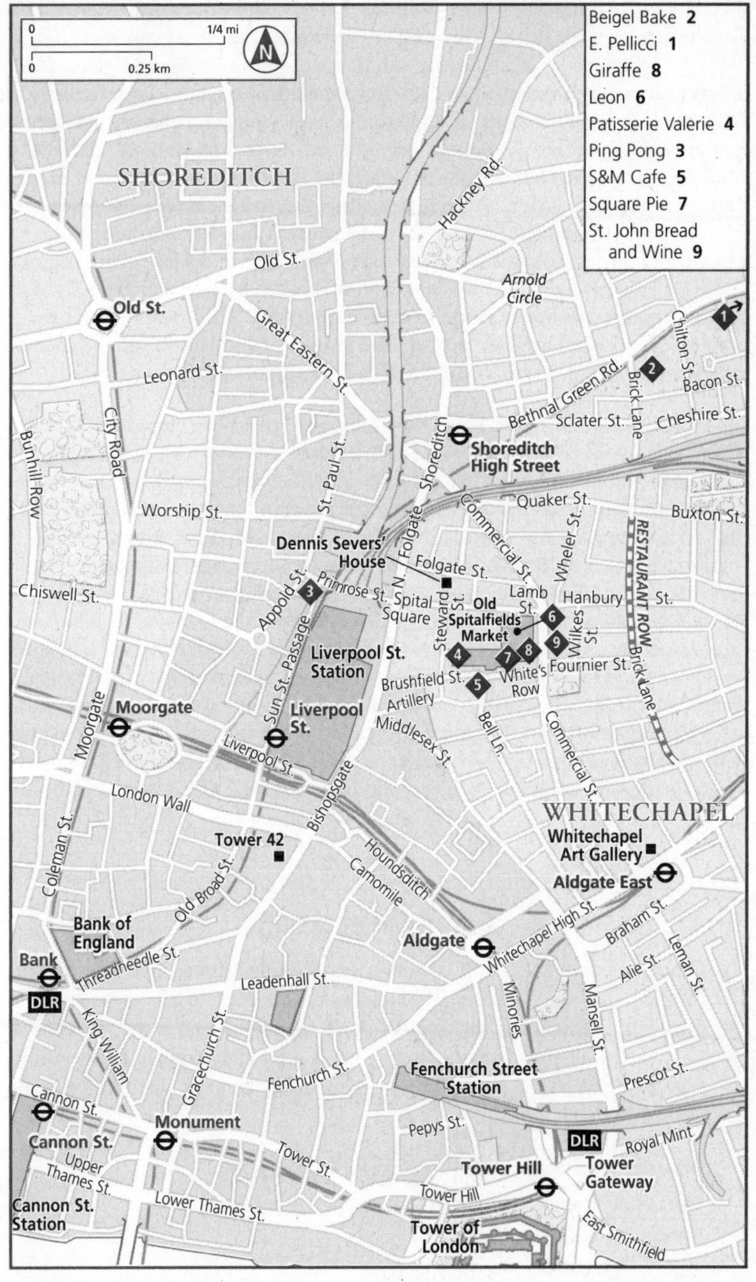

0
1/4 mi
0
0.25 km
N
Beigel Bake 2
E. Pellicci 1
Giraffe 8
Leon 6
Patisserie Valerie 4
Ping Pong 3
S&M Cafe 5
Square Pie 7
St. John Bread and Wine 9
SHOREDITCH
Hackney Rd.
Old St.
Arnold Circle
Old St.
Great Eastern St.
Leonard St.
Bethnal Green Rd.
Chilton St.
Brick Lane
Bacon St.
Sclater St.
Cheshire St.
Bunhill Row
City Road
St. Paul St.
Shoreditch
Shoreditch High Street
Quaker St.
Buxton St.
Worship St.
Folgate
Commercial St.
Wheler St.
RESTAURANT ROW
Dennis Severs' House
Folgate St.
Chiswell St.
Appold St.
Primrose St.
N.
Spital Square
Steward St.
Lamb St.
Hanbury St.
Old Spitalfields Market
Wilkes St.
Sun St. Passage
Liverpool St. Station
Brushfield St.
White's Row
Fournier St.
Brick Lane
Artillery
Moorgate
Moorgate
Liverpool St.
Middlesex St.
Bell Ln.
Commercial St.
Liverpool St.
London Wall
Bishopsgate
WHITECHAPEL
Coleman St.
Tower 42
Houndsditch
Camomile
Whitechapel Art Gallery
Aldgate East
Old Broad St.
Bank of England
Aldgate
Whitechapel High St.
Braham St.
Leman St.
Bank
Threadneedle St.
Alie St.
DLR
Leadenhall St.
Minories
Mansell St.
King William
Gracechurch St.
Fenchurch St.
Fenchurch Street Station
Prescot St.
Cannon St.
Pepys St.
Monument
Cannon St.
DLR
Royal Mint
Upper Thames St.
Tower St.
Tower Hill
Tower Gateway
Tower Hill
Cannon St. Station
Lower Thames St.
Tower of London
East Smithfield

It's a tad out of the way (10-min. walk north of the Tube, opposite Vineyard Walk, or 15 min. east of the British Museum) in Clerkenwell, but that's why it's a find. The decor is beyond fab—a Romanesque fun house of plaster murals and gnarled chandeliers overseen by a massive mask of Zeus adorned with tendrils of metallic fabric. ("But he looks more like Jesus Christ with the Statue of Liberty's hat on," cracked my waitress one day.) Even without a deal, you can have three courses and wine for around £13, and even less before 7pm when the £10 three-course special is in effect. Rarely has paying so little afforded such dignity: The menu changes, but on one visit, I received an astounding 22 mussels in my mussels marinier (shallots, garlic, and white wine) for my piddly £2—and yes, they were fresh and well sauced. Mains are just as generous. Possibilities may include a duck and leek parcel with braised red cabbage and ginger and honey sauce; fillet of salmon with spicy coconut potatoes; or a hearty roast lamb or baked red pepper. It's a favorite of journalists from the *Guardian* offices nearby. Sunday is roast day: £6.50 including potatoes and vegetables.

££–££££ Hand-in-hand with the gastropub trend is "nose-to-tail" eating. That's when your chef doesn't waste a single part of the animal, resulting in tastes that were commonplace to his agrarian English forefathers (heart, cockscomb, marrow, whole pigeon) but are new to most Western tongues. Most places charge, um, an arm and leg for it, but you can sample it at **St. John Bread & Wine** (96 Commercial St., E1; ☎ 020/7251-0848; www.stjohnbreadandwine.com; Mon–Fri 9am–11pm, Sat 10am–11pm, Sun 10am–10:30pm; reservations recommended; AE, MC, V; Tube: Aldgate East), a lower-priced offshoot of the fancier St. John restaurant. Walls are simple white, chairs are plain wood, and the kitchen staff is serious about good food, no matter its form. The menu changes every few hours from traditional breakfast to daring dabbles, but before 7pm, expect plates for about £6 (after 7pm, prices zoom to around £15 a plate). Experience dishes like cold lamb with chicory and anchovy, smoked sprat (sardines) with horseradish, and laverbread (made with seaweed) with oats and bacon. A meal here can be an adventure

Grape Expectations

Many popular restaurants don't have licenses to serve alcohol, but they will allow you to bring your own ("BYO"). Most places charge a £1 to £3 "corkage fee" for the privilege. Fortunately, the English don't tolerate a bad quaff, so even the cheapest bottles of store-bought stuff (£3–£7) are highly drinkable. You can pick up some excellent hooch on the go at the following common High Street chains:

Oddbins (www.oddbins.com)
Majestic Wine Warehouse (www.majestic.co.uk)
Marks and Spencer (www.marksandspencer.com)
Threshers (www.threshergroup.com)
Sainsbury's (www.sainsburys.co.uk)

(ever eaten dandelion?), but fortunately, because of the sensible prices and the fact that most plates are designed to be shared, trying something you don't like won't hit your wallet too hard. St. John also makes terrific homemade bread, so if your palate fails, your hunger still won't prevail.

££–£££ Finding something for everyone in your group can be a tall order, but then again, what's taller than a **Giraffe** (kids) (Crispin Place, Spitalfields Market, E1; ☎ 020/3116-2000; www.giraffe.net; Mon–Fri 8am–11pm, Sat 9am–11pm, Sun 9am–10:30pm; AE, MC, V; Tube: Liverpool Street)? This cheerful, contemporary chain—like an enlightened Friday's for the new century—has quickly become ubiquitous based on a rangy menu that includes big salads, burgers, Southeast Asian stir fries and noodle bowls (all mostly around £9), cocktails, and seven much-ordered brunch options (£6–£7.50) available until 4pm daily. Normally, restaurants that try too many genres don't do well, but here, the food is generally satisfying, non-greasy, thoughtfully sourced, and successful. The staff is supernaturally friendly in a theatrical way that Europeans rarely are (maybe they're lifted by the cheerful world music playing throughout). Children are especially well-treated: Look around the airy dining room during the day, and you'll see a forest of helium balloons swinging from each kid's chairback. Check out the same room after dark, and it will be transformed into a candle-lit cafe. Weekdays from 5pm to 7pm, a meal of a starter and a main is £6.95. There are additional locations at Southbank Centre (Tube: Waterloo), the Brunswick Centre near the British Museum (Tube: Russell Square), 6 Blandford St. in Marylebone (Tube: Bond Street), 7 Kensington High St. (Tube: High Street Kensington), and 29–31 Essex Rd. (Tube: Angel).

SOUTHWARK & BOROUGH, INCLUDING AROUND WATERLOO STATION

There's plenty to eat along the south bank of the Thames, which is increasingly lined with mid-level places, mostly chains such as Wagamama or coffee cafes.

£–££ One of those amazing discoveries, the **Southwark Cathedral Refectory** (London Bridge, SE1; ☎ 020/7407-5740; Mon–Fri 8:30am–6pm, Sat–Sun 10am–6pm; no credit cards; Tube: London Bridge) is on the Thames-facing side of the 900-year-old church. Wholesome as a church should be, it concentrates on freshly made soups (like coriander and carrot), sandwiches, quiche, and pasta and stir fry that are made-to-order (all £3–£7). This is no sloppy potluck; desserts are wickedly massive, and even the salads' honey-mustard dressing is made from the real stuff, not bottled junk. Try the elderflower presse, a typically English cordial. The Anglican Church, being modern, displays work by local artists, sells wine by the bottle, and even makes cute napkins with the church's logo on them.

££–££££ It's easy to go overboard at **Yo! Sushi** (kids) (Belvedere Rd., County Hall, SE1; ☎ 020/7928-8871; www.yosushi.com; Mon–Tues noon–10pm, Wed–Sat noon–11pm, Sun noon–8pm; MC, V; Tube: Westminster or Waterloo), on the street behind the London Eye box office, because it's one of those fun conveyor-belt sushi places—you know, you sit at a bar and grab what you want to eat as it cruises

Binging at Borough and Beyond

Londoners are lucky to have Southwark's extravagant **Borough Market** ★★★ (8 Southwark St., SE1; ☎ 020/7407-1002; www.boroughmarket.org.uk; Tube: London Bridge), a rich atmosphere that combines Victorian commercial hubbub with glorious, farm-fresh flavors. About a dozen vendors sell their countryside meats, cheeses, and vegetables all week long, but the market blooms beneath its metal-and-glass canopy Thursdays from 11am to 5pm, Fridays from noon to 6pm, and Saturdays from 9am to 4pm, when up to 130 additional vendors unpack and the awe-inspiring scene hits full swing. The best time to arrive is Thursday or Friday ahead of the lunch crowds; Saturdays are plain nuts.

If there's any country that has wholesome farming down, it's England, and this market is their showplace. If you go when you're hungry, you will dream about its wares for months after returning home. Work up an appetite at **Gorwydd Caerphilly,** which revitalized a nearly forgotten cheese variety—unpasteurized, consumed young, with a thick rind and a lemony taste—and now makes it on its 100-acre Welsh farm (around £2 per 100g/3½ oz.). The **Northfield Farms** stall attracts quite a queue with organically raised beef and lamb burgers, or even ones made of stilton cheese, for £3.50, and **West Country Venison** does deer burgers (£3.50), but the most popular dish at the market is unquestionably the grilled chorizo sandwich at the **Brindisa** booth facing Stone Street; make sure you get yours with oil-drizzled piquillo peppers from Spain (£3.50). My visits to London aren't complete unless I have one. Roast, a hugely popular £19-a-dish restaurant upstairs, shows off its skills until 3pm at its **"Roast to Go"** counter, which charges sharply reduced prices (£5) for its mouthwatering meats like salt beef with pickles or pork and crackling for £5. At **Maria's Market Café,** the moon-faced proprietor slaves over a stove making fresh bubble (kind of a mushy version of home fries) that brings office workers from far and wide (it's £1 on a roll). Enjoy the rich chocolate bonbons of **Dark Sugars** (its delectable truffles, £5.50 for 100g/3½ oz., include offbeat ingredients like chili, dry apple cider, gin, and white chocolate with nutmeg) on the premises, but don't have any sent home; I have twice heard stories of credit cards being charged without the treats being received. Like almost everything at Borough, it's food you can only enjoy in London.

by. Servings are colored according to how much they cost (the decent ones are £2.20–£5). Kids love it. But the protein fix is refreshing for a bread- and noodle-obsessed city, and the fish is fresh. Just take some advice your meal should have heeded: Don't get hooked. Three plates makes for a moderate lunch, and four could spell disaster for your day's spending. Beyond this location, there are ones at 5–14

Seating at the market is limited, which is why many people bring their booty to the benches in the yard of the nearby Southwark Cathedral (p. 119), or to the Thames beyond it.

Outside at 9 Stoney St., wash it down with whatever unusual brew is on tap this month at the **Market Porter,** which is known for daring microbrews. Put your feet up by its double-sided fireplace. Overhead by the Bedale Street market entrance, not far from the market's **Bedales** wine bar, check out the hand-painted wooden panel listing the 90-year-old rent structure for stalls. Got room left? Good—there are a few dozen more stalls to sample. And don't neglect the Green Market, which fills a yard across Bedale Street.

Borough is the best food market, while plenty of others sell mostly produce and raw meats (not so useful for tourists), but there are markets within reach of central London where you can buy cooked foods for a few quid. One of the largest is the **Notting Hill Farmers' Market** (Behind Waterstone's at Kensington Place at Kensington Church, W8; www.lfm.org.uk; Sat 9am–1pm; Tube: Notting Hill Gate), good for ready-made fish pie and chicken soups and near the simultaneous Portobello Road market. The newly created **South Kensington Market** (Bute St., SW7; www.lfm.org.uk; Sat 9am–1pm; Tube: South Kensington), lined with French cafes, often has vendors selling cooked sausages, breads, and organic juices and jams, and not far away at the same time, **Partridges Food Market** ★ (Duke of York Square, SW3; www.partridges.co.uk; Sat 10am–4pm; Tube: Sloane Square), run by a ritzy grocery, hosts some 150 foodie-targeted stalls selling Moroccan food, teas, Thai meals, Caribbean cuisine, and other refined tastes. Office workers use the **Whitecross Weekly Food Market** (Whitecross Street, EC1; www.whitecrossstreetmarket.co.uk; Thurs–Fri 11am–5pm; Tube: Old Street) for cheap Latin food—new to Britain—and curries, little cakes, and cooked sausages. On Sundays, the crowded **Brick Lane UpMarket** ★★ (91 Brick Lane, E1; www.sundayupmarket.co.uk; Sun 10am–5pm) does a wide range of international food, cooked at kiosks. It also sells original fashion items made by Whitechapel artists.

St. Paul's Church Yard (Tube: St. Paul's); the Brunswick Centre (Tube: Russell Square); the Trocadero at 19 Rupert St. (Tube: Piccadilly Circus); Selfridge's at 400 Oxford St. (Tube: Bond Street); Harrods at 102–104 Brompton Rd. (Tube: Knightsbridge); Harvey Nichols at 102–125 Knightsbridge (Tube: Knightsbridge); and St. Pancras, Paddington, and Victoria stations, among other spots.

VICTORIA & CHELSEA

Check the map on p. 123 for more chain outlets in the area, and don't forget that Victoria Station, the busiest train station in the U.K., is well-stocked with inexpensive eats.

££-£££ The one-room, canteen-style **Jenny Lo's Tea House** (14 Eccleston St., SW1; ☎ 020/7259-0399; Mon–Fri noon–3pm and 6–10pm, Sat 6–10pm; no credit cards; Tube: Victoria) is one of the few low-priced restaurants among the dwindling budget hotels of the Ebury Street area, but it comes with a pedigree; the proprietor's late father operated the expensive Ken Lo's Memories of China around the corner. Jenny does Cantonese/Szechwan, and does it quickly, but with less spice than in China, and with more noodles and dumplings, to suit British taste. Soup noodles (like chicken, Chinese mushrooms, and cabbage, £6.50) are large enough to perform as a complete meal. Jenny cares about her dishes, refusing to add MSG, but she won't reshape your view of Chinese food. Mains are £6 to £10.

KENSINGTON, KNIGHTSBRIDGE & EARL'S COURT

When you're near the major museums, the closest inexpensive food options are found either in those institutions' on-site cafes or among the corporate establishments on Old Brompton Road, which leads southwest from the South Kensington Tube station house. One block west of there, block-long Bute Street is like a mini-Paris, lined with several French patisseries with outdoor cafe seating.

££ Serving Indian food in a stylish environment of fire engine–red walls and clear glass, **Masala Zone** ★ (147 Earl's Court Rd., SW5; ☎ 020/7373-0220; www.masalazone.com; Mon–Fri 12:30–3pm, and 5:30–11pm, Sat 12:30–11pm, Sun 12:30–10:30pm; MC, V; Tube: Earl's Court) is another affordable minichain. It's also smart enough not to sacrifice Indian authenticity or spice for a modern personality; its slogan is "real Indian food at unreal prices." Among the wholesome marquee items are the *thalis* (£8–£11), the working man's lunch of breads, stews, and sauces served on a large platter; and *masala dosa,* a cone-shaped bread sheaf stuffed with a potato-based filling—think of it as Bombay bubble. Mains are £7 to £8; before 6:30pm, two courses are £8.35. Locations are also at 48 Floral St. (Tube: Covent Garden), 80 Upper St. (Tube: Angel), and 9 Marshall St. (Tube: Oxford Circus).

££–£££ Some chains just do things better than others, and **Bella Italia** ★ (60 Old Brompton Rd., SW7; ☎ 020/7584-4028; www.bellapasta.co.uk; daily 8am–11pm; AE, MC, V; Tube: South Kensington), decorated in a mild, urban-Tuscan style, is one of the winners. It's the best Italian-style chain among the many vying for your attention. Flavors here simply strike the right balance. Roasted vegetables (£2.75)—a medley of courgettes, onions, peppers, squash, and sage—arrive neither too oily nor too hot. The pastas taste exactly as advertised and span from £6.25 to just over £89 for noodles with meatballs, chicken, duck, pancetta, and so on. There are also nine personal pizzas (£5.95–£8.50) to choose

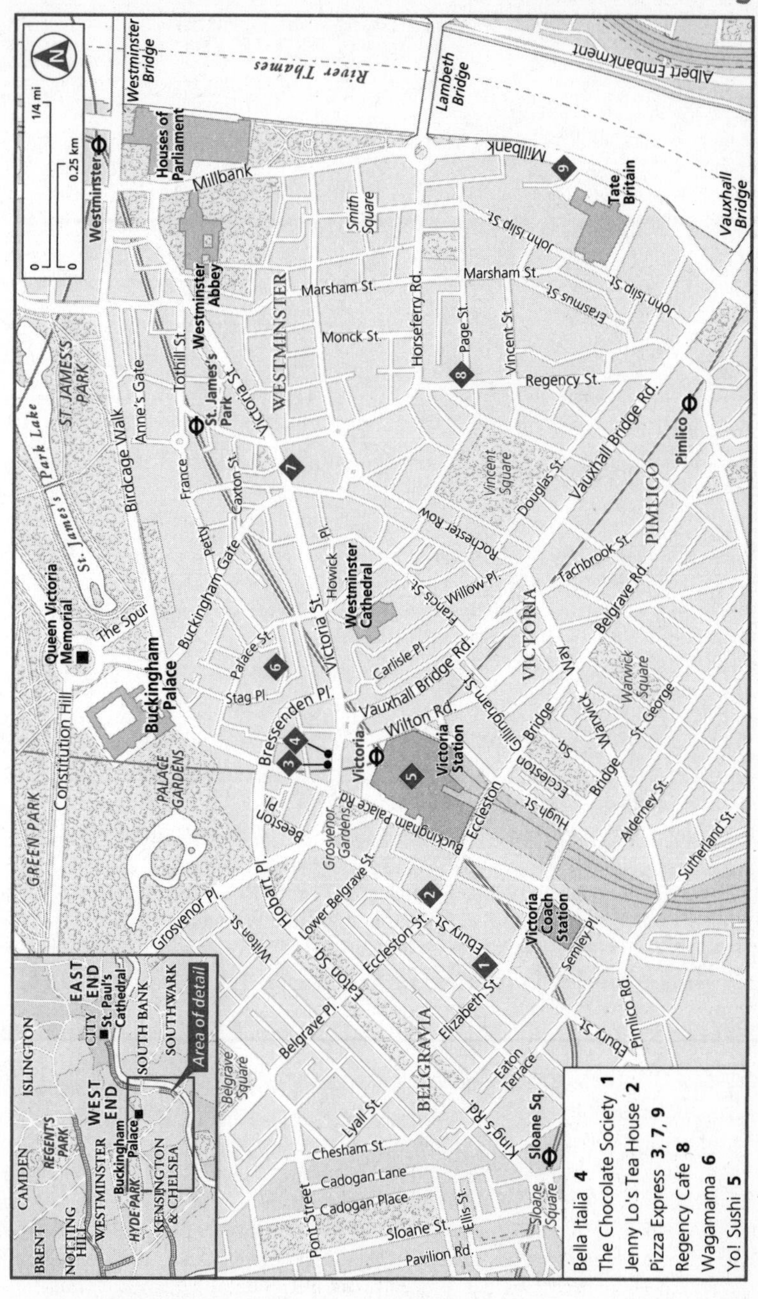
Bella Italia 4
The Chocolate Society 1
Jenny Lo's Tea House 2
Pizza Express 3, 7, 9
Regency Cafe 8
Wagamama 6
Yo! Sushi 5
Area of detail
CAMDEN
ISLINGTON
BRENT
NOTTING HILL
WESTMINSTER
REGENT'S PARK
HYDE PARK
WEST END
CITY
EAST END
St. Paul's Cathedral
Buckingham Palace
SOUTH BANK
SOUTHWARK
KENSINGTON & CHELSEA
0.25 km
1/4 mi
River Thames
Albert Embankment
Westminster Bridge
Lambeth Bridge
Vauxhall Bridge
Houses of Parliament
Westminster
Millbank
Westminster Abbey
Smith Square
Tate Britain
John Islip St.
Marsham St.
Erasmus St.
Horseferry Rd.
Page St.
Vincent St.
Monck St.
Regency St.
WESTMINSTER
Tothill St.
St. James's Park
Victoria St.
ST. JAMES'S PARK
Park Lake
St. James's
Birdcage Walk
Anne's Gate
France
Petty
Caxton St.
Buckingham Gate
Queen Victoria Memorial
The Spur
Buckingham Palace
Constitution Hill
GREEN PARK
PALACE GARDENS
Palace St.
Stag Pl.
Bressenden Pl.
Howick Pl.
Westminster Cathedral
Carlisle Pl.
Francis St.
Willow Pl.
Rochester Row
Vincent Square
Douglas St.
Vauxhall Bridge Rd.
Pimlico
PIMLICO
Tachbrook St.
Belgrave Rd.
VICTORIA
Wilton Rd.
Victoria
Victoria Station
Gillingham St.
Warwick Way
Warwick Square
St. George
Eccleston Bridge
Eccleston Sq.
Hugh St.
Alderney St.
Sutherland St.
Beeston Pl.
Buckingham Palace Rd.
Grosvenor Gardens
Eccleston
Grosvenor Pl.
Hobart Pl.
Lower Belgrave St.
Wilton St.
Eaton Sq.
Eccleston St.
Ebury St.
Victoria Coach Station
Semley Pl.
Elizabeth St.
BELGRAVIA
Belgrave Pl.
Belgrave Square
Pimlico Rd.
Eaton Terrace
King's Rd.
Sloane Sq.
Sloane Square
Lyall St.
Chesham St.
Cadogan Lane
Cadogan Place
Pont Street
Sloane St.
Ellis St.
Pavilion Rd.

Kensington Dining

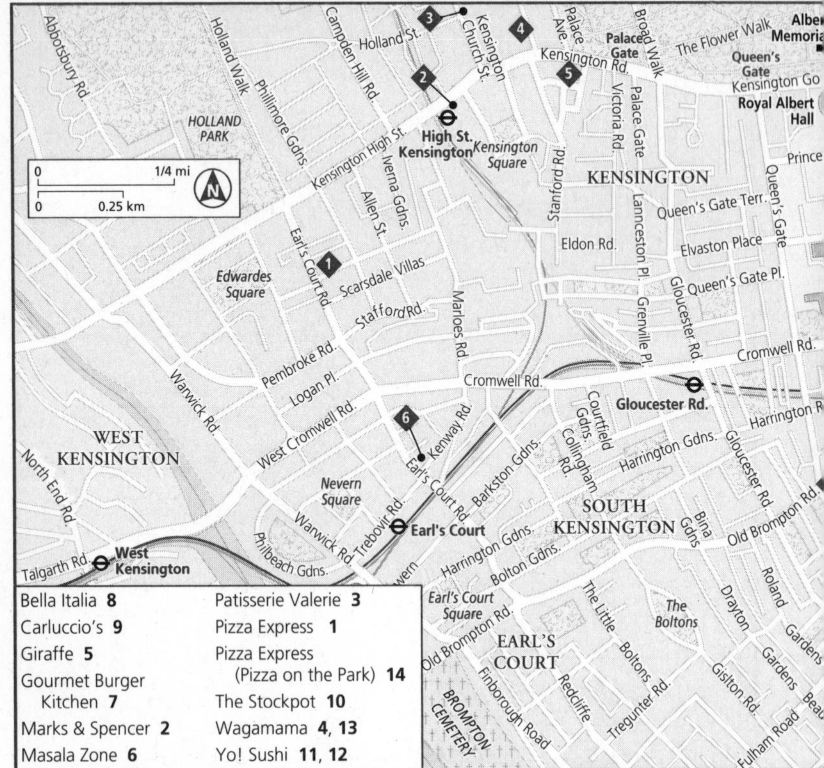

from, all delicious. Although this location is near the big museums, there are 14 others, including 1 Cranbourn St. (Tube: Leicester Square), 30 Henrietta St. (Tube: Covent Garden), 64–66 Duke St. (Tube: Bond Street), 25 Argyll St. (Tube: Oxford Circus), and 152 Victoria St. (Tube: Victoria).

BAYSWATER, PADDINGTON & NOTTING HILL

£–££ Ideal for a quick bite when you're Notting Hill way, **Manzara** (**24 Pembridge Rd., W11; ☎ 020/7727-3062; Mon–Sat 8am–1am, Sun 8am–11:30pm; AE, MC, V; Tube: Notting Hill Gate**) is overlooked as another storefront kebab house by the hordes that pass it on their way to Portobello Road. Inside, it's not much more attractive, with a shiny interior more appropriate to a fast-food joint than a place serving palatable Mediterranean grub. Get past that, though, and you'll taste a wide range of well-seasoned Turkish dishes, including many vegetarian options. The marinated chicken and lamb with rice uses top-quality meat, and the spicy aubergine dip has a kick stronger than striker Cristiano Ronaldo's. My favorite is its long, rectangular Turkish pizza, or "pide." You'll pay a £5 minimum to eat in, but considering that the minced lamb and spinach and feta are both £7, that's not hard to manage.

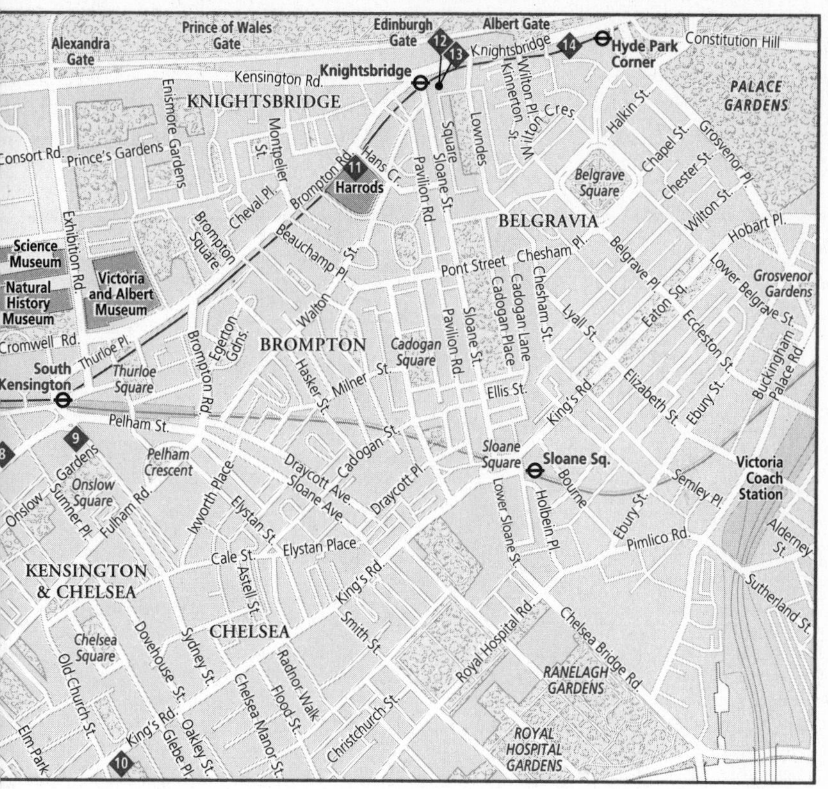

££–£££ For exotic cuisine served by friendly, family-run restaurants, Edgware Road is about as good as it gets near the center of London. **Kandoo** (458 Edgware Rd., W2; ☎ 020/7724-2428; daily noon–11:30pm; AE, MC, V; Tube: Edgware Road) is an unassuming little bit of Persia, proudly embellished by its owners with homey touches like a little dining garden out back. Breads are baked to order in a handmade, tiled oven in the front window, while the many dishes, mostly lamb- and chicken-based, come out of the back kitchen. Mains (around the £10 mark) are cleanly flavored and suffused with just the right amount of garlic, mint, saffron, or tarragon. Monday through Thursday from noon to 4pm, a set lunch of a starter, naan, and a main costs £8.50, including a soft drink (by itself normally £1.70). The chance to taste Iranian cuisine, let alone stuff this carefully done, makes it worth the shuffle up Edgware Road.

££–£££ Burmese cuisine isn't common even in the world's most multicultural cities. Another standout on Edgware Road, **Mandalay** ★★★ (444 Edgware Rd., W2; ☎ 020/7258-3696; www.mandalayway.com; daily noon–2:30pm and 6–10:30pm; AE, MC, V; Tube: Edgware Road), barely 30 seats and deceptively plain, revels in the coconut milk, lemongrass, turmeric, and garlic that distinguishes much Asian cooking, but it replaces the cloying cloves and cardamom of

Bayswater & Notting Hill Dining

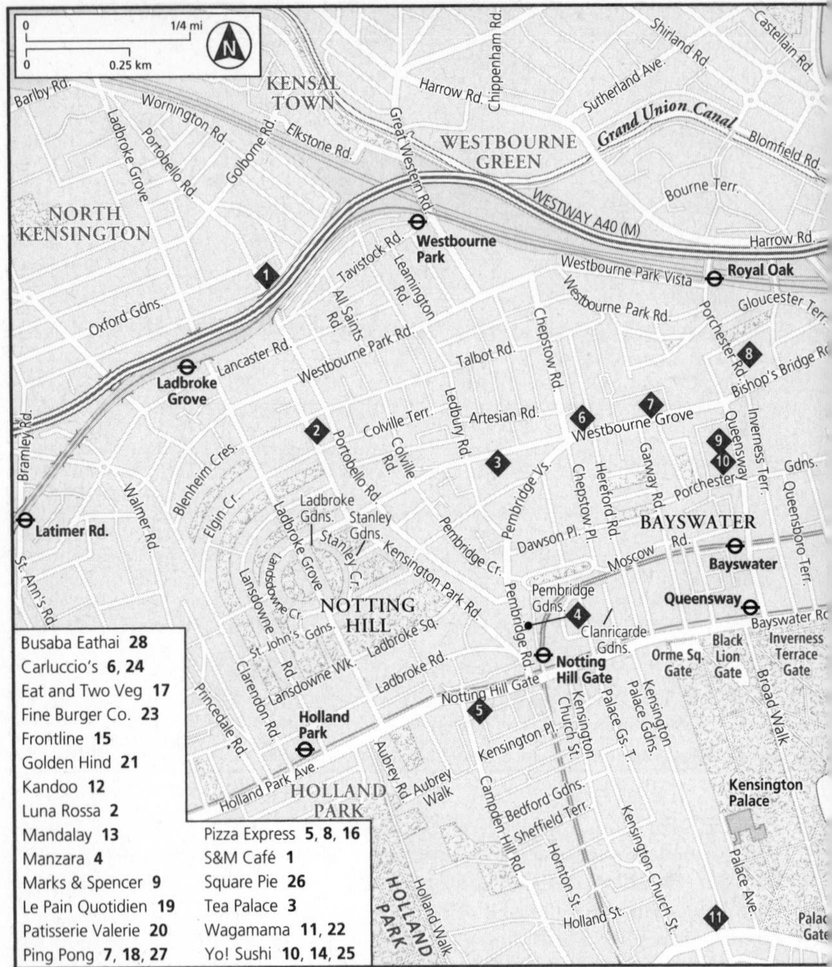

Indian cooking with an array of dried prawns and fish sauces. Traditional dishes, all multilayered with flavor, include *ohn-no khaukswe* (turmeric-yellow soup with noodles, veggies, and prawns, £5.90) and the *laksa-esque sett-na-myo-hin-cho,* called "dozen ingredient" soup on the menu (£2.90). Ask for some *balachaung* (£2.90), which is a blend of onion, dried prawns, garlic, and chili, fried together and applied as a condiment or spice to just about everything. The twice-cooked fish curry (£6.50) is a customer favorite, as are the calabash fritters (£2.40 for two). The owners are proud of their cuisine, so if you show an interest, you'll be rewarded with a whistle-stop tour of their country's best plates. Book ahead.

££–£££ Forgive its cheesy interior, tarted up like an old piazza. It's the cheesy pizza you want at trattoria **Luna Rossa** (kids) (**190-192 Kensington Park Rd., W11;**

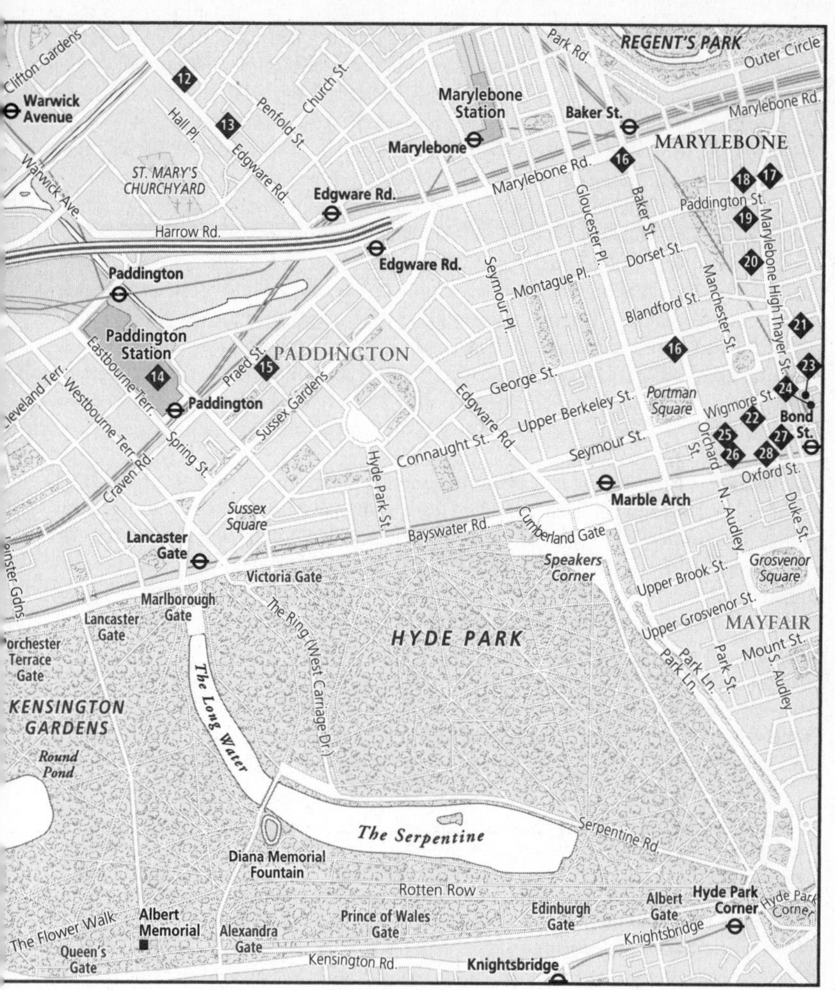

☎ 020/7229-0482; www.madeinitalygroup.co.uk; Mon 6–11:30pm, Tues–Fri noon–4pm and 6–11:30pm, Sat 11:30am–11:30pm, Sun noon–10:30pm; MC, V; Tube: Ladbroke Grove), 1 block behind Portobello Road. It's baked in rectangular sheets and arrives on ridiculously long wooden planks that, once they're placed precariously across your table and between your chairs, will have everyone in your party diving for new positions like an Italian version of *Twister.* This regressive bit of fun appeals to young residents of Notting Hill, to say nothing of their kids (who are treated like gold by the wait-staff), but if you don't want pizza, plenty of pastas are on the menu, too. The wine list is pricey, and things get noisy, but it's a good time.

£££–££££ Frontline ★★★ (13 Norfolk Place, W2; ☎ 020/7479-8960; www.thefrontlineclub.com; Mon–Sat 8am–11pm; AE, MC; Tube: Paddington) functions as a base for war correspondents, so its walls are adorned with emotional still images from more than 60 years of international events, and proceeds go toward fostering fair independent journalism. But it's not like people eat here out of charity. Frontline maintains the warm, airy vibe of a place that could charge twice what it does, with leather banquettes, oversize hanging lampshades, and white tablecloths. The knockout dishes are smart, with a modern British flair and seasonal variations: leek and potato soup; fish pie; parsnip, sage, and onion tart; and pear sorbet. I'm all about the shepherd's pie (£13 at dinner, £9 before) with a side of creamed leeks (£3). The owners also price their excellent wine list about as low as you'd find it at wine shops. Mains are £11 to £18, making this a splurge, but the quality of the cooking and the aspirations of the club make it one well spent. There's a set meal (starter, main, dessert) for £15 early weekday evenings and most of the day on weekends. Its club room has lectures on modern news issues.

£££–££££ I think fish and chips is generally better in the north of England than in London, and it's always better to get it from a place dedicated to it than from a pub. But **Golden Hind ★ (73 Marylebone Lane, W1; ☎ 020/7486-3644; Mon–Fri noon–3pm and 6–10pm, Sat 6–10pm; MC, V; Tube: Bond Street)**, which has been in business forever (since 1914) and has the spare look of a mid-century caff, is highly rated by connoisseurs of fish and chips. Although a dinner here is a splurge (a starter plus a main total around £15), it's worth a stop because you'll get haddock, plaice, or cod, done perfectly crispy. Round things out with a few Greek specialties like mussels, plus desserts (traditional spotted dick—steamed suet pudding with currants—served with custard) just like Mum's. If you don't want your fish fried, you can get it steamed with herbs. Bring your own booze; everyone else does.

The M&S Break

Marks & Spencer department stores can be your stomach's salvation. Head straight to the basement of almost any outpost of the British chain, where you'll find a spacious wonderland of ready-to-eat hot dishes, sandwiches, and soups, all usually well under the £5 notch. You'll find a large slate of seasonal food including wraps made with non–genetically modified ingredients, ice cream made with Channel Islands milk, fresh produce, fair trade coffee . . . you get the idea. M&S' stand-alone **Simply Food** stores sell many of the same items. For BYO dinners, M&S sells inexpensive (under £5) but well-selected wines, too. Responding to the popularity of M&S's foods, grocery giant **Sainsbury's** now produces its own impressive line of prepared foods. M&S's largest store is at 458 Oxford St. (Tube: Marble Arch). Other handy branches include 173 Oxford St. (Tube: Oxford Street); 10 Cardinal Place, off Victoria Street (Tube: Victoria); and Simply Food at Euston, King's Cross, Liverpool Street, Marylebone, Paddington, Victoria, Bond Street, and Waterloo stations.

BRIXTON

££ Because of its colonial past, London hosts huge numbers of settlers from the islands. For some of its best Jamaican food, try the cheek-by-jowl **Bamboula** (12 Acre Lane, SW2; ☎ 020/7737-6633; www.walkerswood.com; Mon–Sat 11am–11pm, Sun 1–9pm; MC, V; Tube: Brixton). Standouts include curried goat, red pea soup, stir-fried callaloo (a spinach-like leaf), and of course, jerk chicken served with a mountain of beans, rice, and sweet plantain. Among its surprises is Guinness Punch, an egg-noggy sipper made with nutmeg, milk, and the Irish stout. Reserve ahead or squeeze in before 12:30pm for lunch and by 7pm for dinner. Also, the wait-staff is on island time, so you won't get in and out in a hurry. Bamboula is opposite Lambeth Town Hall, a two-minute walk south of the Tube.

FIFTEEN PUBS YOU'LL LOVE

Pubs are the beating heart of British life, and they have been for centuries. Hundreds are scattered throughout the city, but you might be shocked to learn that many of the oldest premises have been so well-loved (or so well-bombed) that most of their original features are gone. Countless other bars (All Bar One, Ha! Ha! Bar) sport modern design, which may disappoint those looking for a richer atmosphere. Many other pubs, particularly in the suburbs, are called "locals"—places that cater to a neighborhood clientele.

Beer in England usually has a higher alcohol content than many varieties you may drink at home. It's also often not chilled—it's not warm, just not ice cold—as intensely as it usually is where you live. Mixed drinks are also served, but don't expect a generous pour as measures are rigidly standardized across the country. As for those hooks under the tables or the bar, they're for your coat.

The following pubs, all centrally located, should do you right. Be they truly ancient, stunningly beautiful, happily situated, or simply charming, they're all authentic and unlikely to let you down. All of them serve food of some kind (burgers, meat pies, and the like) for at least part of the day; you usually order at the bar, where you receive a numbered tag for your table so that servers can find you. Pubs commonly charge under £3 for a pint, the favored serving size of about 20 American ounces. Pints are usually cheaper than bottled beer.

Few pubs meld abundant history with an enviable location as perfectly as the three-story **Anchor Bankside** (34 Park St., SE1; ☎ 020/7407-1577; Mon–Sat 11am–11pm, Sun noon–9:30pm; MC, V; Tube: London Bridge), whose Thameside patio in sight of St. Paul's dome is perhaps the most agreeable (and popular) spot in London at which to sit a spell with a fresh-pulled pint. There's been a tavern here at least since the 1500s, when Londoners ferried to Southwark by the hundreds to experience bear baiting, gardens, brothels, and Shakespeare (the playwright surely would have known the place). Diarist and royal confidant Samuel Pepys is said to have watched London burn to the ground from the safety of this shore in 1666, and another Samuel, this one Johnson, may have kept a room here while he compiled the first English dictionary. The industrial Anchor brewery that subsumed it for 200 years was cleared away in the 1980s, and a spacious (but always crowded) riverside terrace was added. Beer snobs kvetch that it has become a tourist draw, but that's all right with me; it's certainly historic, and pubs have always been getaways for the common man of the day.

Having a beer in **The Argyll Arms** (18 Argyll St., W1; ☎ 020/7734-6117; Mon–Sat 11am–11:30pm, Sun noon–10:30pm; MC, V; Tube: Oxford Circus) can feel like drinking in a bejeweled, red velvet box. That's thanks to the many acid-etched glass screens that subdivide the space into dignified drinking areas. Originally installed in 1895 to prevent brawls between the working and middle classes at a time when even subway rides were segregated, the screens somehow survived the 20th century. It's one of the prettiest pubs in London, and its location southeast of Oxford Circus (by several of the Tube's exits), makes it an easy stop.

A laid-back, wood-lined, and easy-to-find pub situated east across the road from the entrance to the National Portrait Gallery, **The Chandos** (29 St. Martin's Lane, WC2; ☎ 020/7836-1401; Mon–Fri 11am–11pm, Sat–Sun 11am–midnight; AE, MC, V; Tube: Leicester Square or Charing Cross) has an upper-floor Opera Room, spacious and furnished with sofas. Big and relaxed, with lots of people who come for a drink before dashing out again, it looks older than it is (it was renovated in early 2006), but it's zero-attitude and makes a solid pre- or post-show choice.

The simple corner beerhouse **The Coach and Horses** (29 Greek St., W1; ☎ 020/7437-5920; Mon–Thurs 11am–11pm, Fri–Sat 11am–11:30pm, Sun noon–10:30pm; MC, V; Tube: Leicester Square), in the thick of Soho's tourist crowd at Romilly Street, dates to the mid-1800s, and although several pubs in London bear its name, few others share its history as a hangout for inebriated journalists. Stay downstairs for better prices.

A onetime haunt of actor Edmund Kean, who drank himself to an early curtain, **The Coal Hole** (91 Strand, WC2; ☎ 020/7379-9883; daily noon–10pm; MC, V; Tube: Charing Cross or Embankment), rebuilt in 1904 in the Arts and Crafts style, is still a hangout for performers at the adjoining Savoy Theatre. Use the entrance in back, by the stage door, to access the clubbier lower level.

The 17th-century charmer **The Dove** (19 Upper Mall, W6; ☎ 020/8748-9474; Mon–Sat 11am–11pm, Sun noon–10:30pm; AE, MC, V; Tube: Ravenscourt Park) houses many legends: that Charles II would cheat on his queen by sneaking off with Nell Gwynne here (probably false); that the composer of "Rule Britannia" lived, and died prematurely, upstairs (true); that dissolute artists Graham Greene, Ernest Hemingway, and Richard Burton all got wasted here (so very true, along with many other imbibers commemorated on the walls). It's a prototypical English pub with character, down to the low ceiling crossed by dark oak beams, brick facade, and open fire. But it's the terraced Thameside location that makes it endure. Sitting outside and watching the river, you'll understand why Hammersmith was a favored retreat from the city for so many centuries. Arrive early on weekends to snare a seat.

Unquestionably one of the most important ancient pubs still standing, **The George Inn** (77 Borough High St., SE1; ☎ 020/7407-2056; Mon–Sat 11am–11pm, Sun noon–10:30pm; AE, MC, V; Tube: London Bridge) traces its lineage to at least 1542, when a map of Southwark first depicted it; the Tabard Inn, from where Chaucer's pilgrims left in *Canterbury Tales,* was then a few doors south (it's gone now). The oldest part of the current structure, a galleried wood-and-brick longhouse, dates to 1677, after a horrific fire swept the district. It later functioned as an 18th-century transit hub, and its courtyard was encircled on three sides with a tavern, a hotel, stables, wagon repair bays, and warehouses. Shakespeare knew it, and Dickens memorialized it in *Little Dorrit,* but the rise of a railway nearly saw it destroyed, and only one side of the former complex survives. The National Trust now protects it. Sip an ale in the low-ceilinged timber-and-plaster chambers, or sit in the cobbled courtyard and soak up the echoes of history.

The Grenadier (18 Wilton Row, SW1; ☎ 020/7235-3074; Mon–Sat 11am–11pm, Sun 11am–10:30pm; AE, MC, V; Tube: Hyde Park Corner), it's said, was the Duke of Wellington's local bar and the unofficial clubhouse for his regiment, hence the battlefield artifacts on display, from old trumpets to lanterns. This tiny plank-floored pub/restaurant, pretty as a picture in a cobbled mews, comes off like a boozer in some tiny upcountry village, with only 15 places at its island bar, part of which is still faced with its original pewter top. The clientele these days skews toward an international mix of students and visitors. The pub is less known for its resident ghost (a soldier) than for its freshly mixed bloody marys, nicely tart with a giant celery stalk. Find this secret place by heading down Grosvenor Crescent from Hyde Park Corner station, hanging a hard right upon arriving at Belgrave Square onto Wilton Crescent, and taking your first right on Wilton Row.

Too tiny and thronged to supply much respite, **The Lamb and Flag** (33 Rose St., WC2; ☎ 020/7497-9504; Mon–Thurs 11am–11pm, Fri–Sat 11am–10:45pm, Sun noon–10:30pm; Tube: Covent Garden or Leicester Square), is nonetheless the epitome of a city pub, tucked as it is down an atmospheric brick alley and blessed with an original fireplace. It has been known throughout its 375 years as both the Coopers Arms and The Bucket of Blood, and its building is said to be Tudor in origin. No one can prove it, since it was heavily rebuilt in the 1890s. You'll find it on a lane just east of the intersection of Floral and Garrick streets. But you probably won't find a place to sit unless you start drinking after lunch.

McGlynn's Free House (1-5 Whidborne St, WC1; ☎ 020/7916-9816; Mon–Sat 11am–11pm, Sun 11am–10:30pm; AE, MC, V; Tube: Russell Square or King's Cross St. Pancras) isn't hundreds of years old, or even important, but it fulfills the image of a "local" where the neighborhood folks hang out in peace and the landlord welcomes new faces. Its coal-blackened brick corner building, painted in old-fashioned green and red trim, is hard to find (it's southwest of Argyle Square in King's Cross), which accounts for some of its appeal. Its street is so quiet that, unlike at most London pubs, you'd actually consider loitering at one of its outdoor picnic tables in summer. It's the sort of place with a few "pokie" gambling machines jangling in the corner, and a rugby or football game on the TV every afternoon. The food's retro, too: Monday to Thursday from 6pm to 8pm, you can get a curry, rice, and a pint of beer for £6.80, and there's a regular menu. Because it's a "free house," it can serve a range of ales from a variety of sources, unlike many other pubs, which are controlled by breweries.

The enchanting **Old Mitre** (1 Ely Court, off Ely Place, EC1; ☎ 020/7405-4751; AE, MC, V; Mon–Fri 11am–11pm, closed weekends; Tube: Farringdon or Chancery Lane), suspended between streets and seemingly between centuries, was once part of a great palace mentioned by Shakespeare in *Richard II* and *Richard III.* The medieval St. Etheldreda's Chapel, the palace's surviving place of worship, stands just outside. This extremely tiny pub (established in 1546 but built in its present form in 1772) has two entrances that feed either side of the bar. The one on the left grants you access to "the Closet," a fine example of a semiprivate sitting area called a "snug." The entrance on the right brings you face-to-face with a blackened stump said to be part of a cherry-tree maypole that Elizabeth I danced around. (Yeah, right, drink another one.) Suck down one of the house specialties: pickled eggs, for less than £1. To locate it, seek a little alley among the jewelry stores on eastern Hatton Garden between Holborn Circus and Greville Street.

There's no pretending that **The Narrow Boat** (119 St. Peters St., N1; ☎ 020/7288-0572; Mon–Sat 11am–11pm, Sun noon–10:30pm; MC, V; Tube: Angel) is historically significant. It's simply a smashing, contemporary place to pass a few hours on a pretty day. Picture windows overlook an attractive basin of the Regent's Canal, where you can watch barges, ducks, and wealthy folks in their waterfront loft conversions. Combine a visit with a stroll along the canal's footpath, and you've got one of the most romantic afternoons London has to offer. Don't confuse it with The Narrow (p. 115), Gordon Ramsay's waterfront gastropub.

The Covent Garden/Leicester Square location is unbeatable, and the ornate exterior and interior of **The Salisbury** (90 St. Martin's Lane, WC2; ☎ 020/7836-5863; Mon–Thurs 11am–11:30pm, Fri 11am–midnight, Sat noon–midnight, Sun noon–10:30pm; AE, MC, V; Tube: Leicester Square) is unmistakably Victorian—ostentatious, just-how-drunk-was-the-designer Victorian, to be precise. Thrill to the Grecian urns in the brilliant-cut glass, the pressed-copper tables, and the nymphs entwined in the bronze lamps. Long a haunt of the city's theatrical community, it's now a suitable pit stop for any West End exploration. The plate meals run the gamut of international offerings—baked asparagus tarts; chicken tikka with pappadum; sausage and mash—usually for under £8.

The facade of **The Sherlock Holmes** (10-11 Northumberland St., WC2; ☎ 020/7930-2644; Mon–Fri 11am–11pm, Sat noon–11pm, Sun noon–10:30pm; AE, MC, V; Tube: Charing Cross or Embankment has a subdued interior and a stock of touristy Holmsian memorabilia (assembled a half-century ago as a tourist gag) that will save you a trip to the similar attractions at the Holmes museum on Baker Street. Note that it's not on busy Northumberland Avenue, but on the street of the same name, which runs just north.

Just the sort of rambling, low-ceilinged tavern you imagine London is full of (and was, once), **Ye Olde Cheshire Cheese** (Wine Office Court, off 145 Fleet St., ☎ 020/7353-6170; Mon–Sat 11am–11pm, Sun noon–9:30pm; AE, MC, V; Tube: Blackfriars, Temple, or Chancery Lane) was built behind Fleet Street in the wake of the Great Fire in 1666, and because of steady log fires and regularly strewn sawdust, it still smells like history hasn't finished passing it by. In later generations, it played regular host to Dr. Samuel Johnson (who lived behind on Gough Square), Charles Dickens (who referred to it in *A Tale of Two Cities*), Yeats, Wilde, and Thackeray. You can get pretty well thackered yourself today: There are six drinking rooms (some in a courtyard converted for the purpose in our day), but the cozy front bar is the most magical. Ask to see the Chop Room's oak paneling and furniture or, if you're free-spending, to sample a steak dinner. Don't confuse this place with the Victorian-era Cheshire Cheese pub at nearby Temple.

5 Why You're Here: The Sights of London

What's worth seeing, what isn't

LONDON IS INFURIATING! HOW ELSE CAN YOU DESCRIBE A CITY WITH SO much to see? Unless you have the time and the money to hang out for months, you're simply not going to be able to see even a smidge of a sliver of the amazing things on offer. Even with the best planning, you'll wind up hungry for more.

Put simply: England has been a top dog for the past 500 years, and London is where it keeps its bark. For centuries, many of the world's finest treasures came here and never left. Most cities store their best goodies in one or two brand-name museums. In London, riches are everywhere. You can walk into a place you've never heard of before and see something priceless.

London's brand-name attractions could by themselves occupy weeks of deep contemplation. But the sheer abundance of history and wealth—layer upon layer of it—means that London boasts dozens of exciting smaller sights, too. Even if you daydreamed in high school history, you'll be fired up when face-to-face with the underground bunker where Britain fought for its life in World War II, or the jewel-encrusted crown worn by the country's Kings and Queens back to 1661.

There's lot of other good stuff to do in the city besides sidle past important relics. Also check out my chapters on London's world-renowned parks (p. 219), nightlife (p. 284), theater scene (p. 285), and those little-known, "under-the-skin" activities that help you meet, play, and learn with real Londoners—"the Other London" (p. 197). By the way, sightseeing discounts, such as 2-for-1s, are sometimes offered for Oyster card holders (check www.tfl.gov.uk/microsites/oysteroffers) and at LastMinute.com.

HOW TO BEST USE YOUR TIME

If you have just 1 day in London: First of all, what were you thinking? If you're in town on a layover, didn't you know that most airlines will allow you to stick around for a few days at no charge? Never mind. What's done is done. Eat a huge breakfast and make your way to **The Tower of London** (p. 142) because it usually opens an hour earlier (9am) than most attractions. Spend about 2 hours there, making stops at the **Crown Jewels** and the **White Tower,** and snap that requisite photo of the **Tower Bridge** (p. 180) from the quay outside. Grab a triangle sandwich for lunch (the quintessential London midday meal) and Tube it to Westminster for the **Houses of Parliament** (p. 181) and **Westminster Abbey** (p. 140, allot two hours). Then walk up Whitehall, passing **No. 10 Downing Street.** If you like art, breathe in the atmosphere of **Trafalgar Square** (p. 240), one of the symbolic hearts of the city, before popping into **The National Gallery**

(p. 145) for an hour or two. If you don't care much for paintings, head back to the Thames for a ride on the **London Eye** (p. 137), where you can watch the sun go down on the Clock Tower where **Big Ben** (p. 184) rings. **West End shows** start around 7:30pm (p. 285), and afterward, head to the nearest **pub** and raise a glass to a city where you've barely scratched the surface (see p. 129 for pub suggestions).

If you have just 2 days in London: You're going to have to move incredibly fast, but you'll be able to see some highlights in 2 days. Start at **The Tower of London,** as on the 1-day tour, but stay until lunch—it's still not enough time to see everything, but we're crunched here. Then take the Tube to Mansion House or Blackfriars, where you can hastily appreciate the underside of the Dome of **St. Paul's Cathedral** (p. 151) before crossing the Thames on the Millennium Bridge to binge on modern art at the **Tate Modern** (p. 146). If it's summer, you can catch an evening show at **Shakespeare's Globe** (p. 187), just a few yards east; in winter, any West End theater will show you what modern British performance is all about. Wind up your day with a beer overlooking the Thames at the **Anchor** pub, or at the wooden-galleried **George Inn** (see p. 129 and p. 130).

Start your second day with a pilgrimage to **Westminster Abbey.** Then walk along **St. James's Park** (p. 221) to behold the front of **Buckingham Palace** (p. 161), before heading across **Green Park** (p. 221) to browse the classy shops of **Piccadilly,** including **Fortnum & Mason** (p. 265). Next take the Tube or a bus to Russell Square, where you'll spend the afternoon roaming, but barely getting to know, **The British Museum** (p. 135). Maybe you'll even want afternoon cream tea at its cafe (p. 100). Wind up the afternoon on the **London Eye** or with a stroll past the shops of **Oxford Street, Regent Street,** and **Carnaby Street** (p. 263). Grab dinner at a West End restaurant of your choice, and afterward, stroll past the lights of **Piccadilly Circus,** where you can catch the Tube back to your hotel.

If you have 3 days in London: Follow the itinerary for 2 days in London, but add in one of the city's South Kensington museums, preferably the **Victoria & Albert** (p. 150), and follow that with a walk through **Hyde Park** (p. 219), possibly to see the Diana, Princess of Wales Fountain, and to tour Diana's former home, **Kensington Palace** (p. 160), in adjoining Kensington Gardens. Take the Tube or a bus to Westminster, and dive into the time capsule of the **Churchill Museum and Cabinet War Rooms** (p. 155). Dine in Islington or Marylebone, and follow that up with a long stroll through those neighborhoods.

If you have 4, 5, 6, or 7 days in London: Go through this chapter and place a check mark next to all the attractions that interest you. Put a circle around the ones I've just named above. If you schedule one or two circled check marks per day, you can sprinkle one or two more uncircled checks in the hours surrounding them. Provided the places you choose for each day are located within five or seven Tube stops' distance apart, the commute between them shouldn't chew up your time. Just remember: Attractions are generally open from 10am to 5 or 6pm—to maximize efficiency, do daytime things (museums, attractions) during the day, and leisurely activities (entertainment, long meals) during the evening.

THE TEN BEST: LONDON'S ICONIC SIGHTS

London has no shortage of wonders, but these are the don't-miss attractions that have kept visitors buzzing for years. If you're not keen on seeing some of them—few children would stamp their feet and beg to be taken to the Tate Britain, for example—replace them with something from one of the other categories in this chapter, such as "Attractions that Ought to Be More Famous" (p. 154) or "Attractions with Niche Appeal" (p. 172).

The British Museum ★★★ (Great Russell Street, WC1; ☎ 020/7323-8299; www.thebritishmuseum.org; free admission; Sat–Wed 10am–5:30pm and Thurs–Fri 10am–8:30pm, closed New Year's Day, Good Friday, and Dec 24–26; Tube: Tottenham Court Road or Holborn or Russell Square), founded in 1753 and first opened in 1759 in a converted mansion, may be the museum to beat all museums. In fact, it's the top tourist attraction in the country—more than 6 million people visited in 2007. Those with an interest in classical crafts and antiquities could spend days here. Put on your walking shoes because it's huge.

In many ways, the British Museum is a monument as much to great craftsmanship as it is to the piracy carried out by 18th- and 19th-century wealthy Englishmen, who, on their trips abroad, seized whatever goodies they could find and then told the bereft that the thievery was for their own good. Yet the good taste of these English collectors is unquestionable.

Navigating the British Museum

With more than 250 years of collecting behind it, the British Museum possesses a mind-boggling number of artifacts, and aimlessly trundling from room to room can quickly numb the brain. Free admission forces directors to coax money from your pocket in other ways, such as charging a few pounds for a **map.** Get around that fee by printing the floor plans from the website; these don't pinpoint the location of the highlights but will at least keep you from getting lost in the labyrinth.

Be sure to get a handle on the day's offerings at the Info Desk (at the left of the two-acre Great Court, under a dazzling glass-and-steel canopy installed as part of a £100-million renovation in 2000) as the museum is always humming with a changing slate of talks, tours, and special exhibitions, some of which will require timed tickets. I particularly recommend looking into the excellent (and free) **"Hands On"** demonstrations, at which visitors are permitted to handle artifacts from the collection with an informed curator. Even better are the free **EyeOpeners tours**, which take about 45 minutes and focus on a single room or theme; they run about a dozen times a day. Audio tours come in a few varieties from highlight- to Parthenon-oriented, each £3.50. The Great Court also loans free kids' materials, including activities backpacks, scavenger trail maps, and event guides. **Guided tours** of the Museum's highlights are a steep £8, three times a day. Considering the price, you're better off on your own armed with information from the booklets in the gift shops.

Holdings are grouped in numbered rooms by geography, with an emphasis on the Greek and Roman Empires, Europe, and Britain. It's impossible to choose the *most* priceless item in a welter of priceless items, but if you have only a few hours to see the most famous and instructive selections, you should see the following:

Dominating the center of the Great Court like a drum in a box, the cream-and-gold **Reading Room,** completed in 1857 but closed to the general public until 2000, was once part of the British Library, which shared the site with the museum until 1998. Famous patrons here included Lenin and Karl Marx, who developed their political theories in the room; George Bernard Shaw, Charles Dickens, and Virginia Woolf. On the southern wall (through which you enter), you can read panels on the museum's history. The Reading Room, which still houses some 25,000 books pertaining to the Museum's stash, is usually open from 10am to 5:30pm, but it may be closed or opened longer for exhibitions.

The museum's most famous, and most controversial, possessions are probably the so-called **Elgin Marbles,** which the museum gingerly refers to as **The Sculptures of the Parthenon** (rooms 18 and 19) to disguise their imperialist provenance: They were looted from Greece by Lord Elgin in the early 1800s. These slab sculptures (called friezes and Metopes), plus some life-size weathered statuary, once lined the pediment of the Parthenon atop Athens' Acropolis but were defaced (literally—the faces were hacked off) by invading vandals in the 500s. They suffered further indignities in a 1687 gunpowder explosion. They're laid out in the gallery in the approximate position in which they appeared on the Parthenon, only facing inward. The government of Greece has lobbied for years for their return, but the British have argued that they're better cared for in London. If you've ever seen the smog-burnt portions left behind in Athens, it's easy to see their point, which makes a muddy political issue murkier.

Fragments of **sculptures from The Mausoleum at Halikarnassos,** one of the lost Seven Wonders of the Ancient World, loom in room 21. So colossal are these chunks—a woman, once one of 36 such figures, carved from a single block of stone; a horse's head that measures 2.1m long (7 ft.)—that they call into question everything we think about ancient peoples' limited technology and culture.

The pivotal **Rosetta Stone** (196 B.C.), in room 4, is what helped linguists crack the code of hieroglyphics, and its importance to anthropology can't be exaggerated. Napoleon's soldiers found it while enlarging their fort in Egypt in 1799, but it was nabbed in 1801 by the British. Consider it his first Waterloo.

The grisly array of **Egyptian Mummies** in rooms 62, 63, and 64 have petrified children for years, and on your visit, they'll probably be thronged with school groups as usual. In addition to the wizened, raisin-like corpses, there are painted coffins; the hair and lung of the scribe Sutimose, dating to 1100 B.C.; and scarabs galore. In room 64, check out the body from 3400 B.C., found in a fetal position without a coffin, which was preserved by dry sand. Beside it is another body, 400 years younger, that rotted to bones and soil because it was laid to rest in a basket.

Kids should also love the leather-faced **Lindow Man** in room 50; he was discovered, throat slit, in a Cheshire bog nearly 2,000 years after his brutal demise. Preserved down to his hair and fingernails, he looks like he could spring to life and pound the glass of his case. Nearby (room 49) is the **Mildenhall Treasure,** a hoard of silver Roman tableware unearthed by Gordon Butcher, a Suffolk farmer, as he plowed his fields in 1942; the saga of how Butcher was cheated of his unexpected fortune was chronicled by children's author Roald Dahl.

The **Enlightenment Gallery,** at the east of the ground floor, is the museum's oldest room (1823), from the Greek Revival edifice that replaced the converted mansion and was gradually subsumed by the massive building that exists today. Its towering walls, lined with wood-and-glass cases and stuffed with knickknacks from around the world, give you a sense for how rarified the museum must have felt in the glory days of British conquest and discovery. Case 22 is full of stuff brought back from **Captain James Cook's voyages** to the South Pacific.

Room 70, on the upper floor, holds three remarkable holdings: **The Portland Vase,** a black, cameo-glass jug that's very difficult to make even today; the bronze **head of Roman Emperor Augustus,** found in the Sudan and lifelike to an unsettling degree (it still has its painted eyeballs, as most statues of the time did); and **The Warren Cup,** a First Century silver chalice graphically depicting homosexual sex in relief. The Warren Cup's acquisition in 1999 for £1.8 million caused some juvenile titters; the discomfort of some guests is made all the more amusing by the fact they have to bend over to inspect its indecorous decorations.

Of the several **gift shops** in the Great Court, the one at the back, under the sky bridge and easily missed, has the best selection. There's a **restaurant** above the Reading Room which serves an afternoon tea (p. 100).

The **London Eye** kids ★ (Riverside Building, County Hall, SE1; ☎ 0870/500-0600; www.londoneye.com; £16 adults, £7.75 children 5–15, free under 5, £12 seniors; Oct–May daily 10am–8 pm, June and Sept daily 10am–9pm, July and Aug daily 10am–9:30pm, closed for maintenance in the first week of Jan; Tube: Waterloo or Westminster) was erected in 1999 as the Millennium Wheel, and like many temporary vantage points of the past, it became such a sensation—and a money-minter—that it was never taken down. The skyline will never be the same. It rises above everything in this part of the city (at 135m/443 ft. high, it's the sixth-tallest structure in London, and 1½ times taller than the Statue of Liberty). The 30-minute ride above the Thames affords an unmatched perspective on the prime tourist territory. On a clear day, you can see to Windsor, but even on an average day, the entire West End bows down before you. That's why you should either go as soon as you arrive in the city, to orient yourself, or (my choice), on your last day in town, when you can appreciate what you've seen.

Each of the 32 enclosed capsules, which accommodate up to 28 people, is shared, climate-controlled, and rotates so gradually that it's easy to forget you've left the ground—which means it will upset only the desperately height-averse. Best of all, capsules are fixed to the outside of the wheel, so by the time you reach the top, you'll have true 360-degree views unobstructed by the support frame.

The ticket queue often looks positively wicked, but in fact, it moves fairly quickly, processing up to 15,000 riders a day. At peak times (weekend afternoons and summer), you'll ride with around two dozen new friends, but if you prefer less company, try immediately after opening (before the school groups descend), or after dark. For a stirring view for £4 less, you can always climb to the Stone Gallery of St. Paul's Cathedral, which surveys The City. ***Tip:*** Booking on the Web

London Attractions

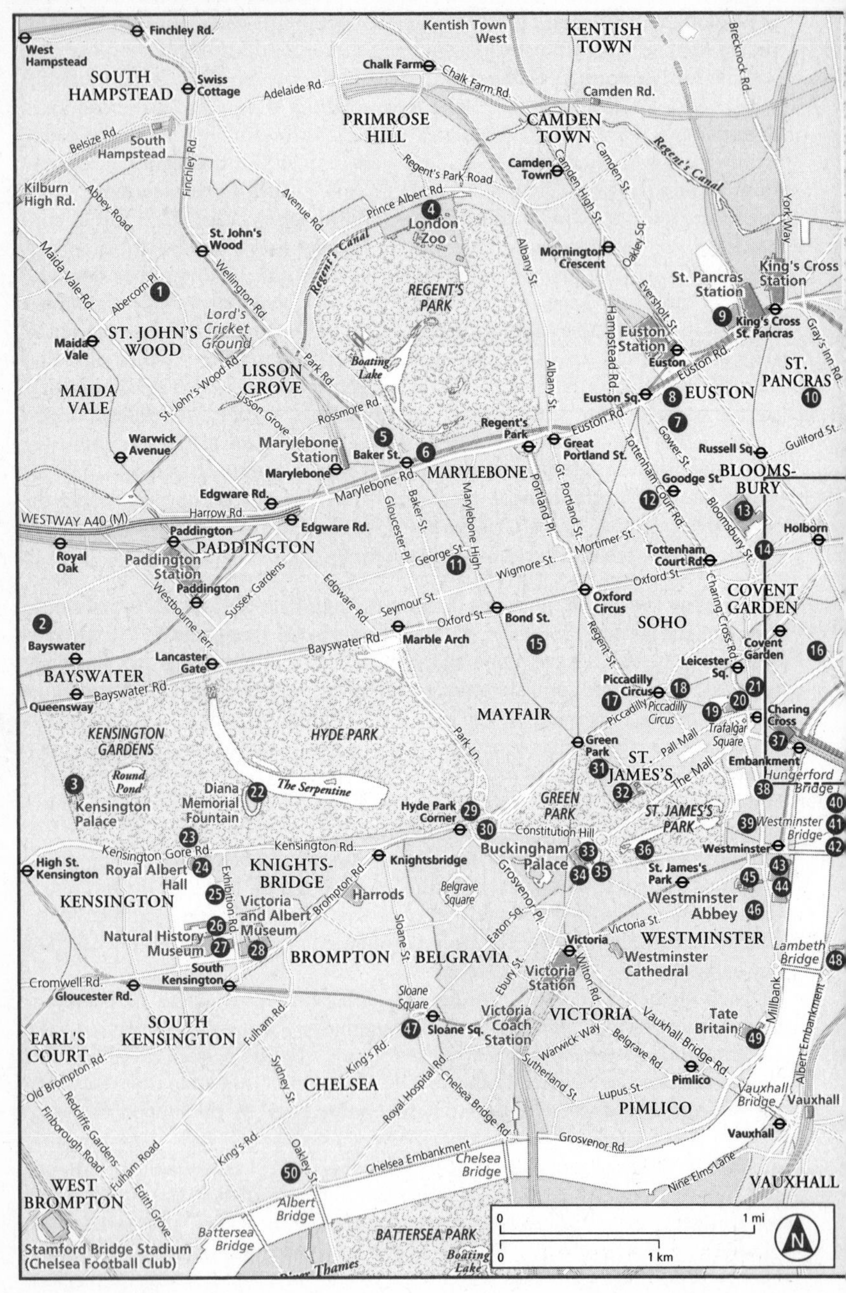

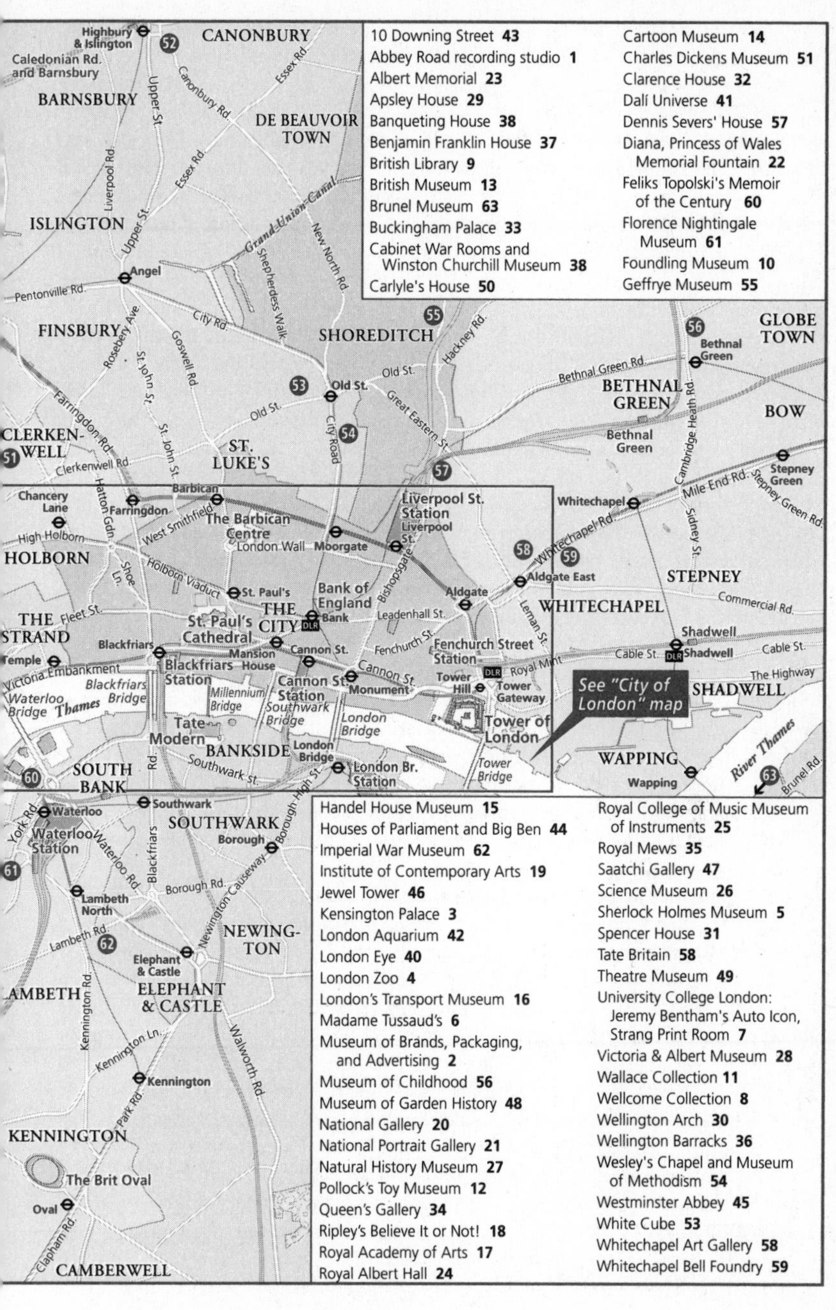
10 Downing Street 43
Abbey Road recording studio 1
Albert Memorial 23
Apsley House 29
Banqueting House 38
Benjamin Franklin House 37
British Library 9
British Museum 13
Brunel Museum 63
Buckingham Palace 33
Cabinet War Rooms and Winston Churchill Museum 38
Carlyle's House 50
Cartoon Museum 14
Charles Dickens Museum 51
Clarence House 32
Dalí Universe 41
Dennis Severs' House 57
Diana, Princess of Wales Memorial Fountain 22
Feliks Topolski's Memoir of the Century 60
Florence Nightingale Museum 61
Foundling Museum 10
Geffrye Museum 55
Handel House Museum 15
Houses of Parliament and Big Ben 44
Imperial War Museum 62
Institute of Contemporary Arts 19
Jewel Tower 46
Kensington Palace 3
London Aquarium 42
London Eye 40
London Zoo 4
London's Transport Museum 16
Madame Tussaud's 6
Museum of Brands, Packaging, and Advertising 2
Museum of Childhood 56
Museum of Garden History 48
National Gallery 20
National Portrait Gallery 21
Natural History Museum 27
Pollock's Toy Museum 12
Queen's Gallery 34
Ripley's Believe It or Not! 18
Royal Academy of Arts 17
Royal Albert Hall 24
Royal College of Music Museum of Instruments 25
Royal Mews 35
Saatchi Gallery 47
Science Museum 26
Sherlock Holmes Museum 5
Spencer House 31
Tate Britain 58
Theatre Museum 49
University College London: Jeremy Bentham's Auto Icon, Strang Print Room 7
Victoria & Albert Museum 28
Wallace Collection 11
Wellcome Collection 8
Wellington Arch 30
Wellington Barracks 36
Wesley's Chapel and Museum of Methodism 54
Westminster Abbey 45
White Cube 53
Whitechapel Art Gallery 58
Whitechapel Bell Foundry 59
CANONBURY
BARNSBURY
DE BEAUVOIR TOWN
ISLINGTON
FINSBURY
SHOREDITCH
CLERKENWELL
ST. LUKE'S
GLOBE TOWN
BETHNAL GREEN
BOW
HOLBORN
THE STRAND
THE CITY
WHITECHAPEL
STEPNEY
SHADWELL
WAPPING
BANKSIDE
SOUTH BANK
SOUTHWARK
NEWINGTON
LAMBETH
ELEPHANT & CASTLE
KENNINGTON
CAMBERWELL
See "City of London" map
River Thames
Tower of London
St. Paul's Cathedral
Tate Modern
The Barbican Centre
Bank of England
The Brit Oval

saves waiting in the ticketing queues, and it gives two other advantages: You can pick your time ahead and you'll save 10% off the price listed above.

If you have to pick one church in London to see, pick **Westminster Abbey ★★★ (Broad Sanctuary, SW1; ☎ 020/7222-5152; www.westminster-abbey.org; £12 adults, £9 children 11–15, seniors, and students; Mon–Tues and Thurs–Fri 9:30am–4:30pm, Wed 9:30am–7pm, Sat 9:30am–2:30pm, closed Sun and occasionally for special events, last admission 1 hr. before closing; Tube: Westminster).** The echoes of history here—the current building dates from the 1200s, but it was part of a monastery dating to at least 960—are simply mind-blowing: Every English monarch since 1066 has been crowned here (with three minor exceptions: Edward V, Edward VIII, and possibly Mary I). Seventeen monarchs are interred here (their deaths date from 1066–1760), as are dozens of great writers and artists. Even if England's tumultuous history and the thought of bodies lying underfoot don't stir your imagination, the interior—in places, as intricate as lace—will earn your appreciation. A visit should take about 3 hours.

Unlike St. Paul's Cathedral, which boasts a stately beauty, the much smaller Westminster is more like time's attic, packed with artifacts, memorials, tombs, and virtuosic shrines. It's easy to feel overloaded after just a few minutes; by the time you've pocketed the change from your admission ticket, you're already treading on the final resting place of poor William Bradford (died 1728 at age 32). It only gets busier from there. Take your time and don't get swept along in the current of visitors. There are dozens of stories to be told in every square meter of this place.

Inside the sanctuary, tourists are corralled clockwise from the North Transept. The royal tombs are clustered in the first half of the route, in the region of the High Altar, where coronations and funerals are conducted. I always find it intense to realize that the most famous rulers of all time are truly *here*—not in story, but in body, a few inches away behind marble slabs. Some are stashed in cozy side chapels (which once held medieval shrines before Cromwellians bashed them to pieces during the Reformation; some vandalism is still visible), but the oldest are on the sanctuary side of the ambulatory (aisle). The executed **Mary Queen of Scots** was belatedly given a crypt of equal stature to her rival, **Elizabeth I,** by Mary's son **James I,** who gave himself only a marker for his own tomb beneath **Henry VII**'s elaborate resting place. James I's infant daughter Sophia, who died aged three days, was given a creepy bassinet sarcophagus in the Lady Chapel.

Only the tombs are labeled, so it helps to have an audio guide (£4). Rentals stop by early afternoon. If you have questions, approach anyone in a red robe; they're "vergers," or officers who attend to the church. They also lead 90-minute tours at least once daily (usually at 10am, but up to five times daily, for £3). If you stump them, you may win an invitation to the atmospheric Library, a creaking loft that smells of medieval vellum and dust, where an archivist can answer you.

The South Transept is **Poet's Corner,** where Britain's great writers are honored. You'll see many plaques, but most (Shakespeare, Austen, Carroll, Wilde, the Brontës) are merely memorials. The biggest names who truly lie underfoot are Robert Browning, Geoffrey Chaucer (he was placed here first, starting the trend), Charles Dickens, Thomas Hardy (buried without his heart), John Gay, Rudyard Kipling, Dr. Samuel Johnson, Laurence Olivier, Edmund Spenser, and Alfred

City of London Attractions

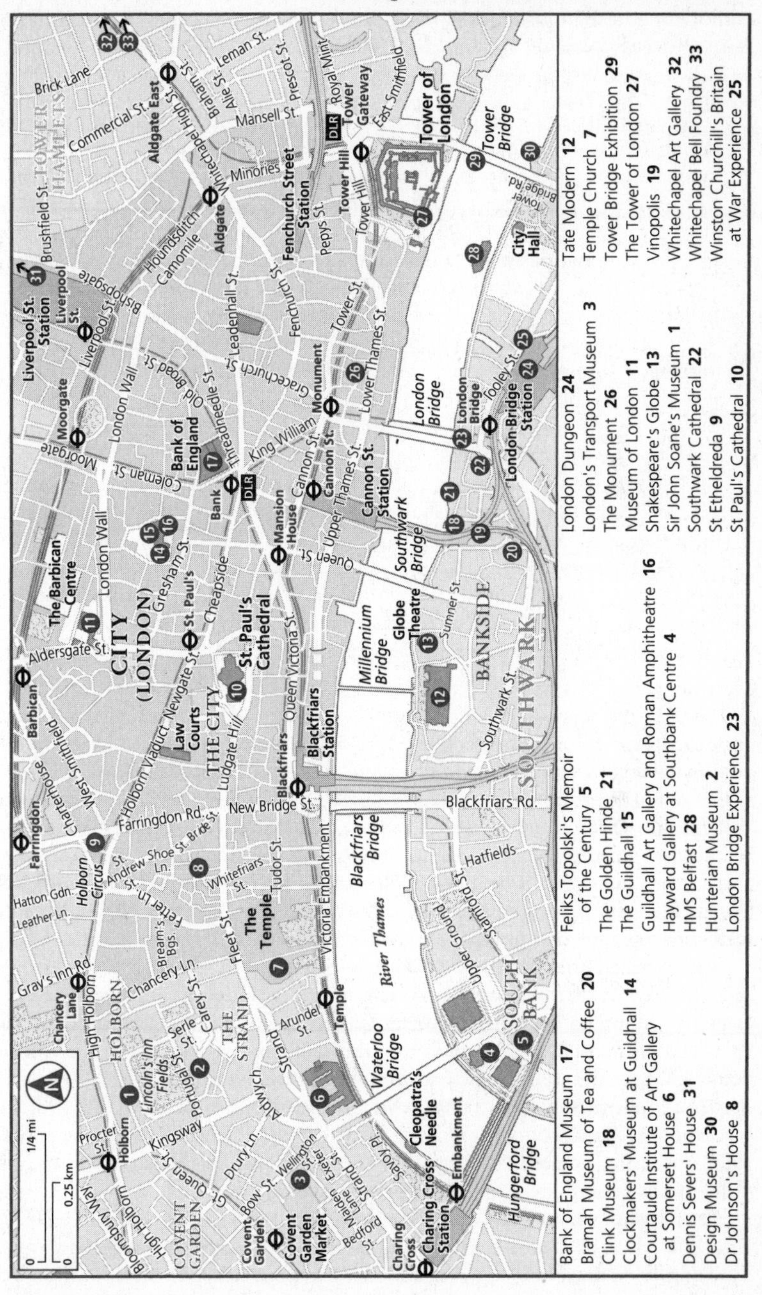

Lord Tennyson. Ben Jonson is commemorated here but is actually buried in the Nave near Isaac Newton and Charles Darwin.

Now for a few Abbey secrets:

- That oak seat between the Sanctuary and the Confessors' Chapel, near the tomb of Henry V, is the **Coronation Chair.** Unbelievably, every English monarch since 1308 has been crowned on this excruciating-looking throne. The slot under the seat is for the 152kg (336-lb.) Stone of Scone, said to be used as a pillow by the Bible's Jacob, and a central part of Irish, Scottish, and English coronations since at least 700 B.C. After spending 7 centuries in the Abbey (except for when Scottish nationalists stole it for 4 months in late 1950), the Stone was returned to Scotland in 1996, where it's on view at Edinburgh Castle. It will return to its slot for every future coronation.
- **Oliver Cromwell,** who overthrew the monarchy and ran England as a republic, was buried with honors behind the High Altar in 1658. Three years later, after the monarchy was restored, his corpse was dug up, dragged to Tyburn (by the modern-day Marble Arch), hanged, decapitated, the body tossed into a common grave, and its head put on display outside the Abbey. (Didn't the Royalists realize he was already dead?) Today his much-abused cranium is at Sidney Sussex College in Cambridge. Cromwell's daughter, who died young, was mercifully allowed to remain buried in the Abbey.
- The **Quire** is where the choir sings the daily services; it comprises about 12 men and 22 boys who are educated at the adjoining Westminster Choir School, the last of its type in the world. The wooden stalls, in the Gothic style, are Victorian, and are so delicate they're dusted using vacuum cleaners.

The Abbey's oft-overlooked **Museum,** beside the Pyx Chamber, contains some amazing treasures, including **Edward III's death mask** (thought to be the oldest of its kind in Europe; it's made of walnut and doesn't ignore his facial droop, which resulted from a stroke), **ancient jewelry** "found in graves" (we know what that means—pried from skeletons), the **fake Crown Jewels** used for coronation rehearsals, 14th-century leather shoes and Roman tiles unearthed on the grounds, and the fateful **Essex Ring,** which Elizabeth I gave to her brilliant confidant Robert Devereux, telling him to send it if he needed her. He tried to, but his enemies intercepted it, and he was beheaded at the Tower of London in 1601. Oops.

Time seems suspended in the **Cloister,** or courtyard. But better gardens are hidden away. At the Museum, head for the corridor to the left and you'll find the fragrant and fountained **Little Cloister Garden,** blackened by 19th-century coal dust, and beyond that to the right, the wide **College Garden,** a tempting courtyard with daffodil beds, green lawns, and five plane trees dating to 1850. The garden has been continuously planted for 900 years, when it grew herbs for an adjacent hospital. Westminster School, started by the abbey's monks in the 1300s, stands nearby. (Incidentally, there haven't been monks in this complex for 550 years, yet Londoners persist in calling it an "Abbey.")

The Tower of London ★★★ (Tower Hill, EC3; ☎ 084/4482-7777; www.hrp.org.uk; £17 adults, £9.50 children 5–15, £14 students/seniors, £46 family of up to 5; Nov–Feb Tues–Sat 9am–5pm and Sun–Mon 10am–5pm, Mar–Oct Tues–Sat 9am–6pm and Sun–Mon 10am–6pm, last admission 1 hr. before closing; Tube: Tower Hill or Tower Gateway DLR) is the most famous castle in the world, a

UNESCO World Heritage Site, and a symbol of not just London, but also of a millennium of English history. Less a tower than a fortified minitown of stone and timber, its history could fill this book. Suffice it to say that its oldest building, the four-cornered White Tower, went up in 1078 and the compound that grew around it has served as a palace, prison, treasury, mint, armory, zoo, and now, a lovingly maintained tourist attraction that no visitor should neglect. It's at the very heart of English history, and exploring its sprawl should take between 3 and 5 hours.

Tickets are sold outside the battlements. Hit the Welcome Centre, just past the Ticket Office, and grab a copy of the free "Daily Programme," which runs down the times and places of all the free talks, temporary exhibitions, and miniperformances. Plenty are offered—the Tower at times feels more like a theme park than a living museum with 1,000 years of history behind it. The prime excursion is the **Yeoman Warder's Tour,** led with theatrical aplomb by one of the Beefeaters who live in the Tower (there are about 100 residents, including families) and carefully preserve it. Those leave every 30 minutes from just inside the portcullis in the Middle Tower. They're engaging, but juvenile—expect bellowing and histrionics, plus a gleeful fetish for yarns about beheadings and torture. (In truth, you can count the people executed inside the Tower on your fingers and toes; it was considered an honor to be killed here, since it was private.) For reasons I'm about to explain, I suggest you double back and join the tour later in the day. If you'd like your history delivered without vaudevillian shenanigans, head to the gift shop on the right after Middle Tower and grab an audio tour (£3.50, but do it early; headsets run out). The official guidebooks (£5) here are pretty good, and they certainly help with orientation.

The key to touring the Tower is to arrive close to opening. At 9am, there's a short ceremony during which the guards unlock the gates for the day. Make a beeline for the two star attractions since intimidating queues form there by lunch: the Crown Jewels, housed in the Waterloo Block at the north wall (farthest from the Thames) and the White Tower, in the center of the grounds.

As you enter the **Crown Jewels** exhibition, you'll see archival film of the last time most of the jewels were officially used, at the coronation of Queen Elizabeth in 1952. After passing into a vault, visitors glide via people-movers past cases of glittering, downlit crowns, scepters, and orbs worn (awkwardly—they're 2.3kg/5 lb. each) by generations of British monarchs. Check out the legendary 105-carat Koh-I-Noor diamond, once the largest in the world, which is fixed to the temple of the **Queen Mother's Crown** (1937), along with 2,000 other diamonds; the Indian government has been begging to get the stone back. The 530-carat Cullinan I, the world's largest cut diamond, tops the Sovereign's **Sceptre with the Cross** (1661). The **Imperial State Crown,** ringed with emeralds, sapphires, and diamonds aplenty, is the one used in the annual State Opening of Parliament. After those come candlesticks that could support the roof of your house, trumpets, swords, and the inevitable traffic jam around the **Grand Punch Bowl** (1829), an elaborate riot of lions, cherubs, and unicorns that shows what it would look like if punch bowls could go insane. Because Oliver Cromwell liquidated every royal artifact he could get his hands on, everything dates to after the Restoration (the 1660s or later). Clearly, the monarchy has more than made up for the loss.

Touring the four levels of the cavernous **White Tower** requires much stair-climbing but takes in a wide span of history, including a fine stone chapel, Norman-era fireplaces and toilets, the gleaming collection of the Royal Armoury (even small children can't help but notice the exaggerated codpiece of King Henry VIII's intricately etched suit from 1540), and some models depicting the Tower's evolution (it's been much altered, but the six smallest arched windows on the White Tower's south side are original to the 11th century). After you're finished in here, you'll have an excellent overview of how the whole complex worked.

Once you've got those two areas under your belt, take your time exploring the rest. I suggest a stop in the brick **Beauchamp Tower** (pronounced "BEECH-um," 1280), where important political prisoners were held and where you can still glimpse graffiti testifying to their suffering. In front of it on Tower Green is the circular glass memorial designating the **Scaffold Site,** where the unlucky few (including sitting queens Anne Boleyn and Lady Jane Grey) are said to have lost their heads. In reality, we don't know exactly where they were killed, but Queen Victoria wanted a commemorative site set, and because of the obvious dangers of displeasing the queen, this spot was chosen.

The **St. Thomas's Tower,** from the 13th century, is closest to the Thames and re-creates King Edward's bedchamber with authentic materials. Beneath it, **Traitor's Gate,** once called Water Gate, originally was used to ferry prisoners in secret from the Thames. Torture was never a part of English law, but it happened here anyway, and the **Bloody Tower** was where some of the worst stuff went down. Don't forget to climb the ramparts for that classic photo of the Tower Bridge. But save the extra quid and skip the Royal Fusiliers Regimental Museum, a dreary hodgepodge of military memorabilia.

Daily at 2:50pm, the guards parade outside the Waterloo Block to the Byward Tower. On Sundays, your admission ticket allows you to attend services at the **Chapel Royal of St. Peter ad Vincula,** the Tower's church, at 9:15 or 11am; otherwise, the only way to get in, and to see the marble slab beneath which Boleyn and Grey's decapitated bodies were entombed, is with a Yeoman Warder's Tour.

Caw, Caw

Ravens probably first visited the Tower in the 1200s to feast on the dripping corpses of the executed, who were taken from Tower Hill (the public execution ground, near the present-day Tube stop) and hung outside the battlements as a warning. You've probably heard the legend that if the ravens ever leave the Tower, England will fall—so seven of the carnivorous birds are kept in cages north of Wakefield Tower, where they are fed raw meat, blood-soaked cookies, and the occasional finger from a tourist dumb enough to stick their hands between the bars. For a more intelligent feeding, the on-site restaurant in the New Armouries building grants three half-price kids' meals for every adult-sized meal.

Hear the Masterpieces at the National Gallery

The National Gallery's audio tours are free (they hold your I.D. as collateral), but don't offer much more information than you could read on the signs, which are awfully straight-laced. Your visit would be best illuminated by some expert input. Check the info desk for daily events, such as the "Ten Minute Talks" about a single work; hour-long 1pm "Lunchtime Talks" devoted to a specific work or artist; storytelling for kids; or the few hour-long guided tours (often at 11:30am and 2:30pm, plus another Wed around 7pm). The displays are usually supplemented by temporary exhibitions, one free and one paid (around £8). The Gallery schedules most family activities for Sundays.

When the bells of St. Martin-in-the-Fields peal each morning at 10am, the doors promptly open to the nearby **National Gallery** ★★★ (Trafalgar Square, WC2; ☎ 020/7747-2885; www.nationalgallery.org.uk; free admission; Thurs–Tues 10am–6pm and Wed 10am–9pm; Tube: Charing Cross or Leicester Square). Don't miss this. It's as relentless as a fireworks show—each famous picture follows an equally famous picture, many of which you'll instantly recognize.

The National Gallery boasts the strongest, widest collection of paintings in the world—a painting of every important style is on display, and it's almost always the best in that genre. The Uffizi in Florence focuses on Italian art, and the Louvre in Paris rambles on with too many second-rate works. If a painter isn't here, though, he isn't worth knowing. There are 2,300 Western European works—mostly royal-owned, originally—which is plenty to divert you for as long as you can manage.

The building was made in 1835; Trafalgar Square was selected because it was considered central, and therefore reachable by poor Londoners. Even today, crowds swell around lunchtime as working people pop in for a free art infusion. As you enter via the main Portico Entrance, gallery areas imperceptibly surge through time in a clockwise arrangement, from 1500 to 1600 paintings, to 1600 to 1700 paintings, to 1700 to 1900 paintings. The sleek Sainsbury Wing, opened in 1991 to house the early Renaissance collection from 1250 to 1500, can only be reached through room 9 (inside 1500–1600) or from the street.

The rooms jumble together, so grab a free Gallery Plan. The best course is to start in the Sainsbury Wing and backtrack, which will order your viewings more or less chronologically. Among the museum's many noteworthy holdings:

Sainsbury Wing

- Piero della Francesca, one of the most sought-after Renaissance painters (there's only one of his works on display in the entire United States), is represented by ***The Baptism of Christ*** (1450s, at press time it was in room 66) with its advanced use of light and foreshortening. The faces of its subjects verge on bemusement, and the dove, representing the Holy Spirit, seems to fly into viewers' faces.

- In his later years, Sandro Botticelli fell under the spell of the hardline reformer Savonarola. He burned many of his finest paintings in the Bonfire of the Vanities and changed to an inferior style, so his best works are rare; ***Venus and Mars*** (1485, room 58), depicting the lovers reclining, is one of them, and it's in a room full of others.

The Main Building

- The Gallery has four Michelangelos. ***The Entombment*** (around 1500, room 8) is unfinished but one of the most powerful. The feminine figure in the red gown is now thought to be St. John, but it's hard to know for sure, since the artist favored strong masculine traits.
- Kids love Holbein's ***The Ambassadors*** (1533, room 4), full of symbolic riddles and famous for a stretched image of a skull that can only be viewed in proper perspective from the right of the painting; and the hideous, porcine old lady in ***A Grotesque Old Woman*** (1525–30), thought to be a satire on ladies who try to look younger than they are.
- Nearby is Hans Holbein The Younger's oil-on-oak portrait of ***Christina of Denmark, Duchess of Milan*** (1538), painted for King Henry VIII when he was wife-shopping. She declined to marry him, and as a happy consequence, survived to 1590.
- The Gallery is rich in Peter Paul Rubens, with some 25 works attributed to him. His ***Samson and Delilah*** (1609–10, room 29) is known for Samson's muscular back and Delilah's crimson robe.
- Edouard Manet's ***The Execution of Maximilian*** (1867–68, room 43) was sliced into five sections after the artist's death, but Edgar Degas reassembled what he could; the missing patches lend the firing-squad scene further tension.

My list of recommendations could continue: George Seurat's almost pointillist ***Bathers at Asnieres*** (1884, room 44), Van Gogh's ***Sunflowers*** (room 45), Leonardo da Vinci's ***The Virgin of the Rocks*** (room 2), Jan van Eyck's ***The Arnolfini Portrait*** (Sainsbury Wing, room 56), a mysterious but fabulously skillful depiction of light that dates to 1434, years ahead of its time. **Rembrandts. Cézannes. Uccellos.** There's so much art here that you may want to go twice during your visit, and the Gallery is so centrally located that you can.

The opening of the **Tate Modern** ★★★ (Bankside, SE1; ☎ 020/7887-8888; www.tate.org.uk/modern; free admission; Sun–Thurs 10am–6pm and Fri–Sat 10am–10pm, last admission 45 min before closing; Tube: Southwark) in 2000 redefined the recreational landscape. Seemingly overnight, Southwark went from an inhospitable no-man's-land, mocked and avoided, to one of the city's favorite promenades. Bankside's chief eyesore, a mammoth power station—steely and cavernous, a cathedral to industry—became as integral to London as the Quire of Westminster Abbey or the Dome of St. Paul's, with more than 5 million visitors annually. The gigantic Turbine Hall, cleared of machinery to form a meadow-like expanse of smooth concrete, hosts changing works specially created by major-league artists, and art hounds of every background recline there as if it were a city park. Even if you don't care for modern art, the building is still a star.

The flow through the galleries, stacked from floors three to six on the river side of the building (the Turbine Hall is alongside them, and can be surveyed from balconies), is sensibly directed, so you won't need much help. Holdings, which focus on art made since 1900, are divided into four areas of thought, loose enough that you never know what sort of witty article waits behind any corner: On Level 3, you'll see Material Gestures (about Abstract Expressionism; free tours at noon) and Poetry and Dream (for Surrealism, probably the most arresting wing; free tours at 11am); and on Level 5, States of Flux (for Cubism and Futurism; free tours at 2pm) and Idea and Object (for Minimalism and pop art; free tours at 3pm). Between those floors, Level 4 hosts two changing exhibitions, which require tickets (£7–£10; check online for what's showing).

The formidable collection, one of the world's best for breadth, is always changing, not just because the museum owns more than it can display (even in this massive facility), but also because countless works come in and out on short-term loans. You could visit once a year and see new stuff each time. Fortunately, the Tate website is always updated with the works that are on display, along with occasional free podcasts to use as tours. It also allows you to locate works on an interactive map and, cleverly, build your own tour based on your favorites.

Some may argue that the curation suffers from over-representation of old-school works and a relative dearth of truly progressive stuff, but I think the selection is approachable even for people normally put off by modern art. On a typical visit, you'll see some seminal items by Picasso, Léger, Braque, and Rivera—and that's just one wing (in this case, States of Flux). True, the descriptions too often dwell on the incestuous culture of the art world, but fortunately, the daring of the pieces themselves speak louder than the curators' self-satisfied descriptions. Who can say which pieces are the most important? Modern art is often a matter of taste, since reputations haven't been cemented by time. But you might recognize some heavy hitters. In room 7 of Material Gestures, you'll find at least two works that critics define as seminal. Claude Monet's hypnotizing ***Water-Lillies*** (after 1916), gives light patterns on water a virtually conceptual character—but not enough to ruffle a classicist's feathers. The painting is considered a harbinger of abstract expressionism. Just as radical for its day was Jackson Pollock's 19-foot-long ***Summertime: Number 9A,*** an insurrection of paint-strewn chaos intended to draw out the artist's unconscious. Joseph Beuys' oversize, haphazard-seeming installation ***Lightning with Stag in its Glare*** (room 6, Poetry and Dream) also wins plaudits, although perhaps its influence is not mature enough to be deeply known.

Modern art can be bewildering, but the Tate's exceptional array of touring aids can make sense of oddity. Just £2 will rent a tremendous multimedia tour of the highlights that plays on a Blackberry-like device that shows you additional images as it embellishes on the works' meaning and context. Collapsible stools, interspersed around the galleries on wall-mounted racks, are another thoughtful touch for those who like to sketch artwork. There are two free daily guided tours of the general collection, usually at 11am and 3pm; ask at the ground floor information desk to find out where they meet. At Level 3's free Family Zone, open on weekends and busy days, kids can pick up an art-related activity, such as a drawing or storytelling kit, and bring it into the galleries with them. The shop, on the bottom floor by the West entrance, is epic.

Some advice: Try to enter the Tate Modern via the doors at its narrow end, facing the west (not the riverside entrance), because that's the most dramatic way to absorb the powerful negative space of the Turbine Hall, although this may not be possible on your visit because the Tate is building a new tower in time for the

2012 Olympics. The glass panels rimming the roof facing the Thames announce the names of the artists currently showing ticketed exhibitions. The sit-down Tate Modern Restaurant on Level 7 can be inhospitable due to crowds (make a reservation online) and high prices—but its panorama of St. Paul's and the Thames is primo, and its fish and chips platter with mushy peas is delicious. It's also £13 at lunch; you can get the same dish for £2 less in the cafe on the second floor, but without that fine view.

Tourists often wonder what the difference is between the Tate Modern and its sister located upstream on the Thames, the **Tate Britain** ★ (Millbank, SW1; ☎ 020/7887-8888; www.tate.org.uk/britain; free admission; daily 10am–5:50pm, until 10pm on the first Fri of the month; Tube: Pimlico). Well, the Modern is for contemporary art of any origin, and the Britain is exclusive to British-made art made after 1500. Not to diminish the quality of the grade-A work on display here, but you won't spot many recognizable masterpieces. Britain has a historic knack for collecting international art, not so much for creating it, so a lot of the work on display is rich with relevance but highly imitative of classical or Renaissance styles. Although the oldest portion of the collection, full of documentary or moralist works by William Hogarth and Joshua Reynolds, illustrate what everyday British life was like centuries ago, it's hard to shake the feeling that, artistically speaking, Britain was playing catch-up with the rest of Europe. That changes when the galleries progress chronologically into the modern era, and works by visionaries such as Francis Bacon and James Abbott McNeill Whistler (granted, not English, but an American who lived in England) reveal the originality and ebullient colors that were latent in the national mind.

The presentation of these galleries is nowhere near as friendly as it is at the Modern. Descriptions are often didactic (works are described, emptily, to be

The Tate-to-Tate Boat

The best way to get between the Tates is not via Tube (a circuitous route) but via the **Tate Boat** (☎ 020/7887-8888; www.tate.org.uk/tatetotate; singles £4 adults, £2 children under 16, unless you have a valid London Transport Travelcard, which reduces singles to £2.60 adults, £1.30 children), a 220-seat catamaran that zips along the Thames every 40 minutes from 10am to around 5pm between the docks in front of the Tate Britain and the Tate Modern. Along the way, it stops by the London Eye and also supplies the only view of Big Ben and the Houses of Parliament that isn't spoiled by angular fences and gun-fondling guards. For hop-on, hop-off service all day, including additional services from the Tate Modern to the Tower of London, buy a **River Roamer** pass for £8 adults/£4 children (£5.20/£2.60 with a Travelcard); family tickets are available. The shipboard decor is by art bad boy Damien Hirst, who fortunately abandoned his famous formaldehyde-dipped sharks for a conservative polka-dot theme. Tate's entertainment!

"questioning" or "explorations") and many paintings are placed at such high levels that glare makes them inscrutable. It's all very good, but a bit too textbook.

Like the Tate Modern, the Tate Britain mounts a respectable line-up of tours and weekend family activities, so it usually pays to go online ahead of time to see what special things are planned and which works are being displayed where. You could fill a Tuesday with the four 1-hour tours that take place then: Art from 1500 to 1800 (11am), from 1800 to 1900 (noon), one dedicated to Turner (2pm), and works from 1900 to present day (3pm). On Tuesdays and Sundays in the early afternoon, a changing "Painting of the Month" is explained. Audio tours are always available for £3.50.

The Tate Britain is also sassy. Online at www.tate.org.uk/britain/yourcollection, you can download the museum's free, wittily written pamphlets, which point out works on funny themes, including "The I'm Hungover Collection" (works about sin, soothing pastorals); "The I'm in a Hurry Collection" (just one painting, a Francis Bacon in room 26, which is a commentary on post-war misery); and "The I Like Yellow Collection." Those are for sport, but there are also must-sees, such as:

- John Everett Millais' sublime ***Ophelia,*** the museum's most popular work, is a delicately painted image (1851–52) of Hamlet's lover drowning herself in a brook as she sings herself to death. Check out the astonishing detail on the leaves and moss, as well as in the refraction effect of the water on her body.
- John Singleton Copley's smoke-filled ***The Death of Major Peirson*** (1783, room 9) was the Duke of Wellington's favorite painting; that figures, since it shows men in uniform. Below it, J. M. W. Turner's trenchant ***The Field of Waterloo*** was painted in 1818, 3 years after the battle; its gloomy piles of corpses, and of bereaved family members searching them, makes the now-unknown battle suddenly vivid and touching. Better than any war painting I can name, it reminds me that real families suffered mightily from wars no one even remembers anymore.
- The oil-on-canvas ***Carnation, Lily, Lily, Rose*** (room 15) depicts children holding paper lanterns so luminous that visitors often halt in their tracks as they pass it. John Singer Sargent (another American who settled in London) is the genius responsible.
- A series of recent eye-catchers is in room 19: The contemplative ***Figure of a Woman,*** by one of the country's most important sculptors, Barbara Hepworth, is somehow both bulky and fluid; nearby is Henry Moore's undulating, semitangled ***Half-figure*** of a female. In a duel between abstract women from the waist up, Hepworth's diffident grace wins—and she did it first.
- The crowning attraction here is the **Turner Galleries,** with their expansive collection of J. M. W. Turners. Turner (1775–1851), the son of a Covent Garden barber, was a master of landscapes lit by misty, perpetual sunrise, and the dozens of paintings and sketchbooks on display testify to his undying popularity. Turner's work is lovely, if sleepy, but the mania for him is a bit beyond me (in Apr 2006, one of his works set a record for British paintings at auction, fetching £20.5 million). Just don't sully his name in these halls; even his crusty paint box and his fishing rod are dotingly preserved.

As a decorative arts repository, The Victoria and Albert Museum, usually called the **V&A ★★★ kids (Cromwell Road, SW7; ☎ 020/7942-2000; www.vam.ac.uk; free admission; daily 10am–5:45pm, until 10pm Wed and Fri; Tube: South Kensington)**, is about eye candy. This means that although the museum occupies a haughty High Victorian edifice more suited to a courthouse or a capitol, it celebrates beauty and style, not politics or history. If it's good-looking, fabulously well-designed, or might look smart on your wall, it'll be here.

The ground floor, a grid of hard-to-navigate rooms, has lots of good stuff, but lots more bric-a-brac (Korean pots, 1,000-year-old Egyptian jugs of rock crystal) that you'll probably walk past with polite but hasty appreciation. The second, third, and fourth levels have less floor space and therefore are more manageable. The second floor is where the special exhibitions, which require paid tickets, are held.

Rooms are arranged by country of origin or by medium (ironwork, tapestries, etc.) but you'll want to see: the **20th Century** (rooms 70–74, level 3), which surprises by including objects you may have once kept in your home (a Dyson vacuum cleaner, Tinkertoys); **Architecture** (rooms 127–128a, level 4), for a nautilus-like preconstruction model of the Sydney Opera House; and endless slices of **medieval stained glass** (rooms 83–84, level 3) Wherever you go, you may use the little stools hanging from pegs on the wall, and if you see a drawer beneath a display case, open it, because many treasures are stored out of the light.

The V&A, which, tellingly, was endowed by the proceeds from the first world's fair (the Great Exhibition of 1851), is very much about fine objects from everyday life, so wandering around the premises, discovering whatever catches the eye, is half the point. Just don't neglect these highlights:

- The seven **Raphael Cartoons** (room 48a), dating from 1515, are probably the most priceless items in the house. These giant paper paintings—yes, paper—were created by the hand of Raphael as templates for the weavers of his ten tapestries for the Sistine Chapel. Before Queen Victoria moved them here, they hung for around 175 years in the purpose-built Cartoon Gallery at Hampton Court Palace. The colors are fugitive, meaning they're fading: Christ's red robe, painted with plant-based madder lake, has turned white—his reflection in the water, painted with a different pigment, is still red.
- None of the sculptures in the sky-lit **Cast Court** (rooms 46 and 46a) are original. They're all casts of the greatest hits in Renaissance art, and they crowd the room like a yard sale. They were put here in 1873 as a sort of World's Fair for the poor, who could never hope to travel and see the real articles for themselves. Like much of the V&A, it was set up for learning, which is why there are so many significant works, such as Ghiberti's doors to the baptistery at Florence's San Giovanni, whose design essentially kicked off the artistic frenzy of the Renaissance. Michelangelo's *David,* floppy puppy feet and all, looks down from his pedestal; he was fitted with a fig leaf for Victorian royal visits. Amazingly, many of these replicas are now in better shape than the originals.
- It's not just that **Margaret Laton's jacket** (room 56) is a gorgeous garment. Its silver-thread embroidery and trim cut will leave you agog, and the survival of such an everyday piece of clothing is highly rare. But what's truly astonishing about the jacket is that it's displayed alongside a 1620 oil portrait

of Margaret Laton herself—wearing the same jacket. The odds against both items surviving and being reunited in the same case are astronomical. Every time I come, I visit the jacket and imagine the long-departed woman who once filled those empty sleeves.

- **Tippoo's Tiger** (room 41) kids is a macabre wooden sculpture commissioned by an Indian sultan in the 1790s. Depicting a life-size tiger in the act of devouring a hapless European, it's rigged with clockworks that cause the tiger to growl and its victim to moan plaintively and weakly bat his arm. It's been a crowd favorite since 1808, when it was part of the East India Company's house museum. Kids will leave either awed or freaked out.
- **The Great Bed of Ware** (room 57), a vast four-poster of carved oak that dates to about 1590, was apparently once a tourist attraction at a country inn, renowned enough for Shakespeare to mention it in *Twelfth Night:* "big enough for the bed of Ware." As you admire it, consider that in those days, bed canopies were installed to protect sleepers from insects that might tumble out of their thatched roofs and into their mouths. Canopied beds, a mark of luxury today, were a sign of a humbler home then.
- The **Ardabil carpet,** the world's oldest dated carpet (copies have appeared on the floors of 10 Downing Street and Hitler's Berlin office alike), is part of a £5.4-million Islamic arts gallery opened in 2006. To preserve its dyes, the carpet is lit for just ten minutes at a time on every half-hour.
- The **Gilbert Collection** of impossibly fine decorative arts (jewel boxes, cameos, silver, fine mosaics, and the like) amassed by a rich enthusiast is so impressive it used to occupy its own museum; in fall 2009, it opens its own suite of galleries at the V&A.

Free 1-hour introductory tours are given at 10:30 and 11:30am, and 3:30pm. The bulk of family events here falls on weekends, including the availability of delightful "Back-Packs," which contain activity sets for kids that engage them in some of the museum's most eye-catching holdings. More goodies for kids are exhibited at the Museum of Childhood (p. 188). Make a side visit to the V&A's western exterior. Scarred during the bombing raids of The Blitz, the stonework was left alone as a memorial. If the damage was this bad in Kensington, just imagine how bad it was in the Germans' main target, East London.

The magnificent spire of the old **St. Paul's Cathedral** ★★★ **(St. Paul's Churchyard, EC4; ☎ 020/7246-8357; www.stpauls.co.uk; £10 adults, £3.50 children 7–16, free children under, £9 seniors, £8.50 students; Mon–Sat 8:30am–5pm, open for worship only on Sun, Whispering Gallery and Dome cleared and last admission at 4:15pm; Tube: St. Paul's)** was a London landmark and part of Old St. Paul's, which was even larger and stood on this site for nearly 600 years before it was claimed by 1666's Great Fire. So when Sir Christopher Wren was commissioned to rebuild London's greatest house of worship, he devoted 40 years to the project and decided to go one further by giving the city a mighty dome—highly unusual for the time. My, how people talked.

St. Paul's cost £750,000 to build, an astronomical sum in 1697 when the first section opened for worship, and now, it costs £3 million a year to run. Wren overspent so much that decoration was curtailed; the mosaics weren't added until Queen Victoria thought the place needed spiffing up. Stained glass is still missing, which allows the sweep and arch of Wren's design to shine cleanly through. Many foreigners were introduced to the sanctuary during the wedding of Prince Charles and Lady Diana Spencer in 1981, but the cathedral also saw a sermon by Martin Luther King in 1964 and Churchill's funeral the following year.

The **High Altar** has a canopy supported by single tree trunks that were hollowed out and carved, and its 15th-century crucifix and candlesticks require two men to lift. (They're nailed down, anyway. As one docent, a half-century veteran of Cathedral tours, lamented, "You'd be surprised what people try to steal.") Behind it is the **American Memorial Chapel** to the 28,000 American soldiers who died while based in England in Word War II. In a glass case, one leaf of a 500-page book containing their names is turned each day. The **organ,** with 7,000 pipes, was regularly played by Mendelssohn and Handel, and the lectern is original. The **Great West Doors,** largely unused, are 27m high (90 ft.) and on their original hinges; they're so well-hung that even a weakling can swing them open. In 2005, the Cathedral completed a £10.8-million cleaning program; a stone panel beside the doors was left filthy to show just how bad things were.

Most people are familiar with the famous 1940 photograph of the **Dome,** lit purely by firelight during the Blitz, which has come to symbolize London's fortitude during Word War II. What most people don't know is that St. Paul's *was* hit, many times—a bomb blasted the floor of the North Transept (photos of the devastation are in the Crypt), and another obliterated the east end. So many people were assigned to stamp out incendiary bombs before they could melt through the Cathedral's lead-lined roof that huge areas of The City were left unmanned—much of London was lost so that St. Paul's could be saved, a bittersweet fact.

Eight central pillars here support the entire weight of the wood-frame Dome; Wren filled them with loose rubble. In 1925, engineers broke them open to find the debris had settled to the bottom, and they filled them again with liquid concrete. If you're fit, you can mount the 259 steps (each an awkward 13cm/5 in. tall, with benches on many landings) to the **Whispering Gallery,** 30m/98 ft. above the floor. Famously, its acoustics are so fine you can turn your head and mutter something that can be understood on the opposite side. That's in theory; so many tourists are usually blabbing to each other that you won't hear a thing, although it is a transcendent place to listen to choir rehearsal on a mid-afternoon. Climb higher (you've gone 378 steps now) to the **Stone Gallery,** an outdoor terrace just beneath the Dome, and catch your breath, if you choose, for the final 152-step push to the **Golden Gallery,** which requires you to scale the inner skin of the Dome, past ancient oriel windows and along tight metal stairs. It's safe, but it's not for those with vertigo or claustrophobia. The spectacular 360-degree city view from the top (85m/279 ft. up), at the base of the Ball and Lantern (you can't go up farther), is so beautiful that it defies full appreciation. For more than 250 years, this was the tallest structure in London, and therefore the top of the world.

If you miss the **Crypt,** you'll have missed a lot. In addition to many memorials to the famous dead (such as Florence Nightingale and plenty of obscure war heroes), you'll find the tombs of two of Britain's greatest military demigods: **Admiral Horatio Nelson** (whose body was preserved for the trip from the battlefield by soaking in brandy and wine; the 72,000-ton weight of the Dome is borne by the walls of this small chamber), and **Arthur Duke of Wellington** (flanked by

Knowing St. Paul's Like a Local

Ninety-minute tours by volunteers, called "supers," cost £3 at most, and leave at 11 and 11:30am, and 1:30 and 2pm. Take one of these instead of an audio tour, which costs a pound more, because the supers are the elder statesmen of the Cathedral; many have been associated with it for decades, going back to the hairy days of the 1940s. You can also worship here; see p. 151.

flags captured on the field of battle; they will hang there until they disintegrate). To the right of the OBE Chapel, in **Artists Corner,** there's a monument to poet **John Donne** that still bears the scorch marks it suffered in Old St. Paul's during the Great Fire (they're on its urn, and it was the only thing that survived the conflagration), and you'll find the graves of the artists **J. M. W. Turner** and **Henry Moore,** plus **Christopher Wren** himself, who rests beneath his masterpiece. "I build for eternity," he once said, and so far, so good: In 2010, the cathedral will celebrate 300 years since its completion. If you're hungry, scope out the cafe, since it's one of the cheaper options in this neighborhood. ***Tip:*** Buy your tickets online ahead (you'll need a printer) and you can save 50p.

The National Portrait Gallery (kids) ★ **(St. Martin's Place, WC2; ☎ 020/7312-2463; www.npg.org.uk; free admission; Sat–Wed 10am–6pm, Thurs–Fri 10am–9pm, last admission 45 min. before closing; Tube: Leicester Square)** could be considered the documentary companion to the National Gallery; everything inside depicts a famous Brit. On paper, that concept sounds like Field Trip Hell. But actually, you'll be surprised how the best works capture the sparkle of life that made their subjects such charismatic history-shapers. Here, the names from your high school textbook flower into flesh-and-blood people. The longer you stare, the more life they seem to have.

I find the ancient kings and queens have the most heft, partly because it's hard to wrap my brain around the fact that in many cases, the actual people posed in the same room as these very canvases. One of the most instantly recognizable paintings is the **Ditchley portrait of Elizabeth I,** in which the queen's jeweled gown spreads like wings and Her Majesty firmly glares at the viewer under stormy skies. Right away, it becomes clear that many artists are slyly commenting on the disposition of their sitters. The troublesome **Henry VIII** is shown in several likenesses. One is an especially delicate paper cartoon, by Hans Holbein the Younger (for a mural at Whitehall—a rare survivor from that palace), in which the king suspiciously peers out with flinty grey eyes—hinting at a shiftiness that His Majesty probably couldn't recognize in his own likeness, but that all who knew him caught. One painting of **King Edward VI,** painted when he was nine, is executed in a distorted perspective (called anamorphosis) that requires it to be viewed from a hole on the right side of its case. You'll also find no fewer than six **George Washingtons** (he was born an Englishman, after all), and one of the only authoritative images of **Captain James Cook,** painted in Cape Town by a Swiss draughtsman on the explorer's fatal voyage.

Fortunately, the portraits don't stop when people started snapping photos. The 1982 oil-on-canvas image of **Margaret Thatcher,** as viewed from below her gunship-grey podium at the Conservative Party Conference in Brighton, is a fearsome and not-very-fond representation of the Iron Lady. In contrast, a 1950 sitting-room portrait of **Queen Elizabeth II** with her parents, **King George VI** and the **Queen Mum,** mines Rockwell-esque, just-us-folks imagery (Mum's about to pour tea, Dad's smoking) to make the Royal Family seem as normal and as middle-class as The Cleavers. The modern portraits tend to change often because there's simply not enough room to show everything. Just about everything can be printed as a poster and purchased at prices starting at £5.

To start, take the escalator to the top floor and work your way down, which takes about 2 hours. The oldest works (Tudors, Jacobeans, Elizabethans) will come first, and you'll progress forward in time—adding photography when canvas fatigue sets in. Frankly, it helps to have a little historical knowledge so that these pictures ring some bells, so consider visiting near the end of your trip, when many of these names will be fresh in your mind from your tours. The £2 audio guide can be dull at the start, but by the end, it uses archival recordings of the famous people you're looking at, which is cool. Bring along kids; the front desk loans free rucksack tours (pick Tudors, Victorians, or 20th-century) for those aged 5 to 11.

The Portrait Gallery isn't the sort of place where you'll spend half your day, but it's a sleeper favorite. Also consider it for its pre-theatre menu (£15 for two courses, £18 for three) served from 5:30 to 6:30pm in the rooftop cafe, which has a terrific view taking in Nelson's Column and Big Ben's tower.

ATTRACTIONS THAT OUGHT TO BE MORE FAMOUS

Housing one of the most precious collections of books, maps, and manuscripts in the world, the permanent "Treasures of the British Library" exhibition at **The British Library** ★★★ (96 Euston Rd., NW1; ☎ 087/0444-1500; www.bl.uk; free admission; Mon and Wed–Fri 9:30am–6pm, Tues 9:30am–8pm, Sat 9:30am–5 pm, Sun 11am–5pm; Tube: King's Cross St. Pancras), displayed in a dim, climate-controlled suite of black cases and rich purple carpeting, is a dazzler. I think it's the most incredible museum in town, and I make a point of going during every visit, if I can. I will never understand why it isn't always mobbed.

The collection holds approximately 150 million items, and adds 3 million each year, so when it puts the cream (about 200 items) on display, prepare to be floored. On a recent visit, I encountered a dejected-looking visitor staring into space from an upholstered bench. His wife came over and asked what was wrong. "There's too many things to see," he said. Indeed—a small portion of the trove includes:

- Two of the four known copies of the Magna Carta from 1215.
- The Beatles' first lyric doodles for the songs that became "Yesterday," "A Ticket to Ride," and "I Wanna Hold Your Hand" (containing an early line, happily revised: "let me hold your thing").
- The Diamond Sutra, the oldest known printed book, which was found in a Chinese cave in 1907 and was probably made by woodblock nearly 600 years before Europeans developed similar technology.

- The *Codex Sinaiticus,* one of the two oldest Christian Bibles in existence (the Pope has the other).
- Charlotte Brontë's handwritten copy of *Jane Eyre.*
- A Mozart score for the glass armonica, and Chopin's *Barcarolle in F Sharp Major* (you can listen to the final works on headphones, too).
- A letter by Queen Elizabeth I, The Virgin Queen, about whether she would get married; and beside that, Sir Thomas More's last letter to Henry VIII.
- An early 11th-century copy of *Beowulf* on vellum, in Old English; it's the only surviving manuscript copy.

Touch-screen "Turning the Pages" displays allow you to thumb through some of the prettiest specimens as if they were open in front of you. Leaf through the Sultan Baybars' Qur'an, written in gold; take a peek at Leonardo da Vinci's sketches of musical instruments; browse Lewis Carroll's complete hand-drawn copy of *Alice in Wonderland* that was presented to the girl herself; and read the 15th-century Golf Book, each page a major illuminated work of art.

You can't handle books unless you're an accredited scholar, but the Library encourages anyone to hang out in its public spaces, regardless of credentials. In addition to the Treasures, rotating and permanent exhibitions are on display. For example, the hall off the cafe contains the huge **Philatelic Exhibition,** 500 vertical drawers containing thousands of stamps from around the world. You can also see a manageable display by the **Centre for Conservation** about how these books deteriorate and what's done daily to preserve them.

Head to the info desk to pick up a free guide and events info; the librarians schedule frequent talks and occasions to inspect unique items from the stacks (including, oddly, non-bibliophilic objects such as locks of Napoleon's hair and the ashes of the poet Shelley). Ask about audio tours of the cache (£3.50) and of the building's design, narrated by its architect, Sir Colin St. John Wilson. The cafe on the ground floor is one of the city's best-kept secrets, considered by those in the know to serve the best cappuccino in town.

I find most war-related attractions to be stiff and barely related to the drama of the events they purport to address. So because I recommend it highly, you can appreciate how fascinating the **Churchill Museum and Cabinet War Rooms ★★★ (Clive Steps, King Charles St., SW1; ☎ 020/7930-6961; www.iwm.org.uk; £12 adults, free for children under 16, £9.50 seniors/students; daily 9:30am–6pm, last admission 5pm; Tube: Westminster)** must be. This was the secret command center used by Winston Churchill and his cabinet during the most harrowing moments of Word War II, when it was looking like England would soon become German. We may regard the period with nostalgia now, but the abject terror of life then cannot be exaggerated; a staggering 30,000 civilians were killed by some 18,000 tons of bombs in London alone and more than 65,000 innocent people were killed in Britain as a whole. Here, in the cellar of the Treasury building, practically next door to 10 Downing Street and Parliament, the core of the British government hunkered down in secret.

When the War ended, the bunker was abandoned but stayed a secret in case hostilities flared up again. In the 1970s, historians found everything left just as it was in August 1945—from pushpins tracing troop movements on yellowed world maps to rationed sugar cubes hidden in the back of a clerk's desk. Although the

Altar Your Plans: These Churches Are Divine

I know, I know—in Europe, where so many historic sights are ecclesiastical, it doesn't take long before Church Fatigue sets in. But don't give up on God yet. Some of these houses of worship have been altered by well-meaning preservationists, falling bombs, or the ravages of time, but all possess dense histories that set them apart.

Southwark Cathedral ★ (London Bridge, SE1; ☎ 020/7367-6700; www.southwark.anglican.org/cathedral; free admission but £4 donation suggested; Mon–Fri 8am–6pm, Sat–Sun 9am–6pm; Tube: London Bridge). Pick up an antique panoramic map of London and look next to old London Bridge on the southern bank. See that church with the square Early English tower? The one flying a pinnacle, and tending to the destitute river men? It still stands. Called St. Saviour's until its elevation to an Anglican cathedral in 1905, the retro-choir, choir, and choir-aisles, dating to the 1200s, constitute the earliest surviving Gothic building in London, but the roof and nave were rebuilt in the mid-1800s. Its Refectory (p. 119) is a choice place for lunch. It's included in the walking tour on p. 242.

Temple Church ★ (Temple, EC4; ☎ 020/7353-3470; www.templechurch.com; free admission; hours vary, so call ahead, but opening days are Wed–Sun; Tube: Temple or Chancery Lane). A well-kept secret until a decoy plot twist in *The Da Vinci Code* put it on the tourist circuit, the Temple Church was consecrated in 1185 by the Knights Templar, who were Crusaders. Famous for its life-size effigies of knights, it was bombed in 1940 and rebuilt, but that's not why the columns are leaning—the originals did, too.

hideout functioned like a small town, with sleeping quarters for the Churchills and 526 others, kitchens, radio rooms, and other facilities that would enable leaders to live undetected for months on end, it feels a lot more like your old elementary school, with its painted brick, linoleum walls, and round clocks.

If the Cabinet War Rooms are old-school, the connecting **Churchill Museum,** opened by the Queen in 2005 after an expense of £6 million, is surely the most cutting-edge biographical museum open at this moment. Exhaustively displaying every conceivable rarity (Churchill's bowtie, his bowler hat, and even the original front door to 10 Downing Street), it covers the exalted statesman's life from entitled birth (interestingly, his mother was an American blue-blood) through his antics as a journalist in South Africa (where he escaped a kidnapping and became a national hero), to, of course, his years as prime minister. Although the entire museum is atwitter with multimedia displays, movies, and archival sounds, the centerpiece will blow you away: a 15m-long (50-ft.) Lifeline Interactive table, illuminated by projections, that looks like a long file cabinet and covers every month of Churchill's life. Touch a date, and the file "opens" with 4,600 pages of rare documents, photos, or, for critical dates in history, surprise animations that

The church stands in the Middle and Inner Temples, and lawyer's chambers surround it like a little litigious village.

St. Etheldreda (14 Ely Place, off Charterhouse St., EC1; ☎ 020/7405-1061; www.stetheldreda.com; free admission; daily 8:30am–7pm; Tube: Farringdon or Chancery Lane). Britain's oldest Catholic church, built from 1250–1290, would have baked in the Great Fire were it not for a sudden shift in the weather. In *Richard III,* Shakespeare mentioned the succulent strawberries that once grew in its garden. The jeweled cask to the right of the high altar contains a piece of the hand of Etheldreda, a 7th-century saint. and beneath the hall is an undercroft that once doubled as a tavern; the singing and brawling often disrupted services upstairs. Around back is the sublime Mitre House Tavern pub (p. 131), a perfect mid-day hideaway. The Crypt Café is cheap but only open weekdays from noon to 2:30pm.

Wesley's Chapel (49 City Rd., WC1; ☎ 020/7253-2262; www.wesleyschapel.org.uk; free admission; Mon–Sat 10am–4pm, Sun 12:30–1:45pm, last admission 30 min. before closing; Tube: Old Street). John Wesley, the 18th-century founding father of Methodism, constructed this chapel as his London base in 1778 on a plot St. Paul's Cathedral was using as a dump. It's one of the few city churches to come through the War virtually unscathed. Wesley's final home, pulpit, and resting places are all here, as is a small **Museum of Methodism** in the crypt. Across the street in Bunhill Fields is a nonconformist cemetery containing the earthly remains of Daniel Defoe, William Blake, and John Bunyan.

temporarily consume the entire table (select the days for Hiroshima bombing or the Titanic sinking to see what I mean). It's a breathtaking design that injects learning with play. It's too bad the addition of the Churchill Museum has caused admission to soar, but I still think the expense is worth it.

The history of London is the history of the Western world, so the miraculous cache of rarities from everyday life in the **Museum of London** ★★ (London Wall, EC2; ☎ 087/0444-3852; www.museumoflondon.org.uk; free admission; Mon–Sat 10am–5:50pm, Sun noon–5:50pm, last admission 5:30pm; Tube: Barbican or St. Paul's) wouldn't be out of place in the greatest national museums of any land. But here, they're cataloged in a place that most tourists, judging by the name, might assume will be lame. Well, it's not. This huge storehouse, smartly presented, contains so many forehead-smackingly rare items that by the time you're two-thirds through it, you'll start to lose track of all the goodies you've seen. When it comes to the history of this patch we call London, no stone has been left unturned—literally—because exhibits start with local archaeological finds (including elephant vertebrae and a lion skull) before continuing to 3,500-year-old spearheads and swords found in the muck of the Thames. Voices from the past come alive again in chronological order: There's a 1st-century oak ladder that was discovered preserved in a well, painted wall plaster from a Roman bath, loaded gambling dice made of bone in the 1400s, a leather bucket used in vain to fight the Great Fire of 1666, and far, far more. The biggest drawback here is that you need to budget a few hours, otherwise you'll end up in a mad rush through the entire lower floor covering the Great Fire to now. You don't want to miss the Victorian Walk, a kid-friendly re-creation of city streets, shops and all, from the 1800s (grab a card at its entrance so you'll know what you're seeing). You can't miss the Lord Mayor's state coach, carved in 1757, which garages here all year awaiting its annual airing at the Lord Mayor's Show in November. The museum, which overlooks a Roman wall fragment outside, is easy to combine with a visit to St. Paul's, and sells one of the best selections of books on city history. ***Warning:*** The lower floor, which covers 1666 to the present day, is under renovation until 2010. Its displayed artifacts, including the Lord Mayor's Coach, will return then.

If you dig the Museum of London, the **Museum in Docklands** ★★ kids (West India Quay, Canary Wharf, E14; ☎ 087/0444-3857; www.museumindocklands.org.uk; £5 adults, free for children under 16, £3 seniors/students; daily 10am–6pm, last admission 5:30pm; Tube: West India Quay DLR or Canary Wharf), which opened in 2003, gives a similarly lush, ultimately redeeming treatment to life on the river in London's East End. Many of the city's other museums would have you believe that London was always a genteel bastion of graceful gentlemen. This place tells the real story of the working men who sweat to put the teacups into more privileged, manicured hands. The history of the Docklands is one of grubby boatmen, unsavory profiteering from the slave trade, and painful Word War II bombings, so studying it only came into vogue once the skyscrapers arrived. Housed in a brick rum-and-coffee warehouse from 1804, the three-floor museum, strong on plain-speaking explanations, traces the history of working on the Thames starting with Anglo-Saxon times. You can inspect an intricate model of the medieval London Bridge, which like the Florentine Ponte Vecchio was stacked with homes and businesses but clogged the river's flow so drastically that it was a threat to life. You'll also roam "Sailortown," a creepy warren of quayside alleys, all shanties and low doorways, meant to evoke the area's early 19th-century underworld. Finally, the spotlight shifts to the harrowing 1940s, when the whole area was obliterated by fire from the sky and forced to reinvent itself as a corporate citadel. The whole circuit takes several hours. There's also a play area for kids, Mudlarks, and a ticket is good for repeat visits all year.

Although it looks like a kingly mansion on the Thames, **Somerset House** (Strand, WC2; ☎ 020/7845-4600; www.somersethouse.org.uk; Tube: Temple), at the river south of Covent Garden, is actually an aggregation of civil buildings in a palatial costume; Londoners used to troop here to register births, deaths, and to research family histories. Now, a portion is open to the public as a terrific art museum. The masses don't visit it, but art historians consider **The Courtauld Institute of Art Gallery** ★★ (☎ 020/7848-2526; www.courtauld.ac.uk; £5 adults, £4 children/seniors/students, free admission Mon 10am–2pm; daily 10am–6pm, last admission 5:30pm) one of the most prestigious collections on earth. Its small two-level selection is supreme, with several masterpieces you will instantly recognize. Among the winners are Manet's scandalous *Le Déjeuner sur l'herbe,* depicting a naked woman picnicking with two clothed men and the artist's *A Bar at the*

Folies-Bergère, showing a melancholy barmaid standing in front of her disproportionate reflection. There are multiple Cézannes, Toulouse-Lautrecs, and Tahitian Gauguins. Degas' *Two Dancers on a Stage* is popular, as is Van Gogh's *Self-Portrait with Bandaged Ear.* Especially rare is a completed Seurat, *Young Woman Powdering Herself,* which depicts his mistress in the act of dressing and initially included his own face in the frame on the wall—he painted over it with a vase of flowers to avoid ridicule. Somerset House's central courtyard, beneath which lie the foundations of a Tudor palace that once stood here, has a walk-in fountain that delights small children, and it's the scene of both popular summer concerts and a winter ice rink. The terrace overlooking the Thames (from across the street) can be enjoyed for free. The former King's Barge House, where visiting boats were once able to moor inside the building (before the embankment landlocked it), houses the newly created **Embankment Galleries (£8 adults, free children under 12, £6 seniors/students; daily 10am–6pm, Thurs until 9pm;)**, devoted to changing fashion and design exhibitions.

It's hard to imagine London without its wheeled icons: the red double-decker bus, the black taxi, and the Tube. **London's Transport Museum ★★ (kids) (Covent Garden, WC2; ☎ 020/7379-6344; www.ltmuseum.co.uk; £8 adults, free for children under 16, £6.50 seniors, £5 students; Sat–Thurs 10am–6pm, Fri 11am–9pm, last admission 45 min. before closing); Tube: Covent Garden)** is the best of its kind in the world and a draw for visitors who are enchanted by the trappings of the Underground system and red double-decker buses. In this soaring Victorian-era hall, which takes about 2 hours to tour, the development and evolution of the city transit systems are traced with impeccable technology (lots of video screens and illuminated boards) and detail (there are even fake horse apples beneath the antique carriages). Besides some pedigreed vehicles, such as Number 23, a steam locomotive that powered the Underground in its earliest and most unpleasant days, there's also plenty of the system's famous Edwardian and Art Deco posters, many of which are so stunning they could qualify for an art gallery. Illustrators and designers will appreciate the background on Johnston, the distinctive and oft-imitated typeface created by Frank Pick in 1916 for the Underground that could now be considered London's unofficial font. Along the way, you'll learn a great deal about the shifts in everyday London life, and you'll likely feel a twinge of embarrassment about the state of your own town's public transportation. Although the museum pleases trainspotters to no end (especially its book shop, overloaded with resources on rolling stock), it's just as interesting for little kids, who get to try their hands at operating simulator buses and trains. School groups of wild, listlessly chaperoned children are common here—they bang away at the video starter buttons and storm through the old Tube cars, pushing grown-ups aside—so you might want to come late Friday afternoons after they've gone. The museum will try to trick you into adding another £2 on your admission as "gift aid" (translation: "We couldn't really afford the lovely £22-million renovation we recently completed), but the prices I list are the true ones.

Small but devastating, **The Foundling Museum ★★ (40 Brunswick Square, WC1; ☎ 020/7841-3600; www.foundlingmuseum.org.uk; £5 adults, free for children under 16, £4 seniors/students; Tues–Sat 10am–5pm, Sun 11am–5pm; Tube: Russell Square)** tracks the history of the Foundling Hospital, which took in thousands of orphans between 1739 and 1953. This was a period in which kids were treated

It's Free!

All of the following attractions charge no admission fees. Not a shabby lineup! You could line up a whole vacation's worth of free activities:

Free all the time:

The Bank of England Museum; The British Library; The British Museum; Guildhall, including the Clockmakers' Museum; The Hunterian Museum; Kenwood House; Museum of Childhood; Museum of London; The National Gallery; The National Maritime Museum; The National Portrait Gallery; The Natural History Museum; The Old Naval College, Greenwich; The Queen's House, Greenwich; The Saatchi Gallery; The Science Museum; Sir John Soane's Museum; The Tate Britain; The Tate Modern; The V&A; The Wallace Collection; The Wellcome Collection

Free part-time:

Courtauld Institute of Art Gallery (Mon 10am–2pm); Guildhall Art Gallery (daily after 3:30pm, Fri all day)

like rubbish: For example, in 1802 a law was passed limiting the time children could work in mills—to 12 hours a day. By that measure, it's clear that the benefactors, who seem needlessly harsh today, were truly helping kids by locking them in this borderline prison. Don't miss the heartbreaking cases of tokens that mothers left at the doorstep with their babies; these tiny objects, into which a lifetime of hopes were imbued, never made it to their children's hands lest they compromise a mother's anonymity. Also take the time to listen to the oral histories by some of the last kids to be raised by the Hospital; at the time of recording, they were elderly but still obviously quite shaken. Upstairs is the Hospital's modest but solid collection of 18th-century English works (Hogarth, Reynolds, Gainsborough), which believe it or not was one of the first permanent art exhibitions in the world. The museum arranges absorbing events, such as concerts, tastings of old beer recipes, and meetings with the last living pupils of the Hospital. The composer Handel loved the Hospital so much that he bequeathed many of his papers to it, including a score to his *Messiah* that was written as a benefit for the facility in 1754; it's on public display. The exercise grounds are now a kids-only park called Coram's Fields; see p. 220 for more info.

TEN TREMENDOUS HOUSES

These palaces and mansions are noteworthy for their architecture and furnishings. For houses that function more like museums to the notables who lived in them, such as Handel or Dickens, look in "Attractions with Niche Appeal" (p. 172).

Although modern people know **Kensington Palace** ★ (Kensington Gardens, W8; ☎ 084/4482-7777; www.hrp.org.uk; £12 adults, £6.15 children 5–15; £11 seniors/students including a free audio tour, online reservations £1 less; Mar–Oct daily 10am–6pm, Nov–Feb daily 10am–5pm, last admission 1 hr. before closing;

Tube: High Street Kensington) as the place where Lady Diana raised Princes William and Harry with Prince Charles from 1984 to 1996, it's been a royal domicile since 1689, when William and Mary took control of an existing home (then in the country, far from town, which inflamed William's asthma) and made it theirs Handsome and haughty, with none of the symmetry that defined later English tastes, the red-brick palace is not as ostentatious as you might expect.

The main tour, a walk-through of important rooms, starts off with a few chambers showcasing ceremonial dress and royal outfits (the Queen's 1957 Norman Hartnell gown, embroidered with Napoleonic bees and French wildflowers in pearls, defies reason). Then it's on to the State Rooms, including the Red Saloon, through which 140,000 people passed in the fortnight after Diana's 1997 death. The walk-through includes the magnificent King's Staircase, lined with delicate canvas panels whose perimeters are rigged with tissue paper slivers designed to tear as a warning of shifting or swelling. The staircase is considered so precious that it was only opened to the public in 2004, 105 years after the rest of the palace first accepted sightseers.

Queen Victoria is well memorialized here: take a peek at the Cupola Room in which she was christened; cases of her toys, including a wax doll that was beheaded and repaired in a childhood incident in 1828 (surely the last time a British sovereign caused a decapitation); and the bedroom where she learned of her ascension, at age 18, in 1837. Near the tour's end, over the fireplace in the Gallery, is a working Anemoscope, which has told the outside wind direction since 1694, and a map of the world as known in that year. You'll also get a chance to see a dozen of Diana's most glamorous gowns, which were made a permanent part of the tour after a temporary exhibition of them proved to be a blockbuster.

At press time, the tour included a walk through the rooms of Queen Elizabeth's sister Princess Margaret, who lived in Apartment 1A, raising orchids and collecting seashells in a plainly decorated flat (the poor thing), from 1960 until her death in 2002. You won't see the apartments in which Diana lived. Unseen parts of the palace are "grace and favour" flats loaned for free by the Crown to people in thanks for past services, and it's for their privacy that some windows remain shaded. Within a decade, it's estimated, the entire palace will be opened to visitors.

I'll be honest. If you were to fall asleep tonight and wake up inside one of the State Rooms of **Buckingham Palace** ★ **(Buckingham Palace Rd., ☎ 020/7766-7300; www.royalcollection.org.uk; £16 adults, £8.75 children 5–16, £14 seniors/students; late July to late Sept daily 9:45am–6pm, last admission at 3:45pm; Tube: Victoria)**, you'd think you're in any number of sumptuous old mansions. Is it opulent? No question. But if ever gilding, teardrop chandeliers, 18th-century portraits, and ceremonial halls could be considered standard-issue, Buckingham Palace is your basic palace. Queen Elizabeth's mild taste in decor—call it "respectable decadence" of yellows and creams and pleasant floral arrangements, thank you very much—is partly the reason. Remember, too, that much of this palace was built or remodeled in the 1800s—not so long ago in the scheme of things—and that the Queen considers Windsor to be her real home.

All tickets are timed and include an audio tour that rushes you around too quickly. The route threads through the public and ceremonial rooms (nowhere the Royal Family spends personal time, and besides, the Palace is open only two

Two Hybrid Galleries/Historic Homes

Upon entering **Sir John Soane's Museum** ★ (12 Lincoln's Inn Fields, WC2; ☎ 020/7405-2107; www.soane.org; free admission; Tues–Sat 10am–5pm, candle-lit nights the first Tues of the month 6pm–9pm; Tube: Holborn), a doorman will politely ask you to hold your bags to your chest. With good reason: These two town houses on the north side of Lincoln's Inn Fields are so overloaded with furniture, paintings, architectural decoration, and sculpture, that navigation is a challenge. The Georgian architect, noted for his bombastic neoclassical buildings (the Bank of England) as much as for his aesthetic materialism, bequeathed his home and its contents as a museum for "amateurs and students," and so it has been, looking much like this since 1837. It's as if the well-connected eccentric has just ducked out to purloin another Greek pilaster, leaving you to roam his creaking wood floors, sussing out the *objets d'art* from the certifiable treasures. His oddball abode is a melee of art history in which precious paintings jostle for wall space like they're at a junk shop: look sharp for three Canalettos (which often fetch $10 million at auction) and a J. M. W. Turner (ditto). Ask to join a guided tour of the **Picture Room,** built in an 1823 expansion, so you can watch its hidden recesses be opened, revealing layer upon buried layer of works (such as William Hogarth's 8-painting *The Rake's Progress* series), filed inside false walls. The museum thoughtfully provides two free MP3 tours online that help make sense of the untidiness. You have to wonder how Soane could legally acquire antiquities such as the sarcophagus of Seti I, carved from translucent limestone, much less what kind of damage is being caused to it by parking it in a packed cellar crypt with barely more notice of its priceless status than a terse descriptive sign (which is more than most works receive here). Mostly, a visit reminds you of the unseemly way in which wealthy Englishmen used to stuff their homes with classical art as a way of stocking up on a sense of righteousness.

If Soane's museum is the life's work of a packrat, its upper-class analog **The Wallace Collection** ★★ (Hertford House, Manchester Square, W1; ☎ 020/7563-9500; www.wallacecollection.org; free admission; daily

months a year, when they're in Scotland) at the back of the palace. Highlights include the 50m-long (164-ft.) **Picture Gallery** filled mostly with works amassed by George IV, an obsessive collector; the 14m-tall (46-ft.) **Ballroom,** where the Queen confers knighthoods; the parquet-floored **Music Room,** unaltered since John Nash decorated it in 1831, where the Queen's three eldest children were baptized in water brought from the River Jordan; and a stroll through the thick **Garden** in the back yard. It's definitely worth seeing—how often can you toodle around the spare rooms in a Queen's house, inspecting artwork given as gifts by some of history's most prominent names? But it's no Versailles.

10am–5pm; Tube: Bond Street), in Marylebone, showcases the fruit of an absurdly rich family's unerring tastes. Yet it's got the dignity of a boutique museum. A little bit V&A (decorative arts and furniture), a little bit National Gallery (paintings and portraits), but with a French flair, the Wallace celebrates fine living in an extravagant 19th-century city mansion, the former Hertford House. Rooms drip with chandeliers, clocks, suits of armor, and furniture, usually of royal provenance, and there's not a clunker among the paintings. While other museums were stocking up on Renaissance works, the Wallaces, visionaries of sorts, were buying 17th-century and 18th-century artists for cheap, and now its collection shines. You might recognize Jean-Honoré Fragonard's *The Swing,* showing a maiden kicking her slipper to her suitor below. Peter Paul Rubens' *The Rainbow Landscape* is also here; its sister painting, *Het Steen,* is at the National Gallery. Thomas Gainsborough's *Mrs. Robinson 'Perdita'* depicts the sloe-eyed actress in mid-affair with the Prince of Wales; she holds a token of his love, a miniature portrait, in her right hand. If she exudes a suspicious mood, it's for good reason—the Prince dumped her before the paint was dry. Some upstairs rooms are done up in spectacular furnishings from the days of the French kings, while at the Ritblat Conservation Gallery, in the cellar, you can try on a replica suit of armor to test its weight. Also check out the room to the right of the foyer at the top of the hour, when a mid-18th-century musical clock, festooned in a golden starburst, chimes one of 14 tunes. The Wallace makes for a gentle break from an Oxford Street shopathon—these people knew *real* power shopping. The museum asks for donations, but you could put the money to buying a guide instead. The £3 audio tour highlights the same paintings as the meaty £7 printed guide. Kids should grab a free trail map, which leads them to the most attention-holding works. The Wallace Restaurant, in the covered courtyard, has an exemplary atmosphere but stupidly high prices, although its French-styled afternoon tea is a reasonable £15.

Tip: Since the Palace is only open in high summer, it's smart to book timed tickets ahead; online that's free, but the phone adds £1.50 per ticket. If you're in London any time other than August or September and spot the Union Jack flying above, you'll at least know the Queen is home. So near, yet so far.

If I had to pick just one palace to visit in London, I'd select **Hampton Court Palace ★★★ (East Molesey, Surrey; ☎ 084/4482-7777; www.hrp.org.uk; £13 adults, £6.65 children 5–15, £11 seniors/students, £1 discount online; Apr to late Oct daily 10am–6pm and late Oct to Mar daily 10am–4:30pm, last admission 1 hr. before closing; National Rail: Hampton Court)** because there's so much more to do than look at golden furniture. A 35-minute commuter train ride from the center of town, Hampton Court looks like the ideal palace because it defined the ideal: The red-brick mansion was a center for royal life from 1525 to 1737, and its forest of chimneys stands regally in 24 hectares (59 acres) of achingly pretty riverside gardens, painstakingly restored to their 1702 appearance. The Crown still stocks many of the 70 public rooms with rare art.

Visitors come looking for vibrations left by Henry VIII during the 811 days he spent here (yes, that's all; he had more than 60 houses), and the extras are so thick that this palace could fill a whole day. Get a "Daily Programme" of the day's events, which usually total more than a dozen and can include tours by costumed docents, Tudor-style cookoffs in the old kitchens, Shakespeare plays in the hammer-beamed Great Hall or the gardens, and detailed explanations of the grounds' history and upkeep. Those are usually free, and so are eight audio tours (four for adults and four recorded expressly for kids). Such satisfying perks also help rekindle some of the history that was snuffed out by successive remodeling—styles seem to change from room to room, starting out Tudor and ending up Queen Anne, but the decor is always over-the-top. Whatever you do, don't neglect to head into the gardens and to lose yourself in the Northern Gardens' shrubbery **Maze** (another £3.50), installed by William III; kids giggle their way through to the middle of this leafy labyrinth. There are metal rods in the hedges to prevent you from cheating. The well-mannered **South Garden** has the Great Vine, the oldest vine in the world, planted in 1768; its grapes are sold in the gift shop in August.

Transportation: From April to September daily, you can take **London River Services** (☎ 020/7930-2062; www.tfl.gov.uk/river or www.wpsa.co.uk) all the way from Westminster pier in central London, the way Henry VIII did on his barges, but it's a slow-going commitment of £14 single/£20 return, and tides sometimes play such havoc with schedules that your arrival time may fall too late to see much. Always call to ask what the water's doing, and consider taking the train out and the boat back. Trains leave twice an hour from Waterloo station, take 35 minutes, and let you off across the river from the Palace.

The Queen dictates who in her family lives at which palace, and she herself lived at the four-story **Clarence House** (Stableyard Rd., SW1; ☎ 020/7766-7303; www.royalcollection.org.uk; £7.50 adults/seniors/students, £4 children 5–16; early Aug to early Oct daily 10am–5:30pm, last admission 4:30pm; Tube: Green Park), a part of St. James's Palace, just before she took the throne. Her mother dwelled here for nearly half a century until her 2002 death at age 101, and now it's chez Charles and Camilla, as well as the official roost of William and Harry, at least until they marry. Prince Charles, having a keener sense of public relations than perhaps any royal before him, recently decided to open the house, where royals have lived since 1827, to tourists during the summer months when the family is away. You won't get to poke around the Prince's medicine cabinet on your hour tour since you can only tour the ground-floor public rooms, which still feel like an old lady's house despite being recently renovated. It feels much more like a grand town house than a mansion fit for a future king and reflects the Windsors' homey, cluttered decorating style, heavy on paintings of horses and light on the gilding and glitter. You'll find it about a third of the way east down the Mall from Buckingham Palace.

The Time-Machine Museum

My personal favorite home tour, the one I'll do again and again without tiring, is the very special **Dennis Severs' House** ★★★ (18 Folgate St., E1; ☎ 020/7247-4013; www.dennisseversh ouse.co.uk; reservations required only on Mon evenings [£12], open 1st and 3rd Sun of the month noon–4pm [£8] and noon–2pm on the Monday following 1st and 3rd Sun [£5]; Tube: Liverpool Street). The opening schedule is complicated, but I'll clean it up for you: Go on Monday after dark for "Silent Night." As you approach this humble-looking town house on a dark street in Spitalfields, the shutters are closed and a gas jet burns. You're admitted by a manservant who speaks very little. He only motions you to explore the premises, room by room, silently and at your own pace. Suddenly, you're in the parlor of a reasonably prosperous merchant in the 1700s, and the owners seem to have just left the room ahead of you. Candles burn, a real fire pops in the hearth, the smell of food wafts in the air, and a cat sleeps contently in the corner. Out on the street, you hear footsteps and hooves. Room by dusky room, without rules or guards, you explore every corner overflowing with the implements of everyday life of the age. Wherever you go, it's as if the residents were just there, leaving behind toys on the stairs, beds unmade, tobacco in bowls, spilled mulled wine, buttered toast and tea growing cold on the table, and cosmetics half-applied. The effect gives you a powerful sense of the period. As you go, printed signs encourage you to assemble the clues in front of you and envision the residents. By the time you reach the last of ten rooms, the attic, you'll have accompanied the house and its changing occupants through its decay into a slum.

This house was dragged down by its declining neighborhood until the late 1970s, when an eccentric American named Dennis Severs purchased it for a pittance, dressed it with antiques, and invented this imagination odyssey—he called it "Still Life Drama" and a "game." Other museums are half-empty and unrealistically neat, but the Severs House is intentionally unlike any museum in the world, designed to make the past come alive through the power of suggestion and imagination. It reassembles life as a messy reality, not as a pretty picture stage managed by researchers and roped off from interaction. As the curators put it, *"Whether you see it or you don't, the house's ten rooms harbour ten 'spells' that engage the visitor's imagination in moods . . . Your senses are your guide."* Reservations are required, and visitors are spaced far enough apart so that they don't often run into each other and spoil the illusion of time travel. The house's daytime hours have much less of the brain-teasing magic that makes Monday's "Silent Night" one of London's most invigorating diversions, particularly for romantics.

Death Takes a Holiday

If you're a major musical star, stay away from London! It seems a disproportionate number of singers have met untimely ends here. These houses aren't open to the public, but their grim pasts make them infamous:

June 22, 1969, 4 Cadogan Lane, Belgravia; Tube: Sloane Square

Judy Garland overdosed on barbiturates and expired in the bathroom of the two-room flat here. The public outpouring of grief, and its suppression by police, resulted in riots in New York City and is credited with starting, or at least fueling, the gay rights movement as we know it today.

September 18, 1970, 22 Lansdowne Crescent, Notting Hill; Tube: Notting Hill Gate

In a basement flat of the Samarkand Hotel, **Jimi Hendrix** washed down nine Vesperax sleeping pills with alcohol. An ambulance was summoned from St. Mary Abbots Hospital, Kensington, but arrived too late for the virtuoso guitar player. The plot thickened 26 years later, when the last person to see him alive, girlfriend Monika Dannemann, was found asphyxiated in a car in Seaford, East Sussex, not long after being accused in court of keeping secrets about Hendrix's final moments.

July 29, 1974 and September 7, 1978, 12 Curzon Place, Mayfair; Tube: Hyde Park Corner

"Mama" Cass Elliot of The Mamas and the Papas was found dead in between solo performances at the London Palladium in a flat owned by songwriter Harry Nilsson, who wasn't home. Contrary to lore, she didn't die by choking on a ham sandwich but from a heart attack brought on by morbid obesity (she was 165cm/5'5" and weighed 108kg/238 lb.).

Four years after Elliot's death, **Keith Moon,** drummer of The Who, died in the same flat. His undoing: chlormethiazole edisylate, a prescribed anti-alcohol drug. Horrified that two of his friends should die while borrowing his apartment, Nilsson quickly sold it to Moon's bandmate Pete Townshend.

Most kings and queens don't have modern-day followings, but eccentric King George III comes close. He's the ruler who, during his reign from 1760 to 1820, lost his American colonies and gradually went crazy from suspected porphyria: see the movie *The Madness of King George* for the tragic tale. **Kew Palace and Queen Charlotte's Cottage** (Royal Botanic Gardens, Kew, Richmond; ☎ 084/4482-7777; www.hrp.org.uk; to get onto the grounds, admission to Kew Gardens is required: £13 adults, free children under 17, £12 seniors/students; admission to the house is an extra £5 adults, £2.50 children 5–16, £4.50 seniors and students; Kew Palace: Mon 11am–5pm, Tues–Sun 10am–5pm, last admission 4:15pm, closed Oct to late Mar; Cottage: June–Sept Sat–Sun 10am–4pm; Tube: Kew Gardens) was where he lived. Well, sort of. He lived in this smallish red house, 10km (6⅓ miles) southwest of London, while his dream home, the Castellated Palace, was being built just to the east. His son hated that never-finished building so much (critics said it looked like a French prison) he blew it up with gunpowder as soon as he could, but the getaway he built for himself in Brighton, an Indian folly, was even weirder. But this secondary crash pad near the Thames, where George III's wife Queen Charlotte died, survives, although it's really only the size of a standard manor house. It reopened in April 2006 after a decade-long restoration, carried out with scientific exactitude, and takes about an hour to tour. The little Queen Charlotte's Cottage, an imitation of a humble village home, was probably built for a zookeeper of a long-gone menagerie. Even if you have a Historic Royal Palaces pass, you still must pay entrance to Kew Gardens (p. 184), making this one expensive time capsule. It's also so distant from the West End that it will chew up most of your day.

This is how you'd be rewarded if you became a national war hero: **Apsley House ★ (149 Piccadilly; ☎ 020/7499-5676; www.english-heritage.org.uk; £5.50 adults, £2.80 children, £4.40 seniors/students, including an audio tour; late Mar to Oct Wed–Sun 11am–5pm, Nov to late Mar Wed–Sun 11am–4pm; Tube: Hyde Park Corner),** with Hyde Park as a backyard and Buckingham Palace Gardens as a front yard, was the home of Arthur Wellesley, who in 1815 defeated Napoleon and became the Duke of Wellington and later, prime minister. The mansion, still in the family (they maintain private rooms), was filled with splendid gifts showered upon him by grateful nations, but he never seemed to get his nemesis off his mind. One dining room–table centerpiece, 22m (72 ft.) long in the form of an Egyptian temple, is beyond fabulous, and it was once Napoleon's. Aspley's art stash, which was largely looted by the French from the Spanish royal family and never went home, includes a few Jan Bruegel the Elders, Diego Velazques' virtuosic *The Waterseller of Seville* (I can understand why it was the artist's favorite work, since just looking at it makes me thirsty); and Correggio's *The Agony in the Garden,* in a case fitted with a keyhole so the Duke could open it and polish it with a silk hanky. In the grand staircase stands a colossal nude Napoleon that the little emperor despised; the Duke got hold of it, too, as yet another token of victory. The whiff of faded masculine glory pervades the place like cigar smoke, both fascinating and sad. The Duke and his best friend lived here together after their wives died, and in the cellar, you can see the Duke's own death mask, together with that of his most bitter rival, Napoleon Bonaparte. I get the feeling that in other circumstances, they would have been buddies. If you're also visiting Wellington Arch across the street, a joint ticket will save £1.90.

A home so lush that its current owners are the Rothschilds, who host diplomatic and corporate events here that make the world go round, **Spencer House ★ (27 St. James's Place, SW1; ☎ 020/7499-8620; www.spencerhouse.co.uk; £9 adults, £7 children under 16/students/seniors, no reservations accepted; Sun 10:30am–5:45pm, closed Jan and Aug; Tube: Green Park)** is the only surviving London mansion with an intact 18th-century interior. Tours of the ground floor and a portion of the first floor are on Sundays only, conducted by very proper guides employed by the Rothschild banking group, who are prone to peering down their noses at weekend sightseers. The home was begun in 1756 as a love nest by Diana Spencer's ancestors (and, by extension, the future king's), and the lavish gilt and carved decor repeatedly invoke the symbols of fidelity and virility. War damage spooked the Spencer clan, who moved out in the 1920s, and since then, they've gradually transferred the most precious elements to their estate at Althorp, 193km (120 miles) north of the city, and replaced them with equally fantastic facsimiles—the fireplace library, for instance, took 4,000 hours to carve. Expect your jaw to drop: three Benjamin West paintings are on loan from the Queen, a chair in the Palm Room has a companion in the Museum of Fine Arts in Boston, and the original Painted Room suite was once at the V&A.

ATTRACTIONS WHERE LONDONERS TAKE THEIR FAMILIES

Many major cities have their own equivalent of the **The Natural History Museum** (kids) ★ (Cromwell Rd., SW7; ☎ 020/7942-5000; www.nhm.ac.uk; free admission; daily 10am–5:50pm; Tube: South Kensington), but few have an equal. You know: a hall of dinosaur bones, countless cases of colorful rocks, a taxidermist's menagerie of stuffed wild animals, and endless, depressing reminders of just how many animals are on their way to being snuffed out for eternity. The commodious NHM, good for several hours' wander, has all that, of course, and more. Organization is a cut above, since pathways through exhibits are clearly marked and plenty of plain-speaking signs and hands-on exhibits for kids are placed at their eye level. Even the dinosaur bones (in the Blue Zone) are supplemented by scary robotic estimations of how they sounded and moved. The mock-up of an average middle-class kitchen infested with various vermin (the Green Zone) is a visitor favorite, as is the Red Zone (the Earth Galleries), a multimedia display about how the planet works. It could all take hours, and that's before you consider the welcome new addition of the **Darwin Centre** (☎ 020/7942-5011; free admission; 45-min. tour; ages 8 or older). Seen only by tour, its goal is to bring visitors face-to-face with the scientists behind the scenes; book a place to see some of the 22 million archived and bottled specimens (including those that came back on the *Beagle*) on 27km/17 miles of shelves.

Even if you don't give a hooey about remedial ecology, the 1880 Victorian building that houses the museum is a landmark worth seeing. It crawls with carved monkeys whimsically clinging to the terra-cotta and plants growing across ceiling panels. Kids under 7 can borrow free Explorer backpacks with pith helmets, binoculars, and activities themed to Monsters, Primates, Birds, Oceans, or Mammals; they tend to run out early on weekends (call ☎ 020/7942-5555 for kid info); and those 7 to 14 should look for the free Investigate hands-on lab in the basement (afternoons are less crowded). Daily Nature Live talks are given at 12:30pm on a huge range of topics, they're streamed and archived online, too. The Museum's brainiacs even cultivate a garden and pond (the Orange Zone; open Apr–Oct) that attract a huge range of English creatures and flowers. So many family-oriented events, many free, happen here that it takes a quarterly 20-page guide to publicize them all; they are also touted online under "What's On".

Around the corner from the Natural History Museum and across the street from the V&A, the mammoth **Science Museum** (kids) ★ (Exhibition Rd., SW7; ☎ 087/0870-4868; www.sciencemuseum.org.uk; free admission; daily 10am–6pm; Tube: South Kensington) is really two museums, one old-style and one far-out, that have been grafted together. So many interesting exhibitions are on display

Lifting the Veil on History

Like British food, British museums have their own parlance:

- The **collection** is all the stuff the museum owns. Often, not all of it is on display at once.
- An **exhibition** is only shown for a short period. Often, these require paid tickets, even if the museum's collection is free.
- When museums talk about **access,** they mean facilities for patrons with limited mobility, sight, or hearing.
- **Audio tours** are recorded narrations, while **multimedia tours** are hand-held devices that play recordings and show pictures.
- **Trails** are maps that guide you to highlights on a given theme.
- **Blue Badge Guides** pass a rigorous testing process to be accredited. They're the upper echelon of guides.
- **Blue Plaques** (www.blueplaque.com) are disks affixed to historic sites that explain their importance, however obscure.
- **Concessions** are reduced prices for senior citizens or students.
- Also, you'll come across cases shrouded in dark fabric or cases lined with drawers. That's not to keep you from touching them. It's to protect their contents from light. Feel free have a look at the precious artifacts within—just make sure to cover them again.

here that I always seem to run out of time. The old-school section, split over six levels (four huge, two small), is an embarrassment of riches from the history of science and technology. Exhibits are similar to what lots of science museums have, but in almost every case, they display the most original or most rare specimen available: 1969's *Apollo 10* command module; "Puffing Billy," the world's oldest surviving steam engine; and a 1950 computer pioneered by Alan Turing. The quieter upper floors are full of subjects like model ships and early computers (second floor), a history of veterinary medicine (fifth floor), and aviation (including the *Vickers Vimy,* the first plane to cross the Atlantic without stopping, third floor).

The high-concept wing buried in the back of the ground floor is easy to miss, but seek it out. A hyper-cool, cobalt-blue, humming, multileveled cavern dedicated to interactive games and displays, it bears little relation to the mothballed museum you just crossed through. The Antenna exhibition (ground floor) is exceptionally cutting-edge, and updated regularly with the latest breakthroughs; past topics have included biodegradable cell phones implanted with seeds and robots controlled by a lamprey fish's brain signals. The interactive exhibits of Launchpad (third floor; heat-seeking cameras, dry ice, and the like) enchant kids. Science-lovin' adults should check out the Dana Centre, the museum's fancy venue for talks (p. 205).

The museum doesn't always score. Corporations sometimes sponsor fawning sections (BP on energy, for example) and the gift shop (mostly mall-style toys) and

Maritime Greenwich: History's Theme Park

While you're in Greenwich, about 30 minutes east of Central London, take in the few other attractions that, along with the National Maritime Museum, comprise **Maritime Greenwich** (www.greenwichwhs.org.uk; Tube: Cutty Sark DLR), a UNESCO World Heritage Site. Situated on a picturesque slope of the south bank of the Thames, Greenwich once was home to the Greenwich Palace, where the Old Royal Naval College stands, and it was where both Henry VIII and Elizabeth I were born. The last part of the palace to be constructed, The Queen's House (1616, Inigo Jones), still stands, but most of the grounds were rebuilt in the late Georgian period as the equally palatial Royal Hospital, a convalescence haven for disabled and veteran sailors. So many of these treasures are owned by the state that many entrance fees are waived; you can play the whole day without paying more than a few pounds. Stop by the Visitor Centre, alongside the *Cutty Sark,* for background information.

Cutty Sark ★ (King William Walk, SE10; ☎ 020/8858-3445; www.cuttysark.org.uk; £5 adults, £3.70 children under 16, £3.90 seniors/students; daily 10am–5pm, last admission 4:30pm, free guided tours before 3:30 weekdays; DLR: Cutty Sark). This handsome wooden ship, launched in 1869, is the only tea clipper left in the world, and a symbol of English economic muscle. Against the odds, it still has nearly all of its fabric and riggings—a 2007 fire didn't consume them because they were in storage for a restoration that was already underway. It reopens in 2010, but check ahead to see how prices and hours have changed.

Old Royal Naval College ★ (Greenwich, SE10; ☎ 020/8269-4747; www.oldroyalnavalcollege.org; free admission; grounds daily 8am–6pm, buildings daily 10am–5pm, Royal Chapel opens Sun at 11am for worship; DLR: Cutty Sark). This 1696 neoclassical complex, the work of Wren, offers

guidebook disappoint. I also don't recommend spending £7.50 on its gimmicky (and unspecial) IMAX 3-D cinema or £4 on its SimEx motion simulator rides.

You might be put off by the name, however, **The National Maritime Museum** ★★ (Romney Rd., Greenwich, SE10; ☎ 020/8858-4422; www.nmm.ac.uk; free admission; daily 10am–5pm; Tube: Cutty Sark DLR) actually isn't as, ahem, dry as most would expect. Since so much of Britain's history from the 17th to 20th centuries was transacted via the high seas, this place, the largest maritime museum in the world, isn't just about boats and knots. The facility has an endless supply of Smithsonian-worthy artifacts that would do any museum proud. Highlights include a pocket watch of a *Titanic* passenger, stopped at 3:07am; a bottle, half full of port, from the wreck of the *Royal George,* which killed 900 people in 1782; and, most ghoulishly, the bloodstained breeches and bullet-punctured topcoat two main sights: the Painted Hall and the Chapel. The Painted Hall has incredible paintings by James Thornhill that took nearly 2 decades to complete. It was the setting for the funeral of Admiral Nelson—check out the electrified diorama of the event in a side room. The Chapel, in the Greek Revival style, is the work of James Stuart. Tours by accredited guides run daily at 11:30am and 2pm (☎ 020/8269-4799; 90 min.; £4 adults, free admission for children under 16).

The Queen's House (Romney Rd., SE10; ☎ 020/8312-6565; www.nmm.ac.uk; free admission; daily 10am–5pm; DLR: Cutty Sark) is connected to the National Maritime Museum by a colonnade. This Palladian home, elegantly decorated, was a pet project for Inigo Jones, who took 22 years (1616–38) to complete his commission. Its nautilus-shaped Tulip staircase, plus other rooms, are considered to be haunted by an unknown specter, so have a camera ready.

The Royal Observatory ★ (Greenwich Park, SE10; ☎ 020/8312-6565; www.rog.nmm.ac.uk; free admission; daily 10am–5pm; DLR: Cutty Sark), commanding a terrific view from atop the hill in Greenwich Park, is yet another creation of Christopher Wren (from 1675). The Empire's most important house for celestial observation, it still houses significant relics of star-peeping, and its collection of clocks includes the very ones that cracked the mystery of measuring longitude, which ushered the English Empire to worldwide dominance. The Prime Meridian, located at precisely 0° longitude, crosses through the grounds (the equator is 0° latitude), enabling you to have a foot in two hemispheres at once. You can also see a live image of Greenwich, naturally projected through a pinhole onto a table, in the museum's Camera Obscura. In the old days, the red Time Ball fell precisely at the same time everyday so that the city could relay the message and set their clocks; it still drops each day at 1pm.

that Admiral Lord Nelson wore on the day he took his fatal shot. It's a museum so complete it even has the North Pole itself—the Arctic location shifts magnetically from year to year, and the museum has the first, obsolete one, planted in 1831 by Captain James Clark Ross. The pole is on exhibit near relics from Sir John Franklin's ill-fated 1848 Arctic expedition, including lead-lined food tins that likely caused the explorers to go mad and die. Also excellent is the Atlantic Worlds display, which plumbs the British role in the slave trade, something few London museums touch upon. It's not all so gloomy, though; you'll spot figureheads, models, antique instruments, and entire wooden vessels. Weekends are full of free kids' events (storytelling, treasure hunts) that bring suburban London families pouring into the gates, and the fun Greenwich Market is running nearby then, too. A new planetarium, sheathed in bronze, opened in 2007 (£6 adults, £4 everyone else), but as state-of-the-art as it is, it's still a planetarium.

ATTRACTIONS WITH NICHE APPEAL

ARCHITECTURE

Back in 1677, it was the tallest thing (61m/200 ft.) in this part of town and therefore a world wonder. **The Monument** ★ (Monument St. at Fish St. Hill, WC4; www.themonument.info; £2 adults, £1 children; daily 9:30am–5pm; Tube: Monument or Bank) was erected to commemorate the destruction of the city by the Great Fire in 1666. Its 61m (200 ft.) height is also the distance from its base to the site of Thomas Farynor's bakery in Pudding Lane to the east, where the conflagration began. Today, there's only one thing to do in this fluted column of Portland stone: Climb it. The spiral staircase of 15cm (6-in.) steps, which has no landings, gradually narrows as it ascends to the outdoor observation platform—a popular suicide spot until 1842, when a cage was installed. They'll tell you it's 311 steps to the top, but they're lying. It's 313 if you count the two before the box office. (Sissies can watch live pictures of the view from the base.) Go on a pleasant day unless you'd like a good wind-whipping. Check out the metal band snaking down the north side; it's a lightning rod, and it crosses along an inscription, in Latin, that blamed Catholics for starting the fire (the insult was chiseled off in 1831). The column was closed at press time for a refurbishment slated to last until early 2009, so check ahead for current prices and hours, which before renovation included discounted package deals with the Tower Bridge Exhibition.

Wellington Arch (Hyde Park Corner, Apsley Way, W1; ☎ 020/7930-2726; www.english-heritage.org.uk; £3.30 adults, £1.70 children 5–15, £2.60 seniors/students; late Mar to Oct Wed–Sun 10am–5pm, Nov–Mar Wed–Sun 10am–4pm; Tube: Hyde Park Corner), built between 1826 and 1830, was intended as a triumphal entry to Buckingham Palace and stood some meters northwest, in the vicinity of the grassy patch east across the street from the Lanesborough Hotel. Tales of its relocation and the switch from Wellington's original statue on top to a smaller statue (*Peace descending upon War,* the largest bronze sculpture in Europe) are told in the little museum inside, which also discusses the period when the Arch served as the city's smallest police station. If you buy a joint ticket with the Duke of Wellington's Apsley House, across Piccadilly, you'll save about £1.90; you can take an elevator up with the admission price.

The quiet, minor **Jewel Tower** (Abingdon St., SW1; ☎ 020/7222-2219; www.english-heritage.org.uk; £3 adults, £1.50 children 5–15, £2.40 seniors/students; Apr–Oct daily 10am–5pm, Nov–Mar daily 10am–4pm; Tube: Westminster), built around 1365, is one of only two remnants left over from the 1834 fire that ravaged the Royal Palace of Westminster. This stone three-level tower, once a moat-side storehouse for Edward III's treasures, has walls so thick it was later considered an ideal setting for taking accurate measurements. Curators now use it for displays about Parliament, across the street, and weights-and-measures standards. Check the glass case by the window, which halfheartedly lays out incredible relics dug up nearby (a 1,200-year-old sword, a 16th-century wine bottle stamped Royal Oak Tavern) as if they're about to go out with the trash.

ART

The glorious palace of Whitehall was home to some of England's flashiest characters, including Henry VIII. In a wrenching loss for art and architecture—to say nothing of bowling history, since Henry had an alley installed—it burned down in 1698. But if you had to pick just one room to survive, it would have been the one that did: **The Banqueting House** ★ (Whitehall at Horseguards Ave., SW1; ☎ 084/4482-7777; www.hrp.org.uk; £4.50 adults, £2.25 children under 16, £3.50 seniors/students, including audio tour; Mon–Sat 10am–5pm; Tube: Charing Cross or Westminster). It was designed with Italianate Renaissance assurance by Inigo Jones and completed in 1622, which means Henry never set foot in it, but another fateful king set his last foot in it: In 1649, Charles I walked onto the scaffold from a window that stood in the present-day staircase, and met his doom under an axe wielded by Cromwell's republicans. The reason to come here is to gape at the nine grandiose ceiling murals by Peter Paul Rubens in which the king is portrayed as a god. They give you a bold clue as to why the rabble would want to see His Highness brought low. Thoughtfully, mirrored tables help you inspect the ceiling without craning your head to behold why Charles lost his.

Dulwich Picture Gallery ★ (Gallery Rd., Dulwich Village, SE21; ☎ 020/8693-5254; www.dulwichpicturegallery.org.uk; £5 adults, free for children under 18, £4 seniors/students; Tues–Fri 10am–5pm, Sat–Sun 11am–5pm; National Rail: West Dulwich Station) would be more famous were it not for one fact: Reaching it requires a 15-minute train ride from Victoria station and a 15-minute walk from the local station. Fortunately, such effort lands you in a pretty village-like enclave of South London. The Gallery, which keeps one of the world's most vital collections of Old Master paintings of the 1600s and 1700s, was once a household name. Magnanimous collectors bequeathed it to become England's first public art gallery (opened 1817), designed with a surplus of space and light by Sir John Soane (who left us his own cramped, dark museum; p. 162). A visit is almost indescribably serene. Soane's skylight system was so novel that it more or less invented the private-gallery genre—you'll see shades of it in the Getty Museum in Malibu, California—and the collection was so well-assembled that after it opened, Britain wasted little time in creating its own National Gallery.

Some might argue that it's worth more than a half-hour, but for most people, that's enough for the genteel, little-known **Estorick Collection** ★ (39a Canonbury Square, N1; ☎ 020/7704-9522; www.estorickcollection.com; £3.50 adults, £2.50 children/seniors/students; Wed–Sat 11am–6pm, Sun noon–5pm; Tube: Highbury & Islington), memorable for its tranquil ambiance in a Georgian house on one of the city's most pleasing residential squares. The narrow collection—modern Italian art, especially Futurism—was established by an American political scientist and art dealer, and its walled garden is a blissful place to enjoy a coffee in fair weather. You don't even need to pay admission to do that.

A gargantuan modern-art achievement, The **Feliks Topolski's Memoir of the Century** (www.felikstopolski.com; free admission; Tube: Waterloo), in the railway arches near Royal Festival Hall, is an arresting 183m-long (600-ft.) painting on 211 separate wood panels that chronicles the 20th century's main events. The artist may sound like the ringmaster of a flea circus, but in fact, he was a respected Polish-born genius with works at the Tate whose objective was to "bear witness" through his evocative drawings, and he worked on this installation, which is like Picasso's *Guernica* on acid, from 1975 until his death in 1989. At press time, it was closed for a badly needed restoration, so check on its new hours.

Royal Academy of Arts (Burlington House, Piccadilly, W1; ☎ 020/7300-8000; www.royalacademy.org.uk; free admission; Sat–Thurs 10am–6pm, Fri 10am–10pm, last admission 30 min. before closing; Tube: Piccadilly Circus or Green Park),

Britain's first art school, was founded in 1768 and relocated to Burlington House, a Palladian-style mansion, in Victorian times. Only a few of its restored 18th-century rooms, the six John Madejski Fine Rooms (Tues–Fri 1pm–4:30pm, Sat–Sun 10am–6pm; free tours at 1 and 3pm Wed), can be toured without an admission fee, but what's displayed there is worth a half-hour: John Singer Sargents, Thomas Gainsboroughs, Stanley Spencers, and even Winston Churchills (the old bulldog was good at everything). The paintings change regularly, but they're always strong. Charles Darwin's *Origin of the Species* papers were delivered for the first time in the Reynolds Room on July 1, 1858; the space now displays 20th-century paintings. Beyond those, you'll pay £7 to £10 for whatever exhibition is on. The museum's biggest event is the annual **Summer Exhibition,** which since the late 1700s has displayed the best works, submitted anonymously; careers have been made by it.

BIOGRAPHY

The Benjamin Franklin House ★ (36 Craven St., WC2; ☎ 020/7839-2006; www.benjaminfranklinhouse.org; tours (required) cost £7 adults, free for children under 16; reservations are required; 5 timed tours daily, Wed–Sun noon–5pm; Tube: Embankment or Charing Cross), the only residence of the portly politico left standing in the world, opened as a sort of architectural preserve in 2006. Astonishingly, Franklin lived here without his family, in a boarding house by the Thames, for 16 years—much longer than many Americans realize—and it was only the Revolution that forced him to pack up and move back to the Colonies. For much of his life Franklin was a fervent loyalist and British imperialist who, even as late as 1775, felt that the differences between Britain and the Colonies could be settled in "half an hour." Tours are conducted by a young actress playing Polly Hewson, the daughter of Ben's landlady, who tells wistful tales as recordings chime in with other voices from her memory. The rewards of a tour are mixed. On the one hand, the spiel crowds out questions, exhibits are sparse (one exception is the ghoulish deposit of human bones in the backyard, likely left over from dissections by Franklin's doctor neighbor), and there are few kids' activities. But on the other hand, it's rare for a famous home of this age to have survived into our lifetimes. It's also humbling to see how this legendary man made do with such small quarters; his study is no larger than the smallest London hotel rooms. The worn back wooden staircase, on which the he got his exercise when French trollopes weren't available, is so well preserved it feels ghostly.

The former home (from 1834–1881) of writer Thomas Carlyle and his exacting wife Jane, **Carlyle's House** (24 Cheyne Row, SW3; ☎ 020/7352-7087; www.nationaltrust.org.uk; £4.75 adults, £2.40 children; mid-Mar to late Oct Wed–Fri 2–5pm, Sat–Sun 11am–5pm, last admission 30 min. before closing; Tube: Sloane Square, then bus 11, 19, 22, or 211) has been converted into a shrine, with his letters, books, and writing chair all on display. The modest home, which has a walled garden and is an excellent vestige of the middle-class Victorian lifestyle, was a salon of sorts for era scribes like Dickens, Thackeray, Tennyson, and Browning. Because it was opened to the public just 14 years after the writer's death, it feels as forgotten and forlorn as the set of a play after the final curtain. It's a short walk from here to comfortable Battersea Park.

Body of Work: Jeremy Bentham's "Auto Icon"

Like England's own Ben Franklin, Jeremy Bentham (1748–1832) was a renaissance man, a philosopher, a utilitarian, and a subversive. Bentham's progressive worldview helped shape civilized England. Prison reformer, supporter of suffrage and the decriminalization of homosexuality, educator, and pen pal of U.S. president James Madison, Bentham worked tirelessly to enable all citizens equal access to courts and schools. He coined the words international, maximize, and codification.

He was so ahead of his time, he still refuses to stay in the past. Bentham was obsessed with furnishing eternal access to his corpse—the gift that keeps on giving, really—and he stipulated it in his will. Starting years before his death, he purportedly carried around a pair of glass eyes that were intended for his future "Auto Icon," as he called it (auto = self, icon = image), which would represent him forever. After he expired, his body was dissected during medical lectures. A colleague dressed his remains and propped them in a wooden case at University College London in 1850. Bentham's severed head was placed between his own feet.

There his remains remain. His skeleton is hidden by his original clothing and gloves, but unfortunately, his shriveled noggin wasn't preserved with much skill, and kids kept swiping it (in 1975, some hooligans from rival King's College held it for a £10 ransom), so today, to keep it from completely disintegrating, it's stashed in the vaults, along with his long-pocketed eyeballs. It has been replaced by a doughy wax head, which sagely observes the current scholarly crop at UCL from beneath an old straw hat. You'll find this freakshow on the east side of Gower Street between University Street and Grafton Way, opposite the castle-like, red-brick Cruciform Building. Go in the gates, veer right around the flank of the grand portico, and enter the door marked South Cloisters. Once inside, hang a right and head for the stone lions (Tube: Euston Square). Then clear your head, and your own eyeballs, with a visit to the changing exhibitions at **Strang Print Room** (South Cloisters; ☎ 020/7679-2540; www.ucl.ac.uk/museums; Mon–Fri 1–5pm; free admission), UCL Art Collection's rare drawings and prints by masters including Whistler, Rembrandt, and Dürer. The same complex also has collections of Egyptian antiquities, geology, and archeology, at weird hours, so ask if interested.

Although Dickens moved around a lot, **The Charles Dickens Museum ★★ (48 Doughty St., WC1; ☎ 020/7405-2127; www.dickensmuseum.com; £5 adults, £3 children, £4 seniors/students; Mon–Sat 10am–5pm, Sun 11am–5pm; Tube: Chancery Lane or Russell Square)** is his last London home still standing. A museum since 1925, these four floors don't exude many vibes from the old guy;

Diana, Princess of Wales Memorial Fountain

In July 2004, the Queen came to Hyde Park to open a beautiful fountain designed to conjure the memory of the mother of her grandchildren and a longtime thorn in her side, Princess Diana. As designed by American architect Kathryn Gustafson, this graceful o-shaped **Diana, Princess of Wales Memorial Fountain** (between West Carriage Dr., Rotten Row, and The Serpentine, Hyde Park; www.royalparks.org.uk; free admission; Nov–Feb daily 10am–4pm, Mar and Oct daily 10am–6pm, Apr–Aug daily 10am–8pm, Sept daily 10am–7pm. Tube: South Kensington) undulates down a gentle slope, sending two flumes of water rushing and bubbling into a calm collecting pool. At three points, bridges bring you to the center of the space. The fountain may be closed in November for maintenance; check website for details.

One day after opening, the trouble began. It clogged with leaves, flooding the surrounding grass. As originally conceived, visitors would be able to splash in the waters, but that ended when the first three guests slipped and fell—the planners hadn't considered algae growth. So for 5 months in 2005, it closed while an asphalt-like path was laid around it, spoiling lawsuits and the effect alike. After it re-opened, hairline cracks were found in its 545 blocks of Cornish granite. The bill for that? £5.2 million. Londoners have decided they don't miss Di *that* much. A House of Commons committee declared it "ill-conceived and ill-executed." I admit that rather than putting me in a state of remembrance, it puts me into a state of wishing I could ride it on an inner tube. But for all that, the Fountain, which is gated and switches off exactly on time (so don't bother coming outside of its opening hours), makes lovely sounds and attracts some 1 million visitors a year. You can reach it most quickly from the Alexandra Gate at Kensington Gore, Knightsbridge, up Exhibition Road from the trio of great South Kensington museums.

after all, he departed in 1839 after staying less than 2 years here. It could be anyone's humble home. Still, his celebrity got a kick-start while he lived here: *Oliver Twist* and *Nicholas Nickleby,* arguably his biggest hits, were written while he was in residence, a short stroll from the Foundling Hospital for orphans. As you watch the half-hour biographical video and inspect the dusty spreads of his desks, his podium, and installments of his biggest books, an unpleasant realization sets in: Charles Dickens was a compelling character but also a jerk. Tough on his kids and unfaithful to his wife, his greatest possession seems to have been his ego. Ironically, his audience still feeds it, nearly 150 years after his death.

A rare surviving middle-class home from the 18th century (built in 1700) in The City of London, this slouching and brick-faced abode happens to be that of the famous lexicographer: **Dr. Johnson's House** ★ (17 Gough Square; ☎ 020/ 7353-3745; www.drjohnsonshouse.org; £4.50 adults, £1.50 children, £3.50 seniors/

students; May–Sept Mon–Sat 11am–5:30pm, Oct–Apr Mon–Sat 11am–5pm; Tube: Blackfriars). He lived here from 1748 to 1759. If you're hoping to learn a lot about the man, you'll have to spring for a book in the gift shop. Little substance is provided in the house itself, which fortunately merits some mild interest on its own terms (the corkscrew latch on the front door, which prevented lock-picking from above, is an example). The rooftop garret in which Johnson and his six helpers toiled to create the first English dictionary was burned out in the Blitz, ironically, by a barrel of burning ink which flew out of a bombed warehouse; you can still see some scorch marks on the ceiling timbers.

In a hilly Hampstead neighborhood of spacious brick-faced homes, Sigmund Freud, having just fled the Nazis, spent the last year of his life. His daughter Anna, herself a noted figure in psychoanalysis, lived on in the same house until her own death in 1982, after which **The Freud Museum** **(20 Maresfield Gardens, NW3; ☎ 020/7435-2002; www.freud.org.uk; £5 adults, free for children under 12, £3 seniors/students; Wed–Sun noon–5pm; Tube: Hampstead)** was established. The eight rooms of the house and their contents, though original and passionately preserved by Anna (Elektra complex, indeed), are not well explained, so don't expect to learn much about the Freuds' pioneering methods. Still, the house is authentic, and if nothing else, you'll be struck by what a lovely place it must have been for winding down a notable life. Sigmund's study and library, which came from the doctors' famed offices at Berggasse 19, Vienna, were left precisely as they were on the day he died—which he did on a couch, of course.

Here's a pleasant *Messiah* complex: **The Handel House Museum** **(25 Brook St., W1; ☎ 020/7495-1685; www.handelhouse.org; £5 adults, £2 children except Sat (free), £4.50 seniors/students; Tues–Wed and Fri–Sat 10am–6pm, Thurs 10am–8pm, Sun noon–6pm; Tube: Bond Street).** This Mayfair building, the German-born composer's home from 1723 (he was its first tenant) to his death in 1759, has lived many lives—before the museum's 2001 opening, conservators chipped 28 layers of paint off the interior walls to uncover the original grey color. You'll see a 15-minute video on Handel's life, and then move on, often attended by old dears serving as volunteers, to see the few humble rooms. They're furnished with period furniture that wasn't his, but not many artifacts. There's a small alcove where kids can try on period costumes and grown-ups can listen to Handel's greatest works. You're best off coming during one of the house's many concerts, held every week or so in a plain recital room (£7–£9 depending on performance). Handel fans should also investigate the composer's collection at the Foundling Museum (p. 159), where he was a crucial patron.

CARTOONS

The Cartoon Museum **(35 Little Russell St., WC1; ☎ 020/7580-8155; www.cartoonmuseum.org; £4 adults, free for children under 18, £3 seniors/students; Tues–Sat 10:30am–5:30pm, Sun noon–5:30pm; Tube: Tottenham Court Road or Holborn),** a small but well-put-together suite of rooms, puts an emphasis on British artists, particularly political ones. Its 750-odd original illustrations, going from Victorian (Cruikshank) right up to contemporary satirists (Simon Bond's *101 Uses for a Dead Cat*), also has a few faces from the funny papers, including Andy Capp ('e was English, luv) and Dick Tracy.

Public Sculpture

In London's heyday, celebrities weren't rewarded with advertising contracts or reality TV shows. They were carved in stone. A slew of important statues dots the city—so many that you'll stop noticing them within a day or so. Keep your eyes peeled for these notable works, five of hundreds:

Albert Memorial, Kensington Gardens (Tube: South Kensington): Albert, Queen Victoria's German-born husband (and first cousin), was a passionate supporter of the arts who piloted Britain from one dazzling artistic and architectural triumph to another. But when he died suddenly of typhoid in 1861 at age 42, the devastated Queen abruptly withdrew from the gaiety and remained in seclusion and mourning until her death in 1901, shaping the Victorian mentality. The bereaved Queen arranged for this astounding spire—part bombast, part elegy—to be erected opposite the concert hall Albert spearheaded. Some of the spire's nearly 200 figures represent the continents and the sciences, and some, higher up, represent angels and virtues. At the center, as if on an altar, is Albert himself, sheathed in gold. The Royal Parks recently completed a restoration that has the memorial gleaming as brightly as it did on its dedication day in 1872. Tours of the interior go at 2 and 3pm on the first Sunday of each month, March to December (no reservations required; £4.50).

"Eros," Piccadilly Circus (Tube: Piccadilly Circus): Every guide book will tell you that the fleet-footed, winged lad atop the Shaftesbury Monument in Piccadilly Circus is Eros, the Greek god of sex, erected in 1893 by Alfred Gilbert and one of the first to be cast in aluminum. Except they're wrong. The statue is based on Anteros, Eros' brother, the god of selfless love. In fact, the work, which tops a fountain dedicated to a Victorian philanthropist, is officially called *The Angel of Christian Charity.* But Anteros, gallant deity that he is, lets Eros cop all the glory. Until World War II, when he was moved slightly, his arrow pointed up Shaftesbury Avenue; now he aims down Lower Regent Street.

DESIGN

If it weren't such a pain to reach, it might be more celebrated. As it stands, the charming **Geffrye Museum** ★★ (Kingsland Rd., E2; ☎ 020/7739-9893; www.geffrye-museum.org.uk; free admission, including audio tour; Tues–Sat 10am–5pm, Sun noon–5pm; Tube: Old Street, then bus 243 or a 20-min. walk), founded in 1914 as a resource for the furniture industry, is beloved by local families and design students. Especially on fine days from April to October, you'll spot these folks relaxing on the exceptional grounds. (The walled herb garden encourages touch, to release scents, and its period plots are historically accurate, cultivated with plants used in several eras, including Elizabethan and Victorian

Cleopatra's Needle, Victoria Embankment (Tube: Embankment): London and New York are sister cities in many ways. They share the same theatrical shows *(The Lion King, Mamma Mia!, Wicked)*. They share hot restaurants and clubs (Nobu, Bungalow 8). They even share priceless relics. The romantically named Cleopatra's Needles—which Cleopatra had nothing to do with—were originally erected in Heliopolis, Egypt around 1450 B.C., and their inscriptions were added 200 years later. The Romans moved the granite spires to Alexandria, where they were later toppled and buried in the sand, preserving them until Egypt gave them away in the early 1800s. New York's Cleopatra's Needle was installed in Central Park in 1881, but. London's was erected three years earlier. Two sphinx were installed to guard it (some say backwards, since they face the sculpture, not away from it). In 1917, damage from the little-remembered first bout of German bombings, in World War I, scarred the southern sphinx, and the damage was left as a testament. There's a third needle in Paris.

Traffic Light Tree, Heron Quays, Isle of Dogs (Tube: Heron Quays DLR): Paris-born artist Pierre Vivant conceived this sly electrified work, which clusters 75 traffic lights—each one relentlessly and independently cycling through red, yellow, green—atop a stalk, in imitation of a bushy tree. In 1998, the 7.8m-tall (26-ft.) sculpture replaced a living plane tree that suffocated from the mounting traffic around Canary Wharf. It's at the intersection of Westferry, Marsh Wall, and Heron Quay. The surrounding roundabout doesn't make it easy to see up close.

Quantum Cloud, O_2 Dome, North Greenwich (Tube: North Greenwich): Mathematics as art. Antony Gormley worked with an engineering firm, which itself puzzled over fractals and physics, to design the colossal (nearly 30m/98 ft. tall) mass of 3,500 four-sided, 1.5m-long (5-ft.) "tetrahedral units" that appear at first like a random "cloud" of metal rods but, when viewed from the right angle, reveal the ghostly outline of a standing figure within. The 1999 work stands on cast-iron caissons in the Thames, to the east of the O_2 Dome.

times.) The entire complex, a U-shaped line of dignified brick houses built in 1714 for ironworkers, feels removed from the rush of the East End. Inside is a walk through time: re-creations of typical middle-class London homes from the 1600s to the late 20th century, artfully arranged to appear lived-in, and complete with explanations of each item on display, including illuminating information about which pieces were necessary and which were merely trendy. To some, they're rooms full of furniture. To others, the Geffrye is a chance to understand how people of the past lived. You know which person you are.

One building here is a restored almshouse; I recommend booking timed tours to see how charity cases lived back in the day (the 1st Sat and first and 3d Wed of the month; £2 adults, free for children under 16). On weekends, curators plan discussions, lectures, and kid-oriented crafts workshops, which gives the place much more energy than you'd expect from a design-based attraction.

The Design Museum (Shad Thames, SE1; ☎ 020/7403-6933; www.designmuseum.org; £8.50 adults, free for children under 12, £6.50 seniors, £5 students; daily 10am–5:45pm, until 6:45pm in July and Aug, last admission 5:15pm; Tube: London Bridge or Tower Hill), just east of the Tower Bridge on the southern bank of the Thames, is strictly for contemporary top-drawer talent—the cool kids of style. To me, that makes it more of a gallery than a museum. The steep fee also means it's best for devotees of high design, not for average sightseers. Shows are puffed-up explorations of random topics (race cars, urban planning), but if they're sometimes ostentatious, at least they're thought-provoking. Each spring, the museum hosts its prestigious Designs of the Year competition, and mounts mini-shows by each nominee. The gift shop (www.designmuseumshop.com) stocks some wild, strange oddities such as artist-conceived housewares, dolls, and office supplies—how about a cup that makes your hard-boiled egg look like it's wearing pants?

Although many of the products it covers are British in origin—Bovril, Cadbury, and so on—the **Museum of Brands, Packaging, and Advertising** (2 Colville Mews, Lonsdale Rd., W11; ☎ 020/7908-0880; www.museumofbrands.com; £5.80 adults, £2 children 7–16, £3.50 seniors/students; Tues–Sat 10am–6pm, Sun 11am–5pm, last admission 45 min. before closing; Tube: Notting Hill Gate), an illustrator's nirvana, still makes for an interesting overview of the history of product art and logos. There's no denying that many of its Victorian and Jet Age specimens—the sum of a 4-decade-long collecting binge by one man—are marvels of design. Major companies like Kellogg's and Twinings also lend firepower to the pop art. It's a testament to the unheralded beauty of all the tins, boxes, and tubes that our mothers have thoughtlessly thrown away over the ages.

ENGINEERING

In the late 1800s, there was no bolder display of a country's technological prowess than a spectacular bridge. Consider The Brooklyn Bridge or the Firth of Forth Bridge. The **Tower Bridge Exhibition** ★ (Tower Bridge, on the side closest to the Tower of London, SE1; ☎ 020/7403-3761; www.towerbridge.org.uk; £6 adults, £3 children 5–15, £4.50 seniors/students; Apr–Sept daily 10am–6:30pm, Oct–Mar daily 9:30am–6pm; Tube: Tower Hill or Tower Gateway DLR), celebrates one such triumph. The museum is like two attractions in one. The first satisfies sightseers who have dreamed of going up in the famous neo-Gothic towers and crossing the high-level observation walkways. For them, it's a close encounter with a world icon. The second aspect of the museum, delving into the steam-driven machinery that so impressed the world in 1894, will hook the mechanically inclined. The original bascule-raising equipment, representing the largest use of hydraulic power at the time, remains in fine condition despite being retired in favor of electricity in 1976; the raising of the spans is now controlled by joystick from a cabin across the road from the entrance (check the box office or call ☎ 020/7940-3984 to learn when the next openings will be). How could such a proud monument survive the Blitz when everything around it got flattened? Answer: The Luftwaffe needed to keep it as a visual landmark.

Although the engineering contributions of Marc Brunel and his son Isambard Kingdom Brunel are largely taken for granted, they're given their due in the small **Brunel Museum** (Railway Ave., SE16; ☎ 020/7231-3840; www.brunelenginehouse.org.uk; £2 adults, £1 children/seniors/students; daily 10am–5pm; Tube: Rotherhithe). With the help of a shield system they invented, these pioneers executed the first tunnel to be built under a navigable river, but London's soft earth didn't make it easy. It took from 1825 to 1843, and this red-brick building, marked by a chimney, was where steam engines pumped the seeping water out of the Thames Tunnel as diggers toiled. The tunnel, lined with arches and Doric capitals, was a commercial flop that deteriorated into a subterranean red-light district. But it later found new purpose as a part of the Underground's East London Line and new respect through this museum.

FINANCE

At the surprisingly complete **Bank of England Museum** ★ (Threadneedle St., EC2; ☎ 020/7601-5545; www.bankofengland.co.uk/education/museum; free admission; Mon–Fri 10am–5pm; Tube: Bank), the intermittently compelling tale of the B of E is recounted in laborious but generous detail, accompanied by plenty of antiques from the vaults. That's fine if you understand finance, but most people lose the plot pretty quickly. Along the way are some fun oddities, including a million-pound note, printed in the early 19th century for internal accounting. There's lots of expensive swag, such as an iron chest from 1700, heaps of silver treasures, and a gold bar so pure (1 part in 10,000 impure) that it was given to Queen Elizabeth as a coronation gift. It's also fun to watch Her Majesty age on the money over the years. The most popular exhibit is probably a standard gold bar, locked in a clear plastic box, that you're invited to lift.

FOOD

A labor of love by a tea aficionado, **The Bramah Museum of Tea and Coffee** ★★ (40 Southwark St., SE1; ☎ 020/7403-5650; www.teaandcoffeemuseum.co.uk; £4 adults, £2.50 children/seniors/students; daily 10am–6pm; Tube: London Bridge) pays respect to the two imports that held the greatest sway over London's economic history. Covering everything from ancient China to modern times and from teapots to teabags, the museum showcases a hodgepodge of holdings—the assorted pots, cups, and grinders will teach you that you've been brewing things the wrong way. The facilities aren't fancy, but the exhibits are well written and fact packed. The afternoon cream teas in the adjoining shop are some of the most affordable, yet best, in the city. At press time, the museum was closed by the death of its founder, and a subsequent "refurbishment" was set to last until early 2009, so check on times and prices.

GOVERNMENT

The Houses of Parliament (Bridge St. and Parliament Square, SW1; ☎ 087/0906-3773; www.parliament.uk; £12 adults, £5 children 5–15, children under 5 free, £8 seniors/students; July–Aug: Mon–Tues and Fri–Sat 9:15am–4:30pm, Wed–Thurs 1:15–4:30pm, Sept: Mon and Fri–Sat 9:15am–4:30pm, Tues–Thurs 1:15–4:30pm; 75 min.; reservations recommended; Tube: Westminster) are a virtual modern-day castle dedicated to government. Throughout the Middle Ages, this

London's Galleries

In case its top-notch selection of museums hasn't clued you in to the fact, I'll start by saying that London is a world capital for art. No other city in the world has such a breadth of it on display. You won't just find antique fine art; some of today's most exciting, high-priced, and controversial contemporary artists live or work in London, including Damien Hirst (he of the animal corpses in formaldehyde), Tracey Emin (she of the unmade bed as art installation), sculptors Ron Mueck and Rachel Whiteread, and architect Zaha Hadid. The city plays such an important role that a term, Britart, has been coined to describe some of the more experimental work.

Dozens of galleries are sprinkled around town—with concentrations in Mayfair and Whitechapel—and most of them will have something interesting on display. *Time Out* lists many in its Art section; also check the booster organization **New Exhibitions of Contemporary Art** (☎ 020/7839-7832; www.newexhibitions.com), which lists events online.

The most celebrated (or, depending on your viewpoint, reviled) collection of Britart, ranging from self-sculpture in frozen blood to immovable hyper-realistic sculptures of homeless people, belongs to adman Charles Saatchi, who displayed works at his popular gallery near the London Eye until 2005, when landlord disputes drove him out. The impressive collection re-opened in October 2008 at the new **Saatchi Gallery** ★★ (Duke of York Square, SW3; www.saatchi-gallery.co.uk; free admission; Tube: Sloane Square) at the 6,500-sq.-m (70,000-sq.-ft.) former Royal Military Asylum building (1801) in Chelsea, complete with a cafe, bookshop, and massive exhibition halls boasting tall ceilings. The socially critical, eye-bending experiments shown here make the Tate Modern's stuff look tame, and no fan of modern art should miss it.

Another important player on the Britart scene is the **White Cube** (48 Hoxton Square, N1; ☎ 020/7930-5373; www.whitecube.com; free admission; Tues–Sat 10am–6pm; Tube: Old Street), a free gallery with many rotating exhibitions. This influential gallery was set up to provide an unfussy, small, focused space for works. A second space in St. James's opened in 2006 (25-26 Mason's Yard, SW1; Tube: Piccadilly Circus).

The Hayward Gallery (South Bank Centre, Belvedere Rd., SE1; ☎ 087/1663-2501; www.southbankcentre.org.uk; daily 10am–6pm, until 10pm Fri; Tube: Waterloo) is the principal exhibition space of the Southbank Centre. The space hosts some terrific blockbuster shows, usually about

was considered one of the monarch's main homes, only to burn down in 1512 and again in 1834, when it was rebuilt into the Gothic citadel now used for the day-to-day running of the Empire. Guides still refer to it as a "palace" because technically, the Crown still owns it. It's roughly divided into three areas: those for the House of Lords (whose members inherit seats, done in rose); the House of

£10, which have included Ansel Adams, Roy Lichtenstein, 1920s Surrealism, and a 60-artist panorama of modern African art. The Hayward also plans about two talks a month, free with your ticket. Some smaller exhibitions (too bad you missed the coral reef rendered in crochet) are free, and so are frequent music events at its cafe/bar, the Concrete.

Here are some notable galleries with **free** shows, mostly open 10am to 6pm weekdays, 11am to 6pm Saturday, and noon to 5pm Sunday:

The **Institute of Contemporary Arts** (The Mall, SW1; ☎ 020/7930-3647; www.ica.org.uk; Tube: Charing Cross) is a cutting-edge booster of art, films, performance, and evening talks. There's always something challenging or intellectual on display here. **South London Gallery** (65 Peckham Rd., SE5; ☎ 020/7703-6120; www.southlondongallery.org; Tues–Sun noon–6pm; Tube: Elephant and Castle or Oval) or SLG, has also been pushing the envelope in one form or another since 1868 with abstract pieces, performance art, and plenty of talks. **The Wapping Project** (Wapping Hydraulic Power Station, Wapping Wall, E1; ☎ 020/7680-2080; www.thewappingproject.com; Tube: Wapping), in a disused hydraulic power station, makes for an awesome setting, and its installations and performances, which can be pretentious, clearly find inspiration from the impressive space. The **Whitechapel Art Gallery** (80-82 Whitechapel High St., E1; ☎ 020/7522-7888; www.whitechapel.org; closed Mon; Tube: Aldgate East) is one of the city's preeminent contemporary galleries, having been active since 1901 and given the first European airings to names as important as Kahlo, Pollack, and Rothko—the East End is home to more artists than any other neighborhood in Europe, and many of them congregate here at its exhibitions, talks, and films. There's music Friday nights until 11pm.

For photography, **The Association of Photographers** (81 Leonard St., EC2; ☎ 020/7739-6669; www.the-aop.org; Tube: Old Street) highlights photojournalism in its gallery; **The Photographers' Gallery** (5 and 8 Great Newport St., WC2; ☎ 020/7831-1772; www.photonet.org.uk; Tube: Leicester Square) established in 1971, is well-patronized, hosting as many as 500,000 visitors a year, and operates a bookshop and a cafe, and gives plenty of free talks; **Proud Galleries** (Buckingham St. at John Adam St., WC2; ☎ 020/7839-4942; Tube: Charing Cross or Embankment; www.proud.co.uk; Tube: Embankment or Charing Cross) mostly shows high-end vintage shots of rock stars and celebrities.

Commons (by far the most powerful, elected by the people, seats of blue-green, with a chamber dating only to 1950); and a few Royal sitting rooms and dressing rooms (golds, browns, burgundies), which the Queen flits through when she shows up once a year to kick off sessions. The walls of Westminster Hall, essentially England's highest all-purpose events space, were built in 1097, and both William

Wallace (remember *Braveheart?*) and the Gunpowder Plot conspirators were tried in it. The Hall, the only part of the original Westminster Palace to survive an 1834 fire except for the Jewel Tower (p. 172), is cherished for its oak hammer-beam ceiling, Europe's largest, dating to 1399; during World War II, it was saved at the expense of the House of Commons itself. Considering all the ornate mosaic flooring, peaked windows, and statues stacked in niches, you would be forgiven for mistaking the complex for a church. It's certainly the high altar of secular Britain.

Frustratingly, The Clock Tower above the Houses—it contains the 13.5-ton bell known as **Big Ben** plus four smaller bells—is only open to tours for U.K. residents (at least there's a virtual tour of it on the Parliament website). But visiting the rest of the complex is a possibility. Citing security concerns, the government has said that foreign visitors may tour only in summer (around Aug 1–Sept 30), when the government is not in session, leaving it a striking ghost town. Booking ahead is advisable, but you can try your luck for last-minute openings at the ticket office, which opens from mid-July next to the Jewel Tower, across the street from Parliament. Sometimes there are temporary exhibitions set up to explicate the nuances of the British system (one in 2008 commemorated the 1958 act to admit "life peers" to the House of Lords—essentially, including people who weren't born to the upper crust). To learn how to attend a debate (it isn't easy), see p. 198.

HORTICULTURE

The 121-hectare (300-acre) **Royal Botanic Gardens, Kew** ★ (www.kew.org; ☎ 020/8332-5655; daily 9:30am–4:15pm in winter, until 6pm in spring and fall, and 7:30pm weekends and 6:30pm weekdays in summer; £13 adults, free for children under 17, £12 seniors/students; Tube: Kew Gardens) would be a delightful place to stroll were it not for the painful entrance fee. It's not that the gardens and glasshouses aren't impressive—there are plants from around the world, many descended from specimens collected in the earliest days of international sea trade, and all are beautifully maintained to satisfy the upper-class ladies who lunch here. Of the seven conservatories, the domed Palm House, built from 1844 to 1848, is probably the world's most recognizable greenhouse, while the Temperate House (which contains the world's largest indoor plant, the 16m/52-ft.-tall Chilean wine-palm) is the largest surviving Victorian glass structure. The gardeners are among the best in the world; in 1986, they coaxed a bloom from a portea that hadn't flowered in 160 years. Kew's contributions to botanical science, ongoing since 1759, earned it a spot on the UNESCO list of World Heritage Sites in 2003. I just can't get past the offensive price, or how long it takes to get here, some 10km/6⅓ miles from the city. Worse, many of the attractions shut down in winter (including Kew Palace, p. 166), so this is mostly a summer attraction.

The **Museum of Garden History** ★ (Lambeth Palace Road, SE1; ☎ 020/7401-8865; www.museumgardenhistory.org; Tues–Sun 10:30am–5pm; suggested donation £3 adults, £2.50 children/seniors/students; Tube: Lambeth North) was the world's first gardening museum, and today it's a reasonably priced alternative to Kew. Its 17th-century knot garden, in which woody herbs are clipped to make low hedges, contains plants popular in that period, and a special emphasis is given to topiary and to the tastes of John Tradescant and his son, the gardeners to Charles I and II. The distinctive gardens were planted in the disused graveyard of a parish church that served for 900 years before its 1972 deconsecration. Of the estimated 26,000 graves here, including those of Captain William Bligh of *The*

Banksy: Graffiti or Genius?

In the shadowy lanes of The City and the East End, a secret avenger lurks. His name is Banksy, and he takes on corporate greed, government surveillance, the death of beauty, and war. No, Banksy isn't a super-hero. He's a graffiti artist and a London institution, and he tackles his topics with the acerbic aplomb of a political cartoonist. He has hung his own work, unnoticed and without damage, at museums in Paris and New York. He painted "We're bored of fish" over the penguin enclosure at the London Zoo. He even smuggled a hooded figure dressed as a Guantanamo detainee into Disneyland. Who is he? Many people would love to know, not so they can charge him with vandalism, but so they can shake his hand. Every year, someone new is fingered as Banksy, but so far no ID has stuck. Meanwhile, Banksy's satire, identified by its stencil design and often by anthropomorphic rats, has garnered such esteem that after he strikes, local councils don't always rush to remove his work. Wherever his guerrilla art unexpectedly appears in his East End stomping grounds, a temporary art attraction is born. Track the latest installations at www.banksy.co.uk and www.artofthestate.co.uk, and then go on an art safari.

Bounty and Elizabeth I's grandmother, virtually no memorials survive, making the place more poignant.

MARITIME

See also the National Maritime Museum (p. 170) and the *Cutty Sark* (p. 170).

Tucked into one of the few remaining slips that enabled ships to unload in Southwark (another is Hay's Galleria, downstream by the HMS *Belfast,* now converted to a boutique shopping area), **The *Golden Hinde*** (kids) (Pickfords Wharf, Clink St., SE1; ☎ 087/0011-8700; www.goldenhinde.org; £6 adults, £4.50 children/seniors/students; daily 10am–6pm; Tube: London Bridge) is a 1:1 replica of Sir Francis Drake's square rigged Tudor galleon, which circumnavigated the world from 1577 to 80. This 1973 version, which is so tiny you will forever be in awe of what those old explorers could do, made its own circumnavigation in 1980. Self-guided and guided tours are available daily, but it also hosts Pirate Fun Day afternoons (£7 adults, £5 children) for kids as well as sleepovers (£40) during which kids can dress in period clothes, hear tales from costumed actors, and help with shipboard tasks on an imaginary voyage. The 2-hour immersive version, the "Maritime Workshop" (raising the anchor, manning the guns), is £8.50. You need to make reservations for all those events.

If you have a physical limitation that keeps you from climbing ladders, stay ashore and admire **HMS *Belfast*** ★ (Morgan's Lane, Tooley St., SE1; ☎ 020/7940-6300; http://hmsbelfast.iwm.org.uk; £10 adults, free for children under 16, £7.20 seniors/students; Mar–Oct daily 10am–6pm, Nov–Feb daily 10am–5pm, last admission 45 min. before closing; Tube: London Bridge) from afar. It's as if the powerful old warship, upon being retired from service in 1965, was simply motored to the dock and instantly opened as an attraction. Nearly everything, down to the grey-and-red checked flooring and decaying cables, is exactly as it was (although I imagine those mannequins with the bad toupees might have been added), making the boat a fascinating snapshot of mid-century maritime technology. The authenticity also makes it a devil to navigate. Getting around her various decks, engine rooms, and hatches requires dexterity and a well-calibrated inner compass. You can roam more or less as you wish, visiting every cubby of the ship from kitchen to bridge, all the while being thankful that it wasn't you who was chasing German cruisers (the *Belfast* sank the *Scharnhorst*) and backing up the D-Day invasion in this tough tin can. Kids receive a free, thorough activity book that helps them locate and understand the most interesting bits. The price, which jumped 20% in 2 years, is too high for those with a lukewarm interest.

MEDICINE

A treat among London museums—but don't eat first—**Hunterian Museum** ★ **(35-43 Lincoln's Inn Fields (south side), WC2; ☎ 020/7869-6560; www.rcseng.ac.uk/museums; free admission; Tues–Sat 10am–5pm; Tube: Holborn)**, at the Royal College of Surgeons, chronicles the life's work of John Hunter (1728–93), who elevated surgery from something your barber dabbled in to something a saw-wielding "scientist" would, ahem, undertake. It's a ghoulish scene, crowded with thousands of specimens, all tastefully presented in a gleaming two-level hall. See Napoleon III's bladder stone and Winston Churchill's gold dentures, designed to fix his childhood lisp. Most of your time will be spent squeamishly perusing some 3,000 black-lidded jars of human and animal pathology and anatomy (many originally obtained by grave-robbers, a common practice then), plus a bone-grinding collection of crude surgical instruments that could chill even the steeliest physician. Check out the cross-section of a chicken's head that Hunter grafted with a human tooth. Such Frankenstein projects funded his school of anatomy. Cluckers got no respect from Dr Hunter: He also proved that bones grow from the ends by firing a lead shot into the center of a chicken's bone, measuring its location, sewing the poor bird up, and killing it later on for dissection. Upstairs, as part of a history of surgery, you'll find an ill-conceived amputation buzzsaw. In its first use, it became slick with blood, slipped, and lopped off a nurse's hand; both patient and nurse were killed by subsequent infection. Ask the good-humored staff questions, or else catch the weekly free guided tour, Wednesdays at 1pm (book ahead if possible).

A disturbing snapshot of pre-anesthetic treatment in the early 1800s, **The Old Operating Theatre (9a St. Thomas St., SE1; ☎ 020/7188-2679; www.thegarret.org.uk; £5.45 adults, £3 children under 16, £4.45 seniors/students; daily 10:30am–5pm; Tube: London Bridge)** was a space built by St. Thomas's Hospital in which surgeries, mostly amputations and other quick-hit procedures, could be conducted where students could see but few others could hear the patients' agonized screams. When the hospital moved in 1862, it was abandoned and sealed away. It was considered lost until 1956, when an enterprising historian thought to look in the attic space above a church that adjoined the old hospital, and he found the secret surgical space, original stadium-style seating, plaster, and all. It's now the centerpiece of a modest museum delving into medical methods of the early 1800s.

While the Hunterian Museum's glassy galleries harbor some ghastly medical leftovers, mostly European, the similarly highbrow **Wellcome Collection** ★ **(183**

Euston Rd., NW1; ☎ 020/7611-2222; www.wellcomecollection.org; Mon, Wed, Fri 10am–6pm, Tues, Thurs 10am–8pm, and Sat 10am–4pm; free admission; Tube: Euston Square or Warren Street), opened in these sparkling premises in 2007, takes an artier, more sociological approach to the history of dealing with the body. Most of the mementos regarding worldwide science or superstition are displayed in two permanent exhibitions and are selected for their loveliness or curiosity (Greco-Roman phallic amulets, Charles Darwin's cane, abstract art about gene modification), so visitors are more likely to leave quiescent than queasy. That unexpected historical chronicle is augmented by a couple of changing exhibitions (such as an assortment of skeletons found under London building sites, or a show about wartime medicine). The free events schedule, which can range from walking tours to performance art, is active, with several happenings a month, and kids 6 to 14 can pick up free explorer packs to help them latch onto the curios.

MILITARY HISTORY

I classify the **Imperial War Museum** ★★ (Lambeth Rd., SE1; ☎ 020/7416-5000; www.iwm.org.uk; free admission; daily 10am–6pm; Tube: Lambeth North or Elephant & Castle) as one of London's unexpectedly great museums, in the same unjustly overlooked category as the National Maritime Museum. There's plenty to do here, and not just for military buffs. Instead of merely showcasing obsolete implements of death, the IWM, the latest tenant of the commodious former mental hospital known as Bedlam, takes great care to help visitors understand the sensations, feelings, and moods of soldiers and civilians caught in a variety of past conflicts. In addition to giving visitors an easy-to-grasp background on major wars, the museum has plenty of authentic and surprisingly moving artifacts and well-maintained displays like The Trench, a walk-through mock-up of a muddy fortification in Somme, 1916; The Blitz Experience, a rousing recreation of an air raid shelter under aural assault; a gallery of artworks about the Great War and World War II; and an exceptionally thoughtful Holocaust exhibition. Sure, there are mighty big tanks and guns, too, but the museum is much less about the toys of war than about the people who found themselves mired in battle.

THEATER & MUSIC

A painstaking recreation of an outdoor Elizabethan theater, **Shakespeare's Globe** ★★ (21 New Globe Walk, SE1; ☎ 020/7902-1400; www.shakespeares-globe.org; £11 adults, £6.50 children 5–15, £8.50 seniors/students; daily early Oct to Apr 10am–5pm, late April to early Oct 9am–5pm; Tube: London Bridge) tends to bewitch fans of history and theater, but it can put all others to sleep. Arrive early in the day, since the timed tours fill up, and they're the only way to see the performance area and the foundations of the Rose Theatre, another Shakespearean stage. Get a bad time, and you'll be stuck waiting for far too long in the UnderGlobe, the well-crafted but exhaustible exhibition about Elizabethan theater. Also avoid matinee days, since tours don't run during performances. The open-air theater was made using only Elizabethan technology such as saws, oak framing, pegs, and plaster panels mixed with goat's hair (the original recipe called for cow's hair, but the breed they needed is now extinct). The first Globe burned down, aged just 14, when a cannon fired during a performance caused its thatched roof to catch fire. It took a special act of Parliament, plus plenty of hidden sprinkler systems, to permit the construction of this, the first thatched roof in London since the Great Fire. The original theater was the same size (and stood 180m/591 ft. to the southeast), but it crammed 3,000 luckless souls. Today, just 1,600 are admitted. Who cares if the scene is touristy? It supplies an immediate entrée into the long-lost Elizabethan world.

Horniman Museum (100 London Rd., Forest Hill; ☎ 020/8699-1872; www.horniman.ac.uk; free admission; daily 10:30am–5:30pm; National Rail: Forest Hill), the legacy of a dilettante tea trader that first opened in 1901, is a hike into South London. But this international-minded repository has a cherished collection of 7,000 musical instruments, plus noted stores of items regarding anthropology (masks, puppets, folk art) and natural history (i.e., stuffed animals galore), and a modest aquarium. Trains from London Bridge take about 15 minutes, but you'll be unlikely to take the journey unless it's for the instruments.

Music aficionados should also visit to the little-known **Royal College of Music Museum of Instruments** (Prince Consort Rd., SW7; ☎ 020/7591-4842; www.cph.rcm.ac.uk; free admission; Tues–Fri 2–4:30pm, closed July–Aug; Tube: South Kensington), across the street from Royal Albert Hall. The Museum holds more than 800 instruments dating back to 1480, including Handel's spinet and Haydn's clavichord (gesundheit!), plus about a dozen Stradivarius violins.

In addition to being a great concert venue, **Royal Albert Hall** ★★ (Kensington Gore, SW7; ☎ 020/7838-3105; www.royalalberthall.com; open daily except Wed, times vary; tours run 10:30am–3:30pm; admission to lobby free, tours £8 adults, £7 seniors/students; Tube: South Kensington) is also one of London's great landmarks, and you don't need a seat to enjoy it. Conceived by Queen Victoria's husband Albert and opened in 1871, a decade after his death from typhoid (Vicky was still so distraught that she didn't speak at the opening ceremonies), the hall contains such oddities as Britain's longest single-weave carpet (in the corridors), the Queen's Box (still leased to the monarchy), and a spectacular glass dome (41m/135 ft. high and supported only at its rim). I'll warn you now: You don't go backstage; some 320 performances a year are presented, many with less than 24 hours' set-up time, and sightseers would be in the way.

TOYS

The goodies at the **Museum of Childhood** ★★ kids (Cambridge Heath Rd., E2; ☎ 020/8983-5200; www.vam.ac.uk/moc; free admission; daily 10am–5:45pm; Tube: Bethnal Green) are courtesy of the awesome V&A Museum, which pulls from its considerable collection of toys, clothing, dolls and dollhouses, books, teddy bears, and games to chronicle kiddom through the ages. Children love toys of any stripe, and exhibits are placed at their eye level with simplified descriptions. Some young ones don't grasp the concept—I saw one toddler burst into tears when she saw a crib behind glass that she couldn't climb into. Just as often, though, the outbursts are from parents, who see their youths flash before their eyes at the sight of, say, a slot racer car set sealed inside a museum case. Child-rearing history is also addressed; look for the "Princess Bottle" of 1871, which had a reservoired shape that allowed for quick milk dispensing but also incubated bacteria, a fact that wasn't realized until countless babies died of infections. The MoC's glass-and-steel building is itself an artifact; it began its life in South Kensington as the home of the nascent V&A collection but was re-erected here in the 1860s (the fish-scale mosaic floor was made by female prisoners, many of whom, ironically, were taken from their own children). As you can imagine, there are free kids programs galore—up to five a weekday, more on weekends—and the gift kiosk is piled with tempting knick-knacks costing less than £3.

For lots more antique toys, visit **Pollock's Toy Museum** (1 Scala St., W1; ☎ 020/7636-3452; www.pollockstoymuseum.com; £3 adults, £1.50 children; Mon–Sat 10am–5pm, last admission 4:30pm; Tube: Goodge Street). A few mildewed old apartments were barely altered before being fitted with cases of vintage toys, and, as you thread through the creaking rooms, you might wonder whether you're going into Sweeney Todd's shop to be murdered. It doesn't help that wax-headed dolls stare at you wherever you turn. The collection is exhausting, if not exhaustive: Mechanical cast-iron banks, 1950s rocket toys, puppets, Gollywogs, wax dolls, the 1921 forerunner to G.I. Joe (Swiss Action Man), doll's houses, a board game based on the Falkland Islands invasion that was banned for being in poor taste. Even if you don't care to gaze at dusty dolls, its ground-floor shop, free to enter, has some terrific, hard-to-find toys that don't cost much, including reproduction tins, lots of handmade items, and cardboard theaters—the museum takes its name from the last great printer of toy theaters.

WORLD WAR II

What an odd, homegrown attraction is **Winston Churchill's Britain at War Experience** ★ (64-66 Tooley St., SE1; ☎ 020/7403-3171; www.britainatwar.co.uk; £10 adults, £4.95 children 5–15, £5.95 seniors/students; the website often posts coupons for £1.50 off; daily Apr–Oct 10am–5pm, daily Nov–Mar 10am–4pm; Tube: London Bridge). Because it begins with one of those "you are there" gimmicks—a simulated lift ride to a recreated Tube station shelter—I suspected it might be a tourist trap. But in between its full-color films of London during Word War II and the cases of quirky relics such as a Rent-a-Cake, a cardboard wedding cake couples could borrow during rationing (it had a tiny drawer for a morsel of real cake), I was hooked. The Imperial War Museum is more authoritative and the Cabinet War Rooms more authentic, but I find this reassuringly amateurish place, and its frozen-faced mannequins, queerly moving. Something about the earnest, let's-put-on-a-museum ethic—as if half of London cleaned their attics of wartime memorabilia just to share the story—rhymes with the improvised efforts that got Britain through the war. Still, an interest in The Blitz will help you see past the place's ragged seams. The eerie, windowless atmosphere includes an Anderson Shelter piped with the disturbing sounds of bombs in flight and climaxes in a hokey walk-through of the bombing of a two-story city block, complete with "smoke" and gushing water. Kids might be bored by the ration coupons, but the rubble gets their attention. It charges more than it should, though, and so if you have to pick just one Blitz-related showroom, the Cabinet War Rooms wins.

OVERRATED ATTRACTIONS YOU CAN SKIP

Why list attractions if they're overrated? Because you're going to be exposed to ads touting these places, and some of them are unjustly staples on the tourist circuit. Besides, I'm aware that if you have bored kids in tow, some of the more inauthentic sights might be just the tonic to jolt them back into a compliant mood.

The Queen inherited one momma of a priceless art collection—7,000 paintings, 30,000 watercolors, and half a million prints, to say nothing of sculpture, furniture, and jewelry—but she shows only a tiny fraction at **The Queen's Gallery** (Buckingham Palace Rd., SW1; ☎ 020/7766-7301; www.royalcollection.org.uk; £8.50 adults, £4.25 children 5–16, £7.50 seniors/students; daily 10am–5:30pm, last admission 4:30pm; Tube: Victoria). The few works that are on display (at the southwest of Buckingham Palace; budget 1 hr.) are undoubtedly exceptional (one of the world's few Vermeers, a Rubens' self-portrait given to Charles I, glittering ephemera by Fabergé), but they're not the cream of what she owns. There's more exciting stuff to be had for free at the National Gallery.

Next door to the Queen's Gallery is **The Royal Mews** (Buckingham Palace Rd., SW1; ☎ 020/7766-7302; www.royalcollection.org.uk; mid Mar to Oct 11am–4pm, last admission 45 min. before closing; £7.50 adults, £4.80 children 5–17, £6.75 seniors/students; Tube: Victoria). Most visitors pop in and out of what amounts to the Queen's garage in about 15 minutes. You'll see stables (fit for a you-know-who; they barely smell at all) and Her Majesty's Rolls-Royces (many of which, at Prince Charles' behest, run on green fuels). You'll also overdose on learning about regulations for when this set of harnesses may be used and when that leather must be polished. The Gallery and the Mews can be seen on a joint ticket (£15 adults, £8 children 5–16, £13 seniors/students).

Avoid it like the plague. **The London Dungeon** (Tooley St., SE1; ☎ 020/7403-7221; www.thedungeons.com; £20 adults, £15 children 5–15, £18 seniors/students, discounts on www.lastminute.com; times shift every 6 weeks but are roughly daily 9:30am–6pm; Tube: London Bridge) is a sophomoric gross-out. Costumed actors (future failed actors all) bray at visitors as they lead them through darkness from set to set, each representing another period of English history as a 13-year-old boy might define them. Plague-ridden rubber corpses "sneeze" on passersby, fake organs squirt "blood" during an autopsy, and cutthroat barber Sweeney Todd gleefully commands you to sit in his chair. The climax is a pair of indoor carnival rides. If you dread being picked on by bad stand-up comics, you're going to hate this place. While you're at it, avoid the similar **London Bridge Experience** (2-4 Tooley St., SE1; ☎ 08445/670-492; www.londonbridgeexperience.com; daily 10am-6pm; £15 adults, £11 kids 5-14, £12 students; Tube: London Bridge), which disappoints just as strongly. And like foot fungus, the worthless **Ripley's Believe It or Not!** (1 Piccadilly Circus, W1; ☎ 020/3238-0022; www.ripleyslondon; daily 10am-midnight; £18 adults, £16 seniors, students, £14; Tube: Piccadilly Circus) has spread to London. Its halls of oddities (sample: a portrait of Diana made from lint) are useless and not worthwhile even for the kitsch value.

I don't want to carp, but *carp?* That's the kind of fish you see at **The London Aquarium** (County Hall, Westminster Bridge Rd., SE1; ☎ 020/7967-8000; www.londonaquarium.co.uk; £13 adults, £9.75 children 3–14, £11 seniors/students, 10% discount online; daily 10am–6pm; Tube: Waterloo or Westminster). There's nothing here that you can't see at other, swankier fish zoos.

In the same building, also dependant on not-so-discerning passersby, is the **Dalí Universe** (County Hall Gallery, SE1; ☎ 0870/744-7485; www.daliuniverse.com; £12 adults, £10 seniors/students, £8 children 12 and over,; daily 10am–5:30pm; Tube: Waterloo or Westminster). Unless you're a mad follower of the surrealist artist, this museum is way too costly for what you get—a few notable originals. Besides, there's enough free Dalí at the Tate Modern and the V&A.

Ritual Abuse

I'm only telling you this because I love you: **Changing the Guard** (Buckingham Palace; ☎ 020/7321-2233; www.royal.gov.uk; free admission; 11:30am daily in May–July, and every other day in other months, cancelled in heavy rain; Tube: St. James's Park, Victoria, or Green Park), sometimes called Guard Mounting is an underwhelming use of 40 minutes of your time. Arrive at Buckingham Palace at least 45 minutes ahead if you don't want to face the backs of other tourists. A marching band advances from Birdcage Walk (often, playing themes from *Star Wars, West Side Story,* or ABBA, which comes as a rude shock), then members of the Queen's Life Guard—two if the Queen's away, three or four if she's in—do a ritual change around their sentry boxes. And that's it, give or take some additional prancing for the cameras.

If you must see goose-stepping redcoats, guards patrol all day at both Buckingham Palace and at Horse Guards Arch on Whitehall (which does its own, uncrowded change at 11am, 10am Sun). Or park yourself at the yard of the **Wellington Barracks,** just east of the Palace along Birdcage Walk, by 11am, and catch the Inspection of the Guard that happens before the same guards march over to the Palace for the main event. Then run off and use the day's golden hours for something less touristy.

Ceremony of the Keys (Tower of London; ☎ 020/3166-6278; www.hrp.org.uk; free admission; 9:53pm nightly; Tube: Tower Hill or Tower Gateway DLR), held every night as the Yeomen lock up the Tower of London, has been a routine for more than 700 years—not even German bombs cancelled it. But it's an awful lot of work for not much payoff: You must enter the Tower at 9:30 (several hours after closing time, so you can't combine it with a day's visit) and won't leave until around 10:05pm, even though the whole show takes less than 7 minutes—plus, photos aren't allowed. As for the event, the Chief Yeoman Warder approaches the heavy wooden gate with keys and a lantern, is asked "Halt, who comes there?," passes muster, and locks up the gates to a bugle call. The end. If you want to see that, apply for tickets by mail only with a minimum of two International Reply Coupons (the equivalent of an SASE, available at your post office) to Ceremony of the Keys Office, Tower of London, London, EC3N 4AB, Great Britain; include the names of all attendees with a maximum of six April through October, plus two possible dates that are at least 2 months in advance (three for summer).

The concept is Victorian in nature: Set up a house as if it were really the home of a fictional character, and then charge people to see it. That's the scheme behind **The Sherlock Holmes Museum** (221b Baker St., NW1; ☎ 020/7935-8866; www.sherlock-holmes.co.uk; £6 adults, £4 children under 16; daily 9:30am–6pm;

Cross Abbey Road—Off Your List

The famous zebra crossing immortalized by the Beatles on the cover of *Abbey Road* is located at the intersection of Grove End Road and Abbey Road (just southwest of the St. John's Wood Tube station). Getting your picture taken there is certainly good holiday-card fodder, but it's not all it's cracked up to be. First, it's a pretty long way to come (about 25 min. each way from Leicester Square by Tube) for a snapshot. Second, the spot swarms with cars, so you won't have more than a few nerve-wracking seconds to get your picture taken. Third, the white stripes have been rearranged and repainted since 1969, so it won't even look the same. Last, although EMI-owned Abbey Road Studios at 3 Abbey Rd. is still around, it doesn't have any facilities for tourists—although it does furnish a live webcam of the crossing (www.abbeyroad.co.uk/visit).

Tube: Baker Street), and it has worked for years, even though it's embarrassingly shabby.

Despite a long history going back to its opening in 1828 as a menagerie for members of the Zoological Society of London, **The London Zoo** (Outer Circle Rd., Regent's Park, NW1; ☎ 020/7722-3333; www.londonzoo.co.uk; £15.40 adults, £11.90 children 3–15, £13.90 seniors/students, buy online for a 10% discount; daily 10am to between 4 and 6pm, depending on time of year, last admission 1 hr. before closing; Tube: Camden Town, then 274 bus) is ultimately just a zoo, and a smallish one at that, with few large animals.

The "wine tasting attraction" **Vinopolis** (1 Bank End, SE1; ☎ 087/0241-4040; www.vinopolis.co.uk; prices start at £20 including 5 tastings and a gin cocktail; Mon, Fri, Sat noon–9pm, and Tues–Thurs, Sun noon–6pm, last admission 2 hr. before closing; Tube: London Bridge) is too general to please neophytes and too pleased with itself to satisfy most wine fans. Exhibits are expensive-looking but vacuous, and many of them appear to be influenced by external interests. There are plenty of special tastings, but they'll hit you for £28 and up. The gift shop (free to browse) sells interesting quaffs.

The Clink Museum (1 Clink St., SE1; ☎ 020/7403-0900; www.clink.co.uk; £5 adults, £3.50 children under 16/seniors/students; Mon–Fri 10am–6pm, Sat–Sun 10am–9pm; Tube: London Bridge), themed to a long-gone prison, exists mostly to exploit a touristy obsession with torture. Signs are poorly written and the museum lapses into amateurish, filthy displays of dummies being throttled by random devices. The TV show *Most Haunted Live!* spent the night here looking for ghosts. It didn't find anything worthwhile, either.

Have you ever heard of David Jason? Amitabh Bachchan? Ant and Dec? If your answer is no, you're not going to get much joy out of the ferociously priced **Madame Tussauds** (Marylebone Road, W1; ☎ 087/0400-3000; www.madame-tussauds.co.uk; pricing is complicated based on time of year and time of day, but it peaks at £23 adults, £19 children, £19 seniors, 10% discount online, £13 for entries after 3pm in winter and 5:30pm in summer; daily 9:30am–5:30pm; Tube:

Baker Street). The execution of their wax doppelgangers, which you can usually touch (Will and Harry are behind ropes, girls), is superb. But the focus of this world-famous waxworks is on British celebrities, so you're not going to be consistently engaged. A 5-minute, Disney-esque ride, "The Spirit of London," invokes every conceivable London stereotype, from the Artful Dodger to plague victims. It makes you wonder who the real dummies are here.

WALKING TOURS

London is a walker's city, one where history is accumulated on every block. You could carry a stack of reference books around wherever you go, but isn't taking a walking tour a much better idea? There are so many guides to choose from that you could fill a week with walking tours alone. There are plenty of qualified operators who cater to custom business, but the outfits I list below charge reasonable rates for walk-up business. Also check the "Around Town" section of *Time Out* magazine ,where museums and organizations often announce one-off tours.

The list of **London Walks** ★★★ (☎ 020/7624-3978; www.walks.com), undoubtedly one of the city's best tourist services, is daunting. On weekdays, there are often more than a dozen choices, and on weekends, nearly 25, which means that if you ever find yourself with a few hours to kill, you can always leaf through one of the organization's white timetables (dispensed at every tourist haunt in quantity and downloadable online) and find instant occupation. Every tour (most are £7) departs from a Tube stop, which makes arrangements easy. The marquee tour is probably "Jack the Ripper Haunts," which heads out to the streets of Whitechapel around sunset and, in the pursuit of ghoulish entertainment, deploys considerably more grotesquerie than uncontested facts. I find many of the group's other walks to be more informative, including "The Blitz," "Old Westminster," and "Behind Closed Doors," which includes a visit to the Royal Courts of Justice, guided by a barrister. Other topics that can give you authoritative tours on lesser-visited themes such as Hampstead village, the "Little Venice" near Regent's Canal, and a range of "pub walks" by neighborhood, places few other regular touring companies touch. The group also provides guidance for sightseeing staples such as the British Museum and Westminster Abbey, as well as guided "Explorer Days" of Bath, Brighton, Cambridge, Oxford, and other day-trip favorites (entry fees and train transit are included in the price, which is usually in the mid-£20s; check these ahead because they may go weekly or seasonally). If there's any fault with London Walks, it's that some groups swell to untenable sizes, and many of the guides, although proven knowledgeable when pressed, rely too commonly on canned performance schtick (in fact, many are actors, and then again, histrionics are preferable to a narcotic delivery). The best way to remedy both problems is to pick a tour with narrower appeal; you'll have a better chance to ask your guide questions. Check the website for schedules.

The government gives written and performance-based exams to the experts who lead its excellent **City of London Guided Walks** (City Information Centre, St. Paul's Churchyard, EC4; pro@cityoflondon.gov.uk, www.cityoflondon.gov.uk; £6 adult, free for children under 12, £4 seniors/students; 90 min. to 2 hr.; Tube: St. Paul's), three weekly tours that depart from the tourist info center facing the south side of St. Paul's Cathedral. The experience is less theatrical and denser with facts than what London Walks generally provides, and group sizes tend to be smaller, too. Christopher Wren is the topic Wednesday at 1pm, Fleet Street's messy history (newspapers, Sweeney Todd) are discussed Fridays at 2pm, and Smithfield, once a center of daily life, is Saturdays at 2pm.

Richard Porter, an extensive writer on the Fab Four, has led his **London Beatles Walks (☎ 020/8200-3438; www.beatlesinlondon.com; £7, 2 hrs.)** for nearly 2 decades; the most regular are the Magical Mystery Tour (landmarks in the development of the band; Sun, Wed, and Thurs) and In My Life (landmarks in the members' personal lives; Tues and Sat). You don't have to book ahead.

Like London, Greenwich operates its own official city tours. The Greenwich Tourist Information Centre carefully vets the guides of its **Greenwich Guided Walks (☎ 020/8858-6169; www.greenwichtours.co.uk; £5, £4 seniors/students, free for children under 14; 90 min.)**. There are usually two basic tours daily; the 12:15pm one takes in the main sights plus the Royal Observatory and the Meridian Line, where Mean Time is measured, while the 2:15pm tour omits those in favor of a trip into The Painted Hall and The Naval Chapel, two stunningly decorated 17th-century rooms in Maritime Greenwich.

A pair of accredited guides hone in on niche topics (especially famous women and Jewish heritage) with **Go East London Tours (☎ 020/8883-4169; www.goeastlondon.co.uk; £7)**, which are backed by various local synagogues, Jewish cultural centers, and the Museum in Docklands. The topics of the tours, offered seemingly randomly about twice month, cover the East End in great detail, which is something few other experts do outside of the usual Jack the Ripper fluff. Especially worthwhile are its tours about the Mayfair trappings of the fabulously wealthy Rothschilds family (which now owns the Spencer family's ancestral home, Spencer House) and the "From Rothschilds to Radicals" tour, which gains access to the city's oldest Ashkenazi cemetery, which is usually barred to tourism.

HOP-ON, HOP-OFF COACH TOURS

There are many reasons I don't recommend those hop-on, hop-off bus tours. They're expensive (£22–£24). Also, after 10 minutes of rolling down the streets in these tourist-processing machines, everything you've seen will blend into a miasma of antiquity, and you'll feel hopelessly turned around, not oriented. Third, these tours are like playing Russian roulette, because your experience depends on the skill and brains of your guide and/or the quality of the amplification system, all of which vary per bus and over which you have no control. The sales staff will promise you the moon, but too often, the people who actually run the coaches are limp and bored.

Narrated bus tours make you wait 20 to 30 minutes to catch your next leg, which can add up to hours wasted, and although your ticket will be good for 24 hours, don't expect to catch anything between 7:30pm or so until after 9am the next morning. The big bus tours' day tickets come with one free walking tour (Changing the Guard, Soho, Jack the Ripper) and a hop-on, hop-off pass for the river shuttle boat (although I have heard reports that paying customers may crowd out passholders like you). Unfortunately, both of those perks must be used during the same 24 hours as the bus ticket's validity, demolishing their usefulness.

In sum, London is a walker's city, and you're better off getting an overview on foot or, if you really want a ride, from a window seat on a real double-decker bus, which is £3.50 for the whole day (see p. 14 for the best routes for sightseeing).

Self-Guided Tours for Nothing

An increasing number of attractions and authorities post free audio files of tours on their websites. If you have an iPod or a similar MP3 player, download a few and skip on paying for commercial products. You can't ask questions, but you can fast forward through the boring bits.

Among the best: Visit London's "Live London Like a Local" and "London Area" guides (www.visitlondon.com/maps/podcasts); the Tate museums' audio tours and interviews, including some for children (www.tate.org.uk/podcasts); the leisurely Free Audio London Walks, by an enthusiast, an Anglican priest (http://londonwalks.libsyn.com or www.robert-wright.com); the tours of Sir John Soane's Museum, which are introduced by actor Stephen Fry (www.soane.org/audio.html); a tour of the area around London and Tower bridges by a local improvement group (www.discoverlondonbridge.co.uk); the National Gallery's video-enabled monthly podcast and its somewhat stuffy "Be Inspired Tour" of highlights (www.nationalgallery.org.uk/podcast); and Islington Council's A1 Audio Tours of its neighborhoods (www.islington.gov.uk). The British version of The History Channel (www.thehistorychannel.co.uk) also often has informational narrations with video, and The PodcastDirectory (www.podcastdirectory.com) has offbeat, unguided videos of stuff to see. Other institutions are adding free audio guides all the time, but you may have to hunt around their sites for "podcasts" or "audio tours" to find them.

Those without digital players can simply follow portions of the well-marked Jubilee Walkway, a government-sponsored path embellished with plenty of descriptive panels that snakes for 23km (14 miles) around the city's best sights, including a substantial stretch along the South Bank. Free maps can be printed from www.jubileewalkway.org.uk.

But if you insist, these companies are the respected players, and you can buy tickets at any marked bus stop:

The Original Tour London Sightseeing (17-19 Cockspur St., SW1; ☎ 020/7389-5040; www.theoriginaltour.com; £22 adults, £12 children 5–15, £2/£1 discount online, including a river cruise; daily 8:30am–7:30pm) tours, conducted on open-top coaches, are covered for 24 hours with a ticket. You can catch the bus (four interconnecting circuits that supply solid coverage of the main sights, plus two routes that operate more like shuttles) at any of the 90-odd stops on the routes, but most people begin at Piccadilly Circus, Trafalgar Square, Embankment Station, near Victoria Station, or outside Madame Tussaud's. If you get on elsewhere, you'll probably have to change buses when they reach those points. Live narrators only appear on the Yellow Line, which covers the broadest swath of town, while the other lines are more likely to have recorded spiels.

The Big Bus Company (☎ 020/7233-9533; www.bigbustours.com; £22 adults, £10 children 5–15; daily 8:30am–7:30pm), also on open-top buses, has three circuitous routes, although two of them (Red and Blue) cover much of the same ground with an unpredictable mix of live and recorded narration. It doesn't matter where you get on, but drivers often change at Green Park on Piccadilly, so you'll avoid that wait by starting there. Online booking saves £2 off adult tickets. You can catch this one at any stop, but most people get on at Marble Arch, Regent Street south of Piccadilly Circus, Charing Cross Road north of Trafalgar Square, or under the South Bank Lion at Westminster Bridge.

The one touristy excursion that I *might* come close to suggesting is the tacky **London Ducktours** (kids) (55 York Rd., SE1; ☎ 020/7928-3132; www.londonduck tours.co.uk; £19 adults, £13 children 12 and under, £15 seniors/students 13–17; daily 10am to late afternoon; 1 hr., 5 min.; Tube: Waterloo). Like their forebears that have plied the Wisconsin Dells for decades, these 75-minute tours are conducted in clumsy, American-made DUKW amphibious vehicles, which roll down streets like buses and then plow into the Thames and motor along briefly as boats. Roofed and mostly splashless, these vehicles were developed as Word War II transports. You can't hop off, the narration and information is spotty, and you only see Westminster and Vauxhall, but if you have kids to amuse, it's a dumbed-down option, and if you're going to spend too much money on a guided tour, at least this one gives you novel views.

THE THAMES BY FERRY

It's hard to imagine a time when the Thames was a jumble of delivery boats and when there was just one crossing, but that was indeed the case just a few hundred years ago. It's still possible to travel by boat, and on a beautiful day, there's not a prouder way to go, even if the Tube and buses are always cheaper. To see the most, sail as far as you dare, such as clear to Greenwich. Just keep an eye on the schedule, since unlike the Underground, ferries depart at rigid times.

Piers are served by a variety of boating concerns, and many are convenient to major tourist sights. There are nine docks between the Tate Britain (Millbank Millennium) and the Tower of London/Tower Bridge (Tower Millennium). Other important stops include Westminster Millennium (for Westminster Abbey, the Cabinet War Rooms), Waterloo Millennium (for the London Eye), Festival Pier (for the Southbank Centre and the National Theatre), Bankside (for the Tate Modern, Shakespeare's Globe), Blackfriars Millennium (for St. Paul's Cathedral), and Greenwich (for Maritime Greenwich). Don't make the mistake of wasting money on a trip between piers that are close enough to walk between, such as Waterloo and Festival piers. One-way from Waterloo to Tower takes about 30 minutes, and trips to Greenwich, which pass the spectacular Canary Wharf developments, take about 45 minutes. There's also intermittent service to Kew and Hampton Court (check status at ☎ 020/7930-2062), although, because of tides, a one-way trip of 2½ to 3 hours usually must be combined with a Tube ride.

London River Services (☎ 020/7222-1234; www.tfl.gov.uk/river; day passes £9 adults, £4.50 children) is a branch of London Transport that has fares integrated with buses and the Tube. Typical fares from Westminster are £6.40 to the Tower of London, £7.50 to Greenwich, and £11 for all-day passes (£3.20/£3.75/£5.25 for children). If you've got a Travelcard (or have the equivalent on your Oyster card), you may qualify for a third off on center-city services. You can pick up schedules (about seven runs each way daily) at Tube stations.

6 The "Other" London

Be a local for a day—play how Londoners play, learn how they learn

- Spending an afternoon watching the borderline brawl that is a session of Question Time at the House of Commons of Parliament.
- Showing up at a pub on a weekday evening to pool your trivia knowledge with a table of locals at a "quiz night."
- Building a burrow for hedgehogs and working alongside other eager volunteers as you learn about the surprising array of English wildlife

DON'T BE DAUNTED BY LONDON'S SIZE AND SWELL. IT'S EASY TO GET A glimpse of the "real" London. And by taking part in these activities (and others, see below) you'll discover a hidden perk: In London, a place that welcomes expats and foreign tourists perhaps more eagerly than any other European capital, it's refreshingly easy to mingle. The city boasts many haunts where you'll be welcomed, even as a so-called outsider, and where you'll be brought immeasurably closer to understanding how Londoners live, play, and grow—and why they plausibly claim that their city is the coolest in the world. I call these places the "other" London primarily because most tourists, stuck in the same circuit, miss seeing them. It's their loss—they're missing out on the London locals live every day.

Dive into two or three of these activities in addition to the standard tourist plans you already have. Once you get a taste of how Londoners live here, you'll probably wish you could be one of them forever.

HOW LONDONERS WORK

While you're gallivanting around the city on your vacation, Londoners are working for the man. See how they earn their pay packets—and how it differs from the way you do it back home—by tagging along at their workplaces for a few hours. Just be prepared to feel jealous if you compare vacations with them, too—the British receive 4 weeks of paid leave a year.

GOVERNING THE ISLES

If you enjoy drama and have a taste for a knock-out war of words, you'll get a rise out of watching the debates in the **Houses of Parliament** (☎ **087/0906-3773; www.parliament.uk; Tube: Westminster**). It's as if someone tried to throw a professional wrestling match, but legislation broke out instead. General debates can be downright caustic, with outbursts of jeering. Because procedure frowns on the use of the pronoun "you" in favor of slightly sneering third-person usage, sessions drip with passive aggression even when the object of the debate is standing right there.

Debates are open to everyone whenever the members are sitting (meaning they're working), which happens in both houses (Lords and Commons) Monday through Thursday sometime before noon or at 2:30pm, and some Fridays around lunchtime. You'll be seated one level above, looking through bulletproof glass at the politicians like you might in the monkey house at the zoo.

If you are so lucky as to get inside the House of Commons for the **Prime Minister's Questions** (or his "Question Time;" Wed at noon, 30 min.), you'll be seated mostly with British observers. U.K. residents are given ticket preference to this event through their own government representatives, but leftover spaces are granted to foreigners who line up outside starting in the morning. Inside, you'll witness the cantankerous inquisition of the prime minister (or his seconds) by his opponents whose every contemptuous verbal volley, thinly dressed in a veneer of deferent grammar, is cheered or booed by all in attendance. The MPs get mouthy, but you're expected to be on your best behavior if you don't want to be hustled away for a little unofficial questioning of your own.

Other Question Times, held in both houses and attended by lesser bureaucrats than the PM, are held Monday through Thursday before noon, and it's much easier to get in then because U.K. residents aren't given ticket priority for them. Fridays, when there's not much going on in the Houses, is the easiest day of all to get in for standard debate, and the proceedings wind up by 3pm in the Commons then.

The House of Commons, where elected members battle to pass policy, is more raucous than the House of Lords, where steelier types inherit their seats. Some Select and Standing Committee meetings may open to the public from Monday to Thursday when they are taking evidence, but they're plodding and nonconfrontational, hence their relative unpopularity with visitors. Parliament doesn't sit at all for weeks at a time spread throughout the year, particularly holidays (see the "recess dates" posted online), with the longest gap from late July to early October—you'll know Parliament's sitting when the Union Jack flies from the southernmost tower of the complex.

When entry is possible, it's granted at the St. Stephen's entrance, closest to the eastern end of Westminster Abbey right across St. Margaret Street. Bring your passport to ease the security process. Checks are laborious, and on busy days you may not get into the building until 3:30pm or so, after the best stuff is over. Get there as early as you can, but if you still miss the Prime Minister's Questions, know that you can always tune in on TV.

Parliament sessions are wholly separate from tours of the Houses of Parliament, covered on p. 181, and some public appellate cases are also heard inside.

You can get into the public spaces of **City Hall** (The Queen's Walk, SE1; Mon–Fri 8am–8pm; Tube: London Bridge), surely one of the most radically designed civic buildings in the world. The attraction here isn't watching paper-pushers push papers. It's the fabulist architecture—the building, a boldly idealistic venture leased by the Greater London Authority, looks like a glassy, semi-squashed egg scalloped with internal spiral staircases. The lower ground floor is tiled with the Photomat, an aerial map of the city comprising hundreds of shots taken with a 90-megapixel camera. When London's Living Room on the ninth floor is open, you can also get a free panorama from its wraparound balcony.

The World Comes to London

Those of us who have been fortunate enough to travel broadly can attest to how sadly unusual it is to find places where people of wildly different colors, religions, and nationalities can live together without killing each other. London, though, like New York City, Toronto, or Sydney, is certifiably multi-ethnic—some 300 languages and 45 distinct ethnic communities—and the patchwork gives visitors the rare chance to sample cultures far beyond the borders of their own. Work permits in the EU have fed several recent influxes to the U.K., most notably of an estimated peak (in 2007) of 750,000 Poles, many of whom are heading back now that the Euro is doing better. It's human nature to collect in neighborhoods with your fellow countrymen, especially if you're new to speaking the language, so certain neighborhoods have popped up as new population centers.

Take a few hours to explore the inexpensive restaurants, pubs, and specialized shopping that cater to newcomers who are eager to get a leg up in England—from pubs serving Kenyan mashed maize to Islamic shops selling prayer clocks and *jalabiya* robes. You'll find people of all stripes everywhere, but here's the Tube or rail stop for some of the major concentrations so you can begin your own world travels:

Bangladesh: Bethnal Green, Whitechapel

Caribbean: Brixton, Willesden Junction

Egypt: Shepherd's Bush

Ghana, Nigeria, Congo, West Africa: Seven Sisters, Hackney Central or Hackney Downs (National Rail)

India, especially northern: Southall (National Rail)

Ireland: Kilburn

Kenya: Barking

Kurdistan: Manor House

Lebanon: Shepherd's Bush

Nigeria: Peckham Rye (National Rail)

Persia: Edgware Road

Poland: Hammersmith, Ealing Broadway

Somalia: Streatham (National Rail)

Sri Lanka and South India: Tooting (National Rail)

Syria: Shepherd's Bush

Turkey: Dalston Kingsland and Stoke Newington (National Rail)

Vietnam: Hackney Central or Hackney Downs (National Rail), Old Street

LAW & ORDER

If Question Time whets your appetite for blood-and-guts government drama, then your venue of choice is the **Old Bailey** (Newgate St., EC4; ☎ 020/7248-3277; www.cityoflondon.gov.uk; free admission; Mon–Fri 10am–1pm and 2–5pm; Tube: St. Paul's), also called the Central Criminal Court. It's the most theatrical of the courts, where white-wigged barristers strut and address each other as "my learned friend" as they prove their cases for wizened, crusty judges. The court doesn't provide tours or explanations for visitors—you just walk into any proceedings in session—and even if you had a guide, they wouldn't be able to talk to you inside. So keep your eyes and ears peeled. You're more likely to be privy to the brutal details of criminal cases at this court, although spectators are often asked to leave before the most salacious details are disclosed. Judges enter proceedings carrying a flower—a tradition that began when the notorious Newgate Prison was on this site and men of law, as they visited to defend the accused, needed to disguise the stench of rotting corpses. The current building, topped by a landmark dome and statue of justice, dates from 1907; justice has come a long way from the days when people were simply executed in the street outside. The unadorned public galleries are similar to the balconies in a small theater except with benches. ***Note:*** Cameras, mobile phones, large bags, and children under 14 are banned.

Civil cases are tried at the **Royal Courts of Justice** (Strand, WC2; ☎ 020/7947-6000; www.hmcourts-service.gov.uk; free admission; Mon–Fri 9am–4:30pm; Tube: Temple), which strains to impress in a Gothic style, but in fact is an 1882 amalgamation of 88 courtrooms wherein the country's most important civil cases—the ones too serious to deal with in the counties—are conducted. The interior, with some 5.6km (3½ miles) of corridors and more than 1,000 rooms, is in many ways as ornate as the exterior, although it's possible the trials (mostly libel, appeals, divorce, and other crimes of paperwork), which you can watch from the back two rows of the benches, may not captivate you as thoroughly as the architecture. Pick up a crucial £1 packet of background information and trivia from the tourist-aware folks in the lobby check-in booth; it explains the process, who's who in the courtroom, and even which company fabricates the barristers' white wigs—they're made of horsehair. It's a public building, so you're mostly free to roam, but keep out of rooms marked "In Private" or "In Camera." As at the Old Bailey, cameras, phones, large bags, and kids are forbidden, so if you're planning on dropping by in between other sightseeing, travel lightly that day. Mondays are too noneventful (jury selection and the like) to satisfy, but the court provides 2-hour tours (☎ 020/7947-7684; £6; reservations required) on the first and third Tuesday of the month at 11am and 2pm.

> *"It is not the walls that make the city, but the people who live within them. The walls of London may be battered, but the spirit of the Londoner stands resolute and undismayed."*
>
> —King George VI, 1940

THEATER TOURS

A number of historic, working theaters bring members of the public into their private spaces for a peek backstage. The most popular one is at **Theatre Royal, Drury Lane** (Catherine St., WC2; ☎ 020/7494-5091; £9 adults, £7 children; Mon–Wed and Fri 2:15pm and 4:15pm, Thurs and Sat 10:15am and 11:45am, Sun by arrangement; www.rutheatres.com; Tube: Covent Garden), whose history, from decent to depraved, reaches back to 1663 (although the present building, one of the city's pre-eminent houses for musicals, dates to 1812). Its 75-minute tour is led by a troupe of costumed actors—apparently hired for their ability to amuse children as they imitate characters from the house's history—and it takes in the backstage, front-of-house, two royal boxes, and the under-stage hydraulics system. You'll also see the sealed entrances to tunnels that once snaked all the way to the river so that sailors, the original scenery riggers, could commute from the ropes of their ships to the ones in the fly space. (Which gave rise to the superstition about never whistling in a theater—it conflicted with the sailors' communication method.) Whether you spot one of the storied ghosts is a matter of luck or clairvoyance.

The **National Theatre** (☎ 020/7452-3400; www.nationaltheatre.org.uk; £6 adults, £5 children; up to 6 daytime tours daily Mon–Sat 10:15am–5:30pm; Tube: Waterloo), dating only to the 1950s, is more suited to fans of state-of-the-art theatrics than to people seeking atmosphere. Lasting 75 minutes, the tour shows off the scene shops and backstage areas of this respected, three-house complex where every great British thespian appears at least once in their careers.

Tours of **The Royal Opera House** (☎ 020/7212-9389; www.roh.org.uk; £9 adults, £8 seniors, £7 students/children; up to 3 tours Mon–Fri 10:30am, 12:30pm, and 2:30pm, Sat 10:30am, 11:30am, 12:30pm, 1:30 pm; 90 min.; Tube: Covent Garden) dwell on the theater's illustrious history and tales of the two houses that stood on this plot first (this one's from 1858). Don't expect snooze-inducing stories of plump divas; in 1809, there was a run of civil disobedience here by mobs who were furious at pricing that excluded the poor. I also got the feeling, from the fulsome praise paid for the recent radical restoration (completed in 2000), that lip service was also being paid to donors. You won't see the auditorium if it's being used for rehearsal.

Two other 20th-century West End theaters also run tours for fans: The **Prince Edward Theatre** (Old Compton St, W1; ☎ 084/4482-5138; www.delfontmackintosh.co.uk; £6.25; Tues 11am; Tube: Leicester Square), an established home for musicals including the original productions of *Evita, Chess,* and *Mary Poppins,* offers tours that include design details about the set for whatever show happens to be playing; and **The Prince of Wales** (Coventry St., W1; ☎ 084/4482-5138; www.delfontmackintosh.co.uk; adults £6.25; Fri 2pm; Tube: Piccadilly Circus), currently home to *Mamma Mia!* but previously trod by Barbra Streisand and Mae West, helps tourists appreciate its restored Art Deco features. Since these are working theaters with changing situations, book ahead.

BREWERY TOURS

When in France, you take in the wineries. In London, ale's the word. Reserve ahead for 90-minute tours of **Fuller's Griffin Brewery** (Chiswick Lane S. W4; ☎ 020/8996-2063; www.fullers.co.uk; £6; Mon and Wed–Fri 11am, noon, 1pm,

2pm, 3pm; Tube: Turnham Green), which begin at the brewery-owned The Mawson Arms pub and culminate at a tasting of its well-loved London Pride bitter, a hugely popular cask ale that is also sold worldwide in a pasteurized, bottled form. Records indicate that beer has been made on this site for more than 350 years, and the Hock Cellar is 200 years old by itself. The brewery claims (not uncontested) to be the city's oldest, but what's not in question is that Fuller's has been brewing under its name since 1845. You'll get more information than you can retain concerning how the quaff is made and what makes the specialized equipment work. Kids under 14 aren't allowed, and those under 18 can't taste the wares. It's six Underground stops west of Earl's Court, and it's the last London brewery welcoming visitors; the Young's brewery sold out to developers in 2007 after 176 years. Such are the times, as most manufacturers can't afford to remain in the city.

FOUNDRY TOURS

America's Liberty Bell. Montreal Cathedral's Great Bell. Big Ben himself. Name an important chimer from Western history, and chances are **Whitechapel Bell Foundry (32-34 Whitechapel Rd., E1; ☎ 020/7247-2599; www.whitechapelbell foundry.co.uk; shop open Mon–Fri 9am–4:15pm, toura 2 Saturdays monthly, £8, no one under 14 admitted; Tube: Aldgate East)** cast it. Sure, the Liberty Bell cracked, by which time it was too late to exchange it, but the foundry's craftsmanship is not in question—Guinness verified it as Britain's oldest manufacturing company, established in 1570, with lineage traceable to 1420. Back then, fulsome industries such as metalworking were found in the East End, where the prevailing winds would carry the grime out of town. This foundry, still operating in a brick-front building from the late 1600s, conducts tours of its cramped, messy workshops on one or two Saturdays a month at 10am and 2pm—always when workers are off duty, because flying sparks and molten metal can result in unwinnable lawsuits. However, the 90-minute tours are usually conducted by the dry-witted Alan Hughes, no ringer himself; he's a fourth-generation founder who derisively refers to ship's bells as "noisemakers" because they're not harmonically tuned with educated ears the way his best bells, true musical instruments, are. Hughes and his craftsmen create, repair, and send bells to belfries around the world, and they do it by hand; because commissions are pricey and few, the foundry also deals in oak-handled versions for concerts.

A visit isn't plastic in any way; groups (never larger than 37 but usually around 25, always full weeks or months ahead) dodge piles of metal dust, sand, shavings, and aged workbenches to collect around heavyweight bells cooling in their molds that were poured a day earlier. Every aspect of the craft, from casting to buffing, is given its due at various stations. You'll even learn that the foundry uses a siren to tell workers when it's time for a break. Why? "Well," says Hughes, "When you work in a bell factory. . . ." There's also a small museum and shop (teeny bells, musical scores for handbells), open weekdays, which don't require tickets.

TV STUDIO TOURS

The storied Pinewood and Shepperton movie studios in West London, the settings for the James Bond and Harry Potter films, among many other classics, don't allow tours. The same goes for Elstree Film and Television Studios in northwest

London, which since 1914 has hosted *The Muppet Show, Raiders of the Lost Ark,* and many Hitchcock films. Entertainment buffs mustn't despair, though, because a small alternative studio exists: **BBC Television Centre Tour** (Wood Lane, W12; ☎ 087/0603-0304; www.bbc.co.uk/tours; reservations required; £9.50 adults, £8.50 seniors, £7 students/children 7–15; Tube: White City). It's true that unless you're a regular viewer of BBC-made programming, you won't recognize many of the faces on the tour of these studios in west London, but you will get a fascinating behind-the-scenes glimpse of the country's principal entertainment factory—control rooms, sets, the newsroom (usually standing idle), Studio 8 (once of *Fawlty Towers*), and other trappings of technical production. Britain's studios are less precious than Hollywood's about controlling access to stars, so you may even get to see some live filming, although I wouldn't bank on it. The tour can seem a little patronizing to people who have a modicum of knowledge about production, as most modern kids now have, and it's not often glamorous.

Since it's a large, working studio, the itinerary changes daily, but it usually lasts about 2 hours, sometimes less. For kids under 10 but over 6, there's a kids' version, the CBBC Tour, which includes the set of British children's shows *Blue Peter* (beloved in Britain, mostly unknown outside it) as well as a visit to an educational TV studio; it costs the same as the main tour.

Radio is a vital part of the British culture, and the BBC also has the famous Art Deco **BBC Broadcasting House** (Portland Place, W1; ☎ 087/0603-0304; tours monthly on Sun; reservations required; Tube: Oxford Circus). The 90-minute tours are steeped in wireless lore and cost £3 less than the TV tours. But unless you're a regular listener via the Internet, it will feel like the guides are speaking another language. The **BBC World Service Shop,** containing mostly radio recordings and DVDs, is on the Aldwych in central London (Bush House, Strand, WC2; ☎ 020/7557-2576; www.bbcshop.com; Mon–Fri 10am–6pm, Sat 10am–5:30pm, Sun 12:30–5:30pm; Tube: Temple).

TICKETS TO TV TAPINGS

Of course, there's no better way to understand the singular culture of British TV than seeing a show being made. British production seasons are relatively short—often just a couple of months at a time—so what you'll see depends greatly on when you visit. National programs are produced all around the United Kingdom—for example, *The Jeremy Kyle Show,* like Jerry Springer with heart, is taped in Manchester, and *The Trisha Goddard Show,* like Tyra Banks with a brain, is taped in Kent. But London hosts the lion's share of the popular shows, particularly if they require the participation of celebrities. Although tickets to pretty much every TV show are free, most studios require that audience members be at least 16 years old. The process of taping a show isn't much different from what it is in other major production centers such as Los Angeles or New York City; audiences (which are notably more subdued than American or Australian crowds) are invited mostly for their willingness to applaud or laugh on cue. Situation comedies and many game shows tend to stop and start, so a half-hour show may translate into a 4-hour commitment, but chat shows and panel shows (a popular format in which comics discuss current events) are usually in-and-out affairs. Don't expect free gifts or money for your presence—that's pure Oprah.

Many tapings by the **BBC (☎ 037/0901-1227; www.bbc.co.uk/tickets)**, particularly those with star power, fill up months in advance or work on a lottery system, but it's still usually possible to snag free tickets to something interesting. Some of its most interesting audience-dependent shows, such as *The Graham Norton Show* (which is like Letterman goes blue) are shot in The London Studios, which is near the Thames around the London Eye. Be careful that you don't secure reservations for something shot in other cities.

The other major British networks, which are hipper than the government-subsidized BBC channels, require potential audience members to arrange for tickets through the individual production companies responsible for each show. Each network's website will help you find the right place to make your request. **ITV (www.itv.com/tickets)** hosts regular TV tapings including *Who Wants to Be a Millionaire?*. **Channel 4 (www.channel4.com/tickets)** broadcasts the edgiest material of the major networks, as well as the hottest American imports. Many TV production companies place classified notices of upcoming tapings in *Time Out* magazine.

A few services broker tickets on behalf of producers, and they're good places to check before a trip: **The Applause Store (☎ 087/1987-1234; www.applausestore.com)**; **Clappers Limited (☎ 020/8532-2770, -2771; www.clappers-tickets.co.uk)**, which handles *Loose Women*, an imitator of America's *The View*; **Lost in TV (☎ 020/8530-8100; www.lostintv.com)**, which does the daytime chat show starring the fussy Paul O'Grady, who sits his pet dog on his desk during interviews; **SRO Audiences (☎ 020/8684-3333; www.sroaudiences.com)**, and **TV Recordings.com.** Calls to non-020 numbers will charge higher rates, so try to handle things online. Also, some brokers may entice you with premium memberships promising advance word of popular shows, but as a tourist, the expense of subscribing isn't worth it. You shouldn't have to pay for tickets.

As I mentioned, radio is still huge in Britain, so free tickets are often available for concerts, interviews, and even radio plays that go out on the BBC's many stations. Contact the **BBC Radio Ticket Unit (☎ 020/8576-1227; www.bbc.co.uk/tickets or radio.ticket.unit@bbc.co.uk)**.

HOW LONDONERS LEARN

Londoners seem to adore making themselves smarter. Edifying conversation is truly part of the culture here, and locals' seemingly boundless inquisitive nature has given the city a deserved reputation for intelligent pursuits. As Oscar Wilde, no slouch of a wag, once put it, "The man who can dominate a London dinner-table can dominate the world." He would know, because he too came from another country (Ireland), and he charmed the world. Together with a long-running tradition of free lectures—instituted for the improvement of the lower classes, perpetuated by museums eager to win grants and serve their communities, and now a standard night out for everyone—this affection for discourse translates into dozens of stimulating, expert-led events every night of the week.

TALKS AND MORE

London has a long tradition of associations dedicated to viewing society from a critical distance. The Fabian Society, for example, whose members included George Bernard Shaw, suffragette Annie Besant, and children's writer Edith

Nesbit (a co-founder), played a crucial role in the formation of today's Labour Party. The non-sectarian **South Place Ethical Society,** another such idealistic organization (and the last of its kind in Britain), was founded way back in 1793 as a salon for free thought and artistic advancement. In 1929, it opened its own unfussy auditorium, **Conway Hall** (25 Red Lion Square, WC1; ☎ 020/7242-8032; www.conwayhall.org.uk; Tube: Holborn), which today attracts some 130,000 people a year to a steady bill of talks by authors and politicians, as well as concerts (music by the London Chamber Music Society, classical songbooks, and experimental compositions). Concerts are held almost every Sunday evening from October to April (usually £8–£10), and many other free events are put on during the week, such as Friday night tango dancing on the stage, preceded by an hour-long class. The line-up also sees free lectures, usually on political or agnostic themes (one recent all-day seminar on the protests of 1968 brought in speakers from three continents), often with question-and-answer periods that allow for interaction with thoughtful locals interested in social improvement. The point here is free thought, not barking out black-and-white political passions, so I find the experience enlightening, not enervating. It's located off the northeast corner of Red Lion Square, about 10 minutes' walk east of the British Museum.

Like the SPES, **Gresham College** (usually at Barnard's Inn Hall, off Holborn, EC1; ☎ 020/7831-0575; www.gresham.ac.uk; free admission; Tube: Chancery Lane) has a long, long history of intellectual stimulation for the masses. In fact, its first lecture was held more than 410 years ago based on the work of the Antwerp Bourse. The College retains eight professors on 3-year tenures (in classic disciplines like divinity, math, medicine, law, and music—Christopher Wren once taught astronomy here) but awards no degrees and enrolls no students; in fact, its entire purpose is to share knowledge, which it does through free hour-long lectures, about a dozen each month except in July and August, when the load is lighter. The discourse is heady and enlightening, not Froot Loopy. Topics are as wonderfully varied as those enjoyed by paying college students: 2008 subjects included revelations of Lewis Carroll's little-known contributions as an Oxford mathematician, a comparison of the British and American Constitutions, a dissection of the soundtrack of Hitchcock's *Psycho,* and the physics behind "freak" waves in the oceans. The College regularly engages academics from around the world, too, who plan their presentations for months. It even posts its past events online through transcripts, video, PowerPoint files, and audio recordings. Where else can you find a free college lecture like these? This group is a real treasure.

Around since 2003 and therefore hipper, **The Dana Centre** (Science Museum, Exhibition Rd., SW7; ☎ 020/7942-4040; www.danacentre.org.uk; Tube: South Kensington) is a stimulating find for casually exploring science, culture, medicine,

A Note About Opening Hours

In addition to keeping the regular business hours listed in this section, many places will keep doors open late for special events. To access standard facilities such as libraries or exhibitions, go during regular hours, because only a few rooms may be open during talks and events.

and technology—and how those issues relate to our lives. It's not as dusty as it might sound—events are consciously irreverent, punky, and often laugh-out-loud funny. For instance, once the subject was carnival rides and participants spent half their time being spun, flipped, and jiggled in machines, afterwards holding serious (if woozy) discussions on the physics of g-forces, and the sociology behind the exhilaration of these rides. Other topics have included the latest CSI techniques and whether animal behavior can shed light on human sexual infidelity. Sponsored partly by the British Association for the Advancement of Science and a brain-research group, this endeavor throws a few events a week (usually Tues–Thurs outside of summer) in a purpose-built cafe (open all day) through a back door of the Science Museum. Most events are free but require reservations.

The **Royal Geographic Society** (☎ 020/7591-3100; www.rgs.org; Tube: South Kensington), slightly stuffy and self-satisfied but not academic, is an esteemed club where intrepid travelers can mix with fellow explorers. What's it like to roam China's Silk Road or take a dog trek through the Russian Far East? Experienced hands appear, slides in hand, to report on their adventures and on the state of the world, as do authors who have recently written works. Non-members get last pick of tickets to the most popular events (held evenings and weekends), but a few excellent series are open to all, including "Discovering People," in which a travel luminary (such as Jan Morris, Michael Palin, or Sir David Attenborough) is interviewed, or "Discovering Places," panel discussions on exotic destinations such as Myanmar. Events are mostly free but sometimes cost up to £15, and they break for the summer.

Let it not be forgotten that it was at the British Museum where Karl Marx developed the political theories that would sweep the planet and shape the 20th century. Lenin spent about a year in London, too. In the spring and the autumn, the **Marx Memorial Library** (37a Clerkenwell Green, EC1; ☎ 020/7253-1485; www.marx-memorial-library.org; visiting hours Mon–Thurs 1–2pm; Tube: Farringdon), fittingly, sponsors thought-provoking lectures on socialism and workers' rights that even the proletariat can afford: £1 per edifying session. The rest of the year, authors hold free readings at regular intervals.

Marx's counter-culture ethic thrives at **Housmans Booksellers** (5 Caledonian Rd., N1; ☎ 020/7837-4473; Mon–Fri 10am–6:30pm, Sat 10am–6pm closed Sun; www.housmans.com), the city's preeminent shop (established 1945) for magazines and books on progressive international topics, at which around 10 free readings and talks are hosted a month. Because the store is plugged into the top tier of investigative journalism and civilized protest, the roster is usually filled with respected writers and researchers who aim their messages at the mainstream. Every Wednesday at 7pm, it mounts an event hinging on a monthly theme such as Latin America, Anarchism, and Peace.

Slightly more middle-brow are the author events at **The London Review Bookshop** (14 Bury Place, WC1; ☎ 020/7269-9030; www.lrbshop.co.uk/events; Mon–Sat 10am–6:30pm, Sun noon–6pm; Tube: Tottenham Court Road or Holborn), the retail wing of the literary publication. It does about two brainy author talks a month, mostly free, at its location near the British Museum's front yard.

Very few other world cities support so many diverse, multinational communities with such harmony, and a few organizations aim to share their home cultures with events and talks. The **Institut de Français** (17 Queensbery Place, SW7;

Chatter Box

I can't stress this strongly enough: London museums aren't only for artifacts. They're also community centers. Beyond their exhibitions, nearly every museum offers free or cheap talks at least a few times a month—by professors, authors, archaeologists, you name it. Plenty of post-talk time is usually allotted for questions. And the programs are anything but stodgy: For example, Shakespeare's Globe recently interviewed an American who was pardoned from Death Row about his impressions of *Coriolanus,* and the V&A chatted with comic-book genius Alan Moore.

You could fill a week of entertainment from these talks alone. Many of them are named in *Time Out* magazine in the indispensable "Around Town" section. A few more (usually with small admission charges) are listed in the "What's On" section of VisitLondon.com and at The Lecture List (www.lecturelist.org). Many more are promoted internally at the institutions that host them, so go online at any museum that interests you. Don't be afraid to ask for a line-up at the front desk of any institution. These events are simply part of the culture here.

☎ 020/7073-1350; www.institut-francais.org.uk; Mon–Fri 8:30am–10pm, Sat 10am–10pm; Tube: South Kensington), the country's official French cultural center, is for francophiles, and often, francophones, but French-only talks are flagged as such ahead of time. Not to be left out, the Germans run their own **Goethe-Institut (50 Princes Gate, Exhibition Road, SW7; ☎ 020/7596-4000; www.goethe.de; Mon–Fri 8:30am–7pm, Sat 8:30am–1pm; Tube: South Kensington)**, and the Spanish have their **Instituto Cervantes Londres (102 Eaton Square, SW1; ☎ 020/7235-0353; http://londres.cervantes.es; Mon–Thurs noon–7:30pm, Fri noon–6:30pm, Sat 9:30am–2pm; Tube: Sloane Square)**, though many of its talks are in English. Also consult the **Egyptian Cultural Centre (4 Chesterfield Gardens, W1; ☎ 020/7491-7720; www.egyptculture.org.uk; Tube: Hyde Park Corner)**, in Mayfair, which outside of summer organizes talks on archaeology and Egyptology, as well as the occasional Sufi dance performance.

And, of course, there's the reigning HQ of free London gab. Near the northeast corner of Hyde Park, where Edgware Road meets Bayswater Road, Londoners of yore congregated to participate in grisly public executions. Such displays gradually fell out of favor, and by the early 1800s, the gathered crowds were jeering at hangings instead of cheering them, and the locale's reputation for public outcry became entrenched. An Act of Parliament in 1872 finally legitimized **Speakers' Corner (Tube: Marble Arch, exits 4, 5, 8, or 9)** as a place of free speech, and its tradition of well-intentioned blathering has since evolved into one of the city's quirkier attractions. A century ago, it was where laborers and suffragettes fomented massive social change, but these days, you're more likely to encounter a rogues' gallery of kooks and idealists. Anyone can show up, always on Sunday mornings after 7am, with a soapbox (or, these days, a stepladder), plus an axe to grind, and orate about anything they want, from the Iraq War to Muslim relations to the superiority of 1970s disco—but if they don't have the wit or the facts to appease the crowd, they stand a good chance of being jibed, or at the very least vigorously challenged. In true British style, most speakers refrain from profanity. Even the heckling is usually polite. While audience participation at this scholarly circus can be heated, it's usually based on facts rather than emotion—the American talk radio hosts are not good role models—so bone up on the goods before daring to spar. I wouldn't say it's worth rearranging your schedule to attend, since it's a true grab-bag of gab, but it's a dearly held tradition—and one of the only things to do in the city on Sunday morning, anyway. The blather continues until late afternoon.

AUCTION HOUSE EXHIBITIONS

London and New York City are the world's most important centers for the buying and selling of art and antiquities. But unlike in New York, in London the auctioneers assume any joe off the street could be a potential millionaire, so it's easy to view the lots that are about to go on sale at the two principal auction houses, **Sotheby's** and **Christie's.** Think of them as museums with very short exhibitions. Check both houses' websites for the opening hours of viewings, which are free and usually last between 2 and 5 days. Depending on your luck, you could see the Duchess of Windsor's jewelry, Old Masters paintings, a rare copy of Shakespeare's First Folio, antique teddy bears, or an array of Roman clay pots. Most of the items will pass into private hands within a week and won't resurface again for many years, if ever. Hours change depending on what's open to viewing. **Sotheby's** (34-35 New Bond St., W1; ☎ 020/7293-5000; www.sothebys.com; Tube: Bond Street or Oxford Circus) has a Bond Street flagship that tends to showcase the most newsworthy material that you'll read about in newspapers worldwide. **Christie's** has two London showrooms, both of which lean toward fine art and furnishings, and it displays the higher-profile lots at its King Street location in St. James's (8 King St., SW1; ☎ 020/7839-9060; www.christies.com; Tube: Green Park; or 85 Old Brompton Rd., SW7; ☎ 020/7930-6074; Tube: South Kensington). To actually buy something at auction, see p. 269.

HOW LONDONERS HELP

Few activities are as satisfying or make it so easy to meet locals as volunteering—even if you have only a day to spare for it. This is a messy city with lots of people who could use your help, yet unfortunately, few places allow foreigners to legally pitch in. You can blame that ubiquitous bugaboo that you will hear cited time and again when someone thinks something is too dangerous: "Health and Safety" rules. Other countries let you show up at a soup kitchen and grab a ladle, but the U.K. requires preliminary labor training, which often makes it impossible for tourists to help out, no matter how harmless the activity might seem.

However, some groups might be able to accept temporary services on a strictly unofficial basis. The chances of finding ways to help increase greatly if you can find a task that doesn't involve contact with food, money, or people in need, such as stuffing envelopes. If you run across a place where you'd like to donate time, it doesn't hurt to ask, but expect to be politely declined.

The following agencies, however, **do** accept short-term help from foreigners: **Thames21** (☎ 020/7248-7171; www.thames21.org.uk), an environmental charity, focuses energy on beautifying the waterway, and it hosts about a dozen litter-picking days throughout the year. That sounds kill-me-now dull, but in truth, a river sweep can be a bit like accidental archaeology; at low tide, it's not uncommon to find items in the muddy bed that were left there generations ago. The Museum of London should know; many of the Roman swords in its collection were retrieved from the river, since that's where people once left precious offerings for the gods. You'll be treading old stone stairs and slopes that were laid by people in the days of the great sailing ships. Few tourists think to experience the river in this way, so you'll find yourself grooming the sand with London families. Should you rather not get your clothes muddy on vacation (I can't blame you), in the summer, Thames21 schedules Catch21, free 5-hour **angling coaching sessions,** at different points in the river's course, each of which attracts kids and families from that area. You don't have to release what you catch, but most people do; after all, this is a love-the-river organization. Equipment is provided.

Another prime source of one-day volunteering events such as building burrows for hedgehogs and unique animal viewings (such as Bat Walks, which are evening safaris for bat colonies held in the summer) across the city is the **London Wildlife Trust** (☎ 020/7261-0447; www.wildlondon.org.uk), which works to protect animals, insects, and trees that call the city home. Most of its activities require that you contact the individual volunteer who's organizing it. On summer weekends, two or three events are often held, ranging from hands-on (path clearing and weeding in a tree preserve) to educational (lessons on composting, nature walks). You may need to bring helper items such as heavy boots or binoculars, but your contact can tell you where to find or borrow them.

If you're not so into muddling through mud or picking through thicket, **GO London** (☎ 020/7643-1341; www.csv.org.uk/Volunteer/Part-time/GO) is a sort of clearinghouse for places seeking helpers. You never know what you're going to get, but typical weekend events (about 50 a year) usually include mural painting, garden planting, cemetery tending, and playground cleanups.

HOW LONDONERS PRAY OR MEDITATE

If you can't afford the hefty entrance charges for the city's most visited churches, you can always get in free by attending a service. It may not afford you a look at its historic artifacts or exhibitions, but it will give you ogling time in the main sanctuary, ear time with some unbelievable organs and choirs, and the chance to mingle with a host of native Londoners who regard these world-famous sanctuaries as their spiritual homes. If you think about it, you'll be seeing the following churches the way they were intended to be seen: from the pews, in meditation.

All of London's most historic edifices are part of the Church of England (a kissin' cousin to the American Episcopalian), and most have no sermon, or else very short ones; simply put, they're light on the fire and brimstone. **St. Paul's Cathedral** (St. Paul's Churchyard, EC4; ☎ 020/7236-4128; www.stpauls.co.uk; Tube: St. Paul's), despite being a major tourist attraction, is called a home church by thousands who guard its heritage. This magical sanctuary, one of the world's greatest, provides four to six opportunities for worship every day, including Mattins (7:30am weekdays, 10:15am Sun), Holy Communion (8am daily, plus

Lunchtime Concerts

On every working day at around 1pm at centuries-old churches across the city you'll find an array of free musical shows known as Lunchtime Concerts. Considered part of these houses' ministry to the public, the offerings range from chamber orchestras, to organists, to soloists, to singers, and are usually quite good. The concerts don't come with strings attached or with heavy-handed evangelism. Even better, they're all free, though many request (rightfully) a donation of £3 or £4, which goes mostly to the upkeep of these ancient and crumbling sanctuaries.

Check the outdoor notice boards at any church to see what's lined up, but some notable or historic churches that get in on the act include the prolific **St. Martin-in-the-Fields** (Trafalgar Square, W1; ☎ 020/7766-1111; www.stmartin-in-the-fields.org; 1pm almost daily; Tube: Charing Cross), dated 1726, is famous for its musical prowess; Sir Christopher Wren's **St. James's Church Piccadilly** (197 Piccadilly, W1; ☎ 020/7734-4511; www.st-james-piccadilly.org; concerts generally fall on Mon, Wed, or Fri at 1:10pm; Tube: Piccadilly Circus), begun in 1676—on Tuesday, it hosts an antiques flea market, and Wednesday through Saturday a crafts market; **St. Andrew Holborn** (5 St. Andrew St., EC4; ☎ 020/7583-7394; www.standrewholborn.org.uk; 1:10pm Wed; Tube: Holborn); **St. Mary le Bow** (Cheapside, EC2; ☎ 020/7248-5139; www.stmarylebow.co.uk; 1:05pm Thurs; Tube: St. Paul); and **St. Mary Le Strand** (Strand, WC2; ☎ 020/7405-1929; www.stmarylestrand.org; 1:05pm Wed organ recitals; Tube: Temple), the central church of the Royal Air Force. Many of these churches also host a range of evening concerts, which cost £5 to £10.

A few nonsanctified locales also get in on the act. Slip into the foyer of the **Southbank Centre** (Belvedere Rd., SE1; ☎ 087/1663-2500; www.southbankcentre.co.uk; Tube: Waterloo), which hosts free music from jazz bands to solo instrumentalists weekdays from 12:30 to 2pm.

The London Organ Concerts Guide (www.londonorgan.co.uk) keeps track of upcoming events. In the winter, the **City Music Society** (☎ 020/8542-0950; www.citymusicsociety.org) sets up a range of concerts at churches and halls across town, both at lunchtime and in the evening.

St. Paul's Cathedral (St. Paul's Churchyard, EC4; ☎ 020/7246-8350; www.stpauls.co.uk; last admission at 4pm; Tube: St. Paul's) isn't big on free concerts, but on many afternoons (from 3–6pm), your regular tour may be atmospherically accompanied by orchestral or choir rehearsals; it's a small comfort if you come to the Dome and find that it closes around 4:30.

12:30pm Mon–Sat), Evensong (5pm daily, 5:15pm Sun), and an evening service (6pm Sun). Its organ can send music lovers into near euphoria. The main sanctuary of the Anglican **Westminster Abbey** (Broad Sanctuary, SW1; ☎ 020/7222-5152; www.westminster-abbey.org; Tube: Westminster) hosts evening prayer or

Evensong with choirs from around the world at 5pm weekdays and Sung Eucharist Sundays at 11:15am, plus a Sunday evening service with simple hymns at 6:30pm (but check ahead, since services are sometimes shuffled to smaller, but equally historic, chapels). Holy Communion is daily at 8am, before the tourists arrive.

Good news! Catholics are no longer executed in England. They can freely attend the towering, Byzantine-style **Westminster Cathedral** (42 Francis St., SW1; ☎ 020/7798-9055; www.westminstercathedral.org.uk; Tube: Victoria), the largest Roman Catholic church in England and Wales and 18m (59 ft.) taller than Westminster Abbey farther east down Victoria Street. It's a handsome historic building from 1903 but isn't popular with tourists, so it has the elbow room to plan a fuller slate of Masses: six on weekdays and Sunday, four on Saturday. Best of all, its choir is considered one of the world's best. Notice that I said *one* of the best: The Baroque-style **Brompton Oratory** (Brompton Rd., SW7; ☎ 020/7808-0900; www.bromptonoratory.com; Tube: South Kensington) is recognized as having the U.K.'s best Catholic church choir, and its 1964 organ has been called the finest built in the postwar period. Mass with choir is held on Sundays at 9am. For a defiantly contemporary service that typifies the progressive form of Christianity sweeping England, there's **ChristChurch** (Piccadilly Theatre, 16 Denman St., W1; ☎ 084//5644-8440; www.christchurchlondon.org; Sun 4pm; Tube: Piccadilly Circus), young in both spirit and congregation. I would say the vibe borrows a lot from the casual evangelical churches of America—the last time I was there, the leader wore a golf shirt, and instead of an organ, there was a band. Despite all that, the church is traditional enough to serve coffee after services.

One of the city's most interesting Jewish houses of worship is the little-known **Westminster Synagogue** (Kent House, Rutland Gardens, SW7; ☎ 020/7584-3953; www.westminstersynagogue.org; 11am Sat; Tube: Knightsbridge), which took residence in an otherwise unobtrusive Belgravia town house in 1963. Today it's a repository for some priceless Czech Torah scrolls rescued from the Nazis; the curator lives upstairs. The 4,000-member **West London Synagogue** (34 Upper Berkeley St., W1; ☎ 020/7723-4404; www.wls.org.uk; Tube: Marble Arch) was founded in 1840 as the first Reform synagogue in Britain and is welcoming to outsiders and women. Men are asked to wear yarmulkes during services.

London boasts a sizable Muslim community, but the majority of its houses of worship are not established as casual attractions. Muslims who would like to pray with locals would do well to visit the **London Central Mosque** (146 Park Rd., NW8; ☎ 020/7725-2212; www.iccuk.org; Tube: Marylebone or Baker Street), which accommodates 1,800 worshipers and has established itself as a progressive leader in the city. Its one-time theological rival, the so-called Finsbury Park Mosque, was once a nest of radicalism that counted Richard Reid, Zacarias Moussaoui, and Chechen rebels among its attendees, but this mosque is so open that it gives tours to schoolkids—some 10,000 a year.

Among London Hindus, the Swaminarayan movement claims the most adherents; the breathtakingly gorgeous, many-pinnacled **Mandir** (105-119 Brentfield Rd., NW10; ☎ 020/8965-2651; www.mandir.org; Tube: Neasden, then 112 or 232 bus) in northwest London is the largest Hindu temple outside of India. This fabulous temple was only completed in 1995. Some 5,500 tons of Italian Carrara

Spirits on the Square

America may have invented and popularized the 19th-century spiritualist movement, but London still embraces it. **The Spiritualist Association of Great Britain** (33 Belgrave Square, SW1; ☎ 020/7235-3351; www.spiritualist association.org.uk; Tube: Hyde Park Corner), which has catered to clairvoyants and mediums since 1872, owns a humdrum Victorian town house in tony Knightsbridge, where it holds workshops on the psychic arts. Private sittings are £35, but for just £6, you can attend one of the hour-long "demonstrations," in which a medium stands at the front of the room and reports on the ghosts and psychic vibrations swirling around the few dozen members of the audience. You won't get quivering tables or milky crystal balls; in truth, the plain meeting area is about as spooky as the function room of a Midwestern Presbyterian church, and some guests will be relieved to know that most leaders acknowledge God during their sessions. I've had mediums pick me out of the crowd and tell me things no other person could know, but I've also been singled out to be told my father was an RAF pilot from the Midlands, which was patently ludicrous. Still, on almost every occasion, I have seen evenings here suddenly take an eerily heart-wrenching turn when some visitor became emotional about what the mediums plucked out of the ether—or *appeared* to. Demonstrations take place some afternoons at 3:30pm and most weekday evenings at 7pm, weekends at 4pm. Even if you're a skeptic, it's one of the most electrifying cheap nights out in town. The house is on the southeast side of the square; combine a visit with a drink at The Grenadier pub (p. 131) off the square's opposite side—an appropriate choice, since the pub is said to be haunted.

marble and Bulgarian limestone were carved in India and shipped here, where they were assembled by volunteers—its dome was built without using steel or lead. The Mandir's interior is delicately carved, as complicated and as white as a doily, and is apt to amaze even people generally unimpressed by such virtuosity. The adjoining Haveli, equally astonishing, is an intensely carved wooden structure that includes a massive 50m-wide (164-ft.) prayer hall made without pillars and suitable for simultaneous use by 4,000 souls. The work, done entirely by hand, is eye-popping. Tourists are further encouraged by the presence of a 279-sq.-m (3,000-sq.-ft.) exhibition entitled **"Understanding Hinduism"** (daily 9am–6pm; £2 adults, £1.50 children/seniors), which explains in plain terms how the religion works and how this spectacular house of worship was constructed. ***Note:*** If you're entering either the mosque or the Mandir, shorts or skirts must not fall higher than the knee (although ankle-length is preferable and sarongs are available to borrow); visitors must also remove their shoes.

The **London Buddhist Centre** (51 Roman Rd., E2; ☎ 084/5458-4716; www.lbc.org.uk; Tube: Bethnal Green), open since 1978 in a disused fire station in the East End, is found in a mini community that includes Buddhist-run vegetarian

Pearly Kings & Queens

One of the most iconic symbols of London life is that of the Pearly King and Queen. You've seen pictures: grinning folks in suits outrageously embroidered with white buttons and baubles. The tradition began in the Victorian markets, when traders trumpeted their status by decorating their seams with smoke pearl buttons. A poor street sweeper named Henry Croft evolved this esoteric nomenclature into fully embellished outfits, weighing up to 14kg (30 lb.) and worn to attract charitable donations. Soon the idea spread to a whole league of approved wearers, each with their own suit representing a different borough of London.

Finding a "Pearly" these days isn't easy. Like the bowler hat and the London fog, they're not very common anymore. The tradition is dying out, and costumes are increasingly more likely to be found hanging in a museum than on the back of rightful owners. But these whimsical garments do come out of their closets for special occasions such as funerals, race days, and charity parties. The most important appearance on the annual Pearly calendar is probably the Harvest Festival in early October, when dozens gather for a thanksgiving prayer service (the location changes). Some of those appearances are announced on the official site of the loosely organized **London Pearly Kings and Queens Society** (☎ 020/8778-8670; www.pearlysociety.co.uk), but you can usually find them in the third weekend of every month at Jubilee Market Hall, Covent Garden, from 10:30am to 2:30pm. These figureheads exist mostly to spread goodwill for charity, so get in there and ask some questions. As for Harry Croft, his statue can be seen every day in the crypt at St. Martin-in-the-Fields, Trafalgar Square. Now he looks as if he's made of pearl itself.

restaurants, organic remedies shops, and boutiques with cool gifts made around the world. As with many Buddhist organizations, it's friendly to newcomers and helps them learn the ropes. It conducts meditation classes for beginners every weekday from 1 to 2pm (£1), and on Saturdays at the same time (£5) at 8 Hop Gardens, off St. Martin's Lane in Covent Garden. Tuesday and Wednesday starting at 7:15pm, it hosts drop-in sessions (£7) where you can learn to meditate and get advice from experienced Buddhists. There's also an on-site bookshop, plus a second-hand shop, Sudana (☎ 020/8981-1225).

Every Wednesday and Friday at 12:30pm, **The College of Psychic Studies** (16 Queensberry Place, SW7; ☎ 020/7589-3292; www.collegeofpsychicstudies.co.uk; Tube: South Kensington), set up in 1884 to foster an understanding of higher human consciousness, opens its doors for free meditation sessions, led by the same experts and intuitives who normally charge £30 per course. These guys plumb personal-energy teachings even more than the spiritualists; there are also talks about trances, hypnotherapy, and angels. Think in the vein of best-selling gurus like Joseph Campbell and Carolyn Myss.

HOW LONDONERS AMUSE THEMSELVES

Contrary to their undeserved reputations, Londoners do like a good-natured mix-it-up. Although you'll find them to be near-catatonic on their morning commutes, when the workday's over, they loosen their ties at events like the following.

SUNDAY PARTIES

Sunday afternoon parties, like Sunday roasts (see below), are a long-held tradition for young people. They're often programmed like a party on a weekend night—with DJs, maybe, or dancing—but Sunday parties are more inclusive and cosmopolitan, they cost less, and because some attendees have been raging all weekend, their vibe is more anything-goes. Sunday's a great day to kick back with the locals and watch the day trickle by. Food is usually served—expect lots of hearty farm meats.

Spun off from the popular Big Chill music-and-multimedia summer festivals held in the countryside, the laid-back **Big Chill Bar** (Dray Walk, E1; ☎ 020/7392-9180; www.bigchill.net; no cover; Sun–Thurs noon–midnight, Fri–Sat noon–1am; Tube: Aldgate East or Liverpool Street), in the Old Truman Brewery, is about loafing on fat sofas, making friends at communal dining tables, and grooving to DJs.

More of a modern pub than a club, **The Lock Tavern** (35 Chalk Farm Rd., NW1; ☎ 020/7482-7163; www.lock-tavern.co.uk; no cover; Mon–Thurs noon–midnight, Fri–Sat noon–1am, Sun noon–11pm; Tube: Camden Town or Chalk Farm) calls itself "a tarted-up boozer." In fact, it's the panacea to the overcrowded Camden Lock Market just across the street. Come here on a Sunday to kick back in between bouts of shopping at the thronged stalls. A range of DJs spinning on two floors shows its true indie spirit, and bands plug in after 3pm; there's a roof terrace and a garden, and as if that weren't enough, a traditional Sunday roast is served. The good times start around lunchtime and end around 10:30pm.

PUB QUIZZES

Nothing bonds strangers like swapping useless trivia. The British have a peacock-like flair for displaying their knowledge of semi-useless tidbits. And anything worth doing improves when you add beer. That's why so many pubs throw informal **pub quizzes,** or **quiz nights,** a staple of British social life. It's easy to get

The Roast with the Most

Eel pie? Um, maybe not. Beheading childless wives? No, thanks. But there's one English tradition worth upholding: the Sunday Roast. Rare is the pub that doesn't offer a spread of comfort food, such as meats with the trimmings, Yorkshire pudding (a pastry-like shell), and gravy, washed down with copious amounts of beer. A standard starting price is £8.95, although gastropubs have influenced some places to charge £15 or more. Find a pub with an inviting garden or back room, bring a stack of Sunday papers, and hang out until you're ready for Monday.

involved. You just show up before the game starts, pay as little as £1 or £2, and raise your hand to play. Contestants are generally grouped into teams of two to four, so if you come alone, you may be asked to join a team that's short players. Your first duty will be to give your team a witty name such as a pop culture reference (like Quizteama Aguilera) or something that's embarrassing when spoken (like The Cunning Linguists). An amiable but usually merciless emcee, called the Quiz Master, calls out questions in a variety of subjects. Over many drinks, which complicate the recall process, teams whisper amongst themselves to come up with an answer that is then marked on a piece of paper. At the end of the game, the papers are graded, and the team with the most points gets prizes ranging from free booze to £100.

Despite the fact that I once worked on questions for a TV game show, I never win these. Like any sore loser, I blame the questions. But in truth, my sense of general knowledge is different from the average Brit's: I can name the capital of Saudi Arabia (Riyadh), but ask me which football star has scored the most FA Cup Final goals, and I draw a blank (Ian Rush, but I had to look it up). I recommend recruiting British players on the spot so your team rounds out its knowledge base. The English players are often thrilled to work with out-of-towners because foreigners are often perceived as having exhaustive knowledge of Hollywood films.

Ask about quiz nights, because these events are so common they aren't always advertised conspicuously. Quiz nights generally fall on Sunday afternoons or Monday through Thursday evenings, but always check ahead, because pubs can switch their scheduling faster than they pull a pint. A flashy night is held at the rock-'n'-roll bar **The Boogaloo (312 Archway Rd., N6; ☎ 020/8340-2928; www.theboogaloo.co.uk; Tube: Highgate);** it slots monthly movie quiz nights (called "You're Gonna Need a Bigger Boat," the first Wednesday of the month at 8:30pm; £2; www.film-quiz.com) using clips, soundtrack snippets, and posters with the movie titles removed. If you can name the movie that the night's name comes from, you're already ahead of the game. (It's *Jaws.*) The Boogaloo also throws general-knowledge nights (called "Who Killed Bambi?" usually 7pm Tues, £1). Find more using the enthusiast's database QuizList (www.quizlist.com).

PANTO

If you're in Britain between late November and early January, absolutely do not miss partaking of the peculiar entertainment known as pantomime, more commonly called ***panto.*** A direct outgrowth of *commedia dell'arte* theatrical tradition that arrived in England in the Middle Ages, panto refers not to limber, black-clad mimes but to slapstick musical romps, drenched in mild innuendo, that enrapture children and titillate their more knowing parents. Some pantos are performed in standard West End theaters, but the most rewarding ones are almost always mounted in gorgeous turn-of-the-century music halls located in old, multicultural London neighborhoods, giving tourists a two-for-one sightseeing experience. Most of the time, the headliners are hammy TV personalities familiar only to the British.

One house with a strong panto track record is the **Hackney Empire (291 Mare St., E8; ☎ 020/8510-4500; www.hackneyempire.co.uk; National Rail: Hackney Central),** built as a variety house in 1901, where both Charlie Chaplin and Stan Laurel cut their teeth before decamping to Hollywood. **Theatre Royal Stratford East (Gerry Raffles Square, E15; ☎ 020/8534-0310; www.stratfordeast.com; Tube:**

Oh, Yes You Can: The Panto Lingo

Attending your first pantomime performance can be as bewildering as going to your first interactive *Rocky Horror Picture Show.* It seems like everyone in the audience, including the toddlers, knows exactly when to yell and what to say. Don't worry—the whole point is to have fun, so your neighbors won't judge you or single you out. But you'll certainly impress them if you come in with a little foreknowledge:

- Most pantos pick from a list of about a dozen stories including Jack and the Beanstalk, Cinderella, Aladdin, and Snow White. The tale of Dick Whittington, about a poor boy (and his cat) who seeks and finds his fortune, is one panto you won't see much of outside London. Each company tinkers with the plot to suit the talents of that year's cast.
- The leading man, also called "principal boy," is played by a woman pretending to be a man, usually by wearing revealing shorts or tights.
- The leading lady, or "dame," is a man dressed as a woman, and the campy double entendres fly. The fame of the actor retained for the role is the mark of a high-profile panto. As you can imagine, it's where many obsolete comics' careers go to die.
- The villain should be hissed and booed.
- Whenever one character is being stalked by another, the audience must shout "It's behind you!"
- Whenever the good guy argues with the bad guy (or "the baddie"), the audience takes the side of the good guy and shouts along with the row. The exchange will repeat along the lines of "Oh, no, he isn't," and "oh, yes he is!"
- Two actors in a single costume will portray a horse or a cow.

Stratford), a living theatrical museum (1884), is also respected for putting on a crowd-pleasing, traditional panto; it's easy to reach by Tube. **The Richmond Theatre** (The Green, Richmond; ☎ 087/0060-6651; www.richmondtheatre.net; Tube: Richmond), from 1899, has been known to hire well-known actors such as Simon Callow and Patsy Kensit. **The Old Vic** (The Cut, ☎ 0870/060-6628; www.oldvictheatre.com; Tube: Waterloo), as a serious company, doesn't do panto often, but it attracts major names when it does. In 2005, it retained Ian McKellen for its Widow Twankey in *Aladdin* (quipped the *Guardian,* clearly in the spirit: "We can tell our grandchildren that we saw McKellen's Twankey and it was huge"). Tickets for all shows, which tend to end within two hours to appease restless kids, usually cost between £10 and £25.

THE SING-ALONG *SOUND OF MUSIC*

The family-friendly "Sing-a-Long-a" *The Sound of Music,* a giddy participatory screening of the 1965 classic, was born at the **Prince Charles Cinema** kids (7

Leicester Place; ☎ 0870/0811-2559; www.princecharlescinema.com; £14–£15; Tube: Leicester Square) in 1999 and swept the world. A documentary on the phenomenon even made it onto the 40th anniversary DVD re-release of the Rodgers and Hammerstein musical. Participants—some of whom angle for prizes by arriving dressed as Nazis and nuns, without regard to gender—receive a "magic moment" bag with edelweiss, curtain swatches, and a party popper to deploy at the moment of Maria and the Captain's kiss. Unlike at *Rocky Horror* screenings, newbies aren't tortured with initiation rituals; all are welcome at this goofy lovefest, which includes a pre-show warm-up and onscreen lyrics (as if you don't know the words to "Do Re Mi"). It's an absolute blast—at evening shows, the 4-hour frolic may get risqué, but only slightly—and is held at least once on the last weekend of the month, usually at 7:30pm.

Now and then, the Prince Charles hosts other "sing-a-long-a" versions, such as ones for the hits of ABBA or *Rocky Horror,* plus a newcomer to the repertoire: the 2007 musical *Hairspray*. Believe it or not, there is actually a company that makes its money mounting and touring these events; check out www.singalonga.net to see where else in town one might be playing. While you're on the street and in a cinematic mode, duck into **Notre Dame de France** (5 Leicester Place, WC2; ☎ 020/7440-2643; www.notredamechurch.co.uk; Tube: Leicester Square) next door, where there's a series of dazzling 1960 murals by writer/director Jean Cocteau in one of its side chapels.

SNOOKER CLUBS

Snooker, a close cousin of American-style billiards, is played at "clubs" where gentlemen (as it happens, but not by requirement) can also buy drinks, snacks, and watch TV. An annual membership, which gets you in the door, costs around £10 (although some places have day passes for around £3), and rental of a table goes from £6 to about £14 on a weekday or weeknight. Some central clubs include the **Centrepoint Snooker Club** (103 New Oxford St., WC1; ☎ 020/7240-6886; www.cpsnooker.co.uk; weekdays 11am–1am, weekends 3pm–1am; Tube: Tottenham Court Road), located in the basement of the Centre Point tower, and the **King's Cross Snooker and Social Club** (275 Pentonville Rd, N1; ☎ 020/7278-7079; daily 24 hr.; Tube: King's Cross/St. Pancras), which never closes.

Some clubs take themselves awfully seriously, so knowing the rules of the game will make you more friends. Each club has its own rules for claiming a table—observe the ritual before diving in. Clubs also sometimes insist that non-members arrive with members, an impossibility for tourists, but they're more likely to be lax about the rules on midweek afternoons and evenings.

The rarified snooker culture can be daunting, but for a looser vibe, opt for a casual pool hall such as **The Elbow Room** (89-91 Chapel Market, N1; ☎ 020/7278-3244; www.theelbowroom.co.uk; Mon 5pm–2am, Tues–Thurs noon–2am, Fri–Sat noon–3am, Sun noon–midnight; Tube: Angel; and 97–113 Curtain Rd., EC2; ☎ 020/7613-1316; Mon 5pm–2am, Tues–Sat noon–2am, Sun noon–midnight; Tube: Old Street; and 103 Westbourne Grove, W2; ☎ 020/7221-5211; tables £6–£10 per hour; Mon–Sat noon–11pm, Sun noon–10:30pm), dimly lit but intentionally kitschy and patronized by dilettantes, not by sharks and hustlers.

For info on other sporting activities in London, see Chapter 7.

BATHS

In the old days, few Londoners had running water of their own, so neighborhood baths became a vital necessity. That necessity evolved into a Victorian vogue for Turkish-style baths, the precursor to the modern gym. They're now just an indulgent tradition, priced low enough to encourage continued civic use and often crawling with local characters. Unlike at snooty day spas, they're as social as bars, except the patrons are lubricated not by ale but by chlorinated water. In fact, each one has lounges or small cafes where, once clad in just a towel, people from every walk of life meet on equal footing. **Ironmonger Row Baths** (1-11 Ironmonger Row, EC1; ☎ 020/7253-4011; www.aquaterra.org/islington; Mon–Fri 6:30am–9pm, Sat 9am–6pm, Sun 10am–6pm; Tube: Old Street), an urban escape of low light, dark woods, and quietly gossiping senior citizens, has two pools (£4 or less), but they're not the star attraction. The real draw is the astoundingly cheap subterranean D.I.Y. Turkish Bath facilities, which include a steam room, three hot rooms, plenty of marble slabs for vigorous rubdowns from on-site licensed therapists, nap rooms, and a cold plunge pool. The area costs £7.70 for 3 hours on weekday mornings starting at 6:30am, rising to £13 after noon and on weekends; those prices include access to the main pools. It's men only Tuesday, Thursday, Saturday; women only Wednesday, Friday, and Sunday; and mixed on Monday afternoons, the only time that swimsuits are mandatory.

More ornate, but also more expensive, is **The Porchester Spa** (The Porchester Centre, Queensway, W2; ☎ 020/7792-3980; daily 10am–10pm; Tube: Royal Oak), an Art Deco facility with many of its original period details (high ceilings, green and white tiles, 1920s fixtures) intact and recently buffed up. It boasts two Russian steam rooms, three Turkish hot rooms, a small Finnish sauna, and lots of beds in its rest area. Three hours cost £20 (£6.70 seniors) here, a hot towel treatment is £30, and a Jewish "shmeissing" treatment involving a good going-over by a soapy brush is £25—high, but the environment is transporting. Men-only days are Monday, Wednesday, and Saturday and women get Tuesday, Thursday, Friday, and Sunday 10am to 4pm. After 4pm Sun, it's for couples only.

For a neighborhood feeling, **York Hall Leisure Centre** (5-15 Old Ford Rd., E2; ☎ 020/8980-2243; www.gll.org; daily 7am–9:30pm, women-only Wed; £3.40–£4.10; Tube: Bethnal Green), administered by the local council (Tower Hamlets), is an East London landmark, open since 1929. Locals hang out all day playing cards, nodding off, and swapping stories. Of all the central London baths, it probably sees the fewest tourists. The affordable day spa (£21 for 3 hr. in its various steam and aroma rooms) is among the hottest in town, and following a petition by adoring locals, the facility is enjoying some long-awaited investment and the addition of plenty of activities such as group fitness sessions. The boxing ring was where pugilists Lennox Lewis and Audley Harrison learned their punches, and there are two swimming pools.

7 Outdoor London

Where to get fresh air in a city of green spaces

YOU SHOULDN'T SPEND ALL OF YOUR TIME IN LONDON GAWKING AT masterpieces in museums or learning about old mansions from the talky end of an audio guide. Britain is an outdoorsy country, and its mild weather and topography tempt locals nearly year-round. Many of the things that make British culture famous—its emerald parkland, its invigorating sporting events, and even its picturesque meandering rivers—can only be enjoyed in the fresh air. Inside, you'll find the refined world of the pinkie-lifting, tea-sipping gentry, but under changeable British skies, chased by clouds, rain, and sunshine (often in the same hour), you'll find the England of the everyman.

PARKS

Parks are a significant part of everyday London life, so if you miss loitering in one, you'll miss one of the central pleasures of the city. You'll also have missed sampling the city's oft-overlooked ecology, animals, and the smells of its flowers and trees. There's a reason that English plants have been exported the world over and why English gardens are the envy of every horticulturalist—they're soothing, and they'll help bring you the relaxation you presumably are vacationing to find.

So what's the best park in town? Ask 10 Londoners, and you'll get 20 answers. Like pubs, parks have neighborhood devotees. But there's one given: On any day when the sun pokes even a few warm rays through the clouds, half of Londoners flock to the city's green spaces to lounge on benches, stroll the classical pathways, and lie (usually in full, long-sleeve dress) on the grass. Eight of the city's great parks, the Royal Parks (www.royalparks.org.uk) were originally owned by the monarchy for private use, and, counted together, they comprise some 2,226 hectares (5,500 acres)—which ranks London among the greenest cities on Earth.

Nearly every park posts a detailed map at every entrance, so it's never hard to pinpoint landmarks. (My advice: If you have a digital camera, snap a picture of the map as you enter—you can refer to it onscreen for the rest of your visit.)

FOR RESPITE IN THE CITY CENTER **Hyde Park** (Tube: Hyde Park Corner, Marble Arch, or Lancaster Gate), bordered by Mayfair, Bayswater, and Kensington, is the largest park in the middle of the city. It's the tourist favorite, mostly because of its location and rolling landscape (138 hectares/340 acres) that recalls the English ideal. London itself identifies with the park, since it's home to the famous Speakers' Corner (Tube: Marble Arch, p. 207), a meandering lake called the Serpentine, and the Diana, Princess of Wales Memorial Fountain (Tube: South Kensington, p. 176). The most famous promenade is Rotten Row, probably a corruption of "Route de Roi," or King's Way, which was laid out by William III as

The Orphan Park

Coram's Fields (95 Guilford St., WC1; ☎ 020/7837-6138; www.coramsfields.org; Tube: Russell Square), was set aside in 1739 in Bloomsbury for the Foundling Hospital, a home for orphans. Ringed with impenetrable gates and overseen by pious benefactors, it took in some 1,000 "foundlings" a year and raised them, on little food and even less personal contact, until they were old enough to be shipped off as apprentices or soldiers elsewhere. In an era where 75% of London kids died before age five, even such a loveless upbringing was considered a blessing. George Frideric Handel counted himself as a benefactor and served as its governor, and his *Messiah* became a seasonal chestnut through its annual benefit performances for the hospital. Its southern stone gate, iron bars now clipped to nubs, is where countless desperate mothers once abandoned their unwanted babies along with a few small mementoes that, because of policy, the children never saw. The extent of the long yard, still lined with its original colonnade, was where generations of "foundlings" marched for their daily exercise. In 1936, it was converted to happier usage as a safe space for kids; today, no adult may enter unless accompanied by a child. Coram's Fields is now the scene of joy between parents and children, with a playground, ball fields, a padding pool, and a petting zoo. You'll find it, ghosts long gone, a few blocks east of Russell Square, not far northeast of the British Museum. The poignant Foundling Museum (p. 159) at the back of the park is dedicated to the Hospital.

his private road to town; it runs along the southern edge of the park from Hyde Park Corner. Hyde Park is where many historic open-air concerts, such as Live 8 and shows by the Rolling Stones and Queen, were held, and it's where television screens are erected for overflow crowds during critical national events, such as Princess Diana's funeral.

FOR THAT COUNTRY MANOR FEEL To the west across West Carriage Drive, so close that it might as well be one with Hyde Park, is the more formal **Kensington Gardens** (Tube: Lancaster Gate, Queensway, Notting Hill Gate, High Street Kensington, or Bayswater), which started as the front yard of Kensington Palace (Tube: High Street Kensington, p. 160). It only opened to plebes like us in 1851, and it hasn't yet shed its hemmed-in, snooty quality. Calming but a bit too busy for perfect peace, it's where you'll see George Frampton's famous statue of **Peter Pan** playing the pipes, snapped by tourists who think it sweet but dissed by locals as twee (Tube: Lancaster Gate). You'll also find the **Serpentine Gallery** (west of West Carriage Drive and north of Alexandra Gate; ☎ 020/7402-6075; www.serpentinegallery.org; open daily 10am–6pm, Fri 10am–10pm; free admission; Tube: South Kensington), a popular venue for modern art exhibitions sponsored by heavy-hitting corporations and art patrons. Each year, a leading architect is assigned the task of creating and building a fanciful summer pavilion there; in 2006, it was a giant egg-shaped canopy, and in 2008, Frank Gehry created a spiky jumble. Volunteers sometimes run guided tours of the park's lesser-known design quirks and statuary; check the bulletin boards at each park entrance to see if one's upcoming.

FOR FLOWER-GAZING AND QUEEN-SPOTTING **The Green Park** (Tube: Green Park), south of Mayfair between Hyde Park and St. James's Park, was once a burial ground for lepers, but now is a simple expanse of meadows and light copses of trees. It doesn't have much to offer except pastoral views, and most visitors find themselves crossing it instead of dawdling in it, although its springtime flower beds (which bloom brightest in Mar and Apr) are marvelous. **St. James's Park** (Tube: St. James's Park), the easternmost segment of the contiguous quartet of parks that runs east from Kensington Gardens, is bounded by Whitehall to the east and Piccadilly to the north. Its little pond, St. James's Park Lake, hosts ducks and other waterfowl. The Russian ambassador made a gift of pelicans to the park in the 1600s, and five (one from Louisiana, four from Eastern Europe) still call it home; they're fed their 13kg (28 lb.) of whiting daily at 2:30pm at the Duck Island Cottage. The park has a fine view of Buckingham Palace's front facade. It could best be described as royal—but the real draw is people-watching, since a cross-section of all London passes through here on an average day. Not a place for picnics or ball-throwing, there's little in the way of amenities or activities, unless you count voyeurism, and I do.

FOR ENJOYING THE WEATHER WITH LOCALS Because its wide spaces make it feel miles away from the city, and because it borders some bohemian neighborhoods, I consider **Regent's Park** to be the people's park, best for sunning, Frisbee-throwing, and strolling long expanses. Once a hunting ground, it was very

A Poignant Pocket Park

Little-known **Postman's Park** (west side of St. Martin's-Le-Grand between St. Paul's Cathedral and the Barbican Centre; open 8am–dusk; Tube: St. Paul's or Barbican), is beloved by those lucky enough to have stumbled across it. Hemmed in between buildings, its central feature is the moving **Watts Memorial,** a collection of plaques dedicated to ordinary people who died in acts of "heroic self sacrifice." Have a seat on a bench and ponder John Clinton, 10, "who was drowned near London Bridge in trying to save a companion younger than himself" in July 1894. In 1893, William Freer Lucas tantalizingly "risked poison for himself rather than lessen any chance of saving a child's life and died." The commemorations ceased in Edwardian times, making these forgotten faces seem forgotten once again. Playwright Patrick Marber gave new life to at least one of the fallen; a character in his film *Closer* took her name from Alice Ayres, who in 1885 saved three children from a burning house "at the cost of her own young life." On the silver screen, Alice got to sleep with Jude Law.

The Hidden Park

Sure, everybody knows about London's famous green spaces, but there's one recreation area, which stretches from London's northwest to its east through gentrified lanes and industrial wasteland alike, that few tourists are told about. It's the Regent's Canal, which threads from Paddington through Camden, Islington, and East London before joining with the Thames (26m/85 ft. lower) just before Canary Wharf. It was completed in 1820 to link with canals all the way to Birmingham and feed the city's massive seagoing trade. In those days, barges were animal-drawn and the districts along the waterway were rat-infested and perilous, but today, it's a frontier for development; many of the horse tracks are leafy promenades, and an increasing number of the shadowy old warehouses have become affluent loft condos. Few tourists even know this ribbon of water is here to explore, but locals favor it for biking and walking (some come here to drink strong beer, too—just smile and nod at them). Along the way, you'll even pass some docks where houseboat barges tie up during their trips through England's canals; their owners can often be found hanging out topside, making conversation with passersby in the way intrepid travelers do. Even without a boat, the canal makes for a lovely backdrop for a stroll; the most popular segment is probably the crescent just north of the London Zoo at Regent's Park; the zoo's Snowdown Aviary abuts the water.

Several companies operate ferry service and tours on the leg between Paddington's "Little Venice" system of basins and Camden's popular lock market, among them the glass-sided **London Waterbus Company** (☎ 020/7482-2660; www.londonwaterbus.com; £6.50 single, £9 return), the only

nearly turned into a development for the buddies of Prince Regent (later King George IV), but only a few of the private terrace homes were built; Winfield House, on 5 hectares (12 acres) near the western border of the park, has the largest garden in London, after the Queen. The American ambassador lives there—surprised? In addition to boasting huge amounts of space (195 hectares/487 acres), the park also has the **Open Air Theatre** (☎ 084/4826-4242; www.openairtheatre.org; tickets £10–£15; Tube: Baker Street) for summer productions by the New Shakespeare Company, comedians, an annual musical, and children's theater; fine Italian and English gardens at the southeast corner; and the **London Zoo** (Tube: Camden Town or Regent's Park; p. 192), which is no great shakes as zoos go but still doesn't skimp on the cool creatures, including gorillas and giraffes. Because there's so much to do and so much space to do it in—it can take a half-hour to walk from one end to the other—this is my favorite of the parks in central London. In the center of the park, off the Broadwalk, you'll find an inexpensive, homey little cafe, **The Honest Sausage** (☎ 020/7224-3872; www.honestsausage.com; Tube: Regent's Park or Great Portland Street), that feels like it flew on its own accord from the pastoral British hinterland; its sausages and bacon come from a family-run business in Gloucestershire, and its cake slices are truly generous. It's service to run all winter; the slightly more luxe **Jason's Trip** (☎ 020/7286-3428; www.jasons.co.uk; Apr–Oct; £7.50 single, £8.50 return); and the ***Jenny Wren*** (☎ 020/7485-4433; www.walkersquay.com; Apr–Oct; £8.50 return for 90 min.). The **London Canal Museum** (12-13 New Wharf Rd., N1; ☎ 020/7713-0836; www.canalmuseum.org.uk; admission £3 adult, £1.50 children; Tues–Sun 10am–4:30pm; Tube: King's Cross St. Pancras), in a former icehouse, is devoted to the waterway. Its website provides free downloadable walking tours.

Along the way, keep an eye out for some unusual floating attractions, such as the **Puppet Barge** (kids) (box office only: 78 Middleton Rd., E8; ☎ 020/7249-6876; www.puppetbarge.com; admission £8.50 adult, £8 children), which moors in five different places depending on the season, entertaining local families. In summer, a variety of floating restaurants and cafes also waylay pedestrians; the most striking, the Fen Shang Princess floating Chinese restaurant, is too pricey to commit to, but its pagoda-like presence on the waters at the northeast boundary of Regent's Park makes for a jarring sight. Catch a glimpse of MTV's futurist/modern studio, on the canal at Hawley Crescent in Camden, before putting your feet up a block west with a beer at one of the cafes around Camden Lock Market (at Chalk Farm Rd.; Tube: Camden Town), where you can watch the narrowboat skipper operate the old locks, still functioning after all these years. The industrial swath of canal between Islington and the Docklands is still gentrifying, so it calls more to enthusiasts than to idle walkers.

possible to find local tennis players for a pick-up match at the sports center near the park's southwest corner. The most breathtaking way to enter the park is from the south through John Nash's elegant Park Crescent development, by the Regent's Park and Great Portland Street Tube stations (Tube: Regent's Park, Great Portland Street, Baker Street, or Camden Town). North of the park, just over the Regent's Canal and Prince Albert Road, **Primrose Hill Park** (Tube: Chalk Farm or Camden Town) affords a panorama of the city from its 62m (203-ft.) high top. On weekends, the summit can seem as busy as Oxford Street, and some badly dated signboards help you know what you're looking at, or more accurately, how radically the skyline has changed in 20 years.

FOR PLAYING ROBIN HOOD Northeast London has some of the most untrampled parks. Mostly because its soil is unsuitable for farming, **Epping Forest** (☎ 020/8508-0028; www.cityoflondon.gov.uk; National Rail: Chingford) has for a millennium remained a semivirgin woodland, so it's the best place to get a feel for what Britain felt like before humans reshaped and denuded its land. It's the largest public space around, 19km (12 miles) long by 4km (2½ miles) wide, and containing a universe of diversion—650 plant species, 80 ponds where waterfowl splash, and even some 1,500 species of fungi (but don't eat any of them unless you know what you're doing). Getting lost in the woods isn't likely, since it stretches in a single direction. Henry VII built a timber-framed hunting lodge in 1543 that was inherited by his daughter Elizabeth and, astoundingly, still stands, now as a museum: **Queen Elizabeth's Hunting Lodge** (Rangers Rd., Chingford, E4; ☎ 020/8529-6681; www.cityoflondon.gov.uk; free admission; Oct–Feb Wed–Sun 1–4pm and Apr–Sept 12:30–5:30pm. National Rail: Chingford.). Epping Forest links to the south with Wanstead's network of parks (Tube: Snaresbrook or Wood Street Walthamstow National Rail).

FOR GHOSTS Haunting **Wanstead Park** (Tube: Wanstead) was, from the time of Henry VII to the early 1800s, the site of a grand, 70m-long (230-ft.) manor house, but when its ruling family ran into hard times, the house fell into disrepair and was razed. What's left are a few bizarre outbuildings and the remains of its formal gardens, including abandoned ornamental ponds with names like Shoulder of Mutton, which date to the early 1700s. It's a lilting park, and one of London's least crowded. Any local who meets you wandering this peculiar patch will be fascinated to hear how you, as a tourist, came across this ghostly bit of turf.

FOR SCIENCE NERDS In southeast London, feeling more like an open space near a village than a city park, **Greenwich Park** (www.royalparks.gov.uk; Tube: Cutty Sark DLR) is 74 hectares/183 acres, and was once a deer preserve maintained for royal amusement; a herd of 30 still has 5 hectares (12 acres) at their disposal (keep your distance because they are unpredictable when in heat). On top of its clean-swept main hill are found marvelous city views and the world-famous **Royal Greenwich Observatory** (☎ 020/8312-6565; www.rog.nmm.ac.uk; Tube: Cutty Sark DLR), a mansion-like complex commissioned in 1675 by Charles II. The observatory serves as the intersection point for the Prime Meridian as well as the center of Greenwich Mean Time. It's now a free museum stuffed with the most historic timepieces in the world, including the clocks that cracked the riddle of longitude for navigators, opening up the world to British dominance. Most people combine a visit with the many other museums of Greenwich on weekends, when the markets are hopping. See p. 171 for more info.

FOR KIDS AND RIVER-WATCHERS South London's **Battersea Park** (www.batterseapark.org; National Rail: Battersea Park or Tube: Sloane Square, then 137 bus), a Victorian innovation, is popular for its elaborate children's playground, which is overseen by a youth group from the local government. I love it for its smattering of 20th-century sculpture and its wacky variety: **The Pump House Gallery** (☎ 020/7350-0523; www.wandsworth.gov.uk/gallery; Wed–Thurs and Sun 11am–5pm, Fri–Sat 11am–4pm) has free exhibitions; the adorable Battersea Park **Children's Zoo** (☎ 020/7924-5826; www.batterseaparkzoo.co.uk; admission £6.50 adults, £4.95 children; daily 10am–dusk) boasts monkeys, otters, and strange Australian animals; and its prancing Fountains Display, the Bellagio on the Thames, runs from March to November. The grandest water show happens on the hour. It's one of my favorite parks near town because it's the only park that's right on the river; sitting near its Peace Pagoda, watching the flow, is an easy way to wile away time. Since the Tube doesn't stop here (another source of this area's quiet appeal), it's a good idea to combine a visit with a shopping trip down

FOR VIEWS & BREWS

Frolic with the rich in the 320-hectare (791-acre) **Hampstead Heath** (www.cityoflondon.gov.uk; Tube: Hampstead), in northwest London. Thickly wooded and easy to get lost in, the Heath is a perennial locale for aimless strolls and (it must be said) furtive trysts. If you venture onto the Heath, make an adventure of it, since it has several sublime places to rest your legs, including **Kenwood House** (Hampstead Lane, NW3; ☎ 020/8348-1286; www.english-heritage.org.uk; Tube: Hampstead or Highgate; see p. 160 for more info), a sumptuous neoclassical home from 1640 adorned with miles of gold leaf and important paintings by Reynolds, Turner, Gainsborough, and Vermeer *(The Guitar Player)*; and **Spaniards Inn** (Spaniards Rd. at Spaniards End, NW3; ☎ 020/8731-6571; Tube: Hampstead), a garden pub dating to 1585 that has a pistol ball, said to be fired by the legendary outlaw Dick Turpin, framed above the bar. The Heath's hilltop is another favored lookout point. The Heath isn't considered a park by locals, but a green space. I've never grasped the difference, but since it was referenced as far back as 1086 in the Domesday Book, I can understand if its posh neighbors don't want to inflict such a venerable idyll with a mundane, civic label like "park." I have a friend who tripped in a mud bog here and contracted scarlet fever, which, given the place's history, shouldn't surprise me. Even its diseases are old-fashioned.

Chelsea's King's Road, and then cross to the park via Oakley Street and the handsome suspension Albert Bridge. As you go, look for the signs, dating to the 1870s, asking soldiers to break step as they cross it lest their vibrations damage the structure. Battersea Park has an active events calendar, so check its website for potential diversions.

FOR GREEN THUMBS Not a park per se, but a rewarding oasis nonetheless, the walled **Chelsea Physic Garden** (66 Royal Hospital Rd., SW3; ☎ 020/7352-5646; www.chelseaphysicgarden.co.uk; admission £7 adults and £4 children 5–15; mid-Mar to Oct Wed–Fri noon–5pm, Sun noon–6pm; Tube: Sloane Square) is a 1.6-hectare (4-acre) plot founded in 1673 by the Society of Apothecaries as a garden for healing herbs, making it England's second-oldest botanical garden. Strike up a conversation with a gardener, and you'll learn more about plantings than a professor could teach. The western side is arranged like a living timeline, with plants normally cultivated in the 17th century followed by ones more common to the 18th century. Described by some as "melancholy," this peaceful hideaway is open 4 days a week, 7 months a year. That's not enough!

FOR FORGETTING THE CITY In southwest London, **Richmond Park** (www.royalparks.gov.uk; Tube: Richmond) is the largest open space in the city, at 944 hectares (2,333 acres). Charles I designated it as a hunting park, and to this day, it's home to free-roaming deer (they're testy when they're in heat, so mind the signs as you enter the gates). The Pen Ponds, in the center, are inhabited by waterfowl. The park adjoins **Wimbledon Common,** itself more spacious than the more central parks, and near the tennis tournament grounds. Unfortunately, it takes a lot of work to reach them all: You have to get to the end of a long Tube line plus a 15-minute walk before you see a blade of grass.

STROLLING THE THAMES

Until right after World War II, the Thames was a working river, teeming with coal boats, ships, dockworkers, and the stinking effluvia of the city's residents. It would regularly flood, too, sweeping away hapless children and inundating riverside property—a problem not wholly solved until the late 20th century. It's a lot more placid these days, and a lot cleaner, but it's still the city's spine, and it's the very reason the first settlers chose this particular spot in the otherwise marshy morass. Experiencing a bit of the Thames can bring you in touch with the city's past. And heady talk aside, it's just pretty.

A not-at-all taxing way to see the river is on the **Thames Path** (www.nationaltrail.co.uk/thamespath), a walking route that follows the river for 296km (184 miles) from its source in the Cotswolds to the North Sea. The bits in town wind through some fascinating brown-brick areas that, more than any other parts of central London, recall the river's heyday as a center for trade and industry. Much of the route feels unofficial and is sometimes deserted, so bring along a map if you decide to sample a portion.

URBAN FARMS

England's roots as a farming country go back thousands of years, and it must be hard to break Englishmen of the habit, because the city still maintains a number of urban farms. The main product being churned out these days isn't milk or meat, but memories—city families come to let their kids pet the sheep, stare down the cows, and chill out in a field of green surrounded by sprawl. Because of mad cow disease, your Customs department now frowns upon visits to British farms in the countryside, so city farms (free of the disease) are your best bet for getting nose-to-snout with Britain's famous agrarian culture. Farms can get muddy, so wear closed-toe shoes.

The most popular urban farm is the free, 12-hectare (30-acre) **Mudchute Park and Farm** (Lower Isle of Dogs; ☎ 020/7515-5901; www.mudchute.org; free admission; daily 9:30am–4:30pm; Tube: Mudchute DLR), which, within the incongruous sight of Canary Wharf's skyscrapers, stocks pigs, horses, cows, ducks, dogs, geese, and llamas; there's also a short nature trail. This slice of bucolic life may seem like the city grew up around it, but in fact, the land dates only to the mid-1800s, when dirt was moved here during the building of a nearby dock, and the animals weren't added until 1977. An hour's horse ride is £22 for adults and £18 for children; book ahead.

The free **Spitalfields City Farm** (Weaver St. at Pedley St., E1; ☎ 020/7247-8762; www.spitalfieldscityfarm.org; free admission; Tues–Sun 10am–4:30pm, closed Mon; Tube: Liverpool Street or Aldgate East), another late-'70s creation, is on a former railway depot right behind Brick Lane, and developers have been salivating over the land for years. It's very small (.5 hectares/1.3 acres) but still manages fur-to-face time with Ursula Goat, Bayleaf the donkey, Itchy the pig, a miniature Shetland pony named Tilley, plus a mess of hens, rabbits, sheep, and ferrets. Petting chickens makes for a queer pairing with the many funky art galleries in the same area, but in a way, it makes sense—both attractions were outgrowths of a poor district with cheap land values. That is changing quickly around Whitechapel.

SPORTING EVENTS & ACTIVITIES

When faced with the electricity of a sporting match, the English lose all reserve. And all fashion sense—many red-blooded British men would sooner die than be caught in something other than their team's colors, a sartorial preference that marks them as faithful fanatics both in and out of the stadium. See these untamed creatures in their natural habitats, but be warned: Do not tease the animals. While Americans are content to mingle in the stands with supporters of their rival teams, the English are more likely to sit in separate sections, which some observers think heightens the risk of brawling and has even resulted in price gouging of the visiting fans.

FOOTBALL (AKA SOCCER)

There's no disputing that London is football mad—not unless you want a beer bottle to the skull. It hosts 13 professional soccer teams, more than any other city on earth. Six of the 20 clubs in the Premiership (or primary league) are based in London, and during the season, from mid-August to mid-May, there's barely a pub in town that doesn't get packed during match broadcasts. In the stadiums, grown men sing and cry, crowds by the thousand mock referees, and children are imprinted at a very early age with the team support considered appropriate in their house. As at many professional sporting events, tempers can run high and emotions can fray, but the club owners work very hard to maintain a family-friendly atmosphere, even if they charge prices that could put the average Mum and Dad in the poorhouse. Football is Britain's favorite sport, and it's London leisure at its most essential. Locals will be only too happy to persuade you to their side. Given the ferocious intensity with which many Englishmen regard their favorite team, it would be wise not to appear to favor one side of the match over another. The 2005 and 2006 Premier League champions (the honor went to Manchester United in 2007 and 2008), **Chelsea** (Stamford Bridge Ground, Fulham Rd., SW6; ☎ 087/19841-905 in the U.K. or 020/7915-2900 from abroad; www.chelseafc.com; Tube: Fulham Broadway) is currently enjoying a resurgence in popularity. It even offers daily **tours** (☎ 087/1984-1955; www.chelseafctours.com; not offered on match days; £15 adults, £9 children) through its stadium and its museum, although unless you've got some background knowledge about the team, it may not get your heart pumping. Across town in a brand-new (2006) 60,000-seat stadium, there's the 1998, 2002, and 2004 winners and 2005's runner-up, **Arsenal** (Emirates Stadium, Ashburton Grove, N5; ☎ 020/7704-4040; www.arsenal.com; 90-minute tours £12 adult, £3 children; £6 seniors/students; Tube: Arsenal). For a less frothy fan experience, try **Fulham** (Craven Cottage, Stevenage Rd., SW6; ☎ 087/0442-1234; www.fulhamfc.com; Tube: Putney Bridge), which despite having played for more than 130 years, never seems to place very high or low in the rankings and thus attracts a milder rabble. The *ne plus ultra* of traditional London footie is probably **West Ham United** (Boleyn Ground, Green St., Upton Park, E13; ☎ 087/0112-2700; www.whufc.com; Tube: Upton Park), whose fans are rabidly devoted despite their team's status as a perpetual also-ran. Its stadium is in a middle-class South Asian neighborhood that affords good postgame meals at its authentic curry restaurants. Kick-off for any game falls between 3 and 7:45pm. For all clubs, match-ticket starting prices range from £25 (Fulham) to £35 (Arsenal) for adults for nosebleed seats (you'll pay £60 to be close enough to catch the players' sweat), although for oversold games, Fulham opens some restricted-view seats for £20 adults/£5 children. For sparsely attended matches, West Ham offers a "kid for a quid" deal for which children pay just £1. All clubs make an effort to welcome seniors and children by granting discounts of about £20.

CRICKET

Filling the gap from April to September when the football players kick back in the Mediterranean, cricket is the quintessential colonial British sport. Half the reason to attend a match is to convince fellow spectators to attempt to explain it to you. (It's a little like baseball—and a lot like watching grass grow.) You'll have plenty of time; some games ("test matches"), played by men in white dressed more like sous-chefs than professional athletes, sprawl languidly over 5 days. For a more manageable time commitment, attend an "over match," which takes but a single day. The most prestigious games are played at **Marylebone Cricket Club Lord's Cricket Ground** (St. Johns Wood; ☎ 020/7432-1000; www.lords.org; Tube: St. John's Wood), considered the high church of the sport. If cricket followed tides, Lord's would be their moon; the official Laws and Spirit, rulebooks that together serve as the Bible of the sport, are enshrined on its manicured grounds, as is the 1882 trophy known as The Ashes, a potent symbol of the ongoing rivalry between the Australian and English teams. Lord's one-day prices start at around £20 for adults, £7 for children under 16; if you know the lingo already, consider a tour of the pavilion (☎ 020/7616-8595; no tours on match days; £12 adults, £6 children). Another important venue, **Surrey County Cricket Club** (Kennington Oval, SE11; ☎ 087/1246-1100; www.surreycricket.com; Tube: Oval), also called The Brit Oval, has an enviable situation very close to central London and stages England's final test match of the summer, plus a bunch of one-day games with international teams; those in the Twenty20 series last 3 hours—ideal for dabbling tourists. Tickets to an average match go as low as £12 adult/£6 kids. The look on your face as you puzzle out wickets, googlies, silly points, and leg byes? Worth many multiples of that.

ICE SKATING

From late November through January, the noble courtyard at **Somerset House** (p. 158) is transformed into a public ice skating rink. Lit by torches and warmed by a cafe serving mulled wine and hot chocolate, this is where skaters from around London come to mingle and slide. Before dark, prices are around £10 adults, £7 children for an hour, and after dark they're £13/£7, including skate rental (Strand, WC2; ☎ 020/7845-4600; www.somerset-house.org.uk; generally 10am–10pm during winter; reservations recommended; Tube: Temple).

ROWING

Each year on a Sunday afternoon in late March or early April, Oxford and Cambridge universities duke it out with their good-natured rowing **Boat Race** (www.theboatrace.org) on the River Thames. This is no goofy college rivalry; the

In the Swim

Although there are few days hot enough for most foreigners to crave an open-air swim in London, they don't have to get wet to appreciate the few remaining public outdoor swimming pools, or lidos, sprinkled around town. Many were constructed in the 1920s and '30s, before the dominion of the automobile, to give city families somewhere to cool off on warm days. Most of these Art Deco playgrounds limped, unloved, through several generations in which they lay fallow and suffered demolition, but a few lucky survivors are being embraced again by their communities. For a few pounds (typically £5 or less, plus small charges for lockers), you can spend a summer day with crowds of Londoners. Bring your sunglasses—not because of the British sun, but to shield your eyes from all the alabaster skin. Hours vary, so call ahead.

Among the city's most famous lidos is the **Brockwell Lido** (Dulwich Rd., Herne Hill, SE24; ☎ 020/7274-3088; Tube: Brixton), which attracts a wide variety of people—Caribbean to gay to old dears—and where you can supplement a dip with a class in Ashtanga yoga or Tai Chi—a separate club, the Brockwell Users Group (☎ 020/7738-6633; www.brockwelllido.com), posts schedules for those activities (usually £8 a session) online. The Lido's summer Whippersnappers kids' program (☎ 020/7738-6633; www.whippersnappers.org) entertains the neighborhood's multicultural kids with a Jamaican and English blend of music classes, workshops, and street dancing, all at the pool. **Hampstead Ponds** (Hampstead Heath at Gordon House Rd.; ☎ 020/7485-5757; National Rail: Gospel Oak or Tube: Kentish Town), is fed by the River Fleet, which is otherwise buried under the city, and was originally dug as reservoirs in the 1700s; they're the only lifeguarded swimming facilities in the U.K. that are open every day of the year. From June through early September, you're actually permitted to swim in a marked-off area of the **Serpentine** (☎ 020/7706-3422; www.serpentinelido.com; Tube: South Kensington) in Hyde Park. Lounge chairs can also be rented. It's on the southern bank of the pond, just north of the middle stretch of Rotten Row. One of the few outdoor (and heated) pools open year-round is at the **Oasis Sports Centre** (32 Endell St., WC2; ☎ 020/7831-1804; www.gll.org, in the Camden section; Tube: Covent Garden or Tottenham Court Rd.), which is not historic but, astonishingly, is hidden behind one of the city's busiest central intersections: High Holborn and Shaftesbury Avenue, making it hugely convenient for tourists. There's also an indoor pool; the complex opens at 6:30am weekdays and 9:30am weekends.

big day attracts around 250,000 spectators, plus 7.2 million more who cheer the live TV coverage. It's been held since 1829, and since 1845 in London. The 6.8km (4¼-mile) curvy course runs upstream (westbound) from Putney (Tube:

Putney Bridge) to Chiswick Bridge at Mortlake (National Rail: Mortlake). The race, which only takes about 19 minutes—Cambridge claims slightly more wins, incidentally, although Oxford is on a winning streak lately—is more or less ridiculous, but it makes for an excellent excuse for a quarter-million people to get merry and drunk at the many riverside pubs around Hammersmith.

RUGBY

Rugby is a great English sport, but it's played mostly in the North. The few clubs that play in town are more upper class than in the northern league, and they don't stoke the fires of Londoners' hearts the way football teams do. The top place to catch an international match, from September through April, is **Twickenham Rugby Football Ground** (Whitton Rd., Twickenham; www.rfu.com; National Rail: Twickenham). Games sell out, so reserve ahead by calling the ticket office at ☎ 087/0143-1111. Tickets are generally £10 to £40, but happily, many of the cheaper seats are covered in case of rain. Tickets (around £20–£40) are easier to score for two local teams: the **London Wasps** (Twyford Ave., Acton, W3; ☎ 087/0414-1515; www.wasps.co.uk; Tube: Ealing Common) and the **Harlequins** (The Twickenham Stoop, Craneford Way, Twickenham; ☎ 020/8410-6000; www.quins.co.uk; National Rail: Twickenham).

TENNIS

It's easy watching the **Wimbledon Championships** (Church Rd., SW19; ☎ 020/8971-2473; www.wimbledon.org; Tube: Wimbledon Park) on TV for 2 weeks in late June and early July, but seeing it in person is a trickier matter. Because tickets for the final matches go to VIPs, you're more likely to catch famous players during the early rounds, when the club's 19 grass courts are all in use. Roaming access to all but three of those (surcharges of £38–£93 are levied for Centre, No. 1, and No. 2 courts, and tickets are distributed by lottery the previous summer) can be had for the price of a "ground pass" (which cost, at most, £20). Around 6,000 ground passes are distributed each morning starting at 9:30am, and if you snag one, you'll probably be inside by noon, when matches begin. Another clever way to get in is to bum tickets off people as they get tired and leave for the day (just don't offer money—the organizers hate that because they sell unused tickets, too, for charity). A few more ground passes are resold after 3pm for £5 to benefit charity. On weekdays and rainy days, your chances of getting unfilled seats for the best courts are better, since people are working or huddling indoors. And after 5pm, ground-pass rates dip to, at most, £14, which isn't such a bad deal since matches continue until 9pm. It's all ridiculously complicated, so check ahead to make sure the rules are the same. If you aren't around for the tournament, the **Wimbledon Lawn Tennis Museum** (Church Rd., SW19; ☎ 020/8946-6131; 10:30am–5pm; £8.50 adults, £4.75 children, £7.50 seniors/students; Tube: Wimbledon Park), which was revamped in 2006, is open to the public the rest of the year. It's sort of like a Hall of Fame with an emphasis, of course, on Wimbledon. Roughly double those prices if you want to tour the main courts (not during matches, of course).

8 Walkabouts

Enjoy a unique curbside view of the city's life and history

PAYING FOR A SIGHTSEEING TOUR SEEMS SMART IN PRINCIPLE. YOU GLIMPSE monuments, briefly, and you hear one or two eye-glazing facts about them as you whiz past. But no coach tour, no hokey sightseeing boat, goes at your speed. None lets you spend as much time as you want, chewing over the vibe of what's before you, or allows you to stop for a few minutes and breathe in the atmosphere.

For that, you should be your own leader. With my self-guided walking tours, there's no "hurry up," and you can break away at any moment to chase whatever catches your interest. I supply commentary and point you toward adventure. You get to enjoy the rest.

My walking tours are packed with tales and tidbits, and they're loosely themed—choose the stomping grounds of kings (tour 1), dingy Dickensian back alleys (tour 2), or the London where modern-day trendsetters like Mick Jagger gathered no moss (tour 3). Each one passes important attractions and pubs that you're free to enter as you go, and they all start and end near Tube stations so that the going is easy.

I guarantee you'll go from not knowing much about parts of London to wanting to know more. You'll understand how the city fits together much better than people who sit idling at red lights on coach tours. All without paying a penny.

Walking Tour 1: Westminster, Whitehall & Trafalgar Square

Start: Westminster Tube station
Finish: Trafalgar Square
Time: Allow approximately 60 minutes, not including time spent in attractions
Best time: Be at the starting line just before noon to hear Big Ben deliver its longest chime of the day
Worst time: After working hours, when energy drains out of the area

When most people hear the word "London," this is the area they immediately picture: the Houses of Parliament, the wash of the Thames, the gong of Big Ben, the humble facade of Number 10 Downing Street, and the imperial government buildings of Whitehall. Kings and queens, prime ministers and executioners, scoundrels and assassins—this is where they converged to shape a millennium of world events, at the command center for England and the British Empire. History fans, lace up.

---

❶ Westminster Tube Station

The best train to take here is the Jubilee Line, which was added at great expense in 1999. The station's concrete-grey, 36m-deep (118-ft.) cavern, ascended by escalators from the Jubilee's platforms, is one of the city's finest new spaces, providing a modern-day analog to the majestic space of Westminster Abbey nearby. Portcullis House, where many MPs (Members of Parliament) keep offices, is overhead.

Find your way to the Westminster Underground station, Exit 1, and walk outside.

❷ Victoria Embankment at Westminster Bridge

Once you're outside, you'll see the River Thames in front of you. If you stood here in 1858, in the midst of what came to be known as The Great Stink, you'd have choked on the fumes rising from the fetid effluvia floating in the river below. Until then, the city had no sewers to speak of—only pipes that dumped into the water. The solution was the Victoria Embankment, a daring engineering project, completed in 1870, that saved engineers from having to dig up the whole city. They simply built a new riverbank, laid sewers along it, paired that with new Underground railway tracks, and topped the unattractive additions with a garden and a new road. Destructive, but effective—how Victorian.

Today, the embankments' benches are raised to allow a good view of the water, the lampposts are rococo, and it's dotted with triumphant statuary like Boudicca in her bladed chariot, which you can also see from here. This tribal queen rose up against the Romans; she failed politically but succeeded aesthetically, becoming a potent symbol for English independence.

The bridge in front of you is the iron Westminster Bridge, from 1862, now the oldest bridge in the city. When the first one went up, in 1739, the builders had to contend with sabotage by river ferrymen, who didn't want to see their business wrecked. The final result wobbled anyway—like the Millennium Bridge in 2000—and made people nervous, prolonging the demise of the river ferry. The London Eye had its own tricky birth in 1999; it was constructed lying flat over the river, resting on pontoons, and then it was laboriously hoisted upright and into place. The mock-Baroque building across the river is County Hall—it looks old, but it only dates to the early 20th century, and was once the seat of the London government.

At the bridge's opposite landing, you can see my favorite sculpture in the city, the South Bank Lion. Weighing 14 tons, 3.6m (12 ft.) tall, and eager-eyed and floppy-pawed as a puppy, he was carved in 1837 by the Coade Stone Factory, which once stood behind him, where County Hall stands today. Made of a durable, synthetic ceramic stone formulated by a mother-daughter team, the lion stood proudly for over a century,

Walking Tour 1: Westminster, Whitehall & Trafalgar Square

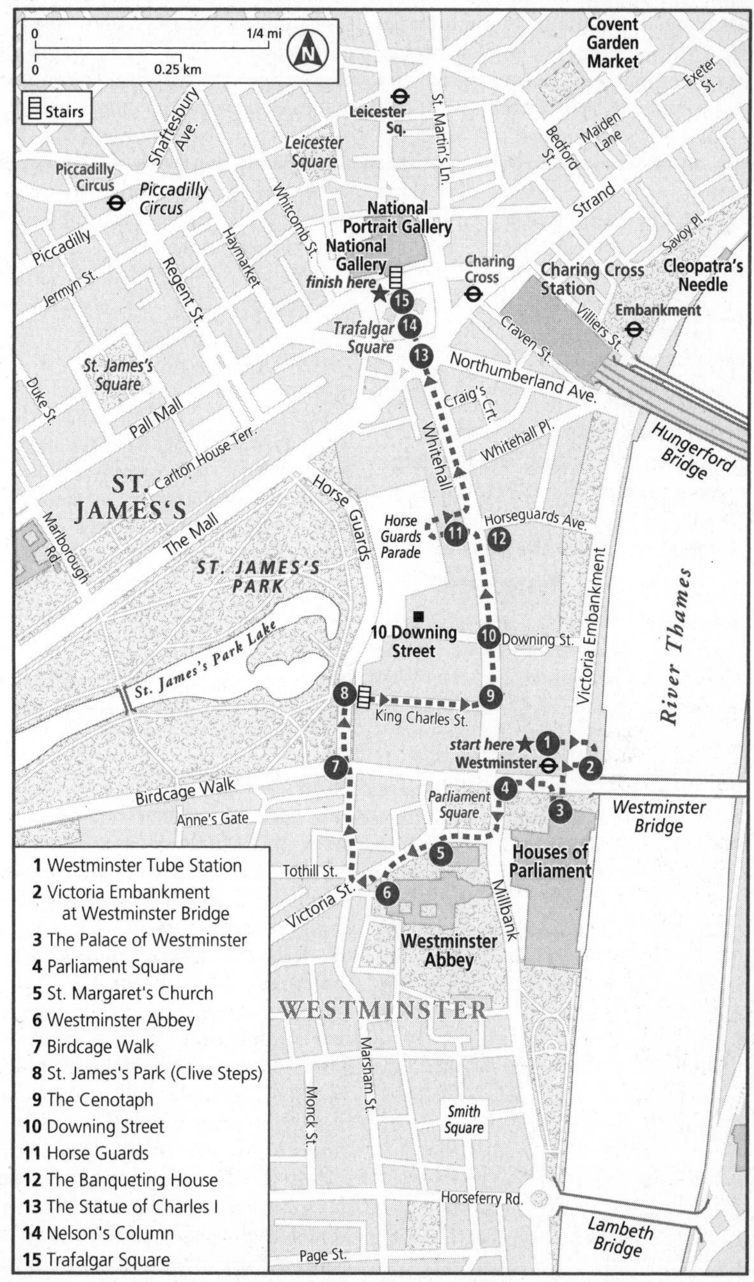

painted red, atop the Red Lion Brewery that was located to the left of the London Eye. Blitz bomb damage destroyed his roost, but at the request of King George VI, he was saved and placed just feet from his birthplace.

If you want, you can run up to the top of the stairs here. A cheap sausage cart is often here, feeding the tourist flocks. The view of Big Ben's Clock Tower is also particularly striking. Because of crowd-control fencing, it's not easy or advisable to cross the street to see the Houses of Parliament up close, but hang on—at the next stop, I'll safely have you nose-to-nose with it.

Go back into Westminster station, head down the corridor, and turn left before the set of four stairs. Leave the station via Exit 3, marked Houses of Parliament. Climb the stairs to

❸ The Palace of Westminster

You're now standing directly underneath the mighty Clock Tower of the Houses of Parliament. Except you aren't, technically. If you want to be precise, you're under St. Stephen's Tower (the name of Big Ben's perch) at the Palace of Westminster (the aged name of the government buildings here). This is as close as you can get to it, so have a good look at the assorted crowns, kings, and crests carved into the facade. These buildings may look like they're from the Gothic period, but in fact they date to 1859, when they rose from the ashes of the old Parliament House, destroyed by a nightmarish fire in 1834. Big Ben, the name of the largest of four bells inside (2.7m/9 ft. in diameter, 13 tons), was named for the portly commissioner of works who oversaw its installation, but there is a bigger bell in town: Great Paul at St. Paul's is 2 tons heavier. Each side of the Clock Tower's four faces is 6.9m (23 ft.) long. Since 1923, the very earliest days of wireless, BBC has broadcast the 16-note prelude (called "Westminster Quarters" and replicated in doorbells around the world) of Big Ben before its six o'clock news summaries using a microphone installed in the turrets. Thanks to a crack that developed in the 1860s, the bell is now slightly off from its original note: E above middle C, but you'd probably need perfect pitch to tell.

This plot of land has been used by royal residents since 1050, when Edward the Confessor built a palace here, away from the hubbub of the walled city. This is therefore one of the oldest sections of London outside The City. Kings ceased living at Westminster as of the reign of Henry VIII, when nearby Whitehall Palace became the main London home, followed by St. James's Palace and currently, Buckingham Palace—but since this land is still government owned, Westminster technically remains a palace.

Head away from the river along the side of the Houses of Parliament until you reach

❹ Parliament Square

The heavy metal bars on the spiked fence that distances you from this building are not there out of mere paranoia; as far back as the thwarted Gunpowder Plot of 1605, the Houses of Parliament have been a target for would-be revolutionaries. Prime Minister Spencer Perceval was fatally shot on the steps of the House of Commons by a former convict on May 11, 1812, and in the Blitz, the buildings were smashed on more than a dozen occasions, including one (May 10, 1941) that caused the near-total destruction of the House of Commons. Watch the security guards sweep the undercarriages of incoming cars with mirrors, and check out the formidable bollards that rise from the ground to prevent unauthorized vehicles from invading the government's seat.

Look across at Parliament Square; a group of protesters is always present, even though their government representatives usually hustle obliviously past them in bulletproofed sedans. Parliament is so embarrassed by the protests against the Iraq War (as of this writing, one man, Brian Haw, has appeared daily since 2001—look for a man in a bucket fishing cap covered with slogan buttons, which the British call "badges") that it changed the free speech laws to require all citizens who wish to protest within a kilometer of Parliament to obtain permission from the police first. As it stands now, Haw is permitted to leave his camp as long as someone is on hand to watch the camp round the clock. The moment it's left unattended, the police will toss it all into a dumpster. Ironically, once the government tried to banish Haw's peaceful protests, free-speech supporters flocked to his side to assist him.

The section of the Houses that juts into the yards, behind the statue of Oliver Cromwell, is Westminster Hall, from 1097, one of the only survivors from the 1834 fire. Charles I, Sir Thomas More, and Guy Fawkes were all condemned to death in the Hall.

Turn left and walk in front of the Houses of Parliament. Use the first crosswalk to your right, heading toward the church. Once at the far side of the church, enter the gate to see the front of

5 St. Margaret's Church

The little side church by Westminster Abbey (p. 140), the one with the four sundials on its tower, is the Church of Saint Margaret, dating to the early 1500s and much changed over the years. Sir Walter Raleigh, who was executed outside the Palace of Westminster, is buried inside, and both the poet Milton and Winston Churchill married their wives here.

You can see the statues of Parliament Square better from here. Probably the most famous one is that of American president Abraham Lincoln, at the western end; it's a copy of one in Chicago by Augustus Saint-Gaudens. The statue of Winston Churchill received a temporary Mohawk made of grassy turf during the anticapitalist protests of 2000. This square, it seems, has always been a home for well-intentioned screw-ups: In 1868, the world's first traffic light was erected here. Gas powered, it blew up.

Follow the footpath to the front of

6 Westminster Abbey

The lawn beside the abbey—yes, the one you just walked across—is in fact a disused graveyard. In a city this old, you simply can't avoid treading on the final resting places of forgotten people. There are an unknown number of plague pits scattered through the city, into which thousands of victims were hastily and unceremoniously dumped to avoid the spread of disease, and several city parks likely had the germ of their beginnings, so to speak, as potter's fields—group graves for paupers.

Although most of the abbey is in the Early English style, the stern western towers above you now were the 18th-century work of Nicholas Hawksmoor, a protégé of Christopher Wren. Hawksmoor's designs are famous for emphasizing the forbidding, angry side of God. Some critics accuse him of using architecture to frighten people into piety. If you're interested, there's a gift shop at the front of the Abbey that you can enter from here, but most of the time the people who use this main entrance in an official capacity do so in either a crown or a coffin. The column in front of the abbey is a war memorial for Westminster School students who perished in the Crimean War—their loss was deeply felt at the time but, sadly, is now mostly forgotten. If you peer down Broad Sanctuary, which becomes Victoria Street, you can see the Italianate tower of Westminster Cathedral, the primary Catholic cathedral of England.

Cross the street to your right (Broad Sanctuary), and cross again at the next zebra crossing. You should be a block west of Parliament Square on Storey's Gate now. Walk straight for about 3 minutes until you find yourself at the corner of St. James's Park. You're at

7 Birdcage Walk

You've just walked past a variety of European Union offices; the proximity to the Houses of Parliament has attracted paper-pushers to take up tenancy around here for centuries. The military has a presence here, too. The road that heads to the left is Birdcage Walk, which leads to the front of Buckingham Palace. Halfway down, you'll find the Wellington Barracks, the headquarters of the Guards Division, where a battalion of one of the Queen's five regiments of foot guards (Grenadier, Coldstream, Scots, Irish, and Welsh) bunks down. There's also a small, curio-packed Guards Museum (☎ 020/7414-3271; 10am–4pm, £3) on the grounds, where you learn that their tall "busby" helmets are made of Canadian brown bearskin. Who knew?

Storey's Gate, which you just walked, was named for the keeper of Charles II's aviary. Birdcage Walk, the street you have now encountered, was named after a royal aviary that was in St. James's Park; until 1928, only the Hereditary Royal Falconer was permitted to drive on Birdcage Walk. The park continues its tradition of hosting bird menageries; the pond is a haven for ducks and geese, and a small flock of pelicans has been in residence since the 1600s. If you do detour down there, just come back to this spot to resume your tour.

Cross the street and walk one block, passing the Treasury Building on your right, until you reach Clive Steps at King Charles Street on the right. Peek into

8 St. James's Park

See if you can spot the lake in the park. The body of water was originally a formal canal belonging to St. James's Palace, the official royal residence from the burning of Whitehall in 1698 to the time Victoria moved into Buckingham Palace in 1837. The old canal was prim and straight in the French style and outfitted with gondolas, a gift of the Doge of Venice. In winter, Samuel Pepys wrote in the 1600s, it would freeze over, and people would frolic upon it using skates made of bone. It was later sculpted into something calculated to appear more random and thus more English. St. James's Palace, which is not open to the public (except for Clarence House, in summers, p. 164), is located on the north (far) side of the park. St. James's Park is essentially the front yard of the palace, and you're standing at its back gate. You might be able to make out a rustic-looking shack just inside the park. That's Duck Island Cottage, built in 1840 as a dwelling for the bird keeper. Not shabby for a servant's quarters.

You'd think that if London were under attack from flying bombers that you'd be much safer if you were a little farther from the Houses of Parliament. Yet in the basement of the sturdy 1907 Treasury Building, Britain's leaders orchestrated their country's "finest hour." Unbeknownst to the world, it was the hideout of Winston Churchill and his cabinet. Famously, but hardly wisely, that daredevil Churchill once went out onto the roof of the building so he could watch one of Goering's air raids slam the city. The cellar, preserved down to its typing pool and pushpins, is now the Cabinet War Rooms, an evocative tourist attraction and a superlative museum paying homage to the bulldoggy prime minister (p. 155).

The imposing building to the left of Clive Steps is the Foreign Office, an important civil office. So who is Robert Clive, the cutlass-wielding subject of this statue on the steps? He was the general who helped the East India Company conquer India and Bengal, partly through a series of underhanded bribes, thus delivering the region into the control of the British Empire for nearly 2 centuries. Don't be too hard on him; the opium-addicted fellow committed suicide by stabbing himself with a penknife.

Walk down King Charles Street and through the arches at the end. You should now be on Parliament Street. Look left, into the center of it. The somber stone column in the traffic island is

❾ The Cenotaph

The Cenotaph (from the Greek words for "empty" and "tomb") is a simple but elegiac memorial to those killed in the two World Wars. A 1919 plaster parade prop that was made permanent in stone by Edwin Lutyens the next year, it was executed with inconceivable restraint when you consider that nearly a million British subjects died in the Great War alone. Its inscription to the "Glorious Dead," coined by Rudyard Kipling, is repeated on other memorials in Commonwealth nations; the Cenotaphs in Auckland, New Zealand, and in London, Canada, are replicas. Uniformed servicemen and -women will always salute it as they pass, and on the Sunday closest to November 11, Britain's Remembrance Day, the sovereign lays the first wreath while other members of the Royal Family observe from the balcony of the Foreign Office. You may see flowers around it, or possibly silk poppies (red flowers with black centers), the national symbol of remembrance.

Walk left up Parliament Street, which soon is renamed Whitehall. In about 30m (98 ft.) on the left, you will reach a black fence with glass lanterns. Stop there and look inside the gates. This is

❿ Downing Street

On the right, by the tree and tough to make out, is Number 10, the official home of the prime minister. It's famous for its lion's head knocker—although to be frank, if you have to knock, you won't be welcome. You used to be able to walk around in there, but Margaret Thatcher had many enemies and sealed the street, so you'll have to make do with peering down the lane. Such security was a long time coming. In 1842, a lunatic shot and killed the secretary to the prime minister, mistaking him for the big man; and in 1912, suffragette Emmeline Pankhurst and friends pelted the house with stones, breaking four windows, in one of many acts of civil disobedience in the fight for voting rights for women. If policemen are preventing you from even approaching the gates, then the prime minister is probably on the move. I've stood on the sidewalks of Whitehall, waiting to be permitted to pass, when suddenly the black gates have burst open, spewed forth an armada of police cars, and the prime minister's Jaguar has blasted onto Whitehall and sped toward the Houses of Parliament as if he'd just robbed a bank.

The lane was laid out by George Downing, the second man to graduate from Harvard University in America and by all accounts a shady individual, a turncoat, and a slumlord. He's one of history's great scoundrels; his underhanded dealings resulted in Dutch-held Manhattan being swiped by the British and the slave trade multiplying in the Colonies. Strange that the most important street in British politics should bear his name.

Downing built Number 10 (then, Number 5) as part of a row of terraced houses in the late 1600s, fully intending for it to fall apart after a few years (instead of actually laying bricks, he just painted on lines with mortar). Yet George II had his eye on the house, and he kicked out a man named Mr. Chicken—further information about him, tantalizingly, is lost to the mists of time—to give it as a gift to the first prime minister, Robert Walpole, in 1730. Instead of taking it as graft, as Downing might have done, Walpole insisted that the house be used by future First Lords of the Treasury, his official capacity. He also connected it to a grand home behind it on Horse Guards, now nicknamed The House at the Back—so now, this deceptive Georgian facade actually conceals 160 rooms. Number 10 is also connected with numbers 11 and 12, and it's even linked to Buckingham Palace and Q-Whitehall, a sprawling war bunker, by long underground tunnels. Many prime ministers elected to live in their own homes, using Number 10 for meetings, but not William Pitt, who moved in upon becoming prime minister at the virtually pubescent age of 24 in 1783. He lived here for more than 20 years, longer than any other prime minister, until his death at 46. Whitehall became a slum in the mid-1800s, and the house fell out of fashion, but then it served as the nerve center for the two World Wars and became indispensable to the British spirit. You can see the original front door, now replaced by a stronger one, on display at the Churchill Museum at the Cabinet War Rooms (p. 155), two stops back.

A little up Whitehall from Downing Street, look for the bronze monument to "The Women of World War II," which depicts no women, but rather their uniforms and hats, which hang on pegs as if they've been put away after a job well done. The implication of this 6.6m-tall (22-ft.) tableau is, of course, that the women went back to the kitchen after briefly filling a more robust societal role. This sly bit of statuary-as-commentary was unveiled by the Queen in 2005. Some 80% of the cost of the memorial was raised by a Baroness who won money on ITV's *Who Wants to Be a Millionaire?.*

Continue up Whitehall, past the monumental government buildings that line it. In about 60m (200 ft.), you will reach another black gate broken by two stone guardhouses. Head inside the yard to view

11 Horse Guards

Built in the Palladian style between 1750 and 1758 on a former jousting field of Whitehall Palace, the Horse Guards is the official (but little-used) entrance to the grounds of St. James's Palace and Buckingham Palace. Two mounted cavalry troops are posted in the guardhouses every day from 10am to 4pm, and they're changed hourly. At 11am daily and 10am Sundays, the guard on duty is relieved by a dozen men who march in from The Mall behind, accompanied (when the Queen is in town) by a trumpeter, a standard bearer, and an officer. Don't make the same mistake of some feckless tourists and try to force the guards to crack up at your shenanigans. It makes you look silly and rude—and they still won't react.

If you think the clock tower arch looks small, you're right. Its designer made it that way so that its proportions would match the rest of the building. You can walk through the clock tower arch (but you can't drive through—only members of the Royal Family can do that) to reach the graveled Horse Guards Parade, the city's largest non-park gathering space. The Parade was once a segment of the canal that's now the lake in St. James's Park, but it was filled in, providing an excellent terrain for state rituals such as Trooping the Colour.

Come back out of the yard onto Whitehall. Across the street you'll see

⓬ The Banqueting House

Built by Inigo Jones, this is not a home but it is the last remaining portion of the great Whitehall Palace. One past director of the Museum of London has called it "the most important and most unassuming building" on this street, and a "slice of genius." Inside is a bombastic ceiling by Rubens depicting the king as a god. That vainglorious posture, and the king's grabs for more power, led to the gory event that happened on this spot on January 30, 1649. If you were standing here then, you would have been in the crowd that watched King Charles I mount the scaffold (wearing two shirts so that he wouldn't shiver—he was no true god, after all), place his head on the block, and be decapitated, handing the reins of the country to a military dictatorship led by Oliver Cromwell. When the executioner held the head aloft, one witness said there was a queasy silence, followed by "such a groan by the thousands then present, as I never heard before and I desire I may never hear again." Charles I was buried privately at Windsor, not at Westminster Abbey, because his deposers (who wanted to rule the country without kings) didn't care to encourage a public scene that could lead to an uprising. (Sounds a little like Brian Haw's troubles are nothing new.) If you want to see what poor Charles looked like, hang on for the next stop. The regicide was somewhat for naught; by 1660, the country grew weary of its leadership and Charles I's son, the hedonistic spendthrift Charles II, was back on daddy's throne. In revenge, the second Charles chose the Banqueting House as the site for his restoration party, and then had the nerve to show up late. England was royal again, and how.

Turn left up Whitehall. As you go, look right as you pass Whitehall Place, and you'll catch a glimpse of the dome of St. Paul's Cathedral.

Take a break

The oldest part of the **Silver Cross** (25-33 Whitehall), the epitome of an everyday pub, has operated as an inn (pub) since 1674. It was recently lavished with a giant expansion, so you shouldn't have trouble finding a seat. The Cross attracts government secretaries and clerks (called "civil servants" round these parts) who nip in for a quick pint, plus a hefty share of tourists from around the world. Find it on the corner of Craig's Court, named for the family that owned the establishment for 135 years.

When you reach the square, cross the street twice so that you're on the oval traffic island, standing under

⓭ The Statue of Charles I

That this bronze statue stands here is a miracle. It's of Charles I, pre-headectomy, and is a precious Carolinian original from 1633. When the king was beheaded, the Royal Family was deposed (permanently, so most people thought) and all their trappings were melted down and broken up for profit. The owner of this statue was commanded to destroy it, but he was clever enough to bury it instead. After the Restoration, it was dug up and placed here in about 1675. That was even before Trafalgar Square existed (the zone was, as an equestrian statue might suggest, used as stables). Charles wasn't a very tall man, and saddling him on a horse goes some way toward making the luckless fellow seem imposing. Someone stole his first sword in 1867, and he went into hiding again during The Blitz, but otherwise, this is one of the oldest things in this part of London that remains in its original place. Its pedestal, unloved and weathered, could use some restoration itself.

This is a good spot, free of traffic and obstructions, to survey your surroundings and take some photos. Look back down Whitehall, from where you just came, and you'll see Big Ben's tower. To the right, the vista through Admiralty Arch concludes in the distance with the grand Victoria Memorial at Buckingham Palace. Important buildings for two Commonwealth nations stand astride Trafalgar Square: Canada House to the left (west) and South Africa House to the right (east; its country's name is inscribed in Afrikaans as Suid-Afrika).

Cross again so that you're on the south side of

14 Nelson's Column & Trafalgar Square

Not long after Charles's statue lost its sword, lightning struck Lord Nelson, who is exposed at the top of his column, and damaged his left arm. The city finally got around to eliminating the bronze bands that held him together in 2006, using the same Craigleith sandstone with which he was constructed in 1843. Since the quarry had closed in the 1940s, craftsmen had to find stone left over from the restoration of a school in Edinburgh. During the work, surveying revealed that the monument is actually 4.8m (16 ft.) shorter than guidebooks have been claiming—it's 51m (167 ft.), not 56m (184 ft.), from the street to the crown of his hat. The man himself is 32m (105 ft.) tall. Why is Nelson so revered? The Admiral sacrificed his life in 1805 to defeat Napoleon Bonaparte's naval aspirations, which secured Britain's dominance over the oceans—and thus pumped untold wealth into London. The column's base is lined with four bronze reliefs that were said to be cast using metal from French cannon captured at the battle that each one depicts. All is guarded by four reclining lions (1867), which serve as mascots of the square.

In the southeast corner of the square, you'll see a stone booth big enough for a single person; that's the city's smallest police station, built in 1926. Once a closet for a phone that was used to summon backup, now it's used mostly to store chemicals for the fountains.

Lutyens, who did the Cenotaph, also designed the two fountains (from 1845 originals), which were ostensibly for beautification but also prevented mobs from gathering in dangerous numbers. Trafalgar Square has long been the setting for demonstrations that turned from protest to unrest, such as infamous riots over poll taxes and unemployment. The English gather here for happy things, too, as they did for the announcement of V-E Day (May 8, 1945), and as they still do for free summer performances.

You may have heard about Trafalgar's Square's famous pigeons. So where are they? Banished for overactive excretion. Until the early 1990s, the square swarmed with them—the fluttering flock was estimated to peak at 35,000—and vendors made a living from selling bird feed to tourists. Eventually, the GLC, London's government, grew tired of shoveling streaky poo off the statues and decided to return the square to its original function as a great public space. They began feeding the pigeons themselves first thing in the morning, and then hired a team of six hawks, tended by a leather-gloved keeper, to patrol the square from 10am to 4pm. The flock, which now number as low as 400, quickly learned to chow down and then clear out for the day; anyone who feeds the birds is subject to a £500 fine.

Head to the other side of the fountains to

⓯ North Trafalgar Square

The GLC made a few other radical changes to the square in 2003, including closing the street to the north, which runs in front of the National Gallery (p. 145), to vehicular traffic. That gave the square a new elevated terrace, from which the views down Whitehall are sublime, particularly at night when landmarks are picked out by spotlights. The GLC also cut a new set of stairs to the Gallery—before then, the square's north side was a grim wall—and beneath the terrace it added the cheap Café on the Square. Suddenly, people really did start hanging out here, and not just to complain.

Most of the statues dotting the square are of forgotten military and noble men; James II is finely crafted, but he looks ridiculous in those Roman robes. The northwestern plinth of Trafalgar Square was designed for an equestrian statue of its own, but money ran out and it stood empty from 1841. More than 150 years later, the naked spot was named The Fourth Plinth (www.fourthplinth.co.uk) and filled by works commissioned from various artists. Sculptures show for 18 months at a time, and so far they've gotten the city talking. Rachel Whiteread mounted a mirror image of the plinth atop itself in luminous plastic. Marc Quinn's marble *Alison Lapper Pregnant* depicted a snow-white, nude woman born with limb deformities and heavy with child. Coming next are Antony Gormley's platter-like necklace for the plinth and Yinka Shonibare's replica of Nelson's ship, the HMS *Victory,* inside a giant glass bottle.

Along the north terrace, by the Café on the Square, look for the Imperial Standards of Length, which were set into the wall in 1876 and moved in 2003 when the central stairs were installed. They are the literal yardsticks against which all other British yardsticks are measured, showing inches, feet, and yards, plus mostly obsolete measures such as links, chains, perches, and poles.

And now, you can reward yourself with a visit to the loo, left of the stairs, and a spot of tea in the cafe. Or, if you crave some more substantial victuals, head over to the street east of the square to St. Martin-in-the-Fields church, finished in 1724. Its combination of spire and classical portico were controversial at the time, but today, it pleases people of all persuasions with its excellent Café in the Crypt (p. 157).

Walking Tour 2: St. Paul's & Southwark

Start: St. Paul's Tube station
Finish: The George Inn, near London Bridge Tube station
Time: Two hours, not including restaurant breaks or attractions
Best times: Weekend days in good weather, when the area is abuzz; Borough Market is most vital on Thursday to Saturdays
Worst times: After dark, when some of the narrow, medieval streets are too dark to see well

It was the best of advertisements, it was the worst of advertisements. Charles Dickens' novels, largely social protests wearing the cloak of entertainment, made readers feel like they had traveled to London when they never left their own armchairs. Trouble is, the city that Dickens has primed visitors to expect—the foggy, coal-smudged metropolis teeming with pickpockets and virtuous orphans—is nowhere to be found. Have the librarians of the world fallen victims to one of the world's most successful smear campaigns? Not at all. Partly thanks to Dickens' work, London simply changed. On this tour, you'll explore what's left of its darker side—from the libertine London of Shakespeare's day to the desperate one Dickens sought to solve with his pen. Along the way, you'll enjoy gourmet food, cutting-edge design, and a beer by the Thames, which conceals a body count of its own.

1 St. Paul's Tube Station

If you just took the Central Line here, you rode what was once called the Central Railway. In the first 75 years of the Underground, train lines were independently owned, and separate tickets were required each time a passenger changed trains. Fares were cumbersome, calculated according to the distance traveled and the class of carriage chosen. When the Central Railway held its grand opening in 1900, in the presence of American wit Mark Twain (who lived in London at the time), it soared above its competitors by dint of several innovations, the most important of which was that anyone could ride as far as they wanted on a flat fare. The so-called "Twopenny Tube," which had one class of carriage like today's Tube trains, was a sensation. Gilbert and Sullivan, swept along, amended a line in their operetta *Patience* from a reference to the threepenny bus to "the very delectable, highly respectable Twopenny Tube." The Central Railway helped democratize public transit and accelerated expansion into the suburbs—even if authorities eventually went back to the old format of charging passengers by distance, not by ride. The St. Paul's station opened on July 30, 1900, as Post Office station—the city's main Post Office was then located across the street on St. Martins-le-Grand (hence the name of Postman's Park, p. 221, just north).

Exit the St. Paul's Underground station and turn left, towards

2 Panyer Alley

Panyer Alley, where you're standing, was named for the basketmakers, or panyers, who once traded here. Look for a plaque on the wall depicting a child sitting on a basket. This plaque,

Walking Tour 2: St. Paul's & Southwark

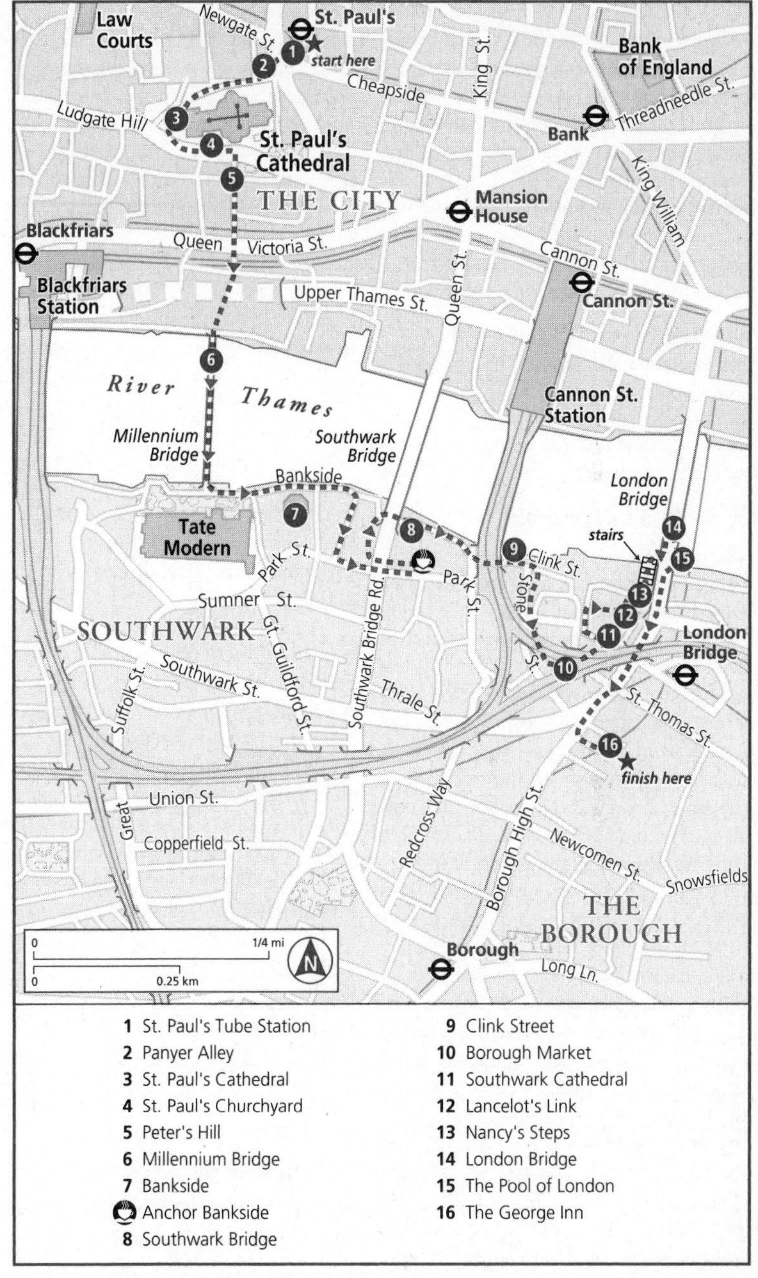

the so-called Panyer Stone, is dated "August the 27, 1688," and reads, "When you have sought / the citty round / yet still this is / the highest ground." The artists behind this stone surely knew that Ludgate is not the highest point in The City; that's Cornhill, which is about 30cm (12 in.) higher. But the sign has been here so long that it would quite literally be a crime to take it down.

Head left, toward St. Paul's Cathedral, and make a right through the pedestrian alley, Paternoster Row, to Paternoster Square. Go through the ornate arch at the left and veer right to the front of

3 St. Paul's Cathedral

The area you've just walked through, Paternoster Row, ranks among the most sacred in London. There have been major houses of worship on the plot of St. Paul's as far back as 604, and for centuries, these narrow surrounding streets have teemed with ecclesiastical scribes and clergy, as well as with untold hordes of desperate supplicants desperate for a handout from the merciful church. By the 1800s, Paternoster Row was known as the center of literary London, first for its publishers—who replaced the scribes—and later for its book market. Yet what you'll see today is an indistinct set of office buildings staffed with financial workers. Even its 23m-tall (75-ft.) column was created only a few years ago to appear older than it is. Why would planners permit the wholesale demolition of such a rich heritage? They didn't. This was Ground Zero of the Blitz. The area was annihilated during bombing raids in 1940. The Germans, recognizing that the destruction of St. Paul's would demoralize a nation that held it as a totem, focused their power on the church, and the spillover devastated everything around it. Every able-bodied firefighter was called to help preserve the cathedral, saving it at the expense of just about everything else.

The stone archway that you passed through, however, is a true antique, although it didn't originally stand here. It's Temple Gate, one of eight ancient gateways to The City of London, which stood where Strand becomes Fleet Street from 1672. It was dismantled in 1878 and was destined for a dump somewhere when a visionary stepped in and brought the stones home. After spending more than a century in the hinterland of his family's Hertfordshire estate, the gate, possibly designed by Christopher Wren, was restored and re-erected here in November 2004. The seven other gates, including Aldgate and Moorgate, were all lost more than 200 years ago.

A statue of Queen Anne, who ruled England when St. Paul's was completed, looks down Ludgate Hill, the street that approaches the Cathedral from the west. In attendance are ladies symbolizing England, France, Ireland, and North America, which she considered her subjects. The statue is an 1886 copy of the 1712 original, which (like Temple Gate once did) now resides, in scabby condition, on a country estate.

Herbert Mason's iconic photograph of St. Paul's dome, snapped during the mighty conflagration that engulfed London after air raids on December 29th and 30th, 1940, was taken from Ludgate Hill. Next time you see that picture, note that it's lit entirely by firelight.

Skirt the right side of the cathedral along the busy street called

4 St. Paul's Churchyard

As they pass the southern yard of St. Paul's, most people notice the agonized statue of Saint Thomas Becket in mid-assassination, designed in 1973 by Edward Bainbridge Copal. But few have a look at the remains of the low stone walls that once encircled the cathedral, or of the metal lumps left behind when the iron fence posts were clipped off. At the end of the building of St. Paul's, Wren complained bitterly to Queen Anne that the construction of the fence around the churchyard was being executed without his consultation, and that its size was out of proportion with his design. Weary of his involvement, she paid him his fee, criticized his work, and sent him on his way. The fence stayed—for a century or two, anyway.

At the crossing, go over the street. Now's a good time to duck into The City of London Information Centre (Mon–Sat 9:30am–5:30pm, Sun 10am–4pm), located inside the wing-roofed building, and stock up on free tourist brochures and timetables.

If you don't need information, turn left. If you do use the information office, when you come out again, turn right. After the patch of grass, turn right again. You should be able to see down Peter's Hill all the way to a white pedestrian bridge over the river. Stroll down

5 Peter's Hill

On the right is the Firefighters National Memorial, which depicts a young man gesturing wildly toward St. Paul's as two others grapple desperately with a hose. It's impossible to exaggerate the devastation caused by the Blitz, both in property and in lives. The superheated firestorms created damage greater in area than those of the Great Fire of 1666. More than 20,000 people were killed, and 1,400,000 left homeless. The names of some 1,000 victims, all volunteer firefighters defeated by the wild blaze and collapsing buildings, are inscribed on the octagonal base. Winston Churchill dubbed this monument "The Heroes with Grimy Faces." For their families, the survival of St. Paul's Cathedral amidst utter devastation remains a testament to their sacrifice. Continue walking straight. After you cross Queen Victoria Street, the glassy building on the left, erected in 2004, is the Salvation Army, which has commanded its members across the world from this spot since 1881. If you're hungry, there's a cheap public cafe in the basement during business hours. Keep going toward the river.

Go onto the

6 Millennium Bridge

You're now on the steel Millennium Bridge, the central city's first new crossing over the Thames since the Tower Bridge in 1894. Its design, which features side-located suspension cables that sag about six times shallower than a conventional suspension bridge's supports do, was a little too advanced for its own good. When it opened, in 2000, and the structure admitted its first pedestrians, it was discovered that their shifting weight caused the bridge to sway. Alarmed pedestrians had to grasp the side rails for support. Engineers closed the 325m (1066-ft.) span, poured in another £5.2 million to solve the issue, and reopened it in 2002. Londoners initially derided it as "The Wobbly Bridge," one of several turn-of-the-century commemorative boondoggles, although they love it now because it has transformed accessibility to the river's southern bank. It's still not perfect—it's plagued by joggers with little regard for idle strollers—but crossing the river here, in view of many of the city's landmarks, young and old, makes for some stirring photos.

Straight across the bridge is the monumental Tate Modern museum

(p. 146), signaled by its factory-like "campanile" smokestack, which from 1952 to 1981 belched exhaust from the Bankside Power Station. Energy has been a fundamental part of the district's character for generations. The Tate's power station replaced an earlier one that dusted everything near it with a coating of soot, and that plant, too, supplanted a foul gasworks that once fed gas to much of the city. Before that, the district was the domain of a legion of coal merchants who shuttled their filthy wares around town in shallow boats. These "lightermen" worked from docks that lined the entire southern shore, where land was cheaper than it was in The City on the northern side. In a way, the building you see before you—only recently transformed into a gallery—is a direct descendant of the way of life that prevailed on the bank back in the 1700s.

How deep is the Thames? The river fluctuates greatly with the tides (which makes it dangerous for swimming), but depending on when you measure around here, it's generally 8.9m (29 ft.) deep at its highest tide and 1.8m (6 ft.) at low tide. The Thames' moodiness is the main reason Southwark, the side of the river where the Tate Modern sits, was for many centuries not even considered to be worth annexing into the city. Until medieval times, the low-lying southern bank was flood-prone and boggy and was instead thought of as an independent borough in Surrey, the county south of London. Londoners made use of the waterlogged land by turning it into gardens, fish farms (the Pike Garden, or Pye Garden, stood pretty much in front of you around the Tate's eastern flank), and romantic nooks you could sneak off to with a lover, but it wasn't until the latter part of the 1700s that people figured out how to drain the water adequately enough to settle the area fully. Simply put, Southwark was where you took a ferry to have a good time. Theaters, bear-baiting pits, brothels, betting halls, and other impure diversions were located there, out of the city's jurisdiction—that is, until the Puritans quashed the fun in 1642, starting the area's next chapter as an industrial center.

Before you completely cross the river, turn back for a stupendous view of St. Paul's dome symmetrically rising from the center of the bridge.

Once you're on the opposite bank, with the river in front of you, turn right. Stand midway between the cluster of town houses and the building with the thatched roof. The path you're on is

7 Bankside

You're now walking along my favorite promenade in the city. It actually continues west, past the Tate Modern, to the London Eye and the Houses of Parliament. When Hugh Grant told Andie MacDowell he loved her by way of David Cassidy in *Four Weddings and a Funeral,* he did it farther along this walkway by the National Film Theatre. On a summer's evening, there's no better place to stroll, people-watch, and appreciate the sweep of the city. I've had many bouts of gratitude here.

As late as the 1960s, the path you're on, which at this place is called Bankside, was a vehicular street bearing two-way traffic, as it had been since the 1600s. Each building on the street owned rights to the docks or water-stairs on the river opposite it, so their tenants were usually people who needed access to the water, such as ferrymen or sailors. The four-story, white house at the left of the blind Cardinal Cap Alley, number 49, was one of them. The house was built around 1710 on the foundations of a pub, the Cardinal's Cap, which itself went up in

1547 to entertain the people who came to Southwark to carouse. Number 49 was home to successive generations of coal merchants, and in the 1930s to the actress Anna Lee (Lila on the U.S. soap *General Hospital*), but not, as the plaque on its front purports, to Sir Christopher Wren as he built St. Paul's. Wren did live nearby, but in a building that was torn down when the power station needed land—this plaque, which hung on that vanished home, was appropriated by a D.I.Y. revisionist in the mid–20th century. Number 49 is just one of countless houses that once lined the river for an unbroken mile along this bank, but it's now one of the last three or four left standing, and it's the only one that has received its own biography, *The House by the Thames* by Gillian Tindall, which recounts the structure's 300-year saga.

To the left of that small cluster of homes, which are stragglers from another era, is the open-air Shakespeare's Globe theater, which made a premature exit in its own era, only to be rebuilt in ours. The circular Globe's stage is even at the same compass point as the 1599 original's. You can learn how it was reconstructed on one of its excellent tours (p. 187).

Southwark may be famous for Shakespeare, but interestingly, the city's theatrical life was only centered here from about 1587 to 1642, while it was illegal to operate a theater in The City proper. Once the laws relaxed, the entertainment venues moved back into town, where they've been ever since.

Southwark was the Elizabethan version of a multiplex, where you could find any amusement to suit you, and the biggest blockbuster was bear-baiting—several bear-baiting arenas were in the area. Even King Henry VIII and Elizabeth I were huge fans; he had a bear pit installed at Whitehall Palace, and she barred Parliament from banning the pursuit on Sundays. One short block past the Globe, between the Pizza Express and The Real Greek restaurants, is a lane called Bear Gardens. Three quarters of the way down this atmospheric, crumbling alley of 19th-century warehouses, you'll find a small courtyard where the Globe Education Centre is today. That's the former location of the Davies Amphitheatre, one of the most popular bear pits, where masses came to enjoy the spectacle of vicious dogs let loose upon tethered bears. Samuel Pepys wrote in his diary in 1666 of attending one such slaughter where he "saw some good sport of the bull's tossing the dogs—one into the very boxes. But it is a very rude and nasty pleasure." Within a month, the north bank of London had burned to the ground in the Great Fire, but Southwark, buffered by the river, was spared that one. (It suffered its own fire 10 years later.)

Under a modern office building in the next street, Rose Alley, lie the foundations of another theater known to have premiered plays by Shakespeare, the Rose. It lasted from 1587 to about 1606. The Swan stood nearby, too, although we may never know exactly where. Ironically, this missing theater gave modern architects their biggest clues about what Elizabethan theaters looked like—they studied sketches made of it by a Dutch tourist in 1596.

Historians think they know where the original Globe stood, and the site, which is now partly covered by protected Georgian homes and Southwark Bridge Road, is marked by a semicircular set of black paving stones. If you'd like to see it, head down Bear Gardens one block to Park Street, turn left and go under the bridge, and just after it, past the buildings on the right, you'll find the arc of stones. Not very suggestive, is it?

In 1949, it was even drearier. It lay behind the locked gate of the decrepit Anchor Brewery, and when American actor Sam Wanamaker (father of Zoë, who played Madam Hooch in the Harry Potter movies) dropped by to pay pilgrimage to the Bard, the indignity of the meager plaque (still there) so enraged him that he resolved to campaign to rebuild the Globe as a living home for England's great theatrical tradition. Which is what came to pass, albeit 4 years after his 1993 death.

Retrace your steps to the riverside. On the water at Bear Gardens, look for a stone seat embedded in the wall of Riverside House. It's said to be the last remaining Wherryman's Seat, dozens of which once lined the Thames. Boatmen, the taxi drivers of their day, would lounge in these perches—this one is 15th century—until someone came along and hired them for a trip across the water. Ferrymen would also court business by shouting destinations to crowds of theatergoers after their plays: "Eastward ho!" or "Westward ho!"

Continue along the river, keeping it to your left. You'll go through a pedestrian tunnel under

8 Southwark Bridge

On the walls of the tunnel, you'll see illustrations of skaters and revelers at the bygone "Frost Fairs" that, starting in 1564, were regularly held on the icy Thames. No matter how many winters you spend in London, you'll almost never see the Thames freeze over. But back then, they had the London Bridge, a few hundred yards downstream. Its 19 arches were so narrow, and its supports so thick, that the river's flow became sluggish, allowing water (and the outhouse filth that churned within it) to freeze. By contrast, during outgoing tides the rush of water through its spans was so fierce that boats frequently capsized, and passengers (few of whom knew how to swim in those days) often drowned. When the bridge was dismantled in 1814, the Frost Fairs melted into history.

Walk past the two modern buildings and take a look underneath Southwark Bridge where it meets the shore. You can still discern the remains of some water-stairs, dating to before the construction of the first bridge here in 1819. These ghostly stairs were once used to convey people and goods to and from the ferries that zipped around the river at all hours. The shoreline once supported dozens of these landings, but gradually, drainage works and fortification of the embankment all but erased most of them. This bridge is the second, dating to 1912, when its central 72m (236-ft.) span was the largest ever attempted in cast iron. The drab hunk of a building to your right is the headquarters of the *Financial Times,* the internationally distributed, orange-hued newspaper nicknamed the *FT.*

Take a break

If you need a breather, few pubs in the city are more idyllic than the **Anchor** (p. 129), which is located here, just before Bankside meets the railway viaduct coming over the river from Cannon Street station. The riverside patio is open in good weather; otherwise, the interior of the pub is charming. This pub was once controlled, as nearly all pubs once were, by a brewery; in this case, it was Barclay Perkins, located just behind it from 1790 until about 1980. Even before brewery ownership, it was a Bankside fixture; in 1666, Samuel Pepys watched the Great Fire rage from here before coming to his senses and hurrying across the river to rescue his possessions from his home in Seething Lane, near the Tower of London.

The pub was declared a slum and nearly cleared after World War II, but preservationists rightly clamored against the move, and it was saved. It has since been respectfully rehabilitated, and it now presents much the same character as it did many years ago, give or take the iPod-rigged bikers who relax here on a summer's day.

After the Anchor, the path jogs inland. Take the first left onto

9 Clink Street

Pass under the railway arch. In a few moments, you've gone from Elizabethan Southwark (theaters, bear-baiting) to Georgian Southwark (coal merchants, breweries). Now you're enveloped by Victorian Southwark, a claustrophobic world teeming with fetid-smelling industry and river rats. You can almost hear the reverberations on this narrow wharfside street. You might even call the sensation Dickensian, and you wouldn't be wrong, since when the writer was 12 years old, his father was thrown into a debtor's prison very near where you're standing, off the Borough High Street.

Prisons were something of a cottage industry for the area; the Clink Street Prison stood here from 1127, when the Bishop of Winchester built it as a lockup for his Winchester Palace, until 1780, when the anti-Catholic Gordon riots saw the dismal hole destroyed. Although The Clink gave its name as slang to all prisons that came after it, no one knows for sure how it got the name itself—Flemish or Middle English words for latch are likely the origin. Suffice to say it was pretty awful. And so is the museum (p. 192) here that purports to tell its story.

In the 1800s, warehousing goods instead of people became this street's stock-in-trade. Look overhead, and you'll see the remains of a pedestrian skyway that once connected the building containing The Clink Museum with a building abutting the Thames; its I-beam was amputated. All around, you'll see hints of the street's past maritime uses, from wooden loft doors to cranes used to hoist crates into upper floors. Today, these spaces house media companies and architects. During the week, you'll see them in their fashionable clothes, staggering across the cobbles in their Italian shoes on their way to mid-afternoon cocktails.

The latter Bishops of Winchester were not nice guys. Henry II (1133–1189) gave them control of this neighborhood, and because it was outside of the jurisdiction of the city, they could pretty much get away with whatever they wanted to. Principally, they cultivated countless brothels and skimmed the profits for themselves—which is how Southwark got its rap as a den of vice. Anyone who annoyed them (heretics, troublemakers) wound up in the Clink, where no one was likely to find them again. Continue down Clink Street. Just before that beveled brick building on the right, you'll see all that's left of the Bishops' palace. This unique geometric rose window, dating to the 1300s when it lit the great hall, was hidden behind a wall until a warehouse fire exposed it again. The three doors below it originally led to kitchens. Double back to Stoney Street.

Turn down Stoney Street and walk under the railway arch. Just past it, on your left, you'll see

10 Borough Market

Stop at the frilly grey portico.

The mood of the neighborhood has changed drastically again. To your left, behind the portico, is Borough Market, a fantasy for the tongue (described in gastronomic detail on p. 281) and the oldest fruit and vegetable market in the city. A market has been held around here since A.D. 43, when Roman soldiers noted passing a market on their way to sack The City. More reliable records date it to 1014, when it served the denizens on the old London Bridge, the city's only river crossing, The market, which hopped around the neighborhood over the centuries, fed from the locus of all the main roads to London from Southern England and Europe, so its wares were the best and most exotic in the city. The cream-grey portico is not original to this place; it's the cast iron Flower Hall of Covent Garden, rescued when the Royal Opera House was renovated and moved here in 2003. If it seems to blend seamlessly with its surroundings, it's probably because it was made around the same time as the rest of the Borough Market structure (1859–60).

The Market still sells grocery staples, but it's best known as a font of gourmet supplies. London's most famous gourmands, including Jamie Oliver and Gordon Ramsay, are often seen milling about the stalls here. The shops across Stoney Street include some of the city's most celebrated coffee suppliers (Monmouth Coffee Company, p. 276) and bakers (Konditor & Cook, p. 275). Park Street, which runs into Stoney Street, looks as quaint as a movie-set version of old England; in fact, it was used in *Harry Potter and the Prisoner of Azkaban*. The Market itself has appeared in films including *Howard's End* and *Bridget Jones's Diary*.

Enter the market. Take your time to explore the 1.6-plus hectares (4-plus acres) of gated stalls and to read the whimsical signs like "Last Christmas, we made 2½ miles of chipolatas!" Astoundingly, this delectable scene is under threat from the advance of a commuter rail plan, Thameslink 2000, which would have part of this glorious area demolished. Railway suits have been lobbying to destroy chunks of the handsome glass-and-steel roof since 1987. Partly because Southwark was never seen as being worth as much as The City, railways have been given license to deface this area since their invention. In fact, the city's first railway, a 6.4km (4-mile) run to Greenwich, plowed its route .8km (half-mile) east of here in 1836. Even after tunneling technology improved, railway men thought nothing of slicing massive brick viaducts through thriving neighborhoods, cutting them off from each other and creating slums. On your tour, you have crossed under a number of railway viaducts built that way, and shortly, you'll see how narrowly one of England's most historic churches averted its own destruction.

Cross the next street and enter the brick arch marked Green Market. Head straight into the grounds of

⓫ Southwark Cathedral

(If for some reason the Green Market arch is closed, just turn left down Bedale Street (it's not marked) and follow it until you see a church appear on your right.)

Before you stands the oldest Gothic church in the city, and the oldest building in Southwark. You'll see its tower appear in nearly every old drawing of the city. In Roman times, it was the site of a villa. Its Christian chapter was begun by the daughter of a ferryman in the 7th century; it was rebuilt in the 850s and again 300 years later. There were once a monastery and a chapel in this yard, where office workers now lunch on gourmet items from Borough Market, but those came and went, too. By the early 1800s, Southwark was crawling with the poor, with factory workers, and with grubby rivermen—people the industrialists didn't have much use for. This place, which by then was limping along as a humble parish church called St. Saviour's, dissolved into dilapidation—it was even roofless for awhile—and we're lucky it wasn't removed completely, because in those days, progress, and not God, was king. The re-routing of London Bridge Road sheared away several small chapels, and in 1863, the railway forced its way alongside the yard—the filth and rumble of the early locomotives must have disturbed worshipers. But by 1905, its fortunes reversed when it was elevated to a cathedral, which now serves 2.5 million across southern London, and in 2000, it was given a lavish cleaning—so much of one that it's hard to discern the true age and sordid past of the place.

The cathedral's entrance is to the left. Go in, go straight across the sanctuary, through the glass doors opposite, up a short flight of stairs, and turn right to the end of the glass-roofed corridor, which traces the line of an alley that was called

⓬ Lancelot's Link

Nelson Mandela opened this building in 2001. Have a look at the display here, which preserves surprising discoveries made in this small area during a 1999 renovation. Look down into the well on the far right, and you'll see the original paving stones from the Roman road that cut through this space in the 1st century. You crossed over this same road several times already today; you were standing above it when you entered Borough Market. Other relics that were found here, piled on top of each other, include a stone coffin, probably from the 1200s, with a carved slot for the head; the foundations of the Norman priory that stood here; a kiln from the 1600s, soot marks intact (bits of the Delftware it made have been found as far away as Williamsburg, Virginia); a lead pipe from the 1800s; and overhead in the wall, an apse and arch surviving from the 1200s. Any one of these items would alone be enough to spark the imagination, but seeing them sandwiched in one tight bunch is truly difficult to wrap your head around. It reminds you that the present really does clothe the bones of the past, and in a city as old as London, history is literally piled, forgotten, under every footstep. As writer Geoff Ryman puts it, "silent as settling snow, experience falls on prepared ground." There's no telling what treasures have yet to be uncovered.

The cathedral has some beautiful painted monuments, including one of the oldest wooden effigies (1280) in England, and is worth a longer visit if you have time. Shakespeare's brother Edmond was buried here in 1607, as was Philip Henslowe, who built the Rose, in an unmarked grave. John Harvard, the founder of Harvard University in Cambridge, Massachusetts, was born the son of a butcher who owned a (long-gone) shop just northeast of the cathedral, and he was baptized here; the Harvard Chapel, off the North Transept, is named for him, and contains the oldest masonry in the building, from the Norman period. Other worthwhile sights include Edwardian stained glass tributes to the Bard's plays, and some of the original ceiling bosses, carved in 1469 and saved when things got bad. How bad? Here's a glimpse: During Elizabeth I's reign, the retro-choir (the part behind the altar) was walled off and rented to a baker. Later on, vestrymen discovered the baker was also raising swine in there.

Halfway back down the hallway, exit the cathedral. Go through the yard into the little lane (it's not marked here, but it's Montague Close; the Thames should be in front of you). Turn right, and just before you reach the overpass, look left for a set of stone steps labeled

⓭ Nancy's Steps

These are popularly held to be the location, in the Dickens novel *Oliver Twist,* where Noah Claypool eavesdrops on a conversation that leads to Nancy's murder by Bill Sykes. In the book, those steps faced the Thames, but these steps are indeed a rare surviving remnant of the same New London Bridge, built here in 1821 as a replacement for the 600-year-old, hopelessly overcrowded London Bridge. The steps that Dickens wrote about were sold in 1968 to an American oilman who had most of the bridge shipped, stone by stone, to Lake Havasu, Arizona, where it remains today. These steps were left behind and attached to this featureless 1973 replacement.

Just so you know, the existing London Bridge was not the source of the nursery rhyme "London Bridge is Falling Down"—that either referred to the burning of a wooden version in 1013, during a skirmish between Danes and Norwegians; or to Henry III's "fair lady" Queen Eleanor, who skimmed the tolls of the medieval bridge for her own purse, leaving its maintenance in a parlous state.

Climb the stairs to the road above. You're now on

⓮ London Bridge

At the top of the stairs, you'll see a pedestal topped by a dragon, the symbol of the city, holding London's crest. You'll see these dragons at several of the city's medieval borders. About 30m (98 ft.) east of here, under modern buildings, is where you would have entered the Stone Gateway, the entry to the disaster-prone medieval London Bridge. For more than 3 centuries, tar-dipped heads of executed criminals were impaled on pikes and stuck atop the Gateway as a vivid warning to would-be ne'er-do-wells.

Turn to the right to use the crosswalk. Go to the opposite side of the street and walk onto London Bridge, over the river. Don't cross the river—just enjoy the view of the

⓯ Pool of London

This section of the Thames, between London Bridge and the Tower of London (you can see it to the left of the Tower Bridge) is known as the Pool of London. It may be quiet now, but for nearly 2,000 years, it was the busiest stretch of water in town, and the heart of international trade. So many goods passed through here that warehouses along the southern bank became known as "London's Larder." During the Industrial Revolution, ships finally became so large that they had to unload downstream, closer to the sea. The section of river in front of you, parallel to this bridge, is where the medieval London Bridge stood.

Across the river from the Tower, you'll just make out an egg-shaped glass building in a grassy expanse. That's the City Hall (2002), designed for use by the Greater London Authority by Norman Foster (who also designed the Millennium Bridge) to be ergonomic and energy efficient, with a huge spiral staircase curling around its atrium and "smart" windows that open on hot days. Just like a politician, it has no discernible edge, and you can't tell if it's coming or going. London mayor Ken Livingstone, a man not known for tact or restraint, called it "a glass testicle." Anyone can have a ball in its public spaces (include a few small exhibitions) from 8am to 8pm, Monday to Friday (www.london.gov.uk).

Turn around and follow London Bridge inland, keeping on this (the left) side of the road. This street becomes Borough High Street. You will pass under another railway arch. Just after you pass a major street forking off to the right (Southwark Street), look for "The George" sign on your side of the street. It marks a passageway to

16 The George Inn

Because the London Bridge was the only crossing to the city from the south for so many centuries, this area became the equivalent of a train depot, and it was dotted with inns, stables, coach yards, and pubs. Everyone going to or coming from southern England or Europe stopped here, often spending the night before pushing into the shoulder-to-shoulder crowds of London Bridge. If you've ever read *The Canterbury Tales,* you'll recall that in 1386, the pilgrims began their journey to the shrine of Thomas a Becket from the Tabard Inn, which was located a short walk farther down Borough High Street, on the left. The George, described on p. 130, is the last survivor from this bustling coaching era. Although the wooden building, which once encircled the entire yard, dates to 1677, the inn was here for at least another 130 years before that, if not longer. We know it was typical of the time because John Stow, in *A Survey of London* (1598), termed it "a common hostelry for travelers." The National Trust took control of it in the 1930s, so it's no longer in danger of being replaced by some disposable office hive. Its outdoor tables are set up in good weather, and a drink here makes a fitting end to your journey through time. People have been drinking beer here for nearly half a millennium—but as you've seen today, the history of inhabited Southwark stretches back many times longer.

Walking Tour 3: Shopping, Soho & *Gimme Shelter*

Start: Oxford Circus Tube station
Finish: Goodge Street Tube station
Time: Two hours, not including shopping or restaurant breaks
Best times: Weekdays, when Berwick Street's market is on and Oxford Street is slightly less crowded
Worst times: After dark, when stores and markets close

All churched out? London is more than stories about dead queens and bloody uprisings. It's always been cosmopolitan, too, and the flash point for trends that ripple out to the rest of the world. Songs first sung at the clubs of Soho soon caused toes to tap on the other side of the planet, and fashion trends born on Carnaby Street remain internationally iconic 40 years later. Bring along your credit cards as we roam some of the city's best shopping streets—packed with stores geared at you, not at some Sloane Square socialite—and then touch upon a few leftovers from

London's recent past, including forgotten air-raid shelters and the settings for some good, old-fashioned sexual scandals. This is the London you found out about from the radio and the runways, not from your social studies teacher.

---

❶ Oxford Circus

Leave the Oxford Circus Underground station using Exit 2. The sidewalks will certainly be busy, so position yourself between the Tube stairs and the balustrade so that you're out of the fray.

You are in the thick of the mile-long Regent Street, which to the right is punctuated by the witches-hat steeple of All Souls Church and to the left curves toward Piccadilly Circus. When the Prince Regent, later George IV, was planning his new pet project, Regent's Park, he decided he also wanted a road to connect his house directly with it. He chose this particular location because, in his mind, it would provide a suitable demarcation line between the gentry of Mayfair, to the west, and the rabble of the traders who lived in Soho, to the east. George tapped John Nash to do the job, completed in 1825. Originally, the sidewalks were covered by stone colonnades, but when those attracted prostitutes, they were removed, and most of the original buildings were later rebuilt—the only Nash original is now All Souls. Even if most of the facades you see now mask more modern buildings, few streets in London impart such a sweeping, uplifting feeling, though few are also as congested with dawdlers from the middle and working classes, folk George wouldn't have preferred.

The other avenue intersecting before you is Oxford Street, following the same line as a Roman road. George's class-centered definition of the landscape has more or less held: The exclusive shops of Oxford Street still lie west of Regent Street, and the downmarket stores tend to be east of it. Look west, left, and you'll spot some of the city's most famous department stores: John Lewis (p. 266), Debenhams, and in the distance, the wedding cake of Selfridges (p. 267). Having a presence on Oxford Circus is considered crucial for brands with mass appeal. On the corner opposite is the smart Swedish clothier H&M (p. 273). A few meters to the right is Topshop (p. 273), another fashion-forward discount chain, which bills itself as the world's largest clothing store—I know of none larger. It's so busy that it refreshes its stock twice a day.

Head right, east on Oxford Street. You will pass Argyll Street on the right. Stroll down Oxford Street. When you pass Ramillies Street, prepare to stop in front of

❷ Marks & Spencer

London has a love-hate relationship with Oxford Street. People come here to shop by the thousands, but they often despair of the crush of the experience. Charles Dickens, Jr., described the street thusly in 1888: "It ought to be the finest thoroughfare in the world. As a matter of fact it is not by any means, and though it is, like all the other thoroughfares, improving, it still contains many houses which even in a third-rate street would be considered mean." We're only going to walk down a sample of Oxford Street. It's usually so crowded, it's all you can probably handle if you're keeping one eye on this book. Keep the other eye out for people propping up day-glo signs reading GOLF SALE. These unlucky individuals are an Oxford Street institution. They're trying to draw foot traffic to

Walking Tour 3: Shopping & Soho

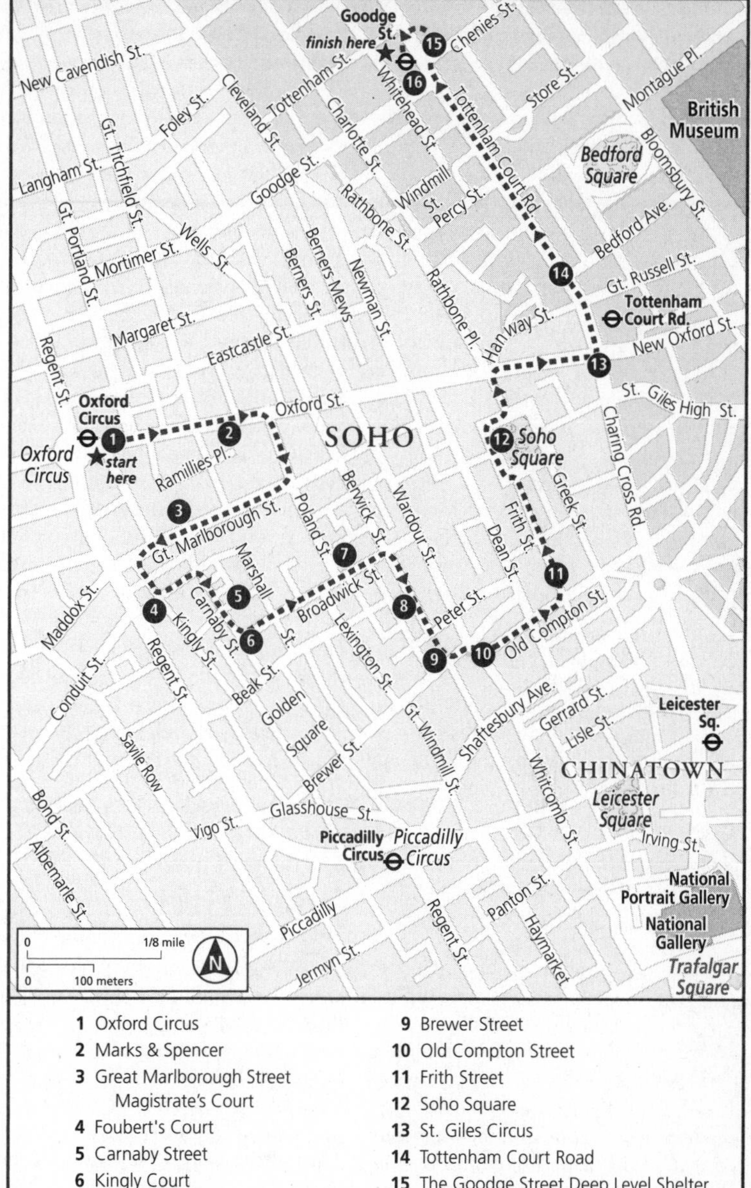

1 Oxford Circus
2 Marks & Spencer
3 Great Marlborough Street Magistrate's Court
4 Foubert's Court
5 Carnaby Street
6 Kingly Court
7 Berwick Street
8 Berwick Street Market
9 Brewer Street
10 Old Compton Street
11 Frith Street
12 Soho Square
13 St. Giles Circus
14 Tottenham Court Road
15 The Goodge Street Deep Level Shelter
16 Goodge Street Tube station

off-street bargain stores selling cut-rate (and cut-quality) sporting goods.

Marks & Spencer (p. 267), or M&S, dates to 1894 and is the favored British department store for the masses, although it's been taking hits from warehouse stores like Tesco. Perhaps proof of its appeal is that the chain can afford to run two giant frontages on Oxford Street; its flagship store is remarkably near here, between Bond Street and Marble Arch Tube stations. For a long time, M&S made a point of dealing in British-made goods, but the pressures of a global market ended that, although it still touts its buying ethics. The store has also been working to replace its stodgy image with one that will attract more style-conscious customers. Its Food Halls (at this store, in the cellar) are well-known as an ideal place to pick up prepared foods, sandwiches, and inexpensive but well-selected wines. Across the street from M&S is the flagship store of music seller HMV. Use a crosswalk if you cross; buses roar along Oxford Street. HMV promotes its latest markdowns (CDs for £4–£6) in the lobby.

Turn right at Poland Street, walk 1 block, and turn right again onto Great Marlborough Street. Walk straight. Soon on your right, at 19-21, you'll see a stout white building that looks like it could repel a tank. That's the former

❸ Great Marlborough Street Magistrate's Court

Charles Dickens worked here as a reporter just before hitting it big as a novelist, and a variety of other big names appeared before the judges here, including the Marquess of Queensbury (defending himself from Oscar Wilde's libel charge) and Christine Keeler (the sex kitten depicted in the movie *Scandal*). When this neighborhood turned bohemian in the Swinging '60s, it began trying a string of drug charges against the likes of Mick Jagger, Johnny Rotten, Keith Richards, Francis Bacon, and, curiously (and coming full circle), the guy who wrote the musical *Oliver!*, Lionel Bart. It's now a stylish luxury hotel, but I suggest you go inside briefly, because much of the old judicial fittings were left intact. You can have a cocktail in one of the old jail cells—now converted into private booths, with Zen stones filling the old toilets—or even peek into Silk, a restaurant slotted into the authoritative Number One court, which still has its witness stand, bench, wood paneling, and vaulted glass ceiling.

Beyond the Courthouse Hotel on the left, you'll see a Tudor-style building of black beams and white plaster. This is Liberty (p. 267), famous for its haute fabrics. It's also famous for its building—it was made in 1924 using wood recycled from junked ships. Liberty's wares are alternately mocked and celebrated, and rarely cheap, but they're usually interesting at the least.

Great Marlborough Street runs into Regent Street. Turn left there and walk the short distance to

❹ Foubert's Court

Times have been better on Regent Street. Wal-Mart–style box stores in the suburbs have put the screws on the destination shops of the city, and this avenue has recently seen a few long-termers lose their sizzle. Dickins & Jones, a department store at the corner you just turned, closed its doors in early 2006 after nearly 170 years of history, having been unprofitable for 4 years. Other upscale frontages, such as an Apple Store, have moved in, but the personality of Regent Street remains in question.

Two doors farther from Foubert's Court, though, at 188-196, is a well-loved holdover from the street's glory days. It's Hamleys (p. 280), one of the largest toy stores in the world. Some 5 million customers pour through its doors every year, but since the sales force is famous for putting on a non-stop show on every floor, it's understandable if many of those customers come to gawp and not to buy. If you go into Hamleys, when and if you come out again, turn right and go back to Foubert's Court.

Walk down the very short Foubert's Court for one block; you'll see "Carnaby" on a metal arch. Go under it and head one block farther. Go right, and now you'll see a much larger arch on

5 Carnaby Street

Yes, those obnoxious arches proclaim your location with a clarion call that proves this street is no longer the mod, super-cool, forward-trending shopping street of the kids in the know. It's more of a mall with an edge. A few names sell products here that are hard to find elsewhere—Ben Sherman, Puma, and All Saints maintain huge stores here—but the days of Swinging London, when men would cruise from store to store trying on hip-hugging black trousers and frilly shirts, are behind it. *Time* magazine spilled the secret of Carnaby Street in 1966, and by the early 1970s, it was pedestrianized as a shopping street, making its hipness a matter of history.

Just after you cross Ganton Street, where Broadwick Street hits Carnaby Street, duck into the passageway on the right:

6 Kingly Court

Clever entrepreneurs are reviving Carnaby Street's mod appeal with this positive development, a retail experiment inhabiting a former timber warehouse. A few niche chains are present, but the stores here are mostly boutiques pushing young designers, which is increasingly rare for London. Now and then, the mini mall produces a new label or product that catches some buzz in the fashion glossies.

Slip out the back door of Kingly Court, opposite its front door, and hang a left on Kingly Street. Three doors in, at number 8, is the Oliver J. Benjamin haberdashery. In the 1960s, it was the fiercely hip Bag 'O Nails pub, where future Wings-mates Paul McCartney and Linda Eastman first clapped eyes on each other. The pub, which saw club performances from the likes of Jimi Hendrix, was also where Fleetwood Mac's John McVie proposed to Christine. Return to Kingly Court.

Retrace your steps out of Kingly Court, cross Carnaby Street, and head straight down Broadwick Street. You'll stop around

7 Berwick Street

A hundred and sixty years ago, this block was a foul slum. French, Greek, and Italian immigrants fled hard times and revolutions by cramming into these tight streets, and by the 1850s, cholera was storming through the over-stuffed city. An 1854 outbreak killed 500 people in barely 10 days. Common wisdom at the time held that the disease was spread through the air—a reasonable conclusion, given how terrible the sewage-smeared city smelled—but a local anesthetist, John Snow, suspected polluted water was the cause. He got permission to inspect the public pump at Broad Street, now Broadwick Street (it's on the sidewalk in the block before Berwick Street) and he found that it was being contaminated with sewage leaking from Number 40 nearby, proving his theory. The saga was recently retold in compelling modern language in the book *The Ghost Map* by Steven Johnson.

Take a break

How grateful were Dr. Snow's neighbors for saving them? Incalculably: They named their pub for him, albeit a century later. It stands at number 39, at Lexington Street, on the site of his practice, and was built as the Newcastle-upon-Tyne in 1867. Raise a pint in his honor here, or if you need caffeine, by Stop 10 we'll be on a prime cafe street.

When you reach Berwick Street, look left. The road here ought to ring a bell for rock fans. Think of this location as the modern-day Abbey Road. It's where, in 1995, Oasis photographed the cover of *(What's the Story) Morning Glory,* one of the seminal CDs of the age. The photographer shot from farther down the street, aiming south, toward where you're standing. (Noel Gallagher, with characteristic eloquence, said he thought the album cover was "s**t.")

And here's another slice of rock history: One miniblock farther down Broadwick Street at number 7, the corner shop covered in striking rust-colored tiles (now Sounds of the Universe record store), was the famous Bricklayers Arms pub. Brian Jones auditioned The Rolling Stones here in 1962, and they held their formative rehearsals upstairs. Across the road at number 6 is Agent Provocateur, a noted lingerie shop. The word "Soho" is probably derived from a hunting cry used when this area was parkland—it's nice to see that some folks around here are still on the hunt.

Turn south on Berwick Street. Walk down it to

8 Berwick Street Market

This is the last great market in the center of the city, and it has been in operation since the 1840s, although vestry records indicate some illicit trading was going on as far back as 1778. London's first publicly available grapefruit was sold here in 1890. Even though many shoppers have migrated to fluorescent-lit grocery stores, you can still buy all manner of fruit, veggies, and everyday staples every day except Sunday. Buy a snack here; these hard-working vendors, many of whom speak fluent Cockney, could use your support. They have been known to cut deals on perishables in late afternoon. Along the storefronts are some interesting punk shops and used music stores, plus a few of the city's last vinyl record shops, which polish up the street's jumble-sale personality.

Pass over Peter Street and under Maurice House, going under the crossover and winding up on

9 Brewer Street

From the late 1700s to the 1950s, Soho was the capital of London sin; it was impossible for a single gentleman to pass unpropositioned from one end of the neighborhood to the other. A 1959 act chased the open salesmanship indoors, to be replaced by drinking joints where men could buy lap time with a lady, and by the 1970s, even those establishments were forced to seek a lower profile or close altogether. By law, today's window displays are not permitted to offer much in the way of titillation, complying with the British reputation (inaccurate in my book) for sexual modesty.

It was in this fleshly carnival that Laura Henderson bought a theater, named it The Windmill, and got around indecency laws, which banned nude dancers, by ensuring that the performers in her naughty entertainment, the Revudeville, never moved a muscle. Famously, the Windmill never closed, not even during the Blitz. The building now houses a common strip joint at Great Windmill and Archer streets, on the other side of the block that's across the street and to the right—don't detour unless you really want to because the tour resumes from here.

This part of Soho is known for its gay-oriented pubs, cafes, and stores, starting with Prowler, a bookshop and naughty video store that's on the corner opposite.

Go left to Wardour Street, make a right and then a quick left. You'll be at the head of

⑩ Old Compton Street

There are a few interesting things to note here. First is the church of St. Anne's, a few yards farther down Wardour Street, on the left. The church was built in 1685, possibly by Wren (then again, which ones weren't?), but everything, save the clock tower, was creamed by the Germans. At night, the fence in front of it is illuminated in the colors of the rainbow flag—a sure sign of the inclusive beliefs of England's progressive clergy. Also, take a look at the far side of the building on the right-hand corner of Old Compton; embedded in its upper floor is the word CHEMIST—the British word for pharmacist—spelled in tile. Like the Berwick Street Market, it's an aging, endangered reminder that, although Soho is now a vivacious district, for many years it was a workaday neighborhood.

Walk down Old Compton Street, Soho's de facto main street, which is busy round the clock. Number 54 is the Admiral Duncan. Dylan Thomas once drank there (then again, where didn't he?), but more recently it has become an important gay pub, and it was here, in 1999, that Nazi sympathizer David Copeland planted a bomb stuffed with 500 nails. When it exploded, it killed three people and injured many more. A bizarre brass chandelier marks the spot. Copeland, an obvious lunatic, also bombed the South Asian population of Brick Lane and blacks in Brixton, but his only fatalities were here. The street's gay clientele has, understandably, been on edge since then, but the street is nonetheless more popular than ever.

On the corner of Dean Street, look right. Down the block on the left, at number 49, is the French House, more commonly called the French Pub. During World War II, it was the drinking haunt of Charles de Gaulle, and it was where the exiled leader formed the Free French government and army. The street beyond the French House is Shaftesbury Avenue, the famous theatrical thoroughfare; many of the side streets between Old Compton and Shaftesbury contain the stage doors for the major playhouses, where famous actors report to work. Now look left, north up Dean Street. In the attic of number 28, Karl Marx dwelled in abject poverty with his wife and several kids, but no running water or toilet. Three of his kids died while he was in residence in Soho in the early 1850s. No wonder he thought communism would be better.

Turn left at

⑪ Frith Street

Bar Italia, the stylish cafe at number 22, is a nightlife landmark of its own (p. 102). But history doesn't stop at the ground floor. Upstairs is where, in 1925, John Logie Baird privately tested a homemade invention he called "noctovision," using a local office boy as a test subject. The next year, he unveiled an improved model for the science nerds of the Royal Institution upstairs in this building. Baird's system, which used a spinning disc, was eventually discarded, but it debuted ahead of American Philo T. Farnsworth's more famous electronic version. Within a decade, the BBC was broadcasting "television"—its new name—regularly. In the 1940s, Baird invented the first color picture tube.

Walk up three doors. For ten months starting in September 1764, the 8-year-old Mozart lived with his father and sister at a house located at number 20 (the building was replaced in 1858). While he was in London, the prodigy amused King George III with his abilities, wrote his first two symphonies, and befriended fellow composer Bach. Another talent of the age, essayist William Hazlitt, lived at number 6; he died in a back room on the third floor. The premises are now an eccentric, enchanting luxury hotel.

Use the gate to head into

⓬ Soho Square

Laid out in 1681, Soho Square was, early on, the fashionable, mansion-lined home of both Charles II's son and the daughter of his grandfather's nemesis, Oliver Cromwell. Later it became the center of the ambassadorial and scientific cliques. Sir Joseph Banks, who made his name collecting exotic specimens as a tagalong on Captain Cook's voyages, moved here in 1777, and in 1799 the square was the scene of the first annual meeting of the Royal Institution, which is now the world's oldest research body. These days, Soho is a center for the music and film industries. Twentieth Century House, the British HQ of 20th Century Fox, is on the southwestern corner. The British Board of Film Classification is also on the square.

In the center of the square, which is technically a private garden even though it's been open to the public for half a century, is a cottage you'd swear was Tudor in origin. In fact, it's an 1895 pastiche made to hide an electrical transformer. Beneath the lawns lie empty air-raid shelters.

Exit the opposite side of the square and go straight down Soho Street. You'll soon hit Oxford Street again. Turn right and head for the next major intersection. Head toward the entrance to the Tottenham Court Road Underground station, which serves the crossing officially called

⓭ St. Giles Circus

We're not too far east along Oxford Street from where we started, but you can see how much less illustrious the shopping is at this end. That's fine if you want a cell phone, knockoff suitcase, or CD (Zavvi, p. 278, is ahead on the left), but this shabby end is not a browser's paradise.

We're approaching the part of town that used to be called "the rookery of St. Giles." It was a notorious slum, a haven for lepers and a source of the plague, which was only cleared through an aggressive program of demolition.

Look across the next major street, and you'll see the 35-story Centre Point development. Built in 1964 with heavy government concessions, it was kept empty for years by its unscrupulous owner, partly to hold out for astronomical rents and partly because doing so would get him off the tax hook, even as the city struggled through a homeless crisis. The charity Centrepoint, which started in the basement of St. Anne's church in Soho and grew into a powerful force in housing issues, derisively took its name from the waste. Critics have assailed Centre Point as an eyesore, and as an emblem of poor urban planning—its inadequate sidewalk has a way of pushing pedestrians in front of buses. Still, it's indisputably one of the landmarks of the London skyline, identifiable from miles away.

You may end the tour here, at the Tube station, which contains some tile mosaics by the great artist Eduardo Paolozzi. Or, if you like, turn right to explore the bookstores on Charing Cross Road. Take a final jaunt up Tottenham Court Road if you want to extend the tour by another 15 minutes.

Turn left and head up

⓮ Tottenham Court Road

I have to admit this blandly developed avenue lacks character, and it isn't my favorite stretch in London, although I seem to find myself walking down it quite a lot. Fans of Andrew Lloyd Webber (anyone?), or at least of T. S. Eliot, will recall that this is the "grimy road" roamed by Grizabella, the "glamour cat" who sings "Memory."

A few spotty points of interest: On the corner, the Dominion Theatre was where, in 1957, Bill Haley and the Comets were the first American rock act to play Britain. This is also known as the city's main district for electronics, but prices here won't be cheaper than they are at home. Soon, on your left, you will see Goodge Street, whose pubs and charity shops are frequented by students who attend the several universities in this area.

Duck into Chenies Street, on your right. At the curving side alley of North Circle, look for the red-striped, rounded buildings on the left, at

⓯ The Goodge Street Deep Level Shelter

In 1939, planners decided to build an express train line beneath the existing Northern Line platforms of Goodge Street. War intervened. In 1942, the unfinished tunnel was allocated to the Americans, and it was under the ground here where General (later President) Dwight D. Eisenhower orchestrated D-Day and announced it to the world, in 1944. There were eight deep-level shelters, and five were open to bomb-shocked civilians; this is one of the most central and best-kept. It retains its ground-level entry blocks, one pillbox and one octagonal, connected by a brick building—thousands of Londoners pass them daily but don't know their original purpose. Since the Cold War, the onetime shelters, now innocuously painted cream with red stripes and named The Eisenhower Centre, have been used for storage. The shelter at Chancery Lane was converted to a telephone exchange, and the one at Stockwell has been decorated, turning it into an improvised war memorial.

Double back onto Tottenham Court Road. Across the street on your right will be:

⓰ Goodge Street Tube Station

Before you end your tour at the Tube station opposite, turn right. This block hosts two of the city's most celebrated furniture stores, Heal's (p. 278) and Habitat (p. 278), both of which, decades before Ikea, provided high-design homewares for affordable prices.

The Goodge Street Deep Level Shelter could originally be accessed from a second point on the west of Tottenham Court Road opposite Torrington Place; some abandoned brick-and-concrete structures and vents linger. Goodge Street Underground station, opened in 1907 and still sporting much of its original tilework, is one of the few in the system that uses elevators, not escalators. You can always use the 136 steps, too—that is, if you still have the juice after your walking tour.

9 London's Best Shopping

The city's most distinctive stores—in the bag

BLAME ELIZABETH I. SURE, THE OLD GIRL LOVED HER BAUBLES AND gold-embroidered bodices (for a glimpse at some Renaissance bling, check out the Ditchley portrait of her at the National Portrait Gallery), but her biggest contribution to English consumerism was probably defeating the Spanish Armada. You see, that established England as the dominant player on the high seas, which in turn opened up channels of international trade never before seen in the West. Ever since the Thames was more jammed with bounty than the parking lot at the mall on Christmas Eve, London has had a hankering for the finer things. Make that an addiction—and not an affordable one, since the richest of the rich flock here to outspend each other. To make matters worse, many of London's stores have been around for hundreds of years, so they're particularly skilled at coaxing cash out of visitors. So before you make a pilgrimage to these shrines to credit, put your window-shopping glasses within easier reach than your pocketbook.

TEN GREAT SHOPPING STREETS

Appropriately for a city obsessed with class, London's prime shopping streets aren't usually defined so much by what they sell as by how much you'll spend to bring home their booty.

New Bond Street (Tube: Bond Street or Green Park): The ultimate high-end purchasing pantheon runs from Oxford Street to Piccadilly, partly as Old Bond Street. Every account-draining trinket maker has a presence, including Lalique, Tiffany & Co., Harry Winston, De Beers, Cartier, Chopard, Boucheron, and Wartski. Asprey's, at 165-169, sells adornments few can afford, but its Victorian facade is a visual treat for all incomes. Sloane Street, in Kensington, has many of the same brands, but Bond Street is still the granddaddy of spendy streets.

The Arcades of Piccadilly and Old Bond Street (Tube: Green Park): Also in the area are several iron-framed, skylighted "arcades" (closed Sun), built by 19th-century blue bloods for shopping in any weather. The best include Burlington Arcade, parallel to Old Bond Street at Piccadilly (silverware, cashmere, objets d'art); the Royal Arcade, south of Burlington Gardens (antiques, art, chocolates); and Piccadilly Arcade, across from Burlington Arcade (men's tailoring; it leads to Jermyn St., once the heart of haberdashery).

Kensington High Street (Tube: High Street Kensington): London's coolest shopping street in the '60s, it's now a hodgepodge of brand names and boutiques.

Store Hours

Stores across the city generally open at 9 or 10am daily and close at 7 or 8pm, although the department stores and Oxford Street shops are often open as late as 8pm. On Sundays, relatively new terrain for British shopping, 11am or noon to 6pm hours are more common; very few places will stay open past then. Expect crowds on weekends, when people pour into town from the countryside.

Oxford Street (Tube: Marble Arch, Bond Street, or Oxford Circus): The king of London shopping streets supports the biggest names, including Topshop, H&M, and a few lollapalooza department stores like Selfridges, John Lewis, and Marks & Spencer. Boy, are weekends crowded! Visit www.oxfordstreet.co.uk for info.

Carnaby Street (Tube: Oxford Circus or Piccadilly Circus): This used to be for the mod crowd, but today such hyperalternative shopping is mostly found on Memory Lane. Instead, expect mainstream choices and a few one-off boutiques. Don't miss Kingly Court, a former timber warehouse converted into a mini-mall for upcoming designers. Visit http://carnaby.co.uk for info.

Floral Street (Tube: Covent Garden): Every lane around Covent Garden (Long Acre, Henrietta St.) is an obvious shopping drag, but they're full of the usual brands. This side street gives respite from the same old tourist tat. Duck in when you want to browse some originals. Visit www.coventgarden.uk.com for info.

Upper Street (Tube: Angel): Islington's chief avenue is emerging as a low-key location for boutiques, vintage outfits, and kitchen-sink junk shops, all pleasantly spelled by unpretentious pubs and cafes. While you're south of the Green, explore the sidewalks of Camden Passage, known for antiques and bric-a-brac.

Tottenham Court Road (Tube: Tottenham Court Road or Goodge Street): Locals sniff, but the street's lower half, between Oxford and Store streets, is their only drag for cut-rate electronics (including voltage converters). North to Torrington Place, pickings shift to brilliantly designed homewares and furnishings at Habitat (191) and London's grande dame of smart styling, Heal's (199).

Cecil Court (Tube: Leicester Square): Distinguished by glazed-tile buildings, matching green-and-white shop signs, and a refreshing lack of cars, this block is a holdout of the antiquarian book trade that once dominated Charing Cross Road, its western anchor. My favorite is Marchpane, at 16, a trove of vintage children's literature. Visit www.cecilcourt.co.uk for info.

King's Road (Tube: Sloane Square or South Kensington): The Chelsea avenue where affluent "Sloaneys" spend is where you go to dream—increasingly, about what King's Road used to be. Most of the truly unique stores have recently been elbowed aside by the same old corporate names.

OUTLETS & SALE SHOPS

Many world-famous designers maintain shops in London, and when, at the start of each fashion season, their newest line comes in, they ship the older items to little-known "sale shops" or "sample sales" where they're unloaded for a song. Most are temporary; for advance word on those, sign up for a free email from the London edition of **Daily Candy** (www.dailycandy.com/london) a few weeks before your departure. *Time Out* also announces big events in its Consume section. But some sale shops pump out deals year-round; a few of the best are listed below. You never know what you're going to find, so check items carefully for hidden damage.

> *"Our primary cultural activity in London was changing money. We had to do this a lot because the dollar is very weak. Europeans use the dollar primarily to apply shoe polish. So every day we'd go to one of the money-changing places . . . and then we'd look for something to eat that had been invented in this century, such as pizza, and we'd buy three slices for what we later realized was $247.50, and then we'd change some money again. Meanwhile, the Japanese tourists were exchanging their money for items such as Westminster Abbey."*
>
> —Dave Barry

Let's start at the top. If you prefer to dress like you're in *Vogue*—showy, original, impractical—then the cutting-edge fashion (Jill Sander, Commes des Garcons, Marc Jacbos) of **Browns Labels for Less** (50 S. Molton St., W1; ☎ 020/7514-0052; www.brownsfashion.com; closed Sun; Tube: Bond Street) will have something to tempt you. When things don't sell at the exclusive Browns store up the road, the outfits move here and permanent discounts are applied. Couture is highly specific stuff, so a visit is hit or miss based on your tastes, but if you're the type who's addicted to £500 frocks, then what a relief it is to me that you'll only have to pay £225. Or, at the very least, you'll have fun trying them on.

While consumers outside the U.K. view Burberry as a dignified brand, in London, thanks to years of plaid overdose by the "wrong" crowd, its primary clientele is mocked as trashy. So the **Burberry Factory Outlet** (29-53 Chatham Place, E9; ☎ 020/8985-3344; www.burberry.com; National Rail: Hackney Central or Tube: Bethnal Green) is in the "wrong" part of town, but nobody back home will know that when you turn up wearing £10 shirts.

The facilities for the **French Connection/Nicole Farhi Outlet Shop** ★ (3 Hancock Rd., E3; ☎ 020/7399-7125; closed Sun; Tube: Bromley-by-Bow) aren't many notches over a woodshed's, but then again, prices aren't much higher than a charity shop's. Discounts for men and women start at 25% off.

For sharp suits at dulled-down prices, try your luck at **Joseph Clearance Shop** ★ (53 King's Rd., SW3; www.joseph.co.uk; ☎ 020/7730-7562; Tube: Sloane Square). The clothes that end up here—lots of grey, lots of updates on classical profiles—were dumped from the lines this season for minor stylistic reasons that probably won't bother you. You'll still look chic for up to 70% less.

An Outlet Mall Daytrip

The region's one true outlet mall, **Bicester Village** ("BIS-ter") (50 Pingle Dr., Oxon; ☎ 01869/32-32-00; www.bicestervillage.com), is 90 minutes west of town, about 24km (15 miles) from the city of Oxford. Jigsaw, the popular High Street clothier, has an outlet here and nowhere else, and DKNY, Nicole Farhi, and Salvatore Ferragamo are among the 80-odd luxury names that send their designer cast-offs here to be snapped up at 30% to 60% off. As with many outlet malls, finds can be spotty, although they do exist. Considering that almost everything for sale here started life at luxury prices, even a modest spree can wallop the bank account. The easiest way to get here is to take a 1-hour train to Bicester North Station from London Marylebone station, which departs about every 30 minutes (£21–£23 round-trip). From the station, you can walk or take a connecting bus (about £1 each way). It's an outdoor mall, which is unfortunate considering some of the best deals fall in January.

Men may also want to raid the **Paul Smith Sale Shop** ★★ (23 Avery Row, W1; ☎ 020/7493-1287; Tube: Bond Street), tucked amidst the pricey stuff around Bond Street, where last season's tees, trousers, and accessories are marked down from £55 to £25, shoes from £110 to £55, jeans from £30 to £19, and hats from £115 to £50. Some of the items are here because they're defective, so inspect carefully.

The expansive, unmissable **Designer Warehouse Sale** (5-6 Islington Studios, N7; ☎ 020/7697-9888; www.dwslondon.co.uk; entry £2; Tube: Finsbury Park or Holloway Road), held over 3 days 12 times a year, pulls an amazing array of brands (at least 100 names for each gender) from across the retail spectrum, including such lush wares as Harvey Nichols and Armani. With a track record lasting more than 2 decades, it's considered one of the best bargain events on the calendar, securing savings from 60% to 80%. Likewise, high-fashion designers who lack their own storefronts (and even those who don't, like Vivienne Westwood and Moschino) bring their castoff samples to **Designer Sales UK** (www.designersales.co.uk), which throws six sales a year (usually at the end of Feb, Apr, June, Sept, Oct, and either Nov or Dec). Deals on original work can be as high as 90% off. Shows are usually held on Brick Lane in Whitechapel. Both of these events require you to join their e-mail list for an invitation, and they charge a little more if you use a credit card instead of cash.

THE SHOPPING PALACES

So venerable is **Fortnum & Mason** ★★★ (181 Piccadilly, W1; ☎ 020/7734-8040; www.fortnumandmason.co.uk; Tube: Green Park or Piccadilly Circus), which began life in 1707 as the candlemaker to Queen Anne, that in 1922 archeologist Howard Carter used empty F&M boxes to tote home the treasures of King Tut's tomb. The *veddy British* department store, which has a special focus on gourmet foods, is renowned for its glamorous hampers, which were first distributed in the days before World War I, when soldiers' families were responsible for feeding their men on the field. Such picnic sets now come with bone china and can cost £300, and the tables of its ground floor food hall are immoderately piled with a cornucopia of such tongue-teasing triumphs as preserved truffles (£15) and fresh Blue Stilton cheese in ceramic pots from £19. Even the bread rolls cost a scalding 50p (albeit in frou-frou flavors like parmesan), although there's something to be said for a store that maintains four of its own beehives for honey (£10 for 8 oz.). Content yourself, as most do, with a wander through the hushed upper-floor departments, which are lit by chandelier, accented by wooden cases, and illuminated by a lotus-like atrium skylight. The fragrance department smells like a rose garden. High tea, taken in the top-floor St. James's tearooms, is no bargain (from £30) but is among the city's most sumptuous.

Under the steerage of its widely reviled owner, the ostentatious Mohamed al-Fayed, **Harrods ★ (87-135 Brompton Rd., SW1; ☎ 020/7730-1234; www.harrods.com; Tube: Knightsbridge)**, a miraculous holdover from the golden age of shopping, has been reshaped into a vertical mall appealing to free-spending, not-too-discerning visitors. Still, based on its prior reputation (or maybe because it's become such a bombastic parody of itself), many visitors prioritize a visit right behind Westminster Abbey or the Tower. Its seven thronged Food Hall rooms are still a glut of exorbitantly priced meats and cheeses, its ornate facade is still emblazoned like a Christmas tree after dark, its endless upper floors are still spiked with racks of gowns and blinding jewelry, but much floor space is devoted to brands you'd find for a third of the price at your local mall (HMV, Krispy Kreme, Starbucks, Coach). The whole artificial environment, from clerks wearing straw hats to the giant "emporium" devoted to the sale of souvenirs (£14 for small gusset bags; £25 umbrellas; teddy bears aplenty), would be more authentic on Main Street at Disneyland than anywhere in the London of old. Of the many escalator banks, the most interesting is the uproarious Egyptian-themed one at the store's center. At its base is a tacky brass fountain memorial to al-Fayed's son Dodi and Princess Diana, who died together in Paris in 1997; a wine glass, preserved from the couple's final tryst, is preserved under glass along with a ring with which al-Fayed claims his son intended to propose to Diana. All in all, if you crave a real British department store experience, visit Fortnum & Mason or Selfridges; if you want to be flabbergasted by the pompous excesses of the jet-set, Harrods is the overly shellacked circus for you.

Absolutely Fabulous' shallow antiheroines Patsy and Edina spoke of **Harvey Nichols ★ (109-125 Knightsbridge, SW1; ☎ 020/7235-5000; www.harveynichols.com; Tube: Knightsbridge)** with the same breathless reverence most people reserve for deities. You'll need the income of a god to afford a single thread of Harvey Nick's women's and men's fashion, and although the store isn't as popular as it used to be, a stroll through this spendthrift's heaven is entertaining. In addition to the lunching ladies on display in the Fifth Floor Restaurant—think of it as a zoo for old money—there's a smart juice bar, Fushi.

Every Englishman knows that if you want a sound deal, you go to **John Lewis ★★★ (Oxford St. at Holles St.; ☎ 020/7629-7711; www.johnlewis.com/oxfordstreet; Tube: Oxford Circus)**, which has a price guarantee; it employs an army of people to scout for the lowest prices in the area, which it matches. That may sound like the gimmick of a low-rent wannabe, but John Lewis, established in

It's Cheaper in England

Believe it or not, even though the pound packs a wallop, some items are still inexplicably less expensive if you pick them up in London.

- **High-quality bedsheets.** £30 to £40 a set.
- **Holiday cards.** £3 a pack. Who's that "Father Christmas" dude?
- **Cereal.** From £1. Bring an empty suitcase if you're weird.
- **Re-released recordings.** Lots of entertainment becomes public domain after 50 years in the U.K.
- **Beer.** A pint of strong ale can set you back as little as £2. Cheers!

1864, is in fact a respected cooperative owned by its employees, and their interest in its success shows in their attentive service and seemingly limitless product line. It also has some exceptional buyers; you'll find things here no other store carries (the bedding department is renowned). Art fans shouldn't miss the building's eastern face, upon which is mounted an abstract cast-aluminum sculpture, *The Winged Figure* (1960), by one of the most important British artists of the twentieth century, Dame Barbara Hepworth.

Liberty (210-220 Regent St., W1; ☎ 020/7734-1234; www.liberty.co.uk; Tube: Oxford Circus), founded in 1875, made its name (and earned much mockery) as an importer of Asian art and as a major proponent of Art Nouveau style. The timber-and-plaster wing looks Tudor, but is actually a 1924 revival constructed from the salvaged timbers of two ships, HMS *Impregnable* and HMS *Hindustan;* the length of the latter ship equals the building's length along Great Marlborough Street. The store's scarf selection is celebrated, as is its selection of fabrics, many of which are designed in-house. Finding your way around saps time but little patience, since the soft wooden spaces are creaky and seductive.

Although its 560-odd locations have been limping along with a deficit of respect from the English people, **Marks & Spencer** ★★ (Flagship: 458 Oxford St., W1; ☎ 020/7935-7954; www.marksandspencer.co.uk; Tube: Marble Arch) is in fact a solid High Street store with solid bargains. Its own-brand clothing, once shoddy and ill-fitting, has been re-envisioned as affordable riffs on well-tailored fashions, and customers are drifting back to enjoy the good buys. One such deal: three pairs of men's underwear for £5. But M&S's crowning achievement is its giant **food halls** ★★★ (usually tucked underneath the store but sometimes a stand-alone shop called **Simply Food**), which sell an astonishing array of prepared meals, soups and sandwiches, and well-selected yet inexpensive wines. M&S is a national treasure, and it's about time the English remembered that.

Aside from Harrods' olive drab sacks, no shopping bag brags louder about your shopping preferences than a canary yellow screamer from **Selfridges** ★★★ (400 Oxford St., W1; ☎ 020/7318-2134; www.selfridges.com; Tube: Bond Street or Marble Arch). It's unquestionably the better of the two stores, since it's not merely a sprawling sensory treat, but it also sells items you'd actually want (unlike Harrods, it doesn't ignore young designers). Since its 1909 opening by an American marketing executive from Marshall Field's in Chicago, Selfridges has pioneered standard department store practices, including placing the perfumes near the front door and inventing the phrase "the customer is always right." Some one million products are for sale, and the beauty department is Europe's largest. The thicket of food counters on the ground floor is mobbed at lunchtime, and the rest of the store is just as popular at other times; some 17 million visits are recorded each year. Given the size of the place, a percentage may still be finding their way out again. Selfridges has traded in history, too; the first public demonstration of television was held on the first floor in 1925, and 3 years later, the store sold the world's first set. During much of the Blitz, Churchill's transatlantic conversations with FDR were encoded via a scrambler stashed in the cellar.

SPECIALTY SHOPS

Although you can find just about anything you want at the palace stores, considering the city is bristling with such excellent smaller shops, why would you want to? You'll run across dozens of winning boutiques as you stroll along, but the following stores count among the city's most interesting and most historic.

ANTIQUES

If you're renovating your home or your look, you'll find few better sources for curios than London, an antique city on a redecorating binge. Once you go back in time about 80 years, you'll find the British style to be quite divergent from the American one, and many accessories and staples will feel like one-of-a-kinds once they're back home. Buying salvage, too, is a clever pursuit here. It requires a hardy budget, specific measurements, and tedious shipping arrangements, but your reward can be incredible finds. You can also find rarities at an auction (p. 269).

More like an upscale junk shop, **After Noah** ★ (121 Upper St., N1; ☎ 020/7359-4281; www.afternoah.com; Tube: Angel) makes its name on vintage toys, crockery, bathroom fittings, cheerful celluloid jewelry, and wooden desks and bedsteads, sadly too large to get home. Its refurbished mid-20th-century telephones are particularly sought-after. There's another location at 261 King's Rd. (Tube: South Kensington), and a small booth on the fourth floor of Harvey Nichols.

The earlier you come, the more you'll find at **Bermondsey Market** ★★ (Bermondsey St. at Long Lane, SE1; ☎ 020/7969-1500; Tube: London Bridge), a weekly event that yields some of the city's broadest inventory (a trove of Edwardian and Victorian ephemera) and most flexible prices. It kicks off before Mother Nature herself rises, at 6am Fridays, and is history by 2pm.

When developers knock down classic buildings, their warm English touches are salvaged by **Blue Mantle** ★ (The Old Fire Station, 306-312 Old Kent Rd., SE1; ☎ 020/7703-7437; www.bluemantle.co.uk: Tube: Borough), the largest antique fireplace showroom in the world.

Military buffs should know about **Blunderbuss Antiques** (29 Thayer St., W1; ☎ 020/7486-2444; www.blunderbuss-antiques.co.uk; closed Sun and Mon, Thurs by appointment; Tube: Bond Street), which has been redistributing war mementos since 1968. Sample steals: bugles encrusted with the Empire's lion and the unicorn for £42, and World War II gas masks from £35. You can even put together a uniform like the ones at the Changing the Guard.

Plenty of tourists swing through the booths in **Camden Passage** (off Upper Street, N1; www.camdenpassageislington.co.uk; Wed and Sat only; Tube: Angel),

Auctions

In Britain, auctions attract customers from all walks of life—they don't rely on cat-stroking Russian mobsters like in some James Bond movie. In fact, it seems like half the shows on British lunchtime TV celebrate *Antiques Roadshow*–style discoveries. Most auction houses, which are located in suburban London, do a heavy business in personal items (as opposed to old office equipment or farm stock) and require a deposit of £10 to £50 before bidding (returnable if you buy something), and skim off 10% to 20% of your total, but if you're the only person interested in an item for bid, you could still walk away with a steal. Make sure you attend the free property viewings, which precede the auctions by a few hours or days. All of the houses below sell antiques, art, jewelry, bric-a-brac, and a steady stream of unexpected finds. Always call ahead or go online to get a sense for the house's character, viewing schedule, rules, and auction times.

Greenwich Auctions Partnership ★★ (47 Old Woolwich Rd., SE10; ☎ 020/8853-2121; www.greenwichauctions.co.uk; Tube: Cutty Sark DLR): High-volume house (700 items every week) in Greenwich, good for items sold without a reserve. Viewings Fridays and Saturday mornings; auctions Saturdays at 11am.

North London Auctions (9-17 Lodge Lane, N12; ☎ 020/8445-9000; www.northlondonauctions.com; Tube: Woodside Park): Between 400 and 700 tasteful items, once installed in lovely homes, go weekly. Viewings Sunday mornings and Mondays; auctions Monday afternoons.

R. F. Greasby (211 Longley Rd., SW17; ☎ 020/8672-2972; www.greasbys.co.uk; Tube: Tooting Broadway, or National Rail: Tooting). A mixed bag, it pawns stuff seized by police and Customs, like bikes and cameras. The furniture, taken for unpaid rent, may depress. Viewings Monday afternoons; auctions Tuesday mornings.

Southgate Auction Rooms ★ (55 High St., N14; ☎ 020/8886-7888; www.southgateauctionrooms.co.uk; Tube: Southgate). Good for items culled from suburban homes. Viewings Saturday mornings and all day Mondays; auctions Mondays at 4pm.

so bargains aren't always very easy to come by. Still, shimmering examples of china, silverware, cocktail shakers, military medals, coins, and countless other hand-me-downs overflow the cases. Despite the name, it's in Islington.

You'll get an incredible selection of fittings and furniture rescued from museums, churches, pubs, and homes at **LASSCo** (The London Architectural Salvage and Supply Company) ★★ (St. Michael's, Mark St. off Paul St., EC2; ☎ 020/7749-9944; www.lassco.co.uk; Tube: Old Street; or Brunswick House, 30 Wandsworth

Rd., SW8; ☎ 020/7394-2100; closed Sun; Tube: Vauxhall), from stained glass to paneling and faucets to wood flooring.

Reasonable but still responsive to sharp bartering skills, **Past Caring** ★ (76 Essex Rd., N1; ☎ unlisted; closed Sun; Tube: Angel) is an overflowing co-op known for its modern-era oddities, like freaky '60s ashtrays and kooky mirrors, coats and belt buckles, and lots of other ephemera.

BOOKS

Few bookstores are as well-realized as **Daunt Books** ★★★ (83 Marylebone High St., W1; ☎ 020/7224-2295; www.dauntbooks.co.uk; Tube: Baker Street), which is lined with oak galleries and lit by a long, central skylight. It prides itself on its travel collection, which is located down a groaning wooden staircase. Everything is arranged by the country it's about—Third Reich histories under Germany, Tolstoy under Russia. It's no slouch in the general interest categories, either. Clerks seem to know what will interest the vaguest browser, and the cashier's desk is always piled with choice curiosities.

For scripts, acting guides, theatrical histories, and performers' biographies, **French's Theatre Bookshop** (52 Fitzroy St., W1; ☎ 020/7255-4300; www.samuelfrench-london.co.uk; Tube: Warren Street), north of lovely Fitzroy Square, is the city's most reliable publisher and supplier.

Labyrinthine **Foyles** ★★ (113-119 Charing Cross Rd., WC2; ☎ 020/7434-1580; www.foyles.co.uk; Tube: Tottenham Court Road), in business for over a century, has thus far survived the onslaught of high rents and low readership. After the 1999 death of its longtime owner, who rang up sales on written slips and kept much of the inventory shrink-wrapped, the store was once again passed to the next generation of the Foyle family, and it caught up with modernity just in time to avoid closure; among other tweaks, it installed a cafe. Now its huge inventory (sold by computer, fully browsable) straddles both popular and obscure titles, and writers favor the store for signings. There are smaller outlets at Selfridges, St. Pancras, and the Southbank Centre, but this is the H.Q.

The librarian leviathan **Borders** (203 Oxford St., W1; ☎ 020/7292-1600; www.bordersstores.co.uk; Tube: Oxford Circus) controls some two dozen London shops as well as the common Books etc. chain, but this is its flagship, carrying some 250,000 volumes. As well as offering plenty of 3-for-2 deals on the latest paperbacks—compare the offers here with the other High Street shops because featured titles differ between stores—it runs a cafe ideal for caffeine infusions and skimming potential purchases. It's active in the author-appearance circuit, too.

Although the Duke of Wellington and the Queen herself are counted among its customers, **Hatchards** ★★ (187 Piccadilly, W1; ☎ 020/7439-9921; www.hatchards.co.uk; Tube: Piccadilly Circus), the oldest bookseller in the city (1797), is also noted for its famous shoplifters: An 18-year-old Noël Coward was apprehended as he stuffed a suitcase full of books. (Characteristically, he talked his way out of trouble.) It has been trading since 1801 at its current location, which means it was selling books before Hardy, Dickens, or the Brontës were writing them. You'll find it not far west of Waterstone's (listed below).

London supports a vibrant protest community—don't forget where Karl Marx fashioned the views that changed the world. Since 1945, the city's pre-eminent store for radical books and current-event journals has been **Housmans**

Booksellers (5 Caledonian Rd., N1; ☎ 020/7837-4473; www.housmans.com; closed Sun; Tube: King's Cross St. Pancras). It also boasts the United Kingdom's largest collection of magazines and newspapers, with some 200 titles on offer at any time, plus stationery and a cafe (free trade all the way). You're not going to find most of the stuff here published back home. I always come away disturbed about all the things I didn't know were going on in the world behind my back, a condition I find intellectually healthy. Every Wednesday at 7pm, someone is booked to speak or debate.

The quintessential secondhand bookstore, cavelike **Keith Fawkes (103 Flask Walk, NW3; ☎ 020/7435-0614; Tube: Hampstead)**, down a side alley off Hampstead High Street, is so crammed it's barely possible to navigate. Those who enter should be prepared to leave, much later, bearing a few unusual discoveries and smelling of yellowed paper. Unlike the filing system, prices are sane.

With no insult to Daunt Books, the world's most comprehensive travel book must be Covent Garden's **Stanfords ★★★ (12-14 Long Acre; ☎ 020/7836-1321; www.stanfords.co.uk; Tube: Covent Garden)**, which since 1901 has peddled globe-trotting goodness, from guides to narratives to fiction with a worldview. Should you accidentally leave your map in your hotel room, beeline to the basement; the floor there is covered with an oversized reproduction of the London A-Z map. There are also reams of maps for purchase, including for walking trails across Britain. You'll find plenty of 3-for-2 deals on the lobby tables.

Built in 1936 as Simpson's clothiers, the Art Deco model for Grace Brothers in the saucy Britcom *Are You Being Served?*, **Waterstone's ★★★ (203 Piccadilly; ☎ 020/7851-2400; www.waterstones.com; Tube: Piccadilly Circus)** is Europe's largest bookshop. Even if Waterstone's is the McDonald's of bookselling, it handles the stewardship of that dubious title with dignity; there are five sweeping floors, an enormous London section, and plenty of easy chairs for browsers and freeloaders. The lobby on the Piccadilly side, lined with beautiful curved plate glass, is where the bulk of bargain books is kept, including the chain's prolific 3-for-2 deals on recent releases. The top floor's panoramic cafe, 5th View, hops after work and into

The Royal Warrant

When you're snooping around the stuffy shops of St. James's or Mayfair, keep an eye out for a royal crest near the store's sign or in the window. That insignia is a seal of approval from someone in the royal family—its presence means that the store counts them as a customer and has done so for at least 5 years. To earn Prince Charles' plumed crest, stores have to do even more, and prove they abide by a sustainable environmental policy. Once a store wins a warrant, it's extraordinarily rare to see it withdrawn, but to its public humiliation, Harrods lost its seal in 2000. But don't ask what goodies these businesses are delivering to the Palace; shopkeepers aren't permitted to tattle. To learn which companies supply the Windsors—say, where the Queen buys her corgis' dog food—search the current warrant holders at www.royalwarrant.org.

the evening. In Bloomsbury, a rambling wood-lined branch is at **82 Gower Street** (☎ **020/7636-1577; Tube: Goodge Street**), which operated from 1936 until the late '90s as Dillon's and serves the students of the nearby universities.

CLOTHING

Unusually, the men's boutique **Albam** (23 Beak St., W1; ☎ 020/3157-7000; www.albamclothing.com; Tube: Piccadilly Circus or Oxford Circus) seeks out well-constructed, in-style clothing (made in the U.K.) but doesn't mark it up by insane factors. Although its prices are similar to those of high-casual chain stores, the store is gaining a following among guys because its clothing lasts longer.

A one-stop for classic items (jeans, jackets, boots, and other casuals), the cavernous **Beyond Retro** ★ (110-112 Cheshire St., E2; ☎ 020/7613-3636; www.beyondretro.com; Tube: Bethnal Green) is a haunt of the poor and stylish, who can put together an off-margin look without overdrawing. It has also opened a second branch in Soho (58-59 Great Marlborough St.; Tube: Oxford Circus).

Dover Street Market ★ (17-18 Dover St., W1; ☎ 020/7518-0680; www.doverstreetmarket.com; closed Sun; Tube: Green Park) is a trendy, fashion-first multi-designer concept, heavy on pretentious industrial architecture, that fuses haute couture (Comme des Garçons, Boudicca) with multimedia art installations, all in a six-story department store–like space with an organic cafe on the top floor. The third floor hosts an outpost of L.A.'s famous vintage store Decades.

One of the first boutiques to move into Upper Street, **Diverse** (294 Upper St., N1; ☎ 020/7359-8877; Tube: Angel) keeps stock changing even as it spotlights white-hot labels such as Marc Jacobs and Paper Denim and Cloth. The clothes are funky, which is to say interesting but not always irresistible.

Only a die-hard clotheshorse would brave the 30-minute train trip to bland Croydon, but for those who dare, the finds at **Fashion Enter** ★ (Unit 2, Centrale Shopping Mall, 21 North End, Croydon; ☎ 020/8681-5014; www.fashion-enter.com; National Rail: West Croydon or East Croydon) may be worth it. Think of it as *Project Runway* in retail form: Fledgling designers, especially cutting-edge students at nearby Croydon College, are given space to hawk their threads.

Clothing samples come off the catwalk and land on the racks of the single-room **Frockbrokers** ★★ (115 Commercial St., E1; ☎ 020/7247-4421; www.frockbrokers.biz; Tube: Liverpool Street), which specializes in eclectic day-to-evening wear, one-offs, and a few vintage pieces. This boutique also sells maternity clothes up to size 24. Some trendy movie stars (Uma Thurman) have been spotted here, but it's not a platinum-card affair.

Because it's been cool for longer than many of its competitors have been in business, **Rokit** (42 Shelton St., WC2; ☎ 020/7836-6547; www.rokit.co.uk; Tube: Covent Garden) has a strong following. Probably the largest collection in the city, Rokit sells retro and vintage threads, shoes, and accessories that are funky and hip-ster-prone, from 1950s industrial uniforms to camouflage to tracksuits. The two other locations aren't as well-stocked: **Whitechapel** (101 and 107 Brick Lane, E1; ☎ 020/7375-3864; Tube: Aldgate East) and **Camden** (225 Camden High St., NW1; ☎ 020/7267-3046; Tube: Camden Town).

Don't laugh: For some reason, in Europe, **The Gap** ★★ (223 Oxford St., W1; ☎ 020/7734-3312; Tube: Oxford Street) is a viable source of truly good-looking, season-aware everyday duds. Its inventory is almost completely different from the baggy stuff it offers in North America. It fits better, too, and doesn't make an endless fetish of the brand's cowboy past. It's definitely worth a look. There's a Gap Kids nearby at 315-321 Oxford St.; as you shop there, consider that the company was embarrassed in 2007 by revelations, hastily resolved, that Indian children were slaving with no pay to make some of its clothing.

As it spreads, the Swedish chain **H&M** ★★★ (261-271 Oxford St., W1; ☎ 020/7493-4004; www.hm.com; Tube: Oxford Street) is becoming an international byword for flashy and of-the-moment clothing bargains. It's where the fashion conscious can find astoundingly cheap outfits—they won't last more than a season or two, but they will turn heads while they do. Some of the chain's biggest European stores are in London. This main store, on the northwest corner of Oxford and Regent streets, has the widest selection, including men's; the location nearby at 234 Regent St. also has a wide range; the outpost a few blocks east at 174-176 Oxford Street only stocks women's and kids'; and the one at Covent Garden (27-29 Long Acre) is small but has a good inventory.

Barry Laden, the force behind **The Laden Showroom** ★★ (103 Brick Lane, E1; ☎ 020/7247-2431; www.laden.co.uk; Tube: Whitechapel), takes chances on eager, young designers when no one else will. Since 1999, this lifelong Whitechapel resident has given counsel and space—a shelf here, a cubicle there—to newbie designers, about 40 at a time. Once you go in, it's tough to leave without something. You'll find one-of-a-kind leather handbags (£20–£30), topcoats (£50), and clothes (skirts from £25). Most items, but not all, are for women.

New Look ★★ (500-502 Oxford St., W1; ☎ 020/7290-7860; www.newlook.co.uk; Tube: Marble Arch) is another reliable High Street chain that does casual wear simply, somewhat fashionably, and cheaply (tops £15–£25, jeans £15–£20). Its specialty is women's clothes, but it does a few men's.

I say, old chap, what happened to all the tweed coats and bowler hats the British men were famous for wearing? They're gathering dust at **Old Hat** ★ (66 Fulham High St., SW6; ☎ 020/7610-6558; Tube: Putney Bridge), where classic British fashion, if that's the term, can be found for cheap (suits from £100).

The hottest store on Oxford Street is currently the giant, perpetually beseiged **Primark** ★★ (499-517 Oxford St., W1; ☎ 020/7495-0420; www.primark.co.uk; Tube: Marble Arch), which teems with young women stuffing shopping baskets with cheap-as-chips, fashionable outfits and outrageously lowballed accessories—finding something for more than £10 would be unusual, and £1 deals are common. Unfortunately, we're also talking about a clientele that discards garments wherever they want, line-ups of bored-looking boyfriends patiently waiting for their ladies to control themselves, and products that may not last more than a year. "The devil wears Primark," mutter the snobs. Arrive before 11am to avoid the mob. The Hammersmith location (1 Kings Mall, W6; ☎ 020/7487-7119; Tube: Hammersmith) is saner but smaller.

After a visit to **Topshop** ★★★ (214 Oxford St., W1; ☎ 020/7636-7700; www.topshop.com; Tube: Oxford Street), you'll no doubt find yourself laden with bags but also in a foul mood—because you'll be furious that they don't have shops like this at home. At this 8,361-sq.-m (90,000-sq.-ft.) store, some 1,000 employees are on hand, many charged expressly with helping shoppers put together a smashing new outfit. The range of accessories is dizzying. It's not just women, either, because the incorporated **Topman** jams with dealseekers, too. Designs are always at the vanguard of youth fashion, yet the prices are defiantly low, which makes this forward-thinking, blockbuster store a primary stop.

Saving Money, Saving Lives

One gratifying way to shop in the United Kingdom is to peruse charity shops, which are secondhand stores—priced like flea markets—whose proceeds go to charity. Because their merchandise is ever-changing, any charity shop at any moment could contain your future favorite outfit or that out-of-print CD you've been hunting for years. For more such shops, visit the Association of Charity Shops (www.charityshops.org.uk):

Cancer Research U.K. (24 Marylebone High St., W1; ☎ 020/7487-4986; www.cancerresearch.org.uk; Tube: Baker Street) puts an emphasis on quality goods, both new and old, and prices are accordingly higher.

Crusaid (19 Churton St., SW1; ☎ 020/7233-8736; www.crusaidshop.co.uk; Tube: Victoria or Pimlico) sells clothes, music, and household goods, and benefits from its upscale neighbors' cast-offs. Its focus is HIV/AIDS concerns.

FARA (841 Fulham Rd., SW6; ☎ 020/7313-0744; www.faracharityshops.org; Tube: Parsons Green) is eclectic and devoted to Romanian orphans. At nearby number 662, it operates a kids' shop.

Oxfam Boutique (123a Shawfield St, SW3; ☎ 020/7351-7979; www.oxfam.org.uk; Tube: South Kensington or Sloane Square) is the trendy (and more expensive) arm of the traditional Oxfam store. Designer clothes are skimmed from area Oxfams and deposited here, sometimes after some clever re-styling. Another high-minded branch is at 245 Westbourne Grove, W11; ☎ 020/7229-5000; Tube: Notting Hill Gate).

Red Cross (69-71 Old Church St., SW3; ☎ 084/5054-7101; www.redcross.org.uk; Tube: South Kensington) is near the wealthy and capricious matrons of Chelsea, who keep it stocked with lush pickings.

Savvy, huge, cheap, and of unexpected extraction like H&M and Zara, the Japan-based, rapidly multiplying **Uniqlo** (311 Oxford St., W1; ☎ 020/7290-7701; www.uniqlo.co.uk; Tube: Oxford Street) is another staple on any sensible Oxford Street shopping spree. It does jeans and tops well, but it's also known for cool socks, and unlike many Japanese clothiers, it sizes for larger frames, too.

For a few years in the 1970s, Vivienne Westwood's **World's End** ★ (430 King's Rd., SW10; ☎ 020/7352-6551; www.viviennewestwood.com; Tube: Fulham Broadway) was the coolest place on the planet. The clock at this guerilla boutique still runs backwards, but London's punk heyday is long over, and Westwood went from rebel to royalty. Never mind the bargains—her Anglomania label is a living museum, but it's not cheap. Still, the fanciful couture inventions, flowing with fabric, are outlandish enough to enchant.

A Spanish chain delivering sophisticated looks for below-market prices, **Zara** ★★ (333 Oxford St., W1; ☎ 020/7518-1550; www.zara.com; Tube: Bond

Street) is a smart stop on any hip shopping spree. It can sell you an entire outfit—one right out of this month's fashion pages—for £60 or less, and this location dresses men and kids, too. The locations at 242-248 Oxford St. (Tube: Oxford Circus) and 118 Regent St. (Tube: Oxford Circus) don't sell for kids.

FOOD

Also take a gander at the markets in the city, listed at the end of this chapter.

English food has been a punchline for so long that even the British were starting to believe the reputation. Enter **A Gold** ★★ (42 Brushfield St., E1; ☎ 020/7247-2487; Tube: Liverpool Street), which looks longstanding because of its vintage fittings but is actually a newcomer. It peddles country comfort food that, it turns out, you can't even find at the English supermarkets anymore, such as Cornish salted sardine filets, Lancashire Eccles cakes, and Yorkshire brack—a kind of fruitcake. Okay, I admit, those names don't help, do they?

Have a hankering for jerky made of beef, ostrich, or kudu (a type of antelope)? **African Enterprises** (Unit 3, The Arches, Villiers St., WC2; ☎ 020/7839-6415; www.africanenterprises.com; Tube: Embankment or Charing Cross) specializes in the stuff, called *biltong,* which is eaten like potato chips in South Africa. You can also try unusual candy bars, groceries, and sodas—the Stoney ginger beer will curl your toes. The store is hidden under the railway arches leading to Craven Street.

Pure powdered cocoa, delectable hand-rolled bonbons suffused with hazelnut, hot chocolate as thick as hollandaise . . . what's not to adore about **The Chocolate Society** ★★★ (36 Elizabeth St., SW1; ☎ 020/7259-9222; www.chocolate.co.uk; Tube: Victoria)? I once had to put my name on a waiting list for its rich, moist brownies. It was so worth it.

The artisan bakers at **Konditor & Cook** ★★ (22 Cornwall Rd., SE1; ☎ 020/7261-0456; www.konditorandcook.com; Tube: Waterloo; or 10 Stoney St., SE1; ☎ 020/7407-5100; Tube: London Bridge; or 46 Grays Inn Rd., WC1; ☎ 020/7404-6300; Tube: Chancery Lane; or Curzon Soho Café, 99 Shaftesbury Ave., W1;

What Can I Bring Home?

On the subject of food, although you should always claim edibles when you pass through Customs, very few things will be confiscated. Most stuff, including baked goods, honeys, vinegars, condiments, roasted coffee, teas, candy bars, crisps, pickles, and homemade dishes, are good to go. But these things will make the inspector dog's nose twitch:

- Meat and anything containing meat, be it dried, canned, or bouillon.
- Fresh fruit and vegetables.
- Runny cheeses, but not firm ones, which make up most cheeses (rule of thumb: if you have to keep it chilled, leave it behind).
- Rice. As if you would import rice.
- Plants, soil, wood, and seeds (non-edible). Ask the nursery whether you need paperwork, because many varieties are permitted. And be warned that officers in Australia respond to wood like it's kryptonite.

☎ 020/7292-1684; Tube: Piccadilly Circus; and 30 St. Mary; EC3; ☎ 084/5262-3030; Tube: Liverpool Street) do a brisk business around holidays, when their adorable hand-decorated cakelets (made with free-range eggs) fly off the shelves and into lovers' mouths. They do lunches (soups, sandwiches), too.

The principles of **Monmouth Coffee Company ★★ (27 Monmouth St., WC2; ☎ 020/7379-3516; www.monmouthcoffee.co.uk; closed Sun; Tube: Covent Garden)** are high—only single farms and co-operatives are used, and the owners often venture to South and Central America to check conditions. That means the beans change seasonally. A second location is by Borough Market (Tube: London Bridge). Yep, you can take coffee through Customs.

Let it be remembered that the common cheddar cheese, before it was blanded down by industrial methods, was the piquant star of Cheddar, England. Farmhouse cheeses from across the British Isles (Crockhamdale, Stinking Bishop, and other types Kraft couldn't cope with) are given their due at **Neal's Yard Dairy ★★ (17 Shorts Gardens, WC2; ☎ 020/7240-5700; www.nealsyarddairy.co.uk; closed Sun; Tube: Covent Garden)**, an upstanding, pure-as-milk cheese wheeler-dealer. Tastings are free, and there's a location at Borough Market (6 Park St., SE1; Tube: London Bridge).

At its shop in the city's legal district, **Twinings & Co. ★ (216 The Strand, WC2; ☎ 020/7353-3511; www.twinings.co.uk; Tube: Temple)** deals in specialty teas, herbal infusions, and coffee blends. There's a tiny museum dedicated to tea. Proof it's old-fashioned: It closes at 4:30pm daily and stays shut on weekends.

HEALTH & BEAUTY

Do I dare to suggest you patronize the ubiquitous High Street brand that has devoured all other drugstores, **Boots ★★★ (multiple locations, www.boots.co.uk)**? Yes, I certainly do. Something like 80% of fragrance sales in the U.K. are conducted over Boots' counters, and the chain's endless 3-for-2 promotions almost always include something worth taking home, be it soaps, razors, or other toiletries. Makeup here costs a few pounds less than at most other stores. The company is steering itself away from the chemical-drenched drugstore rabble, too, with its popular Botanics line. Its triangle sandwiches, sold at some locations, are among the city's least expensive.

You'll catch its fragrance a block away. **Lush ★★ (Unit 11, The Piazza, Covent Garden, WC2; ☎ 020/7240-4570; www.lush.co.uk; Tube: Covent Garden)**, part of a growing international chain, slices fresh soap loaves the way farmhouses cut cheese wheels. If you've come to London with someone you love, its fizzy "bath bombs," which turn even the plainest hotel tub into a fragrant pool, are as effective as Cupid's arrow. Other locations include 1/3 Quadrant Arcade, Regent St. (Tube: Oxford Circus); 202 Portobello Rd. (Tube: Notting Hill Gate); and along platforms 15-19 of Victoria Station (Tube: Victoria).

At the forefront of Britain's powerful environmental movement, **Neal's Yard Remedies ★★★ (15 Neal's Yard, WC2; ☎ 020/7379-7222; www.nealsyardremedies.com; Tube: Covent Garden)** supplies beauty aids, holistic treatments, massage oils, and even make-your-own-cosmetics ingredients, all cruelty-free, clear of toxins, and naturally formulated. Its products—London's answer to the New York beauty boutique Kiehl's—are well respected for their quality as well as for their ethical

The Great Museum Shops

Not all museum stores were created equal. The British Museum's stalls don't have enough space to get truly interesting, and the Science Museum is mostly interested in sending kids home with trinkets. But these exhibitors carry items you won't find anywhere else, and you don't have to spring for an admission ticket to peruse them.

London history: The Museum of London (p. 157) has not just mainstream books but also heaps of vanity pressings, specific to a neighborhood or an era, put together by passionate historians. Running a close second is **London's Transport Museum** (p. 159), which in addition to more tomes on the Underground than you thought possible, carries a busload of gifts themed to the Tube's famous logo and catch phrases.

The arts: It may be a design museum, but the **Victoria & Albert** (p. 150) sells stuff that spans art, history, and design, and it's not picked over. I've found books for £18 that Amazon.co.uk listed for £80. And the **National Gallery**'s (p. 145) Print on Demand kiosk, in the Sainsbury Wing, lets you pull up just about any of its masterpieces and print your own high-resolution poster of it on semi-gloss paper (£10–£25)).

Coffee table books: The Tate Modern's (p. 146) shop, long as a football field, tries to be all things to all art lovers, and it largely succeeds.

World War II: The Cabinet War Rooms' (p. 155) shelves of non-fiction are overshadowed only by its postcards based on propaganda posters.

High design: The Design Museum's (p. 180) envelope-pushing ethic is embodied by its sometimes haughty, always eye-catching library.

Wine: The attached museum is worthless, but the shop of **Vinopolis** (p. 192) sells wine, whisky—even absinthe, the "green fairy" tipple.

standards, and the brand is expanding rapidly across the city. Neal's Yard's primary store is squirreled away between Monmouth Street and Shorts Gardens, just northeast of Seven Dials.

I don't really want to picture Prince Charles lighting a Bluebell Classic candle and anointing his body with a blend of roses, lavender, and jasmine, but the cold fact is that **Penhaligon's** ★ (41 Wellington St., WC2; ☎ 020/7836-2150; www.penhaligons.co.uk; Tube: Covent Garden), established in 1870, is listed as an official supplier to the Prince of Wales. It hand-squeezes and custom designs its own fragrances for both men and women—generally floral-based and gentle—and sidelines in luxury shaving and grooming products. A picturesque location is at 16-17 Burlington Arcade, just east of Old Bond Street (Tube: Green Park).

HOMEWARES

Consider **Habitat** ★★★ (196-199 Tottenham Court Rd., W1; ☎ 084/4499-1122; www.habitat.co.uk; Tube: Goodge Street) not for furniture but for its cheerful linens, kitchen tools, and bath fabrics. In pursuit of the department store's mandate (set by founder Sir Terence Conran) to bring high design to the masses at affordable prices, A-list artists (Tracey Emin, Manolo Blahnik) are regularly recruited to contribute temporary sale items. Although this store is Habitat's showpiece, nice-size outposts are at 208 King's Rd. in Chelsea (Tube: Sloane Square or South Kensington); and 121-123 Regent St. (Tube: Piccadilly Circus).

A stalwart of Tottenham Court Road since 1840, **Heal's** ★★ (196 Tottenham Court Rd., W1; ☎ 020/7636-1666; www.heals.co.uk; Tube: Goodge Street) was instrumental in forwarding the Arts and Crafts movement in England, and its furniture and homewares, which are usually defined by chic shapes, have proven so influential that in 1978 it donated its archive to the Victoria & Albert museum. The kitchen department is popular.

MUSIC & MOVIES

The city's only store devoted to musical theater and standards vocalists, **Dress Circle** ★ (57-59 Momouth St., WC2; ☎ 020/7240-2227; www.dresscircle.co.uk; closed Sun; Tube: Covent Garden) trades in karaoke recordings and theatrical souvenirs. You'll find CDs of classic musicals from the 1950s and earlier for next to nothing: £3, although new releases are easily £10 more. The staff can be crotchety, and perversely, it closes at 6:30pm, an hour before the nightly curtain, making it impossible to shop on the way to a show.

Another eccentric Islington gem, **Flashback** (50 Essex Rd., N1; ☎ 020/7354-9356; www.flashback.co.uk; Tube: Angel) is a cramped shop that, happily, doesn't favor one style of music over another—as long as it's old, it's in, and it's one of the last places in town that knows vinyl.

Once part of a chain that went under, **Fopp** ★★ (1 Earlham St., WC2; ☎ 020/7845-9770; www.fopp.co.uk; Tube: Covent Garden), on a busy corner across from the Palace Theatre, re-opened in 2007 as an HMV-owned prospect to satisfy strong public support. Now it's getting its footing again, and its following praises it for discounting new releases and employing staff that have a clue. Discounts are plentiful, and the stock goes beyond the same old songs.

At first glance, **Steve's Sounds** ★★★ (20 Newport Court, WC2; ☎ 020/7437-4638; Tube: Leicester Square) is just another used CD jumble shop. But look deeper: Music journalists and DJs unload their promotional copies here, so you can find new releases and uncirculated pressings for under-single-digit prices.

I don't get it. Why would any intelligent businessman buy a priceless brand, Virgin Megastore, only to rename it something as mindless as **Zavvi** ★ (14-16 Oxford St., W1; ☎ 020/7631-1234; www.zavvi.co.uk; Tube: Tottenham Court Road)? The basics of the store remain the same. It's still a cacophonous multi-level catch-all for the latest in DVDs, CDs, and video games. The purchasing is gradually going middlebrow, but Zavvi is still the biggest record store in town. The Piccadilly Circus frontage once occupied by the also-departed Tower Records (1 Piccadilly, W1; ☎ 020/7439-2500; Tube: Piccadilly Circus) is similarly stocked. Both stores host celebrity appearances and minigigs, which are publicized on site. The selection and vibe here are better than at the overly mall-ified HMV stores.

Don't Let the DVD Code Crack You

In their aggressive drive to ensure they extract the maximum amount of cash from every economy, Hollywood studios release most DVDs with "region codes." American and Canadian players will only play Region 1 discs, and Australia and South America are zoned Region 4, but the DVDs you buy in the U.K. will be coded Region 2. This is annoying, to put it politely, because many DVDs for sale in Britain—TV shows, documentaries, and so forth—simply aren't available anywhere else. Some experts have warned that region coding is probably a violation of the WTO's free trade agreements. The only legal solutions for now: Buy DVDs marked "All Regions," (sometimes noted as Region 0) or, back home, pick up a "multizone" DVD player that accepts discs from any region. Those are often sold in neighborhoods where recent immigrants have settled.

SHOES

Some of the great value clothing stores also sell enough shoes to fill a smaller store. Topshop (p. 273), especially, has a strong range for both women and men.

When a shoe hits it big on the runways, it soon appears, priced small, at **Faith ★★ (192-194 Oxford St., W1; ☎ 020/7580-9561; www.faith.co.uk; Tube: Oxford Circus).** Styles, all current and wearable, go for £40 to £60, and it also does retro designs, men's shoes, and purses.

Although I look terrible in pumps, I understand that many women aren't above engaging in a little shoe tourism. The legendary Malaysian cobbler **Jimmy Choo** started his luxe line in 1996 with a fashion editor from the British edition of *Vogue.* Today, he designs a couture line that is sold by appointment only at 18 Connaught Place (☎ 020/7262-6888), a location so exclusive it's not posted on the corporate website. If you're not a celebrity or MP's wife, you'll have to content yourself with the flagship store **(27 New Bond St., W1; ☎ 020/7493-5858; www.jimmychoo.com)**, where high-heeled foot candy costs around £350.

The H&M of footwear, **Office ★★★ (6-17 Tottenham Court Rd., W1; ☎ 020/7631-1512; www.office.co.uk; Tube: Tottenham Court Road)** rips off designer styles cheaply but effectively, and its permanent sales shop is smack in the West End, north of the Dominion Theatre. Top shoe labels are sold for peanuts, such as Postes for £15. You'll find lots of women's stuff, less so men's. The company's nearest non-sale shop is at 57 Neal St. (Tube: Covent Garden).

STATIONERY

One of my first shopping stops is always **Muji ★★★ (187 Oxford St., W1; ☎ 020/7437-7503; www.muji.co.uk; Tube: Oxford Circus)** a Japan-based chain that sells an incredible array of nifty, sleekly designed gadgets (futuristic alarm clocks), stationery (pens in rainbow colors, slim pocket-size pads) and containers (clear Acrylic Stacking Pot tubes for vitamins and pills). Much of this book was collated using its E.V.A. Zip Pockets. It even sells cosmetics and clothing. Muji's witty "City in a Bag," an assortment of wooden blocks shaped like the major London landmarks, is a great souvenir for kids (£6). Other locations include 41

Carnaby St. (Tube: Oxford Circus); 37-38 Long Acre (Tube: Covent Garden); Whiteleys Shopping Centre (Tube: Queensway); and 6-17 Tottenham Court Road (Tube: Tottenham Court Road).

Paperchase ★★★ (213-215 Tottenham Court Rd., W1; ☎ 020/7467-6200; www.paperchase.co.uk; Tube: Goodge Street) does for stationery what Habitat does for chairs and tables: imbues them with infectious style, bold colors, and wit. Its journal selection is incomparable. Starting in summer, stock up on holiday cards, not only since they're much cheaper in the U.K. than abroad (about £3 for 8) but also because some proceeds go to charity. There are many so-so branches in this chain, but this three-floor flagship is a big paper cut above.

If you're into office supplies (admit it—it's time to come out of the supply closet), the ubiquitous **Ryman Stationery** ★ (multiple locations; www.ryman.co.uk) chain, which makes an appearance on almost every busy shopping street, is a good place to stock up on hard-to-find stuff like A4 paper, envelopes, and convenient "box files" (strangely absent from many countries' stationers), which are available in a spectrum of sprightly colors.

The racks of **Scribbler** ★ (15 Shorts Gardens, WC2; ☎ 020/7836-9600; www.scribbler.co.uk; Tube: Covent Garden) are devoted expressly to greeting cards, and you'll never see its selections anywhere else. It's a great place to stock up on random, trendy cards none of your other friends will send.

The cotton-fiber content of the paper at **Smythson of Bond Street** ★ (40 New Bond St., W1; ☎ 020/7629-8558; www.smythson.com; closed Sun; Tube: Bond Street) is probably higher than in your bedsheets. The Queen, a one-woman thank-you note industry, buys her paper here.

TOYS

A dream of a toy store, **Hamleys** ★★★ (188-196 Regent St., W1; ☎ 080/0280-2444; www.hamleys.com; Tube: Oxford Circus), is so festive and colorful, it's likely to send your kid into sensory overload. It's one of the world's few department stores devoted just to children, and the only must-see toy store in London now that Chelsea's Daisy & Tom store has closed. The employees, themselves kids at heart, are having a grand time, and their ebullient demonstrations of the latest play technology, conducted spontaneously throughout the store's seven floors, are part of the fun of a visit. There's a cafe on the fifth floor, next to the action figures.

LONDON'S GREATEST MARKETS

Unfortunately, with the inexorable spread of megastores like Tesco, Sainsbury's, and the Wal-Mart-owned Asda, outdoor markets that have been feeding Central Londoners since the Dark Ages are finding themselves extinguished. The following markets solider on, providing a huge range of produce, meats, and cheeses straight from nearby farms, as well as cheap clothing, music, and even kinky underwear. Not every market sells something you can take home, unless you count memories: For example, the Columbia Road Flower Market (Sundays at 8am; Tube: Old Street), is an Eden for English blooms, which get cheaper around 2pm, near closing time. Even if you aren't keen to buy anything, a stroll down one of the market lanes, where stallkeepers bark in Cockney accents and the city's immigrant

Market Hours

Unless otherwise noted, markets are mostly outdoors and generally kick off at around 8 or 9am in the morning and start packing up at around 3pm.

population gathers to resupply, is like a front-row seat to the ongoing opera of everyday life. It's London as it was—and hopefully will continue to be.

Berwick Street Market (Berwick St. around Broadwick St.; daily except Sun; Tube: Piccadilly Circus)

Good for: Fruit and vegetables and basic wares; it's small, but it's the last daily street market in the West End, dating to the crowded days of the 1840s.

Also check out: Interesting punk clothing and record shops along the route.

Borough Market (Southwark St. at Stoney St.; Fri and Sat; Tube: London Bridge)

Good for: Organic and farm-raised meats, cheeses, rare beers, fine produce—the market dates at least to Roman times; wares and the atmosphere are pitched to foodies, not shopping grannies.

Also check out: The artisanal food in the stores along Stoney and Park streets.

Brick Lane Market (Brick Lane between Bethnal Green Rd. and Buxton St.; Sun 8am–2pm; Tube: Aldgate East)

Good for: Secondhand clothes, bike parts that might be stolen—more appealing are the trendy boutiques in the overlooking buildings.

Also check out: Beigel Bake (159 Brick Lane), maker of the city's most beloved bagels (and also of a mean brownie); the artists selling handmade bags, shoes, and cards; the Indian spices and herbs on offer at **Whitechapel Market,** a 10-minute walk southeast by the Whitechapel Tube stop, daily except Sundays.

Brixton Market (Electric Ave. at Pope's Rd.; daily except Sun; Tube: Brixton)

Good for: Exotic produce, spices, halal meats, sold to reggae and hip-hop.

Also check out: Brixton Village, stalls selling African and Caribbean clothes, foods, and homewares; Ritzy's Art Fayre, a designer market, every Saturday.

Camden Lock Market (Camden High St. at Buck St.; daily (but weekends are best); Tube: Camden Town)

Good for: Tourists favor its variety of cheap fashions, sunglasses, music mixes, fresh-made foods, partly in a dockside setting. A 2008 fire destroyed the Canal Market part of it, but there's still of plenty of shopping left in several other connecting areas.

Also check out: Stables Market, on the other side of the railway off Chalk Farm Road, sells vintage clothes, antiques, and pop culture knick-knacks; Electric Market (on Camden High Street) is an indoor fair of cool T-shirts, fake furs, and goth wear, Saturday and Sunday.

Hacking the Tax Attack

First, the good news. When you see a price in England, that's the full price. Tax is always included.

Now, the bad news. That tax is usually charged at a rate of 17.5%. It's called VAT (Value-Added Tax), and it goes to enviable programs such as national health care, so that any British citizen who needs emergency care doesn't have to go into debt to get it.

And more good news. Tourists can often get about 15% of that back. As long as the store you're patronizing participates in the "VAT Retail Export Scheme" (not all of them do) and you get the paperwork from them while you're there (stores have varying minimum-purchase requirements), you can apply for a refund, minus a chunk for administrative fees. The only purchases it doesn't work for are vehicles, unmounted gemstones, and anything (except antiques) requiring an export license.

To get your money back, you must:

- Be a non–European Community visitor to the U.K.
- Complete the tax refund form you got from the retailer (ask for it!).
- Present that document to Customs at the airport the day you leave Britain. You must also have the goods on hand, which means a) you must put them in your carry-on or b) you pack the goods in your baggage but first check in at your airline to pick up your travel documents, then bring your yet-to-be checked baggage to Customs, and then re-submit your baggage at the airline counter once Customs is finished. This process can take anywhere from 5 to 45 minutes, so plan ahead. Your refund will usually be processed on-site by a teller who will take a cut, so if you haven't made any big-ticket purchases, it won't be worth the hassle.

Britain maintains information via ☎ 084/5010-9000 or http://customs.hmrc.gov.uk.

Chapel Market (Islington; daily except Sun; Tube: Angel)

Good for: Cheese, dumplings, meat pies, toiletries—it's a real catch-all working-class market on a street that still looks the way it did 25 years ago.

Also check out: The antithesis of a market, the gleaming N1 Islington mall, dominates the eastern end of the street; it's New London versus Old London.

Greenwich Markets (11A Greenwich Market; www.greenwichmarket.net; Wed–Sun, but best weekends; Tube: Cutty Sark DLR)

Good for: Antiques, crafts, honeys, breads, cakes in village-like setting.

Also check out: The cafes lining the covered Craft Market.

Leather Lane Market (Leather Lane between Clerkenwell Rd. and Greville St.; weekdays from 10:30am–2:30pm; Tube: Farringdon)

Good for: Hot and ready-to-eat food, be it Jewish (latkes, salt beef), Mexican (burritos), or universal (salads); sweatsuits and skirts, shoes, jeans.

Also check out: The classic sandwich shops and "caffs" (diners) on the street.

Portobello Road Market (Sat; www.portobelloroad.co.uk; Tube: Notting Hill Gate or Westbourne Park)

Good for: Antiques, hot foods, jewelry, clothes, tourist tat by the ton.

Also check out: The packed pubs along the route; the galleries and antiques shops in the storefronts, where prices can be better than at the stalls.

Queen's Market (Green St. at Queen's Rd.; Tues and Thurs–Sat; Tube: Upton Park)

Good for: 80 stalls and 60 local stores for gourmands and world travelers, with ingredients from Asia, Africa, Russia, the Caribbean, and elsewhere; international clothes and rugs. Although it's been going for over 100 years, the town's council wants to sell the site to developers.

Also check out: Its defenders' website, www.friendsofqueensmarket.org.uk, which argues their market is 53% cheaper than what's for sale at Wal-Mart.

Riverside Walk Market (on Southwark under the Waterloo Bridge; daily noon–7pm in good weather; Tube: Waterloo)

Good for: Tables of used books, maps, lithographs, and wood engravings.

Also check out: Lower Marsh Market on Lower Marsh between Westminster Bridge and Baylis roads (south of Waterloo station), for a classic produce market.

Spitalfields Market (Commercial St. between Brushfield St. and Lamb St.; www.visitspitalfields.com; daily except Sat; Tube: Liverpool Street)

Good for: Up-and-coming designers and artists, prepared world food, handmade homewares, jewelry, vintage cinema posters. It's the most gentrified market in town, and there are lots of one-of-a-kind clothing items for sale, not all of them affordable. The rollicking success of this market has been one of the major reasons that East London is now considered a prime hip hotspot.

Also check out: The market's theme days, including antiques (Thurs); fashion (Fri); and fine foods (Thurs, Fri, Sun). Trendy boutiques line the market plaza, and they *are* open Saturdays.

Walthamstow Market (Walthamstow Market St.; Tues–Sat; Tube: Walthamstow)

Good for: 450 stalls selling everything, from knockoff clothes to food to Chinese-made batteries—it's the longest market street in Europe.

Also check out: You may not have the energy to see much else in this multicultural neighborhood, since the market is a kilometer long.

10 London After Dark

Do Londoners ever just stay at home at night? Would you?

LET NO ONE TELL YOU THAT LONDON TUCKS ITSELF INTO BED EARLY. Perhaps that was true in your grandfather's day, but nowadays, the U.K. rocks all night. The Tube may shut down after midnight, but the entertainment rollicks until dawn. It's even true of the working sector: In the 1960s, you'd be lucky to find a place to buy a carton of milk after suppertime. Now, some 7 million people work during the night in the United Kingdom, and that figure is expected to double by 2016.

London, simply put, is an entertainment hub. With hundreds of theaters, comedy clubs, and nightclubs, London has more to offer on a single night than many cities can muster in an entire year. Whether your tastes run toward cinema or just plain sin, the city caters to everyone.

That said, London's nights aren't perfect. The city's prevailing liquor laws, to say nothing of a Tube system that often closes after midnight, force even top clubs to sometimes unceremoniously dump their clientele on the streets in mid-toast. Whereas in Spain, Greece, and New York, the night rarely begins before 1am, that's usually when the DJ packs up at many of London's top clubs. Recent changes to the law have only added an extra hour to a few clubs' operations. That can put a crimp in plans since it forces those who can't afford taxis to choose just one or two activities in a single night: dinner, theater, or club. The Night Bus system (p. 15) assuages some of the financial pain, but it's a buzzkill to follow a festive night out with bus-stop curb-gazing.

GETTING THE SCOOP: The best way to know what's going on is to do what the locals do: Hit the newsstand. Londoners turn to their newspapers and magazines for announcements of the latest to see, hear, and do. The most complete listings information for entertainment is published on Saturday. Start with these resources:

- ***Time Out* magazine,** £2.99: The original publication of what's now an international brand, *Time Out*'s 200-odd weekly pages constitute the most comprehensive listing of goings-on, hands down. It should be your first purchase upon landing. New issues come out on Tuesdays.
- **Visit London:** The "What's On" section of its website (www.visitlondon.com) is assiduously updated and, even better, it's free.
- The ***Evening Standard:*** Sold by countless hawkers on pavements around town (50p)—just make sure to pick up the free accompanying lifestyle-centric magazine section, such as *ES* on Fridays; it's usually in a nearby stack. *ES* is also available online for free (http://standardonline.newspaperdirect.com).

- ***Metro:*** Distributed for free in racks at Tube stations citywide, most copies are gone by mid-morning, but commuters leave copies behind on the trains, so look around; it's not considered weird to pick up a pre-read newspaper.

GOING TO THE THEATER

If you leave London without seeing at least one stage show, then you'll have missed one of this city's most glittering attractions. No city in the world has influenced Western culture more than London has. This is where Shakespeare defined great writing and Gilbert and Sullivan shaped modern musical theater. It's where David Garrick, Laurence Olivier, and countless other luminaries earned their enduring reputations as actors. London's influence isn't just in antiquity; the great work continues to this day, and if you doubt it, look at the lists of Oscar, Emmy, and Tony winners from the past decade—nearly every year includes at least a few London exports. Appearing on the hallowed boards of London's great theaters and concert halls has made stars of mere performers, and legends of mere stars. Every year, famous movie actors book short engagements in the West End to cut their stage chops away from career-damaging American critics.

Whenever you hear the phrase "West End" in relation to shows, think of the term as describing the 60-odd top tier of theaters in the middle of town where you catch most of the major tours and the big names. These are the shows that most tourists flock to see, but that doesn't mean they're always the best shows in town—the West End is increasingly clogged with mediocre dramas propped up by Hollywood names and by so-called "jukebox" musicals that are the intellectual equivalent of bubble gum. Look to the smaller houses, often called off–West End, or fringe, for the real innovative fare at much more affordable prices. A surprising number of shows that later go on to worldwide success begin as little shows in little off–West End houses.

THEATER TICKETS FOR LESS

If you are desperate to see a specific show, book tickets before you leave home to ensure you won't be left out. Check with **The Society of London Theatre** (www.officiallondontheatre.co.uk), the trade association for theater owners and producers (established in 1908), for a rundown of what's playing and soon to play, as well as for direct links for online purchase. Keep in mind that while most links will deliver you to ticket sellers such as Ticketmaster, where you will pay a premium of as much as 20% for your booking. Only use that method if you'd be heartbroken to miss a particular show. That website also gives you access to show-specific promotions, such as discounted tickets for families or a coupon for a free program to the show; under "Buy Tickets," click "Special Deals."

Although there are ways to snag cheap unsold seats on the day of the performance (see "Saving on the Stage," below), to make sure you have tickets in hand before your trip, it would be wise to look for discounts in the months before you travel. Given a lead time of a few weeks, the established website **LastMinute.com** sells many shows for half price, as does **LoveTheatre.com** (click "Special Offers"). The site **London.Broadway.com** also sometimes advertises slight discounts, but make sure you see evidence of a price cut, because many of its ticketing offers are, in fact, at regular retail rates. My favorite place to find nearly every available discount is the marvelous website **BroadwayBox** (www.broadwaybox.com/london), which posts a helpful, exhaustive listing of all the known discount codes (often more than 100 at a time) for the West End shows.

Once you get to London, grab a copy of *The Official London Theatre Guide,* dispensed for free in nearly every West End theater's lobby and at all tourist offices; it tells you what's playing, where, for how much and how long, and the location of each theater. Unless you buy tickets for full price directly from the box office of the theater (which, unlike Ticketmaster and its ilk, don't slap you with huge extra fees), there's only one intelligent place to get tickets: **TKTS** (www.officiallondontheatre.co.uk/tkts; booth on south side of Leicester Square; Tube: Leicester Square; Mon–Sat 10am–7pm, Sun noon–3pm; MC, V or cash for tickets, no travelers checks, up to £2.50 per ticket service charge), operated by the Society of London Theatre. It sells same-day seats at mostly half-price for all the major houses. While the white-hot shows won't be represented here, about 80% of West End shows are—every day, TKTS posts a list of its available shows on its website, which is handy for same-day planning as well as for getting an advance idea of the kind of stuff that may be on sale when you get there. When it comes time to make a purchase at the booth, there's a window for matinees and one for evening shows. Musicals range from half price (about £25) to full price (around £55); dance performances are around £18; and plays cost £18–£23, although the prices fluctuate per production. Come armed with a magazine or a newspaper that lists what the shows are about because TKTS offers no descriptions. TKTS operates a second booth at a shopping mall in Hendon, a northwestern bedroom suburb that you, as a tourist, are highly unlikely to visit. (Brent Cross Shopping Centre's Upper Mall; Tube: Hendon Central; Mon–Sat 10am–7pm, Sun noon–6pm; MC, V, no cash or travelers checks).

Soho, Leicester Square, and Piccadilly Circus are dotted with closet-size stalls hawking tickets to major shows and concerts. My advice is strong and simple: Don't deal with them. These places are mostly on the up-and-up, but they are really only for audiences who simply *must* get tickets to their chosen show regardless of cost. They tack on service fees as high as 25% of the ticket's face value. The Society of London Theatre suggests before you give your money to any of these outfits, call the self-policing Society of Ticket Agents and Retailers (☎ 087/0603-9011) to find out who is reputable. Likewise, many theaters offer same-day standby seats, rarely discounted by a penny. And I shouldn't have to warn you about scalpers, called **touts** here, because they often issue counterfeit tickets or abscond with your cash before forking over anything at all. Some sightseeing discount cards also brag about discounts, but their deals are mostly for the longest-running, touristy shows and they don't save you nearly as much as TKTS would—only around £20 off the top price.

BEYOND THE USUAL WEST END FARE

The main West End theaters—the ones you'll see advertised on the sides of double-decker buses—are mostly commercial ventures. They tend to show stuff that producers think will yield big audiences and which, consequently, grind on in interminable runs. That doesn't mean that the slate is comprised entirely of Vegas-style schlock or unadventurous revivals—the West End is still where you find some of the world's most acclaimed talent. But it does mean the shows there are

Saving on the Stage

Apart from using TKTS, how can you save on a show? Try these ideas:

- **Matinees are often cheaper than evening shows.** (Unfortunately, they also cut into your available daylight touring time.)
- **Ask about standing room tickets.** Not all theaters have them, but the Donmar, the National, and the Old Vic, to take three examples, do, and they sell for under a tenner (£10). These are only released once everything else has been sold, so you can't count on them.
- **Buy at the box office** to avoid paying telephone booking fees.
- **Seats at the top of the back of the theater** can cost a quarter to a third of what the seats in the stalls do—but bring opera glasses.
- **In one of the older theaters, you can often settle for a restricted-view seat.** You may have to crane your neck at times to see around the edge of the balcony or a pillar, but you'll be in the room. They cost about a third what top-price seats do. The website Theatremonkey.com posts audience members' theatre-specific opinions about which seats are good and which are rip-offs.
- **If you're a student, some box offices (but not TKTS) may offer you discounts of 20% to 40%.** Make sure you have a recognized ID card with you—see p. 359 about that.

generally the most crowd-pleasing, and enjoy all the positive and negative associations that come with mass appeal.

For challenging work mounted by producers intent on taking artistic risks, look to the many theater companies found elsewhere around town. Many of them have designed and built their own facilities expressly for pumping out fresh shows, and each of them has a devoted following of fans and donors that most tourists, because of the circles they travel in, don't hear about. Because these fringe companies put such a premium on developing quality material, you're just as likely to find a winner off–West End as you are on it. In fact, many West End shows began life as sold-out runs in these smaller houses. What's more, you're just as likely to catch the stars of tomorrow—all at prices that are half what you'd shell out for a West End megamusical that was created by committee.

Soho, Covent Garden & Trafalgar Square

Also see The Barbican Centre (p. 290).

You can't often snag a last-minute ticket to the 250-seat **Donmar Warehouse** ★★★ (41 Earlham St., WC2; ☎ 020/8544-7412; www.donmarwarehouse.com; Tube: Covent Garden) without standing in line for returns. Its productions, mostly limited runs of vividly reconceived revivals, are simply too hip and buzzy. Past coups for this comfortably converted brewery warehouse include the *Cabaret* revival that swept Broadway and appearances by world-class performers such as

Ian McKellen, Nicole Kidman, and highly regarded British actors like Adrian Lester, Simon Russell Beale, and Kenneth Branagh. For edgy productions that are just palatable enough to be popular, it's top of the list. Ten full-price same-day tickets are dished out each morning at 10:30am sharp, with a maximum of two tickets per person. The Donmar has, in the past, borrowed a second West End theater so it can program more shows; through August, 2009, it was scheduled for the Wyndham's (www.donmarwestend.com).

For something challenging, try **The Drill Hall** ★ (16 Chenies St., WC1; ☎ 020/7307-5060; www.drillhall.co.uk; Tube: Goodge Street), a theater-and-cabaret venue with two houses that swing with adventurous works concerning sex, gender, and politics. A two-woman version of *The Marriage of Figaro?* Check. A play about an angry lesbian who fakes a stigmata to get back at the Catholic church? Sure. Appearances by lightly clad performance artist Tim Miller? Yup. Expect short, experimental runs. Money's tighter than it once was here, so, this risky venue is currently on the bubble. Tickets usually cost £5 to £10.

Most of the best stuff mounted by the vaunted **Royal Shakespeare Company** ★★ (☎ 017/8940-3444; www.rsc.org.uk) happens at its 5.6-hectare (14-acre) site (just rebuilt) up in Stratford-upon-Avon, but it does maintain a presence in London: principally, the Novello Theatre on Aldwych (Tube: Temple or Covent Garden), where you'll find a repertory of classic plays put on from November to March by some of the industry's most esteemed actors. The RSC also sometimes books the semi-ruined Wilton's Music Hall (Tube: Tower Hill). While Shakespeare's Globe has built a reputation for approaching old texts with trailblazing new ideas, the RSC is best described as supplying definitive versions of The Bard's work (albeit with some digressions made by splashy directors). The RSC also cultivates the youth market by selling £5 seats, including some of the best in the house, to those 16 to 25. Forty of the 50 seats set aside for each show can be booked in advance.

Booking top-flight visiting artists, the indispensable **Shaw Theatre** (100-110 Euston Rd., NW1; ☎ 087/1594-3123; www.theshawtheatre.com; Tube: King's Cross St. Pancras), which began as an offshoot of the public library, is big on comedy, stand-up, cabaret, and offbeat gigs like classy mind-readers and author talks. You're as likely to see Andrew Lloyd Webber tinkling ivories, Ben Vereen hoofing,

Curtain Time & Pre-Show Wine

- Standard curtain times range from 7:30 to 8pm for evening shows, and matinees start anywhere between 2 and 4pm. Every theater is different, so check your ticket. Nearly all theaters are closed, or "dark," on Sundays.
- Rare is the theater that doesn't sport some kind of bar or cafe facilities—a cultural requirement for pub-raised Londoners—making it easy to make a night of a show. Theater companies with their own buildings (such as the Almeida, the Old Vic, and the Menier Chocolate Factory) often run their own mid- to high-end restaurants.

West End Theaters

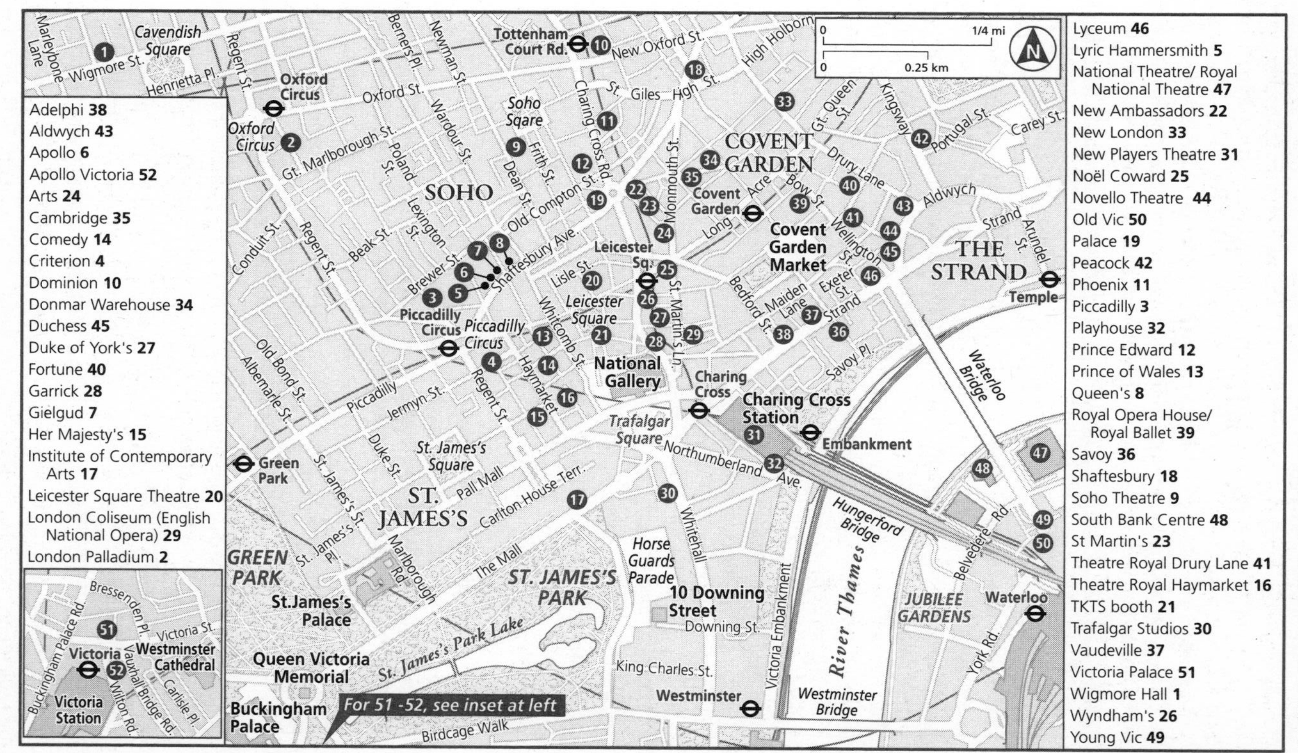

The Do-It-All Venues

In London, the arts are well-funded and well-patronized. These three complexes hum year-round with top-line entertainment not just from here, but from traveling companies from around the world, which consider London a crucial stop on the arts circuit. When I say that something's always happening at these places, I really do mean that you can pick from about a dozen events a week. They're essential.

The Barbican Centre ★ (Silk St., EC2; ☎ 020/7638-8891; www.barbican.org.uk; Tube: Barbican) was built in the 1950s, when earnest but misguided city fathers turned their attentions toward redeveloping a bombed-out crater. The end result was a preposterously forbidding, mixed-use luxury residential/business complex that took more than 20 years to finish. They optimistically planned for lively crowds by adding Europe's largest arts and conference center, too, with a concert hall, two theaters, three cinemas, and two galleries.

You can't always find something going on in all of its venues, and even when things are rocking full-tilt, the bunkered Barbican still feels so windswept it makes *Blade Runner* look like Candy Land, but what does play here is rarely dull. It hosted the first English-language run of the musical *Les Misérables* in 1985, and today is the home of the celebrated theater company Cheek By Jowl (www.cheekbyjowl.com), which often re-envisions classic texts to critical praise. It's nearly impossible to classify the Barbican's fare, since it receives a wide range of the world's great orchestras, singers, and composers, plus a handful of banner festivals each year, particularly in the realm of contemporary music and experimental theater. Its cinemas often screen features fresh from major film festival triumphs, and the long-running Bite festival brings in work from new names and white-hot international producers. When you check out its website (tickets are cheaper online), don't neglect the "Education" section, which lists family events (like sing-alongs) and talks by famous directors, social critics, and (ironically, I think) architects. There are often free exhibitions in the Concourse Gallery, as well as in the foyer galleries.

To reach the main entrance from the Barbican Tube stop, head east on Beech Street, then turn right on Whitecross. Have a wander around this drab concrete carbuncle for a lesson in the dangers of hyperactive urban planning. On the grounds are the Guildhall School of Music and Drama (famous graduates: Ewan McGregor, Joseph Fiennes, and Orlando Bloom), a lake that buffers the noise from the Circle Line running underneath, the

or Elaine Stritch singing as you are Sandra Bernhard ranting or Michael Feinstein crooning. Expect prices from £30 to £60. During the holiday season, it's one of the most central places to catch a panto (see p. 215).

superlative Museum of London, and by the roundabout at London Wall, ruins from old Roman fortifications. Interestingly, those stones are a link to the Barbican's performance history; in Elizabethan times, the area lay just outside the walled city, where theater was illegal, and it therefore was one of the few places you could catch a show. A forlorn artistic outsider: That's been the Barbican for 400 years.

Sadler's Wells (Rosebery Ave., EC1; ☎ 020/7863-8198; www.sadlerswells.com; Tube: Angel) has been a part of the fabric of London life for so long (since 1683) that its current two-house home, dating to 1998, is actually the sixth. Today, you can turn to this Islington establishment to catch some of the world's greatest companies in movement- or rhythm-based performances that transcend language. Its specialties are ballet (Matthew Bourne is a frequent guest artist), contemporary dance, and opera, with plenty of deserving international companies (the Ballet National de Cuba, as an example) and themed festivals (Brazilian samba, Indian theater) rounding out its boisterous, high-minded, multicultural seasons. The company also runs the Peacock Theatre on Kingsway east of the Covent Garden district (Tube: Holborn).

Like the Barbican, **Southbank Centre** (Belvedere Rd., SE1; ☎ 087/1663-2501; www.southbankcentre.co.uk; Tube: Waterloo), a bleak canvas-colored slab, was conceived as a postwar pick-me-up, but age was not kind; despite a peerless riverside location (once the site of the Lion Brewery), it's got a reputation as a forbidding architectural scowl that looks more like a pile of sidewalk curbs than an artistic capitol. It's perkier on the inside, and a recent remodeling has endeared it somewhat to locals. Designers have even made a virtue of the brutalism, naming one of its new cafe spaces Concrete. Hit its website before visiting, because it's chockablock with listings for free and family-oriented events; some 1,000 programs a year go down here at its three concert venues as well as in its huge central hall, which has a cafe and is open to everybody. Dance, classical and contemporary music, the London Jazz Festival, and films fill the bill, but by no means define it—you'll also find readings of new fiction, the Hayward Gallery for art (p. 182), the Saison Poetry Library (Britain's largest collection of 20th-century poetry, with 90,000 volumes), and the classical music mecca called the Royal Festival Hall. At concerts where the onstage choir seats aren't in use, you can often buy them for £6. The complex abuts a particularly pleasant esplanade on the Thames.

The well-heeled **Soho Theatre** ★ (21 Dean St., W1; ☎ 020/7478-0100; www.sohotheatre.com; Tube: Tottenham Court Road), which functions like an ongoing one-building arts festival, doesn't linger over any of its triumphs or its failures for long. With quick changeover (just a few weeks for most shows), it casts a wide net in looking for the latest voices in theater, comedy, cabaret, and wacky stunts (such as young writers given 300 min. to write a play about their youth). There's always something unusual going on. Tickets can be dead cheap; as low as £5, although £10 is the norm. Check its website for discounts.

Another promising potpourri is at **Trafalgar Studios** ★ (14 Whitehall, SW1; ☎ 087/0060-6632; www.theambassadors.com/trafalgarstudios; Tube: Charing Cross), with two spaces (in the gorgeous ebony-and-silver former Whitehall Theatre, located just south of Trafalgar Square) cultivating productions chosen more for their commercial potential than for their artiness. The menu is new plays, carefully chosen revivals, and small-scale comic performances that, it's hoped, will graduate to long runs in other West End houses. Among its recent attractions were Neil LaBute's *Fat Pig* and a revival of *Sweeney Todd* that later swept Broadway.

Southwark

Also see the Southbank Centre (p. 291) and Shakespeare's Globe (p. 187).

In an intimate setting among exposed beams and cast iron columns, **Menier Chocolate Factory** ★★ (51-53 Southwark St., SE1; ☎ 020/7907-7060; www.menierchocolatefactory.com; Tube: London Bridge), a converted you-know-what from the 1870s, is where some of the city's hottest shows have been mounted recently. Its *Sunday in the Park with George* transferred to the West End and later to Broadway, and it produced the U.K. premiere of Jason Robert Brown's chamber musical *The Last Five Years.* Ask about its top-value "meal deal" (about £28), which combines a two-course dinner at its modern English restaurant with a ticket. This company is one of the few to present Sunday shows; it's dark Mondays.

American star Kevin Spacey moved to London to run the **Old Vic** ★ (The Cut at Waterloo Rd., SE1; ☎ 087/0060-6628; www.oldvictheatre.com; Tube: Waterloo or Southwark), although the fruits of his stewardship have been mixed. His choices (generally mountings of talky, meat-and-potatoes drama—stuff actors love to sink their teeth into) have been decent, if not barnstorming. And there's little doubt that under his steerage, the 200-year-old building is pulling bigger crowds than it did before. Those under 25 can snare a few £12 tickets; otherwise, nosebleed seats usually start at £15. Standing room is £7.50.

Beside the Thames near the London Eye, the government-subsidized **Royal National Theatre** ★★★ (South Bank, SE1; ☎ 020/7452-3000; www.nationaltheatre.org.uk; Tube: Waterloo), often simply called The National, is perhaps the country's most noted showpiece for top-flight drama and acting, and the frequent home of the city's hottest tickets. Every London-based theater nut ends up enjoying a show here at least a few times a year. Nicholas Hytner *(The History Boys, The Crucible),* its director, is one of the theater world's luminaries, and he plans a diverse repertoire for its three theaters that runs from envelope-pushing musicals *(Jerry Springer: The Opera)* to classic revivals (the Hugh Jackman *Oklahoma!*) to a huge range of dramas, including world premieres by famous writers cast with household names. Actors consider it a privilege to tread the boards at this modern theatrical complex, and the season runs year-round. Two-thirds of the tickets for every performance in its May-to-August Travelex season (☎ 020/7452-3000; www.nationaltheatre.org.uk/travelex), which usually includes about four plays, are just £10; the rest are £30. The complex's considerable public areas host free exhibitions in art and photography every day but Sunday, and in the same spaces, free hour-long concerts of every genre are programmed at least three times a week, usually in late afternoon. Check out its Platforms series, which features talks and performances by visiting artists and entertainment legends for £3.50. In the summer, its waterfront outdoor space hosts free screenings and performances (from dance to circus); look into its Watch This Space series for what's up. Students aged 15 to 19 can qualify for £5 seats by becoming members of its Entry Pass program.

A rare children's theater that caters to kids without suffering from over-precious programming or a depressing lack of funding, **The Unicorn Theatre** kids ★ (147 Tooley St., SE1; ☎ 020/7645-0500; www.unicorntheatre.com; Tube: London Bridge) is operating on a high note, having opened its very own state-of-the-art facility near the theater cluster of Bankside in 2005. At least two productions, one for each of its theater spaces, run at a time; some are script-based and some sensory-based for younger kids and kids with autism. Many shows are designed to expose kids to other cultures, places, and classic stories for the first time. Everything is carefully classified according to the age for which it's appropriate. If only every city had a kids' facility as lush as this one.

Spry and in top form following a rehab of its theater-and-cafe complex, the **Young Vic** kids ★ (66 The Cut, SE1; ☎ 020/7922-2922; www.youngvic.org; Tube: Waterloo or Southwark) makes a habit of pairing unknown talent with established directors and actors, stepping back, and hoping for frisson. It often achieves it, and if it fails, it doesn't dally long, since it has three theaters (seating 500, 160, and 80) to fill. Odd musicals, plays from other countries, experimental (but approachable) drama—the programming is limber. Around the holidays, it mounts original family shows. It often discounts for students.

North London, Including Islington & Camden

Also see Sadler's Wells (p. 291).

One of the admirable things about the **Almeida Theatre** ★★ (Almeida St. off Upper St., N1; ☎ 020/7359-4404; www.almeida.co.uk; Tube: Angel) is the way it sticks to its guns, mounting intelligent plays (some new, some translated, some unfairly forgotten, many in their European premiers) without much regard for their mass appeal—although it sometimes scores the odd A-list performer. The resulting experience is often thought-provoking and usually satisfying. It's also well-funded enough to have a clean, modern facility (including a pub, although plenty of others are nearby) that any theater company would envy. In the summer, it runs a season of scaled-down opera and musicals. The lowest tier (restricted view) costs £6, but when those go, £15 is the starting point. From Monday to Thursday and for matinees, £10 tickets are set aside for students and seniors.

Making just as much of a lower budget, **Arcola Theatre** ★★★ (27 Arcola St., E8; ☎ 020/7503-1646; www.arcolatheatre.com; Mainline Rail: Dalston Kingsland), set in a former textiles factory, was founded in 2000 and rose to prominence quickly, regularly impressing critics. They must all have cars because Hackney is not a breeze to reach (it requires a change of Mainline trains or a long, long walk from the Tube). The Arcola's shows, mostly by cool contemporary writers (Adam Rapp, Sam Shepard, and names yet to be in lights), run a month each at the most, keeping the bill brisk. On Tuesdays if there are seats available by 7pm, the theater sponsors "Pay What You Can" sales; arrive with some loose change and an obvious foreign accent. Otherwise, you'll usually pay £12.

New End Theatre (27 New End, NW3; ☎ 087/0033-2733; www.newendtheatre.co.uk; Tube: Hampstead) was built in Hampstead as a mortuary, but since conversion to an 84-seat theater in 1974, it has breathed life into countless world premieres, including some written by Jean Anouilh, Richard Curtis, and Anthony Minghella. Its past talent includes Judi Dench and Emma Thompson. Shows only run a few weeks at a time, guaranteeing a varied list of options, from one-man shows to political farce.

Reopened in 2006 after a lavish £29.7-million redevelopment, **Roundhouse** ★★ (Chalk Farm Rd., NW1; ☎ 084/4482-8008; www.roundhouse.org.uk; Tube: Chalk Farm), located in a rehabbed 1846 locomotive shed, picks up on the maverick spirit of neighboring Camden with a frisky lineup of innovative theatrical creations such as musical dramas and spectaculars, many of them given a crowd-pleasing, dance-inflected, shock-to-the-system twist. In the 1960s, it was one of London's most important stages, particularly for counterculture concerts: Jimi Hendrix, Pink Floyd, and The Doors played here. It was the place to catch seminal musicals like *Oh! Calcutta!* and *Godspell* and the scene of triumphs from Peter Brook, Helen Mirren, and Tony Richardson. In more recent seasons, it scored with a limited-run appearance by American agitator Michael Moore and you're just as likely to see one-off comedy events, concerts (The B-52s, Dirty Pretty Things) or author events like the launch of Chuck Palahniuk's latest book. Check out its separate events schedule, which often includes student fashion showcases and career advice for artists, all for free or for as little as £1.

For an ethical challenge, try the **Tricycle** ★★ (269 Kilburn High Rd., NW6; ☎ 020/7328-1000; www.tricycle.co.uk; Tube: Kilburn), which evolved from a simple pub theater to a homegrown arts complex (theater, cinema, art gallery, workshop space, cafe) that now specializes in topical and political theater. It mounted the British premieres of *Ain't Misbehavin'* and four August Wilson plays, and its productions of *Kat & the Kings* and *Stones in His Pockets* transferred to the West End and later to Broadway. It often finds a subversive way to make a nuanced political point; famously, one show hashed out West Bank atrocities while cooking aromatic Middle Eastern dishes onstage. The company's website posts "offers" such as £8 seats that must be booked at least 3 days in advance. On Tuesday evenings and for Saturday matinees, 30 seats are set aside on a "pay what you can basis" for students, seniors, and people with disabilities.

West London, Including Kensington & Notting Hill

The rickety **Gate Theatre** (11 Pembridge Rd., W11; ☎ 020/7229-0706; www.gatetheatre.co.uk; Tube: Notting Hill Gate), a black-box, 70-seat space in Notting Hill, puts a premium on fine acting and on producing international work, such as *Tejas Verdas,* about the horrors of Pinochet's Chile; Mark Ravenhill's *Shoot/Get Treasure/Repeat,* about the effect of war on regular folks; and Eugene O'Neill's rarely mounted, Expressionist *The Emperor Jones.* Its reputation is strong.

You'll find spectacular stuff at the **Lyric Hammersmith** kids ★ (Lyric Square, King St., S6; ☎ 087/1221-1729; www.lyric.co.uk; Tube: Hammersmith), which may look like a fusty Victorian jewel-box theater, but in fact hosts a distinctive mix of multimedia-based shows, avant garde experiments by established writers, and an

Stalls, Circles & Ice Cream

London theater has its own traditions, which you should be aware of:

- Programs are not free; they cost from £2 (for plays) to £5 (for musicals). On top of that, big musicals will also sell a glossy souvenir brochure for £7 to £10.
- Some seats are equipped with plastic opera glasses, which can be rented for the show with a 50p or £1 coin.
- What North American theaters call "orchestra" seats, London houses call the "stalls." And instead of a "mezzanine," they have a "Dress Circle," and above that, "Upper Circle" or "Royal Circle." If there happens to be a third, topmost level, that is the "balcony," or sometimes, the "gallery." And because many theaters were constructed in a class-obsessed era, there will likely be a separate street entrance for each area.
- The break between acts is called an "interval," not "intermission."
- The big snack? Ice cream, sold by ushers (or "attendants").
- Older theaters are required to deploy the "fire curtain," which seals the stage from the auditorium in the event of flames, once during every performance. It's usually done discreetly during the interval.
- A century ago, people were smaller, so there isn't much space in old venues' seats. Leave big bags at the hotel. And ladies, cover your knees, because in the Circles, they will likely be at face-level of the person sitting in front of you.
- Londoners generally do not give standing ovations, no matter how brilliant the performance. If you're pleased, applaud more vigorously.

annual Christmas show to write home about. Its kids' shows are its bread and butter. A second, smaller house, the Lyric Studio, is where the wildest stuff is seen. Tickets range from £10 to £30 for the main house and £7 to £12 for the Studio.

Back in the 1870s, a Dissenters' chapel on the south side of Sloane Square was converted into a theater, and that space evolved into one of the city's most crucial venues, producing eleven plays by George Bernard Shaw, including the premieres of *Major Barbara* and *Heartbreak House.* Still one of the world's leaders in presenting new plays by rising writers, the prestigious **Royal Court Theatre** ★★ (Sloane Square, SW1; ☎ 020/7565-5000; www.royalcourttheatre.com; Tube: Sloane Square) devotes a hefty portion of its schedule to important premieres from the likes of Tom Stoppard and performances from esteemed actors such as Fiona Shaw. Everything I've ever seen here has been memorable in some way, even if I sometimes felt it could use another draft—but the theater does have a proud tradition of fighting censorship of any kind, so perhaps that stubbornness extends to the authors' willingness to hone their scripts. Among the classics launched here were John Osborne's *Look Back in Anger,* and *The Rocky Horror Picture Show,* and past artistic directors include *The Hours* director Stephen Daldry. Investigate

Curtain (and Bottoms) Up!

In the early 1970s, a new form of alternative theatre swept London: the pub theatre. Often just a scruffy front bar equipped with a tatty back room, basic seating on benches or chairs, and tickets from £5, your typical theater pub is often where some of the city's most idiosyncratic, let's-try-this-and-see-if-it-works theater is found. Many of the houses that survive have done so by morphing into crucibles of talent. Today, some of the most respected fringe venues in town are pub theaters, and they have just as much artistic power as many better-heeled West End palaces.

My favorite five pub theaters are:

The Bush Theatre ★★★ (Shepherds Bush Green, W12; ☎ 020/7610-4224; www.bushtheatre.co.uk; Tube: Goldhawk Road or Shepherds Bush) was threatened with closure in early 2008, when budget cuts forced the British government to end funding. Alarmed, name-brand talents such as Judi Dench, Ian McKellen, Salman Rushdie, and Daniel Radcliffe endeavored to save the place, which they did. The Bush, around since 1972, attracts some 40,000 people a year to see its regular slate of brand-new plays by new writers, which in the past have included Conor McPherson *(The Seafarer)* and Jonathan Harvey (whose Bush production of *Beautiful Thing* became a movie), as well as British debuts for Beth Henley, Adam Rapp, and Tony Kushner. It also attracts movie actors (like Joseph Fiennes and Alan Rickman in his earliest days) who want to reconnect with audiences and who don't mind the fact that this shoestring operation concentrates so much on nurturing writers that it lacks wardrobe, make-up or wig departments; each production must organize those on its own.

upcoming shows before leaving home, because the intimate houses sell out quickly if a show catches buzz. Seats are just £10 for any play on any Monday evening (shows change often but usually spotlight new talent); get tickets in advance for its downstairs theater, and from 10am on the same day for the upstairs theater, which has unreserved seating. Frequent readings of new plays are also held for £7.50. Standing room can be had an hour before performances for just 10p, but the discount is so steep because your view will be obstructed.

The East End

One of London's greatest old theaters, the ornate **Hackney Empire** ★ (291 Mare St., E8; ☎ 020/8985-2424; www.hackneyempire.co.uk; Mainline Rail: Hackney Central or Hackney Downs, or Tube: Bethnal Green, then bus D6, 106, or 253 north) was where, once upon a time, you could catch Charlie Chaplin before he became a superstar. It's still a glitter box brimming with life and applause. Several performance spaces are overseen by an industrious management, so there's always something going on here, be it kids' shows, dance, comedy, hip-hop drama, kung fu extravaganzas, short RSC runs—even the occasional Bollywood dance championship. You could say its glory days as a variety hall are back, which suits me

The Etcetera Theatre ★★ (265 Camden High St., NW1; ☎ 020/7482-4857; www.etceteratheatre.com; Tube: Camden Town), above The Oxford Arms pub, programs lots of various, odd, and challenging shows (more than 1,000 productions since 1986—sometimes two different ones a night) in its very small black box. Stimulating and daring the way theater should be, but is it always good? No, but that's what the beer's for.

The King's Head ★★★ (115 Upper St., N1; ☎ 084/4412-2953; www.kingsheadtheatre.org; Tube: Angel). This one is a 115-seater at a 19th-century bar that has more than a whiff of a Wild West saloon about it. Founded in 1970, it boasts alums that include Kenneth Branagh, Clive Owen, Joanna Lumley, Ben Kingsley, Juliet Stevenson, Hugh Grant, and John Hurt—their fading images (younger, braver, poorer) line the walls. This is the city's prototypical pub theater, and it has a potent pedigree.

Landor Theatre (70 Landor Rd., SW9; ☎ 020/7737-7276; www.landortheatre.co.uk; Tube: Clapham North). Basically a large room, this space specializes in palatable musicals and comedy, most of it just £5 to £10.

Old Red Lion ★ (418 St. John St., EC1; ☎ 020/7837-7816; www.oldredliontheatre.co.uk; Tube: Angel). Founded in 1979 above a pub that's popular in its own right as a scene of football-game viewing and evening pint-draining. So if there's nothing good on, you can still get happy. The ORL hires its 60-seat space to a variety of small producers, and also hosts the occasional comedy night.

fine, for as long as pleasure palaces like these survive, London's culture will be rich. Tickets generally start around £10.

OTHER AUDIENCE OPTIONS: DIVAS, CONDUCTORS & TV

The West End is a world-class carnival of theatrical delights, but don't let it overshadow London's strong traditions in the other performing arts. Opera and classical music, and to a lesser extent dance, exert powerful presences on the seasonal calendar. Always check to see if any celebrated international companies are bringing productions to town for a limited run; if they're good enough to warrant an expensive trip across the sea, they'll almost certainly be worth it.

OPERA

Opera's a budget-breaker. Frugal travelers should try the street singers who perform daily at the **Covent Garden Piazza** (Tube: Covent Garden). That's not a joke: Performers are auditioned before being awarded buskers' licenses, so the caliber here is high. Also check to see if there's a touring opera putting down stakes at Sadler's Wells (p. 291). Of course, nothing compares to these institutions:

English National Opera ★★ (The Coliseum, St. Martin's Lane, WC2; ☎ 087/1911-0200; www.eno.org; Tube: Leicester Square). With the Royal Opera entrenched as the country's premium company, the ENO relies on progressive programming (*Nixon in China;* a piece about Muammar Qadhafi) plus opera staples *(Aida, The Barber of Seville)*—all sung in English—and the gloriously refurbished London Coliseum theater (topped with a revolving globe) to pull the posh punters. Tickets start around £19, with seats at the sides of the very-high-up balcony (price code P10) starting at £10 on weekdays, £15 weekends. In an ongoing "Sky Seats" promotion, 12,000 seats in the Dress Circle, excluding Friday and Saturday nights, are £25 off in person or £20 online (www.eno.org/skyseats extra/main.html; ☎ 087/0160-6059). Students and seniors can queue at 10am on the day of performances for unsold tickets at about two-thirds off. Once all seats are sold, the ENO releases standing room at the back of the Dress and Upper circles, not the stalls, for £5.

Opera fans don't need to be reminded of the role the **Royal Opera House** ★★ (Bow St., Covent Garden, WC2; ☎ 020/7304-4000; www.roh.org.uk; Tube: Covent Garden) plays on the world scene, but outsiders might be surprised at how inviting and attractive its home is. No longer a fusty upper-class enclave, the place changed the way it does business in 1999 after a 30-month renovation; now, instead of being open only to ticketholders, the general public are able to enjoy its cafe and panoramic terrace, as well as (for select performances) hear the music outside when performances begin. The main house, which is shared by the equally prestigious Royal Opera and Royal Ballet, was supplemented with a 400-seat space, the Linbury, for chamber opera and dance, as well as the Clore, a Royal Ballet studio seating 180. Standing room for the biggest productions is £10, and the lousiest seats, in its high-up "amphitheatre" balcony, start at £7 and zoom up to £180 for the stalls. Students and seniors can also pay £15 for unsold tickets 4 hours before opera performances.

DANCE PERFORMANCE

London's dance scene has yet to achieve the vibrancy of New York's or Germany's. That's not to say there's nothing to see; it's just that some of the best terpsichorean productions are put on by visiting companies, not by Londoners. The first thing to do is check the schedules at The Barbican (p. 290), Roundhouse (p. 294), Sadler's Wells (p. 291), and Southbank Centre (p. 291), which present a cornucopia of performance genres. To find out about one-off performances, check *Time Out*'s "Dance" section.

The lucky tenant of a gleaming translucent building by the same team that designed the Tate Modern, **Laban** (Creekside, Greenwich, SW8; ☎ 020/8691-8600; www.laban.org; Tube: Cutty Sark DLR) puts on a mixed bill (£3–£15) from hip-hop to Flamenco, as well as works by modernist up-and-comers from its dance school. Many progressive pieces appear here, but they don't run for long.

The Place ★★★ (17 Duke's Rd., WC1; ☎ 020/7121-1000; www.theplace.org.uk; Tube: Euston) is known for contemporary dance—specifically, as the home of the Richard Alston Dance Company, the London School of Contemporary Dance, and the host venue of some 100 companies a year from around the world. Prices start at £5 and don't often go higher than £15, and there are no assigned seats.

Known as the country's premier ballet company, **Royal Ballet** ★★ (Bow St., Covent Garden, WC2; ☎ 020/7304-4000; www.roh.org.uk; Tube: Covent Garden), caters to classicists and attracts the biggest talents in the dance world. It shares the Royal Opera House with the Royal Opera, which means performances have to be shuffled accordingly. The company often mounts smaller, slightly more experimental work in the building's two smaller performance and rehearsal spaces, the Linbury Studio and the Clore Studio Upstairs. Students and seniors can also pay £13 for unsold tickets 4 hours before opera performances.

English National Ballet (www.ballet.org.uk) was created in the 1950s with the stated purpose of touring classical ballet around Britain and internationally, which the world-class company still does. When it's in London a few times a year, it uses the Coliseum (home of the English National Opera, where it uses the same ticketing rules, prices, and contact information) and the Royal Festival Hall (bookable through the Southbank Centre, p. 291).

CLASSICAL MUSIC

Imposing, ornate, and adored by music lovers worldwide, the circular **Royal Albert Hall** ★★★ (Kensington Gore, SW7; ☎ 020/7589-3203; www.royalalberthall.com; Tube: South Kensington) is one of the few performance arenas on earth where, once they have performed there, artists can truly claim to have made it. During the summer, the BBC Promenade Concerts (the Proms) fill this historic, 5,200-seat hall with classical music, but the rest of the year, the space books a hodgepodge of tours, arena-style musicals, the Cirque du Soleil, concerts (the house organ is 21m/69 ft. tall and has 10,000 pipes)—even tennis matches. During summer, RAH's Ignite series of free lunchtime concerts are held most Fridays at noon in its Café Consort, but otherwise, whether there are discounted tickets available is up to the promoter of each show. See p. 188 to tour the hall.

With 900 seats, **Cadogan Hall** ★ (5 Sloane Terrace, SW1; ☎ 020/7730-4500; www.cadoganhall.com; Tube: Sloane Square), is a onetime Christian Scientist church now regularly used by, among many others, the Brodsky Quartet, the Royal Philharmonic Orchestra, and the BBC Proms, which books it during the summer as a supplement to its concerts at Royal Albert Hall. Tickets range widely depending on what's booked, from £10 to £35 for professional musicians, and from £5 for youth orchestras and the like.

In addition to its lunchtime concerts (suggested donation £3.50), **St. Martin-in-the-Fields'** ★★★ (Trafalgar Square, WC2; ☎ 020/7766-1100; www.stmartin-in-the-fields.org; Tube: Charing Cross) evening Concerts by Candlelight (Tues and Thurs–Sat) are popular occasions to flick your Bic to Baroque, chamber, and Early music. Tickets range from £10 to £22, depending on the act and how far back you sit. There are £6 seats without a view of the performance area, but that may work for you because the acoustics are terrific. Wednesdays see Jazz Nights in the church's marvelous budget cafeteria, Café in the Crypt (£5 for general admission, £8 for a reserved place).

Opened in 1901 as a recital hall for the Bechstein piano showroom that was once next door, **Wigmore Hall** ★★ (36 Wigmore St., W1; ☎ 020/7935-2141; www.wigmore-hall.org.uk; Tube: Bond Street) was seized (along with the company)

The English Channels

I'm all for watching a little TV on vacation. TV distills a society's character like nothing else. I can learn more about a place from its news programs and game shows than I can from a week's worth of newspapers—and I find locals would much rather talk about their favorite programs than the woes of the world. Make a point of tuning into these shows, which occupy an important place in pop culture. Double-check airtimes in the newspaper—they tend to hop around:

Weekdays at 3:25pm, Channel Four: Countdown. This long-running game show for brainiacs was given its due as a couch-potato institution in the 2002 Hugh Grant movie *About a Boy*. Its 30-second ditty, played as contestants solve word and math puzzles, is the U.K. equivalent of the *Jeopardy!* theme. Cougarish Carol Vorderman, a Mensa-level Vanna White who drew letters and numbers for contestants for more than a quarter century, left the show in 2008 but remains a pop-culture fixture, even publishing her own line of popular Sudoku books.

Weekdays at 1:45pm and 5:30pm, Channel Five: Neighbours, a squeaky-clean suburban "soapie" set on Ramsay Street launched the careers of Kylie Minogue, Guy Pearce, and Natalie Imbruglia. Made in Melbourne, Australia, it's so beloved in Mother England it might as well be British—in fact, the British market is one reason it's still in production. Its second airing is followed by another bubbly Australian soap, set on the New South Wales seaside (offering lots of opportunity for hot young people in swimsuits), **Home and Away** (weekdays at 6pm, Channel Five).

Weekdays at 5pm, Channel Four: Richard & Judy is a chat show emceed by the First Couple of British gab, married Richard Madeley and Judy Finnigan. They're the British version of North America's Regis and Kelly or Australia's Bert Newton—mainstream, reassuring, and attractive to

as enemy property in World War I. A nasty start, but it soon reopened as one of the world's great chamber concert halls. Today, it's known for ideal acoustics and a roster of some 400 concerts a year. Outside of summer, it hosts Monday lunchtime concerts at 1pm that are simulcast on BBC Radio 3. They're a great value at £8 to £10, as opposed to up to £20 at night.

Also check out the listings for the Barbican (p. 290), the Southbank Centre (p. 291), and the city's lunchtime concerts (p. 299).

FREE MUSEUMS THAT PARTY

Because so many of London's museums cost nothing to visit, special free-entry evenings are not as prominent here as they are in other cities. But that doesn't mean that a few of them don't know how to jam. Londoners use these occasions big-name guests who know they'll be treated with kid gloves. They have also ripped a page from Oprah's guide and started a popular book club.

Monday, Wednesday, Friday, 7:30pm, ITV: Coronation Street, Britain's longest-running soap, and often its top-rated show, has been sudsing along since 1960. "Corrie" is about the goings-on in the fictional industrial town of Weatherfield, near Manchester. William Roache, who plays Ken Barlow, has been on since the start; his character's 1981 wedding drew more viewers than that of Princess Diana and Prince Charles 2 days later.

Weekdays at 7:30 or 8pm (four times a week), BBC One, repeated weekdays at 10pm, BBC Three: EastEnders, set in the made-up borough of Walford, mines the insular dynamic of life in East London. Its doyenne is pub landlady Peggy Mitchell, played by Barbara Windsor, a 1960s soubrette who keeps the years at bay by way of the knife. The cigarette-addicted, put-upon character of Dot Cotton (now known as Dot Branning) is embraced as a cultural archetype by ironic Brits.

Weekdays, 10:30pm, BBC Two: Newsnight is a current events program hosted by journalism icon Jeremy Paxman, who is more willing to grill squirming politicians than America's more deferent news gatherers.

Mid-May, BBC One: For the **Eurovision Song Contest** (www.eurovision.tv), European countries submit and perform a hokey pop song, and then viewers across Europe vote for their favorite. This cheesefest, an annual tradition since 1956, is unbelievably popular, with a worldwide audience peaking at one billion, and it started the careers of ABBA and Celine Dion; *Riverdance* was born during the tabulation interval in 1994. The BBC's host, Terry Wogan, has been increasingly vocal in complaining that Britain now almost always places at the bottom of the pack thanks to a newly formed Eastern European voting bloc.

to limber up after a long day's work with a glass of wine and some framed eye candy.

Visiting a museum during evening hours is also a smart way to unclog your schedule; wherever possible, it frees up time to see museums or attractions that don't have late hours. The only down side to these events is that some institutions tend to close off less popular galleries. Be sure to give yourself enough time; most museums don't admit patrons 30 to 45 minutes before the posted closing.

Wednesday: The venerable **National Gallery** (Trafalgar Square, WC2; ☎ 020/7747-2885; www.nationalgallery.org.uk; Tube: Charing Cross) stays open until 9pm. Some patrons actually take the chance to file past the masterpieces, but many more dally in the bar overlooking Trafalgar Square.

Thursday: The British Museum (Great Russell St., WC1; ☎ 020/7323-8000; www.thebritishmuseum.ac.uk; Tube: Tottenham Court Road or Holborn) keeps its galleries open an extra 3 hours until 8:30pm (and its Great Court stays open until 11pm Thurs–Sat). The **National Portrait Gallery** (St. Martin's Place, WC2; ☎ 020/7312-2463; www.npg.org.uk; Tube: Leicester Square) keeps its doors unlocked an extra 3 hours, until 9pm.

Friday: It's the big night! The **Tate Modern** (Bankside, SE1; ☎ 020/7887-8888; www.tate.org.uk/modern; Tube: Southwark or London Bridge) throws light across the Thames all the way until 10pm, and its second-level cafe and panoramic seventh-level restaurant entertains revelers until closing time. **The British Museum**'s major galleries are open until 8:30, and the **National Portrait Gallery** again closes at 9pm. Across town on the last Friday of the month excepting December, the **V&A's Friday Lates** (Cromwell Rd., SW7; ☎ 020/7942-2000; www.vam.ac.uk; 6:30–10pm; Tube: South Kensington) throw in funky perks such as guest DJs, fashion shows, and a bar—all to changing themes such as Cuban culture or garden design. And on the first Friday of the month, **Late at Tate Britain** (Millbank, SW1; ☎ 020/7887-8888; www.tate.org.uk/britain; Tube: Pimlico) combines drinks, performances, talks, and concerts with a 10pm closing, about 4 hours past the usual deadline.

Saturday: The **Tate Modern** again posts a 10pm closing.

All week: The **Institute of Contemporary Arts** (The Mall, SW1; ☎ 020/7930-3647; www.ica.org.uk; Tube: Charing Cross) is open until 1am Tuesday to Saturday, 10:30pm Sunday, and 11pm Monday. Many of its most popular talks, performances, and screenings are scheduled for the evening. Its bar stays open, too.

COMEDY CLUBS

London's comedy scene—counterintuitively—is dominated by Edinburgh's. Each August in the Scottish capital, hordes of wannabe laughmakers head north for the city's famous festival season, where they vie for awards, audiences, and perversely, that shiniest of brass rings, a major London booking. The rest of the year, it seems that half the stages in town are either helping artists groom material for Edinburgh (June and July's schedules are packed with new shows) or cashing in on its past successes. The fevered competition has created a comedy scene that has less in common with the stand-and-discuss neuroses of New York clubs and more to do with the brittle high concepts of, say, Monty Python or *Little Britain.* You may miss a few local references, but you're sure to appreciate the wit.

The weekly listings magazine *Time Out* runs down what's on, including the many little one-time-only shows (usually £5). All comedy venues serve food and drink (not included in the ticket price, not always required), while shows are usually at 7:30 or 8pm and finish in time for you to catch the Tube home. There's a concentration of options in the Camden Town/Chalk Farm area.

Amused Moose ★ (Moonlighting Nightclub, 17 Greek St., W1; Tube: Tottenham Court Road; or The Arts Theatre Comedy Cellar, 6/7 Great Newport St., WC2; Tube: Leicester Square; or The Cellar Bar at The Washington, 50 Englands Lane, Camden, NW3; Tube: Belsize Park; phone for all venues: ☎ 020/7287-3727; www.amusedmoose.com; prices are usually £8 if you bring along a printout of its online show listings, £9 if you don't) has been around long enough for some of its new talent to be famous, and for old talent to validate it with appearances: Screen comics Ricky Gervais, Dave Gorman, and Mackenzie Crook have all performed here. Its banner show is its Saturday night showcase at the Soho pub Moonlighting—big-name comics like Eddie Izzard or Stephen Merchant sometimes appear here without a peep of advance word to test out new material—but it sometimes books nights at the West End's Arts Theatre or in Camden. The company takes all of August off to decamp for Scotland.

Canal Café Theatre (The Bridge House, Delamere Terrace, W2; ☎ 020/7289-6054; www.canalcafetheatre.com; cover £9; Tube: Warwick Avenue) a space cluttered with candle-lit tables, has up to 14 shows a week, including some sketch and improv outings, but its most famous is "NewsRevue" (www.newsrevue.com) a send-up of current events, running since 1979 but updated weekly, that holds the Guinness record for the longest-running live comedy show; it plays Thursday through Sunday.

Chuckle Club ★★★ (3 Tuns Bar, Clare Market Building, Houghton St., Aldwych, WC2; ☎ 020/476-1672; www.chuckleclub.com; £10; Tube: Holborn), held each Saturday at the London School of Economics, books genuinely funny—and decidedly bookish, very British—comics who share the bill with an equal complement of unknowns. Most of the audience members aren't students, and there are usually five slots for comics (three for professionals and two for newbies) who do 25-minute sets. All this despite its deeply unfunny name.

The 400-seat **The Comedy Store** ★★ (1a Oxendon St., SW1; ☎ 084/4847-1728; www.thecomedystore.co.uk; cover £13–£15; Tube: Leicester Square or Piccadilly Circus) was created in 1979 in imitation of clubs popular in New York. It pioneered the alternative movement that elevated Jennifer Saunders, Eddie Izzard, Ben Elton, and *Whose Line Is It Anyway?* to fame, and it's still considered the best place to catch the odd marquee name, which is why it gets away with charging £15 to £18, although some weekends post midnight shows for £13. Monday nights are for King Gong, an amateur talent night, that's sometimes funny and sometimes dire (£5). On Wednesdays and Sundays, improv comics entertain, while Thursday, Friday, and Saturday are for stand-up.

Downstairs at the King's Head ★ (2 Crouch End Hill, N8; ☎ 020/8340-1028; www.downstairsatthekingshead.com; tickets usually £4–£7; Tube: Finsbury Park) may appear to be an iffy hole in the wall, but in fact it's an admired haunt of well-known comedians who want to try out new stuff, as well as a launch pad for success stories. The best value is "Comedy Try Out Night" Thursdays, when 16 new acts appear (£4); otherwise tickets are £7.

Larger than your average comedy cubby hole, **The Fym Fyg Bar** ★ (231 Cambridge Heath Rd., E2; ☎ 020/7613-1057; www.thefymfygbar.com; tickets £7 Fri, £9 Sat; Tube: Bethnal Green), on Fridays and Saturdays, works hard to book comics (three nightly) who know what they're doing, so this is one cheapie night that ranks higher than many others.

Hen & Chickens ★★ (109 St. Paul's Rd., N1; ☎ 020/7704-2001; www.unrestrictedview.co.uk; cover £6–£12; Mainline Rail: Highbury & Islington), a simple 54-seat room above a pub popular with football fans, used to make its way on new plays, not all of them worthy, but to fill out the seasons, it's been gravitating to one-night-only comedy shows, attracting some top-drawer British names (Jimmy Carr, Danny Bhoy).

Jongleurs ★ (11 East Yard, Camden Lock, Chalk Farm Rd., NW1; ☎ 084/4844-0044; www.jongleurs.com; tickets £15; Tube: Chalk Farm) has 16 locations around the U.K., and so while it brings in names, it also brings in a less discerning, heckle-prone clientele (think bachelorette parties). Basic meals start at £5.95. There are locations in Bow and Battersea, but this one is easiest to reach.

Laughing Horse ★ (☎ 077/9617-1190; www.laughinghorsecomedy.co.uk; cover £5) has roaming shows that spotlight rising (or, sometimes, sinking) performers, which is one reason it puts on one of the cheapest comedy nights in town. Mondays it's in residence at The Blue Posts pub in Soho (18 Kingly St., W1; Tube: Oxford Circus); Tuesdays, it's at the Coach and Horses pub in Soho (1 Great Marlborough St., W1; Tube: Oxford Circus); Wednesdays and Sundays are in Camden at the Liberties Bar (100 Camden High Street, N1; Tube: Camden Town). The rest of the time, its comics appear in single-night runs in harder-to-reach suburbs including Wimbledon and Richmond.

Pleasance Theatre Islington ★★ (Carpenters Mews, North Rd., N7; ☎ 020/7609-1800; www.pleasance.co.uk/islington; Tube: Caledonian Rd.; cover £5–£10), with two spaces squeezed into a former wood warehouse, has stronger ties than most to Edinburgh; it operates the Scottish festival's chief comedy venue. It also presents theater, bringing its total to 180 new shows a year.

CINEMA

Hollywood's latest releases show up across the Atlantic anywhere from a few weeks to a couple of months after they've debuted in North America. Sometimes, they come to London *first*—New Yorkers were outraged in 2008 when *Sex and the City* premiered here several days before it showed up in Manhattan, the city it idolizes. Increasingly, though, the studios' biggest-budget features premiere in London the same week as they do in Los Angeles, to thwart would-be pirates. Major movie premieres are usually held at one of Leicester Square's giant cinemas, including the **Odeon** (24-26 Leicester Square, WC2; ☎ 087/1224-4007; www.odeon.co.uk; Tube: Leicester Square), from 1937, the largest cinema in the country, with seating for about 1,700. But tickets for Leicester Square theaters cost an outlandish £14. For better prices—in even more historic houses—you'll have to look elsewhere. Because so many handsome old cinemas have survived (although boring mall-style cineplexes are steadily advancing), movie-going can still feel like an event. In most theaters, you even select your seats when you buy your ticket.

After many decades during which the country's studio facilities were either closed or overtaken by international film projects, Britain is slowly learning to accept that its homegrown films are worth attending. *Four Weddings and a Funeral* wasn't a success in the U.K. until its distributor advertised that it had hit number one in America first. The release of *Shallow Grave* in 1994 is considered a watershed because it was one of the first U.K.-bred films in years to earn a profit at home. For more information about movies that are funded and filmed in the United Kingdom, check out the U.K. Film Council (www.ukfilmcouncil.org.uk), the government-backed booster association for the film industry.

One of the oldest houses showing movies in London, **Coronet** ★ (103 Notting Hill Gate, W11; ☎ 020/7727-6705; www.coronet.org; Tube: Notting Hill Gate) was built as a small variety house in 1898. In 2004, it was sold to an area church.

History buffs despaired of losing this fine institution, done up in rich reds and woods, until the church proudly revealed that it intended to spruce it up and continue operating it as a cinema. Just more proof that Britain is now a truly secular society. The story gets better: Tickets are normally £7, but on Tuesdays, they're half-price, and on Mondays, students also pay £3.50. The cinema made an appearance in *Notting Hill,* in the scene when Hugh Grant's character wistfully attended a movie starring his estranged girlfriend (Julia Roberts).

One of my favorite ways to spend a Sunday in London is to sack out in front of one of my favorite screens in the world: **The Electric Cinema** ★★★ (191 Portobello Rd., W11; ☎ 020/7908-9696; www.electriccinema.co.uk; Tube: Ladbroke Grove or Notting Hill Gate). The leather seats are softer, deeper, and more private than anything you have at home, and each one is equipped with a footstool, table, and a wine basket—it's a luxurious, romantic way to pass a few hours. The bar in the back of the house sells everything you need, from crudites to booze. Meanwhile, the films, which change daily, hop between first-run (around £15) and well-received art house movies—nothing too obscure—so if there's nothing worth seeing today, tomorrow is another story. Shockingly, this place stood derelict from 1993 to 2001, and only a fierce campaign saved it. It's an institution now; get seated early for the slightly ribald preview reels, which feature a thumbnail history of the building (built in 1910) and young British stars (like Andrew Lincoln from *Love Actually*) in unbilled cameos. Capacity isn't huge, so to get the best spots (such as the private two-seater sofas in the back), it's wise to book ahead. If you don't mind sitting in the first three screens (it's not bad, although there are no footstools), you can save £2 to £2.50 off the price.

Cineasts regard the **National Film Theatre** ★★★ (Belvedere Rd., South Bank, ☎ 020/7928-3232; www.bfi.org.uk/whatson; £8.60; Tube: Waterloo), located a stone's throw downriver from the London Eye, as London's best filmhouse. The programming, by the British Film Institute (BFI), is mind-bogglingly broad and savvy, from classics to mainstream to historic—more than 1,000 titles a year. For example, on a day in a recent July, its three screens unspooled a rare 1924 color

A Jukebox for Movies

One of the coolest, and least publicized, embellishments that came out of the National Film Theatre's recent renovation was the addition of its **Mediatheque** (Belvedere Rd., South Bank; % 020/7928-3535; Tues 1pm–8pm, Wed–Sun 11am–8pm; reservations recommended; free). Without paying a penny, anyone can show up at the British Film Institute's HQ beside the Thames, be seated in a private carrel with a screen for one, don a pair of headphones, and call up one of thousands of films, most of which you'll never find on Netflix. The options are massive, from documentaries about punk rock to 3-minute newsreels from the 1940s to a short glimpse of Stonehenge shot in 1900. My favorite is the deliciously patronizing *A Welcome to Britain,* intended for visiting G.I.s in 1943. A rainy day in London? No problem!

Hooray for Bollywood

A 20-minute train ride out of the city will bring you to several thriving Pakistani and Bangladeshi neighborhoods, where boisterous Indian-made musicals, called Bollywood films, are the dominant diversion. Now and then the major chains like Odeon or Vue Cinemas will screen a random Indian hit, but by and large, the cinemas regularly showing the films are historic 1930s structures that are clinging to life in a tide of advancing redevelopment. Call ahead to ask if the features are subtitled in English.

Belle-Vue Cinema (95 High Rd., Willesden Green Library, NW10; ☎ 020/8830-0823; Tube: Willesden Green). It shows a mix of American and Indian film in Northwest London for £3 to £6.

Boleyn Cinema (7-11 Barking Rd., East Ham, E6; ☎ 020/8471-4884; www.boleyncinema.co.uk; Tube: Upton Park). This 1938 Art Deco house lay derelict in East London for 14 years before re-opening in 1995 as a Hindi venue; it's now said to be the U.K.'s highest-grossing Bollywood cinema. Tickets are £5 except on Tuesday, when they're £3.

Himalaya Palace (14 South Rd., Southall; ☎ 020/8813-8844; www.himalaya palacecinema.co.uk; Mainline Rail: Southall). Built in 1929 in an ostentatious Chinese temple style, West London's Himalaya Palace languished as a market for 18 years before being restored to film in 2000. It shows Hollywood and Bollywood (London's largest screen for the latter) at a standard price of £5.95.

film shot by a British road-tripper, Alfred Hitchcock's *Rebecca,* a documentary on teen-age songwriters from the 1960s, and the 1974 blood-soaked slasher *It's Alive.* As the country's preeminent archive and exhibitor, it also programs plenty of talks, special previews, and retrospectives—even the occasional free screening.

Thought to be the oldest purpose-built cinema in the U.K., the **Phoenix Cinema** ★ (52 High Rd., East Finchley, N2; ☎ 020/8444-6789; www.phoenix cinema.co.uk; Tube: East Finchley) was constructed as the Premier Electric Theatre in 1910; by 1985, despite its handsome Edwardian barrel-vault ceiling, it was nose-to-nose with the wrecker's ball before fans (including director Mike Leigh) rallied. Hollywood is the star here, though plenty of documentaries and Sunday afternoon classics are screened. It also has a liquor license. The £5.75 Monday shows are reasonable considering weekend evening tickets for the same films are £8.75.

Signified by a marquee of silly, Warhol-esque royal portraits (the Prince of Wales in Dame Edna glasses, the Prince of Wales under an afro), the **Prince Charles Cinema** ★★★ (7 Leicester Place; ☎ 0870/811-2559; www.princecharlescinema.com; Tube: Leicester Square) may be irreverent about its future monarch, but its respect for film is unquestioned. It shows second-run films at a steep discount (£4 weekday matinees, £5 evenings and weekends) and programs a lively slate of classic and recent Hollywood movies that deserve to be seen on the big screen. Its greatest claim to fame is its family-friendly "Sing-a-Long-a" *The Sound of Music* (£14), a participatory screening of the 1965 classic (p. 216).

Open since 1911—it retains much original plasterwork and the proscenium arch—the **Ritzy Picturehouse** ★ (Brixton Oval, Coldharbour Lane, SW2; ☎ 087/0755-0062; www.picturehouses.co.uk; Tube: Brixton) had some rough times in the '70s, when it was nearly demolished. With the addition of four screens, a cafe, a bar, and state-of-the-art equipment, it's again the neighborhood's pride, and screens everything from mainstream flicks to art films to documentaries. It also stages Q&As with top directors, including Spike Lee and M. Night Shyamalan. Movies cost £6.50 before 5pm or £8.50 after. For evening shows, family tickets (two adults, two kids) cost £24, or £26 if you have three kids; family tickets before 5pm are £20 to £23.

DANCE CLUBS, MUSIC CLUBS & THE BAR SCENE

Just as many of London's live music venues don't draw a heavy line between the musical genres they present, no rigid division exists between gig venues and dance venues; in fact, many spaces switch from live music to dance in a single evening. That's one of the things that make the city's nightlife so vibrant, but it's also why it's important to check programming in advance.

Students can often get discounts on entry—as if you needed any more proof that education is valued in England. Don't forget to check the restaurant chapter for top pubs (p. 129); gay and lesbian venues are listed at the end of this chapter. If you plan to club nearly every night of your stay, look into buying the £20 Circle Club Card (www. circleclubcard.com), a membership that gets you discounted or free admission and two-for-one drink specials as about 20 places; as long as your combined savings would total more than that initial £20, you could save with it.

LIVE MUSIC, INCLUDING JAZZ, POP, FOLK & ROCK

Dozens of theaters and arenas in town book concerts by recognizable names, but it would be fruitless to list them since they're almost all rented by promoters and don't always have something going on. The better advice is to stay on top of who's playing by checking *Time Out* (www.timeout.com) or *New Musical Express* (*NME;* www.nme.com) magazines. Since big shows sell out months in advance, the best recourse is to book ahead via **See Tickets** (☎ 087/1230-0010; www.seetickets.com); **Stargreen** (☎ 020/7734-8932; www.stargreen.com), which has a small office at 20/21a Argyll St., outside the Oxford Circus Tube station; Ticketweb (☎ 087/0060-0100; www.ticketweb.co.uk; or **Ticketmaster** (within the U.K.: ☎ 087/0534-4444; outside the U.K.: ☎ 011-44-161/385-3211; www.ticketmaster.co.uk), all of which levy fees but let you buy from abroad.

If you want to get into the best shows, you have to book ahead, before you arrive. The most important venues post their schedules and link to ticket sellers on their websites. Check out **Bush Hall** (www.bushhallmusic.co.uk); the **Carling Academy Brixton** (www.brixton-academy.co.uk); the **Carling Academy Islington** (www.islington-academy.co.uk); the **Hammersmith Apollo** (www.hammersmithapollo.net); **Shepherds Bush Empire** (www.shepherds-bush-empire.co.uk);

plus the **Electric Ballroom** and **Koko** (see below). Also give the student union at the **University of London** (www.ulu.co.uk), or ULU, a shot, since the hall books plenty of acts and is open to the public.

The most massive venues—where your favorite artist will look like a tiny, bouncing smudge on the far side of 10,000 sweaty fans—are the cavernous **Earl's Court Exhibition Centre** (www.eco.co.uk) and the just-rebuilt **Wembley Arena** (www.whatsonwembley.com). Sometimes you'll also see big gigs on the sports pitches at **Arsenal's Emirates Stadium** (www.arsenal.com/emiratesstadium) or **Twickenham Stadium** (www.rfu.com/microsites/twickenham), well outside of town. The once-reviled Millennium Dome re-opened in 2007 as a concert venue for around 20,000 spectators (ladies, there are nearly 550 toilets, too). Pretentiously renamed **The O_2** (www.theo2.co.uk), its first bookings, for Bon Jovi and for the Led Zeppelin reunion tour, validated the indoor arena as a worthy venue, and now, everyone from Elton John to Dolly Parton to Tina Turner keeps the place rocking. Don't hope for major deals at any of these venues—this is the big leagues, baby, and prices typically start at £45 for nosebleed seats.

You often won't encounter known acts at them, but London also has a few other landmark stages—good for a beery evening out with the locals. At most, you can catch a variety of song styles at the same place from one night to the next.

King's Cross & Camden

For its championing of unsigned artists, **The Bull and Gate** ★ (389 Kentish Town Rd., NW5; ☎ 020/7093-4820; www.bullandgate.co.uk; cover £5–£6; Tube: Kentish Town), more pub-with-backroom-stage than club, is doomed to fly under the radar jammed with major stages. That means it can charge low covers for a three- or four-act evening.

Launch pad for a thousand indie bands, some that actually ended up soaring (Coldplay, Blur, etc.), **Barfly** ★ (49 Chalk Farm Rd.; ☎ 084/4847-2424; www.barflyclub.com; Tube: Chalk Farm) is a dark, intimate bar/performance space (once called The Monarch) with a good mix of students, musicians, and old-time locals. Because its stage is filled with a smorgasbord of fresh faces and rock-inspired sounds, it's also a place where A&R men are likely to snap up the next big band. Beware the sometimes over-zealous moshers. When the bands wrap up, a house DJ spins for a few more hours while the audience chills.

Particularly midweek, **Dingwalls** ★ (Middle Yard, NW1; ☎ 020/7267-1577; www.dingwalls.com; cover £8–£15; Tube: Camden Town), an ever-popular house of rock, folk, and acoustic guitar, often waives its cover before 7pm. How dignified: Audiences may actually sit at tables to enjoy the music.

Any bar that proudly proclaims itself the birthplace of the '70s ditty band Madness would not on the surface seem to be a place you'd want to enter without prior insobriety. But the **Dublin Castle** ★ (94 Parkway, NW1; ☎ 020/770-0550; www.bugbearbookings.com; cover usually £6; Tube: Camden Town) has street cred. It was the first bar in London to win a late liquor license from the government, so it became an important nightspot. Really no more than a threadbare, greenish pub with a teeny backroom stage, it hosts bands struggling to make it—and a few (Blur, for one, and Madness for two) actually have.

Not to be confused with the upscale Electric Cinema, the **Electric Ballroom** ★★ (184 Camden High St., NW1; ☎ 020/7485-9006; http://electric-ballroom.co.uk;

cover £10–£20; Tube: Camden Town) is one of those dicey, utilitarian halls that never loses the lingering smell of old beer. It has hosted the likes of Sid Vicious, The Clash, and Garbage. Steel yourself for a weeklong roster of punk, goth, industrial, glam, metal, and other genres whose adherents are unlikely to do any more architectural damage to the premises than what's already been done by the ravages of time and neglect. Saturday night is the most accessible, when Shake, a freewheeling disco and '80s event, rolls in. Even though the building is landmarked (it was the first ballroom in London to replace gas lights with electric, hence its name), Transport for London keeps lobbying to bulldoze it so that it may enlarge the Camden Town Tube station.

Much London nightlife is mired in dance music and the illusion of luxury, but as proof that things are finding their way back, try **Green Note** ★★★ (106 Parkway, NW1; ☎ 020/7485-9899; www.greennote.co.uk; closed Mon–Tues; Tube: Camden Town), a welcoming vegetarian cafe/bar where acoustic live sets, from folk to jazz, are booked Wednesday through Sunday. Filled with pillows and upholstered seating, it's a laid-back scene, and prices are sensible (tapas are £3.45–£4.95). Most shows are £5 to £8, but bigger names that require advance bookings (like John Wesley Harding or Carmen Souza) are £9 to £14. Reservations are suggested if you want to eat in the front room (no meat, all organic), but you can swing in just for the shows.

The prime venue for "names," the intimate **Jazz Café** ★★★ (5 Parkway, NW1; ☎ 020/7916-6060; www.jazzcafe.co.uk; cover £10–£25 depending on the act; Tube: Camden Town) keeps the music going from 7pm to 2am, usually in the form of concerts (jazz, soul, bluesy vocalists) by acts with big followings. There's both standing room and cabaret tables; show up early for a good position.

Favored by visiting indie bands, **Koko** ★ (1A Camden Rd., NW1; ☎ 087/0432-5527; www.koko.uk.com; £7 cover; Tube: Mornington Crescent) is a multilevel, 1,500-capacity ballroom that in its former days as a theater saw performances by Charlie Chaplin, and reworked as The Camden Palace in the '70s and '80s, was an epicenter for pop—The Eurythmics, Boy George, and Wham! played their earliest gigs here. Now updated, with steeper-than-average drink prices, Koko hosts Club NME on Fridays, a mélange of live bands, guest DJs, and a tiered dance floor. Often, the first 100 people are admitted for free when the doors open at 9:30pm. In July, it hosts the iTunes Festival, when acts are free.

If you're not a headbanger, the singer-songwriters at **Monto Water Rats** ★★ (328 Gray's Inn Rd., WC1; ☎ 020/7837-7279; www.themonto.com; cover £6; Tube: King's Cross St. Pancras) may appeal more than Camden's squalling pubs. Bob Dylan made his U.K. debut in the back room in 1963, and Oasis braved London audiences for the first time here in 1994. It's little wonder, then, why the record-label scouts brave the grime to listen to the new acts, be they alt-country, rock, or hip-hop. You'll find much of the same genre at an intimate pub, **The Betsey Trotwood** ★ (56 Farringdon Rd., EC1; ☎ 020/7253-4285; www.plummusic.com; cover £5; Tube: Farringdon), which hosts a few singer-songwriters a month—Jason Mraz appeared here early in his career.

A favorite among rock fans, former cinema **Scala** ★★ (275 Pentonville Rd., N1; ☎ 020/7833-2033; www.scala-london.co.uk; cover £10–£13; Tube: King's Cross St. Pancras) is a pleasing place to catch an acoustic or lyrical band; its three levels give nearly everyone a good view of the stage, fostering a sense of intimacy

O_2 Breathes Again

The first time most non-Brits saw the Millennium Dome, James Bond was falling onto it from a hot-air balloon in the opening sequence of *The World is Not Enough* (1999). But the British, alas, were already sick of the thing by then. The £789-million boondoggle, built on a peninsular wasteland on the Thames in East London, was conceived as a showplace for what turned out to be a poorly attended turn-of-the-21st-century exposition. Some elements of the design were clever in theory: The world's largest domed structure, it was and is supported by a dozen 100m-tall (328-ft.) yellow towers, one for each hour on the clock in honor of nearby Greenwich Mean Time. Shuttered since 2000 after a single year of use, this spiky white elephant stood empty and despised as an icon of governmental waste. By 2007, though, a complete refit had transformed the interior of this reject into a stylish go-to spot for nightlife, sports (some 2012 Olympic events will be held here) and entertainment—albeit mostly the big-ticket stuff, heavy on corporate sponsorship—with a 20,000-place arena and a mall for food and clubs. Now the O_2, as it's known, is already a fixture on the city social scene.

Beyond the arena (see p. 308), which sees the biggest names in music, the dome's prime draws, all indoors in a space as large as ten St. Paul's, include:

IndigO_2, (☎ 084/4844-0002; www.theindigo2.co.uk) is considered the "intimate" performance space, although with 2,350 places in an acoustically superior, contemporary room, it's still plenty big, has four bars, and attracts major talent (Prince, Jools Holland). Tickets are £20 to £50 in most cases.

The O_2 Bubble, a second-level exhibition space preferred by blockbuster traveling shows such as 2008's Tutankhamen antiquities display.

appropriate to its capacity of around 1,000 people. Outside of the performance area, a mazelike warren of rooms confuses the drunk ones and hides the shy ones. When it's not hosting gigs by indie bands, it often turns to club nights. Its proximity to King's Cross station puts in easy reach of six Tube lines, but also in the path of potential development over the next few years.

Islington

The Dublin Castle folks also run the **Hope & Anchor** (207 Upper St., N1; ☎ 020/7354-1312; www.bugbearbookings.com; £5–£6 cover for bands; Tube: Angel), and they apply the same winning, if unexacting, formula here: Bands you've never heard of in a guile-free pub setting. Its wee, low-ceilinged cellar space was briefly known for punk bands and for the U.K. debut of Joy Division, but now it's a scruffy but friendly bar where you won't be afraid to spill your beer.

An 11-screen Vue cinema multiplex using digital projection—a rarity for Britain.

The so-called "Entertainment Avenue," a stone street that skirts most of the dome's circumference and is lined with mid- and high-end casual places to eat, including outposts of local favorites S&M Cafe (p. 116) and Pizza Express (p. 94). These places get busy at night before and after major events, but by day, you can often have them nearly to yourself and score some excellent lunchtime deals.

In 2008, the owners of the tried-and-true mega-club Fabric (p. 314) were tapped to create another club under the dome. At press time, the 2,000-capacity place, with two balconies over a dance floor and an auditorium with terrific sightlines, was to be called Matter. Expect a dance floor designed to rattle the bones with its bass notes. The addition puts a stylish, architect-approved spin on London's club scene, which has traditionally squatted in post-industrial spaces. If the success of IndigO_2 and the arena are any indication, methinks the kids'll be alright with it.

Even if you aren't carrying a ticket to see any shows there, it's worth exploring the massive open spaces inside. The bubbly-blue mega-chandelier hanging above the main entrance is enough to blow your mind, and the considerable efforts the facility goes to for a low environmental impact (composting waste, turning cooking oil into biofuel) are appreciated. One of the keys to O_2's explosive success has been the fact the sleek and newly built Jubilee Line station that runs beneath it, making getting to East London fuss-free. But as much as I dig the pretty Jubilee, I suggest another method: Use the **Thames Clipper** (www.thamesclippers.com) ferries (p. 15), which run half-hourly past midnight to and from the Queen Elizabeth 2 dock, just east of the main dome entrance.

Oxford Street & Soho

Many decades have passed since **The 100 Club** ★ (100 Oxford St., W1; ☎ 020/7636-0933; www.the100club.co.uk; cover £7–£21, but check its schedule, since 25% discounts are given in advance; Tube: Tottenham Court Road) was a prime hangout for U.S. servicemen homesick for the jazzy sounds of Glenn Miller and his colleagues. In 1976, after passing through an R&B and jazz period that had Louis Armstrong puckering up for audiences, it sponsored the world's first punk festival, and bands like the Sex Pistols—unsigned at the time—took the stage. This red-walled club still can't decide which era to honor, so it careens between punk, swing, R&B, and jazz.

For a cute little bar for live rock bands that's close to the action of the West End, you could do worse than **The Fly** ★ (36-38 New Oxford St., WC1; ☎ 084/4847-2424; www.barfly.com/theflylondon; cover £5–£7; Tube: Tottenham Court Road or Holborn). The basement, where the teeny stage is, can only fit about 50 people, but that's just right for groovy acoustic sets, and in the roomier ground-floor area, which is light on the seating, DJs are usually keeping the mood cool. Unlike many West End places dishing out live rock music, this place is reasonably priced and actually has street cred; its brother location, Barfly (see above) is one of the city's greats, and its parent company also publishes *The Fly* (www.the-fly.co.uk), an influential new-music magazine.

Unlikely as it is for a chain restaurant, the **Pizza Express** ★★ (10 Dean St., W1; ☎ 084/5602-7017; www.pizzaexpresslive.com; cover £15–£20; Tube: Tottenham Court Road) in Soho and its counterpart, **Pizza on the Park** ★★ (11 Knightsbridge, SW1; ☎ 020/7235-5273; hwww.pizzaexpressclub.com/pop; cover £15–£20; Tube: Hyde Park Corner), both host casual concerts in on-site jazz clubs by acts such as Jamie Cullum, Jacqui Dankworth, and Roy Haynes. Few tourists know that **Ray's Jazz** (113-119 Charing Cross Rd., WC2; ☎ 020/7440-3205; www.foyles.co.uk; free admission; Tube: Tottenham Court Road), a combo record store/cafe, is above the beloved Foyles bookstore, and fewer know that on many weekday nights each month, it gives the gift of free jazz.

For more than 45 years, **Ronnie Scott's Jazz Club** (47 Frith St., W1; ☎ 020/7439-0747; www.ronniescotts.co.uk; £25 for restricted-view weekdays, £30 regular price, up to £45 for major acts; Tube: Leicester Square) has been the standard bearer in London for smoky, intense, American-style jazz, and it honors a long tradition of pairing visiting U.S. greats with local acts. But the old dive got ritzy. After a £2.1-million renovation, the 255-seater began charging extreme prices. Now this old-school club, though credentialed, is a shopping mall for music. Entry prices are dotty (and if you want a table, you have to eat—starters hover around £7), but it's true that the club draws important names, including Wynton Marsalis, Van Morrison, Tom Waits, Cleo Laine, and Mark Knopfler. Shows usually start at around 6:30pm, and the main acts take the stage around 9:45pm—good for catching the last Tube home—although there is sometimes a second house that will force you to take a taxi instead.

Irish and English music is called "roots" here. The postage stamp–size **12 Bar Club** ★★★ (22-23 Denmark Place, WC2; ☎ 020/7240-2622; www.12barclub.com; cover £6; Tube: Tottenham Court Road) is a central place to find it, booking four acts a night (mostly singer-songwriters), and it costs but £3 to £7 to hear all of them. The adjoining cafe/restaurant is blissfully inexpensive (plated meals top out at £4.50). **Enterprise Studios,** nearby at 1-6 Denmark Place, is an affiliated space that hosts a Sunday night open-mic night for artists to show off for two or three songs (5:30–8pm; £3).

Brixton

Plan B (418 Brixton Rd., SW7; ☎ 087/0116-5421; www.plan-brixton.co.uk; cover £5; Tube: Brixton) features a lineup packed with electro, pop, ska, and other Gen Y forms—London's version of American urban styles—and club nights are frequently accompanied by some kind of techno punch such as computerized light walls.

DANCE CLUBS

London's club scene, though ever monumental and influential, is in transition; in early 2008, three of its largest venues, all in the Kings Cross area, were lost to development. Partly to blame is the city's penchant for otherwise empty warehouse spaces, which are at a premium. Now that there's no real hub for clubbing, even popular parties routinely change spaces, and to make a multi-groove night of it, you'll have to trek. The best after-hours fleshpots are scattered across town, and as a consequence, many tourists end up bailing after the first round of clubbing. The revelers who go to after-hours clubs are usually in it for the long haul, which is one reason London's pre-dawn parties have a reputation as some of the most entrancing and transporting in Europe.

Before you go inside any club, do yourself a favor and consult the maps posted on the nearest bus stop to see which Night Bus (p. 15) you should take home. The Tube shuts down after midnight and stays closed until dawn on weekends, and between those hours, black taxis are not easy to find or afford.

The city is speckled with super-luxe, invitation-only, £20-an-entry clubs for the rich and famous (Kabarets Prophecy, Bungalow 8), but most of the action is in smaller venues that appear, make their mark on the scene, and then vanish in a couple of years. Bigger clubs host "nights," which are roving or intermittently held promoted parties, and it's this universe that has spawned international talent like the Pet Shop Boys and Boy George. In the club world, cool venues and hot DJs change temperature every month. What's drawing crowds as of this writing may not be worth their time in 6 months. So grab an issue of *Time Out,* which employs journalists so versed they seem to write in a secret clubbers' language.

King's Cross & Camden

The three-level multi-media nightclub **Egg** ★★ (200 York Way, N7; ☎ 020/7609-8364; www.egglondon.net; cover from £12; Tube: King's Cross St. Pancras or Caledonian Road or Camden Town) is cracking fun, and gets into just about everything, from house (its specialty), retro, soul classics, and live music. It's super-fashionable and likes it that way, although the door policy isn't rigorous. It's the sort of place where both boys and girls can wear baby doll outfits and still fit in; you should ideally look as smart and/or trendy as you can. Fridays are Always Frydaze, a popular mixed night with a minimum of attitude but a maximum of judgment-free revelry, which spins envelope-pushing sounds ranging from bassline to grime. On some weekends it's possible to stay past dawn, which many revelers do in its expansive outdoor garden.

The aforementioned **Electric Ballroom** ★★ (184 Camden High St., NW1; ☎ 020/7485-9006; http://electric-ballroom.co.uk; cover £10–£20; Tube: Camden Town) supplements its concert schedule with crammed dance club nights. Friday is for Sin City (£7), a three-level blend of rock, metal, and glam (dress code: "dress to depress"), while Saturdays are for Shake (£10), for disco and pop. Printing the "club nights" page from its website can save you £2.

Soho & the West End

For those who don't want to pack it in at 1am, one of London's most central after-hours clubs for underground dance is **The End** ★ (18 West Central St., WC1; ☎ 020/7419-9199; www.endclub.com; cover £6–£16, weekdays, before midnight, and advance purchase yield the cheaper prices; Tube: Holborn or Tottenham Court Road), which pounds until 3 or 7am, depending on the night, from a festive DJ booth in the center of the dance floor. The crowd is full of out-of-towners intent on having a good time—for those in the West End, your hotel is a sunrise stagger away.

The City

You have to take yourself seriously to rank at **Fabric ★★★ (77a Charterhouse St., EC1; ☎ 020/7336-8898; www.fabriclondon.com; cover £13–£16; Tube: Farringdon or Barbican)** a three-room former butchery by Smithfield meat market where musicheads hack away at beats to find cutting-edge rhythms. If you're a DJ, playing this 2,230-sq.-m (24,004-sq.-ft.) palace—one of the last superclubs in town—is a career zenith. Fridays are the queue-round-the-block FabricLive, when DJ beats blend with live hip-hop and drum and bass, and Saturdays are more about techno, electro, and underground spinners. In Room One, the groundbreaking Bodysonic dance floor pumps teeth-chattering bass frequencies into the soles of those who dare to move upon it.

Architect-designed, hyper-stylized, and noted for its digital timer counting down the minutes until last orders, **T Bar ★★ (56 Shoreditch High St., E1; ☎ 020/7729-2973; www.tbarlondon.com; Tube: Liverpool Street)** hosts DJs in monthly residencies and never charges a cover to enjoy them. The onetime tea warehouse is low-ceilinged and tracked with exposed ductwork, lending an intimate, easy energy that counteracts the decor, which in a less inclusive place might be considered poseur. By day, it's also a canteen-style restaurant, giving fashionistas their requisite three squares a day: eating, lounging, and vogueing.

One of the city's preeminent venues for live gigs is the 4.4-hectare (11-acre) Old Truman Brewery, a beer factory that's been redeveloped into a casual complex of artist spaces and clubs. Its main draw is **93 Feet East ★ (150 Brick Lane, E1; ☎ 020/7247-3293; www.93feeteast.co.uk; cover £6–£8; Tube: Aldgate East or Liverpool Street)**, which counts the White Stripes and James Blunt among those who have either booked secret gigs or appeared before they got huge. Old-school DJs hang out in the Pink Room (more of a grey-green room, really), but there are lots of stairways, outdoor areas, and dance-floor spaces to explore. Mondays and Fridays are often for free bands, while Sundays are usually an intriguing all-day mix of DJs and experimental visuals. Many people combine a night here with a pilgrimage across to the street to the laid-back **Vibe Bar ★ (91-95 Brick Lane, E1; ☎ 020/7426-0491; www.vibe-bar.co.uk; free most nights, but £3.50 some weekends after 8:30pm; Tube: Aldgate East or Liverpool Street)**, a DJ bar with oodles of live acts, a great many of them free.

Brixton and South London

Held at Plan B (see above), **Fidgit** (www.plan-brixton.co.uk; £6 before midnight, £8 after) is a Friday-night smash-up of funk, soul, house, and hip-cop that, thanks to a late liquor license, stretches until 5am. On Thursdays, the club hosts **Throwdown** (8pm–3am; £5), which starts with a spectacular dance demos and pole-dancing competitions before segueing into hip-hop sets by top DJs.

Dance scenesters either love or hate the **Ministry of Sound ★★ (103 Gaunt St., SE1; ☎ 020/7740-8649; www.ministryofsound.com; cover £14–£20; Tube: Elephant and Castle)**. As London's first megavenue to successfully export a pseudo-corporate clubbing brand, MoS aggravates many of the hipsters it aims to entrance, but to the layman, it's the setting of fabulous sets, a diverse crowd, and top equipment. Garage bands are what it does best, but plenty of techno, acid house, and virtuosic mixes dazzle the scoffers. In spring 2008, when its longtime home club Turnmills closed, trance and electronic dance night **The Gallery**

Swinging London, the Sequel

As Bette Midler once quipped, "When it's three o'clock in New York, it's still 1938 in London." She was being snide, but it's true that the 1940s were far too transformative for London to completely leave them behind, and young clubbers have rediscovered the hedonistic genre that moved their grandparents: swing. Jive at these one-nighters: At **Hula Boogie** (South London Pacific, 340 Kennington Rd., SE11; ☎ 020/8672-5972; www.hulaboogie.co.uk; £7; Tube: Kennington or Oval), in a setting that recalls a U.S. Army base in the Pacific, you can unleash your inner jitterbug to the sounds of the '30s, '40s, and '50s. Whenever an obscure dance is called for (the Hand Jive, for instance), the organizers throw in a free 5-minute lesson, and off you go. Equally retro but slightly sleazier, **The Lady Luck Club** (Platinum Bar, 23-25 Paul St., EC2; www.ladyluckclub.co.uk; first Fri of the month; £10 before 11pm, £12 after; Tube: Old Street or Liverpool Street) parties are down-and-dirty evocations of a 1950s pulp novel; and at the mostly monthly **Virginia Creepers Club** (www.virginiacreepersclub.co.uk; £7 before 10pm, £10 after), 1950s burlesque collides with over-the-top glam—think Bettie Page in elevator boots.

If you fancy swinging of a different sort, here's a swapping party you have to pack carefully for: At the sublimely ridiculous **Swap-A-Rama Razzmatazz** (Favela Chic, 91-93 Great Eastern St., EC2; ☎ 020/7613-4228; cover £3–£5; www.myspace.com/swaparamarazzmatazz; Tube: Old Street), held monthly on the fourth Thursday, if you see someone wearing something you want—boots, dress, you name it—you simply grab it off them. And, of course, you're expected to return the favor—so you shouldn't arrive in your favorite chemise, although you may leave in your new favorite.

Finally, the burlesque revival that swept American cities has bumped and grinded into London, tinged with performance art, at the **Bethnal Green WorkingMen's Club** (44-46 Pollard Row, E2; ☎ 020/7739-7170; www.workersplaytime.net; cover £5–£8; Tube: Bethnal Green), a onetime hangout for blue-collar laborers that now puts on politically incorrect, dirty-and-diverse variety shows, twirling tassels and all. Take *that,* Andrews Sisters!

(www.thegallery-club.co.uk) moved here for its weekly Friday engagement. Saturday is the week's other peak night; squeeze into the balcony bar and observe the energy gushing from the warehouse-like main floor, called "the box."

Okay, so **Roller Disco** ★★ (Renaissance Rooms Vauxhall, off Miles St., SW8; ☎ 084/4736-5375; www.rollerdisco.info/vauxhall; cover £10 Thurs and £13 Fri and Sat, includes skate rental; Tube: Vauxhall) is not exactly a dance club, but it does involve shaking your booty. These long-running nights appeal to those sick of or intimidated by the self-important club scene—crowds lace up their roller

Drinking in the View

If you're going to deviate from the pub circuit to order an expensive cocktail at a cosmopolitan bar, you might as well do it where there's a view.

Oxo Tower Restaurant, Bar & Brasserie (Bargehouse St., South Bank, SE1; ☎ 020/7803-3888; www.harveynichols.com; Tube: Southwark): After work, the penthouse of this affectionately held landmark, once a power station and later a factory for beef-stock cubes, is elbow-to-elbow with media types who are very pleased with themselves. Turn your back to them and enjoy the Thames, eight floors below, with the dome of St. Paul's standing prouder than your cohorts.

Roof Garden at The Trafalgar (2 Spring Gardens, Trafalgar Square, SW1; ☎ 020/7870-2900; www.thetrafalgar.com; Tube: Charing Cross): This outdoor spot's our little secret, since few people seem to know about it. On the seventh floor of this stone hotel the view takes in The Clock Tower at the Houses of Parliament, the London Eye, and Nelson's Column. Even on a Saturday night, it's never very crowded, which may be unjust, but it makes for a romantic outing for the rest of us.

5th View at Waterstone's (203-206 Piccadilly; ☎ 020/7851-2433; www.5thview.co.uk; Tube: Piccadilly Circus): Atop one of the city's best department stores for books, this south-facing cafe takes in Westminster Abbey, Parliament, and Whitehall. The list of international beers is long. Cocktails aren't cheap (£8), but they're as cheap as they get for panoramic bars like these, and as a bonus, you can read any book from the store for free.

Ruba Bar (5 More London Place, Tooley St., SE1; ☎ 020/3002-4300; www.hilton.co.uk/towerbridge; Tube: London Bridge), at Hilton Tower Bridge hotel, is a business-hotel bar with a difference: a ninth-floor, gratitude-inducing vista including the Tower of London, the Tower Bridge, and the HMS *Belfast*. It's not the hippest spot (its signature cocktail is the Rhubarb Daiquiri), but at least you won't jostle with hyper kids.

Vertigo 42 (Tower 42, 25 Old Broad St., EC2; ☎ 020/7877-7842; www.vertigo42.co.uk; Tube: Bank): Because it's atop one of the tallest buildings in The City, and tables command a stellar view of just about everything, this bar deigns to charge £12 for a glass of champagne and £6 for a little dish of almonds. That means it's for special occasions, like for the day you sign your bankruptcy declaration. It's most impressive at sundown and at night, but consider the £15 set lunch (soup, salad, dessert), Monday to Friday, when you can see the jumbo jets on their approaches to Heathrow over South London. It doesn't allow kids, and reservations are mandatory.

skates while three rooms spin disco, hip hop, and house. Needless to say, it's pretty kitschy (prizes are even awarded to those who look the most '70s), so there's no attitude and falling is permitted. On the first Wednesday night of the month, the concept takes a slightly ruder angle with Skate Bitch (www.skatebitch.co.uk), during which funk, soul, and ska prevail.

GAY & LESBIAN

London has the most varied and vibrant gay and lesbian scene in the world. The city boasts more than 100 pubs, clubs, and club nights, and a dozen saunas—beat that, San Francisco or New York! The music seems to crank a few notches louder when the jolly and outrageous **Pride London** (www.pridelondon.org) season rolls along, in late June or early July.

Daily gay-oriented pursuits have traditionally been centered around Soho, where the bars and clubs take on a festive, anyone-is-welcome flair, and after work, guys spill into the streets. For clubbing, Vauxhall has emerged as a center. But as a mark of a truly integrated city, now nearly every neighborhood has its own pubs and gay nights. Where you spend an evening depends on your proclivities and willingness to commute. At most places, there aren't usually cover charges unless an event or show is on, when they're about £5 at bars and £11 for clubs. London's scene is remarkably inclusive—straight women and male friends will almost always feel comfortable tagging along unless they're going to a club specifically designed to attract clientele based solely on their sexual tastes. Lesbians who want to go out at night must usually plan a little because most girls' events take the form of weekly scheduled nights in bars that might cater to other niches during the rest of the week. The Sapphically inclined should turn to Gingerbeer (www.gingerbeer.co.uk) for listings.

The monthly general-interest magazine ***GayTimes*** (£3.50; www.gaytimes.co.uk) rounds up the current addresses, but for a clue about events, grab one of two weekly magazines. The racy **Boyz** (www.boyz.co.uk) includes a thorough day-by-day schedule, which also appears on its website. It's distributed for free at many gay bars. The free **QX Magazine** (www.qxmagazine.com), catering more to the club scene, publishes a less comprehensive diary, but it's still useful, and conveniently for advance planning, you can read a free facsimile of the printed edition every week. *Time Out* also has a weekly "Gay and Lesbian" section that dwells more on clubbing than on well-rounded pursuits.

Soho

Thanks to its cobalt-and-steel design, **Barcode Soho** ★★ (3-4 Archer St., W1; ☎ 020/7734-3342; www.bar-code.co.uk; cover around £4 after 10pm weekends; Tube: Piccadilly Circus), a two-level space on a side street, seems on the surface like a snooty setting, but in reality it attracts a varied crowd of friendly over-25s, and it serves drinks longer than many rivals (until 1am most nights). Its downstairs space does straight-friendly comedy nights on Tuesdays. The bar has also opened a Vauxhall location (Arch 69, Albert Embankment, SE1; ☎ 020/7582-4180; Tube: Vauxhall). From 4pm to 7pm, both bars serve £2 pints.

Candy Bar (4 Carlisle St., W1; ☎ 020/7494-4041; Tube: Tottenham Court Road) is one of London's best-known (and only 7-days-a-week) lesbian bars, and given that there aren't too many girl bars in town, it attracts a wide spectrum of types (even tagalong men), even if its music spectrum seem more narrowed to R&B. Later at night, the basement bar opens. The monthly party **Lounge** (**www.lounge.uk.net**) is another popular lesbian night, but it switches venues, sticking mostly to the West End, so you'll need to make advance plans. At press time, the original promoters of the lesbian Candy Bar had decamped to Ku's top level from Sunday to Wednesday to organize lesbian nights (see www.thecandy bar.co.uk); no telling if either the bar or the promoters were going to change names to avoid confusion.

Come six o'clock in summer, Old Compton Street fills with men in boots, pint glasses, and basso conversation, as patrons from **Comptons of Soho** ★ (51-53 Old Compton St., W1; ☎ 020/7479-7961; Tube: Leicester Square or Piccadilly Circus) and cruisy **Admiral Duncan** (54 Old Compton St., W1; ☎ 020/7437-5300; Tube: Leicester Square or Piccadilly Circus) overflow into an ongoing block party. Both bars cater to an over-30 crowd, and are light on snobbery.

My pick for the best gay bar for no attitude and a mix of every gender and age, **The Edge** ★★ (11 Soho Square, W1; ☎ 020/7439-1313; Tube: Tottenham Court Road) is a stylish-but-warm complex set up to offer something for every mood. Despite having four levels (the top one's for dancing, the candle-lit first floor is loungy), it gets incredibly, uncomfortably crowded with manflesh. The coolest thing about it is its location right on Soho Square, and patrons often duck out to kick back in the park, giving this hotspot a less frenetic vibe than many other trendy places. In summer, sidewalk tables are laid out and fill up quickly.

Friendly Society ★ (79 Wardour St., W1; ☎ 020/7434-3805; Tube: Leicester Square) is a Jetsons-styled basement bar where the patrons are convivial and the music is peppy, light, and diva-rich—think Dolly Parton and Diana Ross. Find it down Tisbury Court, an alley between Wardour and Rupert streets (don't worry—it's not scuzzy). Its owner, Maria, is something of a local star on the scene.

No other dance club in town, gay or straight, comes close to attracting such a pantheon of legendary live performances as **G-A-Y** ★★★ (www.g-a-y.co.uk). Kylie, the Spice Girls, Cyndi Lauper, Bjork, and of course, Madge, all performed here at the height of their fame, and some have been known to drop by unannounced to collect career laurels. Although it goes four nights a week, the big names visit on Saturdays, when 2,000 chipper young things bop until 4am. The event's longtime home, Charing Cross Road's Astoria Theatre, was slated for a late 2008 demolition to make way for a major train project, but the G-A-Y brand is clubbing gold and it's likely to move to another, less beloved venue, so check its website for where. The club also runs a bubblegum-light pre-show hangout, **G-A-Y Bar** ★★ (30 Old Compton St., W1; ☎ 020/7494-2756; Tube: Leicester Square), which is lively most hours of the day with a young, twinkie crowd, who come to chatter, steep in cheery Europop, and watch videos on the plasma screens. You can buy tickets for the big club at the Bar.

Heaven ★★ (Under the Arches, off Villiers St., WC2; ☎ 020/7930-2020; www.heaven-london.com; £4–£8; Tube: Charing Cross or Embankment) is a big, three-level Saturday-night dance blowout, which has been running for ages and therefore isn't too crammed with trendoids. Popcorn is its bustling Monday dance night, but Wednesday's Work! is a crowd-pleaser serving up house, electro, and R&B. None of its nights are groundbreaking; they're simply old-fashioned, straight-friendly, hands-in-the-air dance jams. The independent cabaret-and-karaoke pub **Halfway to Heaven** (7 Duncannon St., WC2; ☎ 020/7321-2791; Tube: Charing Cross), low-key and plain, is so named because it's about halfway between Leicester Square and the Heaven nightclub.

Just south of Shaftesbury Avenue from Soho, three-level **Ku Bar** ★ (30 Lisle St., WC2; ☎ 020/7437-4303; www.ku-bar.co.uk; Tube: Leicester Square) is a manageably sized, pleasantly cruisey, generally laid-back bar and lounge that some nights gives its Klub space over to modest club events and comedy gigs. It's the place you go when you don't want a scene, but you also don't want a dusty cave populated with trolls stuck to their barstools.

Housed in a former postwar girlie bar, **Soho Revue Bar** ★★ (11 Walkers Court, W1; ☎ 020/7734-0377; www.sohorevuebar.com; cover £5–£10) retains its glam-lounge roots with red, showroom-style banquettes, crystal chandeliers, and a roster of burlesque-inspired shows on the stage. When there's not a show, the club pumps with electro and indie music and collects some of Soho's most put-together boys. Wednesdays are Trannyshack, an outrageous pansexual conclave with live drag shows, but it's Circus, on Friday, that attracts style celebs and gets the kids dressing haute.

79 CXR (79 Charing Cross Rd., WC1; ☎ 020/7734-0769; Tube: Leicester Square), a contemporary multileveled cruise bar, dark and bordering on sleazy in the bathrooms, gets busiest after work when the salarymen pour in to mingle. The loft is for socializing and the odd across-the-room flirt.

King's Cross, Camden, and Islington

A fierce following patronizes **The Black Cap** ★★ (171 Camden High St., NW1; ☎ 020/7485-0538; www.theblackcap.com; Tube: Camden Town). This pubby place, which has a roof garden, is centered on its basement performance space, shoulder-to-shoulder during its weekend drag and cabaret shows.

For those who like it dirty, no other large space in the city can compete with **Central Station** (37 Wharfdale Rd., N1; ☎ 020/7278-3294; www.centralstation.co.uk; Tube: King's Cross St. Pancras) for evenings of full-on, sexually charged pursuits, including occasional nights for lesbians. Three floors plus a roof terrace and a cabaret mean there can be cruising events of various flavors going on at once, so it's essential to check its schedule beforehand. Fetish nights aren't the only thing going down in cellar cruise spaces.

South of the Thames

As large clubs close in the rest of town to make way for development, Vauxhall, on the Victoria Line just south of the river, has gradually collected the refugees, in particular gay partiers. The largest party at press time was the go-go boy–filled **Juicy** (£13), held Saturday at **Area** (67-68 Albert Embankment, SE1; ☎ 020/7582-9890; Tube: Vauxhall), a cavernous and rambling club where countless and various boys thump away from 10pm to lunchtime Sunday.

Another hive of activity is **Fire** (South Lambeth Rd.; ☎ 020/7582-9890; www.fireclub.co.uk; cover usually £5–£10; Tube: Vauxhall), which has four rooms (in fact, on some days, there are two events happening in two different areas), four separate entrances, a state-of-the-art sound system, and a tendency to play uplifting or clean-sounding music. Check its website to get a handle on the variety of this week's promoted parties. Should it all get too much, there's a chic chillout bar. Sundays from 11am to 5pm, the popular Later event attracts shirtless revelers who never went to bed the night before.

Although most lesbian events take place as nights, the homey-but-hip **Oak Bar** (79 Green Lanes, Islington, N16; ☎ 020/7354-2791; Tube: Manor House) has a schedule that is about 80% for women. Many weekend events go until 3am, although you wouldn't want to pay for a taxi from Stoke Newington at that hour.

A well-known leather dive with a dress code that changes per the night, **The Hoist** (Arches 47b and 47c, South Lambeth Road, SE1; ☎ 020/7735-9972; www.thehoist.co.uk; cover £6–£10; Tube: Vauxhall), open Friday through Sunday, has been the set for several pornos and isn't for the fainthearted. Or, on some nights, for the clothed.

London's biggest dance club for "bears" (for the uninitiated, those are beefy guys who would never dream of shaving their chests like the young "twinks" do), the spacious, two-chambered **XXL London** (The Arches, 51-53 Southwark St., SE1; ☎ 020/7403-4001; www.xxl-london.com; cover £5–£8; Tube: London Bridge) is not only unusual for having such a large and devoted clientele (who knew there were so many bears running loose in London?), but also for presenting club sounds with minimal attitude. Its arched-ceilinged dance floor (actually the vault's beneath a railway) can get super sweaty when it's packed, but that doesn't bother the dancers, who just strip off their shirts and grind on. If this scene gets you going, also check out **Megawoof!** (www.megawoof.com; first Sat of the month; £10), a party for the same niche (its slogan: "Hunks who funk") held, at press time, in Vauxhall.

Saunas

Chariots (www.gaysauna.co.uk) is like the Starbucks of the tub-and-towel set; there are six locations around the city, all of which cater to professionals who often spend their time chatting and socializing instead of getting down to business. The largest, with the most space for, er, socializing and sitz baths, are **Waterloo** (101 Lower Marsh St., SE1; ☎ 020/7401-8484; Tube: Waterloo), installed in a warren of atmospheric vaults beneath the railway viaducts and popular with businessmen; **Vauxhall** (Rail Arches, 63-64 Albert Embankment, SE1; ☎ 020/7247-5333; Tube: Vauxhall), again under 19th-century railway arches; a teeny one at **Farringdon** (57 Cowcross St., EC1; ☎ 020/7251-5553; Tube: Farringdon); **Shoreditch** (1 Fairchild St., EC2; ☎ 020/7247-5333; Tube: Liverpool Street), popular with Whitechapel hipsters and commuters from Liverpool Street station; and the lower-key **Limehouse** (574 Commercial Rd., E14; ☎ 020/7791-28008; Tube: Limehouse DLR), where you're more likely to meet a genuine East End local. While I would never suggest that skinflints save on a hotel night by crashing at one of these joints (after all, you can't bring luggage), I will submit, with a wink, that you can stay for as long as 12 hours for £11 to £15. **Pleasuredrome Central** (Arch 124, Cornwall Rd. at Alaska St., SE1; ☎ 020/7633-9194; www.pleasuredrome.com; Tube: Waterloo; £14), another under-the-arches, sleekly designed hideaway, never closes, and is one of the few sizable, non-skanky saunas not operated by Chariots.

11 Seven Great Day Trips

Get out of town with few pounds & fewer problems

YOU'VE FLOWN ALL THE WAY TO ENGLAND. IT WOULD BE A SHAME TO MISS seeing some of the sights that make it special—the rolling countryside, the High Streets plied by elderly shoppers, the ageless towns built alongside slow-flowing rivers. You can't get these things in London, but you can sample them in some of the out-of-town places that have played an integral role in the development and culture of London life. Taking an excursion to one of those towns is like getting two experiences for the price of one: You'll see what everyday English life is like, and you'll enjoy world-famous sights such as Windsor Castle, or the quads of Cambridge.

Britain has comprehensive transport, but it's not quick as mercury. Because of traffic and a dearth of superhighways, you can expect a 48km (30-mile) trip to take an hour, so a spot that's 129km to 161km (80–100 miles) each way, such as Stonehenge or Bath, will require you to rise at dawn if you want to buy yourself much touring time at all. Going by bus is often less expensive than by rail, but the inefficient journey will involve narrow roads.

I've chosen seven of the most popular day trips out of London and listed them in order of my preference, which has a lot to do with how manageable they are. Call or go online before you plan your trip to verify open hours. For a variety of reasons, attractions outside of London sometimes limit their hours, and you'd hate to travel out to, say, Windsor Castle and find its gates barred owing to a state visit from the King of Swaziland and his wives.

Although I give highlights for each place, it's simply impossible to provide comprehensive guides to seven additional cities in a book about London. So I also provide a tourism information office contact for each city. All of them will be able, for a fee (£3–£4, plus 10% of the room rate), to hook you up with a bed for the night, should you decide that you'd rather not trek back to London right away. Many close by 4:30pm, and most charge 30p to 60p for a city map, so before you leave home, download and print the free color maps provided by **Visit Britain** (www.visitbritain.com). Museum entry outside of London is between £4 and £6, and colleges and churches charge less than £3, unless otherwise noted.

WINDSOR & ETON

You may have had your fill of palaces in London proper, but you haven't seen the best. A fortress and a royal home for more than 900 years, **Windsor Castle** (☎ 020/7766-7304; www.royalcollection.org.uk; £5 adults, £8.50 children 5–16, £13 seniors/students; Mar–Oct daily 9:45am–5:15pm, Nov–Feb daily 9:45am–4:15pm, closed for state visits) was expanded by each successive monarch who dwelled in

Saving on Your Excursion's Rail Ticket

Train fares listed in this section are provided as a guideline; National Rail pricing schemes are complicated and unpredictable. The good news is that for all of the destinations served by trains, if you return to London on the same day that you leave it, you can pay just a little more than the price of the usual one-way (single) ticket. Rail clerks may call this kind of a deal a "day return." More tips:

- Tickets for travel tend to be most expensive on Fridays, when Londoners head out of town for the weekend.
- You can also find incredible deals (up to 70% off) if you happen to be among the first customers to book "advance" tickets on a given train departure, but that requires planning several months ahead. You can book starting 12 weeks before your journey.
- Prices are highest for "open" tickets with no restrictions, but chances are you won't need to change your itinerary for a day trip, so always spring for the discounted restricted fare.
- If you have a Travelcard for the Underground, it will often enable you to deduct a small amount from your fare to nearer destinations like Windsor. National Rail's phone operators will help you plan routes and hash out your fare questions (☎ 08457/48-49-50 in the U.K., ☎ 011-44-20/7278-5240 from overseas; www.nationalrail.co.uk).
- Sometimes local attractions team up with National Rail to offer discounts on admission if you take the train; ask at the railway box office if deals are on, or check the National Rail website for "offers."

it—more battlements for the warlike ones, more finery for the aesthetes. The resulting sprawl, which dominates the town from nearly every angle, is the Queen's favorite residence—she weekends here—and its history is richer than that of Buckingham Palace. Windsor, just (32km/20 miles) west of London, is no less thronged with tourists and corny souvenir shops, though.

The castle's **State Apartments** are sumptuous enough to be daunting, and a tour through them, available unless there's a state visit, includes entrance to some deeply historic rooms. Around a million people file through every year, so sharpen your elbows. **St. George's Chapel** (closed Sun), a Gothic spectacle built by Henry VIII, is the final resting place of 10 monarchs, including Elizabeth II's father (George VI), mother (the Queen Mum), and sister (Princess Margaret). It's safe to assume that this is where she will wind up one day, too. The palace also has a large complement of Her Majesty's priceless art and furniture collection, including the oft-replicated *Charles I in three positions* by Anthony van Dyck (1635–1636, in the King's Dressing Room); the executed king is buried in the Chapel. In 1992, one-fifth of the castle area was engulfed by an accidental fire; the Queen recounted her despair over that, plus the breakup of two of her children's marriages, in her now-famous "annus horribilus" Christmas speech to the

Greater London Area

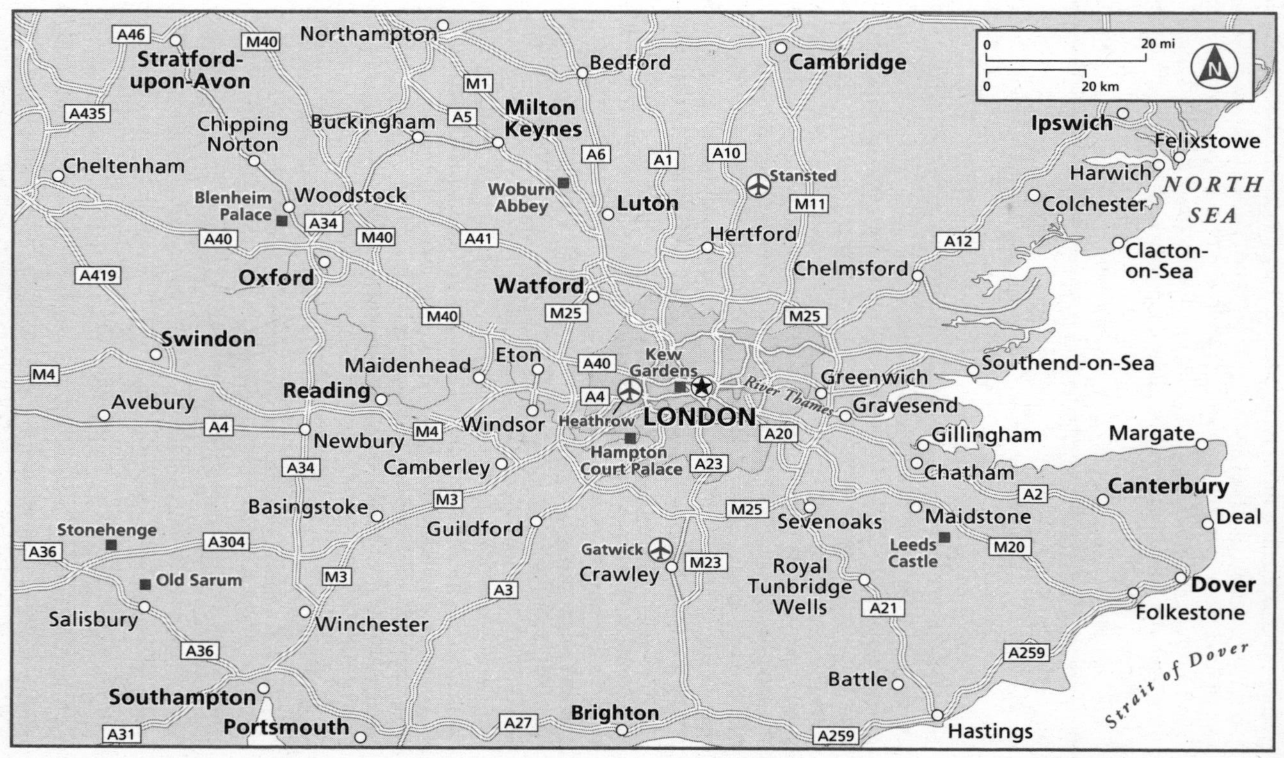

nation, and much effort and funding went into putting everything back to the way it was before. In fact, the Queen originally opened Buckingham Palace to visitors to fund the restoration. **St. George's Hall,** one of the repaired areas, is the Queen's chosen room for banquets. Kids love **Queen Mary's Doll's House,** an extravagant toy built in the 1920s with working electricity, elevators, plumbing, and insanely fine details. From October to March, the tour also includes the **Semi-State Apartments,** George IV's private rooms, considered by many to be among the best-preserved Georgian interiors in England. There's also a **Changing the Guard** ceremony at 11am (on alternate days, Mon–Sat; check the website).

The Castle is the superstar here, but minor supporting roles are played by the succinctly named **Great Park** adjoining it; the 4.8km (3-mile), pin-straight **Long Walk** that culminates with an equestrian statue of George III; and the museum at **Eton College** (☎ 01753/67-11-77; www.etoncollege.com; £4.20 adults, £3.25 children/seniors/students; guided tours Mar–Oct at 2:15 and 3:15pm, £5.50 adults, £4.50 children/seniors/students), a short walk over the Thames (which is narrow at this western remove) from the castle. Eton is one of the most exclusive, most unbelievably posh boys' schools in England. Princes Harry and William are alums, known as Old Etonians, as are kings and princes from around the world. **The Guildhall** (High St.; ☎ 01753/74-39-00; free admission), just south of the castle, was where Prince Charles and Camilla Parker-Bowles had a quiet civil marriage in April 2005; it's no St. Paul's, where in 1981 Charles wed his first wife, what's-her-name, but it is also the work of Christopher Wren (note its delicate arches). The building was apparently designed without the center columns, which made councilors nervous; Wren threw up some columns but left them an inch shy of the ceiling, just to prove that his architecture was sound.

How to get there: The price difference between transport options is negligible, so because riding the rails is quicker, it's got the edge. **Trains** (☎ 08457/48-49-50; www.nationalrail.co.uk; 38–56 min.; £8) go directly from Waterloo station to Windsor & Eton Riverside or from Paddington to Windsor & Eton Central with a change at Slough. Trains requiring no changes leave twice an hour, and trains requiring a change leave a little more frequently. Or take a coach by **Green Line** (☎ 08706/08-72-61; www.greenline.co.uk; 1 hr. 45 min.; £8 single) numbered 701 or 702 from Hyde Park Corner or the Colonnades Coach Station south of Victoria Station.

Tourist information: Royal Windsor (Old Booking Hall, Windsor Royal Shopping, Thames St.; ☎ 01753/74-39-00; www.windsor.gov.uk).

BATH

Easily roamed on foot, Bath, about 161km (100 miles) west of London, is revered as a splendid example of Georgian architecture. The pleasing sandstone hue of its buildings set against the slate-grey British sky, the assiduously planned symmetry of its streets, the illusion that Jane Austen (who lived here from 1800–1805) is taking tea within one of its 18th-century Palladian town houses—Bath's magic comes from its consistent and regal design. No wonder the upper crust of the 1700s found it so fashionable, and no wonder their descendants have not dared to alter it. And no wonder UNESCO inscribed it as a World Heritage Site—a rarity for an entire city. The Romans were the first to recognize the tourism potential of the natural hot springs, which bubble at a rate of 250,000 gallons a day. The steamy **Roman Baths** (Pump Room, Stall St.; ☎ 01225/47-77-85; www.romanbaths.co.uk; £11 adults, £6.80 children 6–16, £9 students, including a free audio guide; Jan–Feb 9:30am–5:30pm, Mar–June 9am–6pm, July–Aug 9am–10pm, Sept–Oct 9am–6pm, Nov–Dec 9am–5:30pm), one of the best-preserved religious spas of that period, were discovered in the late 1800s, and the restoration and accompanying museum are excellent. The Victorians mounted a proud colonnade around the excavation, and water has long been drawn in the adjoining Pump Room; you can drink a glass of the sulfuric stuff if you like, or settle down for a pricey lunch in neoclassical style.

First-time visitors are blown away by the sweep and elegance of The Royal Crescent, a dazzling 30-house development that took some 7 years to complete, from 1767 to 1775. Its first house is now a period museum, **No. 1 Royal Crescent** (1 Royal Crescent; ☎ 01225/42-81-26; www.bath-preservation-trust.org.uk; £5; Tues–Sun 10:30am–5pm, until 4pm in Nov). Robert Adam put up **Pulteney Bridge,** which crosses the River Avon, in 1773, just as a similar bridge in its shop-lined style, the medieval London Bridge, was crumbling. There are walks along the river, too. Bath also hosts about 20 small museums, including the **Museum of Costume** (The Assembly Rooms, Bennett St.; ☎ 01225/47-71-73; www.museumofcostume.co.uk; £7 adults, £5 children, £6 seniors/students; daily 10.30am–5pm, until 6pm Mar–Oct), dedicated to fashion from the late 1500s to today; and the **American Museum in Britain** (Claverton Manor; ☎ 01225/46-05-03; www.american museum.org; £7.40 adults, £6.50 seniors/students, £4 children; Mar–Oct, Tues–Sun noon–5pm), devoted to home interiors, applied arts, and folk art from U.S. history.

How to get there: Trains (☎ 08457/48-49-50; www.nationalrail.co.uk; 90 minutes, twice an hour; £13) leave from Paddington station and let off in Bath Spa, an ugly section of town about 5 minutes' walk from the good stuff. Because they take twice as long and cost nearly £10 more, I don't recommend taking a **National Express** bus (☎ 08705/80-80-80; www.nationalexpress.com; 3½ hr.; £17 single, £18 return), even when special deals are offered.

Tourist information: Visit Bath/Bath Tourist Information Centre (Abbey Chambers, Abbey Churchyard; ☎ 090/6711-2000, from overseas ☎ 011-44-844-847-5257; www.visitbath.co.uk).

OXFORD

Whereas the face of London, 92km (57 miles) east, has been forcibly reshaped by the pressures of war, disaster, and commerce, Oxford was made stronger by them. When plague killed townspeople, the colleges snapped up their houses, and when the Reformation cleaned out the churches, the colleges took their land, too. Academies used the extra space to carve out some of the most beautiful college buildings in the world. Here, the reverence for education borders on the ecclesiastical. Yet Oxford is no cloister; it's a decidedly modern city—thriving, sophisticated, and busy.

Wandering the heart of Oxford's cobbled streets and grey stone alleys and ducking into its colleges to soak up their abject loveliness makes for a happy afternoon, particularly for fans of architecture. Many of the most iconic building clusters in this city of 140,000 (30,000 of whom are students) are collected together in the center of town, and they were built to house the university's nerve center.

The main research library is the flabbergasting **Bodleian Library** (Broad St.; ☎ 01865/27-72-24; www.bodley.ox.ac.uk; free admission, £2.50 tour; Mon–Fri 9am–5pm, Sat 9am–4:30pm), nicknamed "the Bod." It opened in 1602 and has been burrowing under the streets of Oxford, trying to find new places to store its multiplying collection, ever since. The round **Radcliffe Camera** ("Rad Cam"; open via guided tours at the Bodleian) was built in the 1740s to house scientific books. It stands on the north side of Radcliffe Square, and on the south is the **University Church of St. Mary the Virgin** (www.university-church.ox.ac.uk; tower £2.50; daily 9am–5pm, 6pm closing July–Aug), whose spire provides a top view of the city. Other popular viewpoints are from the octagonal cupola above Sir Christopher Wren's **Sheldonian Theatre** (Broad St.; ☎ 01865/72-68-71; www.sheldon.ox.ac.uk; £2; Mon–Sat 10am–12:30pm and 2–4:30pm, closes 3:40 Nov–Feb); and from the 22m (72-ft.), rectangular **Carfax Tower** (Carfax; ☎ 01865/79-26-53; £2.10 adult, £1 children; Apr–Sept 10am–5:30pm, Oct–Mar 10am–4:30pm), the last remaining chunk of the 13th-century St. Martin's Church, located by the crossroads of the city center. The doors between the inner and outer quadrangles of **Balliol College** (Broad St. and St. Giles; ☎ 01865/27-77-77; www.balliol.ox.ac.uk) still bear scorch marks from where Bloody Mary burned two Protestants alive for refusing to recant. **Magdelen College** (High St.; ☎ 01865/27-60-00; www.magd.ox.ac.uk; £4; daily 1–6pm), pronounced "Mauldin," is one of the largest and most peaceful colleges here; its tower is the city's highest point, and its chapel is carved with breathtaking detail.

Oxford, like Cambridge, is comprised of individual colleges that feed off a central university system. Each of Oxford's 39 colleges has its own campus, tradition, character, and disciplines, although many close their grassy inner sanctums to visitors. The largest, and the most popular, college to visit is **Christ Church** (☎ 01865/27-64-92; www.chch.ox.ac.uk; £4.90 adult, £3.90 seniors/students/children; Mon–Sat 9:30am–5pm). Its interiors loom large in children's literature; it stands in for Hogwarts School in the Harry Potter films, and it was where Lewis Carroll (aka mathematician Charles Dodgson) befriended the little girl for whom he wrote *Alice in Wonderland.* Christ Church is the site of the cathedral for the local diocese, and its Meadow, still grazed by cattle, is a delightful place to watch punters on the rivers Isis and Cherwell.

Offering more than just a pretty facade, **The Ashmolean Museum** (Beaumont St.; ☎ 01865/27-80-00; www.ashmolean.org; free admission; Tues–Sat 10am–5pm and Sun noon–5pm), was founded way back in 1683, literally before anyone knew what the word "museum" actually meant. It houses an important hodgepodge of antiquities and art on par with (but on a smaller scale than) the British Museum, including a lantern carried by Guy Fawkes during the foiled Gunpowder Plot; the Anglo-Saxon Alfred Jewel of gold, enamel, and rock crystal; a Stradivarius violin; and assorted Old Masters paintings. **Modern Art Oxford** (30 Pembroke St.; ☎ 01865/81-38-30; www.modernartoxford.org.uk; free admission; Tues–Sat 10am–5pm; Sun noon–5pm) is a well-respected museum for contemporary works. Hovering somewhere between those two places, the **Pitt River Museum** (Parks Rd.; ☎ 01865/27-09-27; www.prm.ox.ac.uk; free admission; Tues–Sun 10am–4:30pm, Mon noon–4:30pm; free; closed for renovation until spring 2009) offers an oft-freakish blend of folk art and anthropology—think shrunken heads and bundles of poisoned arrows brought back by British explorers over hundreds of years. **The**

University Museum of Natural History (Parks Rd.; ☎ 01865/27-29-50; www.oum.ox.ac.uk; free admission; daily 10am–5pm) is a Victorian setting for dinosaur bones, fossilized specimens, and the like.

During the school term (mid-Jan to mid-Mar, late Apr to mid-June, Oct to early Dec), some university buildings required for study (libraries, residence halls) are closed, or they only open on Saturdays. At all times of year, watch out for zooming bicyclists; an unwritten law seems to dictate that they own the city.

How to get there: The least expensive, easiest method is by coach, since companies compete for students with regular buses rolling round the clock. The **Oxford Tube** (☎ 01865/77-22-50; www.oxfordtube.com; 100 min. with no traffic; £12 adult, £9 seniors/students, £6 under 16, same-day return £15/£12/£7.50) bus leaves every 12 to 15 minutes from 6:12am to 9:35pm and around every half-hour or hour at all other times, even in the middle of the night. It picks passengers up near the Tube stations at Marble Arch, Victoria, Notting Hill Gate, and Shepherd's Bush. Judging by the way the owners spell their bus line, it seems they weren't educated in the City of Dreaming Spires, but **Oxford Espress** (☎ 01865/78-54-00; www.oxfordbus.co.uk; 100 min. with no traffic; £12 adults, £6 seniors/children, £9 students, same-day return £15/£12/£7.50) provides a similarly comfortable coach service (including sockets for mobile phone chargers), but with London stops at Baker Street, Marble Arch, and Victoria. Both coaches drop you off at Gloucester Green, in the Oxford city center. Give rush hours wide berth, since many locals commute to London from these parts. **Trains** (☎ 08457/48-49-50; www.nationalrail.co.uk; 1 hr.; £17 single) go from Paddington station to Oxford, sometimes via Reading, and with enough advance planning, fares can be as low as £4 each way.

Tourist information: In addition to selling (yes, selling—not giving) maps and guides, **The Oxford Information Centre** (15-16 Broad St.; ☎ 01865/25-22-00; www.visitoxford.org) offers daily walking tours using accredited guides. Schedules vary, but there's always a daily University and City Tour at 11am and 2pm (£7 adults, £4 children under 16). On summer Saturdays, it runs tours of movie filming sites and an Inspector Morse tour. The Centre also sells self-guided tours that you can download and use with an MP3 player (£5 for three). You can download free maps of the city from Visit Britain (www.visitbritain.com).

CAMBRIDGE

Oxford is a city in its own right, but Cambridge, in the marshes 79km (49 miles) northeast of London, would barely have a pulse without its university. That makes Cambridge manageable. It feels in some ways like a typical English town, with a daily market for crafts and food on its central square, Market Hill. Its best rewards come when you wander through randomly chosen iron gates or along a river path—that's when the inviting little town really opens up. For some reason, the marauding Puritans neglected to smash the 16th-century stained glass windows at **King's College Chapel** (King's Parade; ☎ 01223/33-12-12; www.kings.cam.ac.uk; £5, £3.50 seniors/students/children; Mon–Fri 9:30am–3:30pm; Sat 9:30am–3:15pm, Sun 1:15–2:15pm; extended summer hours)—they probably thought they were just as divine as you will. The chapel's fanned and vaulted ceiling, a work of craftsmanship that stuns even those who care little for such things, was completed at the behest of Henry VII. Its famous choristers sing at services during term time.

The Trade-Off with Escorted Tours

Arranging your own day trips using public transportation will almost always be the most cost-effective method, but there are cogent reasons for choosing a guided coach tour. It's simply quicker to allow someone else to drive you around, making sure you cram a laundry list of major sites into a short time span, and consuming spoon-fed nuggets of information about each place. What you learn won't have much depth, but at least you'll have been.

Problem is, you'll have paid a pretty penny for it: Most tours cost at least £70 a day, not including food. I believe you get a richer experience (and one that doesn't have you idling in traffic and trooping into gift shops all day), when you do it yourself. But some people desperately want to soak up as many sights as they can, even if it means they skim the surface. For them, here are the major players in the coach-tour biz, sold aggressively through the concierges at expensive hotels (who love getting the commissions):

- **Evan Evans Tours** (in the U.K. ☎ 020/7950-1777, in the U.S. ☎ 800/422-9022; www.evanevans.co.uk)
- Gray Line's **Golden Tours** (in the U.K. ☎ 084/4880-6981, in the U.S. ☎ 800/548-7083; www.goldentours.co.uk)
- **Premium Tours** (☎ 020/7404-5100; www.premiumtours.co.uk)

Better yet are the more affordable **London Walks** (☎ 020/7624-3978; www.walks.com), which run frequent "Explorer Days" for just £12. These use public transportation and don't include admission fees, but you'll have a local guide every step of the way to show you how it's all done.

Like Oxford, Cambridge's calling card is the elaborate and ancient architecture of its colleges. Unlike in Oxford, it's easy to venture into the cloistered grounds of many of Cambridge's colleges (the oldest was founded in 1286 after a squabble in Oxford necessitated the establishment of a second educational capital), though doing so usually requires a few quid. The best is **Pembroke College** (☎ 01223/33-81-00; www.pem.cam.ac.uk), the third-oldest in town, distinguished by the oldest gatehouse in Cambridge and by a chapel with an ornate plaster ceiling, which was the first completed work by Christopher Wren (after finishing, the man seemed never to rest again). Unlike many of the colleges, Pembroke never charges visitors to poke around its common areas. In *Chariots of Fire,* sprinters tried to get around the .8-hectare (2-acre) yard of **Trinity College** (☎ 01223/33-84-00; www.trin.cam.ac.uk; £2.50 adults, £1 children; Mar–Oct daily 10am–5pm) in the time it took for its clock to strike 12. Trinity is the largest and most endowed of Cambridge's 31 colleges. Tourists are often told that the wooden **Mathematical Bridge** (1749) spanning the Cam at **Queen's College** (Silver St.; ☎ 01223/33-55-11; www.queens.cam.ac.uk; opening times and fees vary by season and day of week) was constructed using no nails, and when curious students disassembled it to figure out how, they couldn't put it back together without using screws. The college is curiously defensive about the accusation, saying that anyone who believes this story "cannot have a serious grasp on reality." The 12th-century **Round Church** (Bridge and St. John's sts.; ☎ 01223/31-16-02; £2, free for students and children; Tues–Sat 10am–5pm, Sun 1–5pm) is the oldest of four remaining circular churches in England.

Cambridge's storied **Fitzwilliam Museum** (Trumpington St.; ☎ 01223/33-29-00; www.fitzmuseum.cam.ac.uk; free admission; Tues–Sat 10am–5pm, Sun noon–5pm) is a first-rate neoclassical building full of examples of applied arts and Old Masters that a city ten times Cambridge's size (of 108,000) would covet. Mill Lane leads to the River Cam, where you can rent a punting boat for £6 or sit at The Mill pub overlooking the water. (The punting alone will set you apart as a tourist, but if you want to look like a tourist savvy to Cambridge traditions, punt from the back of the boat. In Oxford, they punt from the front.) The meadows along the Cam are known as **The Backs,** and they make for idyllic walks.

The head of Oliver Cromwell, which was impaled outside Westminster Hall in London as a warning against regicide (albeit 3 years after the man died of natural causes), was finally buried within an antechapel (not open to visitors) at Sidney Sussex College in 1960. It's in an unmarked grave, to keep pranksters from pinching the much-abused thing. That's Cambridge in a nutshell: It has many secrets, and history is layered everywhere, but since it's still a working university town, its marvels won't be handed to you the way they are at most tourist sites. You have to wander, wonder, and ask questions.

Keep in mind that colleges aren't open, and street life is at a minimum, outside of term (mid-Jan to mid-Mar, late Apr to mid-June, Oct to early Dec).

How to get there: Nonstop coaches from **National Express** (☎ 08705/80-80-80; www.nationalexpress.com; 2 hours; £14 single) leave hourly from Victoria Coach station; don't get off at Trumpington, but wait for the city center stop. There are trains, but be warned that Cambridge's station is several miles from the city center, so you will need to call a taxi once you arrive; coaches are the smarter way to travel. If you insist, though, **trains** (☎ 08457/48-49-50; www.nationalrail.co.uk; 45–90 min.; £18 single) run by One Railway take 90 minutes, but the First Capital Connect trains take half that time and leave twice an hour. All depart from Liverpool Street station and stop at Cambridge Station.

Tourist information: **Cambridge Visitor Information Centre** (The Old Library, Wheeler St.; ☎ 08712/26-80-06, from overseas ☎ 011-44-1223/464-732; www.visitcambridge.org) sells maps and guides but won't dispense them for free. Cambridge also sells hour-long walking tours on downloadable MP3s (www.tourist-tracks.com; £5 for two). You can download free maps of the city from Visit Britain (www.visitbritain.com).

CANTERBURY

Bath is proper and Salisbury bows to its cathedral, but charming Canterbury, in shape and in spirit, conjures the jumble of a medieval city, battlements and all. St. Augustine established the first cathedral here in 597. Everything is contained within the walled Old City, on the River Stour, in which cars are banned, and strolling tangled, ageless lanes can absorb you so completely that you forget there are other things to see in town. Its three-towered, steeply priced **Cathedral**

(☎ 01227/76-28-62; www.canterbury-cathedral.org; £7 adults, £5.50 children/seniors/students; Mon–Fri 9am–5pm, until 5:30pm during summer, Sun always 12:30–2:30pm), a UNESCO World Heritage site, is the mothership for Anglicanism, and it has been drawing sightseers since Henry II's goons stabbed Thomas Becket to death in 1170; the site of the dastardly deed is still a place for reflection. The pilgrims of Chaucer's *Canterbury Tales* told their tales as they made their way here, to pay tribute to his shrine, and plenty of tourist traps still profit off their exploits. The cathedral's undercroft (cellar) is considered to be the finest example from the Norman period left in the country.

Elsewhere in the city, which is 90km (56 miles) southeast of London in the rolling countryside of Kent, is an excavated portion of the lower-lying Roman town, now the **Canterbury Roman Museum** (Longmarket, Butchery Lane; ☎ 01227/78-55-75; www.canterbury-museums.co.uk; £3, £2 seniors/students/children; Mon–Sat 10am–5pm; varying summer hours). Canterbury is also the home of a university, which gives the old city a noticeable verve and a coziness, to say nothing of funky, student-approved cafes and clothing stores. I love Canterbury, and like nothing more than walking past its old walls, sipping elderflower drinks in its vegetarian cafes, and discovering Old England around every cobbled corner.

How to get there: Coaches go from Victoria Coach station on **National Express** (☎ 08705/80-80-80; www.nationalexpress.com; 2 hr.; £13 single). **Trains** (☎ 08457/48-49-50; www.nationalrail.co.uk; 90 min.; £21 single) go from London Victoria to Canterbury East or from Charing Cross station to Canterbury West. Both stations are equidistant from the town center.

Tourist information: **Canterbury Information Centre** (12/13 Sun Street; ☎ 01227/37-81-00; www.canterbury.co.uk) sells two downloadable audio walking tours for £5.

STONEHENGE & SALISBURY

Construction began about 5,000 years ago on **Stonehenge** (☎ 08703/33-11-81; www.english-heritage.org.uk/stonehenge; £6.50 adults, £3.30 children, £5.20 seniors/students; mid-Mar to May and Sept to mid-Oct daily 9:30am–6pm, Jun–Aug daily 9am–7pm, mid-Oct to mid-March daily 9:30am–4pm), and the first recorded day trips to the megalith were in 1562. Arranged in such a way that it aligns with the rising of the sun during the midsummer solstice, this Neolithic circle of stones is certainly Britain's most important ancient wonder, it's a UNESCO World Heritage Site (together with Avebury, a far less interesting, but still important, line of rocks 39km/24 miles north). Whether its builders, who remain anonymous, worshiped the sun or merely appreciated astronomy is only the beginning of the mystery. We also can only make educated guesses as to how these prehistoric people, using only rudimentary tools, managed to hoist these slabs from Wales to here, and then into place. Even if you don't salivate over such long-ago feats of ingenuity, the distinctive profile of the stones, surrounded by empty plains, "henge" earthworks, and hundreds of lumpen burial mounds, will surely be iconic.

To some, Stonehenge is a circle of rocks. If it's raining, it's a damned circle of rocks. But people still ask to go, and if that's their dream, then they should do it. Just understand that you may not get it, even though the inadequate visitor center has a few bits about ancient practices and theories on how Stonehenge's arrangement may have evolved over time. You're also not allowed to walk amongst the rocks the way visitors once were; you have to stick to a footpath that curves near the circle but keeps the formation at a safe distance, good for pretty photographs but bad for curiosity. Most tourists like you and me are being kept at arm's length (exception: Clark Griswold, who managed to topple them like dominos in *National Lampoon's European Vacation*), but you can apply in advance for a 1-hour pass to stroll among the rocks, timed just before or after the site closes to the public for the day. These passes are never given for Tuesday or Wednesday mornings, and October through February is usually blocked off, too, and slots must be applied for in writing. The forms can be found by searching for "stone circle access" at the English Heritage website, above.

The limited experience (a disappointment for many who trudge 129km/80 miles west of London to have it) is why few people see Stonehenge without passing through Bath on the same day. That itinerary is offered by coach tours; putting it together yourself with trains and buses is not ideal because the connections chew up too much time. Salisbury is do-able, though, since trains headed there connect with a bus (see "How to Get There," below).

The city of Salisbury is defined and commanded by the soaring 120m-tall (394-ft.) spire of its famous **Salisbury Cathedral** (33 The Close; ☎ 01722/55-51-20; www.salisburycathedral.org.uk; suggested donation of £4; times vary but generally daily 7:15am–6:15pm), built with uncommon efficiency between 1220 and 1258 and barely touched since. This early English Gothic masterpiece is considered by many to be the most breathtaking church in the world. After you've seen it, and lost yourself in gazing at it and sighing, the rest of your time in Salisbury will be contentedly spent walking the city's medieval streets, which were laid in a loose grid and give the city a neat, airy character.

How to get there: Trains don't go directly to Stonehenge; the nearest station is in Salisbury, nearly 16km (10 miles) south. So the easiest way to get here is to drive. The rocks are located 3.2km (2 miles) west of Amesbury in Wiltshire on the junction of A303 and A344/360. Or take a half-hourly **train** (☎ 08457/48-49-50; www.nationalrail.co.uk; 90 min.; £27 single) from Waterloo station to Salisbury station. There used to be a cheap public bus to the rocks from there, but it says a lot about the values of the local tourism authorities that they replaced that route entirely with the expensive Stonehenge Tour Bus by **Wilts & Dorset Buses** (☎ 01722/33-68-55; www.thestonehengetour.info; 30 min.; round-trip £11 adult, £5 children, £11 students), which leaves seven times a day between 10am and 4pm from Salisbury station. A few extra buses are tossed in during the summer; check its website for updated schedules.

Tourist information: Salisbury and Stonehenge (Fish Row, Salisbury; ☎ 01722/43-43-73; www.visitsalisbury.com).

STRATFORD-UPON-AVON

Stratford-upon-Avon, often described as a "chocolate box" of a town in the Heart of England, doesn't make an ideal day trip from London unless you're willing to make some decisive sacrifices. Not to be confused with Stratford, the up-and-coming multicultural section of East London, Stratford-upon-Avon in Warwickshire, 144km (89 miles) northwest of London, is lily-white and all about the Bard. If he touched it, or if his descendants did, you can bet it's been turned into a tourist attraction. The problem with a trip to Stratford, besides heaving summer crowds, is that its biggest attraction, the highly respected acting company the **Royal Shakespeare Company** (Waterside; ☎ 01789/40-34-44; www.rsc.org.uk), is hard to see on a day trip. The RSC has three theatres in town where it presents as many as three shows a day. Unless you take the train on a matinee day, seeing a show requires an overnight stay. And matinees are frequently booked out by school trips and group tours; if you intend to catch one, you'll need to book about 2 months ahead so you're not shut out. Even if you are, don't sweat it, because the RSC performs steadily in London, too.

The genuine remainders from Shakespeare's day are set upon by Anglophilic coach tourists like dogs upon scraps. The town of 113,000 is, believe it or not, the second-biggest tourist draw in England, after London, so you can imagine how many shops clamor to sell the most miniature thatched cottages and teddy bears in Union Jack T-shirts. **Shakespeare's Birthplace** (Henley St.; ☎ 01789/20-40-16; www.shakespeare.org.uk; £9 adults, £4.50 children, £8 seniors; Mon–Sat 10am–4pm and Sun 9:30am–5pm, slightly extended hours in summer) is thought to be the home where the playwright was born, but even if it wasn't—subsequent generations' adoration of the writer have colored historical judgment—it's a good, if heavily restored, example of an upscale Elizabethan house. The locals didn't care for it much until P. T. Barnum tried to buy it and ship it, stone for stone, over to America, and suddenly, it became a national treasure. Admission there includes entry to two other historic homes, Hall's Croft and Nash's House, both associated with the Bard's descendents and valued mostly for their Tudor aesthetic. A mile northwest of town, the picturesque thatched **Anne Hathaway's Cottage** (Cottage Lane, Shottery; ☎ 01789/29-21-00; www.shakespeare.org.uk; £6 adults, £3 children, £5 seniors/students; Mon–Sat 10am–4pm, Sun 9:30am–5pm, slightly extended hours in summer), in a quintessential English garden, is where the playwright's wife (not the American ingénue) lived before she married him, and it dates to the 1400s. You can reach the cottage, a rare window into life 500 years ago, along a public footpath from town.

For all the fragrant gardens and twee, humpbacked cottages, it's easy to forget that in Shakespeare's day, Stratford was a squalid, smelly market town. That's not to say that Stratford won't fulfill some stereotypes of a pretty English town. Stratford's popularity is enhanced by its nearness to the surrounding Cotswolds, which you simply won't be able to see comfortably on a day trip from London.

How to get there: The most direct **trains** (☎ 08457/48-49-50; www.nationalrail.co.uk; 2hr., 15 min.; £30 single) go from Marylebone station to Stratford-upon-Avon station. Make sure you don't buy a ticket for plain old "Stratford," or you won't actually be leaving London. Buses run by **National Express** (☎ 08705/80-80-80; www.nationalexpress.com; 3 hr., 15 min.; £16 single) take an hour longer, but cost less. Taking the first bus of the morning (8:30am) and the last bus back (5:45pm) only gives you about 6 hours in town, which is do-able but won't enable you to see even a matinee.

Tourist information: Stratford-upon-Avon Tourist Information Centre (Bridgefoot; ☎ 08701/60-79-30; www.shakespeare-country.co.uk).

12 The Essentials of Planning

Getting there easily, cheaply, safely & with a fat wallet

FIRST OF ALL, RELAX. GETTING TO LONDON ISN'T AS TRICKY AS IT USED TO be. Finding airfare was once the most daunting part, but thanks to the emergence of Web booking, now it's not much harder than finding a cross-country flight. Being ready for the rest (money, electricity, packing) is simply a matter of having the facts.

The only two tools you'll need to get there are a telephone and Web access—and a phone really isn't that necessary. The rest you'll find in this chapter.

WHERE TO FIND TOURIST INFORMATION

Two official information offices, supported by British tax dollars, are set up to help tourists learn what's worth seeing, doing, and eating—all for free. **Visit Britain** (☎ 800/462-2748; www.visitbritain.com), the information bureau for the whole country, has plenty of information to start you off, including consultants you can grill by telephone. Its **Britain Visitor Center** (551 Fifth Ave., Suite 701, New York City, NY, 10176) welcomes walk-in visitors during business hours. But **Visit London** (www.visitlondon.com), the city's hip official tourist bureau, possesses the bigger database by far. It's stocked with more information than you'll know what to do with, including special deals, specialized downloadable guides (restaurants, museums, movie locations, gay life, and so on), newsletters, and reams of to-the-minute listings for upcoming events (walks, festivals, talks, performances). Visit London doesn't maintain an informational phone line, but it strives to answer all e-mailed questions within 36 hours. Visit London and Visit Britain will both send free information packs to prospective tourists; request those online. The two outfits also collaborate on an information center in London on Lower Regent Street, just south of Piccadilly Circus.

WHEN TO VISIT

It's always time to visit London. Even though it's approximately at the same latitude of Edmonton, Alberta, the prevailing weather patterns keep London's weather from being extreme in any way. It gets cold in the winter, but rarely snowed in. It gets warm in the summer, but rarely blisteringly so (in fact, most buildings don't even have air-conditioning). The winter months are generally more humid than the summer ones, but experience only slightly more rain.

The principal art season (for theatre, concerts, art shows) falls between September and May, leaving the summer months for festivals and park-going. A few royal attractions, such as the state rooms of Buckingham Palace, are only open in the summer when the Queen decamps to Scotland. In summer, when the weather is warmest and half of Europe takes its annual holiday, the airfares are higher, as are hotel rates (although corporate hotels crank rates much higher than family-owned places tend to), and the queues for most of the tourist attractions, such as the London Eye and the Tower of London, might make you wish you'd come in March. For decent prices and less crowds, I prefer spring and fall—April and October seem to have the best confluence of mild weather, pretty plantings, and tolerable crowds. Prices are lowest in mid-winter, but a number of simpler sights, such as historic houses, sometimes close from November to March (the Attractions section, p. 133, will tell you which ones do), and the biggest annual events take place during the warmer months.

The table below charts seasonal weather and price shifts.

	Jan	Feb	Mar	Apr	May	June	July	Aug	Sept	Oct	Nov	Dec
Average Temps ° F	40	40	44	49	55	61	64	64	59	52	46	42
Average Temps ° C	4	4	7	9	13	16	18	18	15	11	8	6
Days of Precipitation (more than 0.25mm)	15	13	11	12	12	11	12	11	13	13	15	15
Avg. hours of sunlight (sunrise to sunset)	8.5	10	12	14	16	16.5	16	14	12	10	8.5	8
Typical transatlantic airfare*	$700 to $830	$700 to $830	$700 to $830	$840 to $920	$1000 to $1150	$1180 to $1240	$1180 to $1140	$1080 to $1140	$820 to $1040	$830 to $1000	$760 to $870	$700 to $830

**Use these to see how prices change seasonally. Frequent sales bring prices lower, and vacation holiday periods both at home and in England, such as Christmas or Thanksgiving, can raise prices, and so can fuel rates. These prices include approximate taxes.*

London's Best Annual Events

Festivals and special events are an integral part of London's calendar, and many regular happenings draw tourists from around the world. Find more events at London's city website (www.london.gov.uk/gla/events), at Visit London's site (www.visitlondon.com), and in *Time Out* magazine (www.timeout.com/london). The regular events below are by no means the full list. There are always short-run, one-off events popping up unexpectedly throughout the year, such as the installation of a temporary lawn across Trafalgar Square to promote London parks, open-air rock concerts like the one honoring Nelson Mandela's 90th birthday, and wacky art installations like the "Telectroscope" that offered live, life-size views of Brooklyn in its lens in 2008. *Time Out* and the commercial weblog **Londonist** (www.londonist.com) are good places to find advance word.

January or Early February

Chinese New Year Festival (☎ 020/7851-6686; www.chinatownchinese.co.uk): In conjunction with the Chinese New Year, the streets around Leicester Square come alive with dragon and lion dances, children's parades, performances, screenings, and fireworks displays.

London International Mime Festival (☎ 020/7637-5661; www.mimefest.co.uk): Not just for silent clowns, but also for funky puppets and Blue Man–style tomfoolery, it's held around town in mid-January.

February

Great Spitalfields Pancake Race (☎ 020/7375-0441): Held on Shrove Tuesday (on a Tues in Feb), this is a race through the streets of Spitalfields by skillet-wielding teams of four, who toss pancakes to each other as they run. Winners receive an engraved fry pan. Spectators get a tale to dine out on.

March

National Science and Engineering Week (☎ 020/7019-4937; www.the-ba.net): In the second week of March, the scientifically inclined throw a week of talks and shows to bring kids and adults alike into the fold.

St. Patrick's Day Parade and Festival (☎ 020/7983-4000; www.london.gov.uk/stpatricksday): When you're this close to Dublin and you consider England's long rivalry with the Emerald Isle, you can expect lots of raging Irish pride—parades, music, cultural village, and food stalls around Trafalgar Square. The city also sponsors concerts and craft fairs promoting Irish culture and heritage. It's not just about drinking—it just looks that way.

BADA Antiques and Fine Art Fair (www.bada-antiques-fair.co.uk): Sponsored in mid- to late March by the British Antique Dealers' Association, it's considered to be the best in Britain for such collectors. Some 100 exhibitors move into a mighty tent in Duke of York's Square, in Chelsea, for the 7-day sales event, which is peppered with talks, exhibitions of rarities, fashion shows, cooking demonstrations, and wine tastings. Don't expect a bargain but an education.

Late March or Early April

Oxford and Cambridge Boat Race (www.theboatrace.org): The popular annual event takes less than a half-hour, but the after-party rollicks into the night. See p. 228.

April

London Marathon (☎ 020/7902-0200; www.london-marathon.co.uk): Incongruous as it is to see some 35,000 athletes stagger around town emblazoned with the logo of the margarine-brand sponsor, Flora, the Marathon is still a kick for spectators, and a landmark on the world running scene. (Hotels around town tend to fill up ahead of it.) The starter pistol fires in Greenwich, and the home stretch is along Birdcage Walk and The Mall around St. James's Park. If you want to run, apply by the previous October—and cut out the margarine.

May

Chelsea Flower Show (☎ 084/5260-5000; www.rhs.org.uk): Tickets go on sale in November for this lillypalooza, and they're snapped up quickly. The Royal Horticultural Society, which calls itself "a gardening charity dedicated to advancing horticulture and promoting good gardening" (don't you just *love* the English?), mounts this esteemed show for 5 days in late May on the grounds of the Royal Hospital in Chelsea. The plants, all raised by champion green thumbs, are sold to attendees on the final day, but sadly, foreigners aren't usually able to get their plants past Customs. The event is so celebrated that it is covered on nightly primetime TV.

June

Beating Retreat (☎ 020/7839-5323): Drum corps, pipes and drums, and plenty of bugle calls: This anachronistic twilight ceremony, held for two evenings in early June at Horse Guards Parade by St. James's Park, involves the salute of the Queen (or another member of the royal family) and the appearance of many red-clad marchers. Scholars can trace its origins back to 1554—so in other words, it may not signify much, but for tradition's sake, it's deeply meaningful. It's the nearest relative to the better-known Trooping the Colour, but without the crowds. Reserve ahead.

Hampton Court Palace Festival (☎ 084/4412-2954; www.hamptoncourtfestival.com): High-end niche names (Rufus Wainwright, Van Morrison, Michael Ball) perform early in the month in a temporary theater on palace grounds. Tickets are around £50.

The Royal Academy Summer Exhibition (www.royalacademy.org.uk): Artists have been in a frenzy about this blind competition for more than 240 years. Paintings, sculpture, drawings, architecture—if you can dream it, you can enter it, and if you're one of the most talented, your piece is anointed as the best that year. The show is what the Royal Academy is known for, and although it's not envelope-pushing, it's a seminal event in British art culture and shouldn't be missed if you're in town. All the works are for sale, and proceeds fund the Academy's palatial digs for the rest of the year.

Trooping the Colour (☎ 020/7414-2479; www.royal.gov.uk): Never mind that the Queen was born in April. This is her birthday party, and as a present, she gets the same thing every year: Marching soldiers with big hats. Gee, thanks. Fortunately, the spectacle is extreme, as a sea of redcoats and cavalry swarm over Horse Guards Parade, 41 guns salute, and a flight of Royal Air Force jets slam through the sky overhead. The Queen herself leads the charge, waving politely to her subjects before the riflemen take over in a passive-aggressive show of might. It's the closest thing Britain has to a national day like the Fourth of July, and after such extravagant displays of pomp, no doubt is left that the color has been truly trooped. Held in mid-June, it starts at 10am. If you want grandstand seats instead of standing in the free-for-all along the route, you'll need to send a request by February at the latest to Brigade Major, Headquarters Household Division, Horse Guards, Whitehall, London, SW1A 2AX, United Kingdom. SASEs are required, so you will have to include an International Reply Coupon from your post office so that your return postage is paid. Otherwise, check out the Beating Retreat for a similar, if less elaborate, experience.

Taste of London Festival (☎ 087/1230-5581): For 4 days in mid-June, the city's top chefs and the region's finest farmers convene in Regent's Park for a belly-stuffing gastronomic celebration.

Pride London (www.pridelondon.org): A signature event on the world's LGBT calendar, London Pride pulls some 825,000 revelers, many of them heterosexual, with a buoyant roster of concerts and performances by famous names plus a parade (the U.K.'s largest) in the center of the city. The gay pride week, co-sponsored by the Mayor's office and a number of British corporations (British Airways, Ford, and others), also makes for an excellent excuse for some blowout dance parties. Late June or early July.

Wimbledon Championships (☎ 020/8971-2473; www.wimbledon.org): Why watch on television yet again? Check p. 230 for tips on how to net tickets and be one of the 500,000 to witness it in person. Late June to early July.

Hard Rock Calling (www.hardrockcalling.co.uk): Tickets are steep (around £60) considering the venue is Hyde Park, but the lineup for this 2-day concert is A-list; 2008 names included Eric Clapton, The Police, John Mayer, and Sheryl Crow.

O_2 Wireless Festival (www.02wirelessfestival.co.uk): Also held al fresco in Hyde Park, late in the month or in early July. 2008 names included Morrissey, Beck, Jay-Z, and Counting Crows.

Greenwich and Docklands International Festival (☎ 020/8305-1818; www.festival.org): An ambitious program of free theatrical and musical pieces, many of them developed by artists expressly for the public spaces they're performed in. It's held in late June.

City of London Festival (☎ 020/7796-4949; www.colf.org): Traditional and high-minded classical music concerts are held toward the end of the month in some of The City's oldest buildings.

Meltdown (☎ 087/1663-2500; www.southbankcentre.co.uk/meltdown): An out-of-left-field compendium of contemporary arts held at the end of June at the Southbank Centre, curated each year by a notable such as Patti Smith, David Bowie, and Massive Attack.

June Through August

Coin Street Festival (☎ 020/7021-1600; www.coinstreetfestival.org): Held around Southwark and the South Bank, this festival gives various London communities (Cubans, Turks, the elderly) different days devoted just to them. Food, music, dance, and bright colors seem to be the objective, as does finding new excuses to enjoy the embankment on the Thames.

Watch this Space Festival (☎ 020/7452-3400; www.nationaltheatre.org.uk/wts): A grab bag of free movies, shows, and concerts in the spaces around the Royal National Theatre. Yep, another excuse to strut around along the mighty river.

July

Rise: London United (☎ 020/7983-6554; www.risefestival.org): London's biggest free music festival, which takes over Finsbury Park for a day, promotes cultural diversity and presents a mix of hip-hop, indie, jazz, pop, reggae, comedy, and family events.

Clerkenwell Festival and **Shoreditch Festival:** These modest-sized local festivals, held in mid-July, delve into the traditional culture of each neighborhood: Italian and Roman Catholic for Clerkenwell, and fashionistas for Shoreditch.

The Lambeth Country Show (☎ 020/7926-7085; www.lambeth.gov.uk): A free, old-fashioned farm show overtakes Brixton's Brockwell Park (for a single weekend in the middle of July, anyway) with farm animals, jam-making contests, a fun fair, tractor demonstrations, and Punch and Judy puppet shows.

July to September

BBC Promenade Concerts (☎ 020/7589-8212; www.bbc.co.uk/proms): The biggest classical music festival of the year, held primarily at the Royal Albert Hall, "the Proms" consists of orchestral concerts for every taste. Seats start at £6.

August

The Innocent Village Fete (☎ 020/8600-3939; www.innocentvillagefete.co.uk): Sponsored by a smoothie company, this 2-day festival in Regent's Park (£7.50) is all about music, a dance tent with a DJ, all-natural food stalls (and plenty of Pimm's), kids' activities, ferret races, and flopping around on the grass. Pray for good weather.

Great British Beer Festival (☎ 017/2786-7201; www.camra.org.uk): Just like it sounds: More than 450 British ales are available to try at Earl's Court Exhibition Centre—after all those tastings, you'll be relieved to learn the Tube is within easy reach. It runs 5 days in early August.

Notting Hill Carnival (☎ 020/7727-0072; www.nottinghillcarnival.biz): In August 1958, roving bands of white racists combed the slums of Notting Hill in search of Caribbean-owned businesses to destroy. Two weeks of disgusting race violence, among the worst in London's history, ensued. Resulting community outrage and newly rediscovered cultural pride led to the formation of a new festival, which today is Europe's largest street parade. Originally a party for Trinidadian culture held in a town hall, the Carnival has grown into a powerhouse smorgasbord of cultures spanning the rest of the Caribbean as well as Eastern Europe, South America, and the Indian subcontinent. It attracts some 2 million people during the August Bank Holiday weekend, which includes the last Monday in August. Sunday is kids' day, with scrubbed-down events and activities, but on Monday, the adults take over, costumes get skimpy, floats weave through small streets, and rowdy hordes celebrate into the wee hours.

September

Brick Lane Festival: Inclusive and warm-hearted, this 2-week event was established in 1996 as a less intimidating alternative to the Notting Hill Carnival, although it's held a few weeks later, on the second Sunday of September. Some 60,000 arrive to enjoy food, music, performances, a fashion show by resident designers, clowns, and buskers, mostly in the name of honoring the melting pot that the East End has always been.

The Great River Race (☎ 020/8398-9057; www.greatriverrace.co.uk): Always over too soon, the Race is the aquatic version of the London Marathon, with rowers vying to beat out 300 other vessels—Chinese dragon boats, Canadian canoes, Viking longboats, and even Hawaiian outriggers—on a morning jaunt from Richmond to the bottom tip of the Isle of Dogs, at Greenwich. It's held on a Saturday in mid-September.

The Mayor's Thames Festival (www.thamesfestival.org): In conjunction with the Great River Race, nearly half a million souls attend London's largest free open-air arts festival, which includes more than 250 stalls selling food and crafts (Southwark Bridge is closed for a giant feast), a flotilla of working river boats, circus performers, and antique fireboats, tugs, and sailboats. Sunday sees the Night Carnival, a lavish procession of 2,500 lantern-bearing musicians and dancers crawling along Victoria Embankment (the north bank), crossing at Blackfriars Bridge, and finishing at the Royal National Theatre. Everything is topped off with barge-launched fireworks. It takes place on a mid-September weekend.

Open House London (☎ 020/3006-7008; www.openhouselondon.org): A blockbuster 2-day architecture-appreciation event that goes down every mid-September. More than 600 buildings, all of them deemed important but normally closed to the public, yawn wide for free tours on a single, hotly anticipated day. Past participants have included the distinctive skyscraper headquarters of Lloyd's and Swiss Re (officially "30 St. Mary Axe" but usually called "The Gherkin") and the Mansion House (official residence of the Lord Mayor, completed in 1752). The list of open buildings comes out in August, and some require timed tickets, but for most the line forms at dawn. Open House also organizes summer walking tours.

Dance Umbrella (☎ 084/4412-4312; www.danceumbrella.co.uk): One of the world's best dance festivals, with plenty of standing-room seats for as little as £5; it peaks in late September.

Late September to Early October

London Fashion Weekend (☎ 020/8948-5522; www.londonfashionweekend.co.uk): It's got nothing on its kin in New York or Milan, but at this brief festival, collections from more than 100 designers are put on sale at deeply discounted prices in the hopes they'll build some buzz.

October

Diwali: One advantage of visiting a multicultural city like London is that it affords you the chance to sample major international holidays in an English-speaking environment. One such treat is Diwali, the Indian "festival of light," when Trafalgar Square is transformed with lights, floating lanterns, massive models of the elephant god Ganesh, music, dance, and DJs. It's free and held in mid- to late October.

Origin: The London Craft Fair (☎ 020/7806-2500; www.craftscouncil.org.uk): Over nearly 2 weeks in a purpose-built pavilion in the courtyard of Somerset House on the Thames, a range of disciplines from more than 300 artists is highlighted, from glass to metal, and from furniture to jewelry.

London Film Festival (☎ 020/7928-3535; www.lff.org.uk): An important stop on the cinema circuit, this event, sponsored by the British Film Institute, starts sometimes spills into November.

October or November

State Opening of Parliament (www.parliament.uk): There's not much to see in person—just a white-haired monarch zipping in and out of Parliament in a state coach with a cavalry contingent—but the rest is shown on television. Inside, the goings-on aren't much more transparent; Her Royal Highness reads a speech in the House of Lords that she didn't even write (the prime minister did), to kick off the new season of legislation and establish the ruling party's objectives. She does wear some lush vestments; there's a cavernous room in the Houses of Parliament devoted just to dressing her. You'll be waiting outside.

November

Guy Fawkes Night: In 1605, silly old Guy Fawkes tried to assassinate James I and the entire Parliament by blowing them to smithereens in the Gunpowder Plot. Joke's on him: To this day, the Brits celebrate his failure by blowing up *him*. His effigy is thrown on bonfires across the country, fireworks displays rage in the autumn night sky, and more than a few tykes light their first sparklers in honor of the would-be assassin's gruesome execution. Although displays are scattered around town, including at Battersea Park and Alexandra Palace, I suggest getting out of the city for the weekend nearest November 5, also called Bonfire Night, because the countryside is perfumed with the woody aroma of burning leaves on this holiday. If you can't do that, mount Primrose Hill or Hampstead Heath for a view of the fireworks going off around the city.

Lord Mayor's Show (www.lordmayorsshow.org): What sounds like the world's dullest cable access program is actually a delightfully pompous procession, abut 800 years old, involving some 140 charity floats and 6,000 participants (Pewterers! Basketweavers!) who parade round-trip from Mansion House in The City and head to the Royal Courts of Justice, on the Strand, all to ostensibly show off the newly elected Lord Mayor to the Queen or her representatives. The centerpiece is the preposterously carved and gilt Lord Mayor's Coach, built in 1757—a carriage so extravagant it makes Cinderella's ride look like a skateboard. The procession marks the only time the coach is permitted to venture outside of its air-conditioned garage inside the Museum of London. That's a lot of hubbub for a city official whose role is essentially ceremonial; the Mayor of London (currently Boris Johnson) wields the true power. All that highfaluting strutting is followed by a good old-fashioned fireworks show over the Thames between the Blackfriars and Waterloo bridges. It's held on the second Saturday in November, and it's usually broadcast on TV.

London Jazz Festival (☎ 020/7324-1881; www.serious.org.uk): Some 165 mid-November events attract around 60,000 music fans. Many performances are free, and tickets are distributed by the venues.

Remembrance Sunday: Another chance to glimpse Her Royal Highness. She and the prime minister, as well as many royals, attend a ceremony at the Cenotaph, in the traffic island of Whitehall, to honor the war dead and wounded, of which Britain has borne more than its share. Those red flowers you'll see everywhere—red petals, black centers—are poppies, the symbol of remembrance in Britain. It takes place on the Sunday nearest November 11.

December

New Year's Eve: London doesn't throw massive street parties in the winter, but Trafalgar Square does host a packed, liquor-free midnight countdown. The next day at noon, some 10,000 participants in the annual **New Year's Day Parade** (www.londonparade.co.uk) traipse up Whitehall from outside Parliament, head up Regent Street, and hang a left on Piccadilly, winding up by the Green Park Tube stop. Some 500,000 line the route, but four times that number watch it on TV.

ENTRY REQUIREMENTS FOR NON-BRITISH CITIZENS

For tourism, citizens of the United States, Canada, Australia, and New Zealand only need a valid passport to enter Great Britain, and they don't have to prearrange visas. You will be asked when you are leaving the country, so it's a good idea (but not a requirement) to have your tickets booked before you land. You should also make sure your passport will be valid for the entirety of your stay.

Visa & Medical Requirements

Passport holders from the United States, Canada, Australia, New Zealand, and South Africa do not require visas to enter the United Kingdom as a tourist. The usual permitted stay is 90 days or fewer for tourists, although some nationalities are granted stays of up to 6 months. If you plan to work or study, though, or if you're traveling on a passport from another country, you'll need to obtain the correct paperwork. This information may have changed by the time you read this, so check **UK Visas** (www.ukvisas.gov.uk) for the latest rules.

The United Kingdom does not require any special immunizations of its visitors.

FINDING THE BEST AIRFARE TO LONDON

The central question is *when* are they? London is such a popular destination (it's served by more flights from the United States than any other European city) that plenty of airlines are vying to carry you across. If you're not redeeming frequent flier miles, there are five rules to finding bargains. Flexibility is key to all of them:

1. **For starters, fly on Tuesday, Wednesday, or Saturday, when traffic is lightest.** The main London airports serving transoceanic travel are Heathrow (LHR) and Gatwick (LGW). Fly to whichever one yields the best price. Conveniently, some airlines, like British Airways, have online day-by-day calendars that show you when the best prices fall.
2. **Choose a transatlantic flight that departs after dinner.** This saves you from paying another hotel night, since you'll arrive in the morning. You're also likely to find lower fares, because business travelers like day flights.
3. **Go off-season.** London's weather isn't extreme, so there's really not a no-go month. November through March generally yield the lowest airfares and hotel rates, although the late December holidays and the last week of November (American Thanksgiving) can be busy, too. Summer prices (June–Sept) can soar well over a grand.

4. **Search for fares for or on a weekend.** Presumably because fewer business travelers want Saturday flights or Sunday mornings, many major airlines post lower prices to fly then. You might also save money by booking your seat at 3am. That's because unpaid-for reservations are flushed out of the system at midnight, and prices often sink when the system becomes aware of an increase in supply. But this method isn't foolproof.
5. **Don't buy last-minute.** Barring unforeseen sales, you'll be unlikely to score a major deal.

To get a feel for how much the airlines and mid-priced hotels charge over time, the graphs at Hotwire's **TripStarter** (www.hotwire.com/tripstarter) are illuminating. Follow a visit there with one to **FareCast** (www.farecast.com), which breaks prices down per hour for any day you propose.

Keep your eyes open for sales, too. Individual airlines often send e-mail alerts when the going gets good. Also monitor such sites as Frommers.com, SmarterTravel.com, and Airfarewatchdog.com, which highlight fare sales. Kayak.com's and SideStep.com's FareTracker can send you regular e-mails highlighting upcoming prices from your home airport.

Most times of year, the least expensive way to reach London is with an **air-hotel package,** which combines discounted airfare with discounted nights in a hotel. I swear by them, and smart travelers do, too. The best air-hotel packages invariably cost several hundred dollars less than what you would pay if you booked both of these components separately. If you find a good air-hotel deal, then your worries about both airfare and lodging will be over, leaving you to plan the real fun. A box introduces you to the major players on p. 38. Most air-hotel deals will allow you to fly back days after your hotel allotment runs out, and at no extra charge. Remember to time your price searches by the cheaper days of the week that I name above, and keep in mind that singles always have to pay a little more, typically $130 to $200. Even considering that, solo travelers could save money.

Then it's a matter of which airlines you check. **Air India** (☎ 800/223-7776; www.airindia.com), which goes from Chicago and Toronto, is known for consistently cheap prices. (Opt for non-refundable, restricted-fare tickets for the best prices.) These airlines schedule regular flights to London, and many produce e-mail newsletters that might alert you to deep discounts: **Air Canada** (☎ 888/247-2262; www.aircanada.com); **American Airlines** (☎ 800/433-7300; www.aa.com); **British Airways** (☎ 800/247-9297; www.ba.com); **Continental Airlines** (☎ 800/231-0856; www.continental.com); **Delta Air Lines** (☎ 800/241-4141; www.delta.com); **Northwest Airlines** (☎ 800/225-2525; www.nwa.com); **United Airlines** (☎ 800/538-2929; www.united.com); **U.S. Airways** (☎ 800/622-1015; www.usairways.com); **Virgin Atlantic Airways** (☎ 800/821-5438; www.virgin-atlantic.com). Many airlines now tack on an extra fee for booking by phone, so try to reserve online.

Primary websites that collect quotes from a variety of sources (whether they be airlines or other websites) include **Kayak.com, Mobissimo.com, Lessno.com, Ebookers.com, Orbitz.com, Travelocity.com, SideStep.com, Qixo.com,** and **Expedia.com.** Always canvass multiple sites, because each has odd gaps in its coverage because of the way they obtain their quotes; for example, at press time

Kayak.com and SideStep.com would show you American Airlines quotes that came from Orbitz.com, but not prices quoted directly by American, which might have been lower. Travelocity allows you to see if there are better prices for flexible travel dates, while SideStep won't. Check a few of those sources and then compare your best price with what the airline in question is offering, because that price might be lowest of all. Some sites have small booking fees of $5 to $10, and many force you to accept non-refundable tickets for the cheapest prices.

If you're hitting a wall, search for transatlantic itineraries that allow for one or two stops, since routes that include stops in Paris or Frankfurt (on Lufthansa or Air France, say) can produce hidden bargains. Since the 1960s, **Icelandair** (☎ 800/223-5500; www.icelandair.com) has enticed intrepid travelers onto flights to London that stop in Reykjavík long enough for them to take a delicious dip in the famous Blue Lagoon, which is near the airport. That cool detour often saves you $200 off the going nonstop airfare. It flies from six North American cities in summer; fewer in winter. Also look at **Aer Lingus** (☎ 800/474-7424; www.aerlingus.com), which stops in Dublin; some of its routes are seasonal.

Some travelers are flexible enough to use alternative booking sites such as **Priceline.com,** where buyers name their own price for tickets and hope the airlines take them up on their offer; and **Skyauction.com,** which functions like eBay for tickets. Travelers who plan to head to multiple international cities on their trip should get a free quote for their entire itinerary from **Airtreks** (☎ 877/247-8735; www.airtreks.com), a travel agent that specializes in multi-city tickets. You'll still want to compare its quote with your own fare research, though.

No matter which airline you go with, prepare yourself for added taxes and fees, which are usually $450 or higher round-trip from the USA—London's airport fees, which account for about $300 of that, are high, and gas prices don't help.

By the way, if you despise flying, there is still a single ocean liner making the 6-day trip between New York City and Southampton, which connects by rail to London in about an hour. That's the magnificent *Queen Mary 2* on the Cunard line (☎ 800/728-6273; www.cunard.com), which makes the run from late spring to early fall. Fares start around $1,500 per person, including all your food.

BOOKING A PLACE TO STAY

For tips on booking online and bargaining, go to p. 68 and p. 78, and for information on renting an apartment or staying in a private home, go to p. 28.

SWAP, MEET: HOME EXCHANGES

You'd be surprised how many Londoners are dying to visit your own stomping grounds, and if you make contact with the right people, you can swap houses at an agreed-upon time (sometimes simultaneously). It sounds strange, but it tends to work and nothing tends to get stolen because swappers often become good friends. Not just that, but their neighbors will often pop by to check up on you, so you have a built-in social circle (and source of insider advice). You can truly live like a local when you swap homes, and quite a few people end up doing it year after year.

Plenty of exchange clubs exist, and because London's an interesting place, it's pretty well represented in all of them. Which club should you choose? Well, since almost all of them are pitched to specific clientele with their own set of tastes, that's for you to decide. Here are the biggies, in alphabetical order:

Digsville.com (☎ 877/795-1019): For $45 a year, this popular and well-designed site allows users to see photos of their prospective swap and even read feedback from others who have traded with its owner.

Geenee.com (www.geenee.com): The owners of this newcomer have visited every flat and rated them with a star system, and members rate each other, eBay-style. The fee (often waived to boost membership) is $75 upon joining, and $120 for the first exchange, but after that, exchanges are free forever.

HomeExchange.com (☎ 800/877-8723): When *The Holiday* came out, this club's listings shot from 6,000 to more than 20,000. This is important because the more members, the more potential swaps. It breaks searches down by interest, including for seniors and long-term stays. It costs $100 a year to list.

Homelink.org (☎ 800/638-3841): Popular with British and Australian travelers (with 13,000 members in 72 countries), this service, around since 1953, costs $110 per year with Web access; printed directories are $60 more.

Intervac (☎ 800/756-4663; www.intervacus.com): Intervac has been around for half a century, but its old catalog system has migrated to the Web. Its claim to fame is that some 80% of its listings are international (52 countries are represented), which means (as it puts it), "you compete with fewer Americans for overseas properties." Access to all international listings is $95 a year.

There are additional exchange sites for special interest groups, designed to provide safe haven for travelers with particular needs. **SabbaticalHomes.com** caters to academics; **Independent Living Institute** (www.independentliving.org) is a free database maintained by a Sweden-based advocacy group for people with disabilities; **HomeAroundtheWorld.com (☎ 020/7564-3739)** is for gays and lesbians and costs £39 for 2 years; and **SeniorsHomeExchange.com** is for those over 50 and costs $79 for a 3-year listing.

Or you could roll the dice with a website like **CouchSurfing.com,** on which folks with spare space angle for temporary visitors. That's free, but there is no vetting system, so consider the risks that might come with accepting an offer.

TRAVEL INSURANCE—DO YOU NEED IT?

Yes, you do, principally because you're going abroad. Should something unpleasant befall you, you may need to be flown back home on a stretcher, and no matter how much you beg, you can't save money by coming home as cargo. At the very least, you may need to cancel your trip before you leave, and travel insurance can buffer you from a large financial loss.

But does that mean you need to buy some? Not necessarily—you may already have it. Your existing medical coverage may include an international safety net; ask so you're sure. The credit card you use to make reservations may cover you for cancellation, lost luggage, or trip interruption; again, ask your issuer. Most hotels will issue refunds with enough notice, but a few of the cheap ones won't.

So what else may you want to insure? If your medical coverage and credit cards help, you may want special coverage for **apartment stays,** especially if you've plunked down a deposit, and any **valuables,** since airlines are only required to pay up to $2,500 for lost luggage domestically, less for foreign travel.

If you do decide on insurance, you can easily compare available policies by visiting **InsureMyTrip.com** (☎ 800/487-4722). Or contact one of the following reputable companies:

- [illegible] **erica** (☎ 800/284-8300; www.accessamerica.com)
- [illegible] **ion** (☎ 800/873-9855; www.csatravelprotection.com)
- [illegible] 37-2029; www.medexassist.com)
- [illegible] **rnational** (☎ 800/826-4919; www.travelguard.com)
- **Travelex** ([illegible]/228-9792; www.travelex-insurance.com)

TRAVELING FROM LONDON TO OTHER PARTS OF THE UNITED KINGDOM

The British rail system is so comprehensive that many tourists spend weeks on the island without seeing the inside of a car. Considering the high cost of British fuel, the rarity of British parking, and the narrowness of British streets, driving a car is not recommended, but if you are silly enough to do it, make sure you learn how to drive a stick shift before you leave home. Cars with automatic transmissions are inevitably much more expensive than manuals. Driving on the left is easy after a few minutes of pulse-racing acclimation.

But if you insist upon wheels to get out of the city, there are rental garages everywhere, although reserving ahead from home yields the best prices. Try to return your car outside the congestion-charge zone to avoid charges and aggravation. You will find similar rates among **Nova Car Hire** (www.novacarhire.com), **Auto Europe** (www.autoeurope.com), **Europe By Car** (www.ebctravel.com), **Europcar** (www.europcar.com), and **Holiday Autos** (www.holidayautos.com). Also check the major names like Avis, Hertz, and Budget, in case they can do better. Air conditioning, something you won't need, adds about £4 to the daily bill. Fuel, or "petrol," is even more expensive than at home, and although most rentals include unlimited mileage, make sure yours does.

RAIL

The original railway builders plowed their stations into the middle of every town of size, making it easy to see the highlights of the United Kingdom without getting near a car. While the British whine about the declining quality of the service, Americans, Canadians, and Australians will be blown away by the speed and low cost of the system, particularly if you book a month or two ahead. Find tickets to all destinations through **National Rail** (☎ 020/7278-5240; www.nationalrail.co.uk). Make every effort to book as far ahead as possible, since early-bird bookings can yield some marvelous deals, such as £16 for a 4-hour trip to Scotland (£100 last-minute is common). When searching for tickets, always search for trips going or coming from all London stations, not just the ones leaving from the station nearest your hotel, because different destinations emanate from different London stations. Looking for departures outside of rush hour might also help you find better deals. The rail system accepts bookings 12 weeks ahead, but unfortunately, not every train company website accepts international credit cards. You may have to phone, or use the booking website TheTrainLine.com.

I've never run across a case in which the money you'd pay for a **BritRail pass** (☎ 866/274-8724; www.britrail.com) is worth it. Tickets bought reasonably in advance will still be cheaper than what you'd pay for the same trips on a pass (i.e. $265 for only 4 days in 2 months), and few tourists ride the rails with the near-daily regularity and long distances that would make a pass pay for itself. You can get timetables on its site, too. Check prices against the U.S. seller **Rail Europe** (☎ 800/622-8600; www.raileurope.com) because its quotes may vary.

BUSES

The least expensive way to get from city to city in Britain (but not the fastest—that's usually the train) is via coach, and because the country's not very big, it rarely takes more than a few hours to reach anyplace. I know lifelong Londoners who have never ventured as near as Scotland because they find the journey—around 5 hours—too cumbersome. **National Express** (☎ 08705/808-8080; www.nationalexpress.com) is a major carrier with scads of departures, but the best-priced is **Megabus** (☎ 090/0160-0900; www.megabus.com), which serves more than 40 cities, and charges as little as £1 for early bookings, although £10 to £15 to go clear to Edinburgh is a more typical rate. Megabusses once lacked toilets, but now they have them. It accepts bookings 2 months ahead; you'll pay a painful 60p per minute to reserve by phone, so do it online. Both coach services depart from Victoria Coach Station, located very near Victoria railway station.

So what's the best place to hear about inexpensive ground tours? Hostels. Drop into one of the places mentioned in the accommodations chapter; most of their lobbies are practically wallpapered with brochures. Don't neglect their bulletin boards, either, since you may catch wind of a shared-ride situation that'll often cost you no more than your share of the gasoline (in Britain, *petrol*).

COMBO PACKAGES

Some packagers put together dashes to popular European cities (Paris, Amsterdam, Berlin, etc.) that include Eurostar/train/air tickets, B&B accommodations for a night or so, and often some sightseeing. Try **Anderson Tours** (☎ 020/7436-9304; www.andersontours.co.uk), check the travel sections of the London papers, and pick up a copy of *TNT* at hostels.

TRAVELING FROM LONDON TO OTHER PARTS OF EUROPE

Not everyone wants to stick around London for their whole vacation. After all, you've flown all that distance, so why not peck around in Europe a little while you're at it? Hop a train, and you can be in Paris for lunch.

The so-called no-frills airlines began life by shuttling Londoners to the mass resorts of the Mediterranean, but today, dozens of small-scale carriers fly all over the place (see the box below for more info). The main hitch is luggage; most no-frills charge you for anything you check, and some flights (such as a few on Ryanair) don't accept checked baggage at all. And woe to you if you pack more

Flying from London to Europe, Cheaply

There are literally dozens of no-frills carriers, most of which eschew assigned seating, force customers to pay more to book by phone (that is, if they even accept non-Web bookings), and charge sometimes shocking prices for checked luggage. These carriers are lifesavers when they work, but pray for good fortune because they have notoriously lousy customer service should something go wrong.

You'll fly out of London's secondary airports: Luton, Stansted, and Gatwick. They start selling tickets to flights for insanely low prices (i.e. £25 to Spain) and gradually raise prices (i.e. £120 in summer) as more seats are sold. If you don't spring for a ticket without restrictions, which often cost about 50% more, you will find it nearly impossible to change your flight.

The biggest lines for the British market are **Ryanair** (☎ 087/1246-0000 in the U.K. or ☎ 353/1-249-7791; www.ryanair.com), which carries some 42 million passengers a year, and **easyJet** (☎ 08712/44-23-66; www.easyjet.com). Dozens more smaller carriers specialize in flights to mainland Europe. You could check prices with each no-frills carrier in turn, but that'd be tedious. Instead, the following websites, which collect prices from multiple carriers, are good starting points. Many of them list last-minute specials, too, in case you have some extra time but can't decide in advance where in Europe you'd like to go. Just be aware of outlandish extra fees such as for checked baggage, and look into the visa requirements for the country you'd like to visit—you'd feel really stupid if you bought a ticket you can't use.

To expand your search, suss out which no-frills airline destinations are offered from London by checking **WhichBudget.com.**

These websites focus on the major carriers but not many no-frills airlines: **Ebookers.com; Opodo.co.uk; Travelocity.co.uk**.

These websites show no-frills carriers (since each one omits a few airlines, check them all), sometimes with a small ($5) booking fee: **Skyscanner.net, Skylow.com, Dohop.com, Travelsupermarket.com, Whichbudget.com.**

Lastminute.com (☎ 087/1222-5969) does big business in discounted vacation packages that include airfare. Picture a week in a Greek Islands for £220 per person, 7 B&B nights in Tunisia for £350, or 4 nights in Venice for £300 per person—that sort of thing. These don't have to booked days before, either; deals are best about two months out.

than a modest case, because you'll get slapped with often exorbitant excess baggage fees, although some airlines allow you to defray that cost somewhat by reserving your allowance ahead online at a discount. Then there are charges for paying by credit card.

The accumulated extra fees and taxes can often mean you'll end up paying as much for that so-called cheap flight as you would have on the major carriers like British Airways. If you'll be returning to London from Europe before flying back home again, consider asking your hotel if you can leave excess luggage behind for a small fee. See p. 351 for more info on this.

In terms of longer flights to other places in the world, it's useful to learn that because so many Londoners are originally from or have family in Commonwealth nations such as Australia, New Zealand, and South Africa, flights to those destinations can often be had relatively cheaply. Even when you add in the cost of your transatlantic airfare, it might be cheaper to fly via London to, say, Sydney, than if you flew Down Under from your home airport. The travel pages of London's newspapers as well as *TNT* magazine, dispensed for free at most hostels, are brimming with ads for deals on flights, charter or otherwise. In addition to the many search engines mentioned in "Getting the Best Airfare to London" above, try **North South Travel** (☎ 01245/60-82-91; www.northsouthtravel.co.uk), a London-based airfare-finding company that frequently posts such deals as £300 round-trip to Johannesburg and £500 round-trip to Delhi.

RAIL

For trips to northwestern Europe, I prefer the train. It's more dignified, since it doesn't require endlessly juggling luggage, enduring airport waiting rooms, and tucking yourself into puny airline seats. As you watch the countryside roll past your window, you get a real sense for how the land fits together. Plus, thanks to the opening, in 1994, of the engineering wonder known as the Channel Tunnel, you can reach several major European cities within around 2 hours and 15 minutes by high-speed train from London. Unlike taking a flight, you won't need to set aside extra hours and pounds for trips to and from the airports; you'll get on and off in the heart of each endpoint. You can literally ride the Tube and the Paris Métro in the same day—both before lunch. In fact, you can ride both a black taxi and the loops of Space Mountain before lunch, since the Eurostar train alights in the middle of Disneyland Resort, just east of Paris. Eurostar links London's St. Pancras station with Paris, Brussels, Lille, and Calais, and from there, you can go just about anywhere using other trains.

Book via **Eurostar** (☎ 1233/61-75-75; www.eurostar.co.uk; phone bookings are £5 more) itself or the U.S.-based **Rail Europe** (☎ 800/622-8600; www.rail europe.com), which also sells European rail passes. Check both sites, since prices can differ slightly, but do it early, because prices just go up as availability decreases. Obnoxiously, if the Eurostar website detects that your computer is from a non-British country, you will be charged higher prices (i.e. $83 for a one-way versus £30, or $60).You may also find that one-way trips cost more than round-trip ones, so if you only need a one-way ticket, it may be more cost-effective to travel the first leg and throw away the second one. Some people report finding prices on the French railroad's site, SNCF (www.sncf.com), that are about 60% of the ones quoted through British sources, but to see those deals, you must enter your location as France (even if you're reading the site in English). Second-class seats are as nice as an airline's, so don't pay more for First.

BUSES

A few coach companies also travel to Europe, usually navigating the Channel with a ferry ride. Because of the pressure put on the market by mushrooming no-frills airlines, rates are extremely low. You'll pay as little as £21 one-way to Paris via **Eurolines** (☎ 08717/81-81-81; www.eurolines.co.uk; 6–10 hours each way). Brussels is £15 and Prague £38 with a 7-day advance purchase from **EuroBus Express** (☎ 087/0608-8806; www.eurobusexpress.net). It can take all day, sunrise to sunset, to reach Paris by this method, so you can imagine what an ordeal it must be to go all the way to Poland or the Czech Republic on a bus, as do many Eastern Europeans who have settled in London.

Young, social adventurers should investigate **Busabout** (☎ 020/7950-1661; www.busabout.com), a coach system that follows set loops from London to France and Spain, Austria, Belgium, Italy, Croatia, Switzerland, and Germany and the Czech Republic. Passengers can hop on and hop off as they please. Some other companies arrange full-on organized tours of Europe's greatest hits—but never for less than you could do independently; choose one only because you'd enjoy having company: **Contiki** (☎ 866/266-8454; www.contiki.com) is geared toward a party-hearty under-35 crowd, **Tucan Travel Adventure Tours** (☎ 020/8896-1600; www.tucantravel.com) is for social scrimpers, and **Fanatics** (☎ 020/7240-3233; www.thefanatics.com) is for followers of organized sports. Whenever you read a sample itinerary, pay close attention to the departure point; if it's not London (often denoted as "ex. London"), you'll have to find your own way there.

FERRIES

No ferry to Europe sails from London. For those, you'll have to get down to the Southern coastal towns of Folkestone and Dover (for France), or Portsmouth (for Spain). Unless you have your own car, it's hard to use the ports of the France-destined lines; most people take them in conjunction with the coach trip booked from London that I just told you about. Some of the bigger players, many sailing the Channel more than a dozen times daily (from £35 each way with a car and including taxes, 150 min.), are **Seafrance** (☎ 087/1423-7119; www.seafrance.com) and **P&O Ferries** (☎ 08716/64-56-45; www.poferries.com). P&O Ferries does France, too, with a run to Bilbao, Spain, every three days. Portsmouth, a harbor on the Southern English coast, is the country's primary ferry port (mostly to France, but a few to Spain); obtain contacts for the latest operators at its website, www.portsmouth-port.co.uk. Given the proliferation of low-cost airlines, ferry travel has become an outdated and time-consuming way to travel and it's mostly used by people who need to transfer cars.

GETTING TO THE AIRPORTS: RAIL IT

Transatlantic flights almost always land at either Heathrow, the world's busiest international airport, or Gatwick, perhaps the most dissed; with a few minor exceptions, the other three airports (Stansted, Luton, and London City) serve flights from Europe, and they're where the cut-rate flyers tend to go.

Happily, getting to and from all of the airports is easy and relatively painless. Every airport offers some kind of rail connection to the central city, and tickets can be bought at desks in the arrivals halls (although Heathrow Express and

Airport Transportation Options

Airport	Cost/ Avg. time to airport using National Rail	Hours of rail service	Where rail service takes you	Cost / Time to Central London for Tube or DLR	Cost/Avg. time for coach shuttle service to Central London	Cost/ Avg. time to airport by taxi
Heathrow (LHR), HeathrowAirport.com	Heathrow Express: £15.50 single, £29 return, kids 5 to 15 £8.20/£14*/ 15 minutes OR Heathrow Connect: £6.90 single/ 30 minutes	5:10am to 11:40pm	Paddington	£4/ 60 minutes on Piccadilly Line	£4 single, kids 11 to 16 £2, under 11 free, £8 return (www.nationalexpress.com)/ 50–70 minutes	£51–£55/ 70 minutes
Gatwick (LGW), GatwickAirport.com	Gatwick Express: £16.90 single, £28.80 return/ 30 minutes OR First Capital Connect: £9 single/ £17 return/ 30 to 50 minutes	3:30am to 12:30am	Gatwick Express: Victoria; FCC: St. Pancras, Farringdon, Blackfriars, or London Bridge	N/A	£6.60 single, £12.20 return (www.nationalexpress.com)/ 90 minutes	£82/ 70 minutes
Luton (LTN), London-Luton.co.uk	£9.90 single/ £19.80 return plus £1 each way for shuttle bus, 60 minutes	5:15am to 12:45am	St. Pancras, Victoria, or London Bridge	N/A	From £12 (www.easybus.co.uk)/ 60 minutes	£75/ 80 minutes**
Stansted (STN), StanstedAirport.com	£17 single, £24 return, kids 5 to 15 £8/£12/ 45 minutes	5am to 11:30pm	Liverpool Street	N/A	£10 single, £17 return (www.nationalexpress.com)/ 110 minutes	£80/ 80 minutes**
London City (LCY), LondonCityAirport.com	N/A	DLR: 5:30am to midnight	N/A	£3/ 25 minutes on Docklands Light Railway	N/A	£25 to £40/ 20 to 40 minutes

** £1 less if you book ahead online at www.heathrowexpress.com*

*** As if you'd be daft enough to want a taxi after seeing those prices, you're more likely to find one at these airports by booking one ahead. Check www.london-luton.co.uk and www.stanstedairport.com for a list of their latest approved taxi companies.*

Stansted Express give a £1 discount for buying online). You'll rarely have to wait more than 20 minutes for the next train on any of these services unless it's very late at night, so you also don't have to worry about rushing to catch anything. Railpasses (Senior Railcard, 16-25 Railcard, Family Railcard) cover all of these routes, but London Underground Travelcards do not; see p. 14 for more on those cards.

The Perils of Early Bird Fares

Rail service doesn't start until around 5am. So don't book flights that depart at 6am unless you're prepared to a) grab a £60 hotel room near the airport, or b) splash out on a dawn taxi ride. Yes, those low sunrise fares could cost you in other ways.

On the flip side of that, if you fly on a no-frills airline into Luton late at night, particularly if you have a non-EU passport, you'll suffer through their understaffed immigration checkpoints. I once waited 90 minutes to be cleared from an easyJet flight to Luton, and despite landing with plenty of time, I managed to catch the last bus to London that night as it pulled away; otherwise I'd have been marooned at an airport hotel. The lesson: At Luton, arrive as early as you can. Heathrow, Gatwick, and London City are better equipped for bearers of foreign passports.

The comfy, business-class-level **Heathrow Express** (☎ 08456/00-15-15; www.heathrowexpress.com) zooms to Paddington station every 15 minutes in 15 minutes. Express Class, the cheapest option, is plenty plush. Despite its expense, this is one of my routine, surefire splurges, because after a long overseas flight, the last thing I want is to board a Tube train with all my gear. **Heathrow Connect** (☎ 084/5678-6975; www.heathrowconnect.com) is designed to give access to local stations, so it takes twice as long (almost 30 min.—still not long at all) and costs half as much. It uses commuter-style carriages and leaves every half-hour.

Heathrow Express passengers, who arrive at Paddington Station during the morning rush (as transatlantic passengers on overnight flights will) have the benefit of using the station's "taxi sharing" program to reduce the price of an onward taxi trip by a few pounds. Obtain a voucher from the dispatcher at the taxi queue; when there's an accumulation of four or more passengers headed to the same zone, you share a taxi, and tip is included. Otherwise, once you arrive at Paddington, you can hop the Tube system. Keep in mind that if you want to buy the cheapest Travelcard, which is a pass for all-day use, you can only do so after 9:30am.

Gatwick Express (☎ 084/5850-530; www.gatwickexpress.com) runs from Victoria station. You can also get to Gatwick via St. Pancras, Blackfriars, or London Bridge stations on First Capital Connect (☎ 08456/76-47-00; www.firstcapitalconnect.co.uk), in 30 to 50 minutes—service ends just after midnight.

Stansted Express (☎ 08456/00-72-45; www.stanstedexpress.com) runs from Liverpool Street station.

Luton and Gatwick have rail service from St. Pancras station, Blackfriars, Victoria, or London Bridge stations by **First Capital Connect** (☎ 084/5676-4700; www.firstcapitalconnect.co.uk), but it shuts down after midnight. The correct stop is Luton Airport Parkway Station, which is linked by a 5-minute shuttle to the terminals.

City Airport is linked so expediently and affordably by the **Docklands Light Railway** that it doesn't require rail service or coach service.

AIRPORT CAR SERVICES & SHUTTLE BUSES

I heartily encourage you to choose rail over road. Traffic is too snarled and rail service is too snappy. Many North Americans think of cars as the default transportation mode, but not in London. The variety of rail and coach connections means that chauffeured rides of any kind are considered a luxury service, and are priced accordingly. On a weekday, a trip from Heathrow to even the western part of London, to which that airport is nearest, can take 2 hours.

Pay more than you have to and take longer to get there? If you insist. The cheapest coach and van services for each airport are listed in the chart, and they all drop you off at standardized stops such as major train stations. For Gatwick, Stansted, and Luton, in addition to the usual National Express coach options, you have the option of the book-ahead, no-frills **EasyBus** (www.easybus.co.uk). However, it does not always beat the standard National Express seats.

You can eliminate the £4 Tube fare that connects any train or standardized coach service with your hotel by using something like **Dot2Dot** (☎ 0845/368-2368, www.dot2.com), a 24-hour shuttle van service that you'll share with other passengers and goes to the front door of hotels in central London for about £13 to £22 each way. That may be easier than a train-Tube combo, but it costs more and usually takes longer.

PACKING

For your wallet's sake, pack sparingly! I know you've heard that before, but it's really true this time. Most of the airlines serving London have laughably strict weight limits. It's not as easy as it used to be to wink your way through the weigh-in. The airlines are desperate for cash, and they will gleefully charge you for every ounce. In some cases, the scales at check-in are programmed to halt progress if they sense a bag over the limit. So you can't avoid thinking about this.

British Airways, for example, grants coach passengers a puny **23kg (51 lb.).** If you exceed that, you will be smacked with a flat fee of £25. For each flight. That only buys you another 9kg (20 lb.), because bags over 32kg (71 lb.) will be rejected outright. Now, I don't know about the luggage *you* use for big trips, but mine weighs about 15 pounds before I pack a single stitch. When it comes to carry-ons ("hand baggage"), it's got to measure no more than 56cm long by 45cm wide by 25cm deep (22×18×10 in.). You can add to that a laptop bag or a purse for free, although in the past that right has been rescinded. Anything heavier than 23kg (51 lb.), it's said, won't be allowed at all. Don't put anything precious in your checked luggage, because Heathrow's Terminal 5, where you may land, opned in 2008 with an abysmal loss rate.

You must check the rules of every airline you'll be flying. If you'll be taking multiple airlines, stick to the tightest set of restrictions of the lot. Many airlines (even the no-frills) give you discounts for booking your baggage fees at least 24 hours before you get to the airport. For example, British Airways charges £75 per extra bag if you do it at the desk, but it's £60 if done earlier online. BA claims its system empowers passengers by giving them this discount, but that's spin. In truth, it's one more preparation that most of us would rather not be burdened with. And just how do they expect us to weigh our bags again when we're in a guest house, about to return home?

Carried Away?

During periods when the British government deems the potential terrorist threat to be severe, the list of permitted carry-on items may be drastically curtailed. Ever since 2006, for flights within the U.K. and to Europe, no liquids or gels (except essential medicines and baby foods) were allowed; anything questionable, including toiletries and cosmetics, had to be packed in checked bags. (It turned out that the criminals who inspired that policy were not planning to blow up airliners, as was the fear, but were aiming at land-based targets.) Carry-on bags' permitted size varied by airline, but in general they could not be larger than 56cm by 23cm by 36cm (22×9×14 in.). During one tense but brief period in 2006, carry-on items for flights to the U.S. were restricted to travel documents only. Two years later, passengers weren't even required to remove their laptops or shoes at Heathrow's inspection points, while in the U.S. they still are. Requirements change regularly, so keep abreast of the latest rules through the Department for Transport (www.dft.gov.uk) or through your airline.

Despite the fact that these changes resulted in heavier checked baggage, the airlines won't budge on their new, restrictive weight limits.

My advice: Plan for souvenirs by starting with lightweight luggage and packing it as far under the weight limit as you can stand. Weigh it on your bathroom scale so you'll have a sense of how much leeway you've got for new purchases.

If you find that you simply must purchase a second suitcase in London, head to the eastern end of Oxford Street (west of the Tottenham Court Road Tube station), which is lined with ticky-tacky shops selling them at low prices. Many of them also sell plastic-coated, zippered duffels in tartan patterns, which are cheap (a few quid) and will see you through the journey home.

So what *should* you bring? Basically, clothes, very comfortable walking shoes, prescription medications (keep them in their original, labeled containers and bring signed copies of their **prescriptions** for Customs and emergency use even though they're unlikely to be inspected). If you require **syringe-administered medications,** always carry a signed medical prescription.

Pare your toiletries down to the essentials. You're not going to the Congo; you can find staples like toothpaste, contact lens solution, and deodorant everywhere in London—many pharmacies stock many of the same brands you have at home. Women should bring a minimum of make-up; the British don't tend to use very much themselves anyway, so women will fit in better without it. Brits are also more likely to wear trousers or slacks than blue jeans, so limit your denim ration to best blend in. If you plan to go clubbing, pack some fashionable duds—Londoners aren't slouches when it comes to dressing up.

You'll be most comfortable if you dress in clothing that layers well. Even in the depth of winter, London's air can be humid, and sometimes, dressing too warmly can become uncomfortable once you begin to perspire. No matter what the average temperature is (see the box on weather, p. 334), the air can grow cool after the sun sets, so plan for that, too. In the winter, a hat, scarf, and gloves are necessities. A compact umbrella is wise year-round, as is an outer coat that repels water, since you never know when you're going to find yourself out in one of those misty rains that makes the British Isles so lush and green.

Don't bring illegal drugs (duh), and also leave the pepper spray and mace at home; they're banned in the U.K.

MONEY

The British pound (£1), a small, chunky, gold-colored coin, is usually accepted in vending machines, so you can never have too many in your pocket. It's commonly called a "quid." Like money in America, Canada, and Australia, it's divided into 100 pennies (p)—the plural, "pence," is used to modify amounts over 1p. Pence come in 1p, 2p, 5p, 10p, 20p, and 50p denominations. Patterns on the obverse of the £1 and 50p coins periodically change to commemorate various areas or events. Sometimes you'll see large £2 coins, too.

Bills come in £5, £10, £20, and £50 denominations. Every now and then, you'll receive notes made by the Royal Bank of Scotland; don't be troubled, since these are legal tender in London, too.

All prices (including at most B&Bs but not at many hotels) are listed including tax, so what you see is what you pay. No guesstimating required. I don't know why we don't do it that way at home.

When bringing up prices, always insert the word "pounds": For example, £2.50 would be uttered as "two pounds fifty" but not "two fifty." Another issue of cultural syntax: When asking for change (such as from a taxi driver), it's customary to tell the amount to keep and not the amount to return to you. For example, to pay £11 with a £20 bill, don't say, "I'd like £9 back." Say, "Please keep £11." I don't know why. Maybe it sounds more polite to them.

Every visitor should have several sources for money. Cash is king, as they say (Queen Elizabeth isn't jealous—her face is on all the money anyway), but international exchange complicates its acquisition. Each of the following sources should be considered a part of your toolbox, but weigh the pros and cons of each.

CASH

In the old days, visitors had to bring wads of their home currency or travelers checks and then exchange it, bit by bit, as their trips progressed. Some of them would even obtain a fistful of pounds at their bank before they left home.

These days, because of **ATMs,** carrying unseemly sums of money is no longer necessary or advisable. You can pull pounds out of holes in the wall pretty much whenever you please. But it's still wise to bring enough of your home currency to sustain you for a few days, just in case something goes wrong with your plastic. Store it someplace safe, and don't spend it unless you have to.

Before leaving home, warn your bank that you intend to travel internationally so that it doesn't place a stop on your account when international withdrawals start cropping up. You may also need to adjust your PIN, since English banks require 4-digit codes. If you know your PIN as a word, memorize the numerical equivalent, because not all English machines will have letters on their keypads.

Most banks hit you with fees of a few pounds each time you withdraw cash. Your own bank may toss in a small fee of its own (another 2% or 3%, but ask ahead to see what its policy is), so gauge for yourself how much you feel comfortable withdrawing at a time to offset that fee. If you have an account with an international bank chain, it'd be smart to ask whether using their machines exclusively during your visit will result in saving on fees. Similarly, ask your bank if it has any reciprocal agreements with any English institutions; Bank of America has long allowed free withdrawals from Barclays machines.

One institution known to charge international usage fees that are well below the industry standard is **Everbank** (☎ 888/882-3837; www.everbank.com), an FDIC-insured outfit that only hits customers for 1%.

Be very quick when using British ATMs. Not just for safety reasons, but because if you fail to retrieve your card within 10 to 15 seconds, many machines will suck it back up again for "security." Should that happen, you won't be able to get your card back for a day or three.

CREDIT CARDS

All of the major credit cards you use at home will work in England, but because of the red tape they stick to vendors, American Express and Diners Club are not as commonly accepted as Visa and MasterCard.

Europeans are moving toward a system that uses "chip and PIN" credit cards impregnated with a SIM card and requiring a code number to use. This system is meant to protect your account information, and while merchants may decline cards without "chip and PIN" if they belong to locals, they are required to accept them from foreigners. If a clerk asks you to enter your code but your card doesn't require one, just tell them it's an international card and you don't have a PIN. If they still resist, ask them to swipe your card anyway, because processing machines can automatically detect when accounts are international. You may want to bring your passport along at all times so that your identity can always be verified.

Before leaving home, warn your credit card issuer that you intend to travel abroad, otherwise it may place a stop on your account when international charges pop up. This happens to me at least once a year despite the fact that it should be obvious by now to my lender that I travel a great deal. Make a note of your credit card company's phone number, but be sure you have one that isn't toll-free, because those usually don't work from abroad (most companies will accept collect-call charges from abroad, though).

Many credit card companies also levy transaction fees of a few percentage points every time you make a charge abroad. Since those companies sometimes bury the fee in the final exchanged amount, you can't always tell if it's happening. Call your credit card company to ask what its international transaction fee is. One of the few credit card companies that doesn't charge an international fee is **Capital One** (☎ 800/955-7070; www.capitalone.com); **Everbank** (☎ 888/882-3837; www.everbank.com) charges a below-average 1%. Credit unions are less likely to charge high rates, but every one is different.

In addition, many vendors charge their own transaction fee (3% is the norm) for many purchases as a way of defraying the cost of dealing with credit card companies; there's no way around this one. Minimum purchases for credit card transactions are also common, and that's also perfectly legal.

Before You Leave Home . . .

Here's some advice on what to do in the weeks before your flight leaves:

Nuts & Bolts:

- Book a flight and hotel. But you knew that one.
- To ease difficulties in case of theft, make copies of your tickets and passport, one to leave with a friend and one to stash in your luggage. Also consider scanning them and storing the files in a free online e-mail account for easy retrieval on the road.
- Buy the electrical adapters you'll need.
- Warn your bank and credit card lenders that you intend to use your accounts abroad, and double-check that everything's set up to work properly. While you're at it, jot down their international phone numbers (the non–toll free ones) in case of emergency.
- If you plant to use your mobile phone, enable roaming and/or have it unlocked so you can use a British SIM card.
- Book any excess or overweight fees with your airline, if needed.

Activity Planning:

- If you elect to take the Heathrow Express or Stansted Express train, book tickets ahead online (p. 350) and you'll save £1.
- Especially from June through September, reserve the time and date of your tour of the London Eye, Buckingham Palace, the Houses of Parliament, Clarence House, Spencer House, the Ceremony of the Keys at the Tower of London, Trooping the Colour, the Whitechapel Bell Foundry, and special exhibitions that require timed tickets (such as at the British Museum).
- If there's a show or concert you have your heart set on catching, book ahead.
- Check the list of major festivals (p. 334) to see if there might be something unexpected you'd like to attend.

Try not to use credit cards to withdraw cash. You'll pay a currency exchange fee, and worse, you'll be charged interest from the moment your money leaves the slot. If your credit card allows for online bill paying, set up that capability before you leave—at the very least, you can pay off your withdrawals within hours, cutting your losses. Some credit cards companies also allow users to put a surplus of funds in their accounts, which may also cut down on lending fees. Using an ATM card linked to a liquid bank account is far less expensive.

TRAVELERS CHECKS & TRAVELERS CARDS

Now that ATMs are so common and so convenient, fewer and fewer people are using traveler's checks. They'd be more enticing if banks didn't hit you with fees or padded percentages at both ends—when you buy them, and when you cash

What Do Things Cost?

Think of a price that you'd consider expensive—say, something you'd pay in New York City or San Francisco—and then turn it into pounds. It's not pretty. You'll find yourself developing a taste for white bread and water.

Tube rides in the city center for a day:	£5.30; £4.80 using Oyster
Taxi ride, Bloomsbury to Knightsbridge:	£9
Newspaper:	50p
Tube of toothpaste:	£2
Box of tampons:	£2
Package of diapers:	£7–£9
Contact lens solution:	£5.50
Cup of coffee:	£1.40–£2.40 (more for lattes and other variations)
Triangle sandwich:	£1.50–£4
Caff breakfast:	£5–£7
Restaurant lunch:	£7 (cheap restaurant), £11 (moderate/expensive joint)
Restaurant dinner:	£8 (cheap place), £14 (moderate/expansive place)
Bottle of wine:	£5–£11
Beer in a bar:	£2.50–£3
Burger King Whopper:	£3.29
Cocktail in a bar:	£7–£12
Bottle of water:	70p–£1.50
Museum entrance fee:	£5–£9 (when it's not free)
West End musical ticket:	£50 full price, £25 at TKTS
Movie ticket:	£13.50 in the West End, £8.50 in the neighborhoods
Walking tour:	£7
Football game:	£25 (and up)
Theater program:	£2–£5

them. Still, some old-school travelers feel comfortable using them, and I can't blame them for wanting to feel safe. All the major types—American Express, Visa, Thomas Cook—are known quantities in London, although decreasingly so. Using traveler's checks, you run the risk of some places not accepting them.

Creditors have come up with **traveler's check cards,** also called **prepaid cards,** which are essentially debit cards loaded with the amount of money you elect to put on them. They're not coded with your personal information, they work in

ATMs, and should you lose one, you can get your cash back in a matter of hours. If you spend all the money on them, you can call a number or visit a website and reload the card using your bank account information. American Express used to offer a prepaid "cheque card," but it discontinued them. That leaves **Travelex Cash Passport** (☎ 888/713-3424 or ☎ 080/0015-0401 in the U.K.; www.cashpassportcard.com; $200 minimum and $2.50 per ATM transaction), which works anywhere MasterCard does and can be loaded in British pounds, Euros, or American dollars; and **All-Access Visa TravelMoney** (☎ 866/387-7363; www.allaccesstravelmoney.com). That one costs $10 and keeps a little over 1% of everything you load onto it, plus all the regular international transaction fees. It also charges you $4.95 a month if you keep it longer than 7 months. It's not ideal, but it's a relatively safe way to travel with money

MONEY EXCHANGES

Like traveler's checks, changing cash is on the outs, and good riddance, since exchange rates are often usurious. Since ATM withdrawals give much better deals, old-fashioned cambios are few and far between these days, although you'll still find a few upon landing at the airport and around Leicester Square and Piccadilly Circus. If you need to change money, take advantage of the better rates offered by banks during regular banking hours (9:30am–4pm). Money exchange booths are for use only after those hours.

HEALTH & SAFETY

If you don't feel well and you need the advice of a doctor or a nurse, the national health care system operates a free, 24-hour hotline that can help: **National Health Service Direct** (☎ 0845/4647; www.nhsdirect.co.uk). Citizens of many European countries are entitled to free health care while in Britain (see www.dh.gov.uk/travellers for details), but everyone else is not, although clinics have been known to treat tourists and then look the other way rather than embark upon the odyssey of paperwork required to bill them. Still, for non-EU citizens, I strongly encourage getting health or travel insurance. See p. 343 for info on that.

Few places in London are unsafe. Some locals are made nervous by a few parts of the East End, but there's not much evidence of random violence to back that up. Neighborhoods that pessimistically might be called sketchy are usually distant from the Tube lines, and they only feel tense after dark, when shops close. London is like anyplace; simply be sensitive to who's around you and you'll do fine.

The biggest nuisance tourists might encounter—besides tipsy locals—is pickpockets. As chronicled in *Oliver Twist,* London (like all cities of size) is home to a skilled subspecies of crook eager to lift your valuables without your knowledge. Oxford Street and the Tube are the prime picking grounds. Simply be smart about where you put your cash (I prefer my front pocket), and about who's pressing up close to you. If anyone thrusts a map or a wedge of cardboard in your face, bat it away, since they're commonly used to divert attention and hide the act.

I'm almost sorry that I mentioned pickpockets at all because they're not common, and now you'll be worried, but honestly—you'll be fine. Just be aware.

If you're truly concerned about theft, consider assembling a "fake" wallet containing a few expired credit cards and a few quid that you can part with in lieu of your real goods. Keep it in an obvious place like your back pocket, and hide the

Can I Do That?

Some things that are considered sins back home may lead to legal pleasures in London. Which means they're not sinful as long as you're on British soil! To wit:

- The drinking age is 18. But if you're having your first legit night out in London, take it easy, because beers here have higher alcohol content than in most countries. Start with a pint every 2 hours and see how that does you.
- There are no open container laws. That means you can drink beer in public. There were once even bars on some Tube platforms.
- You may smoke Cuban cigars. Get them at any tobacconist and puff away. If you're American, though, don't try smuggling them home.
- Absinthe, the brutal quaff nicknamed "The Green Fairy," is available here. Drink up because American Customs frowns on many versions of it.
- The age of consent is 16 no matter the sexual preference.

"real" one in a money belt or in your front pocket. By the time a villain realizes they got a decoy wallet, they'll be long gone.

Surveillance is the new British national pastime; there are more closed-circuit TV cameras per person than in any other country. Guns are banned—even on most police officers—so you don't often see the kind of violence taken for granted in the United States. Londoners cite increasing knife crime as a problem, but the victims are almost always young men who themselves carry knives. Some male tourists have gotten fleeced at some of the **"hostess bars"** in Soho. If you do suffer a lapse of judgment and accept the barker's invitation to go into one, understand that if you accept the company of a lady, you could receive a huge bill that may be exacted by lunkheaded yobs with tattooed fingers and indecipherable accents.

Should you find yourself on the business end of the legal system, you can get advice and referrals to lawyers from **Legal Services Commission** (☎ 084/5345-4345; www.legalservices.gov.uk). Victims of crime can receive volunteer legal guidance and emotional fortification from **Victim Support** (☎ 020/7268-0200; www.victimsupport.org.uk). In the unlikely event of a sexual assault, phone the **Rape Crisis Federation** (☎ 084/5122-1331; www.rapecrisis.org.uk).

SPECIAL TYPES OF TRAVELERS

ADVICE FOR FAMILY TRAVELERS

London is a dream for families. Something about it captures kids' imaginations—is it the new-sounding accents, or maybe the talk of princesses, or the tales of people getting their heads lopped off? Maybe the appeal is because so many of the stories kids love, from Roald Dahl to Harry Potter to Peter Pan, take place in London. Whatever it is, children are often captivated by the city's attractions, particularly if they've had a hand in helping the family shape its daily activities.

London attractions are eager to cater to the family market. The kingly treatment starts, at many places, with the so-named **Family Ticket,** which grants a low price for parents and kids entering certain sights together, such as a single price for two adults and up to three kids. Always ask about it, because some box offices neglect to post the prices. Single parents and those with a smaller brood aren't left out, because kids under the age of five are almost always admitted for free, and kids under 15 receive hefty discounts off the adult price.

Many museums—and I really, really love this—consider it a badge of honor (and a selling point to fish for government funds) to offer elaborate **kids' activities,** usually for free or for a pittance. For example, the Natural History Museum lends themed "Explorer Backpacks" equipped with a pith hat, binoculars, pens, paper, and a booklet that engages children under 7 in their visit with simple scavenger-hunt activities. Most of the big museums do something similar. Even the smallest exhibitions, such as the Handel House Museum, often offer a nook for coloring, simple hands-on activities, or a rack of little costumes to try on. I daresay parents will get bored of most museums before their kids do. Perhaps the only place where your very young (under 5) children won't be embraced with open arms is the theater—many won't admit little ones.

The **Family Railcard** (www.family-railcard.co.uk) is for at least one adult and one child aged 5 to 15, with a maximum of four adults and four kids on one ticket; at least one child must travel with you at all times. It awards adults 33% off and kids 60% off. Two kids under the age of 5 can travel with an adult for free at all times, even without this card. It's for sale at rail stations.

If you are a **divorced parent** with joint custody of your children, make sure you bring documentation proving that you are entitled to take your kids out of the country; otherwise Immigration may give you a hard time or even deny you entry.

Some resources that offer family-specific travel tips include the **Family Travel Network** (www.familytravelnetwork.com), online since 1995. **Travel with Your Kids** (www.travelwithyourkids.com) specializes in tips for international travel, and it also maintains a section just about London's finds. **The Family Travel Files** (www.thefamilytravelfiles.com) rounds up tour operators and packagers geared to families, but its suggestions aren't always the most economical or efficient.

Babysitting: **Top Notch Nannies** (☎ 020/7259-2626; www.topnotchnannies.com) normally brokers child-minders—usually Australians or Eastern Europeans—to wealthy London families, but it also runs a sideline, **Brilliant Babysitters,** which starts with a £10 booking fee and then charges about £8 an hour on weekday evenings and £9 an hour on weekends.

The weekly *Time Out* magazine, on sale wherever you turn in London, includes a section on kids' activities. Of course many events and sights that aren't expressly kid-specific might enchant your offspring, so plumb the other sections, too.

When it comes to buying baby supplies, this vocab primer should help: Pacifiers are called "dummies," diapers are "nappies," and a crib is a "cot."

ADVICE FOR STUDENTS

My advice boils down to: Have your ID ready to go, and always mention that you're a student, because it'll save you cash, including on trains to other cities. Attractions gladly offer discounts of around 50% for full-time students, but your high school or university identity card may not cut it in a place where clerks may not have heard of your school. Before leaving home, obtain a recognized ID such as the **International Student Identity Card** (ISIC; www.istc.org or www.myISIC.com) so that there's never a question of your eligibility. Those under 26 who are not in school can obtain a **International Youth Travel Card,** also through ISIC, which performs many of the same tricks as a student discount card.

Even before buying airline tickets, those under 26 should consult with a travel agency that specializes in the youth market and is versed in its available discounts: **STA Travel** (☎ 800/781-4040; www.statravel.com) is a big name.

ADVICE FOR TRAVELERS WITH DISABILITIES

London can be very hard going. The city can't seem to strike the right balance between preserving old buildings and making sure they're accessible to all. With the laudable exception of the Docklands Light Railway, only a slim selection of Tube stations offer lift service, and those with plenty of escalators still require passengers to climb several flights of stairs. It's shameful. The situation is so scrambled, and positive changes so slow, that you'll need to do a bit of research. For guidance on the transport system's facilities for people with disabilities, including free detailed maps, contact **Transport for London Access and Mobility** (☎ 020/7941-4600; www.tfl.gov.uk and search for "accessibility"). On the bright side, most **taxis** are wheelchair accessible; look for the illuminated chair symbol by the "for hire" sign. The government has also set up the **Disabled Persons Transport Advisory Committee** (www.dptac.gov.uk), which supplies transportation information online. The website for **Nationwide Disabled Access Register** (www.directenquiries.com) tattles about the accessibility features of a wide range of facilities, from attractions to car renters.

Generally speaking, the more expensive a hotel is, the more likely it is to be wheelchair accessible, but of course, you should always call ahead (as you probably already do anyway) to make sure. Two of the few low-cost lodgings with provisions for guests in wheelchairs are the YHA Thameside and the easyHotel in Kensington, both listed in the Accommodations chapter.

Most resources for travelers with diabilities prefer to disseminate their research via the Web or through publications. **Artsline** (☎ 020/7388-2227; www.artsline.org.uk) helps distribute information about accessible entertainment venues, including which ones have infrared hearing devices for rental; it also welcomes calls. Blind or partially sighted travelers will find useful advice from the **Royal National Institute of Blind People** (☎ 020/7388-1266; www.rnib.org.uk). **Tourism for All** (☎ 084/5124-9971; www.tourismforall.org.uk) is a charity that passes accessibility information to older travelers as well as to travelers with disabilities.

Two organizations publish guides that may assist in planning: **Access in London** (www.accessproject-phsp.org) is updated about every 7 years—the most recent version, available for a suggested donation of $5, is from 2003; and every January, **The Royal Association for Disability and Rehabilitation (RADAR)** (☎ 020/7250-3222; www.radar.org.uk) puts out *Holidays in Britain and Ireland,* a list of 1,500 accessible accommodations and entertainment centers nationwide.

The British agency **Can Be Done** (☎ 020/8907-2400; www.canbedone.co.uk) runs tours adapted to travelers with disabilities.

Wheelchair Travel (☎ 01483/23-76-68; www.wheelchair-travel.co.uk) rents out self-drive and chauffeured chair-accessible vehicles (including ones with hand controls), provides day tours, and arranges city sightseeing in vehicles that accommodate up to a dozen people. Car rental runs from £46 a day.

The **London Disability Arts Forum** (☎ 020/7739-1133; www.ldaf.org) plans exhibitions and events by and for artists with disabilities.

ADVICE FOR GAY & LESBIAN TRAVELERS

On November 18, 2004, the British government passed the Civil Partnership Act, which allowed gay and lesbian couples the same civil rights afforded to mixed-gender couples, including in matters of inheritance, pensions, and next-of-kin privileges for hospitalizations—basic entitlements still denied to people in the United States. That goes a long way toward explaining the culture's prevailing attitude toward same-sex couples. Public displays of affection are received with indifference in the center of the city, although in the outer suburbs couples should show more restraint. Gay bashings are rare enough to be newsworthy, but it's true that an element of society can, once full of ale, become belligerent Particularly in parks at night, be aware of your surroundings and give wide berth to gaggles of drunken lads. This advice, of course, holds irrespective of your sexuality.

The website **Queery** (www.queery.org.uk) lists gay and lesbian social events and festivals and is partnered with the **London Gay & Lesbian Switchboard** (☎ 020/7837-7324; www.llgs.org.uk), a counseling hotline.

For nightlife planning, the best sources for information (among many less handy glossy lifestyle magazines) are the **Boyz** (www.boyz.co.uk), which publishes a day-by-day schedule on its website. The free **QX International** (www.qxmagazine.com) lets anyone read a free facsimile of its printed edition every week, so you can plot a course through the hotspots while you're still at home. Both publications are distributed for free at many London gay bars. This guide's overview of gay nightlife begins on p. 317.

ADVICE FOR SENIORS

Don't hide your age! Seniors in England are usually classified as those aged 60 and over, and they're privy to all kinds of price breaks, from lower admission prices at museums to a third off rail tickets (but you first have to apply for the **Senior Railcard;** www.senior-railcard.co.uk). If you lived in London, you could get even more, such as free Tube rides forever. How's that for generational respect?

You may hear seniors being referred to as OAPs, which stands for Old Age Pensioners. That acronym is falling out of use, perhaps because it's rare to find a solvent pension fund anymore. Don't be automatically offended if you're also referred to as a "geezer," though—in England, it means a fun-loving (if sometimes rowdy) bloke or dude of any age.

Help for Women Travelers

A true club and not an agency, **Women Welcome Women Worldwide** (☎ 01494/46-54-41; www.womenwelcomewomen.org.uk) is for female travelers, and membership costs £35 a year; at press time, there were more than 550 women registered in the United Kingdom who were eager to meet and host traveling women from around the world. The entire point of the organization is to broaden lives by connecting members with other members from foreign cultures, so if you avail yourself of this group, you'll be seeing London with someone who wants to treat you like a friend and take an active interest in your experience.

If you're over 50, you can join **AARP** (601 E Street NW, Washington, DC, 24009; ☎ 888/687-2277; www.aarp.org), and wrangle discounts on hotels, airfare, and car rentals. The well-respected **Elderhostel** (☎ 800/454-5768; www.elderhostel.org) runs many classes and programs in London designed to delve into literature, history, the arts, and music. Packages last from a week to a month and include airfare, lodging, and meals.

STAYING CONNECTED

INTERNET

Especially if you bring a wireless-enabled laptop, getting online in London won't challenge you. This place is full of international travelers—and therefore, places to get online. Most hotels are wired or wireless; at hotels, rates run from £10 to £20 a day, although £12 is probably the average, while at guesthouses, it's often free. Countless Internet cafes and coin-gobbling kiosks can be found around town (even, sometimes, in phone booths), and inns often have a system for your use. Libraries are reserved for residents.

Because of rampant wireless access (even McDonald's is rolling out wireless at its London locations), there aren't many Internet cafés left. The most common is **easyInternetcafé** (www.easyinternetcafe.com), part of the day-glo empire that brought you easyJet and easyHotel, which operates spaces filled with row upon row of flatscreen terminals. Rates fluctuate according to how many people are present, but usually hover around £1 for 30 minutes. These places are fairly filthy, understaffed, and crawling with gaming youth (keep a close eye on your bags), but they're open until 10pm or midnight, and you can usually find a seat. There are three West End locations of note: east of Trafalgar Square (456-459 Strand; Tube: Charing Cross), at 358 Oxford Street (Tube: Bond Street), and inside the Whiteleys Shopping Centre on Queensway (Tube: Queensway).

TELEPHONES

Long-distance telephone cards, the cheapest mode, are available at newsagents and post offices. After you hook into your card's system by way of a toll-free number, a price of 10p for the first minute and 4p for subsequent minutes would be typical. Don't use them in your hotel room, since even "free" 0800 calls can cost there.

The majority of London's rapidly vanishing **payphones** are operated by BT (British Telecom), and they are costly. The minimum charge is 40p (nothing under a 10p coin accepted, and phones don't give change), which buys a 20-minute call for local and national numbers. You can imagine how outrageous an international call would cost from the same machine. Anytime you call a mobile phone in Britain, the fee will be bearably higher, although under the British system there is no fee to *receive* a mobile call. Some payphones accept credit cards at a premium: £1.20 to start and 20p per minute for local and domestic. Full charge breakdowns by country and call duration are searchable at **British Telecom** (www.payphones.bt.com/publicpayphones). Stick to payphones on the street if you can, since phones at many pubs and hotels legally jigger their phones to charge at a higher rate—the price must be posted on the phone.

Mobile phone service grants a fairer price, but it takes some doing to arrange. Apart from renting a phone while you're in London (an undertaking that I wouldn't

Dial-a-Guide

Local calls start with 020. If the number is close to the center of town, the next number will be 7, otherwise, it will be 8, or in rare cases, 3. The main toll-free prefixes are 0800, 0808, and 0500. Numbers starting with 07 are usually for mobile phones and will be charged at a higher rate. Numbers starting with 09 and are premium-rate calls that will usually be very expensive (i.e. £1.50 per minute) and may not even work from abroad.

From Home:

- When dialing a number in this book, precede it with your country's international prefix (in the U.S. and Canada, it's 011), add the U.K.'s country code (44) and drop the first zero in the number.
- You often can't reach 0845, 0870, and 0871 numbers (charged at 10p a minute or less) from abroad, and when you can, you're charged more; if you have to call one from abroad, I suggest using the Web instead to get information. The 0845 prefix enables some companies to make a little money for every call received. As you can imagine, this profiteering leads to putting customers on hold. Unfortunately, many of the same companies are too cheap to offer local numbers that non-Brits can use. Whenever possible in this book, I've found a local number that you can reach.

From Britain:

- Dial 00 first to signal you're making an international call. Then add your destination's country code (Australia: 61; Canada: 1; New Zealand: 64; United States: 1) and last, the area code and number.
- The main toll-free prefixes are 0800 and 0500.
- 0845 numbers are charged at a local rate; 0870 at the national rate.
- If you call a toll-free number located back home, you'll still pay international rates for it.

recommend to the casual visitor), many tourists who already own quad- or tri-band mobile phones from T-Mobile or AT&T go the easy route and simply enable the international **roaming** feature of their service. That will work, but your phone company will bleed you for it. I advise doing this only as an emergency tool or if you have deep pockets, since you'll end up paying as much as $2 per minute and other administrative fees, even if you just call another location in London.

What's worse, mobile phone providers have a nasty trick up their sleeves: Once they know that your phone is abroad (they're alerted the first time you turn it on, even if you don't make calls), they charge obscene international rates every time someone calls you—even if you don't answer. Even if those callers don't leave a message. Even if your phone's *off,* because as far as your phone provider knows, you're abroad and so all attempts to reach you are routed as such. Tell everyone you know not to call you abroad unless they absolutely have to. Also jot down the time and number of every single call you make, since mobile phone companies commonly bill customers for calls they didn't make and then blame it on bad information sent by the foreign company that handled the call.

If you do have a quad- or tri-band phone that uses the GSM system—and ask your company if you don't know, because you might without knowing it—you can hop into pretty much any mobile phone shop (they're everywhere) and buy a cheap **pay-as-you-talk** phone number from a mobile phone store. You pay about £2 for a SIM card, which you stick in your phone, and then you buy vouchers to load your account with as much money as you think you'll use up (no refunds). That will give you a British number, which you can e-mail to everyone back home, that charges local rates (10p–40p per min.), not crazy international ones, for your calls. Just remember to call your provider before you leave home and have them give you the code to "unlock" your phone so that the British SIM card will function in it. That service is usually free. U.K. mobile providers with pay-as-you-talk deals, all comparable, include: **Vodafone** (www.vodafone.com), **O2** (www.o2.co.uk), Orange (www.orange.co.uk), **T-Mobile** (www.t-mobile.co.uk), and **Virgin Mobile** (www.virginmobile.com).

To pay even less, just send text messages to the folks back home. The English send well over a million text messages a month; they know, as you should, that for quick communications, they're cheaper than even a local call.

If you'll be traveling with a laptop and you'll have broadband Web access where you're staying (two big "ifs"), consider downloading a free Internet phone service such as **Skype** (www.skype.com), which will allow free calls to anyone who also has the program, worldwide. You'll have the option of being able to buy cheap credits enabling you to make phone calls to regular phones using your computer. Using a USB headset gives you the best call quality (and call privacy), but that's one more thing to pack.

RECOMMENDED BOOKS & FILMS

Lots of movies and books are set in London—too many to count. But the recommendations that follow give a sense of the city's everyday life. The city is the star in these picks, not just a setting.

HISTORY

London: The Biography, by Peter Ackroyd is a doorstop covering every epoch. *The London Compendium,* by Ed Gilnert, serves as a street-by-street catalog (maddeningly indexless) of little-known facts. For a witty tour of London oddities by way of the places on its version of the Monopoly board, try *Do Not Pass Go,* by Tim Moore. *The Pax Britannia Trilogy,* by Jan Morris, is a three-volume saga of the rise and fall of the British Empire. A *Survey of London, Written in the Year 1598,* by John Stow offers an eyewitness account of the reign of Elizabeth I. Gillian Tindall's *The House by the Thames* spins the story of Southwark's changes by tracing the history of a town house that survived them all. *The London Scene: Six Essays on London Life,* by Virginia Woolf, is a quick read in which the writer profiles the city in the early 20th century. *The Subterranean Railway,* by Christian Woolmar, details the Tube's tortured creation.

FICTION

Charles Dickens' *Oliver Twist* regards the woes of the Industrial Revolution while his *A Tale of Two Cities* is set in London and Paris in the late 1700s. *The Complete Sherlock Holmes,* by Arthur Conan Doyle, proves useful if you want to understand the most elementary Holmsian references. In *The End of the Affair,* Graham Greene captures the psychosis of living in London during the Blitz. *Hangover Square,* by Patrick Hamilton, showcases the malaise of the prewar years. Unlike its film adaptation, Nick Hornby's *High Fidelity* is set in London, and it provides an accurate snapshot of modern city life. *Saturday,* by Ian McEwan, is about a man confronting his views in a post-9/11 city. *London: The Novel,* by Edward Rutherfurd, tells the city's tale as an epic saga. *1984,* by George Orwell, was inspired by the writer's post-Blitz malaise in Islington. *253,* by Geoff Ryman, is an unusual work tracing the inner thoughts of 253 Londoners as they ride a doomed Bakerloo line train. *White Teeth,* by Zadie Smith, offers a comic portrait of the city's modern Asian immigrant families.

FOR KIDS

A Little Princess, by Frances Hodgson Burnett, is a twee but time-proven rags-to-riches tale. *The Story of the Amulet* and *The Story of the Treasure Seekers,* by E. Nesbit, collects sassy stories of magic, set in Edwardian London, that cut a pattern for J. K. Rowling's *Harry Potter* series, which is steeped in the British school milieu. The *Mary Poppins* series centers around a practically perfect nanny and some quintessentially West London stories about the upper-middle-class.

MOVIES

Gad-about-town Michael Caine hits on every London lass in *Alfie* (1966). Two young lads fall in love in the gritty Thamesmead project of southeast London in *Beautiful Thing* (1996). Judi Dench plays a wartime burlesque theatre owner (warning: Bob Hoskins naked) in *Mrs. Henderson Presents* (2005). *About a Boy* (2002) features Bayswater, the London Zoo, Regent's Park, and Channel 4's *Countdown.* In *The Elephant Man* (1980), Shad Thames, south of Tower Bridge, stands in for darkest Whitechapel. *Four Weddings and a Funeral* (1994) was made at the Chapel at Greenwich's Royal Naval College and the South Bank Centre, among other spots. *Withnail & I* (1987) shows Camden Town in the '60s not as a bohemian paradise, but as a bittersweet trap of poverty. *Frenzy* (1972) is a Hitchcock hatchet job filmed mostly around Covent Garden. *The Madness of King George* (1994) was shot around Windsor, Eton, and Syon House. Watch *Notting Hill* (1999) to see Hugh Grant pine in London's swankiest 'hoods. *Secrets and Lies* (1996) showcases an authentic clash of residents of many cultures, with a pivotal scene set in a caff. *Sliding Doors* (1998) is a clever "what if" fantasy shot all over town. Don't call it stupid; *A Fish Called Wanda* (1988) definitely bears renting and was mostly shot in Clerkenwell and the East End (Ms. Cody's dogs met their hilarious ends at 69 Onslow Gardens in South Kensington). Check out *The Italian Job* (1969) for a car heist classic every Briton can quote.

The ABCs of London

Area codes See p. 363 for info.

ATMs/Currency Exchange See "Money" on p. 353. The city's main American Express office is at 30-31 Haymarket, SW1; ☎ 020/7484-9610; Tube: Piccadilly Circus.

Business Hours Offices are generally open weekdays between 9 or 10am and 5 or 6pm. Some remain open a few hours longer on Thursdays and Fridays. Saturday hours for stores are the same, and Sunday hours for stores are generally noon to 5 or 6pm. Banks are usually open from 9:30am to 4 or 5pm, with some larger branches open later on Thursdays or for a few hours on Saturday mornings.

Drinking Laws Legal drinking age is 18.

Electricity The current in Britain is 240 volts AC. Plugs have three squared pins. Foreign appliances operating on lower voltage (those from the U.S., Canada, and Australia use 110–120 volts AC) will require an adapter and possibly a voltage converter, although the range of capability will usually be printed on the plug. Most modern phone or iPod chargers and laptops can handle the stronger current with only an adapter. A few hotels, but not many, will provide a bathroom plug for a simple appliance such as a shaver.

Embassies and Consulates As a capital, London hosts foreign diplomats. Many offices are open only in the morning. **Australia:** Australia House, Strand, WC2B 4LA; ☎ 020/7379-4334; www.uk.embassy.gov.au; Tube: Temple. **Canada:** Canadian High Commission, 38 Grosvenor St., W1K 4AA; ☎ 020/7258-6699; www.canada.org.uk; Tube: Bond Street. **Ireland:** Passport and Visa Office, Montpelier House, 106 Brompton Rd., SW3 1JJ; ☎ 020/7225-7700; www.embassyofireland.co.uk; Tube: Knightsbridge. **New Zealand:** New Zealand House, 80 Haymarket, SW1Y 4TQ; ☎ 020/7968-2730; www.nzembassy.com/uk; Tube: Piccadilly Circus. **United States:** 24 Grosvenor Square, W1A 1AE; ☎ 020/7499-9000 or 020/7894-0563; www.usembassy.org.uk; Tube: Bond Street; no walk-ups admitted; you must phone ahead for an appointment.

Emergencies The one-stop number for Britain is ☎ 999—that's for fire, police, and ambulances. See "Health & Safety" earlier in this chapter for more info.

Holidays Banks and most businesses close on Christmas Day (Dec 25) and Boxing Day (Dec 26). Good Friday and Easter Monday are public holidays. There are three bank holidays, on the first and usually the last Mondays in May (how they fall depends on the year), and the last Monday in August. Museums are generally closed on public holidays, but business is usually booming on bank holidays.

Hospitals In the U.K., the ER is usually called A&E, for "Accident and Emergency." If your need for care is urgent, dial ☎ 999 rather than risk going to a medical center that doesn't offer A&E. **Charing Cross Hospital,** Fulham Palace Road, W6; ☎ 020/8846-1234; Tube: Hammersmith; **Royal London Hospital,** Whitechapel, E1, ☎ 020/7377-7000; Tube: Whitechapel; **Soho NHS Walk-In Centre,** 1 Frith St., W1; ☎ 020/7534-6500; Tube: Tottenham Court Road; **St. Thomas's Hospital,** Westminster Bridge Road, SE1; ☎ 020/7188-7188; Tube: Lambeth North, Waterloo, or Westminster; **University College Hospital,** 235 Euston Rd., NW1; ☎ 084/5155-5000.

Libraries Library services are not available to nonresidents of London. The main British Library is at 96 Euston Rd., NW1; ☎ 020/7412-7332; www.bl.uk; Tube: King's Cross St. Pancras; Monday, Wednesday to Friday 9:30am to 6pm, Tuesday 9:30am to 8pm, Saturday 9:30am to 5pm, Sunday 11am to 5pm.

Mail At press time, postcards cost 50p to send to Europe and 56p anywhere else.

Most light letters will cost 50p to 81p, depending on their weight. For price updates, consult www.royalmail.co.uk. Stamps can be purchased at many newsagents, supermarkets, and at any post office; most are open 9am to 5:30pm weekdays, plus 9am to noon Saturdays.

Newspapers and Magazines London offers more publications than one would think a city of its size could support. The broadsheets, ordered from left to right, politically speaking, are: *The Guardian, The Independent, Evening Standard, The Daily Telegraph,* and *The Times*. The salmon-colored *Financial Times* covers business. The tabloids are fluffier and more salacious, and they include *The Sun* (which has published photos of topless "Page Three Girls" since 1970), *The Mirror, Daily Star, The Daily Mail* and *Daily Express;* few of those deliver news as most people would define the term. Most have a weekend or sister publication; *The Guardian*'s is called *The Observer. The Sunday News of the World* is notoriously gossipy, as is the muckraking *The People. Time Out* publishes a thorough weekly listing of events and entertainments; new issues go on sale Tuesdays. International publications such as the *International Herald Tribune, Time, Newsweek,* and *USA Today* are widely available. Some 1.3 million copies of the flimsy *Metro* are handed out for free on the Tube every weekday morning. Other popular magazines include *Heat* (celebrity gossip), *Radio Times* (TV listings and celebrity interviews), *Hello!* and *OK!* (fawning celebrity spreads usually planted by publicity agents), *Q* (music and entertainment), and *NME* (music).

Pharmacies Every police station keeps a list of pharmacies that are open 24 hours. Also try **Zafash,** open 24 hours, 233-235 Old Brompton Rd., SW5; ☎ 020/7373 2798; Tube: Earl's Court; and **Bliss,** open daily 9am to midnight, 5-6 Marble Arch, W1; ☎ 020/7723-6116; Tube: Marble Arch. For nonemergency health advice, call **NHS Direct** at ☎ 0845/4647.

Safety See p. 357 for info.

Smoking Smoking is prohibited by law in any enclosed workplace, including museums, pubs, public transportation, and restaurants. If in doubt, ask permission.

Taxes All prices, except some hotel tariffs, are listed including taxes.

Telephone directory assistance Call ☎ 118-500 or go to www.bt.com.

Time Zone London is generally 5 hours ahead of New York City and Toronto, 8 hours ahead of Los Angeles, 11 hours behind Auckland, and 9 hours behind Sydney. It is 1 hour behind western continental Europe.

Tipping Waiters should receive 10% to 15% of the bill, unless service is already included—always check the menu or ask your server if service is included because traditions are changing. At pubs, tipping isn't customary unless you receive table service. Taxi drivers should be tipped about 10% of the fare. Service staff at fine hotels should be greased with a pound here and there, but staff at B&Bs and family-run hotels don't expect tips. Bartenders and chambermaids need not be tipped.

Toilets London doesn't have enough of them. Washrooms can be found at any free museum in this guide, any department store, any pub or busy restaurant (though it's polite to buy something), and at Piccadilly Circus and Bank Tube stations. Train stations also have public toilets, some of which may cost 20p to 50p. Also keep an eye out for spray-cleaned, coin-operated (50p) Automatic Public Conveniences, or APCs.

Index

See also Accommodations and Restaurant indexes, below.

GENERAL INDEX

ACCOMMODATIONS

RESTAURANTS